# DESTINY'S CHILD

## Gaius Julius Caesar

D. J. Anley

Published 2007 by arima publishing

www.arimapublishing.com

ISBN: 978 1 84549 200 7



www.destinyschild-gaiusjuliuscaesar.com

Cover image credit to Musée du Louvre, Paris



Printed and bound in the United Kingdom

Typeset in Garamond 11/14



Swirl is an imprint of arima publishing.

arima publishing
ASK House, Northgate Avenue
Bury St Edmunds, Suffolk IP32 6BB
t: (+44) 01284 700321

www.arimapublishing.com

## *Author's note*

The whole conception of this, my first novel, came from a conversation with my seven-year-old daughter Jessica, who, after discussing her latest school project on the Romans, asked how Caesar came to be famous. When I asked her what she meant she replied,

"Well, how did he become powerful? Are you born to be so powerful and famous or does it just happen when you get older?"

This innocent comment sparked a chain of events that lead, five years later, to what you have read today.

In my search to answer the question of destiny I stumbled across a story so rich and vibrant that it screamed out to be told. Ask anyone if they know who Gaius Marius and Sulla were, and they shake their heads in perplexity, and yet, without the part these two titans played in shaping the late Roman Republic and the undoubted effect they had on Caesar's childhood, Gaius Julius Caesar might have remained a shadowy figure in history.

All the historical content in this book was found through laborious research and I have endeavoured to be historically accurate whilst writing a fictional story, around factual evidence. I apologise for my failing if I am found to be wanting in this area.

The characters in this story all lived in Caesar's time and much of their interaction has been recorded. The main political and social events in Caesar's young life did in fact happen. His relationship with Gaius Marius was commented upon and recorded for posterity, as was his dealings with Sulla. Some of the words quoted in this story, according to records, were spoken by the great men themselves. The prophecy did exist, and rumour abounded that Marius tried to prevent Caesar from usurping his place in history by forcing him into the priesthood.

The relationship between Caesar, Marcus and Aemi are slightly more tenuous and their early relationship is not recorded. Marcus did die at the hands of Catalus Caesar, in revenge for the suicide of his father under Marius's short reign of terror. History records that Marcus was cut into pieces and offered up on the alter as a sacrifice to the gods. Aemi is recorded as Caesar's Master of Horse in later years and he remained a staunch ally even after Caesar's death. Sources mention that they were childhood friends, and Marcus was related by Caesar through Gaius Marius so perhaps they were all friends after all?

The relationship between Marius and Sulla is thankfully well recorded by their contemporary peers. That these two men brought Rome to her knees and threatened the very end of the empire is not in dispute. Their actions and disregard for the Mos Maiorum paved the way for later Roman generals, including Caesar, to supersede the Senate in power, and, as is common knowledge, the Roman Republic ceased to exist after Caesar's death.

As for the question; 'Are the great historical figures of our time destined from birth to take their place as stellar examples of human power and greatness in the annuls of time?' I have still not reached a conclusion.

That I was destined to write this book, I have no doubt.

D. J. Anley
March 2007

This book is dedicated to:

*Jessica and Mark.*

*'You have been by inspiration, and my rock,
and will always be my greatest loves.'*

and
*Joan and Terry*

*'You kept the faith'*

# CHAPTER ONE

*"In war, events of importance are*
*the result of trivial causes."*
*(Gaius Julius Caesar)*

## ROME: January- March 90BC

*Senior Consul: Lucius Julius Caesar*
*Junior Consul: Publius Rutilius Lupus*

Three boys sat side by side, their sandaled feet hanging over the edge of the precipice. The Tarpeian Rock was the execution place of Rome; over seventy feet below were the jagged rocks that had hastened the end of many a guilty man, condemned for their crimes against Rome and thrown mercilessly to their death.

"Father says that after Lucius Appelius Saturnius caused the riot in the Forum and all those innocent people were killed, Gaius Marius should have taken Saturnius straight here and thrown him off instead of giving him sanctuary in the Senate House. Saturnius was a traitor to Rome and he deserved to die a traitor's death, but your uncle insisted that they stand trial for their crimes and because of that they escaped proper Roman justice." Thus spoke young Marcus Aemilius Lepidus, only son of the renowned and powerful senator of the same name and called Aemi by his friends, both of whom sat next to him now.

"My uncle was trying to do the decent thing!" retaliated the second boy. Shorter by a head than the other two, his dark hair and complexion closely resembling his uncle, Marcus Marius Gratidianus defended Gaius Marius against this criticism. He picked up a small rock and angrily threw it out into space. All three boys watched as it spun in the air and fell down into the abyss below them before smashing onto the rocks.

"I wonder if the traitors bounce when they hit the bottom, or do they just splat into pieces?" Aemi mused, staring down to where the rock had landed.

But Marcus was not going to let the last comment go easily. "Gaius Marius was unfairly blamed for the death of Saturnius and his followers. He gave them sanctuary in the Senate House to keep them safe until their trial could be heard. How was he to know that a group of senators' sons would climb onto the roof, rip off the tiles and stone Saturnius and the others to death inside the building! That's Patrician justice, is it?"

The third boy until now had kept quiet. He was used to his two friends bickering with each other but the arguments usually finished as quickly as they started. This time however he knew that Marcus would not back down easily and if he didn't do something the two boys would end up in yet another fight.

"Marcus, you are correct to say that our uncle was not to blame for that incident and it is wrong of people to keep bringing it up after nine years, but to blame the deaths on Patrician noblemen is also wrong. There is no evidence that they were to blame; the culprits were never found. It is my opinion that it is as unfair to blame men of Patrician families as it is to blame our uncle Gaius Marius, therefore you are both in the wrong and should stop this argument before it goes any further."

Marcus Marius shrugged his shoulders and a smile crept across his lips. Within seconds, both he and Aemi lay on their backs roaring with laughter, much to the bemusement of their friend.

"Oh Caesar, you're so funny, especially when you don't mean to be!" Aemi said, finally sitting up to catch his breath. "You just have to be an advocate when you grow up, you know. Everything's so logical to you and you put your argument over so well! But yes, the argument must stop, eh, Marcus?" Marcus nodded in agreement and both boys smiled at Gaius Julius Caesar, their friend.

Caesar did not smile but his dark eyes twinkled with amusement just the same. He and Marcus were the same age, ten, but whilst Marcus was short, stocky and dark after his Italian parents, Caesar was tall, lithe and fair-haired, a true Patrician Roman. Aemi was the eldest at eleven and was also fair-haired, though his was tinged with a hint of red and he had bright green eyes. He was the same height as Caesar and came from one of the ancient Plebeian families of Rome, the Amelii.

Caesar watched his two friends, as they lay side-by-side, playfully poking each other in the ribs and giggling, the argument forgotten as quickly as it had started. He smiled inwardly to himself as, true to form, Aemi began to complain that Marcus was being too rough and Caesar mused that whilst Aemi might be the eldest of the group, in many ways, he behaved as the youngest. Life for Aemi was trouble free. Nothing he did was ever serious and his days were one big playground of fun, to be enjoyed at every moment. Marcus, Caesar thought, looking at his cousin who was now flicking dust into Aemi's face to annoy him even further, was the opposite. He was a serious boy and very sensitive to insults, whether about him or his family. Quick to anger, thoughtless to the consequences of his actions, Marcus was often getting into fights with other boys and very often Caesar and Aemi had to intervene to prevent him from receiving a serious beating.

Caesar smiled as Marcus rolled quickly out of Aemi's reach to avoid the angry punch aimed at him for throwing dust into Aemi's face. Three years they had been the best of friends and for three years he had been the peacemaker between Marcus and Aemi. From the moment he had been invited by his Aunt Julia to join the lessons at his Uncle Marius's house where his cousin and Aemi were being privately tutored by the best pedagogue in Rome, Caesar had found himself in the middle of the continual battle that was their friendship. Aemi was the son of a prominent senator who lived next door to Gaius Marius and was deemed a suitable companion for Marcus to associate with when he had first come to live with his uncle. Although Caesar and Marcus were cousins, they had not met until Marcus was sent from his hometown in Arpinium, to live with Gaius Marius in Rome in the hope that he would follow in his uncle's footsteps and have a successful military and political career. Indeed Marcus showed promise that one day he would make a very good soldier for he excelled in training at swordplay, the javelin and riding. In the classroom, however, he showed little interest in learning anything other than the battle tactics of famous Roman generals in history. Marcus loved living with his uncle, whom he worshipped, and nothing was surer to anger him than the insults about Gaius Marius being of Italian birth and a New Man, (non-Roman), in the Senate, even though by this time Marius had been Consul no fewer than six times, a record no Roman had ever achieved.

Caesar understood that Marcus sometimes felt inferior to his Patrician cousin and Aemi's illustrious and wealthy family, for birth and breeding formed a significant part of how a person fitted in to Roman society. Of course, it didn't help that Aemi took every opportunity to remind Marcus that he was not "Roman", and their precarious friendship had lasted solely because of their love for Caesar.

Aemi threw himself down on the ground next to Caesar and scowled at Marcus, who was busy foraging for more rocks around the old cypress tree.

"He always takes things too far!" he muttered, brushing dust from the front of his tunic.

Caesar turned and looked at Aemi appraisingly. "Perhaps if you stopped baiting Marcus you might have an easier time of it. You know he is stronger than you and he will not stop until he has bested you. You have only yourself to blame, you know, Aemi."

Aemi grunted and picked imaginary bits of dust from his arms.

"Anyway, it is far too hot to be arguing," Caesar said, wiping away the sweat that was running down his forehead.

It had been the hottest day so far that year and the boys had spent a stifling morning in the classroom with Alexander, learning to read and write in Latin and Greek, and studying arithmetic and history. The afternoon, as always, had been spent on the Campus Martius, a huge open area just outside the city walls to the north of the Servian Gate. Traditionally the armies trained there before leaving for foreign wars, and returned to the Campus if they were awarded a triumphant march through the streets of Rome to celebrate a victory over an enemy. The youth of Rome also trained there, learning their battle skills from retired legionaries or gladiators that had won their freedom and chose to teach their fighting skills to others. Gaius Marius had hired the services of an ex-gladiator to teach the boys the skills of the gladius, the short sword used by all Roman legionaries and officers, the pillium, a long spear that could be thrown either from foot or from a horse's back, and wrestling, which came into use in hand-to-hand combat. They were also taught to ride a horse, as officers in the army always rode into battle and the boys, when they reached seventeen, would be expected to join the army as junior cadet officers. For all three boys this was the best part of their day where they could run around in the warm sunshine, laugh, shout, scream and use up the youthful energy that had built up throughout the morning in the formal atmosphere of the classroom.

Today however, it had been too hot to train for long. It was summer and the temperature was over one hundred degrees. The horses had been sweating even before they had been ridden, and all the boys had felt too uncomfortable and sleepy to make much of an effort in their training. Finally, the chief instructor had decided to call a halt with the training for the day and the students were sent home. Caesar, Marcus and Aemi had decided to climb the Palatine Hill, the highest point in Rome, to sit at the Tarpeian Rock, a favourite haunt of the boys.

The breeze on the hill was refreshing and offered them relief from the heat and stench of the cramped city below. The earlier argument now behind them and peace restored, Aemi lay flat on his back, allowing the cool breeze to flow over him. Marcus had returned to sit on the edge of the cliff top, throwing stones down to the bottom and watching them smash in little pieces. Caesar sat staring out at the view below him, marvelling at the number of people who were milling around the streets and market place even though the heat was unbearable.

"How long has the Tarpeian Rock been used to kill people?" Marcus asked.

"Centuries," Caesar muttered. He was concentrating on the scene in the market place below him where a man had lost control of a herd of goats and they were now rampaging around the stalls, causing mayhem.

"Actually I know a bit about this," Aemi said, propping himself lazily onto one elbow. "When Romulus was King of Rome there was a war with the Sabine tribe and they attacked Rome in force. They managed to capture the daughter of Spurius Tarpeius, one of the governors of Rome. She was called Tarpeia and because Spurius would not surrender the citadel that was here on top of the Palatine, the Sabines flung Tarpeia off these rocks to her death. The Romans won the battle in the end of course, and the rocks were named after Tarpeia to remember her death." Aemi rolled over on to his back and laughed. "There, you see, I do remember some of the things Alexander teaches us!"

"Very impressive, Aemi," Marcus said sarcastically. "But that's not the version of the story I was told when I lived in Arpinium. My tutor said that the Lady Tarpeia betrayed the Romans and all for her love of gold. She told the Sabines that she would open the gates of the citadel if they gave her some of the gold bracelets that they wore on their arms. When she opened the gates, the troops rushed in and battered her to death with their shields to show their contempt for the woman for betraying her city. After the battle she was buried on top of this rock and that's how it got its name!"

"Well, you would have been told that version of the story living in Arpinium, wouldn't you?" sneered Aemi.

Caesar closed his eyes and inwardly sighed as, once again, the harmony of the group was destroyed.

"What's that supposed to mean?" Marcus retorted.

"Well, you Italians can't tell any story about Rome without it having something bad to say about the Romans. Just because you have no great history of your own to boast about, you have to put ours down! You Italians beg to be given our citizenship rights, share our glory and the profits we bring back from war and then you deride our history with stupid stories like that! Romans are greedy. Romans cannot be trusted!"

"Oh, 'you Italians', is it? 'We Romans', is it? You can never resist rubbing my nose in the fact I am not as Roman as you!" said Marcus, getting to his feet.

"Not as Roman as me? You are not a Roman at all. You are an Italian living in Rome and given Roman citizenship. That is not the same as being Roman, I can assure you," Aemi replied haughtily.

"Then I am surprised you bother talking to me at all, let alone call me your friend as I'm just an Italian! Well, I do have citizen's rights the same as you. You are no better than my family and me. My uncle has been Consul of Rome six times and he is Italian. What has your father ever done? I am your equal, Aemi. I will fight in Rome's army just like you and I will enter the Senate at thirty, just like you. Italians are Romans in all but name and you know it yet you still think you're better than us mere Italians. Well, let me tell you that you're not. One day all of Italy will be Rome and Rome Italy, and then where will your petty prejudices get you, Aemi?" Marcus paused to catch his breath.

Aemi simply stared at his friend in disbelief, taken aback by the force of what he had said.

"Marcus, I'm really sorry. I didn't mean to offend you when I said those things. Look, you're my friend and I don't think of you in the same way as I do all Italians. Honestly, I *am* sorry. To me, well, you're as Roman as… well… as Roman as a person can be who is not Roman by birth."

"Aemi," the quiet voice of Caesar interrupted, as Aemi continued to stumble around his apology. "You should shut up now before you make things even worse. I think Marcus understands that you are sorry, don't you?" he said, turning to Marcus who was now standing facing them with his fists clenched in anger.

"I know what he said and I know what he really meant!"

Caesar chose to ignore the tone in his cousin's voice. "You should be more careful how you say things, Aemi. You really do have a habit of saying the wrong thing at the wrong time and it will land you in big trouble one of these days. Now, both of you shake hands and make up. It is too nice a day for fighting. Friends?" he asked, stretching out his arm and curling his fist. Aemi jumped to his feet and did the same, putting his fist on top of Caesar's.

"Friends," Aemi said and looked at Marcus who was still standing with his fists clenched.

"Friends?" Caesar repeated.

Marcus moved forward as though to join his friends but then Aemi ruined it by saying, "Oh come on, Marcus. Make up. Stop being so sulky all the time!"

Marcus pulled away and then with a sudden lunge he head-butted Aemi in the stomach and knocked him to the ground. He jumped on top of Aemi before he had a chance to react and began punching his friend as hard as he could. Aemi retaliated and the two boys rolled around in the dust, grunting with the effort of fighting.

Caesar stood by, watching. He was quite used to these little fights between the other two, it was their way and usually the worst thing that happened was a bloody nose or a few scrapes and bruises. Tomorrow it would all be forgotten and they would be friends again.

Finally Marcus managed to get on top of Aemi and pinned his arm to the ground. Both boys lay still, panting with the exertion; Aemi had a bloody nose. Marcus let go and jumped to his feet, leaving Aemi lying flat on his back.

Wiping the dirt from his eyes Marcus turned to his cousin and said, "I'll see you tomorrow, Caesar." And without a backward glance he walked off across the hill.

Caesar helped Aemi to his feet and brushed his friend down as best he could as Aemi spat a glob of blood onto the floor.

"I told you this would end in trouble," Caesar said, smiling grimly. Aemi grinned back. The fights always ended the same way with Marcus winning and then walking off in a huff.

"Well then, you were right again, as usual," Aemi replied. "I tell you one thing though, Caesar. Marcus may be better than me at many things, but he can never be Roman, no matter how much he tries to be nor how well he fights, and we Romans always win in the end, don't we!"

With a final tug to straighten his tunic, he walked off after Marcus. Caesar hung back for a second and shook his head. "You just never give up, do you, Aemi?" he said to himself, and then, with a wry smile, he ran to catch up with his friend.

The following morning, Caesar made the daily journey from his home in the heart of the Subura district, to the opulent area of the Palatine, and to the home of his uncle, Gaius Marius.

As he walked through the narrow streets he was constantly greeted by shopkeepers and stallholders, and the few people that were out early getting the daily shopping. Caesar was used to the crowds, the noise, dirt and smell of thousands of people living shoulder to shoulder, crammed into small insulae, sometimes seven stories high. He wrinkled his nose as he passed by a side street that was littered with rotting food and excreta that had been thrown from the windows of the apartments to the ground below, and then skipped deftly across the narrow water channel that flowed down the centre of the road. As he passed by one of the smaller forum market places, the noise was incredible, with so many people talking, shouting their wares, bargaining for the day's shopping, children screaming and scampering around the streets in their bare feet, a myriad of languages spoken in this polyglot of Rome. But to Caesar, the dirt and the depravation didn't matter. The Subura was his home and he loved living there. He had friends of many different nationalities, and it didn't matter to them if you were Italian, Plebeian or Patrician; you were accepted for yourself and not for what class you belonged to or which area of the Roman Empire you came from.

Caesar had been born in the Subura. His mother, Aurelia, had been given the large insula as part of her wedding dowry to provide her with an independent income. It was never her family's intention that she and her husband would actually live there, but Gaius Julius Caesar was poor, and until he could earn the money to move his growing family into one of the more salubrious areas of Rome, the Subura remained their home, much to the frustration of their families.

Aurelia had grown to love the area and enjoyed the independence of running her own business and her own life without interference, a luxury few Roman women were afforded. The close community spirit meant that she was never lonely during the months and years her husband was away with his legions, and by dint of her hard-won efforts she now owned one of the best insula in the area.

Caesar and Aurelia were happy, and couldn't imagine living in any other part of Rome. Here they could be whatever they wanted to be with no airs and graces, and secretly, they both dreaded the day that Gaius Julius Caesar would return home and demand that the family move to the Aventine, an area infinitely more suited to the image of a rising politician, for Caesar's father had written in his last letter that when he returned from Gaul he intended to run for the office of Praetor.

A young cavalry officer strolled past Caesar as he walked up the hill towards the Palatine. Caesar glanced back enviously over his shoulder, wishing he was old enough to join the legions and follow in his father's footsteps, and yet this ambition was not forged by a strong desire to be like Gaius Julius, for he hardly knew him. Reminded of his father, Caesar reached back into his memory and tried to recall his face, but it was a blurred, hazy remembrance because he had not seen him now for over a year. This was not an unusual situation for a Roman who made his career in the army, especially those men from the higher social classes, and they could spend months, even years apart from their families. The wives of these men were expected to run the household and raise the children in their husband's absence without a word of complaint; it was the Roman way.

Caesar walked on, musing over how his mother would feel when his father eventually did come home. Young as he was, he knew that his mother found having her husband home on those rare occasions more an inconvenience than a pleasure. Gaius Julius made no secret of his loathing for the Subura and had demanded that Aurelia find somewhere more suitable to raise their child, somewhere that befitted the Patrician Roman gentlewoman that she was. Caesar had lost count of the number of times his mother had promised to begin looking for a new house but as soon as her husband returned to duty, she carried on as though it had never been mentioned. And so it went on, year after year, with Gaius Julius becoming more and more frustrated with his wife but never in Rome long enough to do anything about it.

Caesar shrugged off this impending family trouble and put the return of his father to the back of his mind as he arrived at his destination. He was admitted into the atrium where he was met by the steward.

"The young masters are already in the schoolroom, Master Gaius."

Caesar nodded and made his way down the familiar labyrinth of corridors of the huge villa. On the way he had to pass his uncle's study, and, just as he came level with the door, it opened, and a slave came out carrying a tray of empty goblets. Caesar stopped to allow the slave room to pass and as he did so he glanced in. He could see at least six men standing around the table, all dressed in togas, with the broad purple stripe running down the front and around the hemline, denoting men of senatorial rank. He recognised two of the senators as they were frequent visitors to his uncle's house and their faces were visible from the open doorway whilst the other men had their backs turned to the door. Before Caesar could look further the slave closed the door and hurried away towards the kitchens.

Musing on the strangeness of what he had seen, Caesar made his way to the schoolroom.

All morning their pedagogue, Alexander, worked the boys hard so there was no time for Caesar to hold a conversation with his friends as to what might be happening in the study. By lunchtime the boys were flagging and losing concentration so a halt was called to lessons for the day and Caesar, Marcus and Aemi, gratefully left the hot and stuffy classroom, making their way out into the large garden for some fresh air.

"I hate reading Greek!" Marcus groaned as he sprawled out on the grass under a large cypress tree, its branches offering shade from the mid-day sun.

"You hate reading anything unless it's about battles and wars." Caesar chuckled, as he sat himself down next to Marcus. He was relieved to be out of the classroom as it gave him the opportunity to speak to his friends about what he had seen earlier. "Talking of war, what is going on in Uncle's study? It looked like he was holding a war council judging by the number of senators that were in there with him."

"Yes, I saw quite a few of them coming to your house before I came round for lessons this morning," Aemi said, flopping down beside his friends. "It must be important, even Father has never had that many senators in his study at once. Do you know what's going on, Marcus?"

Marcus looked around to check that there were no slaves near by before he signalled Caesar and Aemi to draw closer.

"Last night I was so hot that I got up for a drink of water. I passed Uncle's study and the door was open just a crack and I could hear voices, so I stopped to listen, obviously," he added with a mischievous grin. "I couldn't see who was in there but I could make out four different voices."

"What were they saying?" Aemi asked.

"I heard one of them talking about someone called Marcus Livius Drusus, and one of the men was saying that people still didn't know who had assassinated him. Then another voice said that it wasn't surprising he'd been murdered because of all the trouble he'd caused, which they seemed to find funny because they all laughed."

"I know that name!" Aemi said excitedly. "I heard Father talking about him over dinner with Mother. Drusus was campaigning for the Italians to be given Roman citizenship. Father said the Senate would never vote in favour of general citizenship for all Italians and that Drusus was wasting his time."

"Well anyway," Marcus continued. "One of the men said he'd been to visit his farm in Etruria, I think it was, and he'd noticed a change in the attitude of the Italian locals. He said he'd felt threatened when he walked through the market place because of the hostility shown him by some of the people in the town and he had been served sour wine and stale bread at the local inn. He said he couldn't wait to return home to Rome."

"That doesn't sound very good, does it?" Caesar said, frowning. "Marcus Livius Drusus murdered before he can get the Italian citizenship law tabled for a vote, and Italians showing open hostility to a Roman gentleman. What else did they say, Marcus?"

"I heard Uncle saying that he could smell war in the air and Rome should start preparing for it."

"War? War with whom?" Aemi exclaimed.

"With the Italians of course!" Marcus snapped. "And keep your voice down."

"The Italians? But why?" Aemi whispered. "Surely they're not planning on going to war against Rome over the issue of citizenship?"

"Think, for once, Aemi," said Caesar impatiently, for he had already worked out that this was no ordinary meeting. "Drusus murdered. Hostile Italians and goodness knows what else that we do not know about. The Italians have wanted general Roman citizenship for years now. They are not content to just have Latin rights. They see themselves as brothers to Rome in every way and cannot understand why they should not be given full citizen rights. They are treated like second-class citizens, which to be honest they are, and their frustration at this injustice has obviously come to a head."

"So you think that they should be granted Roman citizenship then? You just said that it was an injustice," said Aemi suspiciously.

"No, I did not say that, I said *they* call it an injustice," Caesar replied.

"Well, I agree with them and so does my uncle," said Marcus. "There's no real difference between Romans and Italians other than our darker appearance and some of the regional languages some of the Italian tribes speak amongst themselves. We share the same way of life, the same gods, the same ideals. Italians supply men for the armies and pay taxes just like Romans. If anyone deserves the citizenship it is them, and I'd support them in their efforts to get it."

"Would you support them even if it meant going to war against Rome?" Caesar asked quietly.

"It won't come to that!" Aemi exclaimed. "Why would they go to all that trouble just so they can call themselves Roman citizens? You can't fight the very people you want to join! Anyway, they can call themselves what they like, because they will never *be* Roman, will they? They won't go to war against us and if they were stupid enough to try then they'd be defeated. Rome never loses!"

"Oh yes it does, what about twelve years ago with the Gauls? Rome suffered its biggest ever defeat at their hands, and whole legions were wiped out!" said Marcus.

Caesar could hear in the tone of his voice that Marcus was becoming defensive

"We won in the end regardless of our losses," Aemi argued stubbornly.

"Yes, but it was thanks to my uncle, the *Italian*, that we did," Marcus retorted.

"Men will go to war if the cause is important enough, and the Italians may believe that the citizenship is worth the sacrifice of many lives," said Caesar. "To be Roman is to be considered above and apart from every other race of people in the known world. We are a conquering people. We take our civilisation to heathen countries. We bring our justice, our gods, our way of life and we tell these people that it is the best way to live, the Roman way. We give their countries stability and protection from their invading neighbours, and in return all we ask for is a tax payable to Rome annually to help us pay for the legions it costs us to keep in these provinces; to give them the Roman way of life, a better way of life than the one they had before. Rome is great, her empire is expanding all the time and the Italians want to be part of her greatness and to share in her good fortune, but by trying to force us to give them the citizenship they will only set the hearts of the Roman people against them. Rome will never be forced into giving the Italians full citizenship and the Italians must surely know this."

Marcus had been listening intently, but Caesar could tell that he wasn't convinced by what he heard.

"You sound so sure of the greatness of Rome, Caesar, but it wasn't always this way. There's been lots of changes to the way Rome was run. First the kings ruled, then Rome became a Republic ruled by Patricians, and eventually they had to share their power with the powerful Plebeian families. Change had to happen in order for Rome to survive, and that's why the Italians should be given the citizenship. Instead of one small city having all the power, it could be an entire country. Just think how powerful Rome would be then. Together we could rule the entire world!" said Marcus passionately.

"You think the Italians are the ones to increase the power of Rome?" Aemi snorted.

"Yes, I do." Marcus retorted. "It will happen, Aemi, I know it will, especially if my uncle has anything to do with it."

"Gaius Marius may be Italian by birth but foremost he is a Roman citizen and has served six times as Consul over the years. He will never take up arms against Rome or encourage the Italians to go to war against us," said Caesar firmly.

"Maybe not," replied Marcus. "But I know he supports the Italians and he would grant them all the citizenship if he could, and he makes no secret of the fact that he holds most of the Senate in contempt for treating him so harshly over the years because he is an Italian. Why shouldn't he support their cause?"

"Then we must pray that he remembers where his loyalty lies, because if he takes the Italian side and it comes to war this could lead to the downfall of Rome," Caesar said.

"Never!" cried Aemi. "Rome will never fall. Rome is eternal!"

"You forget, Aemi," said Caesar. "Rome's army is made up of a large number of Italians. We have trained them to fight our way, therefore it would be like Romans fighting themselves, and only great generals like Gaius Marius will be able to give us the advantage. Both sides would be evenly matched in skill and numbers of men. It would be by no means certain that Rome could win this war, the only certainty is that it would tear the whole country apart."

The sudden clatter of galloping hooves along the cobbled street drew the boy's attention away from their discussion. It appeared that the horse had stopped outside the villa because it wasn't long before they heard the faint sound of raised voices coming from over the garden wall from the street behind.

"I wonder what's going on?" said Caesar, cocking his head to one side as he strained to hear.

"Quick, let's go and see!" said Marcus, jumping to his feet.

The boys ran back to the villa, and once inside they made their way along the corridor before finally coming to a halt by the side of a large statue of Venus at the edge of the atrium. Caesar could see the group of senators that had been with Gaius Marius in the study, now standing together, looking towards the main door where raised voices could still be heard.

The three boys crouched down out of sight. They had a good view of the atrium and the senators, and Caesar watched the steward enter with a very dishevelled messenger following close behind. The messenger saluted Marius, who had moved forward away from the group to receive him, handed him a scroll and stepped back, allowing him privacy to read. Gaius Marius opened the scroll without a word and began to read its contents whilst the senators stood silently, waiting.

Caesar could feel his heart pounding against his chest as he held his breath, waiting to see what would happen next.

Marius read quickly and then, rolling up the scroll, he nodded to the messenger. "Tell Lucius Julius Caesar that I shall come to the Senate House directly."

The messenger bowed to Marius and was escorted from the atrium by the steward.

Turning to the waiting senators, Marius spoke. "It would seem that our meeting has been well timed, for events in Italy have overtaken us."

"What is it? What has happened, Marius?" Publius Albinius, one of the senators asked.

Caesar held his breath as he tried to catch every spoken word.

"My brother-in-law, Gaius Julius Caesar, has just returned from Asculum with disturbing news. It would appear that family hostages have been exchanged between several Italian tribes in the north to ensure that they all will remain loyal when they go to war against Rome."

"When they go to war?" exclaimed Albinius.

"Yes. It appears to be the case. Marcus Perganus, the magistrate for Asculum, found out about this conspiracy and he threatened the Elders with the removal of Roman citizenship as a punishment. I am afraid that their answer was to murder him in cold blood in the market place and when they had done that, the residents turned on all the Roman citizens and visitors that were in the city, including women and children, and they slaughtered them all, right down to the last baby."

Caesar saw the senators gasp at the shock of the news. Italians killing Romans, it was unheard of.

"The Senior Consul has called all senators to an urgent meeting in the Senate House as a result of this appalling news; obviously this cannot be allowed to pass unchallenged. I suggest, gentlemen, that we make all reasonable haste to the meeting, but say nothing of what we have discussed today, understand?"

The senators nodded in agreement and then sprung into action; slaves were called, orders shouted, and with a great billowing gust of white togas they left the villa.

Caesar exhaled slowly, allowing his body to slump slowly down to the floor. Aemi and Marcus joined him. The three boys turned to look at each other, their faces reflecting the shock they felt at hearing this catastrophic news. What would this mean for them, for Rome, for everyone in Italy?

"So it's war then," Aemi whispered.

Marcus and Caesar looked at him but said nothing, shocked into silence by the terrible news.

"I had better go home." Caesar sighed, getting slowly to his feet. He peered round the statue to make sure the atrium was now empty of people before he stepped out into the corridor.

"Oh don't go now, Caesar, let's go to the Campus Martius and see what news we can pick up down there. Someone's bound to have heard about Asculum – maybe we can find out some more," said Marcus excitedly.

"I have to go, Marcus. The man who brought the message to Rome is my father. I have to go home and warn Mother that he is back; she will want to be prepared," said Caesar. He could not help feeling a sense of dread at the thought of his father having returned unexpectedly.

"You don't sound too happy that your father is home, Caesar. Don't you like him?" Aemi asked.

Caesar frowned. "I neither like nor dislike my father, Aemi. I do not know him. He is a stranger to me, but he is my father and I must be there to welcome him when he returns home. I will see you both tomorrow," he said, and set off home with a heavy heart.

Over two-hundred senators attended the emergency meeting called by the Senior Consul for the year, Lucius Julius Caesar; a respectable number considering most of the senior families spent the summer months in their villas on the coast, well away from the overbearing heat and stench of Rome.

The city itself was a holiday attraction, with people coming from all over the Empire to visit, making it an unbearable place to live in the summer, with the extra noise and overcrowding in an already overpopulated city.

Sitting alone on the dais, in his curule chair, Lucius Julius Caesar waited as the last few senators filed into the hall. He wondered how the absent Junior Consul, Publius Rutilius Lupus, was faring on his fact-finding mission. Leaving Rome the previous day to visit his vast plantation farm in Grumentium, southern Italy, Lupus had gone to ascertain if the Italian dissent had spread from the north of the country down towards the south.

When it looked as though the last of the senators had arrived, Lucius ordered the guards to shut the huge, bronze doors of the House. The news of an Italian uprising was worrying, and the last thing he wanted to do was to cause panic; this was one occasion when the people of Rome would have to wait to find out what this Senate meeting was all about. As soon as this was done, however, the news spread like wildfire amongst the many frequenters of the Forum. To the people, the closing of the doors signalled only one thing – trouble, and it wasn't long before the area was packed, everyone waiting in nervous anticipation.

Inside the House, meanwhile, Lucius Julius Caesar had wasted no time in reading his report. Stunned silence greeted his final words, as the senators took a moment to digest this astonishing atrocity that had been meted out to their citizens. The slaughter of Roman civilians was unheard of outside a war situation, and to murder innocent women and children was beyond all comprehension, particularly as the traditional allies of Rome had become the murderers.

"Is there any doubt that this report may have been exaggerated, Consul?" Marcus Aurelius Cotta asked.

Lucius looked grim as he shook his head. "I am afraid not, Marcus. A junior legate managed to escape the slaughter and found Gaius Julius Caesar, in Picentum, a few hours later. Caesar felt he should bring the news straight to Rome himself, as the legate died of his injuries soon after imparting the news."

Marcus nodded gravely and resumed his seat.

Lucius took a deep breath and pressed on, for there was no point delaying what was inevitable. "The Senate now has to decide what course of action to take against the inhabitants of Asculanum, in particular, and any other towns in the north that we find to be involved in the conspiracy."

"There is only one course of action open to Rome, Consul: war!" shouted Gnaus Cornelius Dollabella, rising to his feet. "Stamp on the Italian traitors now, before the dissent spreads like a disease throughout all Italy. Show them the might of Rome. Show them we will not be held to ransom or terrorised into giving them the citizenship, because as we all know, that is the issue that lies at the bottom of all this."

"I agree," said Quintus Servillius Caepio, rising to his feet. "I told this house two years ago that Marcus Livius Drusus was stirring a hornet's nest of unrest by championing the Italian claim to be made full citizens, but none of you took any notice, did you? Now look what has happened. Drusus convinced the Italians that it was possible to have the law passed through the Senate, but he was assassinated before he could make that happen. It is his death that has sparked this Italian revolt."

Lucius held his hands up as a silent plea for calm. He threw Caepio a withered look as he did so, wishing that for once he would stop taking the moral high ground, which almost always was the catalyst for argument in the Senate.

"And we all know who killed him, don't we, Caepio!" shouted Lucius Orestes.

"Are you implying that I had something to do with his murder? Because if you are, I shall have you up before the law courts for slandering my dignitas!" roared Caepio, his face flushed purple with rage.

Lucius Orestes held up his hands up in mock submission, but grinned broadly. He had made his point to the house.

The Consul smiled inwardly to himself. Orestes was as sharp as a blade and never missed a trick. How like him to say what most of the House already believed; that Caepio was involved in the murder of Drusus, along with Gaius Marius, but of course, none would dare say it openly.

"Back to the business in hand," he commanded, but was prevented from speaking further by a loud knocking on the bronze doors.

The force of the doors opening pushed the guard back against the wall, as a dishevelled Publius Rutilius Lupus barged his way into the hall. He hurried across the open floor between the tiers towards the dais, and all eyes watched in awe at the sight of the Junior consul in such a state of disarray.

Lucius's stomach tightened as he watched his colleague walk towards him. Judging by his appearance, he did not bring good news.

Lupus stopped in the centre of the room. "I have a message!" he wheezed. Clearing his throat, he tried again. "I have a message from the Chief Magistrates of the New State of Italia." Lupus paused to catch his breath, before pulling out a roll of parchment from the folds of his toga, and, holding it up high for all to see, advanced to the dais, and climbing the steps, handed the scroll to Lucius Julius Caesar. Having completed his duty, Lupus collapsed with exhaustion in his vacant consular chair.

Lucius unrolled the scroll and felt his hands begin to tremble as he stared down at the neatly written Latin words before him.

"Read it aloud, Lucius," Lupus urged. "Read out to this House what these Italians have to say to the Senate of Rome."

Lucius cleared his throat, and taking a deep breath to regain his shaken composure, he began to read from the scroll. *"From Quintus Poppaedius Silo, Chief Magistrate of the new State of Northern Italia, and, Gaius Papius Mutilius, Chief Magistrate of the South. Hail to the Senate and people of Rome..."*

And so it went on. Spelling out the Italians' frustration at the Senate's broken promises to grant general citizenship for all. The leaders of the various Italian tribes were frustrated at being unable to participate in the governing of Rome. After fighting side by side as allies for so many years, yet never reaping the rewards of the large bounty that Rome won, time and again, the Tribes had decided enough was enough. They formally declared that they now belonged to the newly formed state of Italia, which would rule itself, free from Roman interference. No further allied military support would be available to Rome. No more taxes would be paid, and they declared that all Italian slaves owned by Romans were deemed free men. All land that had originally belonged to Italian farmers and landowners before the Punic Wars was once again considered the property of Italia, and no compensation would be paid to the Roman owners for the loss of this property.

This last demand in particular caused complete uproar in the House. All senators owned land and slaves, to run the property in their master's absence, and much of it was in Italy. The majority of a senator's income came from the produce of his land and without it many would be plunged into poverty.

It took some time for Lucius Julius Caesar to restore order to the House, as he fought against his own feelings of anger and disbelief at the unimaginable affront shown by the Italians. This new state of Italia was a flagrant challenge to the authority of Rome, and something had to be done immediately to stop it.

After hours of deliberation a vote was held to decide whether to negotiate with these tribes, or to declare war on them. Not one senator voted to negotiate. The supremacy of Rome was being challenged, and there could be only one course of action.

Whilst the Senate of Rome held a council of war, Caesar was dealing with his own family battles. The first meeting with his father on the night of Gaius Julius Caesar's return to Rome had, as in the past, been very stilted and formal; neither father nor son knew each other well enough to be comfortable. As soon as dinner was over, Caesar excused himself from the room, claiming that he was tired, but in truth he found the company of his father difficult to enjoy, for the man was a stranger to him.

Later that night, lying in his sleeping cubicle, Caesar pulled the blankets over his head to drown out the sound of his parents arguing in the room next-door. As he had anticipated, his father was angry that he had come home to find the family still living in the Subura. Caesar could hear his mother's sobs as she pleaded against the move, but this only increased his father's anger and the argument raged on. Caesar pulled the covers around his head tighter, and wept.

When he rose early the next morning, his father was nowhere to be seen. Caesar made his way to the workroom and found his mother at her loom, weaving what appeared to be the start of a fine red cloak, obviously meant for his father. He noted Aurelia's red, swollen eyes, and, understanding her sorrow, Caesar gave her a hug.

"Where has Father gone, Mother?" he asked, as Aurelia held him in a tight embrace.

"To meet with your Uncle Marius. He hopes to be able to help him with the recruiting of the new legionaries."

"Will Father go to fight the Italians with Uncle Marius?"

"That will be for the Senate to decide, Gaius. Your father says that they are meeting later today to decide who will be placed in command of the army. He hopes to serve as a senior legate to whoever is appointed."

"Does that mean Father will have to go away, Mother?" Caesar tried to keep the sound of hope from his voice for he did not want to appear disloyal to his father, yet, at the same time, he could not bear to hear night after night of arguments either.

"Yes, it does, I'm afraid. I am sorry you may not be able to spend more time with your father, to get to know him properly. It would certainly benefit you to have a man around, now that you are older," Aurelia said, stroking his thick blond hair.

"I do not need my father around to teach me how to be a man, Mother," Caesar said indignantly. "Besides, we do not have anything to say to each other. He knows nothing about me, other than what you tell him in your letters. He is a stranger to me, and though I try to talk to him, I find it very difficult. I am sorry, Mother, truly I am," he said, burying his face into her neck and smelling the warm, comforting sweetness of her perfume.

"I do understand how you feel, Gaius." Aurelia sighed. "But you must try harder to get along with him when he does come home to us. He has told me that he intends to run for election as a praetor once this war is over, which will mean he can stay in Rome for at least a year, if he's successful. That will give you both time to get to know one another," Aurelia said, pushing her son gently away so that she could look at him. "Your father is a good man, Gaius, he is noble and honourable, and a kind husband to me. You will like him when you get to know him, I promise. Besides, you are your father's son and much of what and who you are comes from him. I see more of him in you every day, so, he is not that much of a stranger to you. Look at yourself and you will see much of him."

Caesar struggled to accept his mother's words, for he had seen little evidence of his father's kindness towards her.

"But he wants us to leave the Subura, Mother, and that makes you unhappy. That is not being kind to you, is it?" he answered indignantly.

"Your father wants what is best for us, and leaving here is part of that. I know this isn't the most desirable place to bring up a child, especially a Patrician, and I have been at fault because I ignored his wishes. He is the paterfamilias. His word is law, and I should have reminded myself of that. Instead, I have made him angry when he should have been happy to be home, and I am sorry for it. Pride can be a destructive thing when it hurts the ones you love, remember that, my son. Never let your pride get in the way of doing what is right."

Caesar could not argue against his mother's words, for in truth she was right. His father, as paterfamilias, must be obeyed, and his mother should not have gone against his wishes for so long. Not wanting to add to her pain by arguing, Caesar held his tongue.

"I will remember your advice, Mother," he said, getting to his feet.

"Good, now, run along. I have this cloak to finish." Aurelia turned away and picked up the bobbin that held the finely spun wool she had prepared to make the cloak.

Caesar understood that his mother wanted to be left alone with her thoughts now. Giving her a kiss on the cheek, he quietly left the room.

# CHAPTER TWO

*"It is easier to find men who will volunteer to die,*
*than to find those who are willing to endure pain with patience"*

*(Gaius Julius Caesar)*

## ROME: April-August 90 BC

The rich vibrancy of life that could usually be found in Rome was gone, replaced by a sombre mood, which the declaration of war with the Italians had produced. Dark, drab clothes had replaced the bright-coloured apparel that the people usually wore. Togas had been discarded, and women now wore veils covering their faces, to signify that Rome was in mourning. Gone was the lively chatter and banter of shoppers and stallholders that once reverberated around the market places throughout the day, for food supplies were becoming short and customers were sparse. With the Italian legions blockading the roads leading to Rome, the price of food was high and the people of Rome were beginning to suffer. If the war continued for too long they would starve, and the Senate, mindful of the need to keep the citizens from rebelling, began to sell off large pieces of public land inside the city to the highest bidder, hoping to fill the empty treasury with the money desperately needed to pay the extra men that were being recruited daily into the legions.

Caesar walked slowly down the Vicus Tuscus behind his two friends, deep in thought over these daily struggles that faced them all. Marcus and Aemi were chatting excitedly about the training of the new legionaries that they would be able to watch on the Campus that afternoon, but Caesar was observing the melancholy change in the people around him, a change that very much reflected his own mood that day. The crisis developing inside Rome affected everyone, including his family and friends, in many different ways, and he inwardly groaned as, for the hundredth time, he heard Marcus complaining to Aemi that living with Gaius Marius had turned into a nightmare.

Caesar thought back to the conversation he had with his father and his Uncle Cotta on the subject of Gaius Marius. Expecting to be awarded command of the legions, Gaius Marius had been thwarted by his enemies in the Senate, who had started a whispering campaign that Marius was past his best, that he was old and unwell, and that the time had come to make way for new men to show their skills commanding Rome's legions. Informed that the only position left open to him would be to help with training the new recruits for the legions that were coming in thick and fast, Marius had taken this as an insult to his dignitas, and his anger knew no bounds. Both Caesar's father and his Uncle Cotta had worked together with other Mariian supporters to persuade him to bide his time, but for how long they could keep this lion caged, no one knew.

"It's horrible living at home, you have *no* idea," Marcus complained, as the boys walked across the Forum.

"Actually, I think we do, Marcus." Caesar could not help himself.

Aemi sniggered at his friend's sarcasm.

Marcus scowled, but continued to vent his frustration. "Aunt Julia has taken to slinking around the house almost whispering her orders to the slaves, and constantly warning them to do nothing to upset Uncle. Do you know, yesterday, his body slave tipped a jug of hot water into the bath whilst uncle was in it, and the water scalded his leg. He went mad, claiming the slave was part of a conspiracy to injure him so that he couldn't fight in the war. He had the slave whipped to within an inch of his life and then had him taken down to the harbour to be sold as a galley slave on one of the new warships! Course, that upset Aunt Julia because the slave was a good one; she said he'd always got Uncle's togas gleaming white."

"Well, as no one is wearing togas any more, I don't suppose it matters too much," said Aemi. "Uggh, how much longer do we have to look like this? I hate these foul colours." He plucked distastefully at his dark grey tunic.

"For as long as the war lasts, I suppose," said Caesar.

"Well, I just hope it doesn't go on for too long, because I get my Toga Virilis in a few years time, and I'm looking forward to that."

Caesar laughed. "You will be a man when you are fifteen, whether you are wearing the Toga Virilis or not, Aemi, so stop worrying."

"Yes, thank you, I do know that, Caesar," Aemi snapped. "But the toga gives you that air of authority, don't you think? It says, I am a Roman, the greatest of men."

"I can't wait to be fifteen," said Caesar wistfully. "I hate being a child. I don't feel like one, and, I don't behave as one, *and,* I detest being treated like one." He angrily kicked out at a stone on the ground. "I wish I was old enough to fight now, instead of having to watch the new recruits being trained to fight for the glory of Rome, whilst I get to play with my wooden sword. It is so frustrating!"

"Perhaps it will last ten years, like the Punic Wars did, then we'll have our chance," said Marcus, swinging his arm in the air and stabbing playfully at Aemi in a mock sword fight.

"Oh, and which side would you choose then, Marcus?" said Aemi, as he irritably fought off Marcus's flailing arms. "You could fight on both sides equally, couldn't you, being an Italian with Roman citizenship?"

"Aemi, don't!" said Caesar quickly, sensing trouble ahead.

"There's no question, I would fight for Rome," Marcus retorted, his face reddening with anger.

"Yes, all right, I'm sorry," Aemi apologised. "It's just that you're in such a strange position, having loyalty to both sides, as it were. I wouldn't want to be in your boots. I'd hate that."

"Well I do hate it and you making nasty comments doesn't help either," said Marcus angrily. "There's plenty of Italians with and without Roman citizenship that are against the war, you know. The only thing it will do is to tear this country apart; turn brother against brother, cause widespread famine and thousands of people will die, on both sides!"

Caesar breathed a sigh of relief as they reached the Servian Gate, one of the seven entrances into the city, through the Servian Walls, the ancient fortifications that encompassed Rome. He could see that the Campus Martius was a hive of activity, full of groups of men undergoing training in preparation for joining the legions that would go to war against the Italians. This at least should stop his friends from bickering for a while.

As they made their way towards the stables, they were passed by a century of legionaries, formed into ten sections of eight men abreast, marching as one, with the training centurion screaming orders to "Keep the distances between the ranks", and "Hold those Pilia straight!"

Caesar felt a tingle of pride and excitement run down his spine as he watched the century march past. His whole being cried out that this was what he was meant to do; to be a part of the greatest fighting machine in the world. To conquer new territory - to increase the Empire until Rome had dominated the world.

The tramp of eighty pairs of sandalled feet hitting the dirt made the ground tremble underneath him, the dust kicked up by so many feet swirling in front of his face, sticking to his skin and clothing in this sweaty heat. The faces of the men were set in concentration, lines of sweat running down their necks from underneath the shining bronze helmets that were strapped to their heads. The mass of red plumes on the top wriggled and waved with the motion of the wearer, and the clinking of the metal and leather overskirt that protected the lower part of the body sounded like a metal drum beating to the rhythm of the marching men, whilst the centurion paced up and down beside the ranks, picking at individuals who were out of step or getting too close to the man in front. This was the life Caesar longed for, and it could not come quick enough for him.

As the last line of legionaries marched past, the boys wiped the dust from their eyes, and gazing longingly at the retreating backs of the soldiers, continued on their way.

They were met at the stables by one of the riding instructors called Hinder. Originally from Gaul, Hinder had served in the auxiliary cavalry unit attached to Marius's Ninth legion, and had seen action in both Africa and Gaul, before retiring from the legions and taking up a post as riding instructor to the noble youths of Rome. Caesar was a favourite of Hinder because of his excellent riding skills, and the boy thrived under his tutelage.

Hinder greeted the boys warmly, and, after sending the others off to get their ponies ready, he walked with Caesar to the stable where his pony stood waiting.

"Athos has been waiting for you all morning," Hinder said, patting the head of the pony affectionately. "He is keen to work, I think he smells war in the air and he wants to join the legions!"

"I think you are right, Hinder," said Caesar, gently stroking the soft white coat of his beloved pony. "Is there much more recruiting to be done before the army is ready?"

"We have one legion all ready to leave, which will go out under the command of Pompeius Strabo when he returns from Picentum with more recruits, and Pompeius Lupus has taken five legions, which will make up the Northern Army. Unfortunately for Lupus, he has Quintus Servillius Caepio as his junior commander, much good that will do him." Hinder grunted in disapproval.

"Isn't Caepio very good then?" Caesar asked.

"The only thing Caepio could command is a field of goats! The command should have gone to Gaius Marius, in my humble opinion. He is the only general Rome has that is capable of ending this war quickly. I hear the Consul, Publius Rutilius Lupus, has offered Marius a post as senior legate to Caepio. What an insult to the dignitas of a man such as Marius! I tell you, Gaius, if the Senate keep allowing the personal feuds of senators to get in the way of what is right for Rome, then the gods help us, is all I can say, boy." And still muttering under his breath, Hinder ambled off.

Marcus appeared, leading his pony, followed by Aemi. The boys mounted up and trotted away towards the riding area. They hadn't gone far when Aemi groaned.

"Oh, no!"

Marcus rode up alongside. "What's the matter?"

"Look, over there, it's Catalus Caesar. That's all we need."

Catalus Caesar was the eldest son of the senator, Quintus Lutatius Catalus Caesar, archenemy of Gaius Marius. The son followed his father's footsteps, and was the sworn enemy of young Marius, the only son of Gaius Marius, and to Marcus, as Marius's nephew. Catalus Caesar had just turned fifteen and was now considered a man in Roman society. He stood among his group of friends wearing his new, plain white Toga Virilis of manhood, chatting and laughing loudly. As though he sensed his prey's arrival, Catalus Caesar turned round and watched the three boys riding past. The laughter was exchanged for a sneer, which slowly spread across his handsome Patrician features.

Caesar realised that a confrontation was inevitable and he quickly turned his pony and rode back next to Marcus. "Remember what Uncle said, Marcus," he warned. "Next time you get into a fight with Catalus and his mob you will be in serious trouble. Just ignore them. Don't let them rile you."

"Caesar's right, Marcus," Aemi added. "We can't help you if you get into another fight. My father threatened to have me whipped if I go home with one more ripped tunic and a bloody nose!"

"I didn't ask you to help me last time, did I?" Marcus retorted.

"No, but you're our friend, and we stick together." Caesar replied.

They urged their ponies faster past the group. Caesar prayed that they would get by unmolested, but it wasn't to be.

"Ah, look, boys, there goes the little Italian wildcat!" Catalus drawled. "He wants to be so much like his uncle Marius; another lump of Italian muck for Romans to tread into the ground!"

His friends giggled, and a young boy, aged about eight, called out, "Hey, Italian! Isn't it time you left Rome to join your traitorous relatives back in Arpinium? They will need a hand building their defences before our legions come and smash the lot of you to pieces!"

There was more laughter from the group, and Caesar's heart sank as he saw the look on Marcus's face.

"Who are you to talk like that to me, you little worm!" Marcus shouted back angrily as he pulled his pony to a halt.

"Who am I? Can't you tell a Roman of noble birth when you see one?"

"I have seen more nobility in my cows back home, and they don't smell half as bad as the stench from you!"

"Marcus. Enough!" Caesar warned.

"Try and control your little Italian friend, Gaius Julius," Catalus Caesar called out. "We know he's your pet Italian, but honestly, a Patrician nobleman must learn to rise above the common masses. After all, you will be in charge of men like him one day. It doesn't pay to be friends with those people, you know, especially as they have proved themselves to be traitors!"

Caesar refused to be drawn into the argument and ignored the jibe, but Aemi could not resist.

"Shut your mouth, Catalus!"

Caesar threw him a look of frustration. The last thing they needed was for Aemi to join the argument as well.

"Make me!" said Catalus. "Or would you prefer to set your Italian on to me?"

"I do what I choose. No one tells me what I can and can't do. I am no Roman's lapdog!" shouted Marcus, sliding quickly off his pony and walking towards Catalus Caesar.

"Ooh, look, the little Italian is angry! What are you going to do, boy, murder us like your traitorous countrymen murdered hundreds of innocent Romans?"

Caesar leapt off his pony and joined Marcus. He didn't know what he could do to prevent the argument escalating but he might be able to hold him back from lashing out.

"They were innocent, but you aren't!" Marcus replied, clenching his fists whilst his face turned red with barely controlled anger.

The young boy who had shouted out, stepped forward in front of Catalus Caesar, as Aemi leapt from his pony and joined his friends.

"My father says he is going to wipe you stinking Italians off the face of this country for what you've done!"

"Your father? Another Roman full of wind, is he?" taunted Marcus.

Caesar moved between the two of them and turned to Marcus. "Please stop now, before this goes too far," he pleaded, but the young boy was not about to back down in front of his friends.

"My father," he said, stepping around Caesar and puffing out his chest proudly, "is Quintus Servillius Caepio, junior commander with the Northern army, and he will wipe every Italian traitor off the face of this world!"

Marcus laughed. "Caepio, is it? Yes, Uncle told me all about him. He says he couldn't round up a pen load of chickens, let alone control a legion. The first sign of trouble and he'll come running back to Rome."

"My father is a great officer! The Senate gave him a senior post in this war. What has your uncle been given? Nothing! Nothing, because he is a has-been; an old, useless bag of wind that lives in the past. My father will be ten times the soldier Gaius Marius has ever been, or ever could be," young Caepio boasted.

"If you weren't such a little runt, I'd smash your face into the dirt and make you eat those insults!"

"The Italian boy is making threats now, is he?" said Catalus Caesar, stepping forward.

Caesar felt the sharp dig of an elbow, as Catalus pushed him out of the way to come face to face with Marcus. Peering down his large roman nose, his beady black eyes jeered in contempt. "Threatening little boys is all you can manage, is it?"

Instinctively, Caesar and Aemi took hold of Marcus's arms at the same time.

"Marcus, come on now, we have training to do," Caesar said firmly, knowing that his friend had been pushed too far and was likely to explode.

But Marcus was not going to back down now. "You think you're so much better than me, don't you, Catalus?" Marcus spat, pulling his arm away from Aemi. "You think you are such a man, showing off in your new white toga. Let's see how much of a man you really are!" And twisting out of Caesar's grasp, he lunged at Catalus.

Taken by surprise, Catalus was pushed backwards as Marcus clung onto his toga for all he was worth. Young Caepio, however, was behind him, and couldn't move out of the way in time. Catalus and Marcus barged into Caepio and lost their balance, falling heavily and crushing him beneath them.

There was a loud crack, and Caepio screamed in pain. "My leg! My leg!"

Caesar and Aemi leapt into action and tried to grab hold of Marcus to pull him away, but three of Catalus Caesar's friends intervened and pulled them off, whilst the others stood round, shouting their support for their friend.

Caesar saw Aemi throw a punch, as he twisted out of the grip of his own assailant. Catalus roared with rage and rolled off Caepio, dragging Marcus with him. Marcus continued to hold on tightly and they rolled around the floor in a tussle. Caesar and Aemi once more attempted to wrestle Marcus from the fight, but were forced back by the flailing arms and legs, whilst Caepio continued to scream in agony.

The sound of the shouting boys drew the attention of some young cadets who were standing a short distance away. One of them, a short stocky blond, rushed over to the group, and, pushing his way through, he grabbed Marcus and hauled him off Catalus. "Let go. Let him go!" he commanded Marcus, who was still clinging to the folds of Catalus's toga.

Marcus released his grip, and the cadet dumped him unceremoniously onto the ground. Marcus lay panting in the dust and was immediately joined by Caesar.

"Now look what you have done!" Caesar hissed angrily, as he watched the young cadet pull Catalus up onto his feet. "You are going to be in so much trouble for this, Marcus. Uncle will not be pleased."

Marcus scowled and shoved Caesar's hand from his shoulder, but Caesar knew that once the anger subsided, Marcus would realise the serious implications of what he had done. Caesar looked around for Aemi, as the young cadet turned his attention to the screaming Caepio.

Aemi, who had been involved in a tussle of his own, was busy wiping away the blood dripping from his nose. Caesar beckoned him over, but his attention was drawn back to the young cadet who was speaking to another of his group who had joined them.

"Just be quick about it, the child is losing blood."

Caesar looked at young Caepio and saw that a small dark patch was oozing from under his leg. He groaned inwardly as he realised the boy was seriously injured.

"Ah well, now, if he is bleeding, perhaps the slaves could sort him out, otherwise my toga will get blood on it, and it is terribly hard to remove a bloodstain, you know," the young man said, with a look of distaste.

"By the gods, Cicero. The child is hurt and all you can think about is getting your toga bloody! You will be covered in the stuff once we fight with my father's legions." The cadet retorted angrily.

"I would sincerely hope that is not the case, Gnaus," Cicero replied, with a look of distaste on his face. "I am appointed as a clerk only, on this expedition, and I should be well away from any fighting. I am not a warrior but a man of letters. I do not do killing!" he said huffily.

Caesar could not help but smirk in scorn at this pompous young man, whose high pitched voice pierced the din of young Caepio's cries of anguish, and the excited chatter of the boys around them. The young cadet he recognised as Gnaus Pompeius, son of the renowned General of the same name.

Pompeius looked at his friend with a frown and then a grin spread slowly across his face, revealing his perfect white teeth. He gave him a slap on the back and laughed aloud.

"All right, Cicero, go and do what you do best. Organise the slaves and a long board to carry the lad on, and be quick about it or he is likely to bleed to death."

Young Caepio, whose cries had reduced to mere sniffles, burst into tears after hearing this assessment of his injuries.

Aemi joined his friends, and Caesar took off his necktie and handed it to him.

"So much for staying out of trouble," he said scornfully, as Aemi held the rag to his nose to staunch the blood.

Catalus Caesar meanwhile had been busy brushing the dirt off his toga, a dark scowl on his face, his dignity in tatters and his new toga, to his dismay, torn on one side. "My toga! Look what that filthy Italian brat has done to my toga," he spat at Marcus.

"Come on, up you get, it's time we left," Caesar said, getting to his feet and pulling Marcus up with him. He had no intention of giving Marcus the opportunity to start another fight.

Gnaus Pompeius now turned his attention to Catalus. "So what were you two boys fighting over?" he asked, looking at Marcus, who was brushing the dust off his tunic.

"Boys? Boys! I am no child, Gnaus Pompeius," said Catalus, mortified. "Can you not see that I wear the toga of manhood? I left my childhood behind over two days ago, and I thank you to accord me the respect adulthood gives me!"

Caesar saw the flash of amusement in the cadet's eyes as Catalus spoke. It was apparent that they knew each other, and Caesar sensed that the cadet did not have much time for Catalus.

"All I saw, Quintus, was two *boys* scrapping on the ground. You may be wearing your Toga Virilis but I do not see anything manly in your behaviour. You were fighting with a child! If you wish to be treated with respect like a man, then you had better start behaving like one."

This retort clearly stung Catalus Caesar, who went red with embarrassment.

"So," continued Pompeius, turning to Marcus, "who is this young 'Italian brat', was it?" and grinning, he offered Marcus his hand.

"My name is Marcus Marius Gratidianus, and I may be an Italian but my family have had citizenship for generations, which makes me as Roman as he is!" said Marcus, glaring at Catalus.

"Marcus Marius you say?" Pompeius replied. "Any relation to Gaius Marius?"

"He is my uncle," Marcus answered, puffing out his chest with pride.

"So that is where you get your fighting spirit from." Pompeius laughed. "It takes guts to fight someone older and bigger than you, and win too, by the looks of things."

"He did not win!" Catalus Caesar cried. "I was caught off guard, that was all, and I was about to get the better of him when you stopped me."

"Mmm. Well then, I would like to see what you look like when you lose a fight," said Pompeius. "Anyway, you two," he said, turning serious once more. "Your little argument has cost a young boy a very nasty broken leg. I shall have to report this incident to the training officers, who will no doubt have plenty to say to both of you. You had better come with me."

"I am not going anywhere!" Catalus Caesar said haughtily. "I did not start this fight and it is not my fault Caepio has a broken leg. It was that animal, there, that caused all this. He is the one you should be reporting, not me!"

"Whom are you calling an animal?" said Marcus, and he leaped forward towards Catalus as though to strike him again. Pompeius grabbed the back of Marcus's tunic and held him fast.

"I didn't start anything," Marcus ranted. "It's him!" He lashed out at Catalus but was held too tightly by Pompeius to make contact. "Every time he sees me, he makes comments about my family and friends, calling us Italian scum. Him and his bunch of boot lickers."

"Is this true?" Pompeius asked Catalus.

"I have merely pointed out, on one or two occasions to the boy, that being an Italian is not very popular round here at the moment," Catalus replied haughtily.

"Is that so?" Pompeius said ominously. "I am Italian, as is my father."

Caesar almost laughed out aloud as he saw Catalus squirm with embarrassment. As much as he wanted to get Marcus away to prevent any further arguments, the air of authority that Pompeius displayed fascinated him.

"Ah, yes, well, of course, I didn't mean you or your family, Gnaus, I mean, you are from an old, established family who have always shown themselves loyal to Rome," Catalus grovelled.

"My family have shown no more loyalty to Rome than the Mariians, and their family are as old and as established as mine. It would be true to say, would it not, that Gaius Marius has indeed attained a status unparalleled by any Roman."

"Yes... No... Well, it was not Gaius Marius I referred to, so much as his nephew there. His father is a common corn merchant and it's his sort that is responsible for causing this war, not families like yours," said Catalus, desperate to dig himself out of trouble.

"How can you be certain that this boy's father has anything to do with the Italian rebellion? Thousands of Italians are as appalled at what has happened as Romans," Pompeius continued.

It was apparent to Caesar that Catalus had realised he could never win this argument, for he made no reply.

"Good. I will take your silence to mean that you agree with me then," said Pompeius, smiling once more. "Now I want you to shake hands like men, and let's have no more of this unseemly behaviour. Understood?" he commanded.

Neither Marcus nor Catalus made any move to shake hands, until, seeing the look on Pompeius' face, Catalus stepped forward.

"As the man in this situation," said Catalus, standing up tall and straightening his ripped and dirty toga, "I will offer my hand to you, Marius, as a token of peace between us. Do you accept?" he asked, holding out his hand.

Marcus made no move to accept it, but Caesar prodded his friend in the back and whispered, "Do it, Marcus. Please!"

Marcus stepped forward and lightly shook the hand of Catalus, before turning and walking away to where his pony stood waiting. Caesar and Aemi followed and collected their ponies, which were grazing happily nearby.

"We'd better go back to the stables so that you two can clean ourselves up," Caesar said dryly, as he put the reins back over his pony's head.

The rest of the group now split up and went off in different directions, but Pompeius came over to Caesar and his friends.

"You put up a brave fight, boy," Pompeius said, smiling broadly.

Marcus grinned sheepishly.

"I am Gnaus Pompeius, of Picentum. Pleased to make your acquaintance, Marcus Marius Gratidianus. I hope that when you come of age you will look me up; I could do with men of your courage in my legion."

"Thank you, sir."

"I will, of course, have to report this incident, but I shouldn't be too worried. After all, as Catalus is so keen to be recognised as the adult in this situation, he can take the responsibility for it. So, who are your friends, Marcus?" Pompeius asked, looking at Aemi and Caesar.

"This is Marcus Aemilius Lepidus, and Gaius Julius Caesar."

"Pleased to meet you both," said Pompeius, shaking each hand in turn. "Are you boys looking forward to joining the legions in a few years' time?"

"Oh yes, sir," Aemi said enthusiastically.

"Well, that is commendable, Marcus Lepidus. I am sure you'll do just fine," Pompeius said kindly. "And you, Gaius Julius? Is it to be the legions for you too?

Throughout the confrontation with Marcus, and Gnaus Pompeius's intervention, Caesar had been watching this young cadet with a mixture of admiration and jealousy. He was living the life Caesar ached for; the life that Caesar knew, deep inside, he was destined for. The need to impress this young man proved too great.

"Oh, I shall be a great commander of our legions, one day. I will be a greater general than my Uncle Marius, and men shall say I was the greatest Roman there ever was."

As soon as the words came out of his mouth, Caesar could have died of embarrassment. He blushed to the roots of his pale blond hair and could not look Gnaus Pompeius in the face.

Pompeius raised an eyebrow in surprise and then he smiled and patted Caesar on the shoulder. "Well then, we shall no doubt meet on the field of war as competitors, because, young friend, I have already marked myself out to be the greatest of men. I look forward to watching your progress."

"I look forward to that day too," Caesar replied, all shame forgotten, as he took the challenge of this cadet head on, without a trace of humour in his face.

Pompeius looked down at Caesar and frowned slightly. "You know something; I truly believe you meant every word you just said."

"Indeed I do, sir. Indeed I do," Caesar replied. His dark eyes glittered with defiant certainty as he looked into the wide, honest, aquamarine eyes of Pompeius.

Pompeius laughed aloud, and, bidding them farewell, walked off to join the other cadets who were waiting for him.

The boys mounted their ponies and set off back towards the stables. Marcus and Aemi, thrilled that Pompeius had shown them such attention, chatted over their plans for the future, fighting in the legions of Rome.

Caesar rode slightly behind, deep in thought. He was angry with himself for having told Pompeius of his dreams for the future. It was something he had kept very close to his chest up until now, but there had been something about that young cadet that had prompted such a reply. In Pompeius, Caesar had seen everything he dreamed of being and he had felt a twinge of jealousy that this young man was closer to realising his ambitions than he was. How frustrating it was to be held back by age. Caesar hated being a child more than anything. He felt as though his life was on hold, waiting for the day when he would become a man, and he could begin to plan his future in earnest. Pompeius was there already, and now he had the war with the Italians to prove his worth and pave the way for future glory.

"One day," Caesar said to himself with resolute certainty. "One day, we shall meet, Pompeius, just as you say, on the field of war, and then we shall see who truly deserves to be hailed the Greatest Roman of Them All."

Two days later, Gaius Marius returned home from the Senate in a towering rage; his shouting could be heard in the schoolroom where Marcus, Aemi and Caesar, were completing their morning lessons.

Caesar exchanged a worried glance with Marcus, who raised his eyebrows and shrugged his shoulders to indicate that this was nothing to be concerned about. Marius was often in a mood these days and to hear him shouting was not unusual.

Caesar was directed to finish off his mathematical calculations by a single, pointed cough from the pedagogue, Alexander, but, as he picked up his stylus, the schoolroom door burst open and Gaius Marius strode in, his face looking thunderous.

Without a word he launched across the room towards Marcus, who was too stunned at his uncle's unexpected entrance to do anything. Caesar let out an involuntary gasp of fear as Marius grabbed Marcus by his tunic and physically lifted the boy out of his chair. Julia came running into the room, her face a mask of sheer terror.

"Gaius, no! Leave the boy alone. Please," she begged.

Marius took no notice of his wife as he dragged Marcus, screaming, by the hair, across the floor and out of the room without a backward glance.

Caesar and Aemi sat stunned, open-mouthed in shock at the violence used against Marcus. Neither boy had dared to make a move to help him, for their fear of Gaius Marius was too great.

Julia turned as she fled the room and ordered, "Stay here, all of you."

Alexander resumed his seat and, clearing his throat, he tried to draw the shocked boys' attention back to their books, but it wasn't long before he could see his efforts were in vain. He called a halt to the lesson for the day by dismissing the boys and advising them to go straight home. Caesar and Aemi hastily collected their things and made their way out to the garden.

"Do you think the lessons will be on tomorrow?" said Aemi, as he threw his bag over the garden wall.

"Perhaps we should stay at home until Marcus calls for us. Who knows what has happened to make Uncle react like this."

"It'll be the fight Marcus had. He said he'd not told Marius, and I told him he was an idiot. Better to confess, in my opinion; they don't seem to punish you as bad. I wonder how he found out?" said Aemi. "He was mad, wasn't he? I hope Marcus is all right."

"Mad is an understatement," said Caesar. "Look, I'll call for you tomorrow and we can see what happens from there."

Aemi nodded, and with a leap he cleared the wall and walked away across his garden towards the house.

Caesar had to find the slave that had accompanied him this morning so he made his way back towards the house, but entered the side door into the kitchen area. Usually a busy, lively place, the room was full of frightened-looking slaves, busying themselves quietly, as best they could. Caesar felt a cold feeling of foreboding spread like ice through his stomach.

The steward, seeing Caesar, hurried over. "Come, Young Master, you must leave now," he said nervously.

But Caesar was routed to the spot. He could hear screams coming from inside the main house, and he knew that they were made by Marcus.

The steward gently took Caesar's arm. "Come, Young Master, quickly now."

But Caesar refused to move and pulled his arm away. "What's happening to Marcus? Is he being beaten?"

"The master… he…" But the steward could not finish the sentence, unable to find the words.

"Did you see what happened after Marcus was taken from the schoolroom?" Caesar demanded.

"No. It is not important now. You must leave. Please," the steward begged, glancing fearfully towards the passageway leading from the kitchen to the main house.

"But that's my friend he's beating!" Caesar cried, horrified at the screams still echoing through the house. His shock had now been replaced by anger. He could not stand the thought that somewhere down the passageway Marcus was being punished by his uncle, and he could do nothing to help. "I must go to him."

"No, you must not. My master has the right to punish any person who lives in his house, for whatever reason. He is paterfamilias. His word is law. His actions are accountable to no man. You cannot interfere in his business, it is unseemly!" said the steward angrily, his hand now tightly grasping Caesar's arm to prevent him from leaving the kitchen.

Caesar knew the steward was right. As head of the house, Gaius Marius was the law. No one could challenge him and he could deal with any member of the household in any manner he saw fit. With a sick feeling weighing heavy in his stomach he accepted that there was nothing he could do to help his cousin, and yet, he could not bring himself to leave either. He remained in the kitchen, his eyes transfixed on the door that led into the house, and flinched at every fresh scream that he heard, powerless to help.

Caesar's aunt, Julia, suddenly appeared in the doorway. She looked dishevelled and her face, as white as chalk, glistened with the tears that ran down her cheeks. At first she did not see her nephew standing at the other end of the kitchen and she immediately ordered some of the slaves to fill a bowl with water and to fetch fresh linen.

Caesar gasped in dismay as he realised Marcus must really be hurt. Julia spun round and he saw fresh tears spill down her drawn face.

"What are you still doing here, Gaius?" she cried in horror.

"I'm sorry, Aunt. I came to fetch my slave to escort me home. What has happened to Marcus?" Caesar demanded, pulling his arm free from the steward and running towards her.

They met in the middle of the kitchen and Julia embraced him tightly.

"Your uncle has punished Marcus for his conduct on the Campus Martius." Julia sobbed.

Caesar felt the heave of Julia's body against his chest as she fought to gain control of her emotions. For a few seconds he drew comfort from their embrace, before Julia slowly released her hold, and moved back to look into the frightened and confused face of her nephew.

"He did warn the boy that next time he got into a fight he would be punished, but Marcus went too far this time. To break a poor little boy's leg; Caepio's son, of all people..." Julia's voice trembled with emotion.

"But what is so special about that boy in particular? Marcus didn't hurt him on purpose, Aunt Julia, and it was Catalus Caesar who started the fight," said Caesar, desperate to help his friend in any way he could.

Julia shook her head. "A letter arrived this morning from Quintus Servillius Caepio, the father. He is blaming your uncle for his son's accident, alleging that he told Marcus to attack little Caepio on purpose, in an attempt to bring his father back from the war. As junior commander, Caepio would have to be replaced if he left his army and returned to Rome, and he is claiming that your uncle orchestrated the whole thing so that he could be chosen as the replacement commander."

"But it is not true, Aunt!" Caesar cried in indignation. "Marcus will tell him what really happened. Let me speak to my uncle, I was there, and so was Aemi. We saw what happened and I will swear by all the gods that it was an accident. Marcus did get in to a fight, that is true, and uncle has the right to punish him for disobeying his order to stay out of trouble, but he never intentionally hurt Caepio. It was an accident, Aunt Julia, surely uncle will believe us?" Caesar pleaded desperately.

Julia shook her head. "I am afraid it is much worse than that, Gaius. Publius Rutilius Lupus, the Junior Consul, believes Caepio's version of events, and he has told your uncle that this sort of underhand behaviour will not be tolerated. My husband has been informed that, under the circumstances, he will not be offered any senior position in the northern or southern army, but the Senate may possibly consider giving him a position as a junior legate once the dust settles over this matter."

"But uncle is the best general Rome has ever had! They cannot treat him like this, surely?" said Caesar; aghast at the repercussions the fight had brought on Gaius Marius.

"This is the excuse your uncle's enemies have been waiting for, Gaius. They know that such a post would be an insult to his dignitas and that he could not possibly accept it. There are men in the Senate that would like nothing more than to see your uncle kept out of this war, and now it looks as if they have what they want." With immense effort, Julia pulled herself together, and letting go of Caesar, she dried her eyes with the back of her hand. "Gaius, you must go home now. There is nothing you can do for Marcus. Go home and do not come back here until I send word to your mother that it is safe. Do you understand me? If you come back tomorrow you could make matters worse for Marcus. You must do as I say. Promise me," she said urgently, and glanced at the door as she spoke as though she expected Marius to come though it at any moment. She hastily kissed Caesar on the forehead before turning away to organise the slaves, who waited with the basin of water and linen towels that she had requested.

Caesar had no choice but to leave and he summoned his slave with a resigned flick of his hand. As he walked over to the door leading out to the garden he heard footsteps running down the corridor and a second later a young slave girl burst into the kitchen.

"Domina! Domina!

One look at the girl's distraught face told Caesar that something awful had happened and, instinctively, he grabbed the door for support.

The girl ran over to Julia and grabbed her hand. "Madam, come quickly!"

"Marcus?" Julia gasped.

"No, Domina, not Marcus; it is the master. He has collapsed in his study. I cannot wake him madam. Come, come now, madam!" the girl pleaded, pulling at Julia's hand. But Julia stood immobile; shock and fear seemed to have stopped her ability to react.

"All the gods, save us!" she gasped. "No, not Gaius, please, not Gaius!"

Caesar felt relief flood through him as he realised Marcus was safe even though it was at the expense of his uncle's health.

"Madam, Please!" the girl let go of Julia's hand and ran back up the corridor followed by several slaves.

Springing into action, Julia hurried from the kitchen, and Caesar was suddenly left alone with his slave.

The screaming had stopped moments before, and now all that he could hear was the crackle of flames as the kitchen fire burned brightly. He suddenly became aware that he was in pain and he released his grip from the door, shaking his hands to bring the circulation back into his fingers. Caesar looked across the kitchen to the empty corridor and strained to hear anything that might indicate Marcus was safe, but there was only ominous silence. He would have given anything to be able to go to his cousin now, but he knew that he was neither wanted nor needed.

A hand on his shoulder made him jump, and he spun round to find his slave opening the door.

"We should go," he said softly.

With one last, longing look back towards the empty corridor, Caesar nodded and followed his slave from the house.

*Gaius Marius had suffered a seizure. Asclepios, the finest Greek doctor in Rome, doubted he would last the night but, true to form, Marius remained undefeated and amazed them all by sitting up in bed the next night and allowing Julia to feed him a little broth. He had lost all feeling in his left arm and his left eye remained partially closed, a physical part of the illness that would never fully heal. Asclepios advised Marius to take plenty of rest and so Julia dutifully packed the family off to their villa in Pompeii.*

A few weeks later, following Marius's collapse, Caesar sat with his mother in the dining room, after dinner, when a letter was delivered. He recognised the wax seal as that belonging to his Aunt Julia, and waited impatiently for his mother to read the letter, praying that it would bear some information about Marcus. Aurelia unrolled the small scroll and read in silence. When she had finished, she sighed and placed the scroll by her side.

"Julia has sent word that she is dispensing with the services of Alexander as he will no longer be required to tutor Marcus. She has asked that I make alternative arrangements for your education, Gaius. Yet another problem for me to sort out because of your disgraceful behaviour," she snapped angrily.

Caesar felt his heart sink at his mother's words. Not only would she not accept that he was in no way to blame for what had happened on the Campus Martius that fateful day, but she also held all three boys responsible for Marius's seizure, and now, to make things even worse, this letter implied that Marcus was no longer living with his uncle, for surely the pedagogue would have gone to live with the family in Pompeii until Gaius Marius recovered.

"Mother, may I still have my lessons with Aemi? I do not think his father has arranged a new teacher yet – at least, he did not mention it in his last letter," Caesar added hastily, for he had been forbidden from seeing Aemi.

"Marcus Aemilius is ordered to remain at home as punishment for his part in this awful matter. I do not know when you will be able to see him again, perhaps, never. The decision rests with his father," his mother snapped.

Caesar hung his head for he did not want her to see the bitter resentment on his face. As far he was concerned, they were the victims as much as Gaius Marius, separated indefinitely, and both he and Aemi uncertain of the fate of Marcus.

"You will no doubt be pleased to know that your uncle seems to be making a quite excellent recovery, no thanks to you and your friends. However, I did enquire after Marcus in my last letter to your aunt, and I am sorry to inform you that he has been sent back to his parents in Arpinium."

"Sent home? But for how long, Mother? Is he coming back?"

"Your aunt says that Marcus was sent away before they left for Pompeii. She does not mention when, or indeed if, Marcus will return to live with them. That is all I am able to tell you, I am afraid."

Caesar was crestfallen. His best friend gone without a word and not even the chance to say good-bye. He knew without asking that he would not be able to write to Marcus.

"I understand. Thank-you, Mother." He stood up and made his way to the door.

As he passed through the doorway, his mother called out. "Gaius, I am sorry. I know how much Marcus meant to you."

Caesar left the room without a word and went straight to his sleep cubicle, the only place he knew he would not be disturbed. He kicked the side of his bed in angry frustration.

"It's not fair. It's just not fair! I hate you, Gaius Marius, I hate you!"

# CHAPTER THREE

*"The long smouldering fires of an Italian war were now fanned into flame… all Italy took up arms against the Romans… for they were seeking citizenship in the State whose power they were defending by their arms."*
*(Velleius Paterculus, History, II,xv)*

## ROME: August - December 90 BC

*Senior Consul: Lucius Julius Caesar*
*Junior Consul: Publius Rutilius Lupus*

Gaius Marius sat inside his command tent, poring over one of many dispatches from Rome. The veins in his temples began to throb as he fought to contain his rising indignation, which only increased with the arrival of his senior legate, Lucius Cassius Longinius.

"Listen to this, Longinius," Marius growled. '*Obviously, the new Consuls may see fit to make certain changes to the command structure of the armies, and, whilst I know that you are continuing to do an excellent job in the north, I am sure you will understand that they will want to put their mark on events by making some changes…'* In other words, Strabo and Cato plan to take over command of the armies, just as I'm finishing all the hard work, and then they'll push me out of the way and claim the glory as theirs!" The injustice of the situation was too much and he slammed the parchment letter onto the table in a fit of temper.

"To be fair, Marius, Strabo has been in the war from the beginning, so he's not really muscling in on the action is he?" Longinius replied cautiously.

Gaius Marius looked up scornfully. "And what exactly did Strabo do? Got himself tied up with a siege in Asculum right from the start, and has sat outside its walls ever since, scratching his arse, the cross-eyed oaf!"

Longinius pulled a face but didn't comment further.

"How quickly they forget. It wasn't so long ago that the Senate was pleading with me to take command of the northern army, after both commanders were killed. 'We need you, Marius, Rome can't win this war without you, Marius', and quite right too. I'm the *only* one capable of turning this war around. Without me they don't stand a chance and they know it, even my enemies, though it would stick in their throats to admit it. And now the new Consuls will muscle in and take the glory, and you wonder why I'm angry!"

"Mmm, well, anyway, nothing is certain yet, is it? They don't take up office until January and anything could happen before then." said Longinius, as he sat down opposite his commander. "If you are replaced, then Sulla will be too. I expect the Consuls will divide the armies up between them. Don't take the changes too personally. It is their right to command, after all."

The mention of Sulla, one-time friend and companion, only served to anger Marius further. "Sulla!" he spat. "That snake in the grass should never have been given command of the southern army. What experience does he have? He's got too above himself this time, I can tell you, thinking he can get along without me holding his hand. He owes everything to me; I made him what he is and what loyalty have I seen in return? He's never once written to tell me of his promotion, or to ask my advice, though I am certain he needs it. No, he turns his back on me and simpers up to those bigots in the Senate who think being a Patrician is the answer to everything! Well I'll show him, he won't last long without me. Sulla will lose his command and then he'll come crawling back, begging for a legate's post, you see if he doesn't!"

Longinius made no reply.

The silence spoke volumes for Marius, who looked long and hard at his senior legate. He had long suspected Longinius of secretly holding Sulla in high regard, and he wondered if, like many other senators in Rome who had welcomed his fallout with Sulla, he saw him as a military rival to Marius. Did he secretly support Sulla's rise to power, for there was no doubt that Sulla's star was rising, and his military and political career was taking off.

"Did you want something?" Marius snapped, as he snatched another scroll from the pile and began to unroll it.

"I came to tell you that our supplies are expected within the next day or two..."

"By all the gods!"

"What is it?"

Marius could barely speak he was so incensed with rage. "What is it? Treachery! Betrayal! That's what it is, and from the one who owes me everything," he roared.

Marius felt all self-control leave him, as his fury knew no bounds. "I will kill him for this! By all the gods, I swear it. Sulla is a dead man when I get my hands on him." He jumped to his feet and slammed his fist hard on the table.

"Sulla? Why, what has he done now?"

"This!" Marius thrust the small parchment at Longinius to read.

"Who sent this to you?"

"It says 'a friend'. What does it matter who sent it to me? This may be a copy of the original letter but it's Sulla's words all right. Now I know exactly what that conniving snake is like. How dare he treat me like this? And he's obviously got a cosy little correspondence going with Cotta or he wouldn't be writing this...this... By all the gods, I'll kill them both..."

"Marius, you need to calm down or you'll give yourself another seizure!" Longinius warned.

"I am calm! This is war, Longinius. War between me and Sulla. There is not enough room in Rome for both of us, and he is going to be the one to go. How dare he do this too me?" Marius spat in fury. His face had turned a mottled purple and foaming spittle flecked the corners of his mouth. "And as for Cotta, he's family, and, I trusted him."

"But you can't be sure Sulla wrote the original letter that this was copied from, or that his correspondence with Marcus Aurelius Cotta is anything other than innocent," Longinius said warily. "It could be a forgery, you know, and perhaps someone is purposely trying to make you enemies, because together you form a formidable team. It might be a plan to have you and Sulla at each other's throats in the hope that Sulla would gain enough support to force you into retirement. It's what your enemies want, after all, isn't it?"

"Sulla win? Ha! Never in my lifetime. I could beat that cur with my hands tied behind me. A plan, you say?" said Marius, calming down enough to think straight. He paced the room for a moment muttering profanities under his breath as Longinius looked on warily.

Finally, Marius snatched the scroll back from Longinius and returned to his seat. "I shall make some enquiries to see if there is any truth in what you say. Cotta can be easily sorted, but, if I do find that this letter was written by Sulla's hand, then he is right in what he says; he is going to have to watch his back every minute of every day, for I swear to you, Longinius, Sulla is a dead man!"

Gaius Julius Caesar returned home unexpectedly, to find that, yet again, his instructions had been ignored, and his family was still living in the Subura. Far from engaging in the warm reunion that couples separated by time and distance enjoyed, Gaius Julius and Aurelia rowed constantly, and, between the arguments, an uneasy silence pervaded the home.

With his parents barely speaking to each other, Caesar became the object of his father's attention. Gaius Julius attended his son's lessons, questioning the tutor on his progress and examining past work that his son had completed. At the end of a busy week, Gaius Julius pronounced himself satisfied.

Caesar and his father rode together across the dry, dusty Campus Martius in silence, late one afternoon. Gaius Julius's attention was drawn to a team of auxiliary cavalry practising their military manoeuvres next to the huge parade ground, where several cohorts of newly trained legionaries were being drilled in marching order. The sound of the centurions bellowing voices echoed across the campus as they screamed orders at their men, whilst the great plumes of dust, kicked up by the galloping hooves of a hundred horses billowed and swirled across the plain, obscuring both men, and the city walls, from view.

Caesar took the opportunity of his father's silence to reflect on what had possibly been the hardest week of his life. He had not been able to relax once during the time they had spent together, their relationship being so formal through unfamiliarity on both sides, and this had led, at times, to feelings of bitter resentment that his father had forced his way into his life so abruptly. What Caesar hadn't bargained for, however, was that whilst he resented his father's interference, at the same time he had found himself driven by the desire to impress him. He wanted to show his father how clever he was at his lessons and how skilled at riding and swordplay he had become. Aemi had come closest to the truth when he said that all he ever strived for was to make his father proud of him, and Caesar now realised that this was what he wanted, too. He even found some sympathy for his cousin, young Marius, whose own father, Gaius Marius, was almost impossible to live up to or impress. For the first time in his life, Caesar was beginning to realise that to have love and respect from his father meant something, but when your father was a stranger, the task was made so much harder.

Gaius Julius glanced sideways at his son, and Caesar caught his eye. In that moment, Caesar saw the glimmer of feeling in his father's face, and a strange, warm sensation invaded his body. He felt his cheeks burn with embarrassment and pleasure, as he recognised the feeling as pride.

Gaius Julius smiled, and rode closer so that their bare knees touched. Caesar felt a sharp, tingling sensation as they made a connection, something he had never experienced before because there had been no physical contact from his father as long as he could remember. He bit his lip to stop himself from shouting with joy, "Look everyone, this is my father!"

As if knowing what his son was thinking, Gaius Julius stopped his horse. "I'm sorry," he said, placing a hand on Caesar's shoulder. "I know… I should have made the time, but …"

"It doesn't matter, Father. You are here now."

Gaius Julius nodded, and smiled.

Caesar saw that his father looked relieved, and with it came the realisation that he really did care for him after all.

"Will you stay in Rome long, Father?" Caesar broke the silence with the question that had burned inside him for the last few days. He crossed his fingers as he waited for the reply and prayed it would be the answer he longed to hear.

"I'm afraid I must leave quite soon," Gaius Julius replied, pulling up his horse and turning to face his son. "I could try and explain this in simple terms but you deserve better than that, Gaius. I see that you are an intelligent boy; mature beyond your years, so I will speak plainly,"

Caesar nodded. The sudden disappointment he had felt at knowing his father would leave soon was tempered by the pleasure he felt at this compliment.

"Do you remember last year when Gaius Marius was taken ill? Well, the same thing happened again a month ago. This time the seizure did not cause any physical harm to your uncle, but I believe it may have disturbed his mind to some degree."

"What do you mean, Father? Has Uncle gone mad?"

"No, Gaius, not mad, but he has changed. He is now extremely… paranoid. Your uncle believes that many in the Senate are plotting his downfall. He has very few men around him that he will trust; fortunately, for the moment, I am one of them, but for how long that will last, I don't know. He sees threats at every turn, and he's convinced himself that the man behind it all is Lucius Cornelius Sulla, who was once a close friend and legate to your uncle."

"I remember seeing Sulla, at Uncle's home, some years ago now. He is a strange looking man, isn't he?" Caesar pictured Sulla in his mind. A tall, athletic man, with very pale skin, a shock of unusual red-blond hair, and, unforgettably, a large wine-coloured birthmark that covered half his face.

Gaius Julius gave a wry smile. "Strange he may be, but I hear the women seem to find him extremely attractive. Anyway, someone sent a letter to Marius that was supposedly written by Sulla, and addressed to your uncle Cotta. It has confirmed his worst fears that Sulla has turned against him. The letter wound him up into a terrible rage. He swore to kill Sulla and anyone else he found to be conspiring against him, and I believe, in his current state of mind, that he intends to carry out his threat."

Gaius Julius paused and looked into the distance, lost in his own thoughts.

Caesar waited patiently, his imagination taking flight as he pictured Marius, dark and brooding, an imposing figure, thick-set and muscular, and Sulla, the golden man, tall and lithe, their swords drawn as they faced each other, light and shade, preparing for mortal combat.

Gaius Julius shrugged. "There's no reasoning with Marius; believe me I've tried. So, I returned to Rome as soon as I could find a reasonable enough excuse to get away. Putting anything in writing would be too dangerous, especially if it fell into Marius's hands, but your uncle Cotta needs to know that he is in grave danger."

"But surely, you have put yourself in danger now, Father? If Gaius Marius finds out you have warned uncle Cotta…" Caesar was suddenly frightened for his father's safety.

"I know, but it's a risk I'm prepared to take. I have to protect my family, especially you and your mother. That's all I care about; keeping you both safe."

"But how can we be in danger? What have we done?"

"You are safe enough for now, and will remain so, as long as your uncle Marius does not turn against me. If he did…well, it would be impossible to judge to what lengths he would go to destroy me. He's a very powerful man, even if he has many enemies, and with his mind working the way it does at the moment, who knows what he is capable of. That is why you must be moved away from the Subura before I leave again. You're not safe there; you are isolated from our family and friends who could protect you both if necessary."

"But, Father, people know us and care for us where we live now. They would not let anyone harm us, they treat us as one of their own."

Gaius Julius shook his head. "No, I'm sorry but I can't take that risk. It has to be this way, Gaius. I'm sorry that it's not what you or your mother wants, but there is danger in the air and I cannot go back to my legion knowing that I have not done everything in my power to protect you both. You do understand that?"

"Of course, Father," Caesar replied sadly. He hated to think about leaving his home and his many friends, but he also wanted to prove that he could be mature. "Perhaps one day, when this is all over, we could go back again, Father?"

Gaius Julius smiled, and placed a hand on his son's shoulder. "No, Gaius, this is a hard lesson for you to learn but one you may yet come to value. Whatever happens in life you never go back; only ever look forward."

Caesar nodded, reluctantly accepting the wisdom of his father's words.

"Now, enough talk. I have a horse that is itching to race back home for his feed," said Gaius Julius. As he shortened his reins his horse began to spin and prance in eager anticipation. "Last back to the gates buys the honey cakes for supper!"

And with a swirl of dust and a thunder of hooves, father and son galloped off across the campus.

Two days later, Gaius Julius returned home from a meeting with the Senate, packed his belongings, and bade a hasty farewell to his wife. He had been charged by the Senate to take new orders to Gaius Marius, and he was unable to say when he would return to Rome again.

When Caesar came home to find his father gone, he felt sadness instead of his usual feelings of relief. The few precious days they had spent together had changed their relationship for the better. Caesar had begun to see what kind of man his father really was, and just as his mother had once said, he was beginning to understand himself better because of it.

"So, they want to replace me as Commander, do they? Not Sulla, me! And who *exactly* are the men who voted for this? Come on, Gaius, you were there. I want names. I want the names of every low, rotten, double-dealing, treacherous swine in that meeting. Who voted against me?" Gaius Marius stormed as he paced up and down the room. His stomach was in knots and his head pounded dreadfully but he would not rest.

"Marius, please, listen to me. It was not how you would believe it to be. The decision of the Senate was purely based upon the rights of the Consuls to take command of the legions if they so chose, and admittedly there are concerns about your age and health, but nothing more, I swear," Gaius Julius Caesar said earnestly.

Marius whirled around and strode up to him, pushing his face barely inches away. "My age? I am still in my prime, man! I can still fight with the best of them, and as for my health, that's just an excuse to get rid of me." Spittle flecked Gaius Julius's face as Marius spoke.

"I'm certain that's not the reason for the Senate's decision. If you would just stop for a moment and hear what I have to say..." Gaius Julius pleaded as he wiped the spit from his cheek.

Marius grunted and continued to prowl around the inside of his command tent like an angry, caged lion. Who could he trust to tell him the truth? Gaius Julius was his brother-in-law, but he was also related to Marcus Aurelius Cotta through marriage to Aurelia. Was Cotta conspiring with Sulla, or was that letter just an innocent correspondence, as Longinius had suggested? He rounded on Gaius Julius, his eyes flaming fire.

"I am not ill, I tell you, and I will not have that used as an excuse against me to remove my command. *My command! My army!*" he thundered.

Marius had known his enemies would find any excuse to try and have his command relieved, but he had always had faith that his unsurpassed abilities as a military commander and the power he still wielded in Rome would keep him safe. Now he was faced with the ignominy of being forced by the Senate to retire on the grounds of ill health. His anger knew no bounds.

Lucius Cassius Longinius, who had been present throughout the meeting, intervened. "Return to Rome, Marius, and let them all see that you're not hampered by ill health and old age. Cassius could take up your case, or even Crassus Orator, after all, he spoke up for your appointment before, didn't he? They need to see you in person, Marius. Too many rumours have reached Rome regarding your health and all of them far from the truth, but you can't blame the Senate for thinking you should be recalled if they believe that you are incapable of command. Look, the new Consuls need to make their mark, and what better way than to take control of the armies and finish this war off once and for all!"

Gaius Marius rounded on Longinius, his face almost purple with rage. "That's just it though, Longinius, you oaf! You said 'armies', but it's not. It's only the northern army, *my* army they want to take over, not Sulla's, and we all know why, don't we? This is Sulla's reward for turning his back on me, and going over to my enemies. Well, I am not finished yet, I can tell you! Gaius Marius does not lose, and no one, *no one* tells me when I'm finished. I'm still the people's favourite. My army loves me; they follow *me*, not Rome. They joined in the thousands, just for the honour of fighting for *me*! I am the Third Founder of Rome, First Man of Rome, Consul an unprecedented six times, greater than any Roman who ever…"

His tirade ended in a splutter. Grasping his chest, his eyes rolling, he fell to the floor like a stone and lay twitching, his body in spasm, foam flecked on the corners of his lips.

Gaius Marius, the great man, was felled by the unseen enemy inside his own body.

# CHAPTER FOUR

*The die is cast. Alea jacta est.*
*(Gaius Julius Caesar)*

## ROME: January - June 89BC

*Senior Consul: Gnaus Pompeius Strabo*
*Junior Consul: Lucius Porcius Cato*

The market place thronged with daily life. Shopkeepers and stallholders vied for business, their sonorous voices rising above the chatter of the crowds to draw custom to their shops and stalls that were laid out with colourful wares, fresh food, and exotic fabrics from around the world. Animals stood tethered or crammed into small wicker cages in every available space, their individual voices blended in a cacophony of bleating and crowing, barking and mewing, that drew the little children to gaze in wonder and, more often than not, in mischief, as they poked and prodded the helpless victims. Friends and neighbours stopped to pass the time, exchanging daily news and gossip whilst their elder sons and daughters paraded in their colourful finery; peacocks and butterflies, fluttering and flirting with their potential mates, whilst in sharp contrast, household slaves, too numerous to count, blended silently and shadowy into the background, their daily chore to purchase the food necessary to feed their hungry masters, and children scurried and screamed their way round the best of playgrounds.

Through this melee, an old man limped. That he was past his prime was evident, with his sunken face and lopsided mouth, craggy and lined from years exposed to the sun, and his jowls and eyelids hanging heavy from age. Yet something about his stature drew people's attention. He had once cut an impressive figure, which could still be discerned if you looked beyond the shambling gait; the air of authority and invincibility exuded from every pore of his body, and his dark eyes blazed with an unquenchable fire for life that no amount of disability could ever dampen. The people didn't need to recognise the man to know that deference and respect should be offered, and they parted in silent homage to allow him passage. This man, however, was a familiar sight walking the streets of Rome, and there were few indeed who did not know his name, or that of his young companion, the golden haired apollo, that was always to be found by his side.

Following his second major stroke, Gaius Marius had been forced to return to Rome to recuperate. The seizure had left him physically weak; his left arm and leg partially paralysed and the doctors had warned that he would never fully recover the use of his limbs, but Marius was determined to regain his former health and strength, and would not contemplate defeat. Once he was strong enough, he had insisted on going out for a walk every day to strengthen his legs, and Caesar had been chosen, as part of the family rota, to accompany him.

At first, the people had looked on in sadness and sympathy as they saw what toll the illness had taken on their hero. When Caesar accompanied his uncle he had avoided their gaze, and tried to ignore the whispers, determined to do his duty, and his softly spoken words of encouragement, as Marius struggled to walk the cobbled streets, kept them both focussed on the job in hand. But, as the days and then weeks passed, the people began to take heart that Marius was slowly recovering. Each day he managed to walk a little further, and the dragging of his left leg became more of a pronounced limp. His courage and determination shone through and they applauded him for it. Now, Caesar could walk with his head held high, meeting and greeting the people as they came forward to offer encouragement and good wishes. He never ceased to be amazed at the reception his uncle received from the moment they set foot outside the house, and, what should have been a short walk, invariably took double the time as so many people wished to stop and talk.

As they walked through the market place, nodding and smiling to the many well-wishers of the day, Caesar reflected back on what had been a very difficult few weeks. Given no choice but to do as his family asked, what had started out as an onerous task for Caesar, and one he had very much resented, was now a pleasure and a privilege. Gaius Marius had done nothing to hide his dismay and irritation at his disability, and, at first, he had taken his frustrations out on Caesar at every opportunity. A wry smile played across Caesar's lips as he thought back to the number of times he had returned home after helping his uncle exercise and had pummelled his pillows with frustration, but, the angrier he became at this trial he had no choice but to endure, the more determined he was to see it through to the bitter end.

He glanced at his uncle and smiled, as Marius laughed and thanked a rather pretty young lady who had presented him with a small bouquet of flowers and a promise of prayers for his continued recovery. All things considered, he thought, the relationship with Gaius Marius was the best it had ever been, and more than he could possibly have hoped for.

As they passed through the market place and into a quieter side street, Caesar picked up the conversation from earlier in their walk. "Was it true that the People hailed you Third Founder of Rome after you defeated the Cimbi and Teutones tribes, Uncle?"

He saw the eager fire of victory in his uncle's eyes as Marius launched into the story of his triumphant return to Rome after this victorious battle, and he smiled to himself. It hadn't taken him long to realise that the best way to pass the time with his uncle was to ask about particular battles he had fought, or countries he had visited. Gaius Marius loved to talk about his achievements, especially his military conquests over the years, and there was no more captive an audience than Caesar, who soaked up every ounce of information.

As they crossed the Forum Boarum, it was clear that Gaius Marius was in need of a rest. He was walking very slowly now, his limp had become more noticeable, and he sounded short of breath.

"Let's find somewhere to rest for a while, Uncle," Caesar suggested, afraid that if they continued, he would become ill again.

As Gaius Marius made no reply, Caesar led him along a quieter side street, off the Clivus Publicus, and soon found an old stone bench.

Marius rested his head back against the cool, stone wall behind him. He remained like this for several minutes with Caesar sitting quietly at his side. Finally Marius opened his eyes and heaved a big sigh. "Old age is a terrible thing for a man like me, lad."

He hung his weary head in his hands but not before Caesar had glimpsed the utter despair etched on his uncle's craggy, lined face.

"My mind, *oh* my mind! It wanders from past to present, to places I do not know exist." Marius sat up and rubbed his face as though trying to wash away the torment he was feeling. He stopped suddenly, as though frozen in time, and his dark brown eyes glazed over, seeming to gaze into another, sightless world.

" Sometimes, I see things that are not even there… but yet… they are so *real* to me that I could reach out and touch them," he whispered, stretching out his hand and grasping at the air around him.

Caesar frowned, unsure where this conversation was leading, or if he was expected to say something reassuring to his uncle.

"This damned illness!" Marius cried angrily. "It has crippled my mind, Gaius, I am sure of it!"

Caesar saw that fire burned brightly behind those dark, deep eyes that now seemed to bore into him, searching for an answer to relieve him of this suffering. Marius dropped his gaze and turned away.

"Do you feel this way often, Uncle?" Caesar asked gently. To see him like this was distressing, for Marius had always been so strong, so in control; now, hearing this weakness admitted to him came as a shock.

Marius turned and glanced at his nephew, his eyes bright now with unshed tears. "Oh Gaius," he said, "I cannot bare it. I force my body to heal, that I can do, but my mind, how do I do that? At first, I thought it was just the illness making me like this and it would pass, but now…now I'm not so sure. It's getting worse, boy. Sometimes hours pass and I don't remember anything that's happened; A darkness covers my mind and I can't control it. Other times, it's just brief moments… it passes quickly, and most of the time I'm able to hide it from people… I have no control, *no control*!" Marius hid his face in his hands.

Caesar looked at the shrunken figure of his uncle. The strong, unshakable rock that was Gaius Marius now slumped on a bench in a back street of Rome, admitting his weakness and failure. Tears pricked the back of his eyes as this man he had grown to admire over the last few months, his military idol, fell, crashing from his pedestal, revealing a mere man, an old, weak, vulnerable man. Now, in place of admiration and adoration, Caesar felt pity and regret. Marius had seemed so big, so inviolate, as though nothing could touch him; overcoming crippling illness twice and never once contemplating failure. When Caesar looked at Marius, he had not seen the man; he saw an image of greatness, in his manner, in his achievements; he saw the greatest Roman general, the greatest Roman Consul. Gaius Marius was always so much more than a mere man, and because of this he had suffered from the jealousy and hatred of so many who would never be able to aspire to the heights he had achieved in his lifetime. What his enemies would have given to see the great man now: Broken, vulnerable, old.

Caesar looked away. He did not want Marius to see the pity in his face and he felt ashamed. He wished more than anything that he could have been spared this moment. He didn't want to see the Marius of now. He wanted to keep the image of the man he believed his uncle to be. Now, all the admiration, the wonder and awe he had felt was stripped away, and he would never be able to see him in the same way again.

Marius opened his eyes and sat up straight as though throwing off the pity and despair he had felt for himself moments before. "My mind still thinks I am twenty years old," he laughed. "I still have such a passion and desire to do the things of my youth. I need the army and the army wants me. There are still battles to be fought, Gaius; honour to be won. *That* is what I most desire. I have lived such a life and yet, there is still so much more I would do, if this damned old carcass would let me!"

Caesar felt a surge of relief as passion replaced pity in his uncle's voice to reclaim the fighting spirit of the man.

"Most people would be grateful just to have achieved a small part of what you have, Uncle," said Caesar. "Perhaps, if you stopped being so hard on yourself, you might find that all of this, confusion, is just part of your illness and you will recover and be able to do the things you desire once more. Perhaps it is time to move on, to do other things; let the younger men try and fulfil their destiny, as you have."

"But I am not ready to move on!" Marius snapped. "I still have so much to give to Rome, if they would just let me. All the military experience I have, and yet the Senate won't even ask my opinion on the smallest of matters."

"When you are better they may ask you to return to the campaign, Uncle," Caesar said, trying to give Marius something to hope for.

"No, they won't, not while they have Sulla and his cronies knocking me down at every opportunity. No, Gaius, I have to face it, it's over for me." Marius said bitterly.

"But, Uncle, you are still a senator. You have been Consul six times! Why not run for the office of Censor? That is a very high honour and you can still serve Rome, just in a different way, that's all."

Marius gave a hollow laugh. "Sit in the Senate to be mauled over by those that would have me exiled from Rome herself if they could! No, Gaius, I have had more than enough time in the Senate to know that my place is on the battlefield among my men. They talk straight; act straight. I know where I am with men like that. The Senate is full of self-serving imbeciles who would not know one end of a gladius from another, but if battles were won by talking then there would be quite a few superb generals amongst them." Marius chuckled at his own joke.

Caesar smiled.

They lapsed now into a comfortable silence. Marius appeared to have shaken off his earlier mood and now rested, preparing for the walk home.

Caesar sat quietly, thinking over what had happened and trying to make some sense of it all. Was Marius losing his mind, or was it just the after effects of the seizure causing him to forget things? One thing he was sure of, he could not bare the thought that one day, when he was old and grey, he would become bitter and twisted and full of regrets as his uncle was now. No, he hoped that he would die when he was at the height of the fame and glory that he was certain would be his one day, then history would forever remember him as a man in his prime and not as it would now record Gaius Marius.

"Old age brings with it regrets," Marius said suddenly. "You must make sure that you live each day as if it were your last. Always do what you believe to be right though others may try to persuade you otherwise. Be true to yourself, bring honour to your family, not shame, and above all else, have courage, boy. Even if you stare into the jaws of death itself, never give in to fear, for if you are a leader of men then they will look to you to lead them. You have a responsibility to your men, Gaius; without them at your back you are but a grain of sand in a desert. With them, you can be the wave that washes all before you. You have the army behind you, boy, and you will have the world at your feet."

"I shall remember what you say, Uncle, as I remember everything that you have taught me these past few months," Caesar replied.

Marius smiled. "Yes, I can see that you're a good student. You listen. You don't ask stupid questions. You show a level head and you put your point across well. You'll make an excellent advocate when you're older."

"Oh, no, Uncle, I do not intend to waste my life in the law courts. I intend to be a leader of men, just like you. I shall join the legions and conquer the world, bringing glory to Rome and the Empire!" Caesar replied enthusiastically, his eyes shining with excitement.

Marius's eyes narrowed as he looked at the boy. "I thought your mother said you were expected to become an advocate; that's why you're given special lessons. Is that not so?"

Caesar grinned broadly. "My mother can expect all she wants, but it's the legions life for me, Uncle. That is where my destiny lies and that is where I shall make the name, Gaius Julius Caesar, shine through eternity as the Roman of Romans!"

"Your destiny boy? What do you know of such things at your age?" Marius retorted.

Caesar's smile was replaced by a blush as he realised he had made his uncle displeased, but not understanding why. "It… is a feeling I have, Uncle. I cannot explain it; I have always had it. I know that I am marked out as someone… special, and, I believe my destiny is wrapped up with that of Rome."

Marius turned fully to face Caesar. "You are very full of your own importance, boy, for one so young. History records that exceptional men are few and far between. Why, I myself have achieved more than any other Roman or Italian ever has, and I doubt whether another such man will follow me for many centuries, perhaps never. What makes you, a mere slip of a boy, think you can come close to what I have achieved?" Marius growled.

Caesar hung his head in embarrassment. He realised now that his uncle had taken his dreams as a direct challenge to his own supremacy. He could have kicked himself for being so foolish.

Marius stood up. "Time we got going. I have business too attend to," he said brusquely, and started to limp slowly up the street. Caesar jumped to his feet and took his usual place by his side. They had gone a couple of paces when Marius stumbled slightly. Caesar reached out to take his uncle's arm but Marius regained his footing and pushed his hand away.

"I can manage!" he snapped, and limped on.

Caesar hung back slightly, sensing that the relationship between them had changed. He was used to his uncle's mood swings, and, ordinarily, he would brush his sharp words aside, but this time, Caesar sensed that there was more than just pain or exhaustion making Marius angry. Was he ashamed for admitting to his own weakness? Or had Caesar's dreams of glory touched a raw nerve? Whatever the cause, the closeness he had felt between them had evaporated in an instant, that afternoon, and he wondered if it would ever be the same again.

Back in his study, Marius poured a large goblet of wine before opening the large cupboard next to his desk and withdrawing a small wooden box. He placed it carefully on his desk and sat down. Opening his drawer, he took out a small bunch of keys, selected one and unlocked the small padlock on the box. He withdrew an old parchment book, and placed it down on the desk in front of him with a sigh. He had often wondered when this day would come, but he had never in a million years expected that the person too challenge his immortal reputation would be a cuckoo in his own nest.

Marius drank deeply and felt the warmth of the alcohol course through his veins. He thought back to over fifty years ago, when he was twelve, living in Arpinium with his family on their large estate. His father had taken him up into the mountains for a few days to teach him how to track wild animals. They had gone higher than Marius had ever gone before so that the air was thin and his skin burned from the bright sunshine. He had followed his father around a steep, narrow crevice and they had come upon a large eagle's nest, woven in between some rocks. Inside the nest were nine baby eaglets, scrabbling around, screaming for their parents to bring them some food. Fascinated by these scraggly, fluffy little creatures, he had approached the nest with caution, keeping an eye out for the adult birds in case they were close by and sensed danger to their babies, but he could see nothing in the clear blue of the sky. He sat down on the ground next to the nest, staring at the eaglets, and, to his surprise, one by one; seven of them scrambled out of the nest and clambered over his chest. The last two eaglets squawked angrily at Marius, lunging at him with their tiny beaks and flapping their flightless wings. Between them, Marius and his father had put each of the babies back into the nest and continued on their way, but upon their return to their village, his father had secretly gone to consult the local Sybil, reader of omens and seer of the future. As she spoke, her acolyte hastily wrote down the Sybil's words, to be recorded for all posterity. A second copy was later given to Marius's father, who had kept it hidden from his son. It wasn't until his death, many years later, that Marius had found the small parchment book containing the sibylline prophecy, and he had kept it under lock and key ever since.

Marius carefully opened the first fragile page of the book and read the fading, scrawled writing:

*Nine eaglets can I see,*
*By seven of them, you shall be,*
*Consul over mighty* Rome,
*More than any other man,*
*Greatest of them all, bar one.*

He turned to the next page, gently flattening out the course, dry, faded parchment.

*The eighth eaglet shall full grow,*
*And bring you pain and much sorrow.*
*Your end he will conspire to make,*
*Your very body try to break.*

And the last page.

*The ninth young eaglet, far behind,*
*From noble birth shall grow to be,*
*The greatest eagle of them all,*
*A hairy king of land and sea.*

Marius closed the fragile pages and took another sip of wine. He had been Consul six times now, just as the Sybil predicted, and he knew without doubt that a seventh would be his before his life was done. Over the years, as each consulship came and went, Marius had remembered these words, and wondered who the eighth and ninth eagle could be. He could only surmise was that both men would become known to him in his lifetime. He had an inkling now that Sulla could be the eighth, for no man living came close to being considered his rival, but the ninth, the greatest eagle of them all? Marius had often wondered who it might be, as the jealousy gnawed away inside him over the years, but, today, he was certain that finally, he had come face to face with the ninth eagle. Marius realised that Gaius Julius Caesar was the one. He had not expected the challenger to be one so young, but now the prophetic words made sense. Caesar was far behind in age and he was noble born, for the Julii clan were a most revered and noble Patrician family. But the words that sealed the usurpers identity, the words Marius had never been able to understand, now fell in to place. 'A hairy king' gave the ultimate clue to who this man would be, and it all made perfect sense, for the cognomen, Caesar, was derived from the Latin, caesaries, meaning hairy.

It had to be him; there could be no other. Marius felt it with every fibre of his being. He gulped down the last of the wine and stared into the flames of the brazier, set close by his desk. All he was, everything he had ever worked for was to count for nothing? His place in history usurped by a mere slip of a lad? There had to be a way to prevent this happening, to secure his reputation for all posterity. If anyone had the right to challenge his supremacy it should have been his own son, not the child of a lowly senator whose family had been slowly in decline for centuries until he, Marius, had given them enough money to regain the family honour.

No, Marius decided, slamming the goblet down hard on his desk. He was not going to let this happen. There had to be a way to stop the boy from having the opportunities that would one day allow him to be hailed the greatest Roman; if only he could think of a way to do it, after all, prophecies were not written in stone were they? Who was to say that if someone wanted to, they could change the outcome?

Marius decided to give this some serious thought. The boy could wait, for now, there was plenty of time to deal with him. First he had the eighth eaglet to deal with. If he was right, Sulla was a fully-grown eagle now, fighting for supremacy of the sky, and Marius was not about to sit back and watch the second part of the prophecy become fulfilled. A slow smile spread across his craggy features. He might never get the opportunity to take to the battlefields again; to fight for the glory of Rome, but there was one battle he could still enjoy, a personal battle, his own to command, and this one he had every intention of winning.

Aurelia sat stony faced, staring into the dancing gold and amber flames of the brazier that helped to keep the cold at bay from the living room, as Marcus Aurelias Cotta finished reading the letter.

"He really is most insistent that you move, Aurelia," said Marcus Aurelius, meticulously rolling the parchment letter back into a neat scroll as he spoke. "Gaius insists that you leave here as soon as possible, and, he has instructed me to find a suitable home for you, unless you have already done so?"

"But, Uncle, we are happy here," Aurelia objected. She drew her luminous, dark brown eyes, reluctantly away from the tranquillity of the dancing flame and fixed them on her adversary. "We are safer here than on the Aventine. The people know us and look after us. My husband does not understand. How can he, when he hasn't spent more than six months with his family in the last twelve years? This place, like it or not, is my home."

"I try to understand your reluctance to leave, Aurelia, I really do," Marcus Aurelius spoke kindly, "But you were given this insula as part of your dowry, to run as a business and to give you some personal income, not to *live* in. Why you chose to dwell in this god-forsaken place the family has never understood. No-one *chooses* to live in the Subura, Aurelia, especially not someone of your social standing, and, I might add, it does not reflect well on the family. These people are not of your class; they do not have your status or your breeding. You always said that moving here was a temporary measure until your business was running smoothly, well, that was twelve years ago and you are still here, and now, from the looks of things, refusing to move out. You really do not have much choice, Aurelia. Your husband has been far more understanding than you deserve, in my opinion, and it is time for you to recognise that, as Paterfamilias, he is right to insist that you do as he asks. You cannot defy him any longer. You are not an independent woman and you must do as he requests, or I fear for the consequences, I really do."

"Paterfamilias! Humph!" Aurelia snorted. "I am more Paterfamilias than Gaius has ever been. I have to be both father and mother to my son, and will be to the child that I carry in my womb now. I might as well be a widow for all the time I have spent with my husband."

"You are expecting another child? Does Gaius know?"

"No, he does not. I waited until I was sure, and I haven't found the time to write to him," said Aurelia, blushing as she made her feeble excuse. She caught the frown on Marcus's face as she lowered her long silky lashes to hide the defiance she felt, and braced herself for further admonition.

"Then that is even more reason for you to move, and quickly. Gaius will never allow another son of his to be born here, and, you really should have told him, Aurelia. I am very disappointed in you. I can see that this move will do you good. You have spent too long on your own and you forget your place!"

Aurelia flushed at her uncle's rebuke and pursed her lips tightly to stop herself from saying something she might later regret.

"Aurelia, listen to me," Marcus Aurelius said, sternly now. "For too long you have been allowed to live the life of a woman not of your class. You are more a common landlady than a Patrician noblewoman. It has been unfortunate that your husband has spent so long apart from you, and this, in my opinion, has only been to your detriment, I am afraid. You have been used to a freedom that few woman of your social rank enjoy, and it is not healthy. Your removal from our society is just not acceptable any longer, especially now that you are expecting another child. Young Gaius will be a man soon, and he needs to be with his peers. It is important for him to mix with boys who will one day be his colleagues in the Senate. Now then, no more excuses, Aurelia. You have got to move from here and that is that. Your mother is willing to visit houses for you if you cannot bring yourself to do so, as will I. Gaius is putting his trust in me, Aurelia, and I will not let him down."

Aurelia knew that any further attempt at argument would be useless but the injustice of her position burned bright within her. Biting her lower lip to prevent the tears of frustration rising to her eyes, Aurelia fixed her gaze on the thin band of gold circling her finger; placed there on her wedding day by the man she had loved more than life itself. The ring, once the symbol of independence from her family and unity with her soul mate, now seemed to enslave her finger, as the manacles of slavery hung heavy on the wrists and ankles of those men and women subjugated to a life of servitude by mighty Rome.

"As you say, Uncle, I must do as I am bid by my husband, my master. I must leave the place I know as home; my friends, the kindness of people around me, and I must go to a world where I have slaves to do every little job for me so that I may spend my days sewing and weaving and having dinner and idle gossip with women I neither know, nor care for. I must adopt the life suitable to my status and forget the life I have had for so long, is that it?" she snapped angrily, feeling the weight of defeat hanging heavy on her shoulders.

Before Marcus Aurelius could reply, the door to the sitting room burst open and in skipped Caesar. The look on the faces of his mother and uncle stopped him dead in his tracks.

"Good morning, Uncle, I didn't realise you were here or I…Mother, is there something wrong; it's not Father is it?"

"No Gaius, your father is well, according to your uncle Marcus, who has just received a letter from him today."

"Your father is fine and he sends you his regards."

"Thank all the gods," sighed Caesar. "Does he say when he will be coming home? Has he been involved in any of the battles? I wonder…"

"That's enough questions for now, Gaius," Aurelia snapped. "Your uncle is not here for a social visit but has come to inform me that your father orders us to leave our home as soon as possible."

Aurelia saw the shadow of sadness creep across Caesar's face and instantly regretted her sharp words, for she knew that her son loved his home just as much as she did, and the news would be a bitter blow to his happiness.

"How soon before we leave, Mother?"

"As soon as I, or your uncle, can find a suitable house for us to live in."

"No more long faces now, please," said Marcus Aurelius lightly. "You shall have a wonderful new home to enjoy, Gaius, much nearer to your young friend, Marcus Aemilius, is it?"

"Yes, Uncle."

"And your mother will need the extra space soon, won't you, Aurelia?" he said without thinking.

Aurelia glared at him. She had not told her son that she was expecting a baby and she did not want him finding out like this.

Marcus Aurelius caught the look and smiled apologetically. "Well, anyway…a bigger house won't hurt a growing boy like yourself…" his voice trailed off as he ran out of words to cover his blunder.

Caesar broke the uncomfortable silence by asking, "Have you seen much of Gaius Marius lately, Uncle?"

"Yes, well, what was it you wanted anyway, Gaius?" Aurelia interrupted hastily.

"To ask if I could meet Aemi and go training?"

"As his father has agreed to allow your friendship to continue, I have no objection, but keep out of trouble," Aurelia warned.

Caesar didn't wait for any opportunity for his mother to change her mind. He quickly said his goodbyes before running from the room.

"That was a bit abrupt, Aurelia. Did the boy say something wrong?"

Aurelia sighed and leant back in her chair. The fight to stay in her home had drained her of what little energy she had left. The pregnancy was not going well and she was suffering from almost constant pain and nausea. "No, not really, but I don't want him asking awkward questions, that's all." she replied, subconsciously rubbing her stomach as she spoke.

"What do you mean?"

"It's nothing, Uncle. I would just rather he didn't mention Gaius Marius...It's complicated."

Marcus Aurelius looked intrigued. "Complicated? How so?"

"Oh, you know Marius, he can be very unpredictable... and he made life ...difficult for my son when he was with him. Their time together ended rather suddenly and I don't want him asking questions I would rather not answer." Aurelia answered evasively.

But Marcus Aurelius was tenacious, and was not a man to give up easily when he felt something was wrong. "Is there something you don't want the boy to know? I just assumed Marius was fit enough to do without Gaius now, and that was why I had not seen them together for a while."

"That is what I have told my son and that's all he, and you, need to know." said Aurelia, rather too abruptly.

"Oh come on, Aurelia, you cannot leave me wondering now, can you? So, what did happen then? It's obvious there is something you are not telling me."

Aurelia was too tired to argue and she knew her uncle well enough to know that he would never let the subject drop until he had uncovered the truth. "All right, I will tell you, but, it must go no further, Uncle, do you understand?" Aurelia cautioned.

Marcus Aurelius nodded in agreement and settled down in his chair to listen.

"The last time my son accompanied Gaius Marius on his exercise, something... strange happened, and the next day I had a visit from Julia, who told me that Marius said he had no further use for Gaius, and he was not required to attend the house any more. When I questioned Julia further, I finally got out of her that Marius said my son had ideas way above his station and that he would no longer tolerate his presence. If that wasn't enough, he insists that Gaius is to refrain from visiting their home. And that is all there is to know, Uncle. I have told Gaius that his uncle is well enough to do without him, and that he should stay away to give him some peace."

"I can't believe young Gaius would do or say anything to provoke that sort of response in anybody, Aurelia. Whatever is he supposed to have done? I take it you asked for an explanation?"

Aurelia looked uncomfortable. "Not exactly, but I have a pretty good idea what it could be," she sighed. "My silly son has the notion that he is going to be a great General when he grows up. More than that, he believes that it is his destiny to be called the greatest Roman that ever lived! He says he will be as great as Alexander of Macedonia. Can you believe the insolence of the boy?"

"Have you spoken to him about it? Have you asked him why he believes this?" Marcus Aurelius chuckled with amusement.

"Oh, believe me I have tried, on several occasions, particularly when he was younger. But he insists that he is meant for great things and neither I nor anyone else can change his destiny. Just where he's got this fanciful notion I don't know; it's certainly nothing I have put in his head, that I can assure you! The best I can do, and have done, is to advise him not to speak of it. That sort of talk will only cause trouble for the boy; you know how superstitious we Roman's are. So you see, my guess is he has said something along those lines to Marius."

Marcus Aurelius looked puzzled. "So, what you are telling me is, that you believe young Gaius has spoken to Marius of his aspirations, and, for whatever reason, Marius has got upset with the boy, and that is why he no longer wishes to see him?"

"Yes. I know it sounds stupid, but I can't think what else would make Marius say what he did," said Aurelia.

Marcus Aurelius shook his head in disbelief. "I cannot believe that the daydreams of a boy would cause a man like Marius to react in this way, Aurelia. There must be more to it than that, surely? Did Julia say nothing to enlighten you?"

Aurelia shook her head. "The whole situation was most uncomfortable, for both of us, and what could I say? If Gaius Marius has made his decision then who am I to argue, but…the more I think about it, the more I believe Julia knows more than she is telling me,"

"What makes you think that?"

"We all know how jealously Marius guards his reputation. How many times does he bring up the fact he was hailed First man in Rome, Third Founder, and all the other accolades he has been given throughout his career? He wants to be remembered as the greatest of Romans. Just look at how he treats Lucius Cornelius Sulla, now he sees that he could manage on his own. He derides him in public; constantly reminding everyone who will listen that Sulla only achieved so much because of the help he gave him. He regards Sulla as a threat and he doesn't like it. Perhaps, he sees a similar threat in my son. Marius will not stand having his reputation usurped from under him while he's still alive," said Aurelia.

"You are right in your perceptions of Sulla and Marius," said Marcus Aurelius. "Jealousy has been the cause of that friendship breaking down, there is no doubt. But I find it hard to believe that a man of Marius's age and reputation would consider a mere slip of a boy a threat to his place in history, for that is the conclusion you are arriving at, is it not?"

"I don't know what to think, Uncle, but I do know that Gaius Marius is not in his right mind. He hasn't been the same since the second seizure, so, who can say what is going on inside his head?"

"Now you really are stretching the point, Aurelia. Gaius Marius is as sane as the next man. I will not believe that he is in any way less sound of mind than you or I!"

"I beg to differ with you, Uncle. There are things you don't know. The last time that they were together, Marius admitted to my son that he wasn't as healthy in his mind as people would believe. Feelings of… confusion; not remembering where he is or who he is with, or even what he has said. Gaius was very upset by the incident and I think he suspects that the real reason he has been stopped from seeing his uncle is because Marius is too ashamed by his moment of weakness to see him again."

"I can quite believe that he would be ashamed, if that was the case," said Marcus Aurelius. " For a man of Marius's calibre to admit anything of that nature to a boy, well, I am more inclined to believe that is the reason for refusing to see the boy again rather than an unqualified belief on your part that young Gaius is some kind of threat to Marius."

Aurelia sighed. "Perhaps you are right, I don't know. Nevertheless, I am concerned for my son. If Marius is unstable, and he does have something against him, then who is to say what he might do in the future? My own husband is concerned enough about Marius to want to move us to a safer area, I know, because he told me so. And how you can be so calm, when you yourself are implicated in conspiring with Sulla against him? Wasn't that letter falling into Marius's hands somewhat responsible for the onset of another seizure? If Gaius Marius believes that you have now joined with his enemies, then you are not safe either."

"That letter was a misunderstanding, Aurelia, and as soon as Marius accepts visitors I shall be straight round there to clear the matter up. As for your husband's concerns, I am well aware of them, and, as he has seen far more of Gaius Marius than myself, I can only concede that there may be, and I stress, *may be,* some cause for concern. If there is something wrong with his mind, and I am not saying that there is, but, Gaius Julius must have good reasons for feeling as you say he does, then I think it best that we get you moved closer to the family as soon as possible, and you must keep an eye on your son. If Gaius Marius does see him as some sort of threat for the future then we should do everything in our power to ensure the boy is kept as far away as possible from his uncle. Only the gods know what your son's destiny will be, Aurelia, but we can do our best to ensure that Gaius Marius has no opportunity to change it."

"Lucius Porcius Cato is dead! When? How? This is superb news!"

Lucius Cassius looked at Gaius Marius in surprise. He had expected the news to be welcome, but his howls of laughter were verging on hysteria.

"He was killed in battle, just outside Corfinium, five days ago after the Italian's ambushed his legion." said Cassius, his silky, deep voice resonating around Marius's study.

"Splendid. Splendid news!" Marius sighed and wiped the tears of laughter from his eyes. "So, yet again this war has cost Rome a Consul. Dear, dear, they do fall thick and fast. I don't suppose Sulla has been killed too, has he? No? Oh well."

Cassius glanced at his colleague, Sulpicius Rufus, and pulled a face, taken aback by the behaviour he was witnessing. He had heard rumours in the Senate that Gaius Marius was unstable and suffered unpredictable mood swings, but now he could see it clearly for himself.

"Oh, I'm sorry, my dear Sulpicius, I didn't mean to imply that your cousin's death was welcome," said Marius with a lopsided smirk.

Sulpicius shrugged his shoulders but his narrow, shifty eyes, gazed thoughtfully through his greasy unkempt hair, as Marius paced up and down behind his desk.

"So then, my friends, what happens now? said Marius, rubbing his hands together in glee. "Are the Senate appointing a new commander to take over Cato's legions? This wouldn't be why you are here by any chance, is it?" he asked, smiling confidently.

Cassius glanced nervously at Sulpicius. This was something he had not expected. Their reasons for visiting Marius was to seek his backing for Sulpicius, who intended to run for a position as Tribune in the forthcoming elections for the Plebeian Assembly. They both knew that Marius held a lot of sway with the voting Plebeians, and hoped he would agree to use his influence to get Sulpicius elected. Neither had thought Marius would not know about Cato, or that the Senate had passed full command of the army over to Pompeius Strabo, the surviving Consul.

"Well?" Marius asked, looking at both men.

Cassius swallowed and spoke first. "The ah…the Senate has decided not to appoint a new commander, but to give full command to Pompeius Strabo."

Cassius saw Sulpicius visibly wince as he spoke, dreading Marius's reaction to the news, for his temper had become infamous since his illness.

"I see," replied Marius, his voice deadly calm, but the smile was gone from his face. "And Sulla? What about Sulla?"

Neither Sulpicius nor Cassius wanted to answer this question, both of them fully aware of the enmity between the two men. Sulpicius took the plunge.

"He, um, he stays as commander in the South. He has had some success in the battles he has fought and the Senate are pleased with his progress, so, he remains in command, for now at least."

"I see," said Marius again.

All three men stood in silence. Suddenly, Marius smiled and then began to laugh again.

"Cato dead! Excellent news. Best I've heard in ages. Good. Good," he chuckled to himself as he walked round behind his desk and took his seat. "So then, if you haven't come to give me command of the army, what have you come for?" he asked, indicating with a wave of his hand that they should sit down.

"I have a favour of ask of you, Gaius Marius," said Sulpicius, and he went on to explain in detail his intention to run for the post of Tribune.

Marius listened intently and when Sulpicius finished, he sat quietly for a moment. "All right, Sulpicius, you want my support, but what exactly is in this for me?"

Cassius nodded his silent permission for Sulpicius to continue.

Sulpicius began to outline his plans, but his nervousness caused him to ramble until finally Gaius Marius lost all patience. "Get to the point." he snapped.

"My point, Gaius Marius, is that vast tracts of land owned by these senators have been reclaimed by the Italians since the start of the war. Farms and vineyards have been destroyed, and slaves set free. Much of the property they owned is now wasteland and will provide no income until this war is over, the farms are repaired, and slaves return to the land. So, as that is not going to happen anytime soon, the unlucky senators have had to borrow money to keep afloat. Borrowing the huge amounts they are doing is illegal, and, technically, they no longer qualify financially to be eligible to retain their place on the Senate, which means…"

"Many of these senators are still members of the Senate House, although, the law says they shouldn't be," Marius completed the sentence as a sly grin spread across his craggy features.

"Now do you see where I am leading?" Sulpicius smiled. "I want to invoke these laws, and, in the process, much of your opposition will be removed once they are expelled," Sulpicius explained. "I am also in favour of extending the citizenship to all Italians, as I know you are, and I believe the time is right to put this to the vote and hopefully put an end to this war once and for all."

Marius nodded thoughtfully. "Yes, Sulpicius, you're right on both matters, but I can think of something much more important to me than that."

"Name it, and if it is in my power to give I would do so gladly, Gaius Marius," said Sulpicius with an oily smile.

"This involves both of you," Marius said, leaning forward over the table. "Sulpicius, if I get you the tribunate, I expect you to lobby the assembly to support me. Cassius, as a popular member of the Senate, you can rally support for me there too."

"And, ah, what exactly is it that you require this support for?" Cassius asked pensively.

"What I want," said Marius "Is total command of the army that will go east to fight King Mithridates. Full command. No sharing. My spies tell me that King Mithridates has seen that Rome has become weakened by this war with the Italians and he believes the time is ripe to strike out against the Empire. For years Mithridates has harboured the desire to claim back the lands that once belonged to his ancestors, but, until now, Rome has been too strong. The time is right for him to strike, for he knows he will never have a better chance of defeating Rome. It's now or never for Mithridates, and, I believe he will choose now. This will be the biggest war Rome has fought for years, and I intend to be the one to win it. I will support your laws, Sulpicius, whatever they may be, and I will give you whatever money you need to help to get the support for me from your fellow tribunes," Marius paused and looked thoughtfully at Cassius. "Cassius, I believe you have a daughter of marriageable age, do you have a husband picked out for her yet?"

Cassius shook his head.

"Then I propose an alliance between our families, your daughter and my son. I will give them a house on the Aventine and your daughter will be given money to provide her own income whilst my son is away doing his duty in the legions. Is that acceptable to you, Cassius?"

Cassius didn't hesitate. He had wanted to marry his daughter off for some time, but her rather unattractive appearance had not encouraged many suitors. "Very generous, Gaius Marius, very generous indeed. I would be delighted to see our great families united. You have my consent."

Marius smiled and relaxed back into his chair. "Good. If we're all agreed, that's settled then. Let me summon some wine and let us drink to the future!"

# CHAPTER FIVE

*"Men in general are quick to believe that which they wish to be true."*
*(Gaius Julius Caesar)*

## ROME: July - December 89 BC

Caesar and Aemi hurried through the crowds milling in the Forum Romanum, heading for the Temple of Saturn. Their broad grins and excited chatter only increased as they neared their destination, for this had been a day eagerly awaited – they were going to spend the morning with the Senate, as part of their education, and were to be chaperoned by Caesar's uncle, Marcus Aurelius Cotta, who was to meet them by the temple steps.

The Temple of Saturn was the biggest building in the Forum, with its imposing oblong shape, towering porticos, and shining white marble pillars and steep steps, representing Rome's continued good fortune, towering above all other buildings.

The boys ran up the steps two at a time until they reached the cool shade of the portico. Leaning against a pillar, they stopped to catch their breath, as they gazed out in wonder at the view below. Around the edges of the Forum were small stalls selling food and drink to the hungry businessmen and visitors. Shops built in to the sides of smaller temples and basilicas sold parchment, ink, stylus pens and wax tablets, among other essential supplies a businessman of Rome might need. Moneylenders, dotted around the Lower Forum set up small stalls where those in need of a loan could come and borrow money, for a fixed interest rate. Opposite the Temple of Saturn, the Tribunal housed the law courts, where the Praetors, the main magistrates of Rome, sat to conduct the business of the day. Outside the building people gathered waiting for their petition to be heard or to lodge a complaint. The daily business of Rome conducted at it's heart, surrounded by the magnificent red brick buildings and coloured marble and stone of the Temples, that people, from all over the empire, came to visit in wonder and awe.

Caesar soaked up the atmosphere around him. His spine tingled with the power and energy the people created as they went about their business. Here he was, in the very centre of the Roman Empire, where his ancestors had walked before him, and, where he would walk when he came of age, to join the Senate and begin the journey towards becoming a future governor.

"Look, Caesar, look over there!" Aemi exclaimed, drawing Caesar back from his thoughts.

He looked in the direction that Aemi was pointing and saw a group of six women walking slowly in single file through the crowds below.

"The Vestal Virgins." whispered Aemi, in breathless wonder.

The boys had never seen the priestesses before, and, as Caesar watched in awe, the voice of his old pedagogue rang in his ears, explaining the history and the meaning behind this most revered religious sect. The Vestal Virgins lived in the Domus Publicus attached to the Temple of the Goddess Vesta, which they shared with the Pontifex Maximus, the High Priest of Rome and overseer of the Vestals. They were keepers of the Sacred Flame that burned continually inside the temple. Legend said that if the flame ever went out then Rome would fall. The women were chosen from Patrician families from the age of three to ten years of age and it was considered a high honour for the family if their daughter was chosen to serve the Goddess. They remained a Vestal Virgin for thirty years after which they were free to marry and have children. Until they had served the Goddess for the required thirty years the Vestals were not allowed to have any form of relationship with men. Their virginity was sacrosanct, and if one was found to have entered a relationship with a man, their punishment was to be buried alive and the man publicly flogged to death.

And here they were, the living guardians of Rome's soul. Caesar watched their progress silently as they moved in solemn procession across the Forum. Dressed head to toe in white woollen robes with their faces veiled, the senior Vestal lead the group. The youngest, which Caesar guessed, could be no more than five years of age, was the last in the line and skipped along holding the hand of a slightly older girl in front of her. They passed by the foot of the steps of the Temple of Saturn below where the boys stood, and Caesar could not help but wonder if this was what the gods looked like, with their white robes shining in the sunlight, looking more ethereal than real women. Another flash of white caught his eye and Caesar saw his uncle appear out of the crowd to stand at the bottom step of the temple. His gleaming white toga with the deep purple border and wide stripe running down the front, indicating he was a man of senior senatorial rank, made him stand out from the crowd of multi-coloured tunics and togas. He saw the boys and waved at them to come and join him.

All thought of the Vestal Virgins left his mind as, with a beating heart, Caesar plunged down the steps to his uncle. Aemi struggled after Caesar, desperately trying to keep his toga from sliding off his shoulder as it had already done several times that morning. Marcus Aurelius had insisted the boys wear their best togas for their visit to the Senate House, and Aemi was having great difficult keeping the reams of fabric that were supposed to drape over his left shoulder, from falling down.

Marcus Aurelius greeted the boys warmly and without delay, lead the way towards the house, with Caesar and Aemi following one step behind, as befitted their status when accompanying a senator.

The Senate House itself was a rather small red brick building, set slightly back from the main forum area. Caesar was surprised that a building housing the greatest government in the known world should be so unimposing, but he kept his thoughts to himself as they climbed the white stone steps and stopped at the two huge wooden and bronze doors that stood as solid sentinels, guarding the inner sanctum of the seat of government.

Two guards dressed in red and gold livery, each holding a silver pointed spear, opened the doors. Several senators made their way up the steps and entered, some nodding at Marcus Aurelius as they passed by, one or two stopping for a quick chat.

Finally, Marcus Aurelius turned to the boys. "Now, remember what I told you. Not a word, not a sound out of either of you once the Senate is in session, and take one of these," he said, signalling to his slave who stood nearby. The slave handed each boy a small fold down wooden stool. "These are for you to sit upon," Marcus Aurelius said. "Now, when we enter, you will see the rostrum at the far end of the hall, that is where the Consuls sit; the Senior Consul sits in the chair highest on the rostra, the Junior Consul in the chair slightly lower down. As it is, you are probably aware that the Junior Consul, Marcus Porcius Cato, was killed in action a few weeks ago. His chair will be draped in black cloth until the elections next year. Our Senior Consul, Pompeius Strabo, is with his legions, and does not return to Rome very often, therefore the leader of the house for today will be the Princeps Senatus, Marcus Aemilius Scarus."

Caesar and Aemi nodded eagerly, soaking up everything that was said. Caesar felt little butterflies of anticipation fluttering in his stomach and he smiled nervously at Aemi as his uncle spoke.

"On the left and right of the hall are the stone tiers where we sit during the session. Those men on the bottom tier, nearest the floor, are this year's most senior magistrates. Behind them, on the second tier, sit senators such as myself, who have previously served as Consuls or Censors. Behind us sit the more junior magistrates, the ex praetors and aediles, and at the very back sit the most junior senator's, the ones who have yet to be elected into office but are now old enough to be a member. You two will sit at the back with these men, and, as I always sit on the left of the house, you two can sit opposite me on the right- so I can keep an eye on you both," Marcus Aurelius said with a grin.

"Now, the rules are very strict once the session is under way. Senior senators always have priority to speak first; the first three rows only are allowed to participate in discussions and debates. If a senator wishes to speak, he must stand and wait to be invited by the Consul, or the Princeps Senatus, if the Consuls are absent. If we are required to vote on an issue, then the Senior Consul present will ask the house to divide. Voting for or against will determine which side of the house a senator will go and stand to be counted. The entire Senate votes, including the junior men. It may be, as often happens, that a subject must be debated over several days. Sometimes a senator will be asked to take to the floor. This means that he may leave his place on the tier and come down to the open floor space in the hall so that everyone can see and hear them. If the senator wishes to speak formally and for some time, this then is called giving an oration. There are two or three renowned orators in the Senate at present; Lucius Licinius Crassus Orator, hence the cognomen, is my personal favourite. To hear him speak is beautiful to behold, so clear and precise; every word counts, unlike some who would claim to orate but in fact waffle on for hours until you forget entirely the subject under discussion," said Marcus Aurelius scornfully.

"Is there anything tabled for discussion today, Uncle?" Caesar asked eagerly.

"Apart from assessing how the war is progressing, I believe there is the issue of a new law rumoured to be tabled in the plebeian assembly next week, which has given the Senate cause for concern. Should be an interesting debate as it's about issuing citizenship rights to Etruscan's, though whether there will be any Etruscans left alive after the war is over is another matter." Marcus Aurelius said cheerfully.

"My father says most of the Etruscans joined the new State of Italia when the war first started, and he believes none of them should be awarded the citizenship as they are all traitors to Rome," said Aemi.

"Yes, well, that is your father's opinion, and no doubt the same of many other senators, but this is why we have debates and votes, so that the decision will be decided fairly…" Marcus Aurelius explained. He was prevented from speaking further by the sound of a gong resonating from inside the building. "The session is about to commence, boys, now remember what I told you, and don't attempt to leave the house until I come to collect you." said Marcus Aurelius over his shoulder as he lead the boys through the bronze doors.

The hall was filled with the deep voices of the hundred or so senators talking idly to each other as they arranged their stools on the appropriate tier for their rank. Marcus Aurelius nodded a farewell to the boys and pointed to where they needed to go, whilst he walked over to the left of the house, and, climbing to the second tier, placed his stool down in the space left empty for him. Caesar and Aemi crossed over to the right of the house and slowly walked up the steep stone steps to the very top tier, where they headed for the corner so that they could tuck themselves out of the way. They unfolded their stools and sat down.

Caesar looked around the house, eagerly committing to memory every little detail. The senator's now filled the tiers; all dressed in their white togas, and it was a sight to behold. He had never seen so many together at one time and they reminded him of a flock of swans, gathered together, happily chatting and laughing amongst themselves. He looked up to the ceiling, noting that the hall itself was remarkably light considering it had only four small windows almost twenty feet up above the floor. What daylight they let in seemed to filter down into spots of white light on the floor, the dust in the air reflecting and twinkling through the shafts of light, giving the room an almost heavenly feel. Around the hall large wall scones were lit, allowing a softer yellow light to contrast against the white daylight from the windows. His gaze travelled towards the far end of the hall. The floors and pillars were made of red and cream marble that had been polished to such a degree you could see your refection in them. The dais, where the Consuls' would sit, was a dark blue marble, which provided a stark contrast to the two brilliant purple and gold curule chairs upon it. Caesar's heart beat slightly faster as he looked at the chairs. One day, he thought to himself, one day I shall sit there. A smile of sweet anticipation played around his lips.

Aemi's fidgeting drew Caesar's attention away from the dais, and he continued to look slowly around the room. Placed around the hall at regular intervals, were large white marble busts on heavy ornate pillars. These were the images of the most prominent men of Rome, who, through the centuries, had helped Her to become the glorious empire she was now. Caesar could not recognise any of them, but they all had similar features of Roman aristocrats; the finely chiselled jaw, prominent cheekbones and large, straight noses, an expression of power, grace and wisdom on each face. The forefathers of Rome stared down through their sightless marble eyes on the future generations; stark reminders of the past glory that was Rome's, and guardians of Her future.

The last few senators were seating themselves into position as the large bronze gong, situated at the back of the house, was beaten once more to indicate the session was due to commence shortly. One young senator was making his way hastily up the steps to the back row where Caesar and Aemi sat. He squeezed past several senators that were already seated and put his stool down in the empty space next to Caesar. He smiled in welcome when he saw them and the two boys sheepishly grinned back but did not dare speak.

"I didn't know they had lowered the age for entry to the House," the young man whispered, in a friendly manner. "I am Quintus Aemilius Scarus by the way," he said, offering his hand to be shaken in turn by the boys.

"Gaius Julius Caesar, and this is my friend, Marcus Aemilius Lepidus," Caesar answered. "My uncle is Marcus Aurelius Cotta, and he has allowed us to accompany him today as part of our education." he added, by way of explanation for their presence.

"Ah, a Juliian. Well it is nice to see that we shall have some young Patrician blood coming up in the future. Our family numbers are dwindling with every generation," said Quintus.

"Is your father the Princeps Senatus?" Aemi asked sheepishly, recognising the name.

The young man nodded proudly. "He is indeed, and has been for over twenty years now. The Princeps Senatus is a rank gained by very few Patricians. They act as the leader of the house, and oversee the Senate when the Consuls can't be present. Usually the Princeps are changed every five years, but in Father's case, he is still considered to be the best man for the job and has been re-elected every time. Father has been formally put in charge of running the Senate by Strabo, who says he's too busy to keep popping back to Rome for meetings, especially now Cato is dead." said Quintus, before turning to speak to the young senator next to him who had just whispered a word in his ear.

Caesar looked across the hall to the opposite tier and saw on the bottom steps, nearest the dais, an elderly senator, grey haired and impeccably dressed, sitting ram rod straight on his stool, holding a large sheaf of parchment. As he looked at the man who he identified as Scarus, a messenger approached him and handed over a small sealed wax tablet. The Princeps examined the seal before breaking the tablet open and reading the contents of the message. Caesar saw a look of horror and disgust appear on the senator's face, and then to Caesars surprise, the Princeps Senatus mumbled something briefly to the messenger before pulling the top of his toga over his head and covering his face. Caesar knew this to be the sign of mourning, and felt a lurch of apprehension, wondered what calamity had befallen Rome that would cause the Princeps Senatus to react so. None of the other senators appeared to have noticed Scarus, and Caesar nudged Quintus, who was still talking to his friend. Quintus turned to look at Caesar, who just pointed in silence. Upon seeing his father, a look of dismay crossed his face.

"What is it? What has happened?" Caesar whispered to Quintus.

"Something terrible, from the look of my father," Quintus replied anxiously.

The Princeps Senatus rose to his feet and removed the toga from over his head. Silence fell instantly in the house as Scarus walked slowly from his place on the tier, out into the middle of the floor so that all could now see and hear him. It seemed to take an age for Scarus to compose himself but finally he looked up at the rows of senators and began to speak.

"Senators of Rome, pray silence, for I have news that will tear at the very core of your Roman souls," Scarus paused to collect himself, the final echoes of his voice dying out around the hall. "Disaster has struck us once again, but not from the direction of our once allies, the Italians. Rome has a new enemy in the East, King Mithridates. For many years this snake has lay quietly in the long grass of Asia Minor, occasionally rearing his ugly head to bare his fangs toward Rome, but never before has he dared strike. Now he has, in the most abominable fashion that only a barbarian could do," Scarus paused again as his words reverberated around the echoing hall. Every senator sat as though carved from marble, and held their breaths, waiting to hear the news.

"I have here in my hand a letter, sent by Manius Aquillius, our commissioner in Bythinia, or, rather he was, for he has now fled the region. His report states that King Mithridates has raised an army, over two hundred and fifty thousand strong. He has invaded Capadocia and Bythinia and is making his way steadily west towards Macedonia. Asia Minor has fallen into the hands of this Eastern King." Scarus stopped, to allow the news to sink in.

Caesar looked at the faces of the senators as they digested this calamitous news. Some looked shocked, others angry, many were dismayed that Rome was to be plunged into yet another confrontation before the Italian war had been ended. Aemi, gripped by the drama of it all, sat opened mouthed, gawping at the Princeps Senatus in wonder.

Scarus looked around the room, turning slowly on his heel, taking in their expression, waiting for the murmur of disbelief that whispered in echoes around the hall.

"Friends, colleagues, Romans. It falls on me, as leader of the House, to break the news to this august body, news of horrors, such unimaginable horrors, abhorrent to our sensibilities as a civilised nation. King Mithridates has issued a decree that there is to be a general massacre of all Roman citizens across Asia."

The house erupted at the news. Senators leapt to their feet, shouting and crying, appalled to the very core of their being at what they head just heard. To be a Roman citizen was to be inviolate. To murder in cold blood thousands of innocent people was unthinkable. Never, in the history of the empire had such an appalling catastrophe befallen its citizens.

Caesar glanced at Aemi and saw fear etched on his face.

"What's happening, Caesar? I don't understand. I'm scared." Aemi whispered.

"Sshh, don't be, just listen. It will be alright." Caesar muttered, and instinctively patted Aemi's hand reassuringly before turning his attention back to Scarus. He saw the Princeps Senatus wipe the tears from his eyes and Caesar understood; to have to be the bearer of such news was appalling, and he had no Consul present to share the burden. He stood, a lonely figure in the wide-open space in the centre of the floor, as round him the shouts and cries of indignation resounded, echoing around the high ceiling, which only served to enhance the volume of the senator's dismay.

Finally, lifting his head to face the Senate once more, Scarus shouted, "Order, Order!" raising his arms in the air to signal that calm should be restored.

Slowly, one by one, the senators resumed their stools and a quiet hush descended once more on the house. The atmosphere was electric now, the tension almost palpable in the air as they waited to hear Scarus speak.

Scarus, when he was quite sure he had their attention once more, took another deep breath and continued. "I am sorry to have to tell you that the massacres have already begun."

No-one spoke. Not one senator moved as the news stunned them in to silence and immobility.

"Manius Aquillius writes, that in towns and villages across Asia Minor, the people are killing all Roman citizens. Slaves have been freed on condition that they turn against their masters. Debtors have had all debts cancelled if they report the whereabouts of the families that have gone into hiding to avoid being murdered…" Scarus paused again, reluctant to continue.

Caesar could hardly breathe as his chest tightened with the overwhelming emotion of the moment. He could see Scarus's hand tremble as he steeled himself to continue.

"Manius Aquillius has given us an example of these atrocities in the town of Tralles, where the native residents could not bring themselves to commit the murders demanded by Mithridates. He writes: *'The senior men in the town found as many Italian and Roman citizens that they could find and put them into the Temple of Concord. There was believed to be nearly two hundred citizens in total. They then hired the services of a Paphlagonian thug named Theophilus, to do the killing. It is reported that he entered the temple armed with an axe and commenced the slaughter of every man, woman and child inside. The poor souls that clung to the statues of the God, believing that somehow this would save them, were pulled away before being hacked to death. Those that refused to let go had their hands hacked off before being slaughtered. Not a single person survived.'*

A single, high pitched mourning wail rose and echoed around the hall, then another, and another, and suddenly the whole house was in uproar once more. This time Scarus did not attempt to restore order. There was nothing he could do but watch as the Senate crumbled into a wild, seething disarray of angry, grieving men.

Caesar glanced at Aemi and saw tears running down his friends face, such was the horror and emotion inside the hall. The boys could never have dreamed that this ordinary visit to the Senate would end in them witnessing, first hand, the most traumatic news Rome had received in centuries.

In the midst of the chaos of shouting and wailing men, Caesar saw his uncle Marcus pushing his way through the senators now milling around freely in the hall. Marcus leapt up the steps two at a time until he reached the top tier and signalled for the boys to join him.

Grim faced, eyes shining with unshed tears, Marcus Aurelius called the boys to him. "Come boys, it is time for you to leave," he said, ushering them towards the steps.

"But, Uncle, can't we stay? I would like to see what the Senate will do next," said Caesar gravely. To have witnessed so much and then to have to leave was torture.

"No, Gaius, you must leave now because the Senate will stay to debate for several hours. You have heard far more than you ever should have and I am sorry if the bluntness of Manius Aquilias's report upset you," said Marcus Aurelius, as he noted the tear-stained face of Aemi. "Now, no arguing, follow me." He led the way back down the steps and across the floor to the doors, the two boys following dutifully behind.

Once outside, Marcus Aurelius stopped and turned to the boys. "Go straight home and don't stop to chatter to your friends. What you have heard today must stay private until the Senate decide what is to be done. If this news leaks out to the people we will have riots in the city, and we cannot afford to have trouble here as well, do you understand me? You cannot tell anyone what you have heard," he insisted sternly.

Caesar and Aemi nodded their agreement, and Marcus Aurelius turned to hurry back inside the House.

"Uncle, will the Senate take long to decide what to do?" Caesar asked.

Marcus Aurelius returned to the boys and lowered his voice so he could not be overheard. "It may take several hours to discuss all that we need to, but I am afraid there can be only one outcome. Rome must declare war on Mithridates, of that there is no doubt." He turned on his heel and walked swiftly back inside, the large heavy doors slamming shut behind him.

The boys turned and walked slowly down the steps and into the Forum. Caesar felt as though he were walking in a dream. All around him people were going on about their everyday business, laughing, chattering, arguing, the daily hustle and bustle of a thriving city. Yet hundreds of miles away, people of the same culture and beliefs, people of the same birth and blood, were being mercilessly hunted down and massacred, and the people of Rome did not know. Some of these people now, in the Forum, could have friends or family in Asia Minor, and they carried on in their cocoon of daily life, blissfully unaware that the world as they know it was being smashed, changing their lives forever.

Caesar bowed his head as he walked hastily through the crowds. He could not look at the people around him, for fear that they would see the disaster written all over his face; the pain and anger in his eyes. They would guess that another tragedy had befallen Rome and he could not bear to see their anguish.

Aemi ran to keep up with his friend as Caesar towards a side street where it would be quieter. Neither said a word as Caesar led the way, but he didn't go towards home, instead, he cut around the back of the Forum and headed for the Capitoline Hill. He needed time to think; needed to get out of the claustrophobic atmosphere of the city streets, and this was the place where he could find the space and air that he so badly needed. He made his way along the Via Sacra and onto the Clivus Capitolinus, the steep road that would take him up onto the hill. He could hear the heavy breathing of Aemi as he struggled to keep up, but his friend did not question where they were going.

They reached the top and headed for the quiet solitude of the Tarpeian Rock. Caesar walked to the edge of the cliff and stopped; staring out across the vast city sprawled out before him, whilst Aemi flopped down under a tree to catch his breath. The sun was waning slowly as the afternoon wore on, giving off the first rays of crimson that would gradually envelope the clear blue sky, bathing the city in her golden blanket. Caesar put his hand up to shield his eyes. From where he stood, he could look out east, across the city's vast expanse of temples, public buildings and markets. Turning south, he looked out over the Circus Maximus, the great gaming arena, where his favourite chariot team, the Greens, would race to glory or defeat, and, sometimes, to death. To the right of the Circus was the Aventine; home of the wealthy knights and senators of Rome, and somewhere down there was soon to be his new house. The mass of stylish white painted buildings reflected the sunlight, making the Aventine glow like a light orb against the red brick of the lower city. Turning again he could see the great river Tiber, winding her coils around the edge of the city like a huge mother snake; the natural barrier for Rome's enemies to overcome before they faced the great Servian wall that enclosed the city and protected her. He turned to look east again, out past the city, to the distance. East, where King Mithridates now swept with his army, reclaiming land that once belonged to his fathers in the time before the Romans came and conquered. East, where thousands of innocent people were losing their lives because they happened to be born of the wrong Race. And East, where a huge, new, Roman army would march, to avenge their dead; to face a barbarian army of over two hundred and fifty thousand men, and where, Caesar knew in his heart, his father would have to go.

Caesar's stomach lurched at the thought and for the first time in his life he longed to have his father with him. He wanted to talk to him so much; to tell him what had happened today; to ask him the many questions that were going around inside his head. He wanted to hear his father's words reassuring him that Rome would survive, that she would win this war like so many of the others. He wanted to know that the barbarians would be made to pay for the slaughter of innocents, and, that his father would return home again soon, and everything would be all right. But his father was not here, and now he would not return home again for at least another year, possibly longer. He would almost be a man then, his childhood slipping into a distant memory, a memory without his father in it.

Caesar closed his eyes and tried to picture his father's face, hoping to draw him closer, if only in his mind, but his concentration was broken by Aemi, who had finally got his breath back and was talking in hurried excitement.

"I wonder if they will have a vote on whether to go to war today? What do you think, Caesar? I can't imagine anybody voting against it, can you? If it's true that Mithridates army is over two hundred and fifty thousand men in strength then that means Rome must field an army of forty legions to match him. Forty legions, Caesar! I wonder who the General will be? I wonder if my father will go as a legate? Yours will without doubt, he's an army man to the core, your father, whereas mine is definitely more a politician. Mother says it's because father is better at throwing barbed arrows from his mouth than his hands. I laughed so much when she said that but father didn't. Do you think we will have enough men to make up forty legions? I expect Strabo will have to end his siege now and actually commit his men to some action for a change, it's about time they bloodied their swords isn't it? Then there is all the veterans around the empire, they could be recalled in an emergency, oh, and Sulla! I nearly forgot about him. How many legions does he have under his command? I hate being thirteen! Why can't I be old enough to join the legions now? It just isn't fair! So what do you think, Caesar? Caesar, are you listening to me?"

"What? Oh, sorry, Aemi, what did you say?" said Caesar, forced back to reality.

"It doesn't matter," Aemi said sulkily.

Caesar sighed and walking over to the cool shade of the tree he sat down next to his friend.

"What is it?" Aemi asked.

"I was just thinking about all the poor innocent people that are dying at this very moment, and thinking how absurd life really is," said Caesar sadly. "I mean, you cannot choose where you are born, or who your parents will be, or who your family are, can you? And yet things like that can make the difference between a hard life or an easy life, or, like now, in the east, the difference between living and dying."

Aemi grimaced as the sobering reality of his friend's words sunk in.

"How many men have died in this war, between the Italians and us, I mean? And what has it all been for? Italians wanting the Roman citizenship so much that they were prepared to go to war against the very people they wanted to be accepted by, and do you know what the irony is in all of this, Aemi?"

Aemi shook his head.

"The irony," continued Caesar, "Is that in the eyes of King Mithridates, Romans and Italians are the same people. No distinction. Both singled out to be slaughtered by his army. I wonder how the Italians feel about that? Well, in a horrid sort of way I suppose they have got their wish. They are being treated as equals now, and they will die because of it."

*The Senate declared war on King Mithridates, whose army was crossing Asia Minor at lightening speed, and set about the task of recruiting men to join the legions who would go east to defend the empire. Taxes were levied on the people to raise money, for the Treasury was almost empty from the heavy expenditure of the Italian war which had dragged on now for two years. To compound matters further, the new magisterial elections were due to be held, after a delay of two months, and only a handful of relatively unknown senators had put their names forward for election as Consul. At a time when strong leadership was called for to help Rome through this crisis, the idea of a weakly steered government and the higher taxes forced upon them, made the people restless, and sporadic riots broke out in the streets.*

*Only one man in Rome welcomed the chaos. Gaius Marius sat in his study day after day, listening to the latest news from the many clients who called on him, and secretly revelled in the misery spreading around him. He saw how desperate the situation was becoming, and he knew that it would soon be time to strike.*

The steward announced the arrival of Cassius and Sulpicius and Marius dismissed the clients still waiting in the atrium and took his visitors into the study, locking the door behind them.

"So friends, what news?" he asked, sliding into the great wooden chair behind his desk, and indicating with a flick of his hand that they could sit down.

"The votes for the new Consuls elect have been counted and the result finalised, Gaius Marius. It is not good news for us. I'm afraid," said Cassius.

"Go on," Marius said, frowning.

"The Junior Consul for this year will be Quintus Pompeius Rufus," said Sulpicius nervously.

"And the Senior Consul?"

Cassius took a deep breath. "The Senior Consul, voted in by a huge majority, is… Lucius Cornelius Sulla."

"What!" Marius roared, jumping to his feet. "Sulla… as Senior Consul? But he wasn't even running in the election!"

"I'm afraid he did," Sulpicius said scornfully. "He left his army five days ago in Campania, under the care of his senior legate, and travelled continuously for two nights and three days to get back to Rome in time to put his name down as a candidate. He only told his legate an hour before he left camp. Nobody knew he had any intention of standing for election, well, no-one who could inform me before he actually arrived in Rome, and by then it was too late to do anything about it," said Cassius moodily.

"Of course, the people jumped at the chance of electing someone who had an ounce of credibility, what with the other candidates so unknown and untried, apart from Rufus of course. Before we knew it, the voting had commenced and Sulla was a clear winner at the end of the day." said Sulpicius.

"He was ever fortunate, that one," growled Marius, returning to his chair. He grabbed the silver goblet from his desk and downed the contents in one swallow.

"Gaius Marius. Even you must see that Sulla has had tremendous success in this war, particularly since he took over command of the southern army," said Cassius. "His reputation is riding high amongst senators and the people. The war is all but over thanks to Strabo and Sulla combining forces and working together. The people see Sulla as a hero, and the Senate sees him as a good general who gets results. Of course, we know who he has to thank for teaching him how to be a success," Cassius added, trying to appease Marius by indirectly crediting him with Sulla's success.

Marius scowled at Cassius from under his large, bushy eyebrows. He was in no mood to be humoured.

"Gaius Marius, this unforeseen event does not change our plans in the slightest you know," continued Sulpicius. "The good news is that I have been elected onto the plebeian assembly, and we sit for our first session in seven days time. I'll put my proposal before the assembly as soon as the priest finishes reading the last auspice, I assure you. Cassius can do his part by lobbying support for you in the Senate, and you must continue to show yourself to the people. Let them know that you are fit enough to take command against Mithridates."

"The people love you, Marius," Cassius said. "You are still their hero, and saviour, and never more has Rome needed saving than now! If we all work together on this we will succeed in achieving all that we have planned for. It doesn't matter who the Consuls are, in fact with Sulla out of the way struggling to sort this mess out in Rome, it makes you the only choice to lead the new army doesn't it?"

Gaius Marius could see the sense in this argument and his scowl was replaced by a more thoughtful expression.

"You can rid yourself of one of the Consuls almost immediately," said Sulpicius slyly. "I know for a fact that Rufus is up to his eyeballs in debt. Most of his income is derived from the farms and vineyards he owns around Samnium. My informants tell me that the Samnites freed all the slaves that farmed the land in that area, and the crops were torched. It will take years for anything to grow in that soil again, and rumour has it that it's nearly bankrupted Rufus. I can propose to the assembly that the old senatorial debt law is re-imposed; after all, it's written into the tablets of law but is rarely, if ever, used. That way, if Rufus is declared bankrupt he will have no choice but to resign from the Senate. "

"He's had to borrow heavily from a money lending client of mine. It shouldn't be too hard to persuade him to call in the debt," added Cassius. "Your first job must be to get the debt law passed, Sulpicius, and that will remove Rufus from the Senate. I will have a word with my client and see if he can't call in the loan early. That should get Rufus securely out of the way and give less support for Sulla. Without a Consul to remain in Rome, he will have to stay here himself, won't he?" Cassius smiled triumphantly.

Marius nodded in agreement as a glimmer of hope lit his craggy features.

"Will the debt law affect Sulla too?" Sulpicius asked.

"That is a difficult one," said Cassius. "He hardly owns any property to speak of and he never has much money. I am not aware that he owes much to anyone I know, which means the debt law probably won't affect him. I am going to have to think about this carefully. Sulla appears to have a strong following in the Senate and it's not going to be easy to dislodge him. The main thing is to stop him from being given command of the new army, but removing Rufus may help towards that end. I'm going to have my work cut out in the Senate if I'm going to convince people not to vote to give Sulla the command, if he wants it that is," said Cassius thoughtfully.

A look of pure hatred crossed Marius's face. "Oh he'll want it alright," he said. "Do whatever you have to do, Cassius. I will not lose this command to Sulla. I would rather die first!"

"Then there is nothing more to be said," Sulpicius said, rising to his feet. "We all know what we need to do, so may I suggest we get on with it."

Cassius and Marius nodded. The time was ripe and the plans were made. Now all they had to do was succeed.

# CHAPTER SIX

*"As a rule, men worry more about what they can't see than what they can."*
*(Gaius Julius Caesar)*

## ROME: January- March 88 BC

*Senior Consul: Lucius Cornelius Sulla*
*Junior Consul: Quintus Pompeius Rufus*

Marcus had come home. As soon as Caesar received the news he left his house and ran without stopping, all the way to the Palatine, to the home of Gaius Marius.

Caesar was admitted into the atrium with a warm welcome from the door slave and was directed to the garden, where Marcus was believed to be waiting his friend's arrival. Caesar paused for a moment, for he had not been back to this house since the last day he had accompanied his uncle for his exercise. He was not even sure he should be there, and, for a second, considered leaving, but the temptation to meet his friend after so long was too irresistible, and Caesar set off along the labyrinth of corridors with the excitement of re-union beating hard in his heart.

At the entrance to the garden Caesar stopped. The heavy, grey clouds on this February morning had parted, to allow the winter sun to cast its feeble rays of life giving warmth onto the damp, bare grass. The gold and stone ornamental fountain glittered in greeting as the icy water tinkled and shimmered, pouring forth from the fish's mouth and cascaded into the pool below. But there was only one thing that his eyes were drawn to, for sitting under the tree near the fountain, where he always used to be found, was Marcus. His stomach fluttered with nerves as he studied his friend. Two years absence had changed him immensely. Stockier and long in leg now, Caesar noted the thickened calves and arms that showed Marcus was fast approaching adolescence. The broadened shoulders and muscled neck added to the increasing resemblance to his uncle, Gaius Marius, along with the fop of black hair that would never look tidy, no matter how many times Marcus might brush it. Remembering the merciless teasing he had subjected on Marcus because of his unruly hair brought a glimpse of a smile to Caesar's face, before the shadow of uncertainty replaced the fond memory. It had been two years since they had last seen each other, and neither had known on that fateful day that their friendship would be torn apart. Caesar wondered if things could ever be the same as before, or, had events over the years changed them beyond reconciliation?

Marcus was playing with his bone dice, his head bent low as he studied the numbers. His hand paused suddenly and he raised his head. "Caesar!" he shouted, jumping to his feet, and bounded over like a puppy dog pleased to see its master.

Caesar walked out into the garden, smiling, as Marcus came to halt in front of him. Both boys looked at each other in silence, taking in the changes that the years had made to their appearance. Caesar could see that Marcus was much taller now, though still not as tall as either himself or Aemi, and looking at his friend's dark brown eyes and square jaw, he was struck by just how much Marcus had grown to resemble his uncle. He saw a look of fear shadow Marcus's face and understood that he too worried that time had wrought changes to great to be ignored.

"I missed you, Marcus."

"I missed you too, more than you will ever know."

Caesar held out his hand and clenched his fist in the old friendship greeting and Marcus placed his fist on top.

"Friends?" said Caesar

"Friends," replied Marcus. Then they both hugged and laughed together as the lengthy separation dissolved before them.

"For a moment, I didn't recognise you, Cousin. You must have grown an extra foot since we last met and you look quite the Patrician dandy," Marcus grinned.

"And you are definitely a Mariian; still no sense of style I see."

Marcus laughed as he playfully punched Caesar in the chest. "So, where's Aemi, couldn't he come?" Marcus asked.

"He has gone to the Campus Martius with his father. It was Aemi's birthday last week and his parents bought him a new horse."

"And I bet it was the best one in the yard. I look forward to hearing him crowing over it, unless he's developed a sense of modesty during my absence. Oh well, perhaps we can meet up with him later. You are staying aren't you?"

"Of course I am. We have lots to talk about. It has been too long!" said Caesar, walking towards the olive tree. He wanted to avoid talking about Aemi as much as possible, for so much had happened since Marcus had been sent away, and of all of it, the animosity that had erupted over the Italian crisis between Gaius Marius and Aemi's father, would be the one that could cause problems for the boy's friendship. As it was, Aemi's father had only tolerated his son's continued friendship with Caesar because he was no blood relation to Marius. Marcus, on the other hand was, and now that he was back living with the family, Caesar had doubts whether Aemi would be allowed to continue this old friendship. The visible sign of the two men's animosity toward each other was the ten-foot wall that now separated their gardens.

Marcus looked at the wall, following Caesar's glance. "I see some things have changed since I left," he said. "I suppose it was stupid of me to think that things would stay the same."

"The world doesn't stop, Marcus. People carry on, even in the most difficult of circumstances, but we adapt to change and you will soon settle back in, I'm sure," said Caesar. "Father once told me to always look forward and never go back. There is a lot of wisdom in those words, I think. We've both changed in many ways since we were last together, but that doesn't mean that we can't have a friendship as good as it was before, and it must not suffer just because of what has happened to other people. We shall move our friendship forward, Marcus, together."

Marcus could not help smiling. "Oh Caesar, it's good to be back. You haven't changed you know. Still the voice of reason and still so serious! I can see Aemi has failed to get you to lighten up a bit. Good thing I returned. I'll soon bring some fun back into your life!"

"I am quite capable of having fun, Marcus." said Caesar, slightly offended at his friend's taunt.

"Oh, come on, I was only joking. I wish I could be more like you. You're the most intelligent boy I know, you have courage and daring, nothing frightens you. You keep your head when others panic and you can talk your way out of anything! You're the best horseman I know, and your battle skills will no doubt be just as good. You are handsome; you are Patrician from the noblest of families. Why, you have it all, Caesar. How could you possibly be boring?"

Caesar smiled. "Well if you put it like that, then I forgive you."

"That's very magnanimous of you; another quality to add to your list," Marcus quipped, before tearing off across the lawn with Caesar in pursuit.

Caesar caught Marcus easily, and pulled him to the ground. Marcus fought hard but Caesar won the day, and, after Marcus had begged forgiveness for the tenth time, the boys collapsed in an exhausted heap.

After a few minutes, Marcus wiped the tears of laughter from his eyes and sat back against a tree. "Oh, how I have missed this, Caesar. You, aunt Julia, this house, Rome!"

"And you were missed, Marcus, very much."

The boys settled down under the tree as though it was only yesterday that they had been together. The only difference was the conversation, for they had a lot of catching up to do.

"I never realised how lucky I was to be living here with uncle Marius until it was too late. I tell you, Caesar, the past two years were far worse than any whipping he could give me."

Caesar inwardly winced at the memory of the last time he had been at this house with Marcus. He still remembered the screams of his friend echoing around the house and the awful helplessness he had felt at being unable to help him.

"Was it truly bad, that last day? I heard you, Marcus, but they wouldn't let me come and help. I am sorry I let you down." Caesar said miserably.

Marcus stared at the grass for a moment, the silence between them filled with memories of the traumatic events of that day.

"It was bad, Caesar," he replied softly. "I couldn't move for over a week, although Aunt Julia did the best she could. Luckily I was too feverish to know too much about the pain. Then, as soon as I was fit enough to be moved, they sent me home. The scars took a long time to heal. Mother says they will be a constant reminder of the shame I caused her."

"Scars? You mean he lashed you so badly that it has scarred you for life?" said Caesar, horrified.

"Oh he scarred me all right!" said Marcus, pulling up the back of his tunic and revealing the mass of red and white welts that covered his back. Even after two years they still looked sore and angry, the skin raised and pitted. Caesar took a sharp breath. He had never seen anything as bad as the mess on Marcus's back.

Marcus let his tunic drop and turned to his friend. "Let that be a warning to you, Caesar. Never ever do anything to upset uncle."

Caesar saw the pain in his friends face and his heart went out to him; feelings of anger against his uncle's cruelty welled up inside.

Marcus saw the look on his friend's face. "Don't be angry for me, Caesar. It's over now, finished. Uncle Marius had every right to give me that punishment. He was the Paterfamilias and I disobeyed him, so he can't be blamed or judged for his actions."

"Yes I know," Caesar snapped. "But you did not deserve to be punished so severely. He could have killed you!"

"He had the right, Caesar," said Marcus adamantly. "It's not for us to question him. Mother was right, they are a permanent reminder of the shame I bought on my family. I deserved to be punished. Now, forget it, it's over."

"I admire your loyalty, Marcus, but I do not agree with you and never shall. The role of the Paterfamilias is to love, honour and protect his family and, yes, to punish if it is necessary, but to abuse the position and the authority that it carries is wrong. To be the master of your home, your wife and children and slaves, is a privilege that should not be abused. I believe that the use of extreme violence against those that are weaker than you shows a weakness of character, not a strength. You are not a man if you must beat your wife to death, or whip your children senseless; you are a coward! The laws of Rome that allows these things to happen in the privacy of your own home, is wrong. People should not turn away when they know violence is taking place, but they do. A man is the law in his own house. Fine, as long as he does not abuse it, and if he does, then he should be publicly condemned, not just whispered about and nothing done to stop him. When I am Consul I shall change the law. I will not govern a Rome where these things go unpunished. A Paterfamilias must behave with honour and dignity, as a Roman should. Anything less than this must not be tolerated."

"Here, here! I'll vote for you, Caesar, and when I am elected on the Plebeian Assembly I shall make it a capital offence to whip children! And, I shall pass a law that states all children must be given honey cakes every night before they retire to bed…and only the best horses should be used for the training of young Romans, to ride and fight!" Marcus laughed heartily.

"Marcus," said Caesar, solemnly.

"All right, Caesar. I'll shut up." Marcus replied and slapping his old friend on the shoulder, he lay back on the grass and smiled. "Oh, Caesar, it's so good to be home."

Coelia sat in her workroom weaving the thick woollen threads of orange and red that would make a new cloak for her husband, Lucius Cornelius Sulla. She threaded the weaving comb deftly, backwards and forwards through the hanging threads, creating the soft textured pattern of interwoven, rich colours of a commander's cloak.

Coelia had not seen her husband for nearly two years, as Sulla had gone to war as a senior legate for Lucius Julius Caesar. They had only married a few weeks before Sulla took his posting, and they had spent only the briefest time together before he was gone. In the infrequent letters Sulla did send to his wife, he never mentioned when he would be returning to Rome. He would briefly enquire after his wife's health before setting out a list of items he wanted sent out to him, and in his last letter he had requested that she purchase for him a new cloak from a particular shop in Rome that he favoured. Then a week ago, with no prior notice from her husband, the steward had informed Coelia that Sulla had returned to Rome unexpectedly and had been elected Senior Consul. Coelia waited in excited anticipation for her husband to return home, but she waited in vain. The minutes turned into hours, turned into days, and Coelia received no communication from Sulla. Each day she bathed and dressed in the prettiest dresses she owned, applied her make-up and dressed her hair so that she would look her best for him, and each night she took off her fine clothes and removed her make-up before crying herself to sleep. It would not be fitting for a wife to chase after her husband, and Coelia knew that if she tried to contact Sulla he would be very angry, so all she could do was wait and hope that today would be the day he would finally walk through the door.

To keep herself occupied, Coelia decided to weave the cloak herself, certain that it would be a welcome surprise, and it made her feel as though she was doing something useful to while away the time. The line of dyed red wool spun from her basket as another row of pattern was completed, and Coelia sighed to herself, allowing her mind to drift.

For as long as she could remember she had loved Sulla. As a young girl she had seen him often around Rome, and he was always the talk of the women's circles for he was considered to be the handsomest, eligible, noble born bachelor in the city. Then he married a young Patrician girl called Julia, and broke the hearts of many women. Sadly, Julia died shortly after they were married and Sulla immersed himself in his career, leaving Rome to fight with Gaius Marius in Africa. On his return, Coelia's father, a not particularly prominent but extremely rich senator, had approached Sulla with the offer of marriage to his daughter, recognising that the young Patrician was set to become a rising star in the legions, and the cash starved Sulla had readily agreed. Coelia had been the happiest girl in Rome the day her father told her that she was to marry Sulla, for he did not know that she had worshipped him from afar. The fact that she was already in love with the man she was to marry was an unusual situation for a Roman woman to be in, and Coelia's friends had found it hard to hide their jealousy that she was to be matched to the man of her dreams. Her happiness was short lived however for far from wanting to remain in Rome and begin his political career, Sulla had jumped at the chance to serve Lucius Julius Caesar, and after the briefest of goodbyes, he left his heartbroken wife to live alone in his large house, with only slaves to keep her company. Coelia had hoped she might be carrying Sulla's child so that she could keep herself occupied by caring for the baby but it was not to be, and she spent many a lonely night weeping into her pillow, longing for her beloved to return to her and to have the child that she so desperately desired. Now, upon hearing of his return, Coelia convinced herself that her husband must be very busy as Senior Consul, attending to urgent business in Rome, for what other reason would keep him from her? She shook her head to rid her mind of the tiny doubts and worries that could not help but creep into her mind. No, today he would come to her. Today her love would return and they would fall into each other's arms just as she had imagined that moment, so many times before.

Coelia bent down to pull some orange wool from the basket, when she heard voices coming from the atrium. She froze, and a deep-throated laugh sent her heart soaring at the realisation that her husband had come home to her at last! She rose quickly and patted her hair to make sure it was tidy, then smoothed the wrinkles from her dress before she flew to the door and wrenched it open, just as Sulla was reaching for the handle on the other side. Husband and wife came face to face for the first time in two years.

Coelia stood, rooted to the spot, as she drank in the beauty of his face. He had changed from how she remembered him; he was more tanned from being exposed to the elements for so long which helped to soften the mulberry red birthmark that ran from the corner of his left eye and covered his cheek, and his red blonde hair now resembled spun gold. His body was also leaner and more toned.

Sulla stared at his wife, the soft brown eyes, and long, black eyelashes so thick that they reached up to caress her finely shaped eyebrows. Her creamy, delicate skin and shining black hair pulled away from her face were unchanged from when they had last met.

For a second, Coelia saw a softness of recognition in his pale grey eyes, before a cold, hard shadow crept across his handsome features. Her stomach lurched in fear.

"Lucius!" she said breathlessly. "You are home at last. It is wonderful to see you after so long, my love." She gazed lovingly and expectantly at Sulla but he made no reply. Why did he not smile at her, throw his arms around her and kiss her a thousand times? She had dreamed of this moment for so long, but this was nothing like it should have been.

Sulla continued to look at her, his face an implacable mask.

Coelia took the initiative and tentatively reached out to take his hand. "Lucius, what is wrong?" She gasped, as he pulled his hand abruptly from her. Tears welled up into her soft brown eyes as she searched in vain for the look of love that she longed for.

"This is for you," Sulla said abruptly, pulling a roll of parchment from under his cloak and handing it to her.

She took it without a word but did not attempt to open it. Her eyes remained fixed to his cold, unemotional face. "What is this, Lucius?" she whispered, her voice shaking with fear.

"Read it and you will see. It explains all that you need to know."

Coelia's hand gripped the parchment tightly but her eyes did not leave his face. The tears now rolled gently down her soft cheeks and traced the smooth elegant line of her neck. Sulla abruptly turned from the doorway to leave.

"Lucius!"

Sulla turned to face his wife, his face set hard against her tears.

"Tell me," she said, her eyes pleading in silent agony.

"If you insist," he snapped. "I have divorced you, Coelia. As from this morning you are no longer my wife. I have lodged all the official papers with the magistrate and the divorce has been accepted. I have allowed you to keep the dowry you entered our marriage with, and it will be enough for you to buy a new home. You may keep your maid, and you can take the cook; I never could stomach the drivel he called food anyway, so he is no loss to me. I am leaving Rome for a few days and when I return I expect you to be gone from this house."

Coelia searched his eyes for any sign that would tell her he didn't mean these bitter words, but what she saw made her tremble in fear. His pale eyes were almost white now, his pupils shrunken to tiny dots. Hatred radiated from them, but it was not hot passionate hatred with Sulla but the cold, hard, unforgiving kind that sent shivers down the spine of even the most hardened man who witnessed Sulla when he was really angry.

Coelia swallowed, trying to keep her composure whilst in her head she was screaming; No! "May I ask why you have felt the need to divorce me, Lucius? In the brief years that we have been married I have been nothing but a true, loyal and faithful wife to you. What have I done to deserve this shame you bring upon me now?"

Sulla's face twitched. The birthmark that covered his left cheek turned a dark shade of purple, as the rest of his face grew pale with barely suppressed anger. All she saw was contempt. She knew Sulla hated weakness in anyone and found the pathetic whining of women particularly hard to stomach. Coelia was making things worse for herself every minute that she kept him standing there, but she could not let go so easily.

"As you insist on making me explain myself to you, woman, I have divorced you on the grounds of baroness. You cannot dispute it as the facts speak for themselves. It is my right as a man to expect my wife to bare me children, and you have failed to provide me with any. I have every right to divorce you and no man will criticise me for it. Now, enough has been said. I am leaving, and when I return, you will be gone, Coelia, do I make myself clear?"

The tears were falling thick and fast now, splashing over her pretty, rose coloured dress. Coelia felt a surge of anger rise inside of her. This was so unfair, she was being punished for something she did not deserve and he knew it. She could see in his eyes that this was just an excuse to be rid of her. Did he love someone else she wondered?

"Baroness? Lucius, in all the time we have been married you have only spent a few weeks with me. You have not been a husband to me long enough to claim that I am barren! Who is she that has turned your heart against me? Who is she that is responsible for breaking my heart? I love you, Lucius, I always have. I would bear you a child, lots of children if you would but give me a chance. Please, Lucius, please do not bring this shame upon me. No man will touch me if you divorce me for this. I will end up a lonely old maid, childless and alone. What have I done to deserve this Lucius? Tell me!" she cried in anguish.

"Enough!" he hissed, leaning forward and grabbing her tearstained face with one hand and squeezing it hard. The pressure was like a vice, so tightly did he hold her. His eyes blazed icy hatred, his lips contorted into thin slivers as he bared his teeth at her. "You are divorced. You will accept my reasons or I will have you flogged and thrown out into the street in disgrace. I shall tell everyone that I found you had entered a relationship with another man while my back was turned. You will be ostracised from your friends, you will be thrown into the gutter like a common whore! You are not capable of bearing children because I say that you are not. What happens to you now is no concern of mine. You are no longer my responsibility. I never want to hear from you, or see you again. Now, I suggest you go to your room and start packing, your time, and my patience, has just run out!"

With a final squeeze to Coelia's face he pushed her back in to the room and slammed the door, before turning and walking from the house and out of Coelia's life.

The steward announced Aurelia's arrival. Julia slipped gracefully from the couch as her sister-in-law entered the room and walked forward to embrace her with voluminous folds of silk billowing around her voluptuous, well-rounded figure.

"Aurelia, how nice to see you. This is an unexpected pleasure. Come, sit down, I shall get a drink brought for you. Wine? Water?" Julia said, fluttering around her guest.

"Water will be fine, Julia, thank you," said Aurelia, sitting stiffly on the edge of a near by chair.

Julia summoned a slave and requested a glass of water to be brought immediately, before reclining once more on her couch. "It is wonderful to see you Aurelia," Julia said cheerfully, as she carefully re-arranged the swathes of material to avoid creases. "I was saying to my husband only the other day that we must ask you and young Gaius to dinner. We do not see nearly as much of you as we should, and with my dear brother away yet again you must be terribly lonely down in the Subura all alone," Julia chirped away, barely pausing for breath.

"I am fine, Julia, and we are quite happy in the Subura, as I tell you almost every time we see each other," said Aurelia stiffly. As much as she loved Julia, Aurelia found her sister-in-law extremely irritating at times, and today she was not in the mood for tittle-tattle.

"I have come on a matter of some delicacy, Julia," Aurelia spoke quickly, before Julia had the opportunity to interrupt. "I think we need to talk."

Julia looked perplexed as she settled herself down to listen and Aurelia wasted no time in getting to the point of her visit. As she spoke, Julia's face turned pasty white, and, by the time Aurelia had outlined her concerns, Julia was visibly upset.

"The point is, Julia, I believe that for whatever reason, known only to your husband, my son stands in danger if he remains around him. He has taken against the boy even though he owes him a debt of thanks for all the hours my son spent helping him to recover from his illness. I don't know why he would seek to hurt Gaius, but I cannot ignore my feelings in this matter, and I believe it would be better for all concerned if Gaius stayed well away from Gaius Marius, and this house." Aurelia paused, waiting for Julia to respond and expecting her to jump to her husband's defence, but Julia simply burst into tears.

It was several minutes before Aurelia could calm Julia down enough to get any sense from her.

"I am sorry, Aurelia, truly I am," Julia sobbed. "You are right, of course you are. My husband is not himself these days and I do not understand what has happened to him," Julia dabbed at her eyes with the hem of her shawl. "He gets angry so easily now, over trivial things. Things he would have laughed at before now turn him into a monster. Oh Aurelia, his rages are a terrible sight to behold. I am so frightened and I hide in fear of him. He became worse after punishing Marcus. The poor boy was nearly flayed alive, and I believe my husband would have beaten him to death if he hadn't been taken by a seizure. Since then, his rages are more frequent and far worse in ferocity. His eyes glaze and he foams at the mouth, he gets so angry! The slaves are terrified of him and I live in fear that he will strike me too, one of these days. Oh, Aurelia, what am I to do?" Julia sobbed despairingly.

Aurelia sat beside Julia and held her hand, rubbing it soothingly to calm her down. "Have you tried talking to him? Does he recognise that he is ill?"

"Oh I've tried, Aurelia, on many occasions. At first he would get upset and beg my forgiveness, promising that he would try harder to control his temper, that he would take more rest. He said he felt well in himself but he did admit to occasionally forgetting what he had just said or done. He says it happens when you get to his age and it's nothing for me to worry about. Absent-mindedness is not an illness he says, and that is it. After Marcus, he swore to me that he would never let anything like that happen again, and I believed him. For weeks he was as kind and gentle as he always was, but slowly he changed again, and, now, he is the worst he has ever been."

"So you have noticed his behaviour deteriorating over time. I was beginning to think that you were choosing to ignore what was happening to your husband, Julia."

"He doesn't sleep much, either," Julia continued. "Every night is the same, pacing up and down in his study for hours, talking to himself and when he does sleep he has nightmares. He has taken to sleeping in a separate cubicle so that he doesn't disturb me, but I still hear him, Aurelia. I lie awake worrying about him, wondering what I can do to bring back the man I love. I miss him, Aurelia," Julia sobbed again.

Aurelia felt a twinge of guilt at having caused her sister-in-law so much pain, but she needed to get to the bottom of the problem between Gaius Marius and her son. "What are his nightmares about?" Aurelia asked. Perhaps they held a clue.

"Sulla. Always Sulla. He rants and raves in his sleep as though he is with him. Betrayal, hatred, lies; he says these words over and over. He shouts at him in his dreams, telling him he will never get command."

"Command…of the legions? Do you think that is what's worrying your husband? Now that Sulla is Consul, he can have his pick of commands, whilst Gaius Marius is left behind?" Aurelia was beginning to make sense of Julia's ramblings. Marius wasn't mad through illness: he was obsessed. Obsessive hatred and jealousy can turn a man insane. It would certainly account for this behaviour. "Julia, listen to me, this is important," said Aurelia, grasping Julia's hands in her own and forcing Julia to look at her. "Does your husband talk about my son in his dreams? Does he mention Gaius?"

Julia thought for a moment and then shook her head. "No, I don't think so. The only other thing he dreams of is the prophecy. I don't recall young Gaius being spoken of. Why?"

A strange feeling passed through Aurelia. Somewhere, in the back of her mind, events of the past were beginning to come together. "The prophecy? What does he say, Julia, think. It's important!"

Julia twisted her face, trying to recall when she had last heard Gaius Marius talk about the prophecy in his dreams.

"I don't know, Aurelia, I… something about stopping it… I don't know. It didn't make sense and I did not understand. Is it important?" asked Julia worriedly, dabbing her eyes again.

Aurelia felt the colour drain from her face as the realisation of truth began to form in her mind. "Julia, do you know what the prophecy said?"

"Of course. The Sybil said my husband would be Consul seven times."

Aurelia frowned, instinctively knowing that there was more to be told. "Think, Julia, please, is there anything else?"

"I don't remember Gaius telling me any more. He just used to laugh about it every time he was elected Consul again and say, remember the prophecy? It was a joke between us, nothing more."

"So why would your husband want to stop the prophecy if all it foretold was that he would be Consul? That makes no sense. There has to be something else; something Marius does not want to come to fruition."

Julia shook her head. "I am sorry, Aurelia, if there is then I don't know of it. Why are you so interested anyway? What has the prophecy got to do with all of this?"

"Because Julia, I'm beginning to believe your husband was told more in the prophecy than he has told you. What if the prophecy speaks of my son; that Gaius is going to rival Marius in some way? I think he realised the person spoken of in the prophecy was my son, on the last day they were together, because Gaius told me he had spoken of his dreams to be the greatest general, the greatest Roman, you know, the things he has been saying since he could talk. He said that Gaius Marius had got angry with him and walked away. Could this be the real reason your husband refused to have anything further to do with my son after that day?

Julia paled at Aurelia's words and the shadow of fear crossed her face for a second, before she gave way to tears again, but not before Aurelia had seen the look in Julia's eyes. She knew something, Aurelia was sure now. Something she had said made sense to Julia.

"Julia?" she said, shaking Julia's hand to force her attention. "Julia! Listen to me. You must tell me everything you know do you hear me? Everything. This is important!"

Julia dabbed at her eyes once more and seemed to shrink in size like a frightened, cornered animal.

"Julia?"

Julia nodded her head and sighing, she looked at Aurelia. "My husband has always been obsessed with his reputation, as you know. The more he was honoured over the years the more desperate he became to hold on to it. He wants his name to stand amongst the greatest men in history. That day, your son did speak about his hopes and ambitions and something he said made my husband very angry. He would not tell me what had happened in any detail but I learnt enough to make me believe that he sees your son as a threat. I didn't want to believe my fears and so I put them away. After what you have told me today I find it almost impossible to admit this, but I think you might be right."

"I knew it!" said Aurelia, relieved to finally be able to make sense of what had happened.

"I am sorry, Aurelia, truly I am. Gaius is a boy with his head filled with silly dreams, as you say. I don't understand how a child could make my husband worry, when there are men like Sulla in a much better position to threaten his reputation. I can only think as you do, that this prophecy has foretold more than I am aware of and that he believes, for whatever reason, that it is your son it speaks of."

"Do you believe he would hurt Gaius?"

"No! Oh no, Aurelia, I do not believe so, truly. But perhaps we should keep young Gaius away from him as much as possible."

"Which brings us back to why I came here in the first place. It is going to be difficult to keep them from meeting, now that Marcus has returned," said Aurelia.

"I know, and I am sorry, but what can I do. Marcus is my husband's nephew. It is not for me to send the boy away again. He agreed Marcus could return as a favour to his sister. What possible reason could I give now for wanting him gone?" said Julia desperately. "I will find ways to keep Marcus occupied and away from Gaius, if you can do the same, Aurelia. We may not be able to stop them meeting all together, but we must be able to limit the amount of time young Gaius spends here in this house."

"It is a start at least," replied Aurelia thoughtfully. "Until we can think of something better, or the situation changes with your husband."

"Situation? What do you mean, Aurelia?"

"I mean that I think Gaius Marius might well be planning to gain command of the legions again. We can't tell what will happen, Julia, so we must wait and see, but one thing I know for certain, you must open your eyes to what is happening to your husband and stop pretending to yourself that nothing is wrong. He is ill, and there is nothing you can do to help him if he will not help himself. Keep me informed of anything, anything at all, that might give us an idea what it is Gaius Marius is planning to do, for he must be planning something, or, why else would Cassius and Sulpicius spend hours locked away in his study?"

Julia blew her nose. "You have been a true friend to me, Aurelia, and I honour you. I give you my word that I will not let my husband harm your son; by all the gods I swear it. But please don't think too unkindly of Gaius Marius. He cannot help this illness he has. Please do not judge him on the man he is now but rather remember the man he was, as I shall."

Aurelia embraced Julia, and hoped that she would continue to be strong once she had left. It had been hard to force Julia to see what her husband had become and it would have been so much easier to let her carry on believing Marius would change back into the man she was obviously devoted to, but Aurelia had her own family to think of. Her son was going to need both women's help if he was to escape any retribution Marius might be planning, that was, if she had guessed right, and he was spoken of in the prophecy. Aurelia gently pulled away from Julia's embrace. "Where are the boys now?"

"I believe they are in the garden," Julia replied, rearranging her dishevelled hair and smoothing her dress.

"Then I think it's time I find Gaius and take him home," said Aurelia, getting to her feet. "We must be strong, Julia. Together we can help each other and get through this," she added, leading the way from the sitting room to find her son.

# CHAPTER SEVEN

*"What we wish, we readily believe,*
*and what we ourselves think, we imagine others think also."*
*(Gaius Julius Caesar)*

## ROME: March – July 88 BC

*Senior Consul: Lucius Cornelius Sulla*
*Junior Consul: Quintus Pompeius Rufus*

Sulla returned to Rome and to an empty house. He wasted no time in ordering the steward to remove every last trace of his wife for he wanted no reminders of Coelia; she was in the past now and he was moving on. There was no time for regrets of any kind.

Standing now, in his oak panelled dressing room, his thoughts were on the meeting ahead. It was to be his first as Consul, and the agenda was full, with only one topic for discussion; the continuing problem of the Italian War. Strabo was doing well with his legions, mopping up the last remaining bands of Italians who refused to lay down their arms, and, until they could be defeated or brought to heel, he knew that Rome could not concentrate all her efforts on going after King Mithridates, who was now in complete control of Asia and looked likely to invade Macedonia. Time was against him and he needed to end this domestic war quickly. Sulla had his sights firmly set on commanding the war in the east, and, whilst he was Senior Consul, he would be assured of that position, therefore, he could not afford to stay in Rome any longer than was absolutely necessary.

The slave put the finishing touches to Sulla's toga, and, with the final drapes hanging to perfection over his left arm, Sulla turned to the full length mirror for a final inspection, dismissing the slave with a flick of his hand. As he patted and preened his hair to perfection, he couldn't help but smile. By sunset tonight he would be married to Caecilia Metella, the nineteen-year-old daughter of Senator Metellus Dalmaticus, head of one of the most politically powerful families in Rome. With Caecilia at his side he would truly walk amongst the great men of Rome; doors would be opened for him, and opportunities offered that would otherwise pass him by.

It was Metellus who had finally convinced Sulla, five years ago, to distance himself from Gaius Marius, if he wanted to climb the Cursus Honorum, the political ladder of Rome. Sulla wrinkled his fine, Patrician nose as he thought of him. Marius was by now becoming something of a social and political leper, with many enemies in the Senate, and Sulla would find advancement difficult if he was seen as an ally to Marius.

A feline sneer crinkled at the edges of his lips as he thought of those senators who had suddenly courted and feted his attention since being elected Consul. He was not stupid, he realised the motive behind the marriage offer and he knew he would be expected to sacrifice Marius for his own advancement but Marius had treated Sulla with contempt, and Sulla's dignity could not stand these public putdowns any longer. Now, he welcomed the chance to break away from his old mentor, to form a reputation based on his own abilities and not from the reflected glory of Marius.

A slave knocked and entered the room. "Senator Metellus Dalmaticus has arrived master."

Sulla nodded and took one last appraising look at his reflection. This was the moment he had been waiting for; to enter the Senate House as Consul of Rome, and he had every intention of making this a memorable year.

Waiting for Sulla in the atrium stood a group of the most politically powerful men in Rome, known in the Senate as the Optimates, a name given to reflect their political leanings. The most prominent member of the group was Proconsul Quintus Lutatius Catalus Caesar, and with him were Proconsul Marcus Antonius, Proconsul Publius Licinius Crassus, Senator Gnaus Metellus Dalmaticus and Senator Gnaus Cornelius Dollabella. When Sulla entered the room and saw the calibre of men waiting with Metellus, his heart swelled with pride. This was a moment to be truly savoured for he had looked up to these men for many years. They were among the cream of Roman society: Rich, powerful, political heavyweights, three of whom had already served as Consul in previous years. That these men should now be standing in his home, waiting upon him, was an honour and a privilege. Sulla felt that he had truly arrived at last. "Welcome," he said, extending his arms wide, "to my humble home. I cannot tell you how touching it is to be met by so many of my esteemed colleagues. I only hope I am worthy to fill this august role of Consul, which others of you have already accomplished with such success."

Catalus Caesar stepped forward and formally shook Sulla's hand. Not as tall as Sulla but twice as wide, reflecting the good living he indulged in, Catalus Caesar was middle aged with a receding hairline. "I have not had the chance to congratulate you on your election victory, Sulla, but it is most welcome news for all of us, I do assure you," he said, smiling graciously as he shook Sulla's hand vigorously.

"Here, here," said Publius Licinius Crassus stepping forward to shake hands. Crassus was a small stocky man in his forties, with short, dark, wavy hair, pulled forward to cover his ears. He was the brother of the renowned senator, Marcus Crassus Orator, though Crassus was the first to admit he had not inherited his brother's talent for great speeches.

Catalus Caesar stepped back and waved a tall thin man forward to meet Sulla. "Have you formally met?" he asked Sulla. "No, well, may I introduce, Proconsul Marcus Antonius.

Antonius stepped forward and grasped Sulla's hand firmly.

"I remember your year as Consul, with Albinius Postumus," said Sulla. "The games you held for the people were simply wonderful; I do not think the people stopped talking about them for weeks afterwards."

Antonius smiled appreciatively but made no reply.

A quiet man this, thought Sulla, as Antonius stepped back to allow the next man to pay his salutations.

Dollabella strode forward, a great big bear of a man, his huge hand held out to greet Sulla. Sulla winced in pain as Dollabella crushed his hand in a vice like grip, shaking it warmly. "Sorry," Dollabella laughed, as he saw the expression on Sulla's face. "Don't know my own strength sometimes. Welcome, Sulla. Heard great things about you from Lucius Julius Caesar. I hope we may serve together soon?" Dollabella boomed in his deep throaty voice.

"Thank-you, I look forward to it. We must talk, soon," Sulla nodded.

"And of course, you know Metellus," said Catalus Caesar, laughing. "He'll be your father- in- law this time tomorrow. You have done well for yourself, Sulla. A very pretty maid you'll have for a wife!"

"I think we have all benefited from this betrothal," replied Sulla pointedly. He was not going to play the grateful poor relation for anybody.

"Quite so, quite so," Catalus Caesar laughed again. "Now, before we leave for the meeting, Sulla, there is something of importance we wish to discuss with you."

Sulla frowned. He realised now that there was a motive behind the meeting of these powerful men. He dismissed the slaves that were standing in the corner, awaiting orders from their master. "Speak freely, please."

"Are you aware, Sulla, that during the last meeting of the Plebeian Assembly, Sulpicius tabled two new laws for discussion at the next meeting, which will be held three days from now?" Catalus Caesar asked.

"I am aware that Sulpicius intends to push for all Italians to be given the citizenship, yes. I presume that is one of the laws he hopes to win a vote on, and, in my opinion, I think he's right. This war has gone on far too long. We've already capitulated and given the citizenship to all but the rebels who still hold out against us, but, they must know that they'll never win, and I'm sure Strabo will have no trouble dealing with the last few pockets of resistance. We need to concentrate all our efforts on the real enemy, Mithridates. If he is not stopped soon he'll be half way down the Italian peninsular before we rally our legions."

"I agree that the Italian war should end sooner rather than later, but as for giving away our citizenship to all the Italians, in my opinion, it is as though we are rewarding them for being traitorous curs!" Dollabella spoke heatedly. "I can see you have got your love of the Italians from Gaius Marius."

Sulla's face reddened with anger. He resented this jibe about his relationship with Marius, especially after he had worked so hard to distance himself from the man.

"I admit that I have learnt a lot of things from working alongside Gaius Marius, but being an Italian lover, as you put it, is not one of them," Sulla retorted. "My opinion is based on the facts, Dollabella, and they speak for themselves. If we don't end this war soon, there will be no Rome to be citizens of. And for the record, I do not need Gaius Marius to tell me what to think. I am no mans puppet, is that understood?" Sulla said, looking at each man in turn to drive the point home. He was only too aware of the political games these men played, and he held no illusions that he fitted neatly into their plans somewhere, for they had spent a long time working to bring him over to their side, away from Marius. Whilst Sulla did not have a problem with their motives, after all, he had benefited greatly from their support, he was intent on proving that he was the master of his own destiny and would not tolerate being dictated too.

"I am sure Dollabella meant no offence by his remark," Marcus Antonius said hastily, looking disapprovingly at his colleague. "I, for one, will support your recommendations in the House today; I assume that's why you called the meeting?"

Sulla nodded, glaring at Dollabella, who in turn dropped his gaze to the floor.

Catalus Caesar coughed pointedly. "Yes, well, anyway, Sulpicius tabled another law to be voted on. He wishes to reinstate an old law from the tablets that says any senator in debt by more than twenty- thousand sesterces should be expelled from the House, and exiled from Rome, if, he refuses, or cannot pay his debts."

"But, surely, that means over half the men in the Senate will be expelled. The house will not be able to function without them!" Sulla felt his stomach tighten at his news. What use would his consulship be if there was no Senate to lead?

"Precisely, Sulla, and that is exactly what Sulpicius intends. He has even gone as far as to call his proposal, The Anti-Senate Law," said Catalus Caesar.

"But why drag up this old law now. Surely he knows that this war with the Italians has plunged most of Rome into debt in some form or other? With no income generated from their farms, many senators are stretched financially. What is he up to?" said Sulla, his mind spinning.

"He is trying to be another Saturnius, and turn Rome on its head, that's what!" said Dollabella angrily.

"Yes, and who was behind Saturnius, supporting him and giving him money?" Crassus asked rhetorically.

Sulla felt the blood slowly drain from his face. "Are you telling me that you believe this is all down to Gaius Marius? That he is involved in trying to destroy the Senate?"

"Who else could it be, Sulla?" said Catalus Caesar. "Who has always pushed for Italians to be granted citizenship? Gaius Marius. And what law is Sulpicius tabling first- Italian citizenship. Who hates the Senate enough to want to destroy it, and, has the money to do so-Gaius Marius. Sulpicius law number two!"

"But why?" said Sulla frowning. "Why go to all those lengths? Marius has never done anything to Rome but support her, even fighting against the Italians when he really agreed with their sentiments for going to war in the first place. No, Marius would have to be mad to want to destroy the Senate; to bring Rome to her knees, especially now with King Mithridates attacking the Empire."

"But that is exactly it, Sulla, you said it yourself. Gaius Marius would have to be mad. Gaius Marius *is* mad! You have been out of Rome for the past two years, but surely you must have heard the stories about him? He suffers delusions, obsessions, violent rages, and his dubious connection to Sulpicius is well known. Face it, Sulla; the man you knew has gone. The seizures he suffered have warped his mind. Nothing is beyond that man these days, nothing, and, I would bet my entire fortune that he is the one behind Sulpicius now," Catalus Caesar said passionately.

Sulla paced the floor, hands behind his back, as he considered Catalus Caesar's words. "I still don't understand what Marius's reasons would be for wanting to harm his beloved Rome? She is everything to him. His achievements as Consul, as General, are testimony to his love and loyalty for her! No, I simply cannot agree with you."

"Sulla, Listen!" Catalus Caesar replied angrily. "Marius has every reason to want to destroy the Senate. It's true that many of us have, over the years, done everything we could to stand in his way, to stop him from achieving the things he has. He is, after all, only an Italian. Those accolades given to him are meant for Roman men! He was not bred to govern this empire, as you, or I, and our fathers, and their fathers before them. We, the Patricians, and, admittedly some of the ancient Plebeian families, are the ones who sit in the Senate by birthright. We are the Fathers of this great city, and along comes this Italian nobody and starts to take over. Of course we're not just going to sit back and let him walk all over us. He is not fit to lick the bottom of my boot! He has no breeding, no family history to tie him to Rome. By all the gods, man, he had to buy himself respectability through his marriage to a Juliian. He is nothing. Marius knows this, and that is why he has spent so many years fighting the Senate. He wanted to be accepted and he never was. How could he be? He is an outsider, the champion of the common man. Frankly, he has done well to get as far as he has, considering the opposition we put in his way."

"That's an understatement," Marcus Antonius commented dryly.

"Yes, alright, Antonius." Catalus Caesar snapped. "Though it pains me to admit it, Gaius Marius has, well, he has achieved more in his lifetime than most of us, but, how much of that was bought with his huge wealth? How many men did he have to bribe to be elected Consul so many times, that's what I'd like to know?"

"He has the support of the people, they always voted for him," said Marcus Antonius.

"Exactly! And that is what makes him so dangerous," added Crassus. "We must not underestimate the support he still has from the people. He is still capable of turning them against us. The very last thing we need right now is a civil war. We must tread very carefully."

"None of you have answered my question," said Sulla impatiently. He was still pacing the floor, brow furrowed, trying to make sense of what his colleagues were telling him. "What exactly is he after? That is, providing it's him behind all this, and I have heard nothing to convince me of that."

"You, Sulla. Marius is after *you*! He wants to destroy *you*, and to destroy *us*!" said Catalus Caesar passionately.

"*Me?*" said Sulla incredulously.

"Yes, *you*! He hates you, Sulla. He hates you with a passion that goes beyond reason. He is obsessed with your downfall, and, I believe he would do anything to achieve that. He nurtured you when you were young. He gave you opportunities, he treated you as a son, but he never wanted you to achieve things on your own. He made you and he wanted to control you. Marius believed you were nothing without him, and you have proved him wrong. You are a threat to him now. You challenge his reputation more than any other because he was the one to teach you, can't you see? He is insanely jealous of you, and it has consumed him to such a degree that he would do anything, *anything* to destroy you!"

"So, Marius would bring down the Senate by exiling goodness knows how many senators from Rome, just to get at me? No. I'm sorry, Catalus, it's you who are obsessed with Gaius Marius. You in particular have gone out of your way over the years to bring him down at every opportunity. I don't deny that I have distanced myself from him and that there is no love lost between us any more, but to tell me that he hates me enough to destroy Rome? No, it's you who are mad, not Marius!"

Catalus Caesar threw his arms up in the air in exasperation and turned away from Sulla. He could not believe that he still refused to accept Marius was behind Sulpicius and the new laws.

Marcus Antonius quietly stepped forward to face Sulla. "Sulla, what Catalus says could be true. I understand that you find this hard to accept, but Marius has changed. He's not the man you knew anymore." He took Sulla by the arm and looked him squarely in the face. "Listen to me, Sulla, Gaius Marius has never truly been accepted by any of us that matter in Rome and has never held the Senate in high regard. He does not make friends; he buys them with his vast wealth. Marius uses people to get what he wants, any way that he can. When his command was withdrawn from the northern army, Marius saw that as a final insult to his dignitas. He says that we crippled him by withdrawing his command and caused him to have the second seizure. It's only his hatred for us that has driven him to get over the illness, and, to add insult to injury, you were given command of the southern army. In his eyes you betrayed him; you threw all that he had given you back in his face. Marius believes you should have refused the command and insisted it was given to him as the more senior General, but you didn't, and understandably so. Now can you see? His hatred was double edged, against you and against the Senate, and then you suddenly appeared and you won, by a landslide victory, the office of Senior Consul. He knows you were supported by our political party, so he sees that you have turned against him and joined his enemies; More betrayal. As Senior Consul, you have the right to command the legions over any other man in Rome. Gaius Marius will not stand by and watch that happen; we know this for certain. He wants to command the legions and he wants to go against Mithridates; that is fact. He hates us, and, he hates you. Bring down the Senate with this debt law, and you go down too…"

"Leaving the way open by popular vote of the people, for Marius to take command of the army and fight King Mithridates and be proclaimed the saviour of Rome one more time," added Crassus.

Sulla looked deep into Marcus Antonius's eyes, searching for any sign of doubt, but all he saw was the honest face of a senior senator whom Sulla knew was considered to be one of the most honourable men in Rome. Sulla realised that he spoke true. This quarrel with Marius had gone way beyond anything he could have imagined; Sulla realised he was going to have to fight for his very life.

"So, what do Rufus and I have to do to prevent these laws being passed?" he sighed resignedly.

Catalus Caesar sighed in relief. "You must suspend all public business immediately, until further notice, then the tribunes cannot hold a lawful meeting, or vote. That will give us some time to work on a way of stopping Sulpicius." Catalus Caesar said firmly.

"Then we must not delay further," said Sulla resolutely. He finally accepted the word of these illustrious men and understood that any loyalty, any feelings of friendship he had for Gaius Marius could no longer exist. To all intense and purposes Marius had declared war by his scheming and plotting, and if he did not act fast, Marius was likely to succeed in bringing him down. The beast had shown himself for what he truly was; it was Marius or Sulla, there could be only one allowed to survive.

Turning on his heel, his face set in determined resolution, Sulla led the way from his home towards the Forum, and, to the meeting of the Senate.

"I envy you that animal," Caesar said to Aemi, as he deftly slid down the bottom of his pony. "I am sure if Father were in Rome he would agree that I am far too big for Athos and he would buy me a horse, but I have no chance whilst he's away."

Aemi brushed the dust from his tunic as he led his horse towards the stables. The ride had been long and hot. The Campus Martius was turning into a desert, as the dry, arid heat of summer approached, which made an uncomfortable ride. Stable slaves took charge of Aemi's horse and Caesar's little white pony and the boys headed to the well to quench their thirst.

"Can't you ask your mother?" Aemi swilled some of the water around his mouth and spat it onto the floor. "Surely she could arrange something with the horse master here. He could find you a fine horse, just like mine."

Caesar shook his head. "Mother is barely talking to me since we argued the other day. Was it so unreasonable to question why I was forbidden to visit Marcus at my own uncle's house? I wouldn't mind if she could give a valid reason, but all she would say was, that is how things stand, and I am to do as I am told. What kind of explanation is that, I ask you? No, I just have to accept that I'm stuck with Athos until Father returns to Rome."

"You can always ride Beacephalus, you know. Any time, just take him, I don't mind."

Caesar smiled at his friend in gratitude. "I'm truly grateful for your kind offer, Aemi, but if you are in a generous mood then there is something much more important I would ask you to do." He paused for a moment, avoiding Aemi's gaze as he steeled himself to ask the question that had been burning inside him since Marcus returned to Rome. He took a deep breath. "I want you to make friends with

Marcus. It's so difficult for me. You are my best friends, and, I want to spend time together, the three of us, the way it used to be. Please Aemi, won't you make the effort?"

Caesar saw the cloud cross Aemi's usually sunny face and he felt a sinking feeling as he anticipated his friend's reply.

"That was a long time ago, Caesar, and people change; situations change. It's not that simple, and you know it." Aemi scuffed the ground with his boot, his eyes looking anywhere but at Caesar.

"But it can be, if our friendship means anything to you, Aemi. I know a long time has passed, but it was always the three of us against the world, wasn't it? We did everything together, and we could again. It's hard for me too, now that I can't see Marcus as easily as before, but we manage, you just have to adapt to the changes, that's all."

Aemi looked sullen, and turned to walk away, but Caesar blocked his path, refusing to let him pass.

"Walking away won't solve anything, Aemi, and you have to talk about this sometime, you know! Why not now? Come on, Aemi, what are you scared of?"

"I'm not scared," Aemi scowled. "You just refuse to understand, that's all, and I don't want to argue with you, especially not about Marcus. Look, our friendship was a lifetime ago. Back then, when we were younger, what happened between our families didn't matter. Who we were, Patrician, Plebeian, Italian, didn't matter, but, it does now. Marcus was sent away and I missed him the same as you, but that's when things began to change for us, between our families, I mean. The Italian War changed everything, and when Father argued with Gaius Marius, and he built that huge wall between our two houses, I knew, that day, that there could be no going back. That wall is the end of everything before that day, and my friendship with Marcus is part of that. Father hates Gaius Marius, and I can't say as I blame him much either- you have no idea what it's like living next to that man, Caesar. He rants and raves like a mad man…"

"Perhaps he has good reason to, if men like your father are always plotting against him," Caesar retorted.

"You see! I knew this would end in an argument between us," Aemi cried. "Every time you want to talk about Marcus we end up arguing. Is it any wonder I don't want to discuss this?" He pushed roughly past Caesar and walked off towards the stable block.

Caesar followed in silence, fighting back the rising frustration. If he had any chance of winning Aemi round then he had to remain calm, or Aemi would use his anger as an excuse to walk away. They stopped at Aemi's stable and Caesar watched as his friend stroked the bold, fine nose of his horse.

"Tell me that you don't like Marcus, and I'll shut up." Caesar said, pressing his back against the warm stone of the stable wall and squinting against the bright sunlight that shone full on his face.

"What do you mean?"

"It's quite simple, Aemi, either you like Marcus, or you don't. Forget everything else, just answer me that one question – yes or no?"

Aemi sighed deeply and hid his face in the horse's mane. "Yes…no…it's not that straightforward, Caesar!"

"Yes, it is, Aemi. All I've heard is your excuses about your father and Marius hating each other, but that's not the real reason, is it? So, come on, tell me. Is it because Marcus is Italian, is that it?"

Aemi blushed to the roots of his red hair and turned away.

"It is, isn't it?" Caesar looked bemused. "Marcus has always been an Italian, and, granted, you two have squabbled over your differences in the past, but it never came between your friendship. How can you turn against him now, Aemi? He's still the same person; the boy you laughed with, fought with, stuck up for when he got himself into fights…he's not just an Italian, Aemi, he's Marcus, our friend!"

"But he *is* an Italian, and that's what makes everything so much harder now, especially with the war and everything…"

"And when this war is ended the Italians will all have Roman citizenship, which will draw them even closer to us than they already are! What excuse are you going to find then, Aemi? I can't believe you would judge Marcus in such a way. It shouldn't matter if he came from a Germanic tribe and painted himself blue, if you liked him, and considered him your friend. Perhaps we shouldn't be friends either, if you want to start using social class as a reason for not liking someone!"

"What do you mean by that?"

"I mean, I am Patrician, descended from one of the founding royal families of Rome, whilst your family were mere wealthy merchant Plebeians who gained their status through trade. My name alone speaks for itself and all that it stands for, whilst you will always have to justify yours. So, now that we have established that you and I are also different in social status, do you still believe your argument against Marcus stands, or do you think, just maybe, you can look beyond your ignorance, and admit to liking Marcus simply for who he is?"

Aemi made no reply and both boys remained silent for a while, letting their anger cool before the disagreement got out of control. Aemi scuffed the dirt with his toe and Caesar gently stroked the horse's neck.

"I wish he hadn't come back," Aemi mumbled.

"I know," Caesar sighed.

Still neither boy would look at each other.

"Father says that I am to have nothing to do with Marcus and I can't go against him. You can understand the position I'm in, can't you?" said Aemi pleadingly.

As much as he hated to, Caesar had to agree that Aemi really didn't have any choice in the matter.

"I'm sorry, Aemi, I do understand, and I didn't mean to argue, with you, of all people, but what do I tell Marcus? He has been back a month now and he keeps asking why he hasn't seen you. I can't keep making excuses to him, can I? Marcus is going to have to be told sooner or later."

"Told what?"

Caesar spun round, his eyes widened in dismay as he saw Marcus standing before them, and judging by the look on his face he had obviously overheard the last part of the conversation.

"Told what, Caesar?" Marcus asked again. "Aemi?"

Aemi said nothing as his face turned red with embarrassment.

Caesar took a deep breath. It was time for Marcus to know the truth. "That Aemi's father has ordered him to stay away from you."

Marcus looked at his cousin and then to Aemi. His cheeks turned red with embarrassment and anger, and Caesar noticed that his fists were clenched together, a sure sign of his impending explosion.

"It's not Aemi's fault, Marcus. He must do as his father orders; he has no choice."

"Is that so," said Marcus, continuing to look at Aemi. "Is it really your father that stops you wanting to be my friend, or, is that just an excuse, Aemi? Come on, tell me for old times sake."

"It is true, yes," Aemi replied, glancing quickly at Caesar before looking back at the ground. "We can no longer be friends, Marcus. I'm sorry," he mumbled.

"Not as sorry as I am," Marcus retorted. "You have changed whilst I have been away. The Aemi I knew would never have turned his back on me just because his father said so! What's the matter Aemi, have you turned soft or something, or maybe the real reason is that it's not seemly for a Plebeian of such high social standing to be seen consorting with a lowly Italian like me!"

"Marcus, stop!" Caesar interrupted. "It's as Aemi said; his father has ordered him to keep away from you, and he has no choice but to do as he is told."

"No choice? Of course he has a choice. He'll come of age soon, a man in his own right. He can do as he pleases then."

Caesar saw a sly smile spread across Marcus's face, and he wondered what Marcus was planning now.

"What say we keep our friendship secret till then, Aemi? When you are a man you can have whomever you want as your friend, and there's nothing your father can do about it. It could be just like the old times."

Caesar held his breath. Marcus was pushing for confrontation and placing Aemi in a very awkward position.

"No," Aemi said suddenly, looking directly at Marcus for the first time. "I will not go against my father, now, or when I come of age. What we had as friends has gone and there's nothing I will do to change that. Too much has happened between our families for us to continue as before. Our friendship is over, Marcus," said Aemi firmly.

Caesar could see Aemi's hands shaking as he spoke, and he felt a twinge of sadness that he had witnessed the end of this friendship. He watched Marcus intently, waiting to see what he would do. Two years ago Marcus would have lost his temper and he and Aemi would have ended up fighting, but time had obviously changed him because Marcus simply nodded once, then turned on his heel and walked away.

Caesar watched as Marcus disappeared from view and then he turned back to Aemi, who looked pale and shaken. "Are you all right?"

"No, not really," Aemi replied, rubbing his hands quickly across his eyes. "Sweat," he said defensively.

But Caesar had already seen the tears, and he realised that through all Aemi's excuses and protestations he really did care about his friendship with Marcus, even though he would never admit it, not even to himself. To sever this friendship had cost Aemi dearly.

"That's it then," said Aemi sadly.

"Yes. That is it."

The two friends walked slowly homewards in silence. For the first time since their friendship began, Caesar felt that something had been irrevocably lost between them. The innocence of their childhood had left them, that afternoon, on the training ground of Rome's warriors. Two years ago, it had not mattered to them what was happening with the rest of the world for theirs was full of laughter, fun and games. It had not mattered who was Italian, Patrician or Plebeian, all that mattered was their friendship, their secret handshakes and pledges to be friends forever. But they were Roman, growing up at a time of immense change, where allies turned to enemies; where the struggle for power in the Senate spilled out into Rome itself, affecting the lives of innocent people. For Caesar and his friends, manhood was but a year away, and, for Aemi it would come even sooner, and with it would come all the things that would change their lives forever. The time had come for them to begin that journey, following separate paths, together, yet worlds apart.

Rome had taken their innocence and would draw them inexorably into a world of politics, war, family duty, and tradition. They could not change it: they could not escape it; that was how it was, for a child living in a Roman world.

The Consuls made their way in a stately fashion, preceded by their lictors, to the rostra in the Forum, opposite the Senate House. The chief lictor mounted the rostra and blew his horn, summoning the crowds to attention. Many of the two hundred senators that had attended the Senate meeting followed silently behind, whilst others remained on the Senate House steps to afford themselves a better view of the large crowd that was beginning to drift towards them. As Sulla climbed the steps onto the rostra, he noticed Cassius, and several senators known for their loyalty towards Gaius Marius, slip away down a side alley, away from the Forum. He smiled to himself. No doubt they were hastening to take the news to Marius that his plans were foiled. It had not been easy, and he had faced stiff opposition from Cassius in particular, who had argued against disbanding the meeting, but his protestations had been to no avail.

At a sign from Sulla, one of the lictors nailed a notice to the pole in front of the rostra so that the people would be able to read the senatorial decree. Sulla stood calmly, surveying the hundreds of faces around him. The Forum was, as usual, full of people going about their daily business, but Sulla was looking for a certain group of men in particular. He had been warned, before the start of this mornings meeting, that a large number of Marius's old veterans had gathered in the Forum, some of them openly carrying batons, and Sulla looked at them now with contempt as he finally spotted them, mingling furtively amongst the crowd. What a shabby looking lot, he thought, as the rough looking men pushed and shoved their way deep into the crowd to be nearer the front of the rostra. He signalled for the horn to be blown again and silence fell as the crowd waited to hear why they had been summoned.

Sulla stepped forward and took a deep breath, casting his eyes across the crowd of people below before beginning.

"People of Rome. I, Lucius Cornelius Sulla, Senior Consul of Rome, together with my esteemed colleague, Quintus Pompeius Rufus, Junior Consul," here he waved his hand in the direction of Rufus, who was standing well back, next to Dollabella and Catalus Caesar, who had joined them on the rostra. "Have today declared that the auspices are too unfavourable to allow the House to sit in session. The Senate cannot meet under such ill omens, and we have decided to suspend all public business until further notice, on religious grounds, in an attempt to appease the gods, who have made their feelings clear! That is all I wish to say, people of Rome. Pack up your things and go home, there will be no trading today."

A murmuring started in the crowd. Ill omens and bad auspices always concerned the superstitious people of Rome.

Sulla turned his back to the crowd and signalled for the lictors to lead the way when, suddenly, a man pushed through the crowd and jumped up onto the rostra. Sulla recognised Sulpicius, but he made no move to call the Lictors to remove him, even though they had moved forward with their spears lowered, to protect their Consuls.

Sulpicius and Sulla locked eyes for a moment, and then Sulpicius turned to face the crowd.

"The Senior Consul, Lucius Cornelius Sulla has declared the omens are bad," he shouted loudly, so that the entire crowd could hear him speak. "How does he know this, when he refused to allow the priests to read the auspices in the Senate House before the start of the meeting?" Sulpicius paused to allow this news to sink in.

The people mumbled amongst themselves, clearly confused by what Sulpicius was telling them.

"Who does this man think he is, people of Rome? He is a Consul, not a priest. Who is he to forbid the priests to do their duty? Who is he to decide what the gods have willed? Do you think you are a god, Sulla?" said Sulpicius, turning to glare at Sulla before facing the crowd again. "Now, he suspends all business on religious grounds, he says! What religious grounds? There are none, just his say so! So now none of us can work. *No* courts, *no* assembly's, *no* business! And for *no* reason, other than because our illustrious Senior Consul says so!"

The crowd were getting behind Sulpicius now. Sulla watched them intently and saw the signs of discontent and anger on their faces. The muttering became louder, but still Sulla chose to do nothing but watch and wait to see what Sulpicius would do next.

"People of Rome, listen to me!" Sulpicius shouted. "I know why the Senate have suspended all business, and it has nothing to do with any religious grounds. They know that I have two laws that I intend to place before the Plebeian Assembly, and they seek to prevent this meeting from going ahead. The Senate are trying to prevent a lawful vote from being held, and I'll tell you why. My first law, people of Rome, is an old law, one that has been allowed to drop into obscurity over the years, but one that I feel should be resurrected in your interests. I intend to remove from the Senate, every Senator that is in debt by more than twenty thousand sesterces. The law states, that no Senator shall owe money to a money lender or another member of the House, yet, I tell you, people of Rome, these fat, rich, corrupt Senators who make the laws that govern you, take no heed of the laws that govern them! They borrow money whenever it suits them. Over half the Senate are in debt up to their eyeballs. Do they get expelled? No. One rule for us, and one for the fat cats of the Senate!" Sulpicius paused.

Dollabella stepped forward, making a lunge for Sulpicius, but Sulla grabbed his arm and pulled him away.

"No, you fool, let him finish," Sulla hissed under his breath. "How else are we to know what Marius is really planning?"

Dollabella swore under his breath but made no move to return to Sulpicius, turning instead to rejoin his fellow senators at the rear of the rostra.

"People of Rome," Sulpicius continued. "One of the worst offenders is standing on the rostra before you! Our very own Junior Consul, Quintus Pompeius Rufus. He is in debt by over a hundred thousand sesterces, and yet he has been elected Consul! How much more proof do you need that these senators think themselves above you and above the laws of Rome?"

Sulpicius turned to look at Rufus, but found that he had managed to slip away without being noticed by the crowd. Realising what was coming Rufus had ordered his lictors to remain on the rostra whilst he slipped down the back steps, removed his purple toga, and vanished un-noticed down a side street.

Sulpicius turned once more to face the crowd, delight written all over his face. "He has fled! He has fled, people of Rome, in disgrace, because what I tell you is the truth!"

People in the crowd began to shout abuse at Sulla and the remaining senators on the rostra now. Whipping themselves up into a frenzy of hatred against the privileged class, Sulla, Dollabella and Catalus Caesar, represented everything the people hated in Rome.

The chief lictor stepped over to Sulla and murmured in his ear but Sulla shook his head and remained standing firmly in his place at the centre of the rostra. A large tomato, hurled from somewhere in the crowd, hit the floor with a splat at Sulla's feet, spraying his toga with red juice. Sulla didn't even flinch as he fixed his gaze on Sulpicius, his birthmark throbbing deep purple; a visible sign to those that knew him that he was angry.

Sulpicius had the crowd exactly where he wanted them and wasted no time in driving home his advantage. "People of Rome, listen to me!" he shouted over the howling abuse from the crowd below him. "The second law I wish to put before the Assembly is one that is close to your hearts. It affects your lives, your families, and your children. The Italian war must be ended, and soon. I propose that full citizenship should now be given to *all* Italians. It is time to end this poverty and famine that the war has brought to Rome. It is time to bring your sons home! We need to free our legions from this domestic war to defend us against the real enemy of Rome, King Mithridates."

Groans rose from the crowd as they remembered the massacre of hundreds of innocent Roman and Italian citizens.

"We need your sons to fight the hardest war Rome has faced since the Germanic tribes invaded our homeland ten years ago. We need a man who can lead our army to victory; a man who has spent his lifetime in the service of Rome, fighting for Rome. There is only one man capable of saving our empire from the eastern barbarian King!"

Sulla tensed. He had not expected Sulpicius to talk about the war. This was a new twist of events. He realised that it was time to act now, before Sulpicius carried the crowd too far. He made a sign to his lictors and within seconds, four officers surrounded Sulpicius, preventing him from having any further communication with the crowd.

As Sulpicius struggled to free himself, Sulla stepped forward to face the people, raising his arms to call for quiet. But the people were in no mood to listen to their Consul. He was now the object of their hatred and anger, and a mass of rotten fruit and other small objects were thrown towards him. Some missiles hit their target, others smashed onto the rostra, splashing lictors and senators alike, with the foul rotten juice.

Dollabella ran forward to Sulla, his arms over his face to protect himself from the rain of missiles falling all around them. Sulpicius was ranting and raving in fury at being prevented from talking to the crowd, kicking and pushing at the lictors who still held him firmly in a tight cordon.

"It's no good, Sulla, you've left it too late, they'll never listen to you now. Come away, get off the rostra while you still can!" Dollabella yelled over the screaming mob.

"No. Never! He is not getting the better of me!" Sulla snarled, turning to look at Sulpicius, who was struggling frantically.

A large, rotten tomato smacked into the side of Sulla's head, exploding over his face and toga.

"Don't be foolish, Sulla! It's over for today, can't you see that man?" Dollabella shouted angrily, and he grabbed at Sulla in an attempt to drag him away.

Catalus Caesar leapt forward to help, struggling to protect his face from the coins and other hard objects now being thrown at them.

The six lictors that were not engaged in holding Sulpicius formed a ring around the three senators, in a vain effort to protect them from the worst of the blows.

As they struggled to pull Sulla across the rostra, eight burley veterans suddenly appeared from behind them, batons drawn, and set about the group of lictors holding Sulpicius. The lictors around Sulla drew their swords and plunged after the veterans in an effort to aid their comrades.

"No violence! I said, *NO VIOLENCE*!" screamed Sulla to the lictors, and he vainly tried to pull the nearest one away from the fight that had spilled out across the rostra.

Batons and swords clashed as an all out battle between lictors and veterans ensued, with several more veterans leaping up to join the fighting.

Dollabella tried to pull Sulla away from the violence around them, but Catalus Caesar, realising it was a losing battle, made off across the rostra, and down the steps, heading for the safety of the Senate House, where several other senators who had stood watching the events unfold, now ran.

Sulpicius managed to break free from his capturers, who were now involved in hand to hand fighting, and ran to the front of the Rostra.

"Marius for General!" he screamed. "Down with Sulla!"

The crowd took up the chant, as Sulpicius ran back and forth across the rostra, screaming and waving his arm to whip the crowd into frenzy.

The veterans, that made up a large majority of the crowd, realised it was time to do what they had come for. Taking out their concealed batons and swords and raising them in the air they chanted, *"MARIUS. MARIUS!"*

The crowd, which was now over a thousand strong, took up the chant. Gaius Marius was the people's hero and Rome's saviour; he was the man to lead the legions east, to avert disaster and wreak vengeance on the poor innocents that had been massacred.

Dollabella manhandled Sulla to the back of the rostra, but Sulla continued to struggle against him. He was Consul. How could he ever live it down if he fled from the trouble like a whipped dog with its tail between its legs?

Dollabella had reached the steps that would take them down the back of the rostra but he stopped suddenly. Coming up the steps menacingly towards them, were a group of veterans, grim faced, swords and batons ready in their fists.

Sulla saw them now and stopped struggling against Dollabella. They both turned and ran across the rostra to the far end, looking for a means of escape, but, surrounding it from all sides, was the crowd, many with weapons, and all chanting, *"MARIUS! MARIUS! MARIUS!"*

The rostra itself was swarming with men engaged in hand to hand fighting; lictors and veterans, slugging it out. Blood covered the floor; bodies of killed and injured men lay all around. Sulla and Dollabella, the only two men not involved in the fighting, were now cornered like rats at the far end, and the gang of veterans that had climbed the steps now drew closer, forcing their way through the mass of writhing, fighting men, their eyes fixed firmly on their prey.

"Save yourself, Dollabella!" Sulla screamed, realising that this was where he was going to meet his end. At least he would die as Consul, he consoled himself. He had made it in the end. Shame it had to end this way, and he didn't even have a sword in his hand to die fighting!

Those were the last thoughts that went through Sulla's mind before blackness descended on him, and he knew no more.

Caesar and Marcus dashed for cover as the fighting spilled out from the Forum into the market place. Running an errand for his mother had given Caesar the opportunity to meet up with Marcus, but unfortunately for them they had walked straight in to the trouble. Terrified at the sight of hundreds of men swarming the streets, batons flailing, hitting out at anyone who got in the way, they found cover under a Temple portico.

Caesar watched as stalls and animals were overturned and kicked aside. Shouts of men and women screaming in fear filled the air and he pressed his back against the wall, shaking with sheer bewilderment at the pandemonium erupting all around.

Marcus clung on tight to Caesar's arm. "By all the gods, what's happening? How do we get out of here?" he screamed.

"We can't, not yet! If we move… Aemi!" In the melee and confusion, Caesar spotted Aemi dashing between some overturned market stalls, followed closely by a man wielding a heavy wooden baton.

*"Aemi!"* Caesar shouted, and without a thought for his own safety he leapt from his hiding place and plunged through the crowd with Marcus following close behind.

As he jumped over a pile of upturned baskets and broken wooden stalls, he caught a glimpse of Aemi as he turned down a narrow side ally, with the man still behind him. Caesar and Marcus followed in close pursuit.

They reached the alleyway and Caesar slowed down as he strained to see what lay ahead in the threatening shadows. The cobbles were damp and slippy, covered in mould and slime, for the sunlight rarely ventured into this narrow passageway, and the stench of decay lingered, insipid, in the air, causing Caesar to gag. As his eyes adjusted to the dim light he moved forward cautiously, Marcus clinging on to the back of his tunic.

"Can you see anything?" Marcus whispered fearfully.

"Not yet…wait…there's something down the bottom…Jupiter, it's Aemi… leave him alone!" Caesar screamed, and ran forward.

The man, one of Marius's many veteran's involved in the riot, turned at the sound of the shout, just as Caesar launched himself on his back. He managed to raise one arm just in time to prevent Caesar from getting a hold around his neck, and with a hard shove he smashed him back against the ally wall. Caesar fell to the ground, next to the prone body of Aemi, who lay unconscious on the cobbles. He was winded, but he fought the pain and immediately scrambled to his feet, just as the veteran aimed a blow at his head with the long baton. A battle cry filled Caesar's ears, and the next second he was flat on his face, as Marcus pushed him out of the way and brought the flat side of his training gladius down hard on the side of the veteran's head.

The force of the blow knocked the man to the floor, and, quick as lightening, Caesar grabbed the baton from his hand, and, with one swift blow, brought it down hard on the man's head, rendering him unconscious.

Marcus and Caesar stood silent, their lungs heaving with the physical exertion of the fight, and then, Caesar laughed.

"Now that was fun!" he panted, throwing the baton down contemptuously on top of the veteran.

"Fun? That wasn't fun, Caesar, he could have killed you!"

"But he didn't, did he. Good work, Marcus," Caesar smiled, patting his friend on the shoulder. "Now, let's get Aemi up and out of here before he wakes up," he said, kicking the man in the ribs to make sure he was still unconscious.

"He's…he's not dead is he?" said Marcus worriedly, looking down at the veteran. "We did hit him rather hard."

"Don't worry about him, he's still breathing, and anyway, it was either him or us. Now, let's get Aemi and get out of here." Caesar answered as he knelt down beside Aemi and shook him gently. Aemi groaned and slowly opened his eyes. "Aemi, it's me, Caesar. Come on, you have to get up, quickly." Caesar encouraged his friend, taking one arm to help him get to his feet.

"What…what happened? Oh my head!" Aemi moaned weakly.

Marcus moved round to the other side of Aemi and took his arm. "He's got a nasty gash to his head, Caesar. Shouldn't we try and stop the bleeding first?"

"No time, we have to leave," Caesar grunted as he heaved Aemi upright.

"Marcus? What are you doing here? You shouldn't…" Aemi began, but Caesar interrupted him.

"Marcus saved your life. Now are we going to stand here and argue or do we wait until he wakes up and finishes what he started?"

Aemi looked down and saw the man sprawled on the floor, but before he could say another word, Marcus and Caesar hustled him away down the ally and to safety.

The rioting appeared to have stopped, but the devastation of both people and property was widespread in that small area in the heart of Rome. Caesar led the way through the carnage of dead and injured animals and men strewn around the market place, mixed with broken stalls, cloth canopies and a myriad of goods, smashed and crushed beyond repair. No-one took any notice of the three boys as they made their way slowly around the back of the Forum, to the Campus Martius, and sought out the small temple garden that they used as a meeting place frequently when they were younger. It would be a good place to rest and clean themselves up.

Aemi flopped onto the grass, under the cooling shade of a large acacia tree and groaned in pain from the wound to his head. Marcus joined him but at a distance, eyeing Aemi warily, whilst Caesar set to work, ripping a small piece of material from his cloth belt and dipping it into the cool waters of the fountain. He returned to Aemi and began to sponge the worst of the blood from his forehead.

"I am going to be in *so* much trouble, when I go home," Aemi winced as the water entered his wound.

"Why? You weren't to know what would happen, or that you would be chased by a baton wielding maniac," Caesar smiled as he dabbed at the cut a little to vigorously.

"Ow, steady, Caesar!" Aemi cried, pulling his head away from Caesar's ministrations. "I wasn't supposed to be out at all, Father's orders, but I saw Marcus leaving the house and I wondered…" Aemi blushed and clamped his lips tight shut.

"You wondered, what?" Marcus snapped. "Why should you be interested in what I'm doing anymore?"

Aemi shook his head, and Caesar saw the pain cross his face.

"Keep your head still, Aemi, at least until I finish this."

"So what were you doing then," Marcus persisted, but Aemi refused to reply.

"That should do it," Caesar said finally, wiping the last smears of blood from Aemi's ear, "It's only a small cut, nothing to worry about. Your hair should hide most of it, and, if you're careful, your mother need never know."

"Thanks, Caesar," said Aemi. He was beginning to feel much better now and the headache was subsiding.

"You still have blood on your tunic," Marcus pointed out. "Your mother is going to notice that, alright! Here, take mine," said Marcus, getting to his feet and undoing his belt.

"I couldn't possibly," said Aemi awkwardly.

"Don't be stupid, of course you can," said Marcus. "They are the same colour, so who is going to notice? We can swap them back next time we see each other." Marcus slipped the tunic over his head.

"I…er…I," Aemi stammered.

Caesar realised Marcus had put Aemi in a very awkward situation, and, wanting to avoid any further confrontation today, he said hastily, "No, Marcus you cannot go home in a bloodstained tunic, what would uncle Marius do to you if he thought you had been fighting again? Aemi, you can have my tunic, I can easily slip into my house unnoticed, so I won't be in any trouble, and I can have it washed and returned to you by tomorrow. Your parents need never know," he said, undoing his belt.

Aemi smiled in silent gratitude. Marcus simply shrugged and turned to pull the tunic back over his head. As he did so, Aemi caught site of his back and let out a gasp of horror. "Your back! What happened to your back, Marcus?"

Marcus hastily pulled the tunic down over his body.

"Gaius Marius did that to him, just before Marcus was sent home to Arpinium, for disobeying his order not to get into any more fights," said Caesar, refusing to cover up for his uncle's atrocious behaviour.

"But you never said!" said Aemi; appalled at the injuries he had seen.

"I didn't know how bad it was until Marcus returned to Rome and showed me," Caesar replied, ignoring the angry and embarrassed look on Marcus's face.

"But you still never told me…what, did you think I wouldn't care?" said Aemi angrily.

"Well you didn't, did you?" Marcus snapped. "When I came back, you didn't want to know me anymore, did you, so why should Caesar tell you anything about this?"

"Of course I would have cared, Marcus, what do you take me for?" said Aemi indignantly. "I still do, I mean.... I," he trailed off, blushing in embarrassment.

"What are you saying, Aemi? Are you telling me that you do want us to be friends? After everything you said to me?" said Marcus scathingly.

"Yes... No... I mean... Oh, I don't know. It's all such a mess, Marcus! It wasn't that I didn't like you anymore, or that I wasn't pleased when I heard you had come back, but so much had happened whilst you were away. Your uncle, my father, the war; we just got caught up in the middle of it, you and I. My father insisted I was to have nothing to do with you when he heard you had returned to live with Gaius Marius. He doesn't want me anywhere near him because he says he is twisted and dangerous. The only reason he lets me see Caesar is because he knows Marius isn't fond of him, and won't have him in the house.

Caesar started. "Is that true, Marcus? Has uncle refused to have me in his house? Is that why I can't visit you anymore?"

Marcus shrugged his shoulders. "Aemi seems to know more about it than me. I was told the same as you, which was precisely nothing." He looked intently at Marcus and after a moment he said, "So, you really were telling the truth, you honestly didn't have a choice?"

"Of course I told you the truth, though I admit I might have said it in a nicer way, it's just, well, I didn't really know how to tell you. I knew you'd be angry, and I didn't want to fight with you again. I know we always used to fight, that was our way, and I didn't mind it, honestly. But we've grown up a lot since those days, and scrambling around in the dirt with you is not something I'd like to do anymore."

Caesar's heart was beating fast with anticipation. Could it be that finally, after so long, they could all be friends again, just as it used to be? He crossed his fingers in superstitious hope, and silently prayed, in that little temple garden, for the gods to answer his wish.

"But in my defence, you did make it hard for me to explain, once you began to taunt me about my father," Aemi was explaining. "I just got mad, and then I wasn't going to give you the satisfaction of a proper explanation after that."

Marcus blushed and pulled a face.

"Look, Marcus, I am sorry I hurt you, truly I am," Aemi wanted an end to the arguing. It had been a traumatic day and his head was beginning to pound again.

"I thought you were jealous of me because I had come back and it meant you would have to share your friendship with Caesar again," Marcus muttered bashfully.

"No...well, yes, perhaps a little, but, I was pleased you came back, honestly. We made a pact didn't we? Friends forever, remember? It was always us, the three of us, Marcus. When you left it didn't feel the same anymore, did it Caesar?" Aemi said, looking at his friend for confirmation.

"No, it was never the same without you, Marcus," Caesar confirmed.

Marcus sat down on the ground next to Aemi. "But nothing has changed has it? I mean, your father will never let us be friends so how can we possibly see each other?"

"No, nothing has changed, not until today that is," said Aemi. "You saved my life, Marcus and just now, you offered to give me your tunic, knowing full well that if your uncle had seen you he would have assumed wrongly, that you had been fighting again, and the gods know what he could have done to you. You put your life at risk for me again, for friendship, and I can't turn my back on you now. It doesn't matter what my father or your uncle think about each other, it isn't about them, it's about us, and our friendship; the three of us, that's right isn't it, Caesar?" said Aemi, turning to his friend.

Caesar nodded. " We have all learnt a valuable lesson today; that true friendship always wins through in the end, whatever is done to try to prevent it. We should accept that we are who we are, and that despite everything, we want to be friends and no-one should be allowed to stop that."

"Hear, hear, Caesar, now that was a speech worth listening to!" Marcus grinned.

"Don't worry, Marcus, we'll find a way round this, you know," said Aemi with a sheepish smile.

"Then let us renew our pact," said Caesar. He held out his arm, fist clenched. "Friends forever," he said.

Marcus put his fist on top of Caesar's. "Friends forever." he repeated.

Aemi followed, so that all three fists were pressed together. "Friends forever," he said.

The pact of friendship was sealed once more, and this time the boys were determined that nothing was going to break it.

Sulla woke up to find himself in a cool, dimly lit room that seemed to be strangely familiar to him. As his eyes became accustomed to the gloom, he could see a wall of shelves full to bursting with scrolls. He turned his head slightly, and a searing pain shot down his neck and through his shoulder, causing him to gasp. As his eyes re-focussed, he became aware of the shadow figure of a man standing behind a large desk. Sulla could see his outline; broad across the shoulders, not very tall, the man had a presence that Sulla could feel even though he could not see him clearly. Something about him was familiar… if only he could…"Marius!" Sulla gasped, and immediately another searing pain ripped through his body.

"Well, you obviously didn't come to too much harm if you know who I am," said Gaius Marius, walking slowly round the side of his desk and out of the shadows to stand in front of Sulla. "Cassius, the shutters if you please. I think Sulla is ready to have a bit of light thrown onto his confusion."

A bright shaft of light lit up the room, dazzling Sulla. He blinked rapidly to regain focus. He recognised Cassius, standing with his back to the light from the window, and over by the door were two men whom he did not know, but, who had the unmistakable look of veteran soldiers, just like the ones that had overrun the Forum.

The Forum, the fighting…it was all coming back to him now. The last thing he remembered was shouting at Dollabella to save himself and then struggling with three of the veterans who had jumped on him. Then nothing…until now. Sulla closed his eyes again and struggled to clear his mind. He realised that he had ended up in Marius's home for some reason, but he was certain it was not out of compassion for an old comrade. He opened his eyes once more and this time he attempted to sit up, realising that he was lying on a couch. Pain shot down his left arm but this time he was ready for it, and, gritting his teeth, he managed to prop himself up into a better position where he could see everyone in the room.

Gaius Marius walked towards him, smiling, and offered Sulla a large goblet, full of wine. Sulla took it gratefully for anything to dull the pain in his body was gratefully accepted, even if it was offered by the enemy.

Marius watched as Sulla drained the last drop from his cup, then he re-filled it from the jug he was holding. "A nice wine, this one, from Valeria. I have several vineyards there. I do enjoy a nice drop of home grown wine," Marius said conversationally.

Sulla eyed him warily, but drained his second glass just as quickly. When he was done, he looked Marius squarely in the face. "What do you want with me, Marius? You didn't bring me here to sample your fine wine did you?" said Sulla sarcastically.

Marius laughed. "You haven't changed have you, Sulla? Still direct and to the point as ever."

Sulla made no reply, his eyes as cold as ice, boring into his enemy. Marius turned and walked back behind his desk, slumping down into his chair.

"So, what *do* you want, Marius? Another consulship? Command of the southern army, what?" said Sulla coldly.

Gaius Marius chuckled, and this time Cassius joined in. Inside, Sulla seethed with helpless anger, but not a trace of it showed in his face. Why were they prolonging this?

"Do you remember what happened to you, back in the Forum, Sulla?" Marius asked.

Sulla shook his head and instantly wished he hadn't, as the pain shot through his neck and down his arm again.

"No? I'm not surprised. You did take a bit of a beating, so I'm told," said Marius, a smile playing sadistically around his lips. "Anyway, the crowd were intent on seeing you ripped to pieces, but, my trusty veterans happened to be in the vicinity and they rescued you from the mob. They kindly brought you here to be placed under my protection. The people would never do anything to hurt me, or my property, you see, I am loved by the people, even now," he said.

"My memory isn't that hazy that I don't remember some of it!" Sulla snapped. "Your trusty veterans were planted in the Forum by you, and Sulpicius, and probably Cassius over there!" he threw a contemptuous look in his direction. "You had every intention of causing trouble. It was your beloved veterans did this to me!"

"Don't upset yourself, Sulla," said Marius in honeyed tones. "You are a clever man so I will not insult you by denying that my veterans were indeed sent in to the

Forum, but they did not go there with orders to attack you, or any other senator, for that matter. From what I hear, you brought that all on yourself by suspending public business and enraging the people. No, my boys were simply there to support me. They are a little… upset by the way the Senate has treated their beloved General. Withdrawing my command of the northern army and replacing me with a mere boy! And no, whilst we're on the subject, I do *not* want command of the southern army. The Italian war is all but over, and I don't take people's left-overs, Sulla, you of all people should know that."

"So what is it then? Come on, Marius. Playing games is not your style. Spit it out!"

"Sulla, you are so impatient," said Marius, smiling. "You always were, and that is one of your many faults. You must learn to wait. All good things come to those that wait, isn't that so, Cassius?"

"Indeed it is," Cassius agreed.

Sulla sighed and rested his head back against the arm of the couch. The wine was beginning to work, and, the pain was now becoming bearable.

"Now," Marius continued. "If you are ready to listen to me properly I can tell you *exactly* what it is that I want." He poured himself some more wine.

Sulla waited.

"I want a letter, written by you, as Senior Consul, to the Senate, explaining that you feel, under the circumstances, it would be better for you to remain in Rome and not to go as General with the legions to fight King Mithridates. You will say, that with the Junior Consul now missing, you want to end the Italian war as quickly as possible, to which effect, you are leaving Rome for a while to attempt negotiations with the Samnite leaders personally. As such, you have decided that there is only one man capable of taking our glorious legions east…and that would be me."

Sulla jerked himself up onto his elbow and glared at Gaius Marius. "*You*? You lead the army against Mithridates?"

*"YES, ME!"* Marius exploded in sudden rage, his face turning purple with anger. "And why not? I am the *only* man who can lead Rome to victory. I have proved it time and time again. There is no man alive who can surpass my military skills, I doubt if there ever will be again, and I am *certain* that it will never be *you*!" Marius leaped up from his chair and leant across the desk towards Sulla, froth forming at the lips. "You will do *exactly* what I tell you to do. *You* are in no position to argue!"

Sulla remained calm, his gaze fixed on Marius's furious face. "And what if I refuse to write the letter? What will you do then, Marius, have the Senior Consul murdered? Even *you* would have to be insane to do something like that! I am inviolate; my person is sacrosanct to the gods as the rightfully elected Consul of Rome. No man can touch me, not even you!"

Marius straightened himself and wiped the spittle from his lips before smiling.

"Oh, I won't be the one to stain my hands with your blood, Sulla, there are plenty of men outside this house right now who would sacrifice their soul and a place in Elysium if I asked it of them. They would do it to please me. *Me*! Because I am beloved of the People, and the men who have served in my legions are still loyal to me. I only have to say the word and you would be taken from here and disposed of. No one would ever be able to blame me for your death. Now, you have two choices, but either way *I* win, Sulla. Write the letter and you can go free. I will ensure that you get away from this house and Rome in one piece. Take a holiday, I don't care, just do not come back to Rome until I have left to take up my command. Or, don't write the letter, and you will die, as certain as I stand here before you now. Choose, Sulla, and choose wisely, for though I have no love for you, I have no wish to see you die this way… not unless it is absolutely necessary."

Sulla flopped his head back against the couch and stared up at the delicately painted ceiling. He thought back to a time, years ago, when, as a young, naïve officer, he had first walked into the study of Gaius Marius, and been impressed by the opulent splendour that surrounded him, but now, the vision was tarnished. The opulent wood panelling and intricate designs on the walls looked faded and old, just like its master. He's got me, Sulla thought to himself. If I refuse to do as he says then I am a dead man and no use to anyone. At least alive there is a chance I will be able to stop him. Catalus Caesar was right. Marius is truly insane. The man I once knew so well has been replaced by this demented devil who still believes he is capable of commanding an army.

Sulla's face remained an implacable mask as he thought through his options. Marius, tense and expectant, paced up and down behind the desk.

"Give me the parchment," Sulla sighed, as he gingerly eased himself upright. "Tell me what you want me to write. I have no wish to die because of you, Marius. Take the command. Fight Mithridates, and I pray to all the gods that an arrow finds its way into that stinking, rotten heart of yours. You want to be a hero of Rome, well be my guest. I hope you get what you are looking for Marius, because it's only in your insane, twisted mind that it will exist!"

Marius was prevented from further explosive retaliation by Cassius who moved quickly to his side to intervene. "Let him have his say, Marius, he's a defeated man. His words mean nothing; he has no dignitas left. When Sulla leaves here, everyone will say that he must have bargained for his life, and the shame of that alone will be enough to destroy any career he may want in the future," Cassius smiled maliciously at Sulla.

Marius appeared appeased by Cassius's words as a smile replaced his angry countenance. "You are an irritating little bird, Sulla, trying to fly with the eagles. You couldn't do it then and you can't do it now. So, write your letter and leave. Your odium is beginning to offend me."

Sulla burned with anger inside but wisely made no reply to their jibes, instead, he rose slowly and painfully from the couch and walked to the table, taking a chair opposite Marius. A new scroll of parchment, reed pen and cake of ink, was passed across the table to him.

It didn't take long to write the letter. It was curt and to the point. Sulla would attempt peace negotiations with the Italian rebels before returning to Rome, where he would remain to oversee the end of this domestic war. The command to take the legions east would be transferred to Marius. When Sulla had signed his name, Marius rolled the scroll and sealed it with hot wax. Sulla pressed his consular ring into the hardening wax and sealed his fate.

Gaius Marius handed the scroll to Cassius. "Take this at once to the Princeps Senatus, Scarus. He will be in charge of the Senate during Sulla's absence. Give him my compliments and tell him that I shall attend the next meeting of the Senate to confirm my acceptance of the command that has so graciously been bestowed upon me."

Cassius took the scroll, and, nodding to Marius, he left the study without a backward glance at Sulla. When he had gone, Marius told the veterans to wait outside the room. When they were finally alone together, Sulla rose to his feet, and slowly clapped his hands. "Well done, Marius. You are obviously not as mad as everyone says you are, for you had this all planned, didn't you? Get rid of our Junior Consul through the debtors law, then, engineer to get me here to sign away my rights to command the legions. *My rights,* Marius, *not yours.* Do you honestly think I'm going to stand by whilst you take Rome's army away from me? I'm certain that if the tables were turned, you would never allow this to happen to you!"

Marius smiled. "You can say what you like, Sulla, but there is *nothing* you can do to stop me. Your letter is on its way to Scarus as we speak, giving him the authority to lead the Senate in your absence. You have given command of the legions to me, and the Junior Consul is no doubt packed and on his way out of Rome as we speak, so he can't help you, not that Rufus would have been much use anyway!" Marius sneered.

"I don't need anyone's help, Marius! You forget I had a good teacher for many years. I can play the game as well as you, no, probably better than you actually. I clawed my way up from nothing and on the way I learned many valuable lessons. I am not some wet behind the ears Patrician sop you can push around, I am your equal, Marius and I have time and good health on my side, whilst you…you have both in *very* short supply! Even the Great Gaius Marius cannot beat old age, senility and death."

Marius's nostrils flared, and Sulla saw the unveiled hate radiating from his dark eyes, but the expected outburst did not arrive. Instead, Marius walked round from behind the desk to face him.

"I may die sooner than you, Sulla, then again, I may not," Marius replied with a smirk. His face was so close that Sulla could smell the stench of wine on his breath, but Sulla wasn't intimidated, and the adversaries locked eyes; Marius's dark pits of blazing fire, met the cold, grey, ice flames of Sulla. "I could crush you into dust right now, if I chose too, Sulla, and you know it. Admit it, I *beat you*! You thought I was an old, has been, and I have proved to you today that I am still very much a force to be reckoned with." he said exultantly.

"Oh yes, you got the better of me today, I will admit that, but there are other days, and I will be waiting for you."

They held their gaze for what seemed an eternity; neither man willing to break deadlock, then, Marius spun round towards the door. "Men!" he called, and the veterans came running back into the room, their swords half drawn in anticipation of trouble.

Sulla looked at them with icy contempt. "You won't kill me, Marius, I know you won't. It's not my death you want, is it? No... You want me to watch helplessly whilst you lead my legions off to war. You want me to suffer humiliation and ridicule from my peers, and you want to see my career destroyed, that's right, isn't it, Marius?"

*"THE WAY YOU WATCHED MINE!"* Marius roared, in a sudden fit of temper.

Sulla smiled. Marius was so easy to throw off guard; it was like teasing a small child.

Marius reined his anger in with difficulty. "How right you are, Sulla," he replied, in a calmer voice now. "And I shall enjoy every second of it. I am going to humiliate you, the way you have done me, plotting and scheming behind my back. And when I return, I shall enjoy seeing you outcast from your social peers as I have been for these last few years. You are finished, Sulla, both politically and socially. Remember, I made you, and, I shall be the one to break you, and send you back to the gutter where I found you!" Marius snarled contemptuously.

Sulla merely shrugged as though it mattered not to him. "Well then, it appears the lines are drawn. You intend to destroy me, and I intend to do everything in my power to destroy you. You won't get away with this, Marius. I am still Senior Consul, and I still have command of the southern army. The minute you leave for the east I shall come after you. Wherever you go, I *will* find you. I will hound you every step of the way. I will crush you and drag you back to Rome in chains. Then, I will have you condemned as a traitor of Rome, and then...I shall have the pleasure of personally throwing you from the Tarpeian Rock, and watch, as your rotten body smashes into pieces. The birds will peck out your sightless eyes, and the fish will nibble at your rotten carcass when I have it thrown in the Tiber. You will *never* get to Elysium, Marius, for I will ensure that your soul rots in Hades for all eternity. This much I *swear*, by all the gods I *swear*, Marius, I *will* destroy you!"

Marius laughed aloud, but it sounded hollow to Sulla's ears; it wasn't the laugh of confidence, but the manic laugh of a desperate, mad man.

"Enjoy your dreams, Sulla, because that's all that they are," Marius snarled. "You won't be in a position to follow me anywhere because I intend to make sure you are taken hundreds of miles from Rome, and you will be kept there long enough for me to be well on my way to the East. Did you really think I would just let you walk out of here? I may be mad, but I am most definitely *not* stupid! Take him!" he ordered the veterans. "You know what to do. Lucius Cassius Longinius will be waiting for you at the Colline Gate with an escort. Tell him, all is well, and I shall call for him to join me in Macedonia as soon as I arrive there."

The men seized Sulla and bound his arms roughly behind his back. Sulla struggled, but the pain from his injuries had weakened him. One of the men pulled a strip of cloth from his belt to use as a gag.

"You won't get away with this, Marius!" Sulla shouted. "By all the gods, I swear I will bring retribution down on you, the likes of which Rome has never seen!"

The gag was forced into Sulla's mouth preventing him from speaking further. The men held him firmly between them: there was nothing he could do.

"Goodbye Sulla," said Marius. "The best man has won; just accept defeat." He nodded to the men to take Sulla away.

As they bundled him out of the study, Marius called Cassius back. "Tell Longinius that I have changed my mind. I want Sulla taken to the place where he was to be held, as we arranged, but I do not want him released…I want him dead. Now go."

The veteran nodded and left the study. Marius poured himself a large goblet of wine, but, as he did so, his hands were shaking, and he overfilled the glass. The blood red liquid splashed down his white tunic and onto the floor, forming a pool at his feet. Marius stared down and gave an involuntary shudder. He grasped the goblet and swallowed the wine in one gulp, and then, in a fit of fury, threw the goblet at the wall, smashing it into a thousand pieces.

# CHAPTER EIGHT

*"All bad precedents began as justifiable measures."*
*(Gaius Julius Caesar)*

## ROME: July- September 88 BC

"Well done Sulpicius, well done!" Gaius Marius laughed, as he paced around his study. "Not one Tribune vetoed the vote?"

"No, Gaius Marius," Sulpicius replied, looking smugly at his patron. "All the laws were passed without a hitch, thanks to my powers of persuasion, and your money. The debtor's law has forced over seventy senators to leave Rome already, and I'm sure there will be more to follow; most of them owe money to someone somewhere, especially since the war. We will seek them out, have no fear."

Marius could hardly contain himself. Everything was going to plan now that he had Sulla out of the way. He looked at Sulpicius, lounging, cock-sure, in the chair opposite. His small, weedy frame, was hidden by his extremely voluminous, rather shabby toga, and Marius fought back those feelings of revulsion that he had every time he set eyes on the man. Ruthless and double-dealing he might be, but Marius knew the value of keeping men like Sulpicius, men with no honour, close. Whilst he was useful to his plan, Marius would continue to support Sulpicius, but, oh, for the day when he could finally rid himself of this foul, leech.

"Gaius Marius, is everything alright?"

"What, oh, yes Sulpicius…Any news of our illustrious Junior Consul? Have you found out where he disappeared too?"

"No, nothing as yet," Sulpicius shook his head. "But I do have people out looking for him; he can't have got too far without someone recognising him."

"And the issuing of Roman Citizenship to all Italians, how did that go down with the people?"

"Not well to start with, I admit, but we still managed to push it through. We have a lot of grateful Italians queuing up to enlist as clients. They recognise the effort you went to on their behalf and they are more than willing to return the favour in any way you may see fit."

"Good. Good! Well, get their names recorded and add them to my client list, and make sure you get them listed by towns, would you; it's much easier that way. I like to know who I can rely on for a favour when I need it," said Marius, returning to sit behind his desk.

"I shall get straight on to it," said Sulpicius.

"And now, the real prize for me, Sulpicius. What about my command?" Marius said eagerly, his eyes twinkling with hungry desire.

"You have been voted unanimously as the new commander of the legions going east to fight Mithridates, by both the Tribunate and the Senate. Congratulations Gaius Marius." Sulpicius said triumphantly.

"Excellent! Excellent news!" Marius laughed exultantly as he poured himself a large goblet of wine. Sulpicius looked expectantly, but Marius ignored him and emptied the goblet in one gulp.

"Sulla's letter obviously convinced the Senate then?" Marius said, licking the wine from his lips as he felt the warm surge of victory course through his veins. Oh, this was a moment to be savoured.

"Yes, of course, it was written and signed by the Senior Consul so the Senate had to agree to it, whether they wanted to or not. A few of them asked why Sulla had left Rome in such a hurry, and without his lictors, but Cassius made a splendid speech and said that if Sulla was this unreliable when he was head of the Senate then how could they trust him to lead an army against Mithridates? Sulla's disappearance swung the vote in your favour; there is no doubt about that. Anyway, what did you do with Sulla in the end, you never did tell me?" Sulpicius asked.

"No, I didn't, did I," said Marius, pouring himself some more wine. "The less people that know the better," he said abruptly.

"But you can tell me, Gaius Marius! We are friends after all. Surely you know you can trust me by now. I got you the command, didn't I?" Sulpicius said in an offended tone.

Marius fixed Sulpicius with a contemptuous stare. "Friends! Trust? I have no friends, Sulpicius, and I trust no man. You should know that by now! You are a colleague, and we did some business together, that's all, and *you* are the last man I would ever call trustworthy. You only do what suits you, when it suits you. You would turn traitor in the blink of an eye if it fitted your ends, so don't bleat on to me about friendship and trust because *you,* Sulpicius don't know the meaning of the words!" Marius snorted and shook his head. Men like Sulpicius were two a penny and would sell their soul to the highest bidder just to get a bit of power.

"I am deeply offended by your words, Gaius Marius!" said Sulpicius angrily, rising to his feet. After all I have done for you, and you treat me no better than a common client!"

*"What we did for each other, man!"* Marius thundered, making Sulpicius jump with the ferocity of his voice. "You got what you wanted, too. Hundreds of people to add to your client list, and the chance to put as many of your cronies into the Senate as you can fit, to replace the ones *you* engineered to get rid of. You have the power you so hungrily sought, so go away and play with it!"

Sulpicius was now bright red with anger at being spoken to no better than an insolent child, but arguing with Marius was never an option and he turned to leave.

"Oh, Sulpicius," Marius called after him. "Just one more thing before you go."

Sulpicius stopped at the door and turned to face Marius, who had swiftly moved from behind his desk and was now standing only inches away. His wide, impressive bulk, bore down ominously towards Sulpicius.

"You *ever* tell me again that you are responsible for my being voted commander of the legions, and I will kill you. Do I make myself clear? I owe you nothing, Sulpicius, n*othing*! Now, *get out*!"

Sulpicius did not hang around to argue, but fled from the study and from the house of Gaius Marius as fast as his feet would carry him.

Marius looked at the empty space where Sulpicius had stood only seconds before and began to laugh. Soon he could be heard all over the house, wave upon wave of hysterical laughter. The slaves shivered and redoubled their efforts at work. Julia hurried to her workroom and locked the door.

Sitting under a tree in Aemi's garden to avoid the burning rays of the mid-afternoon sun, Caesar sighed. Aemi had just won his third match in a row of knucklebones, much to Caesar's frustration. He disliked games of chance but he disliked losing even more, and had insisted that they play another game.

"You'll only lose again, Caesar. I'm on a winning streak today with these new bones," Aemi jeered, tossing the white ivory bones into the air and catching them skilfully on the back of his hand.

"Your luck won't hold forever, it's only a matter of time before the odds change in my favour, and then we shall see who is laughing." Caesar said moodily.

"It's not luck, it's pure skill, and you, my friend, just don't have it!" Aemi boasted.

"Tcha!" grunted Caesar. "Just throw them."

Aemi tossed the bones up into the air. Catching the sunlight they twinkled like falling stars. As they began to descend, a loud scream pierced the quiet solitude of the garden.

"What was that?" said Aemi, completely forgetting to catch the bones.

"I don't know, but it sounded like it came from my uncle's house," said Caesar, cocking his head to listen better.

Another scream filled the air and then the sound of several voices shouting.

Aemi and Caesar jumped to their feet, their game forgotten.

A third scream, and this time the sound of something smashing could be heard.

"What in Juno is happening? It sounds like a war's broken out in that house!" Aemi exclaimed.

"Aunt Julia!" gasped Caesar. "I should go round there, she might need me."

"Don't be stupid, Caesar," said Aemi, grabbing his friend's arm to prevent him from leaving. "You can't go round there. Marius will explode if he sees you."

"But I have to do something!" said Caesar, running over to the high wall that separated Aemi's garden from that of Gaius Marius.

"There's nothing you can do, Caesar, leave well alone," insisted Aemi.

There was another sound of something smashing and the unmistakable voice of Gaius Marius roaring in rage.

"I told you, they do this all the time these days. Your uncle is just plain mad!"

Suddenly a boy's voice could be heard shouting. "No, Uncle, No!"

"It's Marcus! He must be in trouble. Marcus… Marcus… it's me, Caesar. Come to the wall," he shouted frantically, hoping his cousin would hear him.

"Caesar? Where are you?"

"Over here, behind the wall. I am here with Aemi. Come to the wall."

Caesar could feel his legs tremble as he waited for what seemed like an eternity for Marcus to arrive. He heard his uncle's voice, roaring in rage from somewhere inside the house and his stomach turned loops of fear.

"I'm here!" Marcus called out. "Can you hear me?"

"Yes, Marcus, what's happening? Are you alright?" said Caesar, pushing his ear up against the wall. "Where is Aunt Julia?"

"She's locked herself into her work room to keep out of his way. He's gone mad, Caesar, completely mad! He's smashing up the house, statues, glass, anything he can find. I can't stop him, Caesar!" Marcus sounded desperate.

"You have to get out of there, Marcus. Get out, before he turns on you or Aunt Julia."

"I can't. I tried to get her to come out of her room but she won't answer me. I can hear her crying but she won't open the door; she's too frightened!"

The sound of more screams and shouts echoed from the house.

"You have to go back and try again, Marcus. You have to get her out of the house. I'll come round to the front. You get Aunt Julia, and we can take her to my mother, she will know what to do." Caesar shouted urgently.

"All right, I'll try," said Marcus, his voice sounding faint as he made his way back towards the house.

"I have to go, Aemi," said Caesar, sprinting across the garden.

"I'm coming with you!"

The boys flew through the house and out of the main door into the street just as Marcus, followed by Julia and the steward, flew out from the house next door. Julia was sobbing uncontrollably, her hair and clothes dishevelled. She was supported by the steward who looked completely terrified.

He saw Caesar and looked relieved. "Take her, Young Master. Go quickly!" and he thrust Julia into Caesar's arms. Marcus grabbed his aunt's arm to help support the weight.

"We will go to my house," said Caesar, putting his arm around Julia's waist to support her better.

"What can I do to help?" Aemi asked.

"Run on ahead and warn mother we are coming," said Caesar, struggling to support his sobbing aunt.

Aemi nodded and sprinted away down the street. A small crowd of people were beginning to gather outside, in the street. Their vain attempts to pretend to be interested in each other, rather than the hysterical scene being played outside Marius's home angered Caesar and he shouted at them to clear away.

"Now, Aunt, listen to me," said Caesar firmly, brushing away the straggled pieces of hair that clung damply to her red, swollen face. You have to walk, you have to help us, and please try to stop crying. People will notice and they will talk. Please try, Aunt," he said, desperately.

Julia was too distraught to pay much attention. The tears flowed feely, and she mewled like a frightened kitten, turning to her nephew for comfort one minute and trying to break free to re-enter the house the next.

"Aunt Julia, please try to calm yourself." Marcus pleaded, as he restrained her from entering the house again.

Caesar was just beginning to despair of ever getting his aunt away when, to his relief, a curtained litter, carried by four slaves, came round the end of the street, led by Julia's steward. Julia was bundled, rather unceremoniously, into the litter and the curtains were drawn to shield her from prying eyes. Caesar told the slaves to head for the Subura.

"What happened?" said Caesar, as they hurried through the crowded streets in front of the litter. Marcus was visibly shaken. His face was pale and drawn, and Caesar could hear his laboured breath as Marcus jogged along beside him.

"We were eating dinner together, and Uncle seemed in a particularly good mood, in fact, since he has been given the command of the legions he could not be happier, he's even been nice to me!"

"So what happened to turn him into a mad man?"

"Uncle had a visitor, Lucius Cornelius Cinna, I think the steward announced him as, and uncle went off to his study to speak with him. They were only gone a short time and then Aunt Julia and I heard shouting coming from the study. I left the dining room and walked out into the atrium as Cinna rushed past me and left the house, and then uncle came out. He was almost purple with rage, Caesar; I don't think I've ever seen him so angry. Foam was coming from his mouth, and he was shouting the vilest words I've ever heard. I ran from him, I am ashamed to say, but if you'd been there you would have understood, Caesar. I was *so* scared. I didn't think about Aunt Julia until I reached the garden and then I heard screaming, so I ran back inside. I saw Aunt Julia rushing into her workroom and I could hear the sound of things being smashed, so, I went and had a look, and there was uncle with his gladius, smashing the heads off all the statues!"

"He was doing what?"

"He was smashing the heads off, and shouting, *I'll kill him*, over and over. I swear, Caesar, he was demented. If I'd walked into that room he would have had the head off my shoulders too!"

"But who was he talking about, Marcus? Who did he want to kill?"

"How should I know? I wasn't going to stay there and ask, was I?" Marcus snapped impatiently.

"No, of course not. Sorry,"

"And so, after he'd finished smashing up the statues, he started on the slaves. They were running all over the house in sheer fright, none of them knew where he would go next. I went to try and get Aunt Julia to leave her room but she was crying hysterically and I don't think she heard me calling her.

"So how did you manage to get her out of the room?"

"I didn't, it was the steward. I ran through the garden into the atrium after speaking to you, and there he was with Aunt Julia. He grabbed me and pulled us both out of the house, and that's when I saw you," said Marcus.

They were entering the Subura district of Rome now. The lack of sunlight threw the streets into shadow, as the walls of the high-rise Insula blocked out the light. This area of Rome always seemed dark and foreboding, and Caesar saw Marcus shudder involuntarily and wrinkle his nose in disgust. He couldn't help but smile because he knew Marcus was thinking how Caesar could actually enjoy living in a place like this, with the streets littered with rubbish and raw sewage.

Marcus put his hand over his nose to try and block out the putrid smell.

Caesar grinned, "You do get used to it you know,"

"No thank-you!" Marcus mumbled from under his hand.

In a few minutes they were home, and Caesar saw Aemi standing by the main door, with Aurelia next to him. He felt a flood of relief at seeing his mother; she could take care of aunt Julia now. The slaves stopped, and Aurelia helped the still sobbing Julia into the house without a word to her son. Caesar and Marcus waited until the slaves had moved away, before joining Aemi at the door.

"Thank all the gods you got here all right, I was frightened Marius might have come after you!" said Aemi, breathing a sigh of relief.

"There's no fear of that," grunted Marcus, still with his hand over his mouth and nose, "He'll still be beheading all the statues; he has hundreds you know!"

Aemi looked perplexed and looked at Caesar for an explanation.

"Later, Aemi," he said, pulling a grim face.

"What will you do now, Marcus? You can't go back there after what has happened?" Aemi said.

"I expect we shall have to wait and see what Aunt Julia wants to do," Marcus replied. "I just hope that she decides to leave him after this. The man is like a wild animal, and, he's completely insane. You have no idea what it's been like living with him. I almost wished I had never come back."

"We had better go inside, Marcus," Caesar said quickly. "Mother will be wondering where we are."

"Oh, she'll be too busy looking after your aunt, and your father," Aemi said casually.

"My father? He's here?" Caesar gasped.

"Oh, yes, sorry I forgot to tell you. He's come home. He…"

But Aemi was left talking to an empty street, for Caesar and Marcus rushed into the house, shutting the door behind them.

"I'll see you both soon then?" said Aemi, to the closed door, and shrugging his shoulders, he turned and began the long walk back to the Palatine.

Caesar stopped short of the sitting room door. He could hear raised voices coming from inside, the loudest of which was the distinctive, deep, melodious voice of his father. Signalling for Marcus to remain quiet, Caesar opened the door slightly and peered into the room. Julia was sitting on the couch crying, with his mother sat next to her talking softly and reassuringly. As he opened the door a little further, he saw the backs of two men. One, tall and tanned, with a mop of gold blonde hair, and dressed in the red and gold military uniform of a Roman officer, his father, Gaius Julius Caesar. The other man was smaller, thinner, with brown wavy hair and a flowing white toga, and as he turned to glance over at the women on the couch, Caesar recognised the man as his uncle, Marcus Aurelius Cotta. He moved slowly through the doorway now, unsure what to do, and watched and waited for someone to acknowledge his presence. Marcus slid quietly in behind him.

Gaius Julius was speaking under his breath to Marcus Aurelius, and Caesar strained his ears to hear what was being discussed. He could see by his stance that his father was far from happy, and his uncle looked decidedly flustered.

"I have tried my best, Gaius, but frankly no-one tells Aurelia what to do. She is her own woman, and she doesn't listen to the family! Every property I have shown her she has found unsuitable for her needs. It's either too big, too small, no garden, wrong street. I cannot force her to move you know!" Marcus answered in a flustered whisper.

Caesar realised immediately what this conversation was about. Left with orders to find a new house, by her husband on his last visit home, his mother had made only tenuous efforts to do as instructed. Now of course, his father was back, and quite rightly, wanted to know why his family had not moved. Caesar's heart sank as he looked at his mother and then at his father. This homecoming was not going to be the welcome event it should have been, for any of them.

Gaius Julius turned to glance at his wife on the couch, and, as he did so, he caught sight of Caesar standing in the doorway. "Gaius!"

Caesar walked in to the room and stood in front of his father. They looked at each other for a moment, drinking in the changes the time apart had made to both of them.

"You have grown, boy," Gaius Julius remarked affectionately. "How old are you now, thirteen, fourteen?"

"I am thirteen, Father," Caesar replied, and felt just a twinge of sadness that his father could not remember his age.

"Of course, yes, well, let me have a good look at you, boy," he said, stepping back to admire his son properly. "You are developing well, I can see that. Good strong calves."

He suddenly caught sight of Marcus who had remained standing in the doorway. "And who is this young man?" he asked, nodding politely at Marcus.

Marcus stepped forward into the room.

"By Jupiter, it's young Marcus Marius Gratidianus, isn't it? Of course it is, you have the look of Marius about you, boy," said Gaius Julius, eyeing up Marcus as he spoke.

"Welcome home, Sir," Marcus bowed politely, but Gaius Julius had already turned away and was looking at his sister and wife huddled together on the couch.

"So then, Sister, what mess have you got yourself into this time? A fine welcome home this has been for me!"

Julia looked up at her brother and burst into fresh sobs of anguish at his harsh words.

"Gaius, she is not one of your legionaries to reprimand, you know!" Aurelia snapped, placing a soothing hand on Julia's shoulder.

"No, she is my sister, and, she has brought her troubles to my house, therefore I have the right to ask," Gaius Julius snapped.

"I am sorry, Gaius, truly I am," wailed Julia.

Not wishing to stand in the middle of the room with the argument raging about him, Caesar beckoned to Marcus and they headed for the small couch in the corner where they would safely remain out of the way.

"Perhaps I could enlighten you, Gaius Julius," Marcus Aurelius interceded. Luckily for Julia, Marcus had been visiting Aurelia when Gaius Julius had unexpectedly returned home. They had only had a matter of minutes together before Aemi had arrived to warn them that Julia would be arriving at any moment. If anyone could calm the situation, it would be Marcus.

"Gaius Marius has not been… shall we say, quite himself lately, and, unfortunately, Julia has suffered quite a distressing time as his wife."

Marcus looked at Caesar and grimaced. "That's putting it mildly," he said under his breath.

"Yes, Marcus, I know Marius has been ill, but surely the reports I have received tell me that he has recovered quite remarkably?" Gaius Julius retorted impatiently.

"Ah…well, yes and no, I'm afraid. Physically he is well, and he is fitter than he has been in many a year due to the amount of training he has been doing down on the Campus Martius, but mentally… well, that is quite a different matter altogether."

Julia sobbed louder.

Caesar and Marcus exchanged knowing glances.

"I am sorry, Julia," said Marcus Aurelius, "but Gaius has to be told the truth. We cannot pretend that your husband is… balanced in the mind, when clearly he is not." Marcus Aurelius turned back to Gaius Julius. "Marius has been suffering from fits of ill temper for some time now, and the level of violence he displays is increasing as a consequence. He is very…unpredictable, to say the least, and one has to be very careful what you say to him now. Aurelia will back me on this, won't you, my dear? She and your son have both been the victims of Marius's strange…whims."

Gaius Julius frowned. " So, now there's something else I don't know about. You should have told me all that had been going on here, Aurelia," he said, admonishing his wife.

Aurelia flushed. "I didn't want to concern you, Gaius, and I promised Julia that I would not speak of this to anyone, besides, I solved the problem without needing your help," she added with a wilful glance at her husband.

"How?" he demanded.

"Neither I, nor our son, visit Julia at the house anymore. Marcus and Julia come here if they want to, and that way we can avoid any confrontation with Gaius Marius. It is much safer this way."

"Much safer? By all the gods woman, what has been happening whilst I've been away?" Gaius Julius raised his voice in frustration. "I am still head of this family, and yet I am the last to know about things that are of great concern to me! Now, all of you better tell me *exactly* what has been happening, and I mean all of it! Boys," he said, looking around for Caesar and Marcus. "Go and get yourselves cleaned up and then tell the cook to sort out some food for you. You are to remain in this house until I say otherwise, but you are to refrain from returning here until you are called, understand?"

Caesar and Marcus hastened from the room without a word, as Gaius Julius turned to his wife.

"And then, Aurelia, you and I can have a talk about why I find my wife and my son still living in this cesspit!"

*Sulla had escaped his captors, and wrote immediately to his friend Marcus Aurelius Cotta, detailing his abduction from Rome, and laying the blame firmly at the door of Gaius Marius. Marcus delivered the letter straight to the Senate, as Sulla had requested. An emergency meeting was held, but all did not bode well for Sulla. After hours of speeches and deliberations, the Senate came to the conclusion that Gaius Marius could not be brought to answer for this alleged crime until Sulla returned to Rome, in person, to lay the charges of abduction and treason before them. Marius was allowed to retain his command and he continued to recruit men for his legions, convinced that he would be hundreds of miles away in Asia, fighting Mithridates, before Sulla or the Senate could stop him.*

*The question on everybody's lips was where was Sulla? He had not been seen since he disappeared from Rome, and apart from his letter confirming that he was still alive, none of his friends had heard a word.*

Sulla retired to his commander's tent; exulted at the response his men had given him. He flung his toga on the floor and fell back exhausted onto a nearby couch, laughing with the sheer madness of it all. For weeks he had been on the run after escaping captivity, expecting to be killed by the orders of Marius at any moment, but Fortuna smiled on her son, and Sulla arrived tired and weary, but resolved to fight another day, at the base camp of his old legion. Now, here he was, the leader of twenty-nine thousand men, and he was going back to Rome alive, and seeking revenge.

"You made the biggest mistake of your life by not killing me when you had the chance, Marius!" Sulla said out aloud to himself. "Now I am coming to get you, and by all the gods, I swear, I will destroy you!"

A polite cough made Sulla start, and he looked over to see his senior legate, Lucius Hortensius, standing at the canvas doorway of the tent.

"Lucius, come in, come in," waved Sulla, beckoning him forward into the room. He called for his slave and ordered wine to be prepared, along with extra oil lamps to be lit, as dusk was setting in and the light was fading fast.

"Well, that did go well, didn't it?" he said, accepting his goblet of wine from the slave and drinking deeply.

Lucius however, did not drink from his cup, but stood to attention, looking warily at Sulla.

"I'm afraid your officers don't share the same enthusiasm for this venture, Sir," he said, blushing slightly, and looking down at his cup to avoid Sulla's icy gaze.

Sulla's eyes narrowed, the smile froze on his lips as the words sank in. He dismissed the slave before he answered, and rearranged the oils lamps that had been hastily left on the table. Once he was content that everything was to his satisfaction he approached his legate. "Oh, how so, Lucius?" he said, his voice dangerously low.

"The Officers feel, well, we…we do not think that marching on Rome is a good idea, in fact, we believe it must not be allowed to happen, Sir. Rome is our city; our families and friends are there. We are officers of Rome, the legions belong to the Republic, and we do not consider ourselves enemies of Rome…and…we will not be part of any plan that could harm her."

As Hortensius spoke, Sulla's eyes had narrowed to slits of ice-cold shards of fury. They bored into the hanging head of Lucius Hortensius, who, throughout his speech, had not once raised his eyes to look Sulla in the face.

"Is that the opinion of you all?" Sulla asked, fighting hard to contain his fury.

"It is, Sir, well, all except Lucullus. He says he will stand with you, wherever you lead."

"Indeed," said Sulla, turning to pace the room. He could feel the elation draining from his body as he weighed up this unexpected turn of events. "So, I have one quaestor willing to support me, out of all my officers, is that what you are telling me?"

"Yes… Sir." Hortensius stammered.

Sulla felt his blood begin to boil with angry frustration. To have escaped capture and death had been traumatic enough, but he had bet his life that his old legion would have supported him. Now, after everything, he was to be abandoned by his officers, and thrown back on the mercy of Marius and the Senate of Rome. Well, this was not going to happen. Not to him, not after everything he had fought for. The spineless idiots would pay for their disloyalty.

"Tell me, Lucius, did I at any time during my speech to the men, mention anything about going to war with Rome?"

"No, Sir, not in so many words you didn't, but…"

"So your argument about refusing to go to war against Rome doesn't really stand, does it?"

"Well, no, I suppose…"

"Just, no, will suffice, Lucius," said Sulla, pacing around Hortensius. "Did I say I would go against the Senate, defy them and take Rome by force?"

"No, Sir, but your tone…"

"My *tone* Lucius? What are you saying? You and the other officers refuse to support me because of my *tone?*"

"Well, no, not exactly your tone then, but…"

"Oh, come on, Lucius, *spit it out man*!" Sulla burst out angrily, circling closer around Hortensius.

"I…We…"

"You do not have a reason, do you, Lucius? Not a valid reason. You stand here, blustering and stuttering like an idiot and you expect me to listen to you!" he almost shouted in Hortensius's ear, making him jump in fright.

Sulla stopped behind Hortensius and leant close to his ear, his voice now no more than a vicious hiss. "You do not know what I want really, do you? You have no idea. Well, I will tell you something, shall I, Lucius? I will tell you what I want, *right* now. I want y*ou* and the rest of the yellow-bellied officers that have hidden behind your shirt tales, to pack your bags, and leave my camp… *tonight* !" He moved away from Hortensius, who remained frozen with fear. "Then I, and my legions, will strike camp first thing tomorrow and leave for Rome, where I will resume my rightful place as the Senior Consul. I shall have Gaius Marius and his supporters of my abduction shackled in chains and put before the courts before they know what has hit them, and then, I shall personally push each and every one of them off the Tarpeian Rock, when they have been found guilty of their crimes against the lawful Consul and Rome. And after I have done all that, I shall take my place as the rightful commander of the legions and we shall go east, and we shall wipe King Mithridates off the face of the world!" Sulla paused for breath, before continuing. "And *you,* Lucius, *you* and the rest of my so called loyal officers, will spend your days begging in the streets of Rome, for I shall see to it, personally, that none of you will ever earn another sesterces as long as you live!"

Hortensius was shaking with fear now, for Sulla's cold rage was terrible to behold, that, and the thought of what the future held in store for him.

Sulla walked up to Hortensius and pushed his face up close, his pale grey eyes cold as ice; not a hint of emotion in them. "Are you clear now, Lucius, about what I want? Are you able to go back to your colleagues and tell them *exactly* what I said? Well?"

"Yes, Sir." Lucius Hortensius stammered, his voice shaking along with the rest of his body. "I am sorry, Sir. We thought…"

"*Thought! Thought?* You are not paid to think, you are paid to do as your General commands!" Sulla roared. "*I* am the only one allowed to think; my rank allows it, my dignitas allows it! Now look where your thinking has got you, Lucius, and *think* about this. *Think* about how you are going to tell your wife you are unable to pay the rent on your house. *Think* about how you will explain to your children why there is no food on the table, and why they will not have new clothes. And *think* about where you will go to beg for your next sesterces, to fill the starving bellies of your family, Lucius! Then, *think* about how you betrayed me; you, and the rest of those stinking cowards, and see if that will pay to put bread on your table and a roof over your family's head. Now *GET OUT*!"

Lucius Hortensius literally ran from the tent, dropping his goblet of wine, and forgetting to pick up his helmet. The other officers crowded around the shaking form of Hortensius and groaned in dismay as he repeated Sulla's words. Some of the men dashed straight to their tents and hastily packed their things, hoping to escape before Sulla had a change of heart and decided to kill them all for insubordination. The remaining few remained huddled in a group, wondering if there was any way they could go to Sulla and beg for his forgiveness.

Lucius Hortensius did neither. He took himself off, away from the camp, into the woodland nearby, took his gladius from his belt and thrust it through his belly, for the shame he felt at betraying his commander, and the shame he had brought on his family, back home, in Rome.

Lucius Cornelius Sulla rode at the head of six legions; twenty-nine thousand men, battle hardened and disciplined, and totally loyal to their General.

The mid-day sun beat down unmercifully on their helmeted heads causing the sweat to run in rivulets down their dust stained faces, but these men, used to harsh conditions, kept marching ever onwards, their hob nailed boots beating a steady marching rhythm through the open countryside, and creating a dust cloud that could be seen for miles around.

His senior legate, Lucius Licinius Lucullus, and a personal guard of twenty men, accompanied Sulla at the front of the mile long column. As they rode slowly down the road, scouts from his advance party cantered out of the heat haze towards the marching column. They came to a halt in front of Sulla, their sweating horses fidgeting with nervous energy, as they relayed the latest information. After commanding the legions to halt, Sulla ordered the centurions to allow their men to break ranks and rest. The sun was at its hottest now, and the men could do with a well-earned break, food and water. In a matter of moments, the rigid marching formation of eight men abreast disintegrated into a mass of bodies, as the weary men found a space by the roadside to sit down.

Sulla remained sitting on his horse, with Lucullus by his side. A slave appeared with two goblets of cool water, and the two men drank gratefully.

"What do you think they're after?" Lucullus asked Sulla, as he stared down the road. The scouts had reported two senators, plus entourage of twenty guards, approaching from the west.

"I expect they're envoys, sent by the Senate to ask what I'm doing. I imagine the officers I dismissed scuttled back to Rome with tales of my intention to return at the head of an army so it's only natural the Senate will want to know what's going on. If Marius is anything to do with it he'll have them believing I intend to take over the city," Sulla replied casually, as he stared intently into the distance. He was under no illusion that Marius would be doing his best to discredit him as he wallowed in captivity, awaiting Sulla's return.

"And are we? I mean, do you intend to attack the city, only, you've never really made your intentions clear," said Lucullus nervously.

Sulla turned to his senior legate and his pale eyes hardened. "I am marching *to* Rome, not *on* Rome, Lucullus. I just happen to have rather a large bodyguard, that's all. After what happened to me I have every right to protect myself, don't you agree?"

Lucullus nodded vigorously, his red feather plume bouncing backwards and forwards on top of his gold crested helmet. "Absolutely, Sulla, but…when we arrive outside the gates of the city, what do you plan to do then?"

Sulla gave a sly smile. "Well, that all depends on what happens between here and Rome. I think I shall wait and see what these two have to say before I make my decision," he said, nodding in the direction of the road.

Lucullus turned and saw two dark shimmering shapes riding out of the heat haze towards them.

A short while later, Gaius Julius Caesar and Marcus Aurelius Cotta stood facing Sulla, whilst the escort of guards were sent to rest under the shade of some nearby trees. Sulla made no move to dismount from his horse and Lucullus remained silent, next to his general.

"It's good to see you again, old friend," said Sulla, smiling warmly at Marcus Aurelius before turning his gaze on Gaius Julius. "And you are?"

"Senator Gaius Julius Caesar."

Sulla smiled again, but not with the warmth he had shown Marcus Aurelius. "Ah yes, Gaius Julius. I believe I had the fortune to spend a delightful evening in your wife's company, a few years ago now, a beautiful woman if I recall. And you have a son; a strange little fellow if I remember rightly. It was at the home of Marius; he's your brother-in-law, I believe?"

"He is," Gaius Julius replied coldly.

Sulla continued to look at Gaius Julius in an appraising manner, his cold eyes showing no emotion. He could see the effect he was having, by the way Gaius Julius's face flushed as he glanced at Marcus Aurelius for support.

"Well then, Marcus," said Sulla abruptly. "I would like to think that you had made the journey from Rome to see for yourself that I am alive and well, but the presence of Gaius Julius, and that rather large guard you have with you suggests otherwise, so, would you like to tell me exactly what it is you do want?"

"Now Sulla, of course it's a pleasure to see you looking so well, and I can't tell you how pleased I was to receive your letter," Marcus Aurelius said cheerfully. "However, I have to say that when you said you had a plan in mind, I wasn't expecting something quite like this," said Marcus Aurelius, keeping his tone light and non-threatening. "There must be six legions behind you. Are you planning to march on Rome? Surely there must be a misunderstanding here, Sulla, please tell me that is so."

Sulla's smile was chilling. "Marcus, of course I'm not marching *on* Rome, whatever made you think that, old friend. No, I am merely marching *to* Rome, well, that is the plan at the moment, but I suspect they may have to change, depending, of course, on what you have to say. I am, after all, the Senior Consul, and my place is in Rome. As I explained in my letter, I did not leave through choice. Gaius Marius had other ideas, but, with Fortune smiling on me, I find myself able to return to my beloved city after all. Surely you do not expect me to just walk back into the city without protection, do you? I would be killed before I reached the Forum!"

"Of course you must return, Lucius, the Senate, and the People, want their Consul back. Indeed, in anticipation of your concerns, Gaius Julius and myself are here to offer you that protection. We can bring you safely back to Rome, Lucius, so, why not leave your legions here, or, return them to their garrison, whichever is best for them. You know you can trust me now, don't you, and I can guarantee your safety. What say you old friend?"

Sulla looked thoughtful for a moment, and Marcus Aurelius looked on hopefully.

"I trust you, Marcus, you know that, but your companion here is the brother-in-law of my enemy. How do I know that he is not one of Marius's men, sent to slip a dagger under my ribs as soon as he gets the opportunity?"

Gaius Julius stiffened and his face flushed with suppressed anger at the insult Sulla inferred.

"Gaius Marius is my brother-in-law, not my friend. If I were to slip a blade between your ribs I would do so because the Senate ordered me to do it, or, I chose to do it, not because Gaius Marius wants it. As it is, you have nothing to fear from me; it is as Marcus says, we are here to give you protection, not to have you killed."

"I am sure Lucius Cornelius did not intend to insult your dignitas, Gaius," said Marcus Aurelius hastily. "But, you must understand his reluctance to trust anyone after what happened to him."

Gaius Julius shot Sulla a thunderous look but made no response to Marcus Aurelius.

Sulla made no attempt to apologise. "Tell me what the Senate demands of me, Marcus. I assume you do have orders for me?"

Marcus Aurelius swallowed; his throat had suddenly become very dry. "As it happens, there was a meeting of the Senate yesterday, and a decision was indeed reached regarding your return to Rome," he paused.

"Well? Come on Marcus, out with it!" Sulla snapped impatiently.

"The ah…the Senate agreed that you should return to Rome as soon as possible, but without your legions, of course. You are…required to give a full account of yourself as to why you left Rome at a time of considerable crisis… but, Sulla, there really is nothing to worry about, all of this is a mere formality of course, it just sounds terribly formal," he added hastily. "I'm certain that once the Senate has heard from your own lips what happened to you, then appropriate action can be taken against Gaius Marius and his associates in this matter. All you have to do is come peacefully with us now, and, I assure you, this whole situation can be resolved to everyone's satisfaction."

Sulla laughed. "Return peacefully, Marcus? You make it sound as though I've declared war on Rome. How absurd is that! My only argument is with Gaius Marius, and for a very good reason!" said Sulla.

"Lucius, you must understand that in marching on Rome with six legions…"

"*To* Rome," Sulla corrected.

"To Rome then, with six legions, that the Senate and People have every right to be concerned. Hand your men over to Lucullus here, and return with us now. Prove to Rome that you mean her no harm!" Marcus Aurelius pleaded.

"Who has Marius in custody?" Sulla asked.

"Custody? Why, no one. He hasn't been detained," said Marcus Aurelius, forgetting for a moment that Sulla probably did not know that his orders had not been carried out.

Sulla's face clouded and his birthmark began to throb a deep purple, the most obvious sign that he was angry. "Do you mean to tell me that, after receiving my letter informing them that Marius was to be detained for treason, the Senate have done nothing? I am the Senior Consul. I ordered his detention, so why was it not carried out?"

"We need evidence, Sulla, you know that. You cannot order a man's liberty to be taken without some form of evidence," said Gaius Julius firmly.

"I sent you a letter explaining what had happened. Is the word of a Consul not evidence enough?" Sulla fumed. He could not comprehend what he was hearing. That the Senate had taken it upon themselves to ignore his order was beyond reason.

"You forget, Sulla, that you also sent a letter telling the Senate that you had left Rome on business, and, that the command of the legions was to be passed over to Marius. It had your seal on it; it was written in your hand." Gaius Julius replied coldly.

"But I explained that. I was forced to write that letter by Marius. I was taken forcibly from Rome by his henchmen, and I have no doubt that the intention was to kill me, if I hadn't managed to escape in time. As soon as I was able, I addressed that issue in my subsequent letter!"

"Lucius Cornelius, please understand, the Senate did not know what to believe, and Gaius Marius denies any involvement, of course. You are the only one who can change all this by returning to Rome and speaking to the Senate in person. The little matter of you leaving Rome against constitutional law can be resolved to everyone's satisfaction if they see you, and hear you; then they will have to believe you, as we do, isn't that right?" said Marcus Aurelius, looking at Gaius Julius for confirmation.

Gaius Julius nodded in agreement.

"So, Marius was given command of the legions, is that what you are telling me?" said Sulla, ignoring Marcus Aurelius.

"Yes, he was." Gaius Julius replied.

"Was the command withdrawn after my second letter?"

"No it was not. He is still legally commander of the legions."

"And he was not taken into custody, as I expressly ordered?"

"No…but…"

"And the Senate are now arguing that it is infact *I* who have broken the law, by leaving Rome without their permission?"

"That's just Cassius and his cronies taking the opportunity to make trouble for you, Sulla. If you…"

"Do you seriously expect me to return to Rome, Marcus, with no real protection, whilst Marius is free and surrounded by legions, half of which are no doubt full of all his veterans. They would do whatever he asked of them; indeed, it was men like that who abducted me from Rome in the first place. You expect me to leave my legions behind and walk straight into the lion's den!" Sulla gave his horse a sharp kick in the ribs to stop it from pawing the ground, but the animal startled, and leapt forward, narrowly missing Gaius Julius.

"May I remind you, Sulla, that these men are not *your* legions, they are Rome's, and they are not to be used against Her, or, any individual you happen to be enemies with!" Gaius Julius retorted angrily, as he put a respectful distance between himself and Sulla's horse.

"Is that so!" Sulla snapped, spinning his horse round in tight circles to calm it down. " Lucullus, call the Centurions here, now!"

"Now, Sulla, please let us not be hasty," said Marcus Aurelius, fanning the dust clouds created by the trampling feet of Sulla's horse, away from his face. "We are not against you, and, neither is the Senate. We are here to ask you to return to Rome with us. Let's sort this out peacefully. Come with us, convince the Senate that you speak the truth!"

Over twenty centurions came running towards them now, with Lucullus cantering beside them. Sulla turned his horse to face his men as they drew to a halt in front of him. The escort of men accompanying Marcus Aurelius and Gaius Julius sensed trouble and ran over, closing protectively around them.

"Sulla, please…listen to me!" Marcus Aurelius pleaded, calling above the heads of his guards.

But Sulla paid no heed. "Centurions, I ask you again. Do you follow me to Rome willingly, or would you rather return to Capua and await further orders from Rome?"

"We follow you, Sulla," they called out in unison.

"These men, that stand before you, have been sent from the Senate to demand my return to Rome, alone. I am being asked to send you back to your camp, under the command of Lucullus, until the Senate decide what is to be done with you, whilst I return to answer for my crime of leaving Rome when the city was in crisis. The Senate do not believe that I was abducted on the orders of Marius, or, that I was forced to write a letter handing over command of the Legions to him. I did write that letter, but with a sword at my throat, and a pain in my heart! So now, Marius sits in Rome, in command of *my* legions! As Senior Consul, *I* am entitled to lead the battle against Mithridates. The Senate are treating *me* as though *I* am the traitor!"

The men muttered their disapproval, shifted their swords restlessly in the scabbards hanging from their waist, glaring menacingly at the senators.

"It is my intention to return to Rome, but I will not go alone, for if I do I shall surely be murdered before I am able to state my case against Marius. I have given you the facts as I see them men, now it is up to you to decide. What say you?"

The senior centurion stepped forward and held out his sword towards Sulla. "My sword is yours to command, as are the men that serve under me, General," he said.

"Ay, and mine," said another. Within seconds all the men surrounding Sulla raised their swords and cried, "*Sulla, Sulla*!"

Gaius Julius and Marcus Aurelius knew that they had lost the battle to convince Sulla to return with them peacefully, and the situation was now looking decidedly dangerous for them to remain. They hurriedly mounted their horses, but, as Marcus Aurelius straightened his cloak, a rock skimmed past his face, grazing his cheek, whilst another struck his horse on the neck, causing the animal to spin round in fright. More rocks followed, thrown by the angry centurions who were determined to show their displeasure for the way their beloved general was being treated by Rome. Gaius Julius turned his horse, using his arm to shield his face, and grabbed at the bridle of Marcus Aurelius's horse. Their guards were doing the best they could to protect their charges but were under heavy missile attack themselves. Gaius Julius spurred his horse into a gallop, dragging Marcus Aurelius with him, as the thunderous chant of hundreds of men shouted, "*SULLA, SULLA, SULLA*!"

Sulla waited until the envoys were out of sight and then he thanked his men for their support. After ordering the legion to fall in, ready for the next stage of their journey, Sulla turned to stare wistfully along the empty road.

Lucullus, who had been watching the drama unfold from the sidelines, rode over to join his General. The smile on Sulla's face faded, as the dark shadow of sadness marred his fine features.

"Are you alright, Sir?" Lucullus asked.

"No, not really," Sulla sighed. "I didn't want this, Lucullus. I didn't imagine for a moment that the Senate would turn against me in favour of Marius."

Lucullus remained silent.

"I don't know who I can trust anymore. Marcus Aurelius was one of my oldest friends, yet even he sides with the Senate against me. They think I want to make war on Rome. They are scared of me! When have I ever done anything other than be a true and loyal son to Rome? They are not prepared to do anything against Marius, who is more of a danger to Rome than anyone has ever been. Why can't they see that, Lucullus, why?" Sulla cried in frustration.

"They are scared of him, Sulla, there can be no other explanation. Everyone knows Marius is going insane, but he still has power, and that is a very dangerous combination. There is no one in Rome strong enough to stand up against him, and until you return, Marius will continue to do whatever he chooses. I am certain that once you return to Rome you will be able to convince the Senate that you speak the truth and they will come to see Marius as he truly is, a demented, obsessed old man."

Sulla looked at Lucullus and smiled weakly. "I hope you are right, I truly do, for the only outcome if they don't, is war. Rome is not big enough for Marius and myself. The time is fast approaching when people are going to have to decide where their loyalties lie. One of us will be the loser, for there can be no other outcome."

Lucullus shook his head in despair, for his general was right. Rome was not big enough for two titans like Sulla and Marius, but would there be a Rome left after those two men had stopped fighting over her? He watched in concern as Sulla rode his horse towards his men. Sulla could phrase it how he liked, but Lucullus knew; they were now marching *on* Rome.

*A second set of envoys met Sulla on the road to Rome. They came with strong demands from the Senate. Hand the legions over to Lucullus immediately, and return to Rome or any further refusal on Sulla's part, would be considered an act of hostility against the City and people of Rome. The legions were ready for the envoys this time, and they stoned them all to death, leaving one barely alive to return to Rome with their answer. Their General, the legally appointed Senior Consul, was coming to Rome, and he would not be alone!*

A single brazier provided both heat and light in the commander's tent, throwing eerie shadows over the occupants, as they listened despondently to Senator Marcus Tullius Decula's account of his last day in Rome. Sulla lay slouched on his couch, his face shrouded in gloom. He picked idly at a plate of food that lay on the small table by his side, but he had little appetite tonight.

"As soon as the guards returned with the news that your men had murdered the envoys, the Senate was called for an emergency meeting and Cassius wasted no time in pressing for a vote to declare you an enemy of Rome. Unfortunately the senators did not take much persuading, as many were still undecided as to your true intentions, but the death of the envoys made up their minds for them. The vote was carried against you, Sulla, and Cassius argued that Gaius Marius should take command of the legions he had already recruited to fight King Mithridates, and use them to defend Rome against an attack from you," Decula said, his hands shaking as he downed his fourth glass of wine.

Sulla said nothing. His gaze lowered, his pale lashes hid the sadness that only his eyes betrayed, whilst his face remained an implacable mask to those around him. That the Senate could believe he was willing to attack Rome, sent a sharp pain right to the very core of his soul, and he did not trust himself to speak.

Lucullus shot a concerned glance at Sulla. "And the Senate voted in favour?"

"No, no, fortunately Cassius pushed them a bit too far by mentioning Marius. There are many senators who believe Marius is unstable, and a liability, and they don't want to grant him any more power than he already has. No, fortunately this motion was rejected, and it so enraged Cassius that he left the House and sought out Sulpicius, who wasted no time in going to the rostra. He told the crowd that you had ordered the envoys to be killed, and that you had proved you intended to march on

Rome with your legions. He managed to whip the crowd up into a frenzy of fear and anger against you, and then he told them that the Senate had refused to allow Gaius Marius to defend the People and the City. When they heard that, the people went wild. As soon as our meeting was over, we wasted no time in leaving the House as quickly as we could. Sulpicius saw us leaving and pointed it out to the crowd, calling out the names of the senators, like me, that openly supported you. The crowd set upon us like a pack of savage dogs and I was one of the lucky ones to escape with my life. I saw Marcus Flaccus fall, and the crowd tore him apart; I'm certain he didn't survive. I managed to avoid capture, and fled to my home, where I took my horse and left Rome, to come and seek sanctuary with you."

Sulla rose from his chair and paced up and down, walking in and out of the shadows, deep in thought.

"Did you come across any more of Sulla's supporters on the road here?" Lucullus asked.

Decula shook his head. "No, not one, but I was probably the first to leave Rome. There will be more men on their way here; I have no doubt, for where else would they go? Rome is not safe now for any man who is known to be loyal to Sulla."

Sulla turned and smiled briefly at Decula. "Any man who seeks my protection shall have it, and gladly, though I cannot guarantee their safety once we reach Rome. I was hoping to avoid a conflict with the Senate, but, as I'm now declared an enemy of Rome, I can see that I'll have to fight my way back in!" He sighed, and grabbed a goblet of wine from his desk. He downed the contents in one gulp, and then, in a sudden fit of temper, he hurled the goblet at the table, smashing it to pieces. A slave burst into the tent on hearing the noise.

"*Get out!*" Sulla shouted, and the slave turned and ran from the tent. He turned to Lucullus. "Take Marcus to your tent, he can bunk in with you for tonight, then tell the guard to keep their eyes open for any more refugees from Rome. They are to be made comfortable and their needs seen to, but, I don't want to be disturbed again tonight, I have decisions to make," he said curtly.

Lucullus and Decula rose quickly from their chairs and left without further ado; the look on Sulla's face was enough to tell them that their presence was no longer needed nor desired.

Once he was alone, Sulla poured himself another goblet of wine and lay down on his bed, his mind turning over the events in Rome that Decula had described. He was now declared an enemy of Rome, he, the Senior Consul! And now there was the possibility of legions being gathered in readiness to defend Rome against him. How had it come to this? Would his men fight their own brothers in arms if they were asked too? Sulla rose from his bed and walked to the far corner of the tent, to the small wooden shrine that was hidden behind a silk curtain. Behind its ornately carved doors was a selection of gods, personally favoured by Sulla. He opened the door and reached for his favourite, the Goddess Fortuna, which he placed on top of the shrine between the two small oil lamps that were constantly lit. He knelt down in front of the statue and closed his eyes.

"Oh, Goddess Fortuna, queen amongst the gods, hear this prayer from your favoured son. You, who have ever been mother protector to me, watched over me, and favoured me amongst all other men, help me to face the ordeals I must now endure. Look over me and protect me. Send me a sign, O, Fortuna, that what I do receives your blessing. I place my life into your hands, so guide me to your will. Protect me from my enemies so that I may continue to worship you, as I worship no other. O, Mother Fortuna, hear my prayer!"

# CHAPTER NINE

*"If you must break the law, do it to seize power;*
*In all other cases, observe it."*
*(Gaius Julius Caesar)*

## ROME: September – December 88 BC

Gaius Julius Caesar burst through the door into the atrium, knocking the steward flying in the process.

"Aurelia! Where is your mistress?" he asked hurriedly, but he didn't wait for the poor steward to answer as he ran towards the inner courtyard and out into the small peristyle garden, in search of his wife.

"Aurelia… Aurelia!" he shouted, searching the outer verandas of the garden. Fear knotted his stomach as he realised that she might be out at the market, unprotected and alone. How would he ever find her in time? He heard the sound of hurrying footsteps, and Aurelia burst through a side passage and out into the garden.

"What is it, Gaius? What's happening?"

Gaius Julius rushed over to his wife. "Thank the gods!" His relief was enormous, but he didn't have time to saver the moment. "Get your things together, clothes, jewellery, all our valuables, anything you will need of importance for the next few days," he said, breathlessly. "Tell the steward to send the slaves to the house of Marcus Aurelias. Where is Gaius?" he asked, looking around in the hope of seeing his son.

"Why, husband, what has happened?"

"Sulla is marching on Rome," he snapped. "Now, where is Gaius? Gaius!" he shouted.

"He has gone riding with Aemi, but…"

"Gods!" Gaius Julius cursed, the gnawing fear returning to his belly. "That's all we need. We don't have time for this!" And he strode back into the atrium with Aurelia hard on his heels. "Well, don't just stand there, woman, go and get your things. I'll meet you back here in a moment. Now hurry!"

"But, Sulla can't be marching on Rome. You said yourself, he would return here peacefully, and there would be no trouble! I don't understand, Gaius, and, where are we to go?"

Gaius Julius rounded on his wife. "Look, Aurelia, we don't have time to stand around discussing this," he cried impatiently. "The negotiations failed, and Sulla is marching on Rome. He has six legions, and he doesn't intend to stop until he reaches the Forum. Gaius Marius is already getting as many men as he can find to defend the city. It's war between them, Aurelia, and there is nothing the Senate can do to stop it. Now, twenty-nine thousand men are going to come pouring through the gates of this city in a matter of hours, and the Subura stands between them, and the Forum. Do you want to be here whilst there's fighting all around you? No, then I suggest you stop asking questions and for once in your life *please* do as I have asked."

"But, where are we going, and what about Gaius? We have to find him before the fighting starts. Oh, and Julia, what about Julia? We can't leave her all alone in that house!" Aurelia cried.

Gaius Julius spoke through gritted teeth, his fear turning to anger as his temper frayed to breaking point. Grabbing Aurelia's arm, he literally dragged her along the passageway towards their bedroom. "We are going to your parents on the Aventine, and I shall send a slave to find Gaius. As for my sister, she is on her own. She chose to remain married to that man, so she can suffer the consequences! Hey, you there!" he called to a passing slave. "Go to the home of Marcus Lepidus and find my son. Take him straight home to Marcus Aurelius Cotta, as soon as you find him, and if he's not there then look down the Campus Martius. Don't return until you find him, do you understand?" he ordered.

"Yes master," said the slave, and bowing briskly, he ran off out of the house.

Gaius Julius flung open the door to the bedroom and pushed Aurelia inside. "Now, hurry, Aurelia, time is running out!"

Mancurio, head slave at the stables, approached Caesar and Aemi as they prepared to mount their horses. "Sorry boys, but you're going to have to return your animals to the stables and leave the Campus as quickly as possible." he said, looking extremely agitated.

"But why, Mancurio, what's happening?" Aemi asked.

"The Campus is being closed to the public until further notice, now come on, off you get," he grumbled.

"What's the hurry, Mancurio?" Caesar asked, as he slid off his pony and led it back towards the stables.

"We have to clear the Campus before the army arrives," said Mancurio, in a low voice, looking around to make sure he could not be overheard. He had a soft spot for Caesar and he didn't mind sharing this information with the boy.

"Army, what army? Has Pompeius Strabo returned from Etruria?"

"No, young master, not Pompeius," Mancurio replied, opening the stable door for Caesar. He leant over the door conspiratorially. "Lucius Cornelius Sulla is on his way to Rome, with six legions!

"Sulla!" Caesar gasped. "But he was supposed to remain in his camp, forty miles from here, at least, that is what father told me yesterday."

"Well he hasn't. From what I hear the talks with the Senate failed. He's on his way here as we speak and we've been told to close the Campus just in case he changes his mind and agrees to a meeting. The scouts say he's only five miles from the gates of the City!"

"*Mancurio*... Stop gossiping and get a move on!" the horse master general shouted from across the yard. Mancurio shot off like a whipped dog, leaving Caesar to finish un-tacking his pony alone.

"Ready?" Aemi appeared at the stable door.

"Just a moment," Caesar replied, slipping the bridle from his pony's head. "Aemi, you will not believe what Mancurio just told me..."

"*Caesar*!" Marcus came running across the yard towards his friends. "Sulla...marching...uncle getting men together...fight in Rome...very bad!" Marcus gasped.

"Catch your breath and try talking slower," said Aemi, unable to understand a word that his friend was saying, but Caesar knew exactly what Marcus meant.

"Gaius Marius is preparing to fight Sulla, is that what you are saying?" he gasped.

"Sulla? What are you talking about, Caesar?" said Aemi. "He's in camp isn't he? Father's supposed to be going with a group of senators to meet with him, to discuss terms for his return to Rome!"

"No, he isn't, that's what I was going to tell you before Marcus arrived," Caesar replied. "Mancurio just told me, Sulla is only five miles from Rome and that's why they are shutting the Campus Martius."

"I was in the house..." Marcus panted. "when a messenger arrived. Uncle went mad, and I could hear him shouting that he didn't have enough time to organise any resistance to stop Sulla. He thinks he won't stop outside Rome, but will force his way into the city! He's gone off to organise the People to defend the city!"

"You must have heard wrong, Marcus. How can Sulla be marching on Rome? It's impossible...it's unthinkable...it's...well, it can't be true!" said Aemi, with a hint of panic in his voice.

"I know what I heard, Aemi. Uncle can't give Sulla a chance to get back into Rome and accuse him of being a traitor. He is going to attack Sulla whilst he's off guard, hoping to kill him before he can enter the city; that's what he said, because I heard him!"

"Where is uncle now?" Caesar's head was spinning. He wasn't sure if it was fear or excitement that turned his stomach into knots as he listened to this unbelievable turn of events.

"He's gone with Young Marius to the Esquiline Gate to organise men to defend the Wall. Sulla is coming from the east, so that's the side of the city uncle will try to defend first."

"He's taken Young Marius with him? What's happened to Aunt Julia?" Caesar's thoughts immediately went to his aunt, who he knew, would be beside herself that her husband, and her only son, were preparing for battle.

"Oh, she pleaded with them not to go, but they refused to listen. What shall we do, Caesar...Aunt Julia's hysterical...She begged me to try and find Young Marius, to talk him into going home before it is too late, but, I thought you could help me, so I came here first."

"Of course I will," Caesar said, without hesitation. "If we go to the Esquiline Gate we might be able to find him, and, find out exactly what's happening, then, perhaps, we can persuade him to talk Uncle out of fighting Sulla."

"We? You mean, us?" Aemi asked tentatively.

"And if we can't…do you honestly think Uncle would listen to him" Marcus ignored Aemi.

"If we can't, then we have to hope and pray to all the gods that Sulla does not want a confrontation." Caesar hurried back inside the stable and slipped the bridle over his pony's head.

"You can't be serious!" Aemi exclaimed. "What if he wants the fight with Marius?"

"Then we better make sure we can run fast, because if Sulla does come through the gates then Rome is going to be overrun by six legions of very angry soldiers!" Caesar pushed Aemi out of the way as he led his pony out of the stable.

"I'm not sure about this idea of yours, Caesar," Aemi said, warily.

"Not scared, are you, Aemi?" Marcus sneered.

"No, I am not. All I'm saying is…"

But Caesar knew that they had no time to argue. Time was of the essence, and every minute they delayed, Sulla was closing the distance on Rome. The thought never entered his head that what he proposed to do was both foolish, and extremely dangerous.

"Look, are you with us, or not, Aemi, because we have no time to lose. Marcus and I are going to find Uncle, whether you come or not, so what's it to be?" said Caesar sharply.

"Well, of course I'll come," said Aemi, indignantly. "I never said I wouldn't, all I was saying was that it will be dangerous."

"Good, then get your horse and let's get going. We can move quickly, and, it will be safer than on foot."

"Get up behind me, Marcus," said Caesar, vaulting onto his pony and reaching an arm down to pull his friend up.

Aemi appeared with his horse, and seconds later the boys were ready to go.

"To the Esquiline Gate," said Caesar, kicking his pony into action, and the boys cantered off across the Campus Martius. As he rode, Caesar felt exhilarated. This must be what it feels like riding into battle. A grim purpose and determination filled his mind, to the exclusion of all else as he entered the city.

They rode down the Via Flaminia, directly towards the centre of Rome; turning left near the Forum, they urged their horses through the crowds.

"Uncle must have spread the word that Sulla's on his way," said Marcus, over Caesar's shoulder. "I am surprised the people are not panicking. They seem remarkably calm."

"Perhaps they don't believe the word of mad Marius, anymore. They probably think he's having a funny turn," Aemi said, steering his horse around a cart that was stuck in a rut of the ill repaired road.

They soon reached the crossroads of the Subura Major, close to the Esquiline Gate. Familiar with the area, Caesar turned his horse down a side street, in the hope that they could get closer by avoiding the crowds that were now streaming down the main roads, but they were just as packed.

Caesar called a halt. It was impossible to continue on horseback now, for the people were packed together wall to wall, all with one purpose, to escape the Subura. The sense of panic was palpable in the air, and the boys struggled to keep their animals under control. Children screamed and cried in fear as they were pushed and trodden over, whilst their mother's shouted at them to keep up and stay close. Carts and barrows were abandoned as the people salvaged all that they could carry on foot, in their desperation to reach a safer area of the city.

"We will have to leave our horses," Caesar shouted over the din of the panicking people. "I know a place where we can leave them safely." He led the way down a narrow side street and under an archway into a wide courtyard. Along three sides were rows of stalls, where several horses stood. Caesar called out, but no slave appeared, so he led his pony into an empty stall and tied him up. "They'll be safe here, I know the owner, and he should recognise my pony if he comes back," he said.

Aemi put his horse in the stall next to Caesar's, and the boys set off on foot for the last part of their journey. Caesar led his friends through a labyrinth of side alleys that only a lifetime of living in the Subura enabled him to do. As he hurried along, he tried to think ahead. Young Marius, the only son of Gaius Marius, had always been as bull headed and stubborn as his father, and Caesar had very little liking for him. If they managed to find him at all, how could they possibly convince him to go home? Caesar didn't hold out much hope, but the thought of his aunt Julia drove him onwards.

As they drew nearer to the Servian Wall, the ancient fortress that circled the oldest parts of the city, the boys could see men moving about on the ramparts, high above them, and, as they got closer still, they could see that the men were positioned at intervals along the Wall, all looking east; the direction Sulla was expected to come from. Finally, after much pushing and shoving, the boys managed to get to the bottom of the tower next to the Esquiline Gate, which was locked and manned by several men. The Gate, standing over fifteen feet high, towered over them, a solid mass of wood and iron, the eight foot bolt drawn firmly across, to prevent anyone entering, or leaving the city. The men gathered around the base of the wall were ordinary citizens of Rome, and they carried an odd assortment of weapons, for most had grabbed the first thing that came to hand when they answered the call to arms, from Marius. Without exception, they all looked fearful and agitated.

"What do we do now?" said Marcus, looking around for any sign of his uncle or young Marius. "They could be anywhere!"

"My guess is they will be up there, somewhere between here and the Viminalis Gate," said Caesar, craning his neck back to look up at the towering wall before him. "Both gates look east, and that's the direction Sulla and his legions will come from.

If he does skirt round the city to the Campus Martius, Uncle will have time to cut across the Quirinal and be there in time to meet Sulla when he arrives."

"But if they are up on the wall, how are we going to reach them?" said Aemi, gazing up at the vast expanse of stone that stretched over one hundred feet into the air.

"We go up," said Caesar, a look of grim determination on his face.

"What?" Marcus and Aemi looked horrified.

"We go up, onto the wall. We can make our way along the walkway until we find Uncle, or Young Marius; they will have to pass us at some point if we are up there."

"We can't go up there!" Aemi gasped, "At the very least, the guards will send us down the moment they see us."

"No they won't, not if we tell them we have an urgent message for Gaius Marius. We tell them we are family, and that Aunt Julia has asked us to get a message to her husband or son. They won't dare stop us; they wouldn't want to risk the wrath of Gaius Marius would they?"

"I hope you're right, Caesar, because I don't fancy being manhandled by a bunch of thugs up there." said Marcus, looking rather pale now.

"Well, we have to try, Marcus, so come on, time is running out." said Caesar, and he made his way to the small wooden door at the base of the tower.

They slipped inside unhindered, and began to climb the narrow circular stone staircase that wound its way up the inside of the tower. They stepped through a small archway at the top and saw men placed along the wall as far as the eye could see, but they were all looking out over the parapets, and did not notice the boys.

"This way," said Caesar, and he set off along the narrow walkway, Aemi and Marcus following closely behind.

The walkway was the width of two men, and, the boys had to walk in single file. The parapet was just taller than Caesar's head, and over a foot deep, carved from large blocks of red stone. Every five feet a small, rectangular widow was carved out of the stone, part of the defence network that allowed defenders of the wall to view the enemy safely, and to launch their arrows or spears if they came under attack. After passing the main bulk of men gathered near the tower, the number thinned sufficiently that the boys were able to stop, and, standing on tiptoe, take their first look over the parapet, to the plains spread out below them.

"By all the gods!" Caesar breathed in wonder at the sight that met his eyes. Marcus and Aemi stared in silent wonder.

The vast, undulating plain spread out before them, as far as their eyes could see. The straight road of the Via Labicana, that led from the Esquiline Gate, out across the countryside, stretched like a dormant snake, winding its way gently across the landscape, out across the horizon, to the world beyond. Smaller cart tracks led off in various directions from the main road, twisting round trees and small houses that were dotted around. The olive groves and ploughed fields added a myriad of colour to the dry, brown scenery, contrasting sharply with the bright blue, cloudless sky, which stretched endlessly before them.

"It's beautiful!" Marcus exclaimed breathlessly.

Caesar shielded his eyes from the glare of the sun and stared out at the horizon. "Where are you?" he muttered, as he strained his eyes to see into the distance. The heat from the sun created a haze that made the ground before him ripple and dance. He scanned along the horizon from south to east, looking for signs of movement, in particular, the huge dust cloud that indicated a Roman army was on the move; thousands of studded boots, scuffing up the dried dust as they marched along. He could hear his father's words ringing in his ears, describing life on the march for the legions, and how, in particular, one could see an army hours before it ever arrived, just from the clouds of dust that it created. Caesar stuck his finger up to test the direction of the wind and found that it was blowing directly from the east, which meant he would see the dust cloud before the legion. He continued to search the horizon for those tell tale signs, but he could see nothing on the roads at all. Usually it would have been swarming with people, animals and wagons, the daily life of Italy passing to and from the city, but the road was empty, the people gone, or in hiding, as though the world outside Rome was holding it's breath, waiting. He turned his head to look northeast. He was aware that his friends were chattering excitedly, but he ignored them, concentrating on trying to see through the heat haze.

Suddenly, his perseverance was rewarded. A small dot on the horizon caught his eye as it moved and shimmered in the heat. Caesar strained to see, holding his breath to keep perfectly still. The dark, grey shape seemed to be growing before his eyes, spreading slowly across the hill in the distance. "The dust cloud!"

"What did you say?" said Marcus, who was standing next to Caesar.

"Dust cloud," Caesar repeated, louder now. "It's the dust cloud of the legions. Sulla is coming!"

Aemi gasped. "What, you can see him? Where? Show me!" he said excitedly, straining to see over the parapet.

But Caesar had already moved away from the edge of the wall. "We don't have time, we have to find Uncle, or Young Marius, as quickly as possible. Follow me," and he ran off along the walkway.

A few men turned to look at the sound of running feet but none of them attempted to stop the boys as they sped past. They came to a narrow section of the walkway and Caesar slowed down to a walk. On his left, the city side, there was a small opening, and as he passed, he glanced down to see a narrow stone staircase that ran steeply down the side of the wall, finishing in the Suburan Forum below.

"Sulpicius!" Marcus said, as he too looked down into the forum, and there, on a raised dais, stood Sulpicius, addressing the huge crowd of men that were gathered about him. Caesar was too high up to hear what Sulpicius was saying to the crowd, but whatever it was, the people were not responding, indeed, some were moving away, sloping off down side alleys away from the forum.

"What's he doing?" Aemi said.

"I bet my lucky bones that he's trying to rouse the men to take up arms and defend the city," said Marcus.

"Well he isn't doing a very good job of it, is he, judging by the number of men who are leaving," said Caesar, for there were noticeably more men leaving the forum than remaining with Sulpicius.

"Can you see Uncle anywhere?" said Marcus, gazing down at the crowd.

"No, but I imagine he will not be too far away. Come on, we better get moving."

*"Sulla is coming! Sulla is coming!"*

Immediately men began to run. Those standing along the wall ran in both directions, towards and away from the Esquiline Gate. A large man pushed past the boys and made his way to the top of the steps. "*Sulla! Sulla!*" he bellowed at the crowd below.

Caesar glanced down over the wall and watched, as the crowd broke up, men scattered in all directions, pushing and shoving in their haste to get away. These men were not going to stand and fight; they were now running for their lives, leaving Sulpicius alone on the dais, screaming for the men to return and defend the city.

"Come on," Caesar shouted, and began to push his way through the men that were coming towards him. "Keep your eyes peeled for Uncle, or Young Marius, they must be a long here somewhere."

"Look!" Aemi gasped. He had stopped to peer over the parapet, intrigued to see if Sulla's legions were visible yet. "By all the gods, look!"

Caesar and Marcus joined him, standing on tiptoe so that they could get a better view.

In the distance, a thick grey cloud swirled up into the sky, a solid mass, hanging heavy in the air, but getting visibly bigger every minute that they watched it. A bright glint of metal on sunlight made the cloud sparkle intermittently, the first sign that there were indeed men out there, and as Caesar watched, the horizon was filled with a grey, glinting mass; a mass that was moving inexorably towards Rome. Every hair at the back of his neck stood on end as he watched the scene unfolding before his eyes, and he suddenly became conscious of Aemi's shaking body, as his friend pressed up close in fear.

"*Hold your positions, stand fast I say*!" a commanding voice bellowed from further along the wall.

"Young Marius!" Marcus cried, recognising the voice.

"Quickly, we have to get to him before he disappears again!" Caesar called behind him as he took off along the walkway in the direction of the voice.

The wall was getting crowded now, thick with men lined up, facing the plain and the enemy before them.

"Gaius! Gaius!" Caesar shouted, as he caught a glimpse of his cousin over the heads of the men around him.

Young Marius turned at the sound of a boy's voice, and saw to his surprise, Caesar running towards him. "Cousin! Come to join the fun?" he asked jovially, as the boys reached him. "I might have known you would have been with him," he said scathingly to Marcus, who returned the comment with a scowl. "Still following him around like a lost puppy, I see!"

Young Marius had never made a secret of the fact that he resented Marcus coming to live with his family, and never missed an opportunity to have a dig at the boy. He glanced at Aemi. "And you too, Lepidus. Now I wonder what your papa would have to say if he saw his precious son was still friends with a Marius? Still, perhaps the son has more sense than the father, eh?" he said slyly.

Aemi puffed out his chest in indignation. "I am my own man."

"Really. So you have come of age and wear the Toga Virilis do you?" Young Marius retorted sarcastically.

Aemi blushed, "Well, no not yet but…"

"Why are you here? Who gave you permission to come up onto the wall?" he said, scowling at the three boys.

Caesar stepped forward to face his cousin. "Your mother is beside herself with fear, for you, and uncle, and she begs you to return home now, peacefully, before it is too late."

Young Marius snorted with contempt. "My mother pleads for our return? What does she know about anything? Father and I will come to no harm, for we have men, many men who are willing to fight to stop Sulla from taking over the city. We fight for freedom, for the Republic. If Sulla enters Rome, he will declare himself Dictator, and bind Rome to him in chains of humiliation and subservience! The Omens are good, and all bodes well for us this day, so you boys, run along home, and tell my mother to keep to her own business, and we will return when our own is done!"

Caesar felt his heart sink as Young Marius spoke because it was obvious that nothing short of a miracle would change his mind. He had to gain some time to work out what to do next.

"How do you know Sulla intends to take the City, has he said as much?"

"He doesn't need to! Sulla's actions speak for themselves; Murdering envoys, refusing to remain in camp after he had been directed to do so by the Senate, marching on Rome with six legions, shall I go on?"

"My father says that Sulla is only marching too Rome with his legions for protection against men like Uncle, who would see him removed as Consul and exiled from Rome. Surely if this is so, then he has every right to protect himself, particularly in view of what happened to him?"

"And what does your father know of such things?" Young Marius snorted derisively.

"He has spoken to Sulla, and, he believes he is acting in self defence only. Your father is trying to frighten the people of Rome against their lawful Consul by feeding them lies, and, trying to make them believe that Sulla is a threat to their safety, with evil intentions, when that is simply not so."

"You are a child, what do you know!" Young Marius retorted, for want of anything better to say.

Caesar's face reddened at the insult, but he pressed on, undeterred. "Cousin, your father, is ill. His actions are not those of a reasonable man, and he has this all-consuming hatred for Sulla. Now, he is trying to turn the people against him, not because Sulla truly poses any threat to us, but because he knows that when Sulla returns to Rome, he will denounce Uncle for treason, and, he is likely to win. Your father will be shamed, and exposed for what he is, what his illness, and jealousy, and hatred have made him, and all because he wanted the chance to lead the legions against King Mithridates. Gaius Marius is about to plunge this city into civil war to get what he wants, regardless of the cost in lives. If you allow him to continue, then there will be a war, and it will be of his making, not Sulla's, and Sulla will win! He has six legions with him, whilst you have, what? Some old veterans that are still loyal to your father, and a few citizens who are only prepared to fight to save their own skins, not because they believe in the righteousness of what they do. You have to stop him, Cousin, before it's too late. You have a duty as a citizen of Rome, and as a son who cares for his father; you will both surely be killed if Sulla enters the city. Please, Cousin, please find your father and leave Rome. Stop this now before it is too late. Save Rome, and save your father from himself!"

Young Marius bit his lower lip so hard that bright red pearls of blood oozed from between his teeth. Caesar watched, and understood that his cousin fought with his knowledge that what Caesar had said was true, and, the overwhelming loyalty to his father. Caesar's heart was pounding so hard that he felt light headed, and he steadied himself against the wall of the parapet. Just as he thought he couldn't bare the anticipation a second longer, Young Marius stepped forward and placed a friendly hand on Caesar's shoulder.

"I salute you, little cousin, and I take back my insult, but though the words you speak are true, I cannot betray my father. What you ask of me is impossible, though I know in my heart that it would be the right thing to do. I must stand beside father, as a loyal son should. It's my duty to protect him, and to do as he bids me, and, if I am to die this day, then I shall die with honour and dignity. That is all a loyal son can do."

"But what about Rome, Cousin? Does She not deserve your loyalty too? Thousands of people will die if Sulla and Gaius Marius engage in battle, innocent people; what about them?"

Young Marius sighed and shook his head. "My heart is torn, I cannot deny it. I would die for Rome. I have sworn the oath of the legions, but I would also die to protect my father. I never thought I would have to choose between them, but the time has come. Father is sworn to engage Sulla in one final battle, and he is prepared to die, if the gods will it. I cannot let him go to his death alone, if that is what his fate must be."

Caesar could see that Young Marius was beginning to waver, but he had said all he could, to appeal to his better judgement. "I understand your dilemma, Cousin, truly I do, but there must be something you can do. Please, Gaius, I'm begging you!"

Young Marius bowed his head for a moment, trying desperately hard to think of a way to salvage both his honour and his conscience.

"Alright," he said decisively. "I will find father and speak to him, but I don't hold out much hope. If he chooses to fight I must stand by him, and we must let the gods decide our fate, but should he agree to leave Rome, I will take him to Cumae, to our villa. I can decide what is to be done once we get there and father is safe."

Caesar gave a huge sigh of relief. He had done all that he could do, and he prayed that Young Marius would be able to convince his father to stop, before it was too late.

"Thank you, truly, I thank you. May the gods look over you and protect you," he said, clasping Young Marius's hand in a firm hold of gratitude.

Young Marius moved closer and embraced his cousin, and, as he did so, he whispered in Caesar's ear. "Take my love back to mother. Tell her that I will do all in my power to look after father, and, if she hears that we have left Rome, she is to follow, and make her way to our villa in Cumae. Can you do that for me, Cousin?"

Caesar nodded as Young Marius pulled apart from the embrace.

"Now, you must leave, it's not safe for you to be so close to trouble," said Young Marius, looking around at the men still lined up along the Wall. "Oh, I almost forgot, your family have gone to the Aventine, to be with your mother's family, for safety. You better go there as soon as you can."

Caesar groaned as the sudden realisation his parents would be going frantic with worry.

"One of your salves found me down in the Suburan Forum. He said your father had sent him to find you. I promised that I would tell you, if I saw you. Now, go, please, Sulla draws near, and, I must find father," Young Marius said hurriedly.

Caesar nodded, "Goodbye, Cousin,"

"Goodbye, Caesar, and as for you," said Young Marius, turning to Marcus,"You are to go straight home to mother and stay with her, do you hear? You stay there until you get word from me that everything is all right, understand?"

"Yes," said Marcus, with a sullen look on his face.

"Remember, Marcus, you are a Marius. It is nothing to be ashamed of. Keep your head high and never, ever deny your family!"

"I won't, Gaius, I promise."

Young Marius nodded, turned, and jogged off along the wall in search of his father.

Aemi and Marcus crowded round Caesar and slapped him on the back. "By all the gods, Caesar, I thought you would never do it!" Aemi laughed with nervous relief.

"It was touch and go; you had me sweating there for a bit," said Marcus as he watched his cousin disappear amongst the men.

"It was a close thing for certain," said Caesar, with a grin. "Now it's in the hands of the gods. Come on, we better get down from here as quickly as we can. Follow me," he said, and set off back along the wall in the direction of the Esquiline Gate tower.

"We are in *so* much trouble," Aemi muttered as he trotted along behind Caesar. Marcus stopped for a second to peer for a last time over the top of the wall.

"Caesar! Aemi, look!" he shouted, pointing over the wall. The two boys ran back to join Marcus and gasped in astonishment at the scene before their eyes.

Across the plain, stretching as far as the eye could see came twenty-nine thousand men that made up the six legions of Sulla's army, now clearly visible, as the heat haze lifted. The silver, gold and bronze of hundreds of thousands of pieces of armour glinted in the sun, dazzling the spectators that stood in awe, watching from atop the walls of Rome. Thousands of tall pilliums bristled above the heads of the legionaries that carried them, so that it looked like a giant porcupine on the move.

As Caesar watched, the column appeared to come to halt, the dust cloud kicked up by thousands of feet, slowly settling, to reveal even more of the army. For several minutes the only visible movement was the legates on horseback, tiny specs, galloping between the legions and giving orders to their men, then, slowly, but with exact precision, the column began to move again, only, this time, it expanded sideways. The legionaries stepped out to stand side by side, spreading and filling the entire horizon with men and horses. The dust cloud covered them from view for a while, but everyone on the wall remained utterly still and silent, transfixed by the sight before them, and fearful of what would happen next.

As the dust cloud settled a second time, the legions had moved considerably closer to the walls of Rome. Now, Caesar could discern the colour of the officer's horses, and the gold Eagles, the pendants on the standards of the legions, were clearly visible at the front of each unit, whilst the mass of Pilliums bristled behind them. The cavalry were also visible, although they remained behind the foot legions. Over a thousand horses stretched out across the plain, shuffling and skitting around with the anticipation of a battle.

It was the most breath-taking sight the boys had ever witnessed. Used to seeing the legions marching to and from Rome in columns of eight men abreast, now they were witnessing the over-whelming sight of a Roman army, in battle formation, but, this time, they were facing their own city; the men hiding behind the safety of the city walls were the enemy.

A groan rose from the crowd of men close to the boys. The fear and anticipation was almost tangible in the air, and Caesar felt a shiver down his spine.

The men on the wall began to panic. Cries and shouts filled the air, as some of them fought to get down through the narrow opening of the tower stairway, which was only wide enough to take one man at a time. Fights broke out among those that were cramming themselves through the doorway, and Caesar watched, as one unfortunate man was pushed over the battlement, falling to his death in the forum below. He did not know what to look at first, the developing mayhem on the wall itself, or the approaching legions, which now appeared to be on the move again, coming ever closer to Rome.

"I don't like this, Caesar," Aemi said, grabbing his friend's arm for comfort. "Don't chicken out now, the fun's just starting!" said Marcus, his excited grin stretching from ear to ear. He stood up on tiptoe to get a better view over the wall.

"We'll go in a minute, we'll never get past the men," Caesar replied, although he to was loath to leave.

"This is madness!" a man shouted across Caesar's head, to his friend, who stood the other side of Marcus, looking over the wall. "How are we meant to stop a whole flamin' army, with the sticks and stones we have? The old man's mad if he thinks we stand a chance against them out there!"

"Well maybe he's got a legion hidden somewhere nearby that'll come and back us up. I heard he was bringing in men from the ninth," his friend replied.

"The Ninth!" snorted a third man contemptuously. "What use would a legion full of spotty kids be to us? My sisters, husbands, sister's, son, is in the Ninth, and he's only sixteen, if he's a day. He can't throw a spear to save his life!"

"Well it might not be the Ninth then!" snapped the second man.

"There aren't going to be any flamin' legions coming to help us, take my word on it. Marius is mad; everyone says so. The only flamin' legion he's got is the one marching around inside his flamin' head!" the first man joked.

"So what're you doin up here, then?" the second man laughed.

"Could do with the money. I was told I'd get a months legionary pay if I came up here," said the first man.

"A month? I only got offered two weeks! Who give you a month?" said the third man.

"Some man of Marius's, down in the forum there," said the first man.

"Well I'm off to get more money then!" said the second man, striding off towards the tower exit. His friends jeered him as he walked away.

"Bring us back some wine!"

"Get some more money for me while you're down there!"

"You're just yella, no stomach, that's your problem!"

The man poked one finger in the air as a rude gesture to his friends, before he disappeared inside the tower.

Caesar smiled. He would eat his boots if these men stood firm against Sulla.

"What's he doing now?" said Marcus, squinting at the legions.

Caesar peered over the parapet and saw three men suddenly gallop away from the main army, heading straight for the wall. They split two ways at the last moment, one riding towards the Esquiline Gate, and, the other two heading north, towards the Viminalis and Colline Gates. The man rode towards the boys' position, before veering off at the last minute to come to a halt a safe distance from the Esquiline Gate. Caesar strained to see over the top of the wall so that he might hear what the messenger had to say.

"Men of Rome," the man shouted loudly and clearly. "Your lawful Consul, Lucius Cornelius Sulla, orders you to open the city gates. He gives you his word that he has not come to Rome as an enemy, and he intends no harm to the People. He has not come to make war, but to talk to the Senate! Open the gates, and he will pass into Rome peacefully, but, if you refuse him entry into his city, then you will pay for your treachery with your lives! So speaks, Lucius Cornelius Sulla!" The messenger savagely yanked his horse's head around and set off at the gallop, back towards the stationary legions.

Mayhem erupted along the wall. Men shouted, in anger and fear, running around with no sense of direction, but all had one burning desire and that was to get down from the wall as fast as possible.

"This is madness!" screamed Aemi, above the din off the panicked men. "We should have left when Young Marius told us to. What are we going to do now?" All the excitement he had felt at the beginning of this adventure had evaporated to be replaced by terror.

"The other staircase, back along the wall. Let's go there, we might be able to get down quicker," Marcus shouted, pointing back along the wall the way they had just come. Caesar nodded, and took off after Marcus, who led the way, with Aemi following closely behind them.

"How are we going to get to the stairs? We can't get across!" Marcus shouted.

"Just wait for a gap and then run through, it's our only chance," Caesar yelled. Aemi was the first to get across the gap and on to the entrance to the staircase that ran down the outside of the wall to the forum below.

"We'll never get down; there are too many men coming up," he shouted across to his friends.

"We just have to wait," said Marcus, who had managed to slip across to join Aemi. "Don't worry, Aemi, it'll be all right,"

Above the din another voice pierced the indiscriminate shouts of the panicking men. *"An army! Another army is coming!"*

Suddenly, men stopped running and hung over the parapet to have a look at what was happening. Caesar took the opportunity to slip across the gap and join his friends.

"Your head!" Aemi gasped, looking in horror at Caesar's face, which was covered in rivulets of blood.

"It's not as bad as it looks," Caesar replied, wiping some blood away from his eyes. He had been pushed into the parapet by one of the panicking guards and hit his forehead on a protruding piece of the wall. "Can we get down yet?" he asked, peering over Aemi's shoulder to look down the almost vertical, stone steps.

They were clear, as many of the men who were initially climbing up to get onto the wall had turned and descended again when they heard that another army was approaching.

"Now; go now!" said Caesar, giving Aemi a shove towards the top step. Aemi clung to the side of the wall and began to take the steps down one at a time. Marcus followed a step behind him with Caesar at the rear.

Aemi had never had a head for heights, and the steepness of the steps, with only the wall to cling on to, and, a sheer forty-foot drop the other side, made him feel sick and faint.

"Come on!" Marcus shouted, urging Aemi ever downwards, but Aemi was beginning to panic, and Caesar could hear his breath coming in small gasps.

"Come on, Aemi, move!" Marcus urged frantically.

"I am!" he shouted back, but took the next step even slower, holding even tighter to the wall with both hands.

"Who is the other army?" Marcus said, turning to look back at Caesar, who was right behind him.

"I don't know; I couldn't hear," Caesar replied. "Come on, Aemi!" he shouted in frustration. But poor Aemi was struggling with every step now. Sweat was pouring into his eyes making it hard to see where to put his feet, and the steps were so narrow that one wrong move would result in plunging to his death below.

They were half way down the steps with only fifteen feet to go, when the roar of voices filled the air from the wall above them, and, a sudden tide of men began to pour down the steps behind the boys. Caesar heard the noise and turned to look back up the steps behind him. "Jupiter! Aemi, Move. Move now, *Move now*!" he screamed at his friend. He realised that if they did not get down off the steps quickly, then the men descending from above would throw them off.

The pressure was too much for Aemi, who now stood frozen, gripping the wall in utter terror.

"Aemi, what in Hades are you doing?" Marcus shouted angrily.

"Can't move...can't...can't," Aemi stuttered.

Caesar glanced behind him and saw to his horror that the men were now only a few feet from him. "Aemi, you have to move. *Hurry!*" he yelled. But Aemi just shook his head and gripped the wall even tighter.

Caesar made the decision; it was either jump from the steps now, or, be pushed off by the approaching men, who, would show no regard for three stupid boys blocking their way. "Jump, jump now, Marcus," he shouted.

Marcus did not argue, he just turned away from the wall and leaped.

Caesar saw him land heavily on the sandy floor below, but wasted no more time. "Jump, Aemi," he shouted.

"*No, I can't!*" Aemi screamed back, totally paralysed with fear, and he vomited down the front of his tunic.

The men were only three steps away from them now.

"You will!" Caesar yelled, and grabbed Aemi's arm. With a mighty yank, he pulled his friend away from the wall.

"*Move, you little...!*" the men, now only two steps away, shouted.

Caesar gave one final heave, and literally pulled Aemi over the edge, as he jumped for his life. They landed with a thud, and Caesar rolled neatly into a ball. He lay winded for a second before he struggled to sit up. He saw Marcus bending over Aemi, who was writhing on the ground clutching his ankle, and he struggled to his feet and went over to his friends. "Is it broken?" he asked, looking down at Aemi's swelling ankle.

"I don't think so, at least, I can't see any bone sticking out," said Marcus, examining the foot. Aemi squealed in pain.

"Aemi, you have to get up. Try and walk," said Caesar, taking hold of his friend's arm. Marcus got hold of the other one, and, between them, they heaved Aemi up onto his feet.

"Aghh!" Aemi screamed, lifting his foot off the ground. "I can't walk, it hurts too much," he cried, catching a sob under his breath.

"Hold him up, Marcus, we will have to support him until we reach the horses, are you ready?" he said to Aemi, who looked as white as a newly bleached toga.

Aemi nodded, and Marcus put Aemi's arm around his shoulder whilst Caesar did the same with the other arm. All around them men were running, shouting, crying. Panic had set in now, and the people of Rome were truly in fear for their lives. The three boys went unnoticed through the crowds, Aemi slung between his two friends, hopping along on his good leg.

Thankfully the horses were not too far away, and, after much jostling and shoving, the boys found their animals still safely tied up in their stalls where they had left them. Aemi was pulled up onto Caesar's horse with much difficulty and many shouts of pain, and Caesar sat behind, to support his friend, whilst Marcus rode Aemi's horse. The boys set off back across Rome, but the journey was slow. Thousands of people were moving in the same direction, trying to get far away from the Subura, believing that Sulla would burst through the Esquiline Gate at any moment. This time, they stuck to the main road, the Clivus Pullius, for the traffic was moving quicker than in the side streets. The road was lined with shops and houses, but instead of the usual hustle and bustle of the neighbourhood, the shops were deserted; doors and windows shuttered up, all the wares usually out on display along the pavements packed up and stored away safely. They dropped down below the Palatine Hill, and skirted around the Circus Maximus, where the roads were less congested, before heading back up the hill and onto the Palatine. The streets around this area were eerily silent, all the inhabitants locked safely away in their homes, waiting and wondering. The sound of horse's hooves passing by prompted several men to peer warily through their windows to see if it was the first sign of Sulla's legions entering the city, and the boys saw the look of relief on their faces as they rode past.

Finally, they reached Aemi's home and wearily helped their friend down from the horse. Two slaves rushed outside upon seeing their young master, and realising that he was unable to walk, one of the slaves gathered Aemi up in his arms and carried him swiftly into the house.

"I'll call tomorrow," Caesar called out to his friend, as the large wooden slammed shut, closing Aemi off from the outside world.

"His father is going to kill him," said Marcus glumly.

"Well, he won't be on his own there," Caesar retorted, as the feeling of dread at what his parent's were going to say to him, settled in his stomach, but first, he needed to see his aunt Julia, to pass on the message from her son.

They led their horses next door and organised a slave to take care of them, before entering the house in search of Julia. The sound of women wailing assaulted their ears as they entered the atrium.

"Aunt Julia," said Marcus, pulling a face at Caesar.

The boys followed the sound to the back of the house where Julia's private sitting room was located. As they entered the room, they found Julia prostrated on her couch with several of her personal slaves hovering around her, mumbling soothing words of comfort to their distraught mistress. Upon seeing the boys, Julia let out a fresh cry, and flung her arms out towards them, indicating that they should go to her for a hug.

"Oh, Gaius, what have you done to yourself?" she sobbed, looking at the bloodstained face of Caesar.

"It's nothing, Aunt Julia," said Caesar hastily, "We are safe and we have seen your son."

Julia clasped Marcus to her bosom and wept with relief. Poor Marcus squirmed with embarrassment and tried to gently prize himself out of his aunt's tight hold.

"I have a message for you, from Gaius," said Caesar loudly, so as to be heard over his aunt's sobs.

Julia instantly released her grip on Marcus, who, quickly pulled back out of her reach and straightened his tunic.

"A message?" she asked, dabbing an already soaking cloth at her eyes.

"Yes, from your son, but you have to stop crying, Aunt, or I will not be able to tell you what he said," said Caesar firmly.

"Are they coming home to me? Are they coming soon?" Julia asked, looking imploringly at Caesar.

He shook his head. "That I cannot say, Aunt, but Gaius has promised to speak to his father and try to convince him to leave Rome and go to your villa in Cumae. He says it is too dangerous for Uncle to stay in Rome when Sulla enters the city. He's outside the gates of Rome now, with his legions, and…"

"And so is Pompeius Strabo, with four legions of his own," said a familiar voice.

Caesar spun round in astonishment. "Father!" he exclaimed, and ran to embrace him tightly.

"Where have you been?" Gaius Julius asked, gently releasing himself from his son's embrace. "I have had slaves out all over the city looking for you, and what have you done to your head, boy?" he said in a stern voice.

"Oh, please, not now!" Julia interrupted her brother. "Gaius was giving me news of my son and husband, please let him continue," she begged.

"He will answer to me first, but for the moment that can wait," he said, looking relieved at finally finding his son. "Get some of your things together, Julia, you are coming with me," he said firmly.

"No, no!" Julia wailed. "My place is here. I must wait for them to return to me. They will come home soon, I know they will!"

"No, Aunt," said Caesar, turning back to Julia. "I have told you, they will not come back here. Gaius hopes to take Uncle to Cumae, to your villa, that is, if he can persuade him to leave Rome before it's too late," he added.

"How long ago did you speak to Young Marius?" Gaius Julius asked.

"Just over an hour ago, Father."

"Then I fear that he did not manage to convince Gaius Marius to leave Rome. The fighting has started."

A wave of frustration swept over Caesar as he heard this appalling news. He had pinned all his hopes on his cousin succeeding, but to no avail. "Father, what did you mean when you said Pompeius Strabo is outside the walls?" he asked. "Is he fighting Sulla? Has he come to defend Rome?"

Gaius Julius shook his head. "No, quite the opposite I am afraid. Strabo has come in support of Sulla. As we speak, he has laid siege to the Colline Gate."

"That must be the other army the men were shouting about, up on the wall," said Marcus, without thinking.

Caesar shot a warning look to his friend to shut up, but it was too late.

"Men? What wall? Where have you two been?" Gaius Julius demanded.

Marcus blushed and hung his head.

"Well, boy?" Gaius Julius barked, making Marcus jump in fright.

"The men on the wall, sir, and… we were coming down the steps from the wall when we heard that a second army had arrived," he mumbled.

Caesar glared at Marcus. Now they would both be in serious trouble.

"The Servian Wall? Do you mean to tell me that you two have been up on the wall itself, with Sulla just the other side?" Gaius Julius exclaimed angrily. "Is this true?" he said, turning his angry glare on his son. "Is this something to do with your injury?"

"Yes, sir, but we had good reasons for being there, we…"

"Enough!" said Gaius Julius, impatiently. "I will deal with you both later, and you can tell me everything, do you understand? But now we have to get Julia away from here before the legions arrive. Marcus, go and organise the sedan chair for your aunt, and wait outside," he ordered.

"Yes sir," said Marcus, and hastened from the room.

Finally, everything was ready, and Gaius Julius helped his distraught sister into the sedan chair, pulling the curtains around her so that people in the street would not see her. He was giving directions to the slaves, when a breathless messenger appeared from a side street and hailed Gaius Julius. Hurried words were spoken before the messenger turned and ran off back down the road. Gaius Julius looked pale; concern now lined his handsome features.

"What is it, Father, has something happened?" Caesar asked, as he joined him in the street.

"I've just been informed that Sulla has broken through the Esquiline Gate, and there is heavy fighting around the Subura," he said, slipping on his helmet. "Gaius Marius has obviously managed to get enough men together to resist Sulla, although I don't know how long they will be able to hold out," he said, as he fiddled with the buckle on his chinstrap.

"So Sulla is attacking Rome after all, even though he said he would not?"

Gaius Julius shook his head, and the red horsehair plume on the top of his gold helmet swayed with the movement. "No, I still believe that Sulla is only attacking Gaius Marius and his supporters. I do not believe he means to harm the People of Rome, or the Senate. Onwards," he commanded the slaves. Gaius Julius stopped as they reached a crossroads, and put his hand on Caesar's shoulder. "You must escort your aunt to your grandmother's house alone, now. I must take this way. Make sure you go straight there, and don't stop to talk to anyone, do you understand?"

Caesar nodded, feeling uneasy, "Yes, Father,"

"I will return as soon as possible; please tell your mother not to worry. Now, you are in charge, so be a good soldier and catch up with the others," he said, ruffling his son's hair.

Caesar looked up at his father. He wanted so much to beg him to stay with them, and, to keep himself safe, but his father expected him to be brave about this and he could not let him down now. Fighting back the tears, he said, "Do not worry, Father, I will look after them until you return."

Gaius Julius bowed his head slightly in approval. "Don't worry, Gaius, I will return, I promise," he said, and turning sharply on his heels he set off towards the Forum.

It was not until the following day that Aurelia received a message from Gaius Julius to say that the fighting was over. Sulla had been victorious, and Gaius Marius and his supporters had fled Rome. The Senate was now working with Sulla to try and restore order, but Gaius Julius cautioned his family to remain indoors until he returned home.

Julia sat in a chair, silently crying over the news that her husband and son had fled Rome, leaving her behind. Marcus looked pale and tired as he sat by Julia's knee, gently holding her hand to offer what little comfort he could. Caesar sat on the floor opposite his mother, his face an expressionless mask, giving her no indication as to how the events of the last two days had affected him, though he too looked tired.

Aurelia folded the letter and rose to her feet. "It is over, at least for now," she sighed. "I think we should all retire and get some rest. The men will return home later today and we must be refreshed and ready for them when they do. It has been a terrible night for us all, and a terrible time for Rome; let us hope that we never have to live through that again." She smiled at her son and then gently coaxed Julia from her chair. "Come, my dear Julia, you need to rest." Aurelia said, as she gently supported her sobbing sister-in-law from the room.

"Do you think she's right, Caesar. Is it truly over?" asked Marcus, getting to his feet and flopping onto the couch where his aunt had sat moments before.

Caesar shook his head and hugged his knees up to his chest as though unconsciously offering himself comfort. "I don't know, Marcus, I wish I could be certain, but whilst Marius is still alive the enmity between him and Sulla will continue. One of them will have to die before Rome can truly be free from these internal squabbles."

"If I was Sulla, I would hunt uncle down until I found him. Do you think that's what will happen?" said Marcus, yawning widely as he snuggled down on the couch.

"I expect so. At any rate he is free to declaim uncle to the Senate, and impeach him as a traitor to Rome. Once he has done that, anyone who finds Marius can detain him forcibly until he can be returned to Rome to stand trial. If I were uncle, I wouldn't stay in Italy; I would get as far away from here as I could, and then wait for the dust to settle before I decided what to do next. Don't forget, he's Gaius Marius;

He doesn't lose. Young Marius will have little luck in persuading him to stay away from Rome. If he lives long enough, then he will come back, if he is half the man I think he is. He still has a score to settle with Sulla, and he will never give up until one of them is dead, don't you agree, Marcus… Marcus?"

But Marcus did not answer; he couldn't stay awake any longer, and had fallen into an exhausted sleep.

*A month after Sulla re-entered Rome, the city was slowly returning to an uneasy calm. The legions that had marched with Sulla were now safely camped some ten miles away, under the temporary command of Lucullus, and Strabo maintained an uneasy watch around the city's parameters with his legion. With no further bloodshed, the People felt reassured that the Senate were once more in control; the annual consular elections had passed without incident, and Sulla was given command of the legions going east against Mithridates. "Mad Marius" was now considered the true enemy of Rome. Sulla wasted no time in sending out search parties to find Marius and bring him back to Rome to stand trial, but so far, the trail was cold.*

Down on the Campus Martius, three boys stood huddled together. Marcus, spat out more blood onto the hard, dried earth of the training ground.

"Hold the rag on the hole, Marcus, it will help stop the blood," said Aemi helpfully, whilst Caesar kept a wary eye on the group of youths standing over by the stables, in case they came back to start some more trouble.

"At least it isn't one of your front teeth," said Aemi, in a vain attempt to re-assure Marcus. "It could have been worse, you know, if your aunt was still here. The steward won't take any notice, especially if you lie low for a couple of days."

But Marcus just scowled, and spat another glob of blood from his bleeding mouth.

Caesar sighed, as he cast a pitiful look at his friend. For the third day in a row, they had gone to the Campus Martius to continue their training after morning lessons had ended, and each time they had been met by open hostility from many of the other young men and boys that trained there. Having an uncle declared enemy of Rome was hard enough, but Marcus bore the brunt of the animosity, whilst Caesar, who was only related through marriage, had received mild taunts, but no physical violence.

"I told you that you shouldn't have come here today, but you wouldn't listen to me, would you?" said Aemi, brushing the dirt from the front of his tunic.

"It was a lucky punch, that's all," Marcus replied angrily, removing the blood soaked cloth from his mouth. "I could beat that Lucius Granius any time, if it was a fair fight, and I told you before, I've nothing to be ashamed of, and, I'm not going to stop coming here because of them!" he added, looking over at the group of boys who were eyeing him warily.

"People don't see it like that though, Marcus," said Aemi. "They can't take their anger out on Marius, so they do it to you as the next best thing."

"They take out their fathers' anger, you mean," Caesar pointed out. "Those boys don't have anything against you personally, Marcus, but between their fathers, and, Uncle Marius, the hatred goes on. They are just reacting to what their families feel."

"Well let them!" Marcus retorted. "I'm not afraid of them, and I'm not going to hide away as though I have committed a crime. I have every right to be here, whoever my relatives are, and they are going to have to put up with it." He glared over at the group and spat out more blood onto the ground in defiance.

"Calm yourself down, Marcus, for all our sakes. I can't get into any more scrapes on your behalf; father would kill me if he knew," said Aemi.

"No one asked you to help, did they? I could have managed well enough on my own, thank-you," Marcus replied sourly.

Aemi flushed with anger. "Well fine, if that's the way you want things to be, next time I'll just stand back and watch as you get pummelled to pieces."

"Please, just stop all this bickering!" Caesar pleaded. "I suggest we leave now, before they return for another go." But he had spoken too late. A group of older boys, some in cadet uniform, were walking towards them.

"Oh no, that's all we need," Aemi groaned. "It's Crassus and his gang."

The eldest of the group of boys walking towards them, at seventeen, Marcus Crassus was the son of one of the wealthiest senators in Rome. An ex-Consul, and senior member of the Senate, he was also a well-known enemy of Gaius Marius. Marcus Crassus the younger, was now a military cadet, serving with Pompeius Strabo's legion, and had been involved in some minor skirmishing when Sulla had marched into Rome. Walking by his side was Catalus Caesar, eldest son of another great senator. Both boys had a deep loathing for Marcus, and Caesar was certain that they were behind a lot of the trouble the younger boys made for him. The group came to a halt in front of Marcus.

"I see you still don't get the message, Marius," Crassus sneered, looking Marcus up and down with contempt.

"And what message would that be, Crassus?" Marcus answered defiantly.

"You are not welcome here on this Campus, in fact, you're not welcome in Rome at all. Go back to Arpinium where you belong, country boy, with the rest of your traitorous family, and stay there. Your presence here offends us," he said haughtily. His friends all nodded in agreement.

Catalus Caesar stepped forward and squared up to Marcus. "Leave here now, Marius, and do not set foot here again! This is a sacred training ground for those that are loyal to Rome. We train to fight our enemies here, and as your uncle has been declared an enemy of the state, along with that traitor son of his, that makes *you* our enemy too. Our greatest wish would be that soon their heads will be on their way back to Rome, for all to see!"

"Shut your dirty mouth, Catalus!" Marcus said, his face red with barely contained anger. The enmity between them went back a long way, and the last time Marcus had fought Catalus Caesar, it had ended in disaster, for young Capeo, who had suffered a broken leg, and for Marcus, who had been whipped to within an inch of his life.

Instinctively Caesar stepped in between them. He knew Marcus blamed Catalus Caesar for what had happened all those years ago, and, when Marcus had returned to Rome, Caesar had dreaded the moment they would finally meet. Now it was here, and Caesar could see that Marcus was spoiling for a fight with his old enemy.

"Go now, Marius, before I make you crawl away on your belly, once I have broken both your legs!" sneered Catalus Caesar. His friends laughed.

"Look, we don't want any trouble, just leave us be," said Caesar.

"I would like to see you try, you stuck up windbag!" said Marcus, pushing Caesar out of the way.

"Oh, Catalus could break your legs and your arms, and your neck, in the time it would take you to feel the pain of the first blow!" jeered Crassus. "He's the junior cadet wrestling champion, and has been for the past two years. No one can beat him, especially not something like you, Marius!"

Without any warning, and before Caesar had the chance to react, Marcus lowered his head and rammed his body into Catalus Caesar, sending him sprawling onto the floor. Marcus landed on top, and immediately head butted him in the face, splitting Catalus Caesar's nose and causing a fountain of blood to cascade over them. It all happened so fast that none of the other boys had a chance to react, so furious was Marcus's attack. Marcus followed up with two well-aimed punches to Catalus Caesar's face, before he rolled off him and slowly got to his feet. Catalus Caesar lay curled on the floor, one hand clutching the right side of his rib cage, the other hand covering the smashed and bloody pulp of his once fine, Patrician nose, and howled in pain.

Marcus hawked up a goblet of blood, left over from his broken tooth, and spat contemptuously at the writhing form of Catalus Caesar. "If this is your champion, then I can't wait to take the rest of you on!" he laughed triumphantly. "Come on then, whose next? You?" he said, lunging threateningly towards Crassus, who backed out of the way. "No Crassus? Well, what about you?" he said, lunging towards another, younger boy, who was part of the group. The boy backed away with his hands in the air, signalling he wanted no trouble.

"Don't!" Caesar placed a restraining arm on Marcus, but was shrugged off.

"Leave me be, Caesar," he said angrily. "If they don't want me here, then one of them is going to have to make me leave!"

He turned to face the group of boys who remained stationary, staring at Catalus Caesar, whose cries of pain had been replaced by agonising groans.

"*I am no traitor to Rome!*" Marcus screamed. "I am *not* my uncle, and I do *not* condone what he did. I am glad Sulla returned to Rome, and I will *not* be forced out by a bunch of bigoted Romans like you! So, *come on*, if you dare. If you want me to leave, then you're going to have to *make me*!"

One of the younger boys stepped forward to Marcus and raised his fists in an act of stupid bravado.

"*Leave him*, he's mine!" Catalus Caesar ordered, and then groaned in agony again.

The boy looked at Crassus, who nodded, and stepped back to join the group.

"Get up Catalus, you fool," said Crassus, prodding Catalus Caesar with his toe in contempt. "Remember who you are, man, and stop crying like a baby!"

Two of the younger boys stepped forward and each grabbed an arm of their fallen hero, tugging him to his feet. Catalus Caesar cried out in pain but managed to stand. They tried to lead him away, but he ordered them to leave him alone, before turning round to face Marcus.

With a great effort, Catalus Caesar managed to straighten himself up to his full height and wiped the blood from his mouth. "Typical Italian scum!" he hissed, venomously. "No honour! Well you wait Marius. You may have bested me today, but I swear, before all the gods, I will have you for this, and when I do, you'll wish that you had thought twice before crossing me. I'll kill you for this, Marcus Marius Gratidianus, by all that I hold sacred, *I swear, I will kill you*!" And with that, Catalus Caesar turned his back on Marcus and hobbled slowly away, surrounded by the rest of his group.

Only Crassus remained behind to face Marcus, and he drew himself up to stand imperiously in front of him now. "You have offended his honour and his dignitas, Marius. You have shamed Catalus in front of his peers, and he will do as he has sworn; I for one pray that I am fortunate enough to be present when he does."

"Let him try, Crassus," Marcus replied scornfully. "I'll be waiting; just let him try!" and he watched as Crassus turned and walked arrogantly after his friends. He turned to Caesar and Aemi, who had remained silent throughout. "Well?" he said triumphantly. "That showed them didn't it? I don't think I'll be having any more trouble from that bunch of gutless fools!"

Caesar looked at Aemi, and then back to Marcus. "Do you understand, Marcus, just exactly what it is you have done?" he said solemnly.

Marcus looked surprised. "Of course I do. I showed them that I couldn't be pushed around."

"No, you haven't," said Aemi. "You've done something much worse than that, Marcus, you have caused a blood feud."

"A blood feud, what are you talking about?" said Marcus, looking perplexed. "I gave Catalus a lesson in never underestimating your opponent, that's all. He only got what he deserved."

Caesar shook his head. "I'm afraid Aemi's right, this is very serious. You have degraded Catalus in front of his friends, and you have, as Crassus rightly said, offended his honour and dignitas. He had no choice but to swear to kill you if he was to retain his honourable reputation. Don't you see Marcus, those were not just empty threats he made you; Catalus has sworn to kill you under oath, and kill you he will, as soon as he gets the chance."

Marcus had lost the triumphant look on his face as he listened to Caesar. "I...I didn't realise it was so serious, I mean, we had a fight, just a fight. He threatened me and he insulted my family, what was I to do, ignore him? What about *my* honour, Caesar?"

"You have no honour, not yet anyway. You have not come of age. Only when you have, can you claim to be defending your honour and dignitas; I'm afraid your argument does not stand," Caesar replied sadly.

"Well…I'll just have to stay out of his way then, won't I? I mean, who knows, he might go off with the legions soon, and with any luck an arrow will find a chink in his mail, or he'll get a spear in his side, anything really, because, if he's dead, then he can't hurt me, can he?" said Marcus, searching for a way to get himself out of this trouble.

"You don't have to worry just yet, Marcus," said Caesar. "Catalus cannot touch you until you come of age, and wear the Toga Virilis. At the moment, you are still a child in the eyes of Rome, and, his honour will not allow him to touch you. Once you come of age, that is when he can come after you, and make no mistake about it, Marcus, he will come."

Marcus looked pale, and slightly panicky. Caesar wished he could do something to make this dire situation better for Marcus, but he knew that there was simply nothing he could do; the die was cast.

"All right, Caesar, well, if what you say is true, then when I come of age we must make a pact, the three of us, to always stick together. He won't try anything with the three of us, will he?" Marcus said, looking desperately at his two friends.

Caesar and Aemi exchanged a knowing look that Marcus did not understand.

"What?" he demanded.

"Sorry, Marcus, but you're on your own in this," said Aemi.

Marcus misunderstood and rounded angrily on his friend. "I see, too much trouble for you, is it? Don't want to go up against your Patrician friends to support an Italian, is that it?" he sneered.

"No, Marcus, you are wrong!" Caesar said, jumping to Aemi's defence. "What he says is right. It is not that either of us does not want to help you, but we can't! The blood feud is between you and Catalus Caesar alone; no one can interfere with that. I'm sorry, Marcus, but that's how it is. Where Catalus Caesar is concerned, you are on your own."

"You see what your stupid pride and temper has done for you now!" Aemi shouted angrily. "I always said it would land you in trouble, didn't I? Well, this time you've gone too far, Marcus. I hope your prayers are answered, and Catalus does meet his end in battle, because if he doesn't then you're going to spend the rest of your life watching your back. It's not *if* he comes to get you, it's *when*!" and Aemi turned and stalked off towards the stables.

Marcus stared open mouthed after Aemi. "Why is he so angry? It isn't him who has got into this mess is it?" he said, looking at Caesar.

Caesar sighed and shook his head. "He's angry because he's scared for you, Marcus, but he will not admit that. We both are. You have made a terrible mistake, and Aemi is right; your temper and pride have led you to this, and your lack of control and poor judgement may well have just cost you your life. This is horrible for us to, you know. We are helpless to protect you, Marcus, and that's why Aemi is angry; you are his friend, and there is nothing he can do to help you, and neither can I."

Marcus hung his head in shame as the reality of the situation began to sink in.

"Perhaps, if I go and speak to Catalus and apologise, he might drop this feud?" he said desperately.

"No, Marcus, nothing you can do will change things. The oath was sworn, and Catalus is committed. I suggest you do as Aemi says and pray to the gods that something happens to prevent Catalus from coming after you. In the meantime, you better work even harder at your fighting skills, because you are going to need them; your very life is going to depend upon it."

Marcus looked at his friend with tears in his eyes. "I'm sorry, Caesar…I," but he could not trust himself to speak further and turned away.

Caesar knew that this was a hopeless cause, but he could not let Marcus go through the next few years in a state of fear and anticipation. "Look, you are not dead yet, Marcus, so come on," he said, putting a comforting arm around his cousin. "Where is that Marian courage you keep bragging to us about, eh? You have the advantage of time, so use it wisely, and who is to say that Catalus will win?"

Marcus smiled bravely, but Caesar knew that inside he felt awful.

"I will have to kill him, won't I? This blood feud…it's to the death isn't it?"

Caesar looked grave as he spoke. "Yes, it is, Marcus; to the death."

Marcus turned away, and then his stomach heaved, and he was sick: sicker than he had ever been in his life.

# CHAPTER TEN

*"I would rather be first in a little Iberian village*
*than second in Rome."*
*(Gaius Julius Caesar)*

## ROME: January-April 87 BC

*Senior Consul: Lucius Cornelius Cinna*
*Junior Consul: Gnaeus Octavius*

Julia left Rome for her country villa in Cumae as soon as she had news that her husband and son had fled the city, but, they never arrived, and after weeks of waiting in vain, she returned to Rome to be with the only family she had left, determined to face the world, but, she soon found that her so called friends had dwindled away, and Julia became as much of a social outcast as her husband.

Only Aurelia visited regularly, now that her husband had bought a new home on the Aventine, and the family had left the Subura behind, much to the relief of Gaius Julius. Heavily pregnant, Aurelia stayed close to home, and Caesar spent as much time out of the house as he could, seeking comfort and peace with his aunt Julia, who in turn relished the opportunity to pamper and fuss over her favourite nephew. Caesar had left home early this morning and he had found his aunt in the work room, busy spinning yarn to make new cloaks for her husband and son in the event that one day, they would return home.

"It is wonderful for Aurelia to have her husband home, especially now that the baby is due," Julia chattered incessantly as she wound the wool onto her spool. "Your father missed out on seeing you as a baby, and I am certain he is looking forward to being there when your new brother or sister is born, especially after losing the baby last year. I wonder, will it be a boy or girl?" she asked, smiling tenderly at Caesar.

"I don't mind, Aunt, as long as the baby, and, my mother, survive," he said, wrinkling his nose and looking rather uncomfortable. Secretly, he had been upset when his mother had told him that she was expecting another child for he had been the only child for thirteen years, and now he would have to share his parents. He soon rationalised that this was not a mature way to feel, and he had tried to be happy for them, but then the fear that his mother might not survive the birth took over, and, the nearer that day came, the unhappier he was. Death rates for mothers and babies was very high, even with the best medical care available, and he knew many friends whose parents had lost several babies, and one or two who had lost their mothers as well. Caesar had not shared those feelings of worry with anyone, keeping them bottled up inside, and preferring not to talk about the baby at all, in case his true feelings were revealed.

Julia stopped winding the wool and placed a tender hand on his arm. "Of course they will survive, Gaius. Your mother is strong and healthy and your father has arranged for the best midwives to be with her when the time comes. I have also made several offerings to the Goddess's, Genita Mana, and, Mata Mutata; they will look over your mother throughout her ordeal. I am sure all the gods will smile down on both mother and child," she said, patting his hand reassuringly.

Caesar sighed. "I'm sure you are right, Aunt Julia." He smiled briefly before concentrating on unravelling the strands of wool he held in his hands.

The door to Julia's workroom opened and in walked Marcus, to Caesar's relief. "I have finished helping Tito, Aunt Julia. May I go out with Caesar now?" he asked, winking conspiratorially at his friend.

"Of course, Marcus," Julia smiled. "Will you be staying for your dinner tonight, Gaius?" she said, looking at Caesar.

"Yes, please, Aunt Julia," he replied, grateful to have the excuse of returning home late. His father was to dine at a friend's house that evening which meant he would be alone with his mother, a prospect he did not relish.

"Good, then I shall see you boys later," said Julia, taking the wool from Caesar as he stood to leave.

Caesar gave Julia a peck on the cheek and he and Marcus left the room swiftly, before she could find an excuse to keep them talking.

"Thanks for rescuing me," said Caesar, as they left the house.

"Why, was Aunt Julia talking about how much she misses uncle again?"

"No, not quite, but she was working up to it, I could tell," said Caesar with a grimace.

"That's all she ever talks about now. Where are they? Will I ever see them again? How lonely she is. Honestly, doesn't she realise that they can never return to Rome? They have been exiled and labelled traitors. The only way Uncle and Young Marius will return is in chains, or in an urn, if someone kills them first."

"I know, and it does get irritating to listen to all of the time, but we have to bare with her, Marcus She is grieving for the loss of her men, and, it is up to us to help her through it. Anyway, if she knew the truth and realised just what they were both capable of then I think it would kill her. Let her live in hope, it does no harm to anyone does it?"

"Mmm, I suppose you're right, as usual, Caesar. Anyway, I'll go on to the Campus Martius, if you collect Aemi, and I'll meet you by the stables," said Marcus.

"We won't be far behind you," said Caesar, turning off to Aemi's home. He waited until Marcus had gone out of sight before he knocked on the door. The doorkeeper showed him into the atrium, where he came face to face with Marcus Aemilius Lepidus, Aemi's father.

A tall, broad man, with white blonde hair and rich brown eyes, Marcus Aemilius Lepidus was a striking looking man. He had an unmistakable aura of wealth, prestige and high status. Traditional in his values, and, a staunch supporter of the Optimate party within the Senate, Marcus Aemilius Lepidus was very definitely the master of this house. Caesar fully appreciated why Aemi both adored and respected his father, with a healthy dose of fear thrown in for good measure, and, it had never ceased to amaze him that Aemi had knowingly gone against his father to persist in his friendship with Marcus, understanding how much he held his father in such high regard.

Marcus Aemilius nodded to Caesar, but showed no pleasure at seeing him. Caesar was made only to aware that whilst his continued friendship with Aemi was tolerated, it was neither encouraged, nor welcomed.

"You will find Marcus in his room," Marcus Aemilius said formally, and, with the briefest of nods, he strode off down a corridor, which led to his study.

"Caesar," said Aemi, who had just wandered into the atrium.

Caesar smiled with relief to see a friendly face. "We are off down the Campus to watch the legions train, do you want to come?"

"Of course I will," said Aemi, "Just give me a moment to tell the steward where I'm going," he said as he disappeared off down another corridor.

Caesar walked out into the peristyle garden to look at the statues whilst he waited for Aemi to return. Like most large roman villas, the ornamental gardens were situated at the centre, open to the elements, with the main buildings encircling the garden on all four sides. He stood admiring the statue of Mars, god of war, when he heard voices coming from inside the atrium, and turned in time to see Aemi's father greeting two senators who had just arrived at the house. Caesar stepped over to the colonnade that bordered the garden so that he would be out of view, just as Aemi appeared running from the other end of the garden. Caesar signalled for Aemi to come quietly, and the two boys crept onto the walkway of the colonnade and closer to the atrium.

"What's happening?" Aemi whispered.

"I'm not sure. Those two turned up just as I came into the garden. I thought they would go to your father's study but it appears as though they have called to give him a message," Caesar replied. The sound of raised men's voices drifted out into the garden.

"Come on, let's get close enough to hear," said Aemi, taking the lead and creeping along the colonnade to the entrance of the atrium.

Caesar followed, but he felt uncomfortable. Spying on their elders used to be fun, but they were at the age now, where, if they were caught, the repercussions would not be pleasant.

Aemi came to a halt by the side of a large statue of Venus and Caesar bunched up close behind him. The conversation in the atrium was loud enough for both the boys to hear.

"How can this be, Fimbria? Are you telling me that Cinna is behind this uprising? But why, what has he got to gain from this?" said Marcus Aemilius Lepidus angrily.

"You can bet your life Marius is behind it," the second senator grumbled.

"We don't have time to speculate, Quintus," Fimbria rebuked his colleague. "The Junior Consul has gathered supporters to go to the Forum. They intend to stop the demonstration, with force if they have to. We have to do something now before more violence erupts on the streets!"

"Where is Octavius now? Do we have time to stop him before it is too late?"

"I don't know. As soon as I heard what was happening I came straight here. If anyone can talk Octavius out of doing something rash, it is you."

"Then let us waste no more time," said Marcus Aemilius Lepidus, and the three men hurried from the house.

"What was all that about?" said Caesar to Aemi, as they came out from behind the statue.

"I don't know, but it doesn't sound too good. I'm going to follow Father," said Aemi, hurrying into the atrium.

"Wait! You can't just rush out there after him, Aemi, you will get into trouble," said Caesar, grasping his friend's arm to hold him back.

"I have too!" Aemi cried, shrugging off Caesar's hand.

"Look, Aemi, think. If you go after your father now, he will send you home. You heard what was said, and, if there is trouble in the Forum then that is the last place he will want you to be." Caesar could see from the look on Aemi's face that this was one argument he was not going to win. "Alright, have it your way, but if we must follow them, then we do so at a distance. We also have to think of Marcus. He has gone ahead to the Campus, and, he'll go through the Forum. We must find him and make sure he's safe."

Aemi reluctantly agreed, and the two boys left the house. There was no sign of the senators, indicating that they had gone at speed down the street.

"They'll be heading for the Forum," said Caesar, and he set of at a run.

"Master Gaius! Master Gaius!" a young slave boy from Caesar's household ran along the street towards them.

"Arausio? What is it? What's the matter?"

"It's your lady mother. Her pains have started and you are to come home immediately."

Caesar's heart sank. "But Marcus…" Caesar was torn between duty to his mother and concern for Marcus, who could be in trouble right now and in need of his help.

"Don't worry about Marcus, I'll find him. You're needed at home," said Aemi, and he gave his friend a reassuring pat on the shoulder. "She'll be all right, Caesar, I know she will."

Caesar prayed that Aemi was right. This was the moment he had been dreading, and there was nothing he could do to help his mother to get through her ordeal.

"I'll pray for you," Aemi shouted, as Caesar and the slave boy ran off down the street.

Meanwhile, Marcus had walked straight into a huge demonstration by Italian citizens, which spread back from the Forum, along the Vicus Tuscus, and into the market area. Hundreds of men were shouting and chanting slogans that Marcus did not understand, but, their faces showed anger and frustration, and the mood of the crowd looked decidedly ugly. Marcus hesitated, wondering if should return to the Palatine, to warn his friends not to come this way, when he saw a man that he recognised from his home town of Arpinium, standing near a market stall close by.

"Antonius, Antonius!" Marcus shouted, pushing his way through the crowd. Antonius turned at the sound of his name being called and his face lit up in surprise as Marcus appeared by his side. "Why, if it isn't young Marcus Marius Gratidianus," he said, ruffling the boys hair affectionately. "I knew you had returned to live in Rome with your uncle, but I never thought I would see you. Rome is a big place, isn't it?"

"Antonius, what's going on? Why are you here, and why are all these men demonstrating?" said Marcus, who was being jostled by the crowd.

"It's wonderful isn't it?" said Antonius, smiling broadly. "Did you ever think to see so many Italians together in Rome at one time? This truly is a sign of change," he said, elbowing a man out of the way to make more room for Marcus.

"But what are you here for? What's it all about?" persisted Marcus.

"The citizenship, and our right to vote, Marcus," Antonius replied. "Senior Consul Cinna, promised all Italians who were granted the citizenship the right to vote, but, the Plebeian Assembly has refused to agree to pass the law. The Junior Consul, Octavius, agrees with the Plebeian Assembly, and the Senate is divided. They can't get away with giving us citizenship but limiting our power to vote. We intend to make them listen to us today, and it looks like we are succeeding, boy. I never dreamed we would get such a turn out; this is truly magnificent!" said Antonius, moving forward with the crowd as it slowly moved towards the Forum."My advice is to go home, Marcus," Antonius said seriously now. "There could be trouble, and this is not the place for a boy to be."

"I will, Antonius," said Marcus who was already tiring of being jostled and trodden on. "I wish you well, and I hope you achieve what you want!" he shouted, as Antonius was hustled forward into the crowd. Antonius raised his hand in farewell and raised his voice to chant with his fellow demonstrators, leaving Marcus to push his way out of the crowd.

He dodged into a narrow side street intending to take a short cut home, but, a noise, like the distant rumble of thunder, caught his attention. Marcus stopped and listened intently. He could hear the fading chants of the demonstrators as they moved towards the Forum, but this other sound was different. Then, he felt a strange vibration under his feet, and at the same time, the rumbling got louder and louder. Almost immediately, a tide of people ran into the side street. Marcus was flattened against a wall, the breath knocked out of him, as panicking men, women and children, fought for space in the narrow street, their sole intention, to get as far away as possible from the impending danger.

The next thing Marcus knew, a large hand grabbed the front of his tunic, and literally threw him backwards. He landed in a heap, and instantly covered his head, as he was kicked and trodden on by scores of trampling feet. His instinct was to crawl for safety, and he groped his way through the sea of legs, searching for an opening to escape. Seconds later he was free, and, as he scrambled to his feet, shocked and dazed, he saw what was causing the panic. Hundreds of men were thundering down the Via Sacra towards him. Many of them were armed, and all had a look of murderous intent on their faces. Marcus leapt out of the way as the tide of men swept by him, pressing up against the wall so as to make himself as inconspicuous as possible, for he knew at times like this, men did not care who they attacked in their frenzy for retribution. Frightened, and unsure how to get away from the trouble, Marcus turned and ran up the side street, out into the lower market place, and headed back towards the Palatine. As he ran along the Clivus Victoriae, he met Aemi coming the other way.

"Marcus, thank the gods that I've found you, are you alright?" Aemi panted, bending over to catch his breath.

"Yes, I am, but what are you doing here? I was just trying to get back to warn you."

"It's a long story, I'll tell you later. I'm looking for my father, have you seen him? I think he may have come this way."

"He ran down there, into the crowd, with two other senators. He's too late, if he was thinking of trying to stop the riot."

Aemi groaned in despair as he looked down the road, his face as white as a sheet. "What's happening, do you know?" he asked.

"The Italians are demonstrating about their voting rights. I met a man that I know from Arpinium, and he told me," Marcus explained. "And then a mass of men appeared back there, armed with batons. They're obviously trying to break up the demonstration but it's turned nasty."

"The senators who were with my father were hoping that he could talk to the Junior Consul, Octavius, to stop this happening," said Aemi, "But he's obviously too late,"

"I'll say," said Marcus. "We better get away from here whilst we can. Where's Caesar?"

"His mother has gone into labour and so he had to go home. We were just on our way to find you when he got the news."

Marcus pulled a face. "Poor Caesar. I know how much he was dreading this. How about we go up to the Tarpeian Rock? We can watch what's happening from up there and it will take our minds off of things."

But what about my father? I can't leave now. What if he gets hurt?"

"There's nothing you can do to help him, Aemi, and anyway, you'd never find him amongst all these men," said Marcus. "Come on, I'll race you!"

Finally, as the sun began to set over the city, Gaius Julius came home. Caesar rushed into the atrium to greet his father and was shocked to see him looking so tired and dishevelled.

"Any news?" Gaius Julius asked his son, as he shrugged his cloak off onto the floor.

"No, not yet, but aunt Julia is with mother and she came from the birthing room a little while ago to say that it would not be long now," Caesar replied, looking anxiously at his father's pale and drawn face.

"These things take time, my son," said Gaius Julius, giving Caesar a reassuring pat on the shoulder. "Come with me, I need a drink." and he led the way to his study, calling out for the steward to attend him.

After ordering wine and food, Gaius Julius collapsed onto the couch in exhaustion, while Caesar took a chair nearby and sat quietly, waiting for his father to recover. A slave entered and placed a jug of wine and water onto the table next to the couch, together with a plate of olives and some hot, freshly baked bread. Caesar dismissed the slave and poured them both a goblet of wine, handing one to his father. "Thank you," Gaius Julius said gratefully, and downed the entire contents in one gulp. "Ah, that's better," he said, wiping his mouth with the back of his hand. "Sit, sit," he said to Caesar, waving him back to his chair.

Gaius Julius heaved himself off the couch and poured another goblet of wine. "Well, what a day this has turned out to be."

"Father, are you all right?" Caesar asked, for he had noticed bloodstains on the front of his tunic.

"What? Oh, that," said Gaius Julius, looking down at the dried blood. "That's not mine, don't worry. There was a bit of trouble down in the Forum earlier, nothing to concern yourself with."

"It looked more than a bit of trouble, Father," Caesar replied, taking a sip of his wine.

"What? Oh Gaius, don't tell me you were down there today! What were you doing?"

"No, Father, I wasn't, honestly. Arausio found me before we... I mean, I was at Aemi's house when two senators arrived, and we overheard what they said, and well..." he tailed off his explanation as he saw the look on Gaius Julius' face.

"You thought you would go and see for yourselves, did you?" Gaius Julius said angrily.

"Well, yes, Father, but we were going to find Marcus too..."

"How many times do I have to tell you, Gaius, this is not a game!" Gaius Julius exploded. "People get killed. Innocent people. When you see there is trouble, you keep away, you do *not* go and find it! Look what happened the last time you and your stupid friends got involved; you nearly got yourselves killed coming down the wall. You were lucky Marcus Aemilius only suffered a twisted ankle, jumping off those stairs. I warned you then, Gaius, if you cannot be trusted, then you will not be allowed to see those boys anymore, do you understand me?"

Caesar lowered his head in shame. His father had made his feelings quite clear before, and he knew he deserved this dressing down.

"I have enough to worry about without you disobeying me, Gaius... you are stubborn, and hot headed, and...Oh, what am I to do with you? What can I say to make you understand, boy?" Gaius Julius emptied his goblet for a second time and immediately poured himself some more wine.

"I am sorry, Father," Caesar said repentantly.

Gaius Julius sighed and returned to the couch. "Everything is turning upside down, Gaius. Rome is falling apart, and I just don't know how this is going to end," he said sadly. "And now, what with your mother, and the new baby… if anything should happen…" he took another gulp of wine. "You are precious to me, son, you and your mother, and the new baby, when it finally arrives into this world." Gaius Julius paused for a moment and looked intently at Caesar. "All I have ever wanted is to protect you; to keep my family safe. It has been hard for me, spending so many years apart from you and your mother."

Caesar shifted uncomfortably in his chair. His father had never spoken to him like this before, and it made him feel uneasy.

"Look, Gaius, today things have happened that have made me realise that nothing ever stays the same, however much you may want it too. People change; they do things that can have a massive impact on everything that you take for granted. Rome is changing, and the stability we enjoyed for so long is crumbling away. Sulla and Marius are ripping this city apart to get what they want, and, it's going to shape our lives in a way we could never imagine. I have come to realise that you must grab your opportunities when you can, because you may never get another chance."

Gaius Julius sighed, and placed his goblet on the floor. Reaching for an olive, he stared at it for a moment, twisting it round with his fingers.

Caesar watched intently, surprised at the emotion his father was displaying. His anger he could deal with, but to see his father so disheartened struck fear in his soul.

Gaius Julius popped the olive into his mouth and chewed slowly as his piercing blue eyes appraised his son. Caesar squirmed uncomfortably in his seat, uncertain what to say or do.

"What I am saying," said Gaius Julius, reaching for his goblet once more, "is that you and I are father and son, and yet we are strangers to each other, in so many ways. I want to spend the time I have left in Rome getting to know you. I want to make up for all the years I was absent, and for you to truly know what it is like to have a father, a real one, not just a name. A boy needs a father to learn from, to look up to and respect. I want to spend the little time I have left, being true to you. It is all I can give you, Gaius, for I have very little else. I am not rich, and you will have to make your own way in the world. What can I give you but my time; to teach you how to become a man, a son I can be proud of. You are a Juliian, and you have a great name to live up too. I have failed, but you, you could bring our family name back to the forefront of Rome. We could be the powerful family we once were, and I want to help you to achieve that, if I can, Gaius."

"But you are a good father to me, and I do respect you," said Caesar, anxious to reassure his father that he had not failed in his duties.

Gaius Julius smiled. "I thank you for those kind words, for I have, in truth, done very little to deserve them, but, I am determined in my mind that by the time we must part again, we shall have come to know each other so much better."

"I would like that, Father, more than anything. And I promise that I will do nothing to disappoint you. I shall be the son you deserve, and I will make you proud- I swear. I shall ensure that our family name will be remembered amongst the greatest men that ever lived. It is my destiny to achieve great things, and the name Gaius Julius Caesar shall never be forgotten!"

Gaius Julius smiled and shook his head. "Oh, you are a strange one, you and your destiny. Your mother used to write about the things you said in her letters to me and how you would drive her to distraction with your ideas of greatness."

Caesar blushed, but he refused to make apologies for what he believed. He knew his mother humoured his aspirations, and his father did not know him well enough to even begin to understand how important these feelings were to him, but his uncle Marius knew, and judging by his reaction, that day in the Forum, when Caesar had spoken of his destiny, took them very seriously.

Gaius Julius sighed. "This baby is taking its time."

A sudden knock at the door interrupted any further conversation, as a slave showed Marcus Aurelius Cotta into the study.

"Welcome, Marcus. Any news?" Gaius Julius asked the slave.

"No, Master, not yet," the slave replied.

"Still waiting then, Gaius?" said Marcus Aurelius jovially.

"For what seems like eternity. You are just in time for some wine," said Gaius Julius. "Please, help yourself to the bread and olives. I ordered them for us, but I don't think we have the stomach to eat yet, do we, Son?"

Caesar smiled at his uncle Cotta, pleased to have his company. "No, Father, not at the moment. Hello, Uncle."

"And how is young Gaius? Looking forward to having a new brother or sister?" said Marcus Aurelius, helping himself to a couple of olives and popping them into his mouth.

"Yes, Uncle," Caesar lied.

Marcus Aurelius sat down heavily into a nearby chair and sighed. "Well, what a day, eh Gaius Julius? Cinna, Octavius, and now a new addition to the Juliian family on the way! If it's a girl you should name her Tempestua, for there has not been a day like this in Rome for a long time!"

"If it's a girl, then she will be called Julia, of course, as tradition dictates," said Gaius Julius with a smile, as he handed a goblet of wine to Marcus.

"Well, of course, with Aurelia as its mother what else could you expect," said Marcus with a chuckle.

"Quite so, Marcus," said Gaius Julius, returning to the couch. "So, why have you come? Are you hoping to wet the babies head?"

"No, no, I will leave that until it has arrived. No, I came to tell you that there will be a meeting of the Senate in the morning. Everyone is expected to go; there are some serious decisions to be made. Octavius has sent messengers out all over Rome. He expects a full turn out."

"That doesn't surprise me," said Gaius Julius. "I expect he and Cinna will have a lot to say after today's events."

"Oh, Cinna won't be there; he's gone," said Marcus Aurelius, looking smug.

"Gone? What do you mean, Cinna has gone?"

"I mean just that; our Senior Consul has gone, left Rome, run away, and I cannot see him returning either," said Marcus Aurelius.

"But he can't just leave Rome! He isn't allowed to leave the city, especially in a time of crisis. That's exactly what he tried to impeach Sulla for, and Sulla was abducted!"

"I know, I know, but the fact remains that Cinna has gone. Do you know that he went through the streets calling on all slaves to join him and his Italian lackeys in the fight against Octavius and his mob? He said he would give the slaves their freedom if they supported him and Marius!"

"He said what?" said Gaius Julius, open mouthed in amazement. "Surely, there is some mistake…I…I find this incredible, Marcus…and, what do you mean, support Marius…what has *he* got to do with this?"

Caesar fought against speaking out. Oh how he would have loved to give his own hypothesis on what had happened, but, he was just a boy, and his opinion was worthless. Instead, he sat very quietly so as not to draw attention to himself, and listened.

"Everything from what I hear," Marcus Aurelius continued. "I don't know all the facts, but, I expect we shall find out everything tomorrow in the meeting. What I do know, is, that Cinna had not changed sides after all. Apparently, he held a stone in his right hand when he made the oath of allegiance to Sulla, once he returned to Rome, which, Cinna says, meant that he was protected when he swore a lie! Can you believe that man? Then he gets himself elected as Consul, and waits until Sulla leaves Rome, before he tries to pass a law to evenly distribute the Italian citizens across the twelve tribes. Many of them are Cinna and Marius's clients, evidently, and they promised to vote in favour of Marius's exile being lifted. It's my belief that the plan was to bring Marius back and then campaign for him to be given command of the legions sent to fight King Mithridates; relieving Sulla of his command of course, only, Octavius got in the way by insisting all the new Italians should be placed into two newly created tribes, which would obviously lessen their voting power. That's why Cinna and Octavius came to blows today, at least, that is my opinion, based on snippets of information I have gathered, and the facts, of course, which speak for themselves." said Marcus Aurelius.

Caesar couldn't control himself any longer. "Why did Cinna flee Rome, Uncle?"

"Ah, now that is a tale to tell, my boy," said Marcus Aurelius, who loved nothing better than explaining things, especially to eager young minds like that of his nephew. "Octavius and his men managed to drive the Italians, who were demonstrating in the Forum, out of the city. It was Romans fighting Italians all over again, just when we thought the civil war was all but over. Cinna managed to escape the main mob, and, as I said to your father, he called on all slaves to join him, but the slaves knew better than to turn to Cinna, and he was left pretty much on his own. I am told he fled the city in disguise, last seen heading for Praeneste with a group of senators loyal to his cause."

"Will the Senate exile him now, Uncle?"

"Almost certainly. Octavius will push for it, of that I have no doubt. Cinna is guilty of treason, for leaving Rome undefended, even though he was responsible for the trouble in the first place, but as Consul, what he did was unforgivable. If we can prove that he conspired to cause a riot then he should be exiled and stripped of his citizenship, his money and property confiscated at the very least. I imagine that is something we shall be discussing tomorrow," Marcus Aurelius said, looking at Gaius Julius.

"And I for one will be voting for the full power of the law!" said Gaius Julius firmly.

Marcus Aurelius looked shrewdly at him for a moment. "Well now, if I were you, I would tread very carefully, Gaius Julius. We are not safe yet; we don't know what Marius will do for one thing, but it will almost certainly involve conspiring against Sulla, and Sulla himself is too far away to help those that might fight his corner. Octavius supports Sulla and would defend any attempt to have his command withdrawn, but, he is a weak Consul, and no match for Marius, should he return. Do not do anything rash, is my advice. I won't be pinning my colours to either banner until I am certain which one will be the victor. I do not intend to place myself in danger because of a personal vendetta between two men, and if you are sensible, you will do the same, Gaius Julius."

Caesar could see the sense in his uncle's argument, and he hoped his father did too.

Gaius Julius said nothing, his brow furrowed as he contemplated these words.

At that moment there was a knock on the door and the steward entered. "The mistress has been safely delivered of a baby girl. She is asking for you, and young master Gaius too."

"A daughter, Gaius Julius. Congratulations!" said Marcus Aurelius, rising to his feet.

Gaius Julius smiled with relief at the news that all was well. "Thank you, Gnaius, we shall be along presently," he said to the steward, who bowed and left the room.

Caesar said a silent prayer to the gods, giving thanks that his mother was safe and well.

"Well, I must be going, I will leave you to your celebrations," said Marcus Aurelius, walking to the door. "Give my best wishes to Aurelia and tell her that I will see her soon, oh, and do not forget what I said. You have a daughter to care for now, and she needs you to stay alive long enough to find the money you are going to have to provide as a dowry fit for a Juliian bride, after all, an illustrious lineage requires a huge dowry for a woman of her status!" said Marcus Aurelius, chuckling heartily as he left the room.

Gaius Julius smiled. "Come on, Gaius. Let's go and have our first look at this daughter of mine that is going to cost me a fortune!"

And placing a fatherly arm around Caesar's shoulder, he led the way from the study.

Young Marius read the letter from Cinna and then handed the scroll back to his father.

"Well, do we go back to Italy, Father?"

"Of course we do," said Gaius Marius. "Like Cinna says, Sulla is hundreds of miles away and cannot help Rome, only Strabo remains with his six legions. If Cinna can get the support of the two legions in Capua, and I can take enough men back with me, we should easily get him reinstated as Consul, and in return, I get command of the legions against Mithridates."

"But, to march on Rome, Father, it goes against the Mos Maiorum, the..."

"What do I care about the Mos Maiorum, or anything else for that matter?" Marius said angrily. "It didn't stop Sulla, did it? What did he care about when he marched on Rome? Nothing, and neither shall I. I will not let any law stop me from claiming what is rightfully mine, and that war *is* mine! Now, no more blathering, either you are with me or against me; Make your choice boy!"

Young Marius looked at his father and swallowed nervously. He thought back to the hard times that had befallen them after their flight from Rome. Riding through the night whilst hiding in empty barns and farms in the day. They had come close to capture in the small town of Minturnae, when the local magistrate had been alerted to their presence in a small house, just outside the edge of the town. Knowing that Marius was condemned as a public enemy of Rome, the magistrate sent a Gaul to kill Marius. As the Gaul entered the darkened room, Marius jumped up from his bed, eyes blazing with anger and thundered, "Do you dare to kill Gaius Marius?" The Gaul had fled the house, convinced that he had seen fire flash from Marius's eyes, and reporting what had happened to the magistrate, he refused to go near Marius again. The magistrate, believing the gods protected Marius, remembered the prophecy spoken of him, that he would be Consul seven times, and so decided to let Marius go on his way unmolested. With Sulla's men hard on their heels, they had travelled across country to the sea, where they stole a small fishing boat and set sail. A storm blew them to a small island, where Fortuna smiled on Marius once more, for several of his friends, and senators that had remained loyal to him against Sulla, were already on the island, and so they hired a ship and sailed to Africa, seeking shelter with Hiempsal, Prince of Numidia.

Throughout the journey, Young Marius had noticed how much his father had changed. His moods were unpredictable, swinging from high excitement bordering on hysteria, to dark, black rages of anger and despair. When his uncle, Gaius Julius Caesar, had recalled him to Rome to be with his father after the second seizure, Young Marius had treated his warnings that Marius was ill and unstable, with contempt. Gaius Marius was a hero to his son who worshipped the very air that he breathed. He had tried to ignore his father's erratic behaviour at first, blaming the turmoil of arguing with the Senate and Sulla, but now he could no longer ignore what was happening, both mentally and physically, and he realised, painfully, that his uncle had been right all along.

Young Marius watched, as his father paced around the room muttering to himself. Once so proud, impeccable in both manners and appearance, the man before him now was a shadow of his former self. Gaius Marius looked old, his face lined and sunken, heavy jowled and puffy eyed. These days, Marius rarely remembered to shave, wandering around with white and grey stubble peppering his face and neck. His hair had grown long and was straggly and unkempt, and his clothes were dirty and torn, but, he refused to change them, saying that he would return to Rome dressed in the clothes he left her in. Some of the men who had joined them in exile had expressed their growing concerns to Young Marius, but he had fiercely defended his father, allying their fears by promising that he would soon return to his former self. He would never admit his own fears about his father to anyone, and he protected him, as a loyal son should, yet, inside his heart was breaking as he faced up to the reality of what his father had become. Now the opportunity had come to return to Rome at Cinna's invitation, but it was not to be the peaceful return that Young Marius had hoped for. He knew that to go back under these circumstances was to be declaring war on Rome; doing the unthinkable, and all his senses screamed against it. But he was his father's son first, and his loyalty had to remain unquestionable. Young Marius consoled himself with the thought that perhaps, by returning to Rome, somehow, this would change his father for the better, by having more of his friends and family around him for support; they could perhaps contain his moods, and keep him stable and safe. He was certain that if he could get him back home to Julia then she would know what to do, she would be able to help her husband as no other could.

Young Marius smiled at his father and shook his head. "No, Father, I do not have to choose. My loyalty will always be to you. My heart and my sword are yours to command. Tell me what you would have me do, and it shall be done," he said decisively.

Gaius Marius looked at his son and tears welled up in his eyes. For a second, Young Marius caught a glimpse of the man trapped inside this decaying mind and body, and his heart swelled with love and pity.

"You have ever been a good son to me, Gaius. I do not know what I would do without you," said Gaius Marius.

Young Marius swallowed hard as he felt pain rise in his chest. What he saw before him was an old, frightened man, fighting to keep hold of reality, fighting a mind and body that was dragging him inexorably towards insanity and ultimately, death. He stepped forward, wanting to embrace him, wanting to protect him as he had been protected for so many years, but as he reached out his hand to touch his father, Marius stepped back abruptly and turned away.

"Call the others," he said brusquely, picking up Cinna's letter. "We have plans to make. I want to leave for Rome as soon as possible."

Young Marius felt hot tears prick the back of his eyes, and, for a second, the image of his mother came into his mind, hugging and soothing him as she always used to when he was hurt or upset as a little boy. He had always hated his mother's tactile love, hating the cuddles and kissing. He had wanted to be hard and strong, just like his father, but for the first time in his life, Young Marius would have given anything to feel his mother's warm and loving embrace.

Gaius Marius turned to stare at his son, who had not moved. "Well?" he said sharply. "What are you waiting for?"

His mother's face faded from his mind, and Young Marius blinked back the unshed tears.

"Nothing, Father. I shall see to it immediately," he said, and picking up his cloak he walked from the room.

# CHAPTER ELEVEN

*"Confidence is that feeling by which the mind embarks in great and honourable courses with a sure hope and trust in itself."*
*(Gaius Julius Caesar)*

## ROME: April-August 87BC

Sulla threw the letter on the floor, and, in frustration, gave a well-aimed kick to his chair, knocking it across the command tent. The guard stationed outside the doorway popped his head through the canvas hangings to see what the disturbance was.

"Get Lucullus and Dollabella in here, now!" Sulla ordered.

The guard's head disappeared instantly, and within minutes Lucullus and Dollabella hastily entered the tent.

"You took your time!" Sulla snapped at his legates, who exchanged nervous glances.

Sulla walked over to the letter and picked it up off the floor. "This arrived this morning," he said, shaking the crumpled scroll at them. "From Catalus Caesar. Rome is preparing for a siege!"

"What? Why?" gasped Dollabella and Lucullus incredulously.

"Cinna and Marius, of course!" said Sulla angrily. "Marius has whipped up support to place Cinna back in the consulship, and Cinna has control of the legions that were stationed in Capua. All that stands between them and Rome is Strabo and Metellus Numidicus with their legions. You realise what this means, don't you?" he said, glaring at the two men.

"We abandon the war and return to Rome?" said Dollabella.

"No, you fool! If we leave now, Mithridates will follow on our heels, and, before we know it, he'll be knocking at the gates of Rome! No, what it means, is, that if Cinna is reinstated as Consul then the first thing he will do is terminate my command here and give it to Marius. Oh, how could I have been so stupid!" he cried, in a burst of rage. "I should never have trusted Cinna. As soon as my back was turned he turns traitor, and now see what he is doing. Rome under siege, and Marius back with his supporters again!" He picked up his goblet of wine and threw it across the tent, smashing it against one of the thick wooden posts that held up the canvas. The impotent rage seething inside him was too much to cope with; he wished it was Marius's head he was smashing to pieces.

"They may not succeed, Sulla. Strabo might hold them at bay until more support arrives. Cinna and Marius could yet be defeated," said Lucullus.

"Well, I shall have to hope that your optimism is rewarded, Lucullus," said Sulla sarcastically. "I intend to win this war against King Mithridates and I am not giving up this command for anyone!"

Dollabella looked concerned. "But if Cinna is the lawful Consul, then he has the right to withdraw your command, and you have no choice but to comply."

Sulla rounded on Dollabella and snarled, "Oh yes, I do have a choice, I simply won't do it. If they want to remove me from this command then they are going to have to come here and make me. We will see who the legions support then, won't we?"

"But you can't make the legions choose between you and the legally appointed Consul!" said Lucullus, looking appalled at what Sulla was suggesting. "You had their support before, when you marched on Rome, but…"

"*To Rome.* I marched *to Rome*, there is a difference!" snapped Sulla.

"*To* Rome, then, but you were the rightfully appointed Consul then, and Marius had abducted you. You had every right to reclaim your office then, but this…this is completely different. The Senate gave you this command, and they have every right to replace you. That is the law, Sulla. That is how it is." said Lucullus firmly.

Sulla glared at Lucullus and his eyes narrowed dangerously as the thought of ripping Lucullus's head from his shoulders flitted through his mind

Dollabella stepped between the two men. "Lucullus is right, Sulla. You cannot contemplate forcing the legions to choose. They are Rome's Legions, not your personal army, and we will not allow you to do this."

Sulla turned his hard, pale eyes on Dollabella, his face purple with barely contained rage, but he remained silent in the face of such strong opposition. Behind his anger, the cold voice of reason told him that if he was to succeed, he needed his senior legates to support him.

Dollabella stood his ground and waited for the expected outburst from Sulla but it never came, instead he simply flung himself onto his couch. "All right, have it your own way, for now," he said, between gritted teeth. "But I will not allow Marius to take command of this army, not now, not ever."

Lucullus swallowed nervously. "This…this animosity, between you and Marius…well, it's gone way beyond a personal vendetta, hasn't it?"

Sulla scowled at him. "Of course it has. He changed that when he had me abducted from Rome and tried to murderer me!"

"Yes, of course, Sulla, and I do understand that, and I stood by you then didn't I?"

Sulla nodded, but continued to glare at Lucullus, who pressed on regardless.

"When you drove Marius from Rome, the Senate supported you, and rightfully so, for what he did was unforgivable, and I hoped, well, we all hoped, that this would be an end to your enmity. Now it appears that Marius has returned, and is intent on gaining command of these legions to fight against Mithridates. He knows that this is his last chance to win glory and honour, the things he values beyond anything else, and you are standing in his way…again. What started as a mere dislike between you has now escalated out of all reason. We are told he is prepared to set an army on Rome, all to get Cinna reinstated, and ensure that he gets this command from you, and you are talking of defying the Senate and proposing to use the legions for your own ends. This is madness, Sulla. Where will it end? Legions fighting legions…their loyalty given to individual commanders. Then what… you win, he wins, but what does Rome win? If you continue this personal war with Marius then you will tear Her apart. Thousands could be killed, not for the glory of Rome, but for the hatred that you two bare each other, and who will do anything, anything, to get what they want, at the expense of everything and everyone else! It is inconceivable that two men could cause the downfall of the empire, but, the way things are heading, the inconceivable looks more like becoming a reality. I am asking you, Sulla, no, I am *begging* you, for the sake of Rome, drop this vendetta against Marius. If you are ordered to give up your command then do so, even if it is to Marius. What does it matter who commands the legions, so long as Rome wins this war against King Mithridates and the empire remains intact? Surely you would not put your own personal pride above the welfare of Rome and her people? I am appealing to you because you are the one capable of stopping this right now. Gaius Marius is sick; he is almost insane, through illness and his jealousy and hatred of you. He is beyond advice, beyond anything, but you, you can stop all this before it goes too far; before you both bring Rome to her knees!"

Lucullus stopped and waited for the expected explosion, but it never came. The three men remained silent. Dollabella shifted uncomfortably, glancing at Sulla and then to Lucullus and back again, waiting for Sulla to respond.

Finally, Sulla sat up and sighed as he rubbed his hands through his hair. "The scouts should have returned by now with news of the enemy's position. Find out what they know and prepare the men to move out. We leave at dawn tomorrow," he said, looking at Dollabella.

Lucullus stared, open-mouthed, as Sulla chose to ignore everything he had said. Dollabella saluted hastily and left the tent but Lucullus remained where he was.

Sulla looked up and frowned. "Was there anything else, Lucullus?"

Lucullus shook his head wearily. "No, Sulla, I have said all that there is to say."

Lucullus saluted smartly and left the tent. The weight of Rome's doom lay heavily on his shoulders.

"So you actually saw the letter he sent Aunt Julia?" said Caesar to Marcus, whilst Aemi lay beside him, listening intently.

As usual, the boys had ended their day of lessons and training by meeting up at their regular haunt, the Tarpeian Rock. The warm summer breeze was cooling, as they lounged lazily under the cypress tree, discussing the day's news. Marcus, however, had shocked his friends by revealing that Julia had finally received a letter from her husband and son, nearly six months after their flight from Rome.

"Of course I saw it, I was with her. She put it in her workbasket after reading it. I knew it was from Uncle, or Young Marius, by the look on her face, but when I asked who the letter was from she told me to go and find something to do. I waited until she went to have her afternoon nap and then I went into the workroom and found it. Young Marius has rubbish handwriting but I managed to read the letter in the end," said Marcus excitedly.

"You were lucky she didn't catch you," said Aemi.

"I was careful, never fear," said Marcus, smiling. "But isn't it astonishing news, Caesar?"

Caesar frowned, looking far from happy. He watched, deep in thought, the men at work in the distance on the city's fortification. Hundreds of slaves toiled tirelessly, repairing the walls with new stone. The city had been on alert, ever since Cinna had been driven out of Rome by Octavius, and the boys watched in fascination as first the huge trenches had been dug in front of the walls, fifteen feet deep in places, and then long sharpened poles had been sunk into the ditches, to prevent anyone from attempting to scale the walls. Wooden catapults had been hoisted up onto the ramparts together with mounds of rocks, placed strategically nearby to be used as missiles in case of attack.

Caesar knew his father was working hard to ensure that there was enough food for the people in the city to live on, if it came to a siege, but, when he tried to question his father about what might happen, he was told in no uncertain terms to keep out of the way. The discovery of the letter was now the closest that they had come to understanding what the adults already anticipated, but never in their wildest dreams could they imagine that Gaius Marius would be returning to Rome, at the head of a small army.

"He didn't say where they were when he wrote the letter did he?" Caesar asked.

"No, nothing like that. I don't suppose he wanted to give their position away, just in case someone else intercepted the letter."

"But he mentioned how many were in your uncle's army; surely that's giving out information," said Aemi.

"Yes, but that is a fact and there would be nothing the Senate or anyone could do about that," said Caesar.

"It certainly explains all the fortifications," said Aemi, looking across at the slaves working on the wall. "Do you think there will be a big battle?" he asked nervously.

"Almost certainly, especially if Gaius Marius is involved," said Caesar.

"What do you think will happen to us? I mean, all of us who are trapped inside the city?" said Marcus.

"That will depend largely on what happens outside the walls I suppose," said Caesar. "If Cinna does attack, then I imagine Strabo will defend the city from outside the walls and Octavius from inside."

"They might not fight though; they might just lay siege to the city instead and starve us into submission," said Marcus.

"They wouldn't do that, would they?" gasped Aemi.

"Why not? Young Marius told Aunt Julia to stock up on food supplies. Why would he say that if he didn't know they would besiege Rome?" Marcus replied.

"This isn't funny any more!" said Aemi, the panic rising in his voice.

"We didn't think it was," said Marcus sarcastically. "The trouble with you, Aemi, is that you never take anything seriously. You just think Rome is invincible, that Romans are untouchable and nothing bad will ever happen to you or your family because your father is a powerful senator. Well, perhaps now you'll realise that bad things happen whoever you are. This battle, if there is one, is going to affect us all, and your pata will not be able to protect you from the feelings of hunger in your belly if my uncle tries to starve Rome into submission!"

"I have to go home now," said Caesar, glancing up at the sun. "Father might be home and I promised that I would be there when he returned."

"I'm going to stay here a little while longer," said Marcus. "I want to watch them hoist that catapult up onto the ramparts."

"I'll walk back with you, Caesar," said Aemi. "I think it is time I had a talk with my father."

"He won't tell you anything!" snorted Marcus derisively. "We're just children, remember. We don't need to know anything of real importance."

"Then perhaps it's about time we proved that we are old enough to be told what is going on, and, that our parents don't have to try and protect us so much," said Caesar. He had realised that the presence of the letter would end the speculation of what Gaius Marius and Cinna were intending to do. The Senate needed all the help that they could get, and Caesar knew what he had to do.

"And how do you propose to do that?" said Marcus.

"By telling them about the letter."

"But you can't!" shouted Marcus. "Aunt Julia will kill me if she finds out I went behind her back and read her private letter."

"She will never harm a hair on your head," retorted Caesar. "I'm sorry, Marcus, but it's like you said to Aemi, this is no game, and if we have information that could help us protect Rome then it is our duty to pass it on," he said firmly.

"But Caesar!" pleaded Marcus desperately.

"No, Marcus, I will not move from this. The Senate has a right to know what Marius is planning and I am going to make sure my father is told everything, as soon as I see him."

"Caesar is right, Marcus," Aemi agreed. "I shall also tell my father. The quicker this information is acted on the better."

Marcus scowled at his two friends, betrayal written all over his face. "He has done it again, even though he isn't even here," he said angrily.

Aemi looked confused, but Caesar understood."Yes, he has, hasn't he? However hard you try to avoid it, Gaius Marius always manages to come between us. If he doesn't do it directly, the trouble he causes for those around him rots through everything, even down to boys like us. The older we become, the harder it will be for us."

"What are you saying, Caesar?" said Aemi.

"The longer this war between Marius and Sulla drags on, the more we and our families are going to be dragged down. Loyalties will divide further, and our lives could change dramatically. The friendship we have had for so many years could be put to the test, as it has been already, but we always managed to find a way around the difficulties. But one day something might happen to us that will split us apart for good." Caesar felt the pain of his words as he spoke. For some time now he had wondered how much strain their friendship could take. Divided loyalties, family pressure and the constant reminder of the social and political differences between them, that once seemed so insignificant and removed from their childhood reality, now whispered faintly in their ears. Fingers of division and suspicion tugged gently at their sleeves, pulling them apart, slowly but surely. Caesar knew that the older they became, the harder it would be to resist these outside influences that would become an intrinsic part of their lives. He had spent many a sleepless night, wondering how their friendship would survive?

"Never! We will always be friends, Caesar," said Marcus emphatically, jumping to his feet.

"Don't say that, Caesar!" said Aemi, with tears in his eyes.

Caesar looked sadly at his two friends, but he knew he was right; he could feel it, deep inside. "I stand by what I have said, though it pains me greatly to think that we three will not always be friends, but we have to face facts. Our childhood is ending and the protection it gave us from the world around us is not going to be there for much longer. Things can happen that will be beyond our control, and our friendship will be tested to the limits; our only hope is that we three are strong enough to resist that happening."

"I would fight to keep it, Caesar!" said Marcus.

"And me!" said Aemi.

"As will I," said Caesar. "Let us pray to all the gods that we never have to put this resolve to the test."

As soon as he returned home, Caesar had delivered the news of the letter to his father who was shut up in his study, immersed in a meeting with three other senators. Gaius Julius praised his son for being responsible, and ordered him to remain at home for the remainder of the day.

"So now we know for certain," said Senator Catalus Caesar, slumping back in his chair. "Marius is marching on Rome, and, my guess is he will collect as many Italians as he can along the way. If Cinna does the same then we shall be in for a hard time of it."

"The defences are in place and most of the wall is fortified. Another few days and Rome will be protected," said Senator Marcus Antonius.

"Let's hope that we have another few days," said Senator Quintus Tullius, cynically. "Cinna is only seven miles from Rome, so our informants tell us. I know he is in camp there but what is to stop him packing up and moving to Rome right now?"

"My guess is he is waiting for Marius to join him," said Marcus Antonius.

"Well, there is nothing for it but we must redouble our efforts and get everything in place as quickly as possible. I think our time has just run out," said Catalus Caesar, rising to his feet. "You have a fine son there, Gaius Julius," he said as he walked to the door. "He will make a good senator one day…providing there is a Senate left after this."

Catalus Caesar opened the door to leave, just as Marcus Aurelius Cotta arrived. They greeted each other warmly.

"Marcus. I'm just leaving, I am afraid," said Catalus Caesar.

"I am sorry to have missed you, Quintus, but actually, I have come for a quick word with Gaius Julius."

"Of course, Marcus, come in," said Gaius Julius, rising to his feet. "We have just finished going over the figures for the food stocks we have placed around the city."

"Then I'm glad I came when I did," said Marcus Aurelius jovially. "I am hopeless with figures!"

Marcus Antonius and Quintus Tullius said their farewells and left with Catalus Caesar.

Gaius Julius poured two goblets of wine and passed one to Marcus. Noticing the harassed look on his face he said, "Trouble?"

"Mmm, could be," said Marcus Aurelius, taking a sip of wine. "I received a letter from Sulla today. Catalus Caesar has obviously been writing to him regularly because he seems to know all that is happening here in Rome."

"Is he coming back?"

"No. No he isn't. He says he is going to remain with his legions. The campaign is going better than expected and he has managed to push King Mithridates back into Macedonia already. He intends to stay out there to keep the momentum going."

"I can see his point," said Gaius Julius. "To leave the east now would leave the empire wide open to attack."

"I agree." Marcus Aurelius nodded.

"So, why do you believe there will be trouble, Marcus?"

"Because in his letter, Sulla says that he is not prepared to surrender the legions over to Marius. He is convinced that if Cinna is reinstated, the first thing he will do is give the command to Marius, if he should ever return to Rome."

" I'm afraid it is no longer if, Marcus, but when," said Gaius Julius, and he proceeded to tell Marcus Aurelius about the latest events.

"This is just the beginning, you realise that don't you?" said Marcus Aurelius, looking very grave. "If Cinna comes back and does as Sulla fears then this really will turn into a war."

"It makes sense that this is what Cinna and Marius are planning, for why else would Marius be returning to Rome? There has to be something in this for him."

"Sulla is adamant that he will never hand over the legions to Marius, even if it means defying the Senate."

"And we all know he is capable of that, so what can we do?"

"Hope that Strabo and the Senate have enough men to stop Cinna and Marius from entering Rome. If Cinna succeeds then we are facing another battle, this time between Sulla and the Senate, and we know from bitter experience that Sulla is more then capable of leading an army to Rome. He has asked me to do him a personal favour," said Marcus Aurelius, changing the subject.

"Oh?"

"He wants me to remove his wife and baby twins from Rome and hide them, just in case Marius and Cinna are successful."

"He really believes Marius hates him so much that he would harm a woman and her babies?"

"Obviously, or he would not have asked."

"What will you do, Marcus?"

"I shall help him of course. Marius need never know, and Sulla will owe me a favour, which may well come in useful one day. Either way, I remain sitting on the fence; it is the safest place to be."

"You play a dangerous game, Marcus. Sooner or later you will have to choose where your loyalties lie."

"Oh, I know, Gaius, but it doesn't hurt to keep them both happy for now does it? There are many men who have openly come out in support of Sulla and been very vocal in their dislike for Marius. I would not want to be in their boots if Marius does return to power; they may well regret nailing their colours to the mast of a man who is too far away to protect them," said Marcus Aurelius wisely. These are dangerous times, Gaius, and my instincts tell me that they are going to get far worse. I wonder if Rome will ever be the same again."

"The Republic has had hard times before and it has always survived. A world without Rome, why, it is inconceivable!"

"But she has never had two men like Marius and Sulla before. They are no ordinary men; they are titans. Two of the most powerful men in the world fighting for control of the legions. Win the legions and you win Rome; She is the ultimate prize, and it is my belief that Marius and Sulla would rather destroy Rome than allow the other to win her."

"No, Marcus, I am sorry but no, what you speak of is not possible. We are a republic, which makes it impossible for any one man to hold absolute power. No, it will never happen." Gaius Julius said adamantly.

Marcus Aurelius could see that he would never convince Gaius Julius that the republic, as they had known it, was indeed in danger of collapsing, if Marius did return to power, so he held his tongue. All he said was, "We shall see, Gaius Julius, we shall see."

Caesar sat in a chair opposite his father, and his mother occupied the couch next to him. The family sat in silence, waiting for the slave to finish re-filling the oil lamps, as the evening light faded to darkness. Caesar looked at his mother but her gaze remained fixed on her husband, her hands composed in her lap, a calm stillness surrounding her. His father, on the other hand, sat twiddling a loose thread from his woollen tunic, a strained, anxious expression on his face, which served only to deepen the sense of foreboding that Caesar felt. When the slave left the room, Gaius Julius spoke.

"You both know that Rome is on the verge of civil war, between the Senate and Cinna, who is demanding to be reinstated as Consul."

Aurelia and Caesar nodded.

"What you are not aware of, is that Gaius Marius is supporting Cinna, and, he is marching to Rome at the head of an army."

Aurelia visibly paled, and glanced at her son, but Caesar avoided his mother's gaze and remained silent.

"I have decided that it is in your best interests to leave Rome. Aurelia, you and the children will travel to Pompeii, a friend of mine has a villa there which he has agreed to rent to me indefinitely."

Aurelia tried to speak but Gaius Julius raised his hand for silence.

"You must leave Rome, Aurelia, tomorrow if possible. Take Gaius and baby Julia, and all the slaves you will need to make your time there comfortable. I don't know how long you will need to remain there, but, I promise, as soon as it is safe, I will let you return," he said firmly.

Caesar's heart was in his mouth. Leave Rome! Leave his father and his friends to suffer whilst he had an enforced holiday hundreds of miles away. He could not think of anything worse, and, as he glanced at his mother, he knew that she was also struggling with her emotions.

"I do not want to leave Rome, Gaius Julius. I do not want to go anywhere. My place is by your side, keeping the home for you, being here when you need me. What kind of wife would I be if I fled Rome at the first sign of trouble?"

"Aurelia, you have always been the best of wives. I have never had to worry that you would not cope when I have been away, but this is not about being a good wife, this is about protecting yourself and our children. I do not know what fate will befall Rome but there will be hard and dangerous times ahead and I would rather not have to worry about your safety here, as well as everything else."

Caesar felt a stab of resentment every time his father said the word children. He was not a helpless child like his baby sister and he had hoped that the past few months would have shown just how grown up he really was.

Aurelia was not going to make it easy for her husband however and she pressed on with her objections. "What about Julia, and Marcus? Am I to abandon them at their greatest time of need? If Gaius Marius does return to Rome and there is fighting then Julia will need all the support I can give her. She has no one else to turn to, and you cannot expect Marcus to look after her; he will never cope alone. They need me here, in Rome, not hundreds of miles away." she said.

Caesar saw the telltale flash of anger escaping her eyes, but Gaius Julius ignored the warning.

"Julia will manage. She has made her choice, and anyway, if the worst does happen and Cinna's return to Rome is successful then she will have the company of her husband and son once more. I cannot be held responsible for my sister, Aurelia."

"And Marcus?" she snapped.

"Marcus is not my concern. If Julia had any sense she would have sent him back to Arpinium long ago instead of fawning over him like a surrogate son!"

Caesar could see that his mother was struggling to think of any other objections she might use to force her husband to change his mind, so he decided to add his appeal to the argument.

"Father, please do not send us away. Mother is right; we should be here for you. We cannot bare to think of you alone, surrounded by danger, without your family to support you," he said pleadingly.

Gaius Julius smiled at his son. "I admire your sentiments, Gaius, but I have been in far more dangerous situations than this in my life, and, I did not have my family round me then, did I? Now, I am not arguing about this any more," he said firmly, looking at his wife. "I have made my decision. You will leave tomorrow."

Caesar looked appealingly at his mother, hoping she would find something that would save them but Aurelia did not even look at him.

"Leave us, Gaius. Do as your father asks," she said, her eyes fixed steadily on her husband.

Caesar rose from his chair and left the room. He could sense that his parents were about to have a huge argument and he was glad to escape so that he would not have to witness it.

When his son had left the room, Gaius Julius turned on his wife, his face flushed with anger. "Look, Aurelia, I know you are not happy, but please, just for once in your life do as I ask, without arguing. I don't want you to leave tomorrow on bad terms!"

Aurelia did not move her eyes from his face. "We are not going."

"Now listen…"

"We are not going, and there is one very good reason why we are not going," Aurelia said firmly.

"No, there is no good reason, Aurelia. Whatever you say I…"

"We are staying to protect our son," she interrupted.

This statement completely threw Gaius Julius, who simply stared at his wife.

"If we leave Rome, we may be putting Gaius at risk. We can protect him better if we all stay together."

"What? What are you talking about? How is Gaius at risk? From what?"

"Not from what, Gaius Julius, from whom. Gaius Marius is the person who could endanger our son's life, and I for one am not prepared to risk it, even if you are. Divorce me if you have to, for defying you, but we are not leaving Rome."

Gaius Julius shook his head in exasperation, completely bemused by what his wife was saying. "Well, you better explain yourself, Aurelia and by all the gods it had better be convincing!"

Aurelia rose from her chair and walked over to the table where a jug of wine and some goblets had been placed. She poured two goblets of wine and handed one to her husband.

"You will need a drink, Husband, for when I have finished telling you what I have to say."

Aurelia told her husband the truth, leaving nothing out. She told him about Marius turning against their son, and the reasons that she believed led up to it; the prophecy, Julia's fears, their mutual agreement to keep Marius from seeing Caesar again, everything. Gaius Julius listened intently throughout, never interrupting his wife, a deepening sense of dread surrounding his soul as every word was spoken. Little things began to fall into place now, things people had said, or more importantly, not said, since he had been home. His sister's reticence to talk about her husband when his son was around; all these little things that made no sense singularly, but now, added together, began to paint a very sinister and worrying picture.

"So you see, Gaius, by removing our son from Rome, we could be placing him in a very vulnerable position, if, as I suspect, Gaius Marius does see him as a threat. It would be much easier for him to arrange some, little misfortune, if we were hidden away in a small villa miles from your protection, than if he stayed here. We do not know how mentally unstable Marius has become since he left Rome, but, if what you have told us is true, and he is marching on Rome, then I think his actions speak for themselves; anything is possible, Gaius Julius. Do you want to be responsible for putting your own son's life in mortal danger?" said Aurelia finally.

Gaius Julius shook his head, torn between what he had seen with his own eyes as far as Marius's mental state was concerned, and now, how this could ultimately affect his own son. "And you say Marcus Aurelius and Julia both think the same? You all believe that my son is part of this prophecy?" said Gaius Julius, struggling to come to terms with what he had heard.

"Yes, Husband, they do. We all do. Without knowing exactly what the prophecy says we cannot know for sure, but, are you prepared to take the risk to find out the truth?"

Gaius Julius slumped back in his chair. An hour ago, everything was settled in his mind, but now? Could he really send his son away knowing that there might be the slightest chance that Marius could come after him, to prevent the prophecy from coming true? How far did this really go? Was there any truth in what his wife believed? How could he ever find out for certain? What was he to do? What?

"Leave me, Aurelia, I have much to think about," he said suddenly.

Aurelia rose to her feet and looked pityingly at her husband. She did not envy him this decision. "Shall I start packing?" she said, opening the door to leave.

Gaius Julius looked hard at his wife. "I don't know, Aurelia. I just do not know."

*Marius and Cinna finally joined forces together with rogue senator and competent legate, Quintus Sertorius. The massive army was split three ways; Cinna and his deputy, Carbo, took the central position and moved towards Rome, capturing town after town and blocking all the main supply routes that led to the city. Quintus Sertorius moved his men to the north east of Rome, and Gaius Marius blockaded the sea routes at Ostia, to the west, thus preventing supplies reaching*

*Rome along the River Tiber. He also captured Antium, Aricia and Lanuvium, small towns just outside Rome, which held the major grain stores that supplied food for the people.*

*Pompeius, commander of the only legions defending Rome, camped outside the Servian Wall, near the Colline Gate, powerless to act against three armies, and so he remained where he was, waiting. The City was now effectively cut off from the outside world. No one could get in or out. The siege of Rome had begun.*

Caesar was woken by a loud clap of thunder. The walls of his sleep cubicle shook, as the air trembled and rumbled overhead. He heard the sound of a baby crying and realised that his sister, Julia, must have been woken by the storm. Throwing back the blanket that covered him he threw on a tunic and padded slowly down the corridor towards the atrium. The sound of the rain clattering on the roof tiles was deafening, and, looking out at the peristyle garden, he could see the water hitting the ground with tremendous force, spraying in all directions.

This was the first rain Rome had seen in months, and Caesar wondered if the crops of wheat that still stood in the fields would survive such a torrential downpour. Then he remembered that, with the siege in full force, the harvested crops would not reach Rome to supply the much-needed grain to feed the people. The mere thought of food made his stomach rumble. The family had been on rations for weeks now, and all the little luxuries he used to take for granted would float, as tempting visions of antagonism, through his mind, as yet another bowl of plain meat and porridge was placed in front of him at meal times. He shrugged resignedly; at least the air was cooler now, after the stifling heat of his airless, windowless cubicle, and he welcomed the fresh breeze that blew into the atrium.

Walking out under the colonnade, that circled the open garden, he sat down on a stone bench, and looked out through the curtain of rain that poured from the roof to the sun baked earth that was once a lush, green, lawn. He pondered on what would happen if the crops were destroyed? The siege had meant that the Senate had dug deep into the reserve stores of grain that was kept to help feed the people of Rome throughout the winter. He knew from his father, that unless the siege was ended soon, the people were in danger of starving, and if the harvest that would supply the food for the following year was destroyed, and the siege continued, then even more would perish.

The noise of the rain splashing on the roof masked the sound of footsteps approaching and he jumped as a voice said, "The storm woke you too?"

Gaius Julius sat on the bench next to his son. "Your baby sister is intent on making more noise than this storm," he said wryly.

Caesar smiled at his father. He knew that he had discovered a new world since the birth of his daughter. Caesar had often heard him say that he could not believe something so small and fragile could cause so much worry and disruption in a house. Caesar, on the other hand, was finding it hard to come to terms with having a sister, although he tried not to show it. He could not help the feelings of resentment, for instance, when he tried to talk to his mother, for invariably the baby would cry and her attention would be drawn to looking after her child, leaving Caesar frustrated and alone. He also felt pangs of jealousy when he watched his father with the baby, tickling her and holding her high in the air to make her laugh. He wished his father could talk about him as a baby, but, of course, he couldn't, because he had never been there. Caesar glanced at his father, and wondered how long it would be before he went away again? A heavy lump caught in his throat at the thought of it. Although his father had been busy these past few months, he had still found time to spend with his son, and slowly, they had begun to know and understand each other better. He wondered why his father had changed his mind so suddenly about sending them away to Pompeii and he longed to ask, but he had never found the right time, and when he tried to ask his mother she had shrugged and said that it was his father's right to decide, and not his to question.

Caesar turned back to stare at the rain, pondering on this question, as Gaius Julius in turn, looked at his son, and, as Aurelia's words rang in his ears, his face clouded over as he wondered what the future had in store for his family.

Caesar glanced up and saw the pain in his face. "Father, what's wrong?"

Gaius Julius blinked and wiped a hand across his face. "Nothing. Nothing is wrong, Gaius, at least nothing an end to this siege wouldn't cure."

But Caesar felt that the look in his eyes had been for him, and nothing to do with the siege. He took a deep breath and steeled himself for his father's rebuke, but he had to ask. "I'm sorry, Father, but I don't believe that is what is troubling you," he said bravely. "I have noticed you watching me a lot lately, and your face is often full of sadness. Have I disappointed you in some way? Am I not the son you hoped for, now that you have come to know me?"

Gaius Julius looked astonished. "No, my son, no! How could you think such a thing? I told you before that I am proud of you. You have proved yourself worthy on many occasions; telling me about that letter for one. You risked your friendship with Marcus to do the right thing, and that shows a high degree of duty and responsibility, indeed, I have come to see that you have a wise head and maturity way beyond your years. No man could ask for a finer son, Gaius, so please, never think that you are unworthy," he said, grasping his son's hand.

"Then what is it, Father, please, tell me."

A loud clap of thunder resounded above them and the rain redoubled its efforts, pounding so loudly on the roof tiles above them that they could hardly hear themselves think. The water poured down in torrents from the roofs, splashing their already damp tunics, and flooding the garden. Water now lapped at their bare feet, but neither of them noticed anything, as Gaius Julius finally resolved to tell his son everything he wanted to know.

When he had finished, Gaius Julius put his head in his hands. Caesar saw the burden of worry and exhaustion lay heavy on his father's shoulders, but he was confused, unsure how he should be feeling at this moment. So much of what had happened over the past few years made sense to him now, and, if anything, he felt a sense of relief that he at least had the answers to all these questions that had been going round in his head for so long.

"Thank you, Father," he said finally, looking at the careworn figure of Gaius Julius sitting beside him.

"I would have given anything to have spared you this, Gaius, truly, but I believe you are at an age where to hide the truth could prove to be more dangerous than for you to know why your mother and I have been so protective of you, especially of late. But you must understand, that we know nothing for certain; this could all be some terrible misunderstanding on our part, yet we have no way of knowing. If your uncle does return to Rome, I must insist that you stay well away from his house, and you are not to visit your aunt Julia, or Marcus. We must do our best to keep you out of his sight, that way, he can't be reminded of your existence so readily."

"Of course, Father, I understand," said Caesar, but his throat tightened and he swallowed hard as he realised how difficult it would be to continue his friendship with Marcus. "May I ask you something?"

"Of course,"

"The prophecy said that Gaius Marius would be Consul seven times, is that correct?"

"Yes, it did. That is actually common knowledge in Rome; Marius boasted about it every time he was elected Consul, but what else was prophesised, only the man himself knows, and he has kept it very close to his chest."

"Then that means that he has one more consulship ahead of him doesn't it?"

"Yes, I suppose it does, but I can't see how he could possibly be elected Consul again, not now."

"But the prophecy has been correct so far, so we must assume that he will indeed be proclaimed Consul for the seventh and final time, which means that he will be successful in returning to Rome with Cinna."

"Who can say…are prophecies set in stone? None of us can know for certain; anything could happen to stop him," said Gaius Julius.

Caesar could hear the uncertainty in his father's voice and he shook his head. "You don't believe that, Father, any more than I do. If it has been prophesised, then so shall it be."

Faint traces of daylight were beginning to show in the sky, though the black rain filled clouds lay heavy over Rome. Another clap of thunder made the very ground shake and the rain burst forth in another torrential downpour. Gaius Julius shivered involuntarily and then sat up straight, his head cocked to one side as he heard voices coming from the atrium. Something in the tone of the voices made him get up to investigate, leaving his son alone.

Caesar was struggling to fight the turmoil that raged inside him. He rose from the bench and walked through the curtain of water pouring from the portico roof, and into the garden. The rain stung his face as he exposed himself to the full force of the elements, the water slicing across his bare arms and legs, so that within seconds he was drenched, but he did not care. What did anything matter when he had finally found out the truth? He stood in the centre of the garden and looked up, just as a jagged bolt of lightening pierced the dark clouds, exploding white light across the sky. Caesar could hardly open his eyes as the rain beat down on his face but he seemed to be enveloped in a warm, thrilling sensation that came with the dawning realisation within him. The realisation that all the years of waiting was finally over hit him hard in the stomach, as though he had been physically punched, and he gasped out aloud. He knew now that the journey was about to begin; all the pieces had fallen into place. All those dreams of fame and glory; that undeniable certainty of greatness that he had carried with him, he now knew to be true. Was this how his hero, Alexander the Great, had felt when he became King, and set of on his venture to conquer the world? Had he ever stopped waiting and hoping? Caesar had never stopped looking for a sign that would prove to him what he believed was real, and now he had it, for in his mind there was no doubt that Gaius Marius believed him to be a threat to his own immortal reputation. That look in his uncle's eyes, the day he had revealed his own beliefs and aspirations, had been fear! Gaius Marius knew Caesar was destined for great things, greater than anything he had achieved, and the people's hero had looked his rival in the face, and he had known.

A smile crept across Caesar's face, and then he laughed, and the laughter kept coming. Not the nervous laughter of a youth who had realised his life was in danger, but the triumphant laugh of one who has seen the future and welcomes it with joy. Caesar knew who he was now. His time had arrived, the journey was beginning, and he embraced it with every fibre of his being.

Gaius Julius watched his son from inside the atrium, as the boy lifted his arms up to the sky, laughing, as all around him the rain hammered down in a relentless torrent. A bolt of jagged lightning ripped across the sky and, for a second, his son was bathed in a golden, surreal light, and Gaius Julius blinked in wonder, for in that moment, he had seen a living god.

"Gaius! Gaius!" he shouted, above the noise of the rain, but Caesar did not seem to hear him.

Another massive clap of thunder exploded directly overhead, shaking the very foundations of the house, and was followed immediately by a second lightning bolt, so bright that it illuminated the sky like a million candles. To Caesar, it was as though the gods were calling him, waking him from the sleep of youth, to the realisation of his future. Welcoming him to their world, and beckoning him forward, to take up those reins of destiny. His mind thrilled with the thought, and a power surged through his body so strongly that the muscles in his arms began to twitch, and his legs felt weak, as the blackness of the sky seemed to be drawing him into it, sucking the very air from his lungs. He was going to meet the gods. He was going forward to accept his destiny!

Gaius Julius ran forward into the stormy deluge as his son fell lifeless to the floor."Gaius! *Gaius*!" He scooped the limp, twitching body of the boy up into his arms. "Gaius, speak to me!"

But Caesar's body just twitched in spasm as though his very soul was trying to force its way out. Soaked to the skin, Gaius Julius carried Caesar back inside the house. "Aurelia… *Aurelia*!" he shouted desperately, as he made his way down the corridor towards his son's room.

"*Aurelia*!"

"From the symptoms you describe I believe that your son has the falling sickness. He needs plenty of rest now, and keep him quiet."

"Are you sure, Doctor? Perhaps it was just the rain and the excitement of the storm?" Aurelia looked worriedly at her sleeping son.

"Has he ever suffered from blackouts before? Fainting fits or uncontrolled spasms of the body?"

"No, never. He is a fit, healthy boy. This does not make any sense; how can this be?"

"The falling sickness is not uncommon, Aurelia, though it usually starts when a person is much younger than your son, that is why I ask if he has experienced anything like this before?"

"No, nothing. Will it happen again? Could he die from it?"

"I will not say no, for I have known people who have never recovered from an attack, but this seems to have been a mild case, from what you describe, although it will hit him harder as it is his first one."

"How often will this happen?"

"There is no pattern to it. It strikes for many different reasons. Asclepios, the great Greek physician, believes that excitement can bring it on, and I am inclined to agree with him. What was he doing before the attack?"

Aurelia looked at her husband. "He was with his father, watching the storm, I believe. He went out into the garden and that is where my husband saw him fall. I'm sorry, there is nothing else I can tell you," she said, looking at Gaius Julius for conformation. He remained silent and nodded that this was so.

"Well, he is safe now. His breathing is strong and regular. Let him sleep, he will feel the better for it. I must leave you now but I will call again tomorrow to see how he is," the doctor said, closing his leather pouch of medical instruments and making ready to leave.

"Yes, of course. Thank you, Doctor. I shall take good care of him, but...what do I tell him when he awakes?"

"You must tell him the truth of course. He must know that this could happen again, and, he should tell his friends and family too, for there are things they can do to help him during an attack. Your son needs to carry a small stick covered in hide with him wherever he goes. This must be placed between his teeth to prevent him biting his tongue during an attack, and, if those that are with him know this, then they could help save his life, for the swallowing or severing of the tongue is the main cause of death in these cases."

Aurelia paled at the thought. "I shall ensure that my son understands."

The door closed and the voices faded away. Caesar opened one eye to see if he was alone in the room, then both eyes. He lay still for a while to let his spinning head settle before he raised himself up onto one elbow. He was in his bed. How had that happened? And what was this talk about the falling sickness he had heard, as he came to his senses? He tried to think back to the last thing he remembered, the storm, the rain, and then nothing. How long had he been lying here, and where was his father?

The door to the room opened and Aurelia walked in, looking tense and drawn. She saw that her son was awake and her beautiful face brightened with relief. She came over to his bed and sat on the edge, rearranging the covers to keep him warm.

"What happened, Mother?" Caesar asked, in a dry, croaky voice.

Aurelia smoothed his fringe back from his eyes. "Hush, now, Gaius, you need to rest. Be calm my son," she said softly, stroking his forehead.

"But what happened? May I have some water please," he said, trying to sit up.

Aurelia walked to the table, poured a small cup of water, and passed it to him.

Caesar drank gratefully, enjoying the cool feel of the water easing his sore throat. When he had drunk his fill he handed the cup back to his mother. "Where is Father?" he asked, as Aurelia returned the cup to the table.

She returned to the bed and sat down again with a concerned look on her face. "You fell, Gaius and your father brought you back into the house. We could not wake you and so we called the doctor, but you are all right, and you should rest," she said, tucking him back under the covers.

"But I feel fine, Mother," he said, trying to sit up. "My head is a little funny but otherwise I am well."

"The doctor said you should rest, and rest you shall, now lie down, Gaius, please," said his mother firmly.

"What is the matter with me, Mother? I heard you talking before with the doctor. What is falling sickness?" he persisted.

"I will explain all to you later, when you have rested," Aurelia replied, as she smoothed the covers down.

Caesar knew it was pointless to argue with her when she spoke in that tone so he resigned himself to being fussed over. "Where is father? I want to see him," he said, when Aurelia had finished.

Aurelia frowned, but Caesar knew that it was a frown of worry and not of anger. "Your father has been called away, Gaius, and no, I do not know when he will be home, before you ask," she said, a little curtly.

"Has something happened, Mother? Is it the siege?" he said, struggling against the tightly wrapped covers to sit up again.

"Do not excite yourself so!"

"Oh, Mother, stop fussing!" he replied in exasperation. "I am not a child and I have told you that I feel fine, so tell me, please!"

Aurelia looked cross and shook her head at her son's wilfulness. "Your father will return when his business is concluded, and getting yourself upset will not bring him home any sooner, now, the doctor said you must rest, and that is what you will do, my boy!" she said firmly, tucking and smoothing the bed covers once more.

"Yes, Mother," he sighed, slumping back onto his bed.

Aurelia left the room satisfied that, for now at least, her son would be safely tucked up in bed and out of harms way.

Caesar huffed in frustration and put his hands under his head to act as a cushion. Memories of the earlier conversation with his father flooded back into his mind and he lay still for a long while, thinking over the events of that morning, then he smiled to himself. The time had finally arrived, the waiting over. Gaius Marius was fighting his way back into Rome to fulfil his prophecy. Would he become Consul for a seventh time? Only time would tell, but whatever he did, Caesar knew with certainty, that his own destiny was somehow wrapped up in the fortunes of his uncle, and, whatever that might be, Caesar couldn't wait to find out.

Gaius Julius Caesar was a very tired and worried man. After two full days of fraught negotiation with Marius and Cinna, as part of a senatorial delegation, he had finally come home to bathe and get a change of clothing before the Senate meeting later that morning. Before he left, Gaius Julius summoned Caesar to his study.

"It looks increasingly likely that Cinna will return to Rome and resume his position as Consul for the remainder of his term in office, and, with his exile lifted, your uncle Marius will return home to Julia, therefore it is important that I remind you to stay well away from his house."

"Yes, Father," said Caesar. Fortunately, he had managed to see Marcus after his father had previously warned him that Marius might return to Rome, and the friends had quickly organised ways and means to continue their friendship, away from the watchful eyes of Caesar's parents.

"I spoke to Young Marius at some length, after I had finished negotiations with his father, and he tells me that Gaius Marius has become increasingly unstable since he fled Rome; I have to say that looking at him, I'm inclined to agree."

"Is he really that bad, Father?"

"The man is a physical wreck, Gaius. Unwashed, unshaven, dirty, ragged clothing, he was almost unrecognisable as the man who left Rome a few months ago. His army consists of Italian slaves; can you believe that? He promised them freedom, and the prize of Roman citizenship if they supported his return to Rome. His moods are very…volatile, and he is most definitely not to be trusted, in my opinion, but I was given little choice in offering him terms to return to Rome. I just hope that the Senate does not live to regret their decision to sue for peace."

Caesar was surprised that he actually felt a sense of pity when he heard how his uncle had deteriorated. The once great man, that he had grown up knowing and respecting, had now all but gone, according to his father, and he wondered if this change would make him less of a danger to himself, or, even more of one?

The study door burst open without warning and in stumbled Marcus Aurelius Cotta, dishevelled and breathless. He collapsed into the nearest chair, his chest heaving as he fought to catch his breath.

"Marcus! What in all the gods has happened?" said Gaius Julius, leaping up from his chair.

"Cinna…Marius…entered the city with army!" Marcus Aurelius gasped, as he struggled to breath.

"What? But we only left them a few hours ago! This is not how it was agreed, Marcus; what has happened to change things?"

"Marius…has led his slave army into Rome. They…they…"

"Just stop and catch your breath, Marcus, I can't understand a word you are saying." said Gaius Julius. "No, stay," he ordered Caesar, who had presumed he should leave, and had moved over to the door.

Caesar returned to his chair. His heart was beating ten to the dozen, through excitement and fear and the shock of seeing his uncle so distressed.

"Cinna and Marius have entered Rome. Cinna left his men on the Campus but Marius insisted on bringing his slave army into the city with him; for protection he said. They marched into the Forum as though they were returning heroes. The People welcomed them with open arms, Gaius, you should have seen them, especially towards Marius, who was always a favourite of theirs," Marcus Aurelius paused to catch his breath before continuing. "I was in the Senate House, trying to convince Octavius to leave, but he refused. He insisted he was a legally appointed Consul and he would not leave for anyone. Then a riot broke out in the Forum, caused by Marius's slaves going on the rampage. We only just managed to get Octavius away in time, but he simply refused to leave the area."

"So where did you take him?"

"He insisted on going to the Janiculum. He says he won't run away from Cinna, though we have tried to explain that his bravery is not in question and it is purely a matter of his safety, but he insisted that his consular chair go with him, and there he sits, in the Janiculum, surrounded by lictors and many of the senators who are loyal to him."

"What of Merula? Did he heed Cinna's warning or has he stayed with Octavius?"

"No. Merula left soon after you did. I expect he's gone to his beloved temple to pray; much good that will do him!" Marcus Aurelius snorted contemptuously. "He never felt comfortable replacing Cinna as temporary Consul, preferring the company of the gods to men."

Caesar recognised the name of Merula. When he had heard that he had been elected to replace Cinna as Consul, after the Italian demonstration went disastrously wrong and Cinna fled the city, Caesar had remarked on the unusual choice of the Senate, for Merula was the Flamen Dialis, a high priest, and he was not supposed to take any part in the politics of Rome. He didn't have time to muse further, as his father continued to question Marcus Aurelius.

"Where is Cinna now? And Marius?"

"At the Senate House I believe, although I did not stop to find out. The slaves are out of control down there and Marius appears to be doing nothing to stop them. They were looting the shops and the forum market place when I left."

"We better get down there now and see if we can't talk some sense into Octavius, before it is too late," said Gaius Julius, throwing off his toga.

"Yes, I rather thought you would say that, and I think we should try and speak to Marius, see if we can't put a stop to his mob looting Rome. He might listen to you, Gaius."

"That's what Octavius thought when he appointed me as envoy, but, where has it got us?" snorted Gaius Julius, as he threw a cloak over his shoulders. "Come on, Marcus, we have no time to lose!"

Caesar stood up. "Father…"

"Gaius, you must stay here, do you understand? Don't leave the house, not for anything. Look after your mother and sister," he said, heading for the door.

"Yes, Father, I…"

"Don't argue, Gaius, just do as you are told!" his father shouted, as he hurried down the corridor, with Marcus Aurelius close behind.

"I only wanted to say be careful," said Caesar, to the empty room.

# CHAPTER TWELVE

*"The life of the dead is placed in the memory of the living."*
*(Marcus Tullius Cicero)*

## ROME: August-December 87BC

Gaius Julius and Marcus Aurelius hurried through the Aventine and down towards the Forum, with several other senators joining them on the way. The nearer they came to the centre of Rome the thicker became the crowds, a melee of bodies, fighting, pushing, shoving, shouting and crying. Shopkeepers looked on in helpless dismay as their shops were plundered by the marauding slaves who were emptying earthenware jars of their contents, smashing and stealing whatever took their fancy. As the senators entered the market place, directly behind the Forum, the devastation became all too apparent. Smashed stalls were everywhere, the goods strewn across the ground, animals wondering around loose or lying dead in warm pools of fresh blood; the flies, not slow to act, swarming around by the hundreds to enjoy the feast. Gangs of slaves were embroiled in fights with the people who had initially welcomed them into the city and now found their livelihoods destroyed and their very lives in peril.

"Oh, this is terrible, terrible!" shouted Marcus Aurelius, above the din of the screaming people. "What has he done to us? By all the gods!"

Gaius Julius remained tight-lipped; his focus was to get through the crowds unscathed and to find Octavius as quickly as possible. If they could just get him away from the centre of this disturbance then Cinna and Marius could concentrate their efforts on bringing order back to the streets. He looked behind, and saw to his dismay, that a gang of angry looking men with staves had waylaid two of the senators that had joined him earlier. He stopped, intending to go back to their rescue but a firm hand grabbed his arm to prevent him.

"Leave them, Gaius. There is nothing we can do!" Marcus Aurelius insisted, and he pulled Gaius Julius onwards through the crowds, towards the Forum.

They rounded the corner of the Temple of Castor and Pollux, and, as if by magic, the shouting stopped. It took a few seconds for the men to realise that a complete change had come over the crowd in the Forum itself, as they continued to push their way through in the direction of the Janiculum, but, sensing that something significant had happened, Gaius Julius pulled Marcus to a halt.

"What's happening?" he said, looking around at the faces of the people. Everyone was stationary, all looking in one direction, towards the lower end of the

Forum. Apart from a low hum of murmuring voices, the crowd was quiet. He strained to look over the shoulders of the men in front of him, but the mass of people was too great, and all he could see was a sea of heads.

"I can't see. There are too many people."

"This way," said Marcus Aurelius, and he began to push his way towards the temple.

The temple steps was packed with men who had the same idea of going higher up to get a better view. Marcus Aurelius shoved and elbowed his way up the steps, apologising as he went, to the men whose feet he trod on or whose ribs he bruised. Finally they reached the top and turned to face the Forum again. The sight that met their eyes made both men gasp in sheer horror.

"By all the gods, this cannot be happening!" Marcus Aurelius cried.

Gaius Julius made no reply. The scene before him was beyond words and beggared belief.

The crowd stretched below him, as far as the eye could see, completely packed with men standing shoulder-to-shoulder; all looking in one direction.

His eyes swept across the crowd to the large white, stone rostra, for centuries the place where great noblemen of Rome had made some of their most notable speeches to the People. It towered above them like a sentinel of the city. The prows of enemy ships taken in battles long past were fixed to the front, as a permanent reminder of Rome's greatest achievements as masters of the sea, as well as land. Tall wooden poles, over fifteen feet high, were spaced at intervals around the edges, usually draped in garlands of flowers or the flags of Rome's victorious legions. Today, however, they were bare, all bar one, and underneath it stood a man.

Gaius Julius swallowed hard, to force back the bile that rose in his throat. The man was Gaius Marius, his appearance no better than a beggar; his long matted hair bedraggled and unkempt, his face dirty and unshaven, his clothes soiled and ragged. There stood this colossus among men, the darling of the People, hailed in his glorious past as First Man in Rome and Third Founder of Rome; He was Consul, General, Husband, Father, and he had a look on his face that was terrifying to behold.

At his feet a large pool of blood lay congealing. Gaius Julius followed the source as he drew his eyes slowly up the red, bloodstained pole, to the top, for there, freshly placed for all of Rome to see, was the head of the Senior Consul, Octavius; his sightless eyes staring out at the People before him, his face set in the calm composure of a man who had faced death without fear. And his lifeblood ran down the smooth surface of the pole, to the feet of the man who had put him there.

The crowd was stunned into complete silence as they watched Marius begin to pace up and down the rostra. Gaius Julius felt Marcus Aurelius stumble into him, but his own legs were like jelly, as his mind fought to comprehend this truly staggering disaster. Never in the history of Rome has such a scene been witnessed before: A Senior Consul murdered, his head displayed like a common criminal for all to see.

A single tear fell, unnoticed, from his eye, as he looked at the faces of the crowd below. Gaius Julius knew what they were thinking, could feel what they were feeling, for he was one of them, and he understood. The Roman people were used to bloodshed, the gladiatorial fights drew large crowds that thrilled to watch the scenes of massacre played out before them in the name of entertainment. They would shout and bay like wild dogs, encouraging the deaths to be more spectacular, more violent; but that was tradition, that was an acceptable part of life in Rome. What faced them all now was something completely different, and they did not know how to react. The life of the Consul was sacred, they were considered to be living gods by the People, surrounded by an untouchable aura of power and invincibility. The Consuls represented Rome; they were the figureheads of the Republic, untouchable, venerated and respected. It was impossible to know how to react, and the People remained awestruck at what they were witnessing.

Gaius Julius became aware for a second of the faint echoes of the fighting and plundering that could be heard in the streets behind the Forum, but before him, in the very heart of the city, over two thousand people stood immobile, in complete silence.

The stark reality of what the last few months had been about hit them all with a force that no siege or clash of weapons could ever have done. Providing there was clear leadership, the People were prepared to let the princes of government fight amongst themselves. Political rivalry was part of Rome and the People understood that, safe in the knowledge that they were protected by the Mos Maiorum.

Gaius Julius stood as still as a statue, the horror forcing inertia. Only his lips moved, as he repeated over and over again, "Mos Maiorum, Mos Maiorum." No other thought could enter his head, for the Mos Maiorum was everything to him, to all the people of Rome. Two simple words formed the world of a Roman. It was the unwritten rules of Rome, signifying the way life should be, and would be, forever more. It was the past, the present, and the future of Rome. The way things had always been, the way things were now, and, the way things should always be in the future. Whatever else happened to Rome, the Mos Maiorum held her together. It was the very idea and essence of Rome, the fabric that held the Republic together. And the Mos Maiorum said that the Consuls' were inviolate; demi-gods, above the law of the common man they could not be harmed in any way by violence of the People.

And now, stuck on a pole at the very heart of Rome was the head of their Senior Consul. And no one knew what to do.

A muttering of fear began to filter through the crowd. What they were witnessing was not just a spectacle of a head displayed on the rostra; it was a challenge to everything that they had known before and what was to be.

"The People look into the face of the unknown and they tremble in fear." Marcus Aurelius whispered , his voice cracked with emotion.

Gaius Julius simply nodded, his mind racing ahead now to what the People would do next. Who would lead them? Did the Senate still exist or had that fallen too? What did this mean for Rome, for the People? And there, in front of them, standing on the rostra showing no fear and in total control was the People's hero, Gaius Marius.

Whenever Rome had been threatened, Gaius Marius had been there to save her. Nothing and no one could defeat him, and so it was to this man that the People turned now. It mattered not who had killed their Senior Consul, or the rights and wrongs of Marius's return to the city; all they knew was, that with Gaius Marius they would find safety and reassurance. The People knew that he would keep Rome safe because they knew he loved them.

A man at the front of the crowd by the rostra lifted his fist high in the air. "*Hail Marius*!" he screamed. "*Hail Marius*!"

Gaius Julius saw the crowd come to life before him as more fists were raised in the air and the cry went up, "*Hail Marius! Hail Marius! Hail Marius!*" A sea of arms before him rose to the sky, saluting the man who stood on the rostra before the people of Rome.

Gaius Julius came to his senses. "Come on Marcus, we have to leave!" he shouted to make himself heard above the roaring crowd, and he turned and began to push his way through the mass of tightly packed bodies and down the temple steps. Marcus followed behind as best he could, and after several minutes the two men managed to find their way into a small side ally that ran down the back of the Forum, away from the crowd.

"What do we do now?" said Marcus Aurelius, completely flustered.

"We make our way to the Senate House and find Cinna of course! Whatever is happening it is madness, and Marius must be stopped," said Gaius Julius, and he set off at a run with Marcus Aurelius in close pursuit.

They skirted round the Forum using the narrow and empty side streets until they came to the back of the Senate House. They went through a side door and entered the hall where over a hundred senators had already arrived; some togate whilst others, like Gaius Julius, wore simple tunics. The correct dress code for senators was completely ignored on this occasion.

Gaius Julius saw his cousin, Quintus Lutatius Catalus Caesar, standing with a group of senators that he recognised, and he made his way over to join them whilst Marcus Aurelius slipped off in a different direction. As he reached the group, Gaius Julius turned to glance up at the dais and saw Cinna, sat on the one remaining curule chair, surrounded by senators welcoming his return to Rome.

"They didn't waste any time!" he said angrily to Catalus Caesar as he joined the group.

Catalus Caesar simply looked contemptuously up at the dais and turned away.

"Have you been outside? Have you seen what's happening?"

"No, not personally," Catalus Caesar replied. "But I have been told."

"What is going on? Why is Marius out there on the rostra alone, parading under the…the head of Octavius, as though he is a conquering hero?" Gaius Julius swallowed at the sickening memory of what he had seen. "The People are chanting his name, hailing him as their saviour! I swear by all the gods the world has gone mad!"

Catalus Caesar nodded sympathetically. "I understand your sentiments, Gaius Julius, but for the present all we can do is wait and see what Cinna intends to do next."

"But why? Why are we waiting? Gaius Marius must be stopped before he whips that crowd into such frenzy that they turn on us! Why is Cinna allowing him to do this? What is going on?" Gaius Julius cried in exasperation.

"Gaius Julius, calm yourself," said Catalus Caesar. "I understand how you feel, but it is in our interests to remain calm and sort this out in the correct manner. Cinna is now our Senior Consul and we, the Senate, allowed him to return under these conditions. He is in charge now and it is up to him to return order to Rome."

"But he isn't doing anything. Look at him, surrounded by all those sycophants!" said Gaius Julius angrily. He could not understand why Catalus Caesar was taking things so calmly.

"Gaius Julius, it is as Catalus says," said Senator Marcus Antonius Orator, calmly. "We gave Cinna back his power of office and we cannot force him to act."

"But he promised that there would be no violence. He swore his return to Rome would be peaceful. Surely he has broken the agreement."

"I am afraid he has not," said Senator Lucius Hortensius, who stood next to Catalus Caesar.

Gaius Julius looked confused. "But…"

"Cinna said that he would not *directly* order violence against any person in Rome, but he could not guarantee that there would not be reprisals. That is why he advised Octavius to leave the Forum before he arrived. But Octavius refused, and well…" Hortensius shrugged and let the rest of the sentence go un-said.

"What about Marius? When I delivered the message from the Senate he was calm and accepting of the situation, and his conditions of returning into the city, so what has happened to change things?" persisted Gaius Julius.

"Gaius Marius never had any intention of returning quietly to Rome." Catalus Caesar said scathingly.

Cinna now rose to his feet to address his audience. "Fellow senators, it has been a long and turbulent day for us all, in one way or another, and so it is time to call this brief reunion to a close. Please rest assured that Rome's troubles are at an end, and I think we should resume on a new and positive footing in two days from now; give the People time to settle down and for daily life to resume. Please be assured that there will be no more violence. I, your Consul, give you my word."

*"For what it's worth!"* snorted Gaius Julius under his breath.

"So, until then," concluded Cinna, and with a casual wave of dismissal, he returned to his chair.

Senators began to drift towards the doors, many relieved that Cinna's attitude seemed to be one of peace and forgiveness. Perhaps his return was not going to be too bad for Rome after all.

As the great wooden doors of the House swung open, their ears were assailed by the chanting of the crowd still gathered in the Forum. "*Marius! Marius! Marius*!

Gaius Julius rushed to the doors. The crowd, if anything, had grown even bigger, and Gaius Marius could still be seen parading around the rostra, soaking up the adulation of the People. Many of the senators collected at the top of the Senate House steps to stare, transfixed, at the scene played out before them. Most had arrived before the head of Octavius had been placed on the pole and they looked on in abject horror at what they saw. Some of them covered their heads with their togas, a sign of shame and mourning, whilst others turned back into the House, unsure of what to do.

Catalus Caesar remained standing in the centre of the floor, his face contorted in repulsion and rage. He turned to Cinna, who was sitting upon the dais.

"Is this what you call a successful return to Rome, Cinna?" he bellowed down the hall at the visibly paling Cinna. "Is that the settled, civilised city you want? *Well?* You have brought Rome to her knees to get what you want, but I bet you did not plan on this, did you?" He flung his arm to point down the Hall to the Forum outside, where the shouting crowd thronged beyond its doors. "Listen to them, Cinna. Can you hear them from where you sit? It's not you the crowd hails as their hero, is it? What have you done to Rome; allowing that mad man to enter our city once again? You think he is your man, you think that by giving him command of the legions in the east that you can control him! *How stupid are you?* Gaius Marius is mad. He is beyond help, beyond reason! Do you honestly think he is going to take any notice of you, once he gets what he wants? If you do, then you are even more of a fool than I took you for, Cinna. Give Marius control of the legions and you might as well wave the Republic farewell. Mark my words, Cinna, and mark them well. You have brought a viper into our bosom again, and the only thing that can stop him now is death; but what destruction, what carnage will he reap before he is stopped? How many lives will he destroy to satisfy his lust for revenge, for there are many of us standing before you today whom he would see destroyed. The blood that mad man will spill will stain your soul forever, Cinna. As you accepted his partnership to help you regain your office, so shall you be partners of death and destruction. Your *odium* is like the stench of a thousand rotting carcasses, Cinna. I hope it was worth it!"

Quintus Lutatius Catalus Caesar ended his tirade with a contemptuous flick of his hand and turned his back on Cinna, who had remained seated, in stunned silence, at this outburst. The senators who had witnessed this explosion of abuse from Catalus Caesar looked uneasy, unsure of what to do next, but Catalus Caesar broke the spell himself by making a great show of arranging his toga into immaculate folds, and then he stalked from the Hall, his dignitas intact, his bearing every inch the aristocratic, Patrician Roman that he was.

The flames of the oil lamps jumped and danced as though they also felt the force of Marius's rage. The man himself paced up and down his study, gnashing his teeth and occasionally punching the air with his fist as Young Marius looked on in dismay. Cinna fidgeted in his chair, unsure of how to proceed. He knew Gaius Marius would not like being told he would have to wait for a vote to replace Sulla as commander of the eastern war, but Cinna had not anticipated that his reaction would be so profound.

"Time, time, time!" muttered Gaius Marius. "I have spent my whole career fighting time, and it is fast running out for me. I *have* to have that command, Cinna and I don't care how I get it!"

"And I assure you that you will, Marius, soon, but we have to go about things the right way. My term as Consul ends soon, and if the newly elected Consuls are pro-Sulla, then any irregularity in your appointment will give them the excuse they need to withdraw the command from you and return it to Sulla again."

Gaius Marius sat up straight; his eyes narrow slits, as he stared at Cinna.

Young Marius tensed; he had seen that look before and it did not bode well.

A smile spread slowly across Marius's face. "I know exactly how to ensure that no man who supports Sulla will get elected into the consulship," he said smoothly, with an evil glint in his eye.

"What, exactly do you mean, Marius?" Cinna asked.

"We remove them, get rid of them… all of them. If they can't vote or stand for election then my success is guaranteed."

Cinna was puzzled, though he had a sinking feeling that he was not going to like what Marius was going to say. "Remove them? I'm sorry, Marius, but I fail to understand what you mean."

Marius smiled broadly, though his eyes were now hard and cold like a snakes.

"Kill them of course. Kill them all, just like Octavius. He got in the way so I had Censorinus cut his head off. Easy!" said Marius, with a smug smile of satisfaction on his face.

Cinna's jaw dropped, his mouth gaping open in surprise. "Surely you can't mean…? Octavius was one thing, Gaius Marius, that was…acceptable to our cause, but what you are suggesting is nothing short of a massacre!"

"If you want to put it that way," said Marius shrugging. "I prefer to think of it as a…cleansing of the Senate. Out with the old and in with the new," he added, with a broad smile. "By removing Sulla's supporters we also remove any possibility of him returning to Rome to cause trouble for us, once I take over command of his legions. On his own he will be powerless. I want to see him suffer!" said Marius getting to his feet. "I want to break him, and return him to the gutter I dragged him from. I want to see him friendless, penniless, no wife, no children, and no legions! And, when I return victorious from crushing Mithridates, I shall see Sulla in chains. I want him on his knees at my feet, begging me to spare his life. I want him to suffer in ways he could never imagine, and then…then, when I see that he truly understands what he has done to me; how he betrayed me, plotted and schemed against me…when I see that in his eyes, then I am going to slit his throat and watch him die, slowly and painfully, while I look in his eyes. He will die knowing that no one defeats Gaius Marius! No one can replace me in the hearts of the People or of the legions. I am and always will be the First Man in Rome, Third Founder of Rome, and I *will* remain for all eternity as the greatest Roman that ever lived!" Gaius Marius laughed exultantly, rubbing his hands together with sheer delight. When he saw the look on Cinna's face he laughed even harder, a wild, maniacal laugh, that sent shivers of fear down Cinna's spine.

Cinna had seen through a window into Marius's soul and what he saw terrified him. He realised that Catalus Caesar was right; he had no control over Marius. How could any man have power over him with what he had become? He truly was insane. Cinna knew that he had made a pact with a serpent, believing he could control it, that it would never turn on him, and now he realised his mistake. Marius could turn on Cinna at any time, and he knew there was nothing he could do to prevent it. He was trapped in this relationship with no way out, and he had burnt his bridges with Sulla as well. Falsely promising not to overturn any of the laws Sulla had put in place during his term as Consul, he had immediately conspired for Marius's exile to be lifted. Now Sulla knew that he was his enemy there could be no going back. Catalus Caesar's vision of Marius proclaiming himself king of Rome flashed before his mind and he felt an overwhelming hatred for Catalus, for being proved right. He, Cinna, had been a fool.

"Very well, Marius, you shall have what you wish, but *only* those that we know are openly supporting Sulla, no one else. This has to be about Sulla, and not an opportunity for you to remove every man that ever crossed you. If you agree to this condition you shall have my support, but only my support. I will not raise a hand to these men as Consul of Rome; there has to be some standards."

"I agree to your terms, Cinna, and, as I anticipated your agreement on this matter, I have already put things in motion. Have no fear, Cinna, there will be no retribution against you for this, after all, those that would complain will not be in any fit state to do so, will they?" he said, smiling triumphantly.

"Then I leave it in your capable hands, Marius," Cinna replied, getting to his feet. "I must take my leave now, I have much to do."

"I will keep you informed of my progress."

"Oh, just one thing," said Cinna, as he opened the study door. "Will Catalus Caesar be on your list?"

"Naturally. He is one of Sulla's most ardent supporters," said Marius.

"Good." said Cinna, and he left the study, closing the door behind him. He smiled to himself as he walked down the corridor. He hated people who proved themselves right at his expense. "Poor, poor, Catalus Caesar. You didn't see this one coming, did you?" Cinna's laugh echoed along the corridors as he left the house.

"But I said to Catalus Caesar, you must watch your back. If Cinna tells Marius what you said about him in the Senate then he will not take that lightly!" said Marcus Aurelius Cotta to Gaius Julius Caesar, as they trudged up the Clivus Publicus on the Aventine towards home. The meeting in the Senate had been a half-hearted affair that morning with less than half of all senators attending, and the meeting had ended earlier than was usual, giving Gaius Julius the rare opportunity to head for home and have dinner with his family.

"But will Cinna take any notice of all the warnings he's had about Marius, whether they come from Catalus Caesar or any other senator?" said Gaius Julius.

"If he hasn't, then he should. He is closing his eyes to the truth if he thinks that he has any control over Marius. That man does exactly what he wants, whatever anyone else might say about it. Oh, I wish Sulla were here. He is the only man capable of stopping Marius," said Marcus Aurelius longingly.

"Have you heard from him lately?"

"No, not since his last letter refusing to give up the legions to Marius."

"And now Cinna is working his way around the Senate, trying to convince anyone who will listen that Marius is the real man for the job. It's going to come to a head soon; it's only a matter of time, isn't it?"

"Well at least Marius will behave himself, until he gets the command at any rate. He won't do anything to upset potential voters, will he?"

"I hope you are right, Marcus, I pray to all the gods that you are. Well, here we are," said Gaius Julius as they reached his house. "Are you coming in?"

"Yes, I think I will. It has been a while since I saw Aurelia and no doubt she will want to show off baby Julia again."

As the two men entered the house, the steward, who looked rather anxious, greeted them. "The mistress would like to see you as soon as it is convenient, Master," he said as he helped remove the cloak from Gaius Julius's shoulders.

"Inform the mistress that I am back and ask her to come to my study," said Gaius Julius, and he lead the way through the atrium.

He had just handed Marcus a glass of iced water when there was a knock on the door and Aurelia entered. "Gaius Julius, I…oh, Uncle, I did not know that you were here," she said breathlessly upon seeing Marcus Aurelius.

"Marcus will be staying for dinner, Aurelia, that is, if you would like to, Marcus?" he said, turning to his friend.

"Love to, thank-you," Marcus Aurelius replied with a broad smile.

"Oh, no…I mean, I am sorry, Uncle, but we have other plans for dinner tonight," said Aurelia with a meaningful look at her husband.

"Why? What plans, Aurelia?"

"This came earlier," she said, handing him a small wax tablet.

Gaius Julius looked questioningly at his wife before he opened the tablet. His face fell as he read it.

"He ordered the messenger to wait for a reply. I had no choice but to accept under the circumstances," Aurelia explained defensively.

"What is it?" said Marcus Aurelius, who had seen the looks on their faces.

"You did the right thing," said Gaius Julius. "We have been summoned to Gaius Marius's home, for dinner, tonight," he said by way of explanation to his guest.

"Summoned?"

"The letter is polite but there is no room for misunderstanding. We are expected to attend," said Gaius Julius with a frown etched across his handsome features. Immediately he began to think if he had done anything that might have upset or angered Marius. Not for one second did he believe that this was simply an overdue family get together.

"Does the letter give you any indication as to what he might want?" Marcus Aurelius asked.

"No, nothing," Aurelia shook her head.

"Then of course you must go. You cannot afford to upset Marius of all people, especially not now, but be very careful what you say to him, is my advice, very careful," said Marcus Aurelius, rising to his feet.

"You do not need to remind us, Uncle, we understand very well what our position must be towards Gaius Marius, particularly as we have our son to think of, though he would not thank us for it," said Aurelia more sharply than she meant to sound.

"What do you mean by that, Aurelia," said Gaius Julius, noting the angry look that crossed his wife's face.

"Your son went out today without telling me! I have told him you will deal with him later. I sent him to his room and that is where he should be now, unless of course, he has taken it upon himself to disobey me again." she replied.

Marcus Aurelius smiled to himself. He had a fondness for Caesar, and the boy's antics over the years had often been a source of great amusement, "He is a spirited boy, Aurelia, and always has been. You can't expect to keep him locked up in this house indefinitely just because you are concerned for something that may never happen. Gaius knows the risks, but he is a bright boy, and he will not do anything to put himself in danger," said Marcus Aurelius lightly.

"I will deal with him later," sighed Gaius Julius. His son's misdemeanour paled into insignificance compared to this latest turn of events. "Now, we had better get ready for our dinner engagement. I will see you out, Marcus," he said, opening the study door and leading the way towards the atrium.

As they walked down the corridor, a loud banging could be heard on the main door. Whoever was knocking was desperate to be let in. As they entered the atrium they heard voices, and then a boys voice screamed, "*Caesar! Caesar, where are you?*"

Aemi came running into the atrium with the door slave close behind him, at the same time as Caesar appeared from one direction and his parents from the other.

"Caesar!" Aemi cried with relief, and burst into hysterical tears.

Caesar rushed to his friend's side. "What is it, Aemi, what has happened?"

"They've taken him! They came…to…our house…and…they took him away!" sobbed Aemi.

"Taken who? Who are you talking about, Aemi?" Caesar demanded, holding Aemi's arms to try and calm him down.

"Father…guards…help him, please!" begged Aemi, turning to look at Gaius Julius.

Aurelia took control, placing a motherly arm around Aemi. "Calm down, Aemi, please. Gaius, take Aemi to the study and get him a drink," she said, and ushered the two boys down the corridor.

"What in all the gods is going on?" said Marcus Aurelius.

"Marcus Aemilius Lepidus taken by guards? I have no idea," Gaius Julius replied.

"It will have something to do with Gaius Marius, no doubt!" said Aurelia as they made their way to the study.

They found Aemi sitting on a chair, sobbing and shaking uncontrollably, whilst Caesar knelt on the floor beside him, talking soothingly to try and calm him down.

Aurelia poured a small goblet of wine and handed it to Aemi. "Here, drink this," she said.

"You have to try and compose yourself, Aemi. I cannot help you if I don't know what has happened," said Gaius Julius sternly.

The sound of an authoritative male voice seemed to shock Aemi to his senses and he looked up at Gaius Julius with big tears rolling down his cheeks.

"Guards…came to our house," he sobbed. "Demanded to see…to see Father. When he came into the atrium they said…they said that he had to go with them. Father refused, and…and they took hold of him. I tried to help him, I swear I did, but they…they pulled me away! I…I had hold of his hand…and they pulled me away!" Aemi broke down in tears again.

"Aemi, please, try and calm down!" said Aurelia, putting a comforting arm around his shoulders.

He nodded and wiped tears from his eyes. "The guards forced father out of the house and there was nothing I could do…I tried, but I wasn't strong enough."

"Whose guards were they, Aemi? Did they say upon whose orders they acted?" said Gaius Julius, dreading the reply because deep down he already knew the answer.

"Marius…they said it was Marius." Aemi wept.

Aurelia glanced at her husband and hugged Aemi tighter to her chest.

"Do you know where they have taken your father, Aemi?" said Marcus Aurelius gently.

"No, Sir. Father shouted for me to get help and then…and then they dragged him away. I came here; it was the only place I could think of."

"And your mother, where is she?" Aurelia asked.

"At the market. She went to buy some new slaves," said Caesar. "That was where I went this morning, to Aemi's house. That's how I know," he said to his mother, by way of explaining his earlier disappearance.

"You were forbidden to go anywhere near the home of Marius!" said Aurelia angrily.

"Not now, Aurelia!" snapped Gaius Julius. The last thing he needed was his own family to start arguing. "I said I would deal with it, and I will, now, Aemi, think, did the men say anything else?"

"No, sir," Aemi buried his face in Aurelia's warm comforting embrace and sobbed his heart out.

"Keep the boy here and I will go and make some enquiries," said Marcus Aurelius, moving to the door. Gaius Julius nodded as Marcus left the room.

"Aurelia, send a slave to Aemi's house to let them know that the boy is here with us. Tell them to find his mother, and to send word when she is home. Aemi will remain here until she sends for him," Gaius Julius ordered.

Aurelia gently prised Aemi from her embrace and stood up. "What are we to do about our dinner with..." she left the sentence there so as not to distress Aemi further by mentioning Marius's name.

"We have no choice but to go," replied Gaius Julius. A deepening dread weighed heavy on him as he realised that they would have to attend this dinner party as though nothing had happened. "Gaius, take Aemi to your room and organise some food for the both of you. Your Mother and I have a dinner arrangement that we cannot get out of so you will have to stay here with Aemi until his mother sends for him. Neither of you are to leave this house, for any reason, do you understand?" he said in a stern voice.

Caesar nodded and began to help Aemi to his feet.

"Should your Uncle Cotta return, tell him that we kept the appointment, he will know what you mean, and tell him to wait for us to return, we will be as quick as we can."

"Yes, Father," said Caesar, and he led Marcus from the study.

Gaius Julius sat on the edge of his desk and sighed. "You better send that message," he said, looking apprehensively at his wife.

"How will we get through this dinner now, knowing what we know?"

Gaius Julius held his arms open and Aurelia stepped forward to embrace him. He ran his hand over her velvet, soft, black hair, and lifted her face to his. "We will get through this together, Aurelia. Nothing will happen to us, I promise. We go, act normally and leave as soon as we are able. We shall say baby Julia is unwell and you are worried about her; that should suffice," he said with a weak smile.

Aurelia nodded, her eyes filled with tears. "I am frightened, Gaius. I am frightened for you and for our son. What is that man up to? What has he done to Marcus Aemilius Lepidus?"

Gaius Julius held his wife close. "I don't know, Aurelia, but I have a bad feeling that it's too late to do anything to help him now."

"How *could* you? How could you agree to this farce of a marriage without consulting me first!" Aurelia stormed, as she walked home with her husband at the end of the evening.

"You weren't there, Aurelia. You didn't see him. You don't say no to Gaius Marius, not any more!" Gaius Julius answered angrily.

"But he is *our* son; nothing to do with him. How *dare* he force you to agree to our son marrying a bride *he* has chosen? Oh, it is all his doing mark my words. What is he up too? What does he get out of this, that is what I want to know?"

"Family alliance. Tying us to Cinna through marriage, making me beholden to him for arranging such a brilliant match. You can't deny that we would ever have secured a girl of such political and social standing without Marius backing us. Cinna is his close friend after all, and I expect he was easily persuaded."

"Yes, I bet he was, but, did Cinna really agree to this match or has he been bullied into it, like we have? He has no more sway over Gaius Marius than the rest of you in the Senate. He is a puppet Consul, with Marius pulling all the strings!"

"Our family, our son, are of high birth, Aurelia, don't forget that. Cinna benefits from this marriage as much as we do, and there is no denying that the match is very suitable," said Gaius Julius, trying in vain to convince his wife that the situation forced upon them wasn't as bad as she believed it to be.

"I do not dispute that Cinna's ancestry makes the family our social equals, Gaius. What I do not like is whose daughter she is, and the fact that you have tied us even closer now to Gaius Marius. My family will be affected by this match too, you know!" Aurelia snapped.

Gaius Julius sighed. "I know, Aurelia, and I will explain it all to your uncle Marcus when I see him, but, you have to understand that I had no choice in the matter. By going against him I would have put us in much greater danger. If Gaius Marius thinks that I support him then we will be safe, and anyway, by allying our son to Cinna's daughter, surely he has proved that he harbours no ill will towards Gaius. Perhaps we have been wrong about him, and there is nothing in this prophecy theory of yours, I don't know, but one thing I am sure of, these are dangerous times, Aurelia, and all I am trying to do is protect my family, surely you can understand that?"

They had reached home, and as they entered the atrium, they were met by Caesar.

"Any news on Aemi's father?"

"No, but Uncle Marcus has been waiting for you. He's in your study, and Aemi went home a little while ago." He looked at his parents and saw, by the look on their faces, that something was wrong. "Mother, what has happened?"

Aurelia undid the broach that held her cloak together. Glaring at her husband she turned away in disgust. "You better ask your father, he is the one with all the answers." she said as she stalked off towards the nursery.

"Father?" said Caesar, looking puzzled.

"Not now, Gaius, it's late and you should be in bed. We will talk tomorrow." Gaius Julius replied as he walked off to his study.

One look at the face of Marcus Aurelius Cotta, and Gaius Julius knew that something truly calamitous had happened. "Well?" he asked.

Marcus Aurelius looked pitiful; his face pale and drawn and his eyes were red from weeping. "Oh, Gaius Julius!" he groaned, and put his head in his hands.

"What has happened, Marcus? Tell me!"

Marcus Aurelius raised his head and wiped a tear from his eye.

"Did you find Marcus Aemilius Lepidus? Where is he?"

"Yes, I found him, well, some of him, at least."

Gaius Julius froze. "What do you mean, some of him?

"I found…I found his head, Gaius. It is on a pole, on the rostra next to Octavius, or, what is left of Octavius,"

"*His head...on a pole*? Marcus, ... are you telling me that Marcus Aemilius Lepidus is dead?"

"Of course he's dead; how else would his head be on a pole?" Marcus Aurelius snapped. "Oh, I am sorry, Gaius, I didn't meant to...Oh, by all the gods, I swear this is terrible, truly terrible," he wailed.

"This can't be happening! Please tell me you have made some dreadful mistake Marcus," said Gaius Julius, desperately wanting to believe that their world was not disintegrating around them.

Marcus Aurelius looked up into his face, and Gaius Julius saw the pain and anguish in his eyes. "No, Gaius, I have made no mistake, and Lepidus is not the only one either."

Gaius Julius folded over, as though he had been physically punched in the solar plexus, "You mean there are *more*?"

Tears ran freely now as Marcus Aurelius nodded, "Oh yes, there are more. Their heads are on spikes around the edge of the rostra, on top of tall poles, for all of Rome to see."

Gaius Julius collapsed into a nearby chair, physically and emotionally stunned by the news. Marcus's words rang in his ears. Senator's heads on poles in the Forum? Surely this was some awful mistake? How could this possibly be happening? But as he looked at the crumpled figure before him he knew that there was no mistake and his eyes welled up with tears at this awful realisation.

"Who are they? How many?"

"Publius Crassus..."

*"Oh no!"*

"...and his eldest son."

*"His son? But..."*

"Attilius Serranus..."

*"No!"*

"Publius Lentulus..."

*"What!"*

"Gaius Nemetorius..."

*"No, please no, not Gaius..."*

"Marcus Baebius..."

*"This cannot be!"*

"And...I'm truly sorry, Gaius, your cousin, Lucius Julius Caesar."

"What? No, no, no, not Lucius, not my cousin, Lucius! What did he do to deserve this? *No, no, NO!*" Gaius Julius shouted, jumping to his feet and pulling at his hair in rage and grief. "*This is madness, utter madness.* What is happening? Who is doing this? *Why*?"

"I have asked those questions a hundred times already, and the only common strand that binds those poor men together was their friendship and open support of Sulla. It's my guess that now Marius is safely back in Rome, he is seeking retribution against those men who supported his exile, and worked against him."

The study door opened and Aurelia walked in to the room.

"*Get out, Aurelia*!" Gaius Julius shouted at his wife.

Aurelia paled at the sight of her husband in such a rage. "Gaius! What…"

"*Get out*! For once in your life do as you're told, woman!" he shouted, and Aurelia fled from the room in tears. Gaius Julius slammed the study door and paced the room.

"Gaius, you should not have taken this out on Aurelia, she did not understand," said Marcus reproachfully.

"Do you dare to tell me how I should treat *my* wife in *my* house?" Gaius Julius stormed. "I am paterfamilias, but no one would believe it, the way my wife and son carry on. All the gods, Marcus, I swear that I have just about had enough. I can't do right for doing wrong. Whichever way I turn I upset someone. Will no one understand what position I am in?" He punched the wall in frustration and blood exploded over his knuckles, but the paid no attention to the pain as he paced up and down the room.

"Gaius, calm down, please. Losing your temper will not change anything," Marcus Aurelius urged.

"What else can I do, Marcus, answer me that? You have no idea! Tonight…tonight I had to agree to *my* son marrying Cinna's daughter; a baby by all accounts. I had to, Marcus; I was given no choice! I agreed only to protect my family but can Aurelia see that? No, she scorns me, and holds me in contempt for being weak. She thinks I should have stood up to Marius and refused the marriage, but what would have happened if I had? Would my head be on one of those poles in the morning? What use would I be to my family then, Marcus, what use?" stormed Gaius Julius, his voice crumbling with emotion. He slumped into a chair, buried his head in his hands and sobbed.

Marcus Aurelius watched, unable to do or say anything to alleviate his friend's pain. "You did the right thing, Gaius, of that I have no doubt. If you had defied Marius then it is almost certain that your fate would have gone the way of the other poor men today, even though you are family."

"I'm sorry for the implications that this marriage means to our families, Marcus, for no one in their right mind wants to be associated with Marius now; I just hope you can forgive me." Gaius Julius cried. It seemed whichever way he turned someone was being hurt.

"What's to forgive? It's not as though you went looking to tie yourself closer to him, is it? Anyway, us Cotta's are a resilient lot and I'm sure we will all come through this unscathed.

"Oh Marcus, Marcus, what am I to do? What is Rome to do? We are all in the clutches of a mad man. An evil, vile creature, ah, words cannot be found to describe him, or what he has done, to all of us." Gaius Julius could not contain himself any longer. He wanted to scream with frustration at the injustice of it all. With one swipe of his arm, he knocked over the small table, next to his chair, sending the wine jug and goblets flying across the room.

"Calm yourself, Gaius Julius, please, this…this violence will solve nothing," Marcus Aurelius pleaded, as Gaius Julius left his chair and paced the room like a caged lion.

"Anything is better than doing nothing, Marcus."

"I understand your frustration, Gaius, but it is brains, not brawn, that will see us through this madness safely, that, and our faith in the gods."

"*The gods*? The gods stood by and watched innocent men be slaughtered, and for what crime, Marcus? What crime did any of them commit, other than to oppose Marius? No, Marcus, there are no gods. We are forsaken; this is the end. If Marius is responsible for this atrocity, then he has ripped the guts out of Rome. The very heart of who we are and what we stand for lies in tatters at our feet! How will we ever recover from this?"

"Gaius, you must have faith, if not in the gods then in yourself, and people like us. Do you think Gaius Marius will go unpunished for what he has done? We must fight; stand together against this tyranny and fight for Rome!"

"How can we fight him? I'm not strong enough; no man is. Face it, Marcus, Marius has won." Pain and defeat lined the face of Gaius Julius, as he stared into the black abyss of the unknown. There was no hope, no salvation; all was lost and he was helpless to do anything about it.

"No, Gaius, you are wrong! There is more than one way to fight. We hold the idea that is Rome in our heads, and in our hearts. If we hold on to that, then Rome will not die; not as long as there is one Roman left who believes in Her. We must wait and gather strength. Lucius Cornelius Sulla will not be away forever. He is the one man we know can beat Marius. We can beat Marius and we shall, truly we shall."

Gaius Julius wiped his tear soaked face with the back of his hand and slumped back in his chair. "And until that day, what? What do we do, Marcus? How do we make sure that our heads do not end up on display in the Forum?"

"You sit on the fence, Gaius. You do nothing to draw attention to yourself, and you accept the match with Cinna's daughter, and act grateful. You cannot let either of them see that you are against this match. You are protected more than most if you ally yourself with Marius and Cinna. Do nothing to make Marius suspicious, and wait until Sulla returns. He is Rome's salvation, of that I have no doubt, and, who knows him better than Sulla? Marius raised him from poverty and taught him everything he knows, never thinking that one day his protégé would turn on him, but he did, and Sulla has the strength and the courage to prevail.

"And then what? Sulla comes back, defeats Marius, and the retributions start all over again, only this time, it's the men who supported Marius who will die. Whichever way you look at it, Marcus, I am doomed!" Gaius Julius groaned in pure misery.

"No, Gaius, that will not happen because once Sulla is back, you can tell him that you supported Marius under duress, and that the marriage was forced upon you; I will back your words with my own; Sulla owes me a debt for saving his family and he *will* forgive you."

Gaius Julius smiled gratefully, but he held out little hope. His life was now in the hands of the gods, and they had forsaken Rome. "What will you do, Marcus? You cannot possibly stay in Rome now; if Marius finds out that you helped Sulla's wife and children escape he will surely kill you!"

"I realise that, Gaius, and under the circumstances I think it best that I leave Rome, tonight if possible, whilst I still have a head on my shoulders to see where I'm going," said Marcus Aurelius dryly.

Gaius Julius frowned. "Where will you go?"

"East, I think would be best. Catch up with Sulla and the legions; I should be safe there. I have no choice now but to climb off that fence and nail my colours to Sulla's flag in the hope that if this does come to a confrontation between Sulla and Marius I am on the winning side. I am sorry to leave you here alone, Gaius, but you know that you have my full support, and sympathy, for the position you find yourself in, and, when the time comes, I swear that I will do all in my power to convince Sulla that you were never a Marian supporter through choice."

"Do you really believe we can do this, Marcus?"

"I do, Gaius, I really do. Now, the time has come for me to say goodbye. I will write as soon as I am able. Tell Aurelia not to worry about me and to look after her mother." said Marcus Aurelius, rising from the chair with a grim smile.

Gaius Julius stood up and the two men embraced.

"I shall miss you, Marcus."

"And I you, but, the gods willing, our separation shall be over soon, and we can all put this nightmare behind us, once and for all."

"Until then, Marcus Aurelius Cotta."

"Yes, until then, Gaius Julius Caesar. Have faith."

The house of Marcus Aemilius Lepidus was in darkness. Wooden shutters were pulled across every window as the household was plunged into mourning, and the only light offered came from the small, clay oil lamps, that flickered dull yellow flames.

Caesar found Aemi sitting quietly in his sleep cubicle and his heart went out to his friend. Aemi's eyes were red and swollen from crying, and his face was gaunt and drawn with grief. In his hand he held a gold signet ring with the family crest protruding proudly from the oval mount in the centre of the band of yellow. Caesar guessed that it was his father's ring.

"A slave brought it back to me this morning," Aemi said, noticing Caesar looking at the ring. He held it up to the light. "It came from father's…father's finger. They found his body earlier," said Aemi, his voice cracking with emotion. "It's mine now, you see…I am paterfamilias. I have to…to take his place and look after mother." Marcus placed the ring into the palm of his hand and caressed it lovingly with one finger.

Caesar watched but remained silent.

"It's funny really; I have not yet come of age, but now I have all the responsibilities of a man," Aemi's laugh sounded hollow.

"I truly am sorry, Aemi," said Caesar, reaching out to touch his friends shoulder. "You know my father would have helped if he could, but it was…too late."

"I know, Caesar, and I am grateful to your family," The weak smile faded as quickly as it came, to be replaced by a grimace. "Do you know, they threw his body in the Tiber…father's body? Our slaves went out and searched all night. They found him and…managed to retrieve this ring before he was thrown in the river. The men who were with my father said, that it was done on the orders of Gaius Marius. They said, that is what happens to men who are traitors, but, father wasn't a traitor, Caesar, *he wasn't!* Aemi cried out angrily before overwhelming sobs engulfed him.

Caesar closed his eyes in despair at his friend was suffering. He wished he could help take this pain away but there was nothing he could do. A surge of anger rose through him at the injustice of it all. How had this been allowed to happen? This wasn't the Rome he knew, where men were dragged from their homes and slaughtered. What had happened to law and order? Who was in control of Rome now? Was this the end of his world, as he knew it? All these questions spun in his mind as he watched his friend, broken hearted, lying on the bed.

Aemi's sobs slowly died away, and he sat up and wiped his face with the sleeve of his tunic. "I feel as though I'm suffocating in here," he said. "Come on, let's go out, I need to get away for a while."

The boys walked through the silent house to the atrium where they met the steward.

"Tell my mother that I have gone out for a while, Crattipas. I won't be long," said Aemi.

"Yes, Young Master, but you should take an escort with you, to keep you safe,"

"I don't need an escort, Crattipas, unless Gaius Marius has taken to murdering children as well, and do not call me young master again, I am the master now, understand?"

The steward bowed low. "Yes, Master."

"Come, Caesar," said Aemi haughtily, as he strode purposely from the house.

They walked with no particular purpose, but the warm sun and fresh air seemed to breathe a little life back into Aemi's pale face.

"I want to be young, just once more, before…before I have to take on all the responsibilities I will have from now on," said Aemi sadly. "Let's go to the Rock and throw stones, like we used to, just one more time."

"All right, but I mustn't be too long; Father's orders," said Caesar, who was risking severe punishment if his father ever found out that he had been so close to Marius's home.

They made their way down the hill towards the Capitol, but as they drew closer they joined a large mass of people walking in the same direction, towards the Palatine Hill.

"There must be a ceremony at the temple, or something," said Caesar, as they mingled with the crowd.

"Let's go and watch," said Aemi. "Yes, I want to go to the temple. I want to ask the gods why they let this happen? Why they left a loving wife without a husband, and a dutiful son without a father. I want answers, Caesar."

Caesar could see that there was no point in arguing. Aemi needed to seek his own way through his grief, and, if going to the Temple helped, then so be it, but, as they approached the steps leading up to the great white marble temple, out from the doors leading to the inner sanctum stepped none other than Gaius Marius, dressed in full military finery. Caesar's heart sank. To see his uncle, today of all days, was the worst thing that could have happened for Aemi. Two other people walked behind Marius, from the darkness of the temple, and Caesar stared in amazement, for joining Gaius Marius, on his left, stepped his son, Young Marius, also dressed in military attire, and to Marius's right, stood Marcus, wearing the brand new army uniform of a junior cadet.

Aemi stopped in his tracks and gasped in astonishment. He could not take his eyes off Marcus. "What is he doing there, standing next to that animal he calls Uncle?" Aemi hissed between gritted teeth. "The traitorous cur! Doesn't he know Marius murdered my Father? How can he stand there, dressed in that uniform as though nothing has happened?"

"We can't blame Marcus for what Gaius Marius has done, Aemi. Perhaps he had no choice but to come here with his fa…with Gaius Marius," Caesar said quickly, hoping Aemi had not noticed his slip of words, for only this morning, he had been informed that Marcus was now the newly adopted, younger son, of Marius. As much as Caesar had wanted to share this extraordinary news with Aemi, he knew that today was not the right time.

All around them the crowd grew silent at the sight of Gaius Marius. Many of the people had seen the carnage of heads displayed in the Forum and rumours were rife that he was responsible for this atrocity.

"Come on, Aemi, let's go," said Caesar, taking Aemi's arm. People around him swore as he elbowed his way through to the edge of the crowd, but Caesar ignored them, his only concern was to get Aemi as far away as possible.

Suddenly, Aemi stopped and pulled his arm away. "Aemi, come on," he urged, but Aemi took no notice as he began to push his way through to the front of the crowd. Caesar had no option but to follow, scared at what his friend might do.

Marcus stared out at the crowd below him in wonder. He was seeing the power Gaius Marius held over the People for the first time, and he was a part of it. He was thrilled to be formally adopted as Marius's son, as he had very little affinity for his own family, back in Arpinium, and he couldn't wait to see the look on Caesar and Aemi's face, when he told them the news. 'You are my son, and from now on you will accompany your brother and I at all times,' Marius had told Marcus this morning, as he handed him a brand new military cadet uniform. These words now rang in his ears, as Marcus stood on the top step of the Capitol Temple, with hundreds of people staring up at him, together with his family, and he felt proud.

Marcus heard the priest declare the reading of the entrails auspicious, and saw how this pleased his father, for the People would read this as a sign that the gods approved. They were preparing to enter the temple to give thanks, when a man broke through the crowds and ran up the steps towards them.

"Gaius Marius, Gaius Marius!"

Marcus saw his father visibly stiffen as the man approached, and he glanced over at his brother, Young Marius, who now stepped forward to block the man from coming any closer.

"Gaius Marius, Gaius Marius, *Please*!" the man pleaded. "I beg you, spare me but a moment of your time!" and he threw himself in supplication at his feet.

Young Marius grabbed the man by the scruff of his tunic and held his head down as several guards ran forward to surround Gaius Marius. Marcus could feel his heart beating hard, and a cold fear made the hair on the back of his neck stand on end.

"Wait, all of you," Marius commanded. "Let Quintus Ancharius speak!"

"Thank you, Gaius Marius, thank you," babbled Ancharius gratefully, lifting his head off the step as Young Marius released his grip. "You are a kind and benevolent man. The gods look on you and smile. You are the chosen one of all the gods; I see that now! I have been blind and foolish to turn against you, you, who are truly the leader of all men. I beg your forgiveness, Gaius Marius. Welcome me back into your fold and I swear, before all the gods, that I will be your most loyal and humble servant. Never again will I turn my face from you. Give me a sword and I will fight by your side. I am yours to command, Gaius Marius. Forgive me!"

Marcus looked on in amazement at the fear and awe his father had inspired in this man, who had begged for forgiveness as though he were pleading to a god. He wondered what his father would do now. Surely he would show mercy to this man who had thrown away his dignitas to humble himself in front of all these people? The crowd watched, enthralled by the scene played out in front of them.

Gaius Marius stepped forward and signalled the man to get to his feet. "So Quintus," he said, looking at this wretch of a senator, who stood shaking in front of him. "You have come to beg for mercy. Did you think that by asking me here, in front of all these people, that you would be safe? You do not trust me?"

"No, Gaius Marius, that is not so. I *do* trust you; you have my complete trust and loyalty!" grovelled Quintus.

"But you did not see fit to give me that loyalty, that trust, before, did you? When I was exiled. When the Senate turned it's back on me. Where was your loyalty then, Quintus?"

"Oh, Gaius Marius, you do not know the anguish and torment and agony of conscience I went through, knowing that you were hunted and defenceless against Sulla, but I am here to make amends and to atone for my failure."

"Mmm, it is not nice being a victim is it, Quintus?" said Marius coldly.

Marcus shivered involuntarily. He had seen that cold glint in his father's eyes before and he knew it spelt trouble.

Quintus shook his head.

"Gnaius!" Marius called out to one of the guards who stood nearby. "How many poles do we have on the rostra?"

"Twenty, Gaius Marius," Gnaius answered promptly.

"Mmm," said Marius as he stared at Quintus, who stood shaking with fear and anticipation in front of him.

"How many are… occupied?"

"Sixteen, at present, Gaius Marius."

"Oh dear, Quintus," said Marius, a wry smile playing at the corners of his mouth. "It looks like your luck has just run out!"

"No, Gaius Marius! Please, I beg you!" pleaded Quintus, realising the fate that awaited him as two guards ran forward and grabbed him by the arms.

"Gnaius, amend that total to seventeen, will you? You know what to do," said Marius, turning his back on Quintus.

"*No*! *No*, Have mercy. *Please*!" screamed Quintus, struggling to free himself from the guards' iron grip.

Gnaius stood in front of the struggling senator, and with one quick thrust of his gladius, he drove it through his heart.

The two guards holding Quintus let go of the body and it slumped to the ground. A pool of bright red blood spread quickly, and began to run down the steps of the temple.

Marcus felt sick and put his hand over his mouth.

Gnaius stepped forward, and with one stroke, he severed the head from the body. Grabbing the hair, he lifted the head up to show Gaius Marius.

Marcus vomited.

Gaius Marius laughed.

The crowd stood silent.

Gaius Marius addressed the crowd. "Look and remember, People of Rome. This is what happens to men who betray Gaius Marius!"

No one moved, no one dared breathe; the tension was palpable in the air.

Gaius Marius turned to Gnaius. "Put the head on the rostra and throw the body in the Tiber."

Four guards picked up the decapitated body of Senator Quintus Ancharius and carried it down the temple steps, with Gnaius following behind, holding the head. A guard handed Marcus a cloth to clean his face and wipe the vomit stains from his uniform.

Gaius Marius turned to gather his sons' to him and glanced at Marcus. "The first is always the worst," he said.

"*MURDERER*!" A voice screamed from the crowd. Marius continued to walk up the steps.

"*MURDERER*. You killed my father!"

"Ignore it," Marius growled, but Marcus recognised the voice. Turning to look down into the crowd he saw Aemi standing on the bottom step looking up at him.

Their eyes met, and Marcus felt the vomit rise in his throat again. Aemi's eyes, filled with pure hatred and contempt, bored into Marcus, and then he spat at the steps in defiance.

"Marcus!" Gaius Marius called sternly from the doorway.

Marcus turned away, tears filling his eyes, and stumbled after his father into the gloomy darkness of the temple.

Caesar pulled Aemi through the crowd and away from the horror of what they had witnessed. His legs were shaking and his heart racing as he made his way towards the Tarpeian Rock.

They reached the cypress tree, next to the Rock, without a word being spoken. Caesar gently guided Aemi to the ground, and sat down next to him. Aemi continued to sit motionless beside him but Caesar saw a single tear slide down his cheek, the only visible sign of emotion from his friend.

"Aemi, Aemi, are you all right?" he asked softly. It appeared that Aemi had gone into deep shock. His eyes were glazed and he made no sign that he heard anything.

"Aemi, it's over, you are safe. Do you understand me?" he tried again, but still Aemi made no response. Caesar decided to let his friend come round in his own time. He walked to the edge of the rock face, and, picking up a small stone, hurled it with all his strength at the jagged rocks below. Gaius Marius, it was always Gaius Marius, ruining their lives, wrecking their friendship without even trying. Aemi had lost his father because of Marius, and they had both lost Marcus to him now, for how could their friendship ever survive this? And, to complete this day of misery, he was pledged to marry some child bride of Cinna, to satisfy the whim of his uncle. Caesar could not blame his father for conceding to Marius's wishes, he understood only too well in what position his father had been placed, and he sympathised. Of course, he had always known that one day he would be told who his parents had decided he should marry, for that was the Roman way, and he could not deny that the families were well suited, but he wished his bride could have been anyone but her; one that would not tie his family even closer to Marius. He picked up another stone and threw it after the first. Why could things not go back the way they were? Caesar, Marcus and Aemi, friends forever, enjoying the adventures of childhood. Now it was ruined, totally ruined...He almost wept in frustration.

"Caesar?"

Caesar turned at the sound of his name and walked back to where Aemi sat, under the tree.

"Tell me this is just a dream, Caesar. Tell me that I'll wake up and none of this will be true. The pain...I feel so empty," Aemi groaned, hugging his knees and rocking himself slowly back and forth.

Caesar sat down beside his friend. "I cannot, Aemi, though I would give anything to be able to tell you otherwise, but you will feel better...in time. We are all in this nightmare together, you, me, and Marcus."

"Marcus! Never mention his name to me again, Caesar, do you hear?" Aemi cried angrily. "He is no friend of mine, not now, not ever. After what his uncle did to my father, to my family; and he stood there next to him in that…that uniform, knowing what that animal had done to me!"

"But we don't know…"

"No, Caesar, *no*! I will not sit here and listen to you trying to defend him, trying to be the peacemaker between us, like so many times before. I don't want to hear it, do you understand? Don't defend him to me! That whole family is rotten. Damned Italians. Look what Marius is doing to Rome: Senators murdered in cold blood, and their heads displayed in public like macabre trophies, as though it's something to be proud of!"

"I'm not trying to defend him, Aemi, I'm just trying to be understanding towards my friend. I too feel shame and disgust at what Gaius Marius is doing, don't forget that he is my uncle too. All I am saying is, perhaps Marcus is as much of a victim in this as we are, and we should not judge him by the actions of Gaius Marius."

"Well don't say any more, Caesar. Don't try to understand, and don't try to justify it either. My father died for nothing but the blood lust of a mad man; they all have, and no doubt there will be more. He won't stop until he has murdered every man who ever stood up to him, or turned their backs on him, or voted against him. If I ever see Marcus again it will be too soon, and don't ever think of trying to talk me round because it won't work. I hate him! I hate Gaius Marius! I hate all that family!" Aemi jumped to his feet and kicked out at a rock lying on the ground as he walked to the edge of the rock face and screamed in rage, and frustration, and grief.

"*It isn't fair*," he cried, turning to look back at Caesar, tears streaming down his face. "*Why* did he have to die? *Why* did any of them have to die? I hate you Marius. *I hate you*!" he screamed, as the tears flowed freely down his young face.

Caesar ran to Aemi and clasped him in a tight embrace. "It will be all right, Aemi, I promise; you will be all right," he said, as the tears welled up in his eyes.

Aemi sagged in Caesar's arms and sobbed. "I want… my… father! I don't …want to… grow up. I… don't want the… responsibility…I want things to be…the way…the way they were!"

The two boys hugged each other, united in their mutual grief, and the knowledge that their childhood had been torn from them and now lay in tatters at their feet. They remained like this for several minutes, taking comfort from each other, until Aemi's sobs died away.

"Come on," said Caesar, releasing his hold on Aemi. "We still have each other, don't we? We can get through anything, and don't forget," he added, smiling through his tears, "I have a glittering future ahead of me, and you promised that you would always be my right hand man!"

Aemi wiped his wet face on his sleeve and gave a brave, watery smile."Yes, you're right, Caesar. It's time to leave my childhood behind me and become the man I have been forced to be. What say we throw those rocks over there, just this one last time, after all, now that I am paterfamilias I am going to have to set an example to you young boys. I can't be seen to be indulging in childish games any more, can I?"

"Now, that's the Aemi I know," Caesar laughed.

Aemi picked up one of the small rocks and walked to the edge. "This one is for Marius; may his soul rot in Hades!" he said, hurling his rock down onto the jagged boulders below.

Caesar threw his rock and watched, as it tumbled and turned in the air.

"And this one…this is for Marcus; for betrayal of friendship and for being a Mariian!" Aemi hurled his rock out into the air after the first one.

"And who is your rock for, Caesar?" said a voice behind them.

Aemi and Caesar spun round to see Marcus standing a few feet away, still wearing the vomit stained cadets uniform.

"*You*!" Aemi shouted and lunged towards Marcus in rage.

Caesar reacted instantly, springing forward and grabbing Aemi's arm. "No, Aemi, don't!" he cried, hanging on tightly.

"Leave me alone, Caesar, this is between me and him!" yelled Aemi, twisting and turning to break the grip on his arm.

"*No! No!*" shouted Caesar, tightening his grip to prevent Aemi getting any closer to Marcus. "What are you doing here, Marcus? Go… you can see how upset he is!" he shouted.

Marcus looked pale but he stood his ground. "I came to say that I was sorry…about what happened. I had no idea, until I heard father talking to one of the guards at the temple."

Aemi stopped struggling. "Father?" he gasped. "Father? You don't mean…?"

"Gaius Marius has adopted me as his son," said Marcus.

"Then you are even more of a traitor! *Son of a murderer*!" Aemi struggled against Caesar's hold.

"*Go, Marcus, please*!" shouted Caesar, whose arms were hurting from holding on to Aemi so tightly.

"*Scum*! *Son of scum*!" Aemi screamed. "I should kill you for what your father has done; see how he likes it, to have someone you cared about murdered in cold blood!" He lunged forward and spat at Marcus, covering the side of his face in phlegm.

Marcus took a step back, his face flushed red with anger and shame, and he wiped the spittle from his face with the side of his hand. "I know you are upset, Aemi but you can't blame me for what Gaius Marius has done! Look, we can still be friends, can't we? It doesn't have to change things between us, not unless you let it."

"Friends? *Friends*? I wouldn't be your friend if you were the last man left in the world! You are no friend of mine, Marcus Marius. You and your stinking family can go and rot for all I care. I hope Catalus Caesar finds you, and soon, and I hope that he cuts you up into tiny pieces and scatters your body on the Campus for all the birds to eat!"

"Marcus, go… I can't hold him much longer," Caesar pleaded, digging his heels into the dirt to hold Aemi back.

"Let him go, Caesar, he can't hurt me. Fighting me won't bring your father back, Aemi," said Marcus scornfully.

"No, but it will make me feel better!" shouted Aemi, and with a huge effort, he broke free from Caesar and lunged forward at Marcus.

Marcus sidestepped neatly and Aemi over balanced and sprawled onto the floor.

"Aemi, don't do this!" shouted Caesar, running towards him, but Aemi jumped to his feet and lunged at Marcus, who moved out of the way again.

"Aemi, stop. You know that I'm the better fighter!" shouted Marcus, but Aemi flew at Marcus, managing to catch his legs and pulled him down onto the floor.

"*Stop it! Stop it, both of you!*" bellowed Caesar, but the boys were flailing around on the floor with fists flying. He could see that whilst Aemi was fighting hard, Marcus was not fighting back the way Caesar knew that he could. As Aemi began to tire, Marcus gave one huge shove and pushed him away, scrambling to his feet.

"You win, you win!" Marcus gasped; holding one hand up in surrender as he backed away and wiped blood from his cut lip with his other hand.

"What's the matter, Marius, lost your stomach for fighting, or have you realised who the better man is, after all this time?" gasped Aemi, rising slowly to his feet and wiping his bleeding nose on the sleeve of his tunic.

Marcus flushed but he made no move to retaliate. "I told you, I concede. You won the day, Aemi," he said taking another step backwards.

"Good, now go! Come near me, or my family again, and I swear, I will kill you, Marius, do you hear me?"

"I hear you, Aemi and don't worry, I won't trouble you again," said Marcus, sucking his lip to contain the blood. "Caesar," he said, nodding curtly at his cousin. Marcus turned on his heel and walked away.

Aemi stood and watched until Marcus had walked out of view. "Did you see that, Caesar? I beat him, I beat Marcus Marius!" he said exultantly. "I showed him, I really showed him."

"Yes, Aemi, you won," Caesar answered sadly. "Did that make you feel better?"

"Oh yes, Caesar. I did it for my father, and for my family's honour. I can't touch Marius, but I certainly made his son pay!"

"Then I'm pleased for you," said Caesar, and, though he knew the truth of the situation, he was genuinely pleased that Aemi had gained some small sense of justice over his father's death. Caesar knew that Marcus had let Aemi win. It was his way of showing how sorry he was for what had happened. It was an act of friendship, but Aemi would never know.

"I'm ready to go home now, Caesar," said Aemi. The laughter and triumph had died in his eyes to be replaced by a hard determination and newfound courage.

Caesar looked at his friend and smiled. "Yes, Aemi, I do believe you are."

*Marcus Aurelius Cotta, hail, from your friend, who remains trapped in this beleaguered city that is Rome.*

*News of the suicide of Quintus Lutatius Catalus Caesar, and Merula, the Flamen Dialis, has sent shock waves through the already depleted Senate, and has been compounded further when several other senators, and wealthy knights followed suit, to avoid the public humiliation of a trial. Everyone knows the accusations are false, but Marius has paid the juries to condemn these men regardless. Those who have stood trial have all ended up on the Tarpeian Rock, their bound bodies are thrown down, to smash on to the jagged rocks below.*

*Those that can, have fled Rome, seeking protection from Sulla. I believe Catalus Caesar sent his son away, to this end, before he committed suicide. He, like many others, have preferred to end their lives, on their own terms, rather than subject themselves to Marius's revenge, and are to be applauded for their courage.*

*Relations between Cinna and Marius are fraught since Marius refused to disband his slave army, but, fortunately for both, the consular elections have kept them busy. Needless to say no other senator dared to place their names on the candidate list, and the vote placed Cinna as the Senior Consul and Marius as Junior Consul.*

*So, it would seem, dear Marcus, that the prophecy has been fulfilled after all. Gaius Marius is Consul for a seventh term, his place in history is assured, but my heart quailed when I heard the news. And so we wait, those of us that are left, and wonder what the gods have ordained for us. I send to you the love of your family, and our prayers that the gods protect you, for you are a good man, Marcus, and you are sorely missed.*

*Gaius Julius Caesar.*

# CHAPTER THIRTEEN

*"I have lived long enough both in years and in accomplishments."*
*(Gaius Julius Caesar)*

## ROME 86 BC

*Senior Consul: Lucius Cornelius Cinna (2)*
*Junior Consul: Gaius Marius (7)*

Caesar stared at the broad, muscular back of Gaius Marius, as he poured wine into three silver goblets, and wondered what this meeting was all about. Marius had sent a summons to Gaius Julius earlier in the day and ordered that he bring his son with him. Under strict orders from his father to say and do nothing that would anger or upset Marius, Caesar sat in his uncle's study, full of apprehension, and waited.

"Here we are," said Marius, placing the goblets down on the desk in front of Gaius Julius and Caesar, before resuming his seat opposite them. "Your good health, brother-in-law," Marius said, raising his goblet in a toast before taking a sip of wine.

Gaius Julius picked up his goblet and drank but Caesar did not touch his. He noticed that his father's hand shook slightly as he held the goblet, the only physical sign that he was uneasy about this meeting.

"Congratulations on your election to the consulship, Marius," said Gaius Julius. "I've not had a chance to speak to you, since you took office."

"Thank you, Gaius Julius," said Marius, smiling smugly. "Though it was a mere formality, as not one senator put his name forward in the elections, so, I suppose you could say the result was inevitable."

Gaius Julius nodded and took another sip of wine.

"Of course," Marius continued. "The prophecy said that I would be Consul seven times, and, as I had already served for six terms in office, I had no reason to doubt that there would not be a seventh."

"Prophecy?" said Gaius Julius lightly. Caesar knew that he was pretending to be unaware of its existence, but by the look on his uncle's face, he knew Gaius Marius was not fooled.

"Oh, come on now, Gaius, surely you have heard the tale; the prophecy made to me when I was a young boy? Everyone in Italy knows of it."

"Well, yes, now that you come to mention it, I do recall hearing something," said Gaius Julius quickly. "But the world is full of prophecies, and, how many of them actually come true, after all?"

"Well this one did," said Gaius Marius. "I often wonder if we are all victims of our own fate, or, can a man have the power to change his destiny, even if it has been prophesised. What do you think?" he said, looking directly at Caesar.

Caesar saw the look on his uncle's face and dropped his gaze back to the floor.

"I…I do not know, Uncle," he muttered.

"Come, come, Gaius, no need to be shy! You always used to talk about your dreams and ambitions; what was it you said to me? Ah, yes, that one day you would be the greatest Roman that had ever lived, isn't that right?" said Marius.

Caesar could feel his eyes boring in to the top of his head.

Gaius Julius coughed nervously and glanced at his son, but Caesar continued to stare fixedly at the floor, refusing to look at Gaius Marius.

"I was young, and foolish. It was the dreams of a boy, that was all, Uncle," he said through gritted teeth. He felt anger and hatred against this man rise inside him but he knew that if he looked at Gaius Marius those feeling would be transparent.

"So, what do you wish for your future now, boy?"

"Only, that I would like to follow in my father's footsteps and join the legions. I would like to see the world before I join the Senate and begin my political career," Caesar replied cautiously, as his father's words of warning echoed in his ear.

"Very admirable sentiments," Marius nodded, sitting back into his chair and taking another sip from his goblet. "Sometimes, however, you can't always have what you want. Sometimes, fate steps in and changes the direction of our lives, whether we want it to or not, isn't that so, Gaius Julius?"

"Indeed it is."

"You see," Marius continued, "I believe that a man's destiny is mapped for him from birth. Some men, like myself for instance, are marked out as…special; the ordinary is not for us. I also believe that it can be in a man's power to change that destiny, if he wants to badly enough. If he knows what his destiny holds then he can, if he so chooses, change it to suit his own ends."

"But surely no man can stand against what the gods have already decided? If it has been written, then so shall it be," said Gaius Julius.

Marius looked at Gaius Julius but Caesar saw a hint of annoyance cross his face.

"Yes, for the…ordinary man, that may be."

Marius sat up abruptly and placed his goblet on the table. "Now, to business," he said bluntly. "The reason that I have asked you here today is that I have decided, with Cinna's approval, to do something honourable for your family."

Caesar glanced quickly at his father, and saw that he had visibly paled. He felt his own anxiety rise in response.

"Gaius Marius, you are most considerate, but…"

"No, no, Gaius Julius," said Marius, holding up his hand for silence. "These have been trying times for Rome, and for me personally. I would like to reward those who have been loyal to me in the same way that I have punished those who betrayed me."

Caesar saw his father swallow nervously. Just what was Marius planning?

"As you are aware, there has arisen a vacancy in the priesthood, after the Flamen Dialis, Merula, saw fit to take his own life; completely against the priestly code, but, well, there we are, it's done now. The position can only be filled by a Patrician of the highest and most impeccable family lines, and, unfortunately for Rome, men fitting that criteria are in short supply at the moment."

Only because you murdered them all, Caesar thought to himself.

"The college of priests were unable to come up with a replacement that was suitable, and so the Pontifex Maximus approached Cinna and myself for suggestions. Fortunately for Rome, I was able to step in and resolve the problem to everyone's satisfaction," said Marius, smiling as he spoke, but Caesar could see that there was no humour in his eyes.

"I am pleased that the Consuls have been able to fill the vacancy so quickly. It is vital that Rome has all her priests in place, and the People's welfare assured," said Gaius Julius. "But, what does this have to do with me, if you don't mind me asking?" he added.

The smile broadened on Marius's face, and he looked slyly at Caesar before sitting back in his chair. The tension in the room was palpable as Caesar and his father waited, with baited breath, for Gaius Marius to reply. Caesar stayed absolutely still, fixing his gaze on the goblet in front of him.

"Well, Gaius Julius, it has not so much to do with you, as your son," said Marius, fixing his eyes onto Caesar. "He has been chosen to fill the vacancy; he is to be the new Flamen Dialis. Congratulations, boy."

Gaius Julius choked on his wine. "My son... Flamen Dialis? But surely there is some mistake? Gaius is only fourteen years old, he is still a child...I mean, please don't think that I am not deeply...deeply appreciative, that you have thought of honouring him in this way, but..."

"No buts, Gaius Julius, and please, there is no need to thank me," said Gaius Marius. I have always taken an interest in your son. I could see that he was a boy of potential and I have always had it in mind to...to help him, any way that I could."

"By making me a priest?" Caesar cried out angrily.

Gaius Julius placed a firm hand on Caesar's arm and squeezed it tightly.

Gaius Marius's smile vanished and he froze, staring menacingly at the boy, their eyes looking directly at each other for the first time.

"It is an honour, boy! You can focus all your ambition into worshipping the king of gods, instead of filling your head with nonsense that you would be king of the Romans!" he spat angrily, his face turning a deep shade of purple.

"But I don't want to be a priest!" cried Caesar, refusing to back down or lower his gaze from his uncle's face.

"Gaius, enough!" barked Gaius Julius. "Your uncle is right, it is an honour, for you, for our family, but surely, Gaius Marius, there must be many men who would fill the position far better than my son," he pleaded.

"I have already told you, Gaius Julius, that there are no suitable candidates. Now, there will be no further discussion as it has already been decided and approved. The boy will assume the title of Flamen Dialis in a ceremony that will be held tomorrow in the Temple of Jupiter, but he will not take office until he comes of age. On that day, he will not assume the Toga Virilis, but instead, he will be initiated into the priesthood as the Flamen, and assume all the duties that are expected of him. Everything has been taken care of; all you have to do is bring the boy to the temple on the fourth hour tomorrow. You may, if you wish, remain to watch the ceremony, it is not a private affair, unlike the full initiation ceremony; after all, it's not everyday that your son is made a high priest of Rome, is it?"

Gaius Julius shook his head, unable to speak.

"Now, a toast I think," said Marius, picking up his goblet, his entire demeanour changing back to one of affability and calmness, "To the new Flamen Dialis, Gaius Julius Caesar. May you live a very, very long, and fulfilled life, in the service of the gods," he said. A malicious smile played at the edges of his mouth, and then he downed the rest of his wine in one gulp.

"To Gaius," said Gaius Julius, raising his goblet to salute his son. He also downed his wine in one.

Caesar sat motionless, his eyes fixed on the face of Gaius Marius. His whole being screamed in defiance and anger and hatred towards this man but he knew that he was beaten. Nothing he could do or say could change what Marius had done to him. He was trapped; his dreams, his ambitions, his life, was over before it had even had a chance to begin, because of this ma and his determination to prevent anyone from challenging his place in history. All he could see was the face of his uncle leering at him, victory blazing in his eyes as he watched his enemy fall, crushed before him.

Caesar's head began to hurt and his vision blurred. The last thing he saw before he passed out was the triumphant face of Gaius Marius.

Caesar woke with a start. As his eyes began to focus he saw his mother and father standing over him. For a second he was unsure of what had happened and then, as his mind grew clearer, the awful truth came flooding back to him.

"No!" he shouted, and he struggled to sit up.

"Gaius, Gaius stop!" Aurelia urged, taking hold of his shoulders and holding him firmly. "You must rest, Gaius. You must rest or you will have another seizure!"

"No, No, No!" he screamed, struggling against his mother's grip. "He is making me a priest, Mother! *He is making me a priest!*"

"I know, my darling, I know."

"I don't want to be the Flamen. I can't be the Flamen, Mother, please Mother, please don't let him make me a priest!" Caesar cried desperately. He dissolved into uncontrollable tears and collapsed in his mother's arms.

Aurelia held her son tightly as his sobs wracked his young body. She glanced once at her husband, who remained standing silently behind her, before she turned to soothe her son, stroking his hair and uttering comforting sounds. Slowly, his sobs subsided and he grew calmer.

"It will be all right, Gaius, shhh now," she said, pulling back a little to look at his tear stained face.

Caesar looked up into his mother's eyes. "How can it be all right, Mother, *how*? He is making me a priest…and not just any priest, but the *Flamen Dialis*. They…they can't do anything, can they? I will not be able to eat what I want… I will have to wear those awful robes…I will never ride my horse again! He…I…Oh, Mother, look what he has done to me!" his very soul wailed in despair.

"I know, I know how you must be feeling, Gaius, but truly, it is not so bad. The Flamen is High Priest of Rome. It is an honour to be chosen. Your life will be spent looking after the welfare of Rome…"

"No, no, you don't know how I feel, Mother!" he cried, pulling back from her arms. "It is no honour for me! He has done this to spite me, to stop me fulfilling my destiny. He has done this to…to stop me from becoming greater than even he could imagine."

Aurelia could not argue because she understood what had happened. Gaius Marius had removed her son from life as effectively as if he had killed him. Tears welled up in her eyes as she looked at Caesar, helpless to save him.

"And you let him do this to me, Father!" Caesar exclaimed, turning to look accusingly at Gaius Julius, the hurt and anger written all over his face. "You sat there and you did *nothing*. You led me to his house like an animal to be sacrificed and *you did nothing*. You say it is for the honour of our family, but, in truth, it was to save your own skin!"

"Gaius, I…"

"No, nothing you can say will change what you have done to me, Father, nothing!" shouted Caesar angrily. "You promised you would protect me. You swore you would never let Gaius Marius do anything to hurt me. *You swore it!*" Tears of frustration rolled down his already sodden cheeks and his breath sobbed with uncontrolled emotion. "Do what you like to me now. Punish me for showing you disrespect, I…I don't care anymore. Nothing…*nothing* you can do to me can make me feel any worse than I already do. Kill me for all I care. You would be doing me an honour, for my life is over; I have nothing worth living for. You let Gaius Marius take my life away, Father, and I will never forgive you. I would rather be *dead*!" Caesar threw himself face down on the bed and howled in utter devastation.

Gaius Julius stood ashen faced at this tirade. The depth of Caesar's despair hit him with a force so strong that he looked physically sick.

Aurelia placed a blanket over her sobbing son, and turned her back to her husband. Gaius Julius was not wanted in this room and he understood why. He left his wife and son together, united in their distress.

Caesar sat in perfect stillness as the Haruspice Priest examined the fresh entrails of the sacrificed bull. He swirled the bloodied steaming mass of innards around in the large copper bowl, staring intently, searching for the signs and omens that only a trained Haruspice could read.

Caesar glanced up towards the grand marble dais, which towered above the temple floor, at the three men who sat upon their chairs, watching the proceedings intently. Seated on a red marble throne on the top platform of the dais was the chief priest, the Pontifex Maximus, who was head of the College of Pontiffs, the main priestly college of Rome. Two steps below on the lower platform the two Consuls sat on their gold and purple chairs. From what Caesar could tell, Cinna appeared to be relaxed, one leg crossed comfortably over the other with his hands placed in his lap, contrasting sharply with Gaius Marius, who was a picture of tension and apprehension. He was leaning so far forward off his chair that Caesar thought him in great danger of toppling off it, so intently was he watching the Haruspice at work.

Caesar turned his head to look left, where among the many Pontiffs and Flamens, the priests of Rome, sat his parents. His father sat pale and stony faced, grimly staring out across the temple as though he were looking beyond the walls to the world outside. Aurelia sat erect and immobile, her beautiful dark brooding eyes fixed firmly towards the dais where she appeared to be watching Gaius Marius. Caesar turned back to look at the Haruspice who had just completed his examination of animal innards and was now passing the bowl to his assistant.

"Well, Marcus, what do you see?" the deep commanding voice of the Pontifex Maximus echoed from the dais.

The priest bowed. "I see no bad omens. The gods are pleased," he answered formally. Then he bowed again to the men on the dais and made his way across the temple to take his seat amongst the College of Augers and Vestal Virgins.

"Lucius Crattipas, did your vigil pass well?" the Pontifex called.

Lucius Crattipas, an Auger, rose from his chair and walked out into the centre of the temple floor. "I spent the night in vigil from sunset to sunrise. No lightning tore across the sky, and no rumble of thunder reached my ears. At dawn a flock of geese flew east towards the rising sun. The auspices are clear; the gods accept this boy as the Flamen Dialis." Crattipas bowed at the dais and then turned and bowed towards Caesar, before returning to his chair.

The Pontifex Maximus nodded and rose to his feet. "Marcus Appaulius. As head of the sixteen pontifices, do you all agree that the signs are favourable and that this child, the Patrician, Gaius Julius Caesar, who sits before you now, fulfils all the criteria necessary to be accepted as the new Flamen Dialis?"

Marcus Appaulius rose to his feet. He hesitated, glancing nervously towards Marius, and then back to the Pontifex Maximus. "We make no objection."

"Gnaus Mentulla. As the Rex Sacorum, what say you?"

Gnaus Mentulla rose to his feet. "I make no objection."

"Octavius Sulpicca. As the current senior priest of the Flamens, what say you all?"

Octavius Sulpicca rose to his feet. "The Flamens make no objection."

"Canuleia. As Chief Vestal, what say you all?"

Canuleia rose graciously to her feet, her body shrouded in the pure white robes of the Vestal Virgins, her face covered with a light silken veil. A soft honeyed voice drifted through the temple. "The Vestals make no objection."

Caesar noticed Gaius Marius visibly relax as the last vote of acceptance was given and a smile of satisfaction spread across his face. The waiting was over; nothing could go wrong now.

The Pontifex Maximus walked to the edge of the dais. "Consuls of Rome, you have witnessed the testimonies of the priests. The omens are favourable. The auspices show that the gods are satisfied. The colleges raise no objection. As heads of the Senate and People of Rome, what say you?"

Cinna rose first as Senior Consul. "I make no objection," he said, and sat down again.

Gaius Marius stood and looked directly at Caesar. "I make no objection…none whatsoever," his voice boomed loudly so that everyone in the temple could hear.

Caesar looked directly at his uncle as he spoke and their eyes locked together. The hatred seemed to radiate from Marius's eyes as he fixed the boy with a look of sheer triumph. Defiance was written all over Caesar's face and he refused to be the one to look away first. He would never let his uncle see that he was defeated. Marius was the first to break the gaze and he sat heavily back in his chair.

"Stand, Gaius Julius Caesar," the Pontifex commanded, and Caesar rose slowly to his feet. He stood tall and straight, every inch noble born, his face a calm mask.

"As you have not yet come of age you will be Flamen Dialis in name only. You will be required to attend the college regularly, where you will undertake instruction in your duties for when you are ready to be initiated into office. On the day of your coming of age, you will attend the Temple of Jupiter, where you will undergo your official inauguration, and you will assume the full duties and life of the Flamen Dialis. Do you understand?"

*What choice do I have?* "I understand."

"Do you accept the position and responsibilities bestowed upon you as the Flamen Dialis?"

Caesar looked directly at Gaius Marius and paused. *I will never forgive you for this.* He waited long enough to make his uncle stiffen with anticipation and then he nodded. "I accept."

"Do you agree to submit your life to the worship of the God, Jupiter, and guard the spiritual welfare of Rome and Her People, until your life ends?"

*My life has ended.* "I do."

"Then by the powers invested in me as Pontifex Maximus, High priest of Rome, I declare Gaius Julius Caesar duly elected and accepted as the new Flamen Dialis from this day forward."

*That's it then, it's over. Condemned to the life of a priest forever. I wish I was dead.*

Everyone in the temple rose to their feet and looked directly at the young boy standing alone in the centre of the temple.

"All hail the Flamen Dialis! Hail Flamen Dialis, Hail!" the people chanted in unison.

The Pontifex Maximus walked slowly down the steps, bowing to Cinna and Marius as he passed. He walked slowly across the floor and stopped in front of

Caesar, bowing formally. Caesar bowed in acceptance, and the Pontifex Maximus moved on through the temple and out the main door.

Cinna and Marius were next to leave, each bowing in turn to Caesar before following the Pontifex Maximus from the building. Then the Colleges, and finally the Vestal Virgins followed, all bowing respectfully to the new Flamen Dialis.

As the last Vestal passed, Caesar was joined by his mother and father, who also bowed respectfully to their son's new office of authority.

"Mother, Father, please!" Caesar whispered, blushing deeply.

"You must get used to it, Gaius, now that you are the Flamen Dialis," said Aurelia, with a smile of pride on her face.

"Yes, but you are my parents, and it feels wrong," he said in embarrassment.

"Not any more it mustn't, for you are higher in rank than us, as High Priest, and the deference must be ours," said Gaius Julius. "At least, when you are not in my house," he added with a smile.

Caesar smiled back. He had thought about what had happened all morning, and the initial anger that he had felt towards his father had vanished. He accepted that his father was as much of a victim as he was himself.

"Come, I have ordered a special meal to be cooked for you tonight," said Aurelia. "You may invite Aemi if you like," she added, as they walked towards the temple doors.

"Thank you, Mother, I would like that," he answered, and wondered how Aemi was going to take the news that he was now a High Priest of Rome, for Caesar had been unable to see him before the initiation.

The family stepped out into the blinding sunlight of the day and Caesar shielded his eyes from the bright glare. As his eyes slowly focussed a dark ominous shadow fell across his face, blocking the sun, and he squinted upwards, to see Gaius Marius standing before him. He involuntarily stepped back and immediately felt the strong comforting arm of his father across his shoulders.

"Gaius Marius," said Gaius Julius in a formal tone of politeness.

"Gaius Julius, Aurelia," nodded Marius cordially. "And of course, the new Flamen Dialis," he said, as a smile spread across his craggy, lined face.

Caesar did not return the greeting but stood firmly next to his father.

"I just wanted to say how impressed I was with your son today, Gaius Julius," said Marius. "He conducted himself most admirably…considering."

"He is a Juliian. What else would you expect," retorted Aurelia stiffly.

Gaius Marius raised a single eyebrow and looked at Aurelia with a hard gaze. "I realise that your son's appointment came as a great surprise to you both, but, the honour bestowed on your family must outweigh any…reservations you may have. The boy is eminently suited to the post; his breeding and acknowledged skill in oration will help to make him a fine example of a Flamen, and, I am sure, ease the burden of his duties. It will not take you too long to memorise all the prayers and rituals you will have to perform, after all you will be doing it everyday, and…" he said, looking directly at Caesar. "…you will have the rest of your life to perfect them."

"I am sure that my son will perform his duties as the Flamen Dialis with honour and dignity," said Gaius Julius, patting Caesar reassuringly on the shoulder. "He understands only too well the concept of duty. He will not disappoint Rome."

"Oh, I am sure he won't," Marius replied, smiling broadly. "Well, I must be off, important matters to see to. I just wanted to wish the young Flamen well; after all, he is my nephew. What kind of uncle would I be if I did not do all in my power to ensure his advancement? Yes, as soon as the subject of a replacement came to my attention I knew instantly that young Gaius was the man for the job. You must be pleased, Aurelia, for it means you will always have your son here in Rome with you. No trudging off with the legions for years on end for him! No, he will remain safely here in Rome, seeing to the religious well being of our city. A comforting thought, don't you think, Aurelia?"

"Indeed," she replied coldly.

Gaius Marius chose to ignore the obvious tone of disapproval in her voice and turned to Gaius Julius.

"Gaius Julius, come and see me in a couple of days, will you? I have a proposition that I think you might like to hear."

"Yes of course, Gaius Marius; I will contact your steward for a convenient time."

"Good, good. Oh, and while I think of it, you must all come to dinner soon. I know Julia would love to see you, Aurelia, and you too, boy. Always had a soft spot for you," he said, looking shrewdly at Caesar. "I will make sure Julia has all your favourite foods, after all, once you are Flamen, your diet will be very limited I understand. Goodness, when the Pontifex Maximus explained all the constrictions surrounding the Flamen Dialis I felt quite dizzy. Yes, a very restricted life; very restricted indeed!" And smiling brightly, Marius bid them farewell and set off down the steps of the temple with a whistle and a spring in his step.

The oil lamps in the study flickered, their flames dancing as if they joined in the celebration as Gaius Marius picked up two goblets and passed one to Cinna and the other to his son. Taking up his own, he raised it high, a look of sheer jubilation on his face. "To victory." he said.

"Victory!" repeated Cinna and Young Marius, and all three men drank deeply.

"Ah, Cinna, what a day, what a day," said Marius, wiping his hand across his mouth. "I can't remember the last time I felt this good. I feel so…alive!" he said, his eyes twinkling with unusual brightness. He leant against his large wooden desk and sighed with sheer satisfaction.

"I am pleased for you, Marius," smiled Cinna. "I knew that if we just waited a little longer then the Senate would come round to our way of thinking in the end. It is indeed a successful day."

"I have to hand it to you, Cinna," said Marius, pouring himself some more wine. "You did it in the end and I'm grateful for your support."

"Think nothing of it, Marius, after all, you came to my aid when I needed it, and I promised you then, that the moment I could legally pass the command to you then

I would do so," said Cinna with a smug look of satisfaction, for today he had persuaded the Senate to pass a vote declaring Gaius Marius the new General of the eastern legions, and recalling Sulla to Rome.

"When do we leave, Father?" said Young Marius, who was excited at the prospect of going off to do battle with the enemy at last,

"As soon as possible. We have Strabo's old legions to prepare first. Quintus Metellus can keep his legions in Italy to stop the damn Samnites from rising up against us once our back is turned. A month from now should see us safely on our way, I should think, and we should be in Macedonia by the summer. We can consolidate our position there, spruce up the legions and push east. Old Mithridates will realise Sulla was a pussycat compared to me, by the time I've finished with him!" Marius said, rubbing his hands together in anticipation.

"Valerius Flaccus has asked to be considered as a senior legate, Marius. I wonder if you could find a place for him on your staff; shouldn't be a problem, should it?" Cinna asked casually.

Gaius Marius paused and looked at Cinna. "You wouldn't be trying to interfere in my right to choose my own staff, would you, Cinna?" he said softly.

Cinna was taken aback at this sudden change in Marius. "Goodness me, no, Marius. I merely suggested…"

"Don't suggest, Cinna. It's not your job to suggest. I am the commander, and I say who my officers will be; got that?" Marius's eyes flashed dangerously.

"Now listen, Marius, I merely proposed a man who I would consider to be a good asset to you, that's all!" spluttered Cinna, outraged at the tone Marius was taking with him.

Gaius Marius snorted contemptuously. "Good asset, is that what you call your spies is it? You don't fool me, Cinna. I know your game."

"Flaccus is *not* my spy, and I will thank you not to take this tone with me! Where is all this coming from?" Cinna cried indignantly.

"Father, I don't think Cinna meant anything other than what he says. Flaccus is a good man. I served under him, and you could do a lot worse than take him with you."Gaius Marius turned on his son, his eyes flashing dangerously. "What would you know, boy! There are spies everywhere. I should know; most of them are mine! But if you think I'm going to take command of the legions and have senior officers who are mere puppets of these schemers in Rome, then you have another think coming. They are *my* legions, *my* men, *my* officers, and they will answer to no one but *me,* is that clear?" he said, turning his gaze on Cinna as he paced the room.

"Quite clear! said Cinna, rising angrily to his feet.

"Father, please! There's no need to get angry. You have the command and you will go east this time. No one can stop you; you are Consul. Sulla can't touch you anymore, and when he is forced to return to Rome, he will be put on trial and ultimately exiled for the crimes he committed against Rome when he marched on the city. He is powerless to stop you now, and, we all support you to, isn't that so, Cinna?"

Cinna nodded and scowled at Gaius Marius, who continued to pace the floor, rubbing his hands together as though he was washing them clean of dirt.

Cinna frowned, noting the frightened look Young Marius gave his father. What was wrong with him? Why was he behaving so strangely?

"Father?" Young Marius spoke gently.

Gaius Marius glanced at his son but he did not appear to see him clearly. Cinna could see that his eyes looked glazed and troubled.

"So little time and so many enemies," he muttered, turning and walking the other way. "They are my legions, *Mine* I tell you! Not Sulla's, no never Sulla's. He stole them from me. Took my men, fighting *my war*!" he hissed between gritted teeth. "I gave him everything and he betrayed me. I treated him like a son and what did he do to me? Lies… betrayal… plotting and scheming behind my back to bring me down. *Me*!" His pacing was getting faster and faster, his hands now moving together furiously.

"Father, please try and calm yourself!" Young Marius begged, realising that something was desperately wrong.

"I had him…so close…and he got away. I should have killed him myself! I trusted others to do the job and they failed me. They betrayed me too. They let Sulla escape. He should never have escaped. He should be dead. *Dead*!" Marius spat the words in pure hatred, flecks of phlegm gathered at the edges of his mouth now and his eyes rolled in their sockets.

Cinna took a step backwards. The sight of Marius was disturbing and frightening.

"I should have stopped him when I had the chance…"

*"Does your Father often have these…rages?"* Cinna whispered to Young Marius.

"…I realise that now. I made a mistake…"

*"Yes…No! There is something wrong…I don't know!"* said Young Marius in a panic.

"…I got the boy though, oh yes, I got the boy…"

*"Can't you do something to stop him?"*

"…I made sure he can never usurp me now…"

*"Like what? I don't know what to do!"*

"…I challenged the gods and I won, I won! Ha, ha, ha, ha." Marius laughed hysterically.

*"Call someone, anyone. Just get him to stop this… this madness!"*

"…No man, *no man* will ever be greater than me. I will be known as the greatest Roman that ever lived…"

*"I can't…what would I say, that he has gone mad? The Consul is mad? I can't do that to him. He will calm down in a minute, I'm sure he will."*

"…The most successful General in history. First Man in Rome; Third Founder…"

*"Well he is mad; what else would you call it? By all the gods, boy, we have to do something!"*

"…I shall be known for all eternity as the Father of Rome!"

"*He will calm down!* Father, Father!"

"...Seven times Consul, seven times, just like the Sybil said. No man has achieved that. No man will ever achieve that again!" said Marius, turning to his son, his face almost purple and his breath coming in short gasps.

"Fetch Mother, please!" Young Marius cried out to Cinna as he tried to steady his father. "And call a doctor, quickly."

Cinna hurried from the study, calling out for Julia as he ran along the corridor.

Gaius Marius was gasping for breath now and his eyes were rolling. Foam covered his lips and sprayed his son with spittle as he continued to try and talk. "I...I...did...it," he gasped, trying to laugh as he clung on to his son's arms. "I...defied the...gods...Sulla defeated...that...boy...out of ... the... way ... A...priest...ha, ha, ha...you should have...seen his...face. Ha, ha, ha. He knew ...he knew I had won...ha, ha, ha."

And the great Gaius Marius collapsed into the arms of his son.

"Father! Father!" Young Marius cried out, as he gently lowered his Gaius Marius to the floor. "Father!" he screamed, as the tears rolled down his face. "Father, speak to me! Please speak to me...Oh by all the gods, *help me someone*...Father, don't leave me! Father, don't go, *Please*!" he wailed in desperation.

But Gaius Marius did not answer. He lay motionless on the floor of his study, his body now still, his voice silent. The man hailed as First Man in Rome and Third Founder of Rome; General, Consul, Husband and Father was dead.

Caesar could not remember the last time he had felt so sad. His father was leaving Rome. Every time the thought entered his mind, a lump came into his throat, and the tears would sting the back of his eyes. He had his bath alone, sending the slaves away once he slipped into the warm comforting water. He remember back to the times he would feel anxiety, even jealousy, when his father had come home, on those short and rare visits, when he was younger. He was always pleased when it was time for his father to leave again, preferring the life with his mother in their cosy insula in the Subura, without a man about to keep a strict eye on him. And then, on one of his visits home, everything had changed. He was ready to know what having a father really meant, and Gaius Julius was ready to be a father to his son. Caesar knew that they had discovered a likeness in each other that had drawn then closer together, and he had begun to recognise parts of himself that belonged to his father. Caesar thought of the year just passed, a year of fear and anxiety for his parents, and anticipation of what could happen to himself. What would he have done without his father there to support him? For all that he was just as helpless against Gaius Marius as the next man in Rome, his father had never wavered in his love and support and protection of his family. Through it all, his father had held his head up high, taken each fresh blow on the chin, and turned these seemingly calamitous events into bearable, acceptable situations for his son, by his love, his patience, and, his conviction that he would protect his family from harm. Caesar recognised that his father had steered his family ship through troubled waters, and now he was about to leave them alone once more. For how long, Caesar had no idea, but now, even the shortest time apart from his father would feel like an eternity.

Shivering from lying in the cold water, Caesar dressed in a clean tunic ready for dinner and made his way out into the main garden at the rear of the house, intending to be alone with his thoughts until he was called.

As he walked along the tree lined path he heard the sound of a child giggling, and he stepped through the dense olive trees to see his father, sitting on the edge of the large marble fountain, playfully splashing water at Julia, who was perched precariously on his knee. Caesar watched as they played together, unaware that they were being watched, Julia laughing uncontrollably, stretching her podgy little arms out before her to prevent the droplets of water from wetting her further. Gaius Julius laughed teasingly and then hugged Julia too him; Caesar saw the look of happiness change on his face to one of sad contemplation, as his little girl snuggled comfortably into her father's safe, warm chest.

Caesar moved backwards so as not to be seen, but the sudden movement in the stillness around them caused Gaius Julius to catch sight of his son.

"Gaius, don't go," he called, and Caesar moved out into the open and walked across to join them at the fountain.

Julia let out a squeal of delight on seeing her big brother and stretched out her arms to him, but Caesar declined to take her from his father, instead tickling her gently under the chin before sitting down on the edge of the fountain next to them.

"You know I am leaving?"

"Yes, Father. Do you really have to go so soon?" Caesar asked, as Julia clutched playfully at his little finger.

"I'm afraid so. Flaccus has been given command of Cinna's legions, and he is setting off for Macedonia to initially take over the command from Lucius Cornelius Sulla. Flaccus needs fresh men to bolster his legions and I have been tasked with the job of recruiting and training these men, before they are sent to join him in the east."

"But why has Sulla been replaced, Father? Surely, once Gaius Marius died there was no longer any need to remove the command from Sulla?"

Gaius Julius shook his head. "Gaius Marius managed to do a great many things in the thirteen days that he was the Consul before his death, and one of those was to withdraw the command from Sulla, and have him declared an enemy of Rome, and an exile. The order was passed mainly because those left alive in the Senate were too scared to oppose him, and, I'm afraid the order stands."

"But why can't Cinna repeal this rule and make peace with Sulla?"

"It's too late for peace between them. Cinna supported Marius, and he allowed the murder of innocent men to go unopposed, many of who were friends of Sulla. He allowed Sulla's house and belongings to be destroyed, and his wife and children had to flee for their lives. Sulla will never forgive these crimes against Rome, and against him personally, and holds Cinna responsible, as much as Marius ever was. The Consuls and the Senate are afraid that Sulla will return to Rome at the head of his legions and seek vengeance for the murders, against those he holds responsible, and that's why there's such a rush to begin the recruiting, for it may be that there will be a second civil war to fight, once King Mithridates has been defeated."

Julia reached for her brother's copper torc bracelet and pulled playfully. Caesar absently removed the bracelet from his wrist and handed it to her.

"Father, may I ask you something?"

"Of course," Gaius Julius replied, hitching Julia over onto his other knee.

"If there is to be another civil war, whose side will you take?"

Caesar watched as his father pondered on the question, and his sister gummed the torc bracelet, as she would do a teething ring.

"I would choose the side that represents the true interests of Rome, in my opinion," his father replied thoughtfully. "I would support whoever will put an end to this continuous blood bath once and for all. We have done nothing but fight continuously for the past ten years and it's draining the Republic of her men. If we continue like this for much longer, Rome will be destroyed, and the Republic will fall."

"And who offers the best chance of saving Her, Father?"

Gaius Julius paused to think for a moment. "In my opinion, it would have to be Cinna. He's not a bad man, though his weakness is his biggest downfall. He has been a victim of misfortune in many ways, and his biggest mistake, by far, was to get himself so heavily involved with Marius. There was no possibility that Cinna would ever be able to control that man, and I think even he recognised it at the end. But Cinna truly does want an end to all this fighting; that I believe with all my heart, and he believes in the Republic, and the traditions and values that have made Rome as great as She is today."

Caesar nodded as his father spoke. "So you believe Cinna wants peace and the Republic restored the way it used to be, with the Senate in control, as opposed to the individual?"

"Yes, on balance I believe he does, and that is how it should be. No one man must ever be allowed to control Rome again; it would be Her downfall, of that I am certain."

"And Sulla, what about him?"

"Ah, now Sulla was driven by his enmity towards Marius, and his desire to forge his own political and military career away from the taint of any friendship with him. Sulla is a hard man, but he lacks the ruthless drive and ambition that Gaius Marius always had. He sees the laws of Rome as things to be ignored, when it suits him, though he claims to be one of the Optimate party in the Senate, who argue for tradition and the Mos Maiorum, but, this contradiction does not win him any new friends, for many in the Senate now fear Sulla as they once feared Marius. He is unpredictable and inconsistent, and he is a man who is not afraid to use the legions to his own personal advantage, which goes against everything the Republic stands for. If ever there was a man who desired to be the sole ruler of Rome, it is Sulla, and unfortunately, there is no man strong enough alive today to stand up against him."

"So if Sulla does march on Rome with his legions, will you fight against him, with Cinna and Flaccus?"

"If that happens, and pray to all the gods that it does not, then yes, I would take the side of the lawfully appointed Consuls of Rome against any man who tried to overthrow them. I just pray that it never has to come to that."

"As do I, Father," said Caesar.

He watched as his father played a gentle tug-o-war with Julia and the bracelet, and he wondered how old she would be before she saw him again. Would she remember this time spent with her father, or, would it become a willow-the-wisp ideal that vanished into the memories of childhood?

"I don't know what I shall do without you, Father," Caesar said sadly, lowering his head to hide the tears that sprang readily to his eyes.

"You will carry on as you always used to, all those years when I was far from home. Your mother is a strong woman, and she will be there for you, every bit as much as I would be, had I been able to stay in Rome, and, you are much older now, so you shall be support for each other, at least, until you have to leave."

A crushing weight settled on Caesar's shoulders at the mention of his fate. "But that's just it, Father. I don't know if I can face the future as the Flamen without you here. I need your support; you make everything seem easy and safe. What will I do without you here to guide me?"

Gaius Julius reached out and grasped his son's arm firmly. "You have the courage to face this, Gaius, and you will not be alone, but, we can't do it for you, my son. This is a journey that only you can follow, and the gods have chosen you to be their voice, here in Rome. Even if I stayed I could not be with you, your daily duties and rituals would keep you busy from dawn to dusk and there would be very little time to spend together. Do not fret, Gaius, I have every faith that you can do this, and do so with honour. When you become the Flamen you will be of age, you will be a man, and you will face what lies ahead with the courage of a man."

Caesar felt slightly ashamed that he had voiced his fear to his father when he should have been showing him how brave he could be, but the dread of facing the future without him there beside him was overwhelming.

"Now, it's time to get this young lady inside for her dinner," said Gaius Julius, lifting Julia into his arms. "Our guests will be arriving shortly and I have to get changed."

They walked in companionable silence back towards the house. Julia, sensing that the mood was sombre, wrapped her podgy little arms around her father's neck and snuggled herself into his chest. As they entered the house they were met by one of Julia's nursery maids who quickly relieved Gaius Julius of his weary bundle and hurried away towards the nursery.

Caesar looked sadly at his father, wishing the evening dinner could have been a private family affair on his last night in Rome. Gaius Julius, seeing the look of sadness on Caesar's face put his arm around his son and drawing him to him, hugged the boy tightly.

"I know how you are feeling, Gaius and I to wish it could be different, but I must go. Be strong, Gaius. Look after your mother and sister for me, and do your duty to Rome." Gaius Julius released his hold and gently tipped Caesar's chin up so that he could see his face. "One day soon you will be the Flamen Dialis of Rome, but never forget who you really are. You are Gaius Julius Caesar, my son."

Caesar smiled weakly and nodded his head. "I will never forget, Father, and I will do my best, always. I will never let you down," he said, his voice cracking with emotion.

Gaius Julius ruffled his son's hair and gave him another quick squeeze. "Oh, Gaius, Gaius, you could never do that."

# CHAPTER FOURTEEN

*"What is the sweetest kind of death?*
*The kind that comes without warning."*
*(Gaius Julius Caesar)*

## ROME 85 BC

*Senior Consul: Lucius Cornelius Cinna (3)*
*Junior Consul: Gnaeus Papirius Carbo*

*The feeling of unease that settled over Rome was not lifted by the election of Cinna, for a second term, and, his close friend, Senator Gnaus Papirius Carbo, as Consuls for the new year. Many Augers reported ill omens on the day of voting, and the People wondered what misfortune would befall them now. Within weeks, their fear was confirmed, when Proconsul, Lucius Valerius Flaccus, who had taken the new legion recruits east to replace Sulla, was murdered by his senior legate, Gaius Flavius Fimbria, a man who harboured secret desires to command the legions himself. His ambition was soon thwarted however, when, after ordering Sulla to relinquish his command and return to Rome, Sulla had refused to take orders from a murderer, and had Fimbria chased from his camp.*

*Relationship between Sulla and the Senate were now at a stalemate, and, unless they could sort out these differences, there would come a time, as the war in the east was resolved, when Sulla would turn his attention back to Rome. With Sulla's previous conduct still fresh in everyone's mind, the city held its breath, and waited.*

Caesar sat on the edge of the Tarpeian Rock and looked out at the city below him. This would be the last time he would ever come to this place, the special place of his childhood, for tomorrow was his birthday. He would officially come of age and throw off his toga of childhood, the official statement to the Roman world that he was now a man. However, there would be no toga Virilis for Caesar, the pure white toga that his friends wore, instead, he would be putting on the purple and saffron striped Toga Trabea, of the Flamen Dialis.

The sun was sinking lower towards the horizon now, bathing Rome in a glorious yellow and orange glow. To Caesar, who sat alone on the rock, the dying sun symbolised the death of his childhood and the death of the life he had always known. Tomorrow the sun would rise in the east as it always did, but, for Caesar, it meant the start of a new life; a life that had been imposed on him, and a life that he dreaded with every fibre of his being.

He sighed, as immense sadness lay heavy within him. He knew that he should be at home now, helping to pack the last of the things that he would take with him to his new life. The home, that after tomorrow, would be a place that he would visit from time to time, for his new home would be the Flaminia, the ancient and impressive house of the Flamen Dialis. He wondered what it would be like to live alone without his family around him, or his friends, just down the road? All he would have for company now were a few slaves and hundreds of dusty books to read.

From the depth of his musing, Caesar suddenly became aware of footsteps and he turned to see Aemi walking across the grass towards him.

"I thought I'd find you here," he said, pulling his white Toga Virilis tightly round him as he sat down.

Caesar smiled but remained silent. They sat together in companionable silence for a while, watching the sun as it sank lower in the sky; the great ball of fire changing to a deep blood red before their eyes.

"It's funny, but the last time we were here I had become paterfamilias, do you remember, Caesar?" Aemi said. "I wanted to come up here one last time, to be the boy I was losing as manhood was forced upon me. We spent many happy times here, didn't we?"

Caesar nodded.

"So, when your mother told me that you had gone out, I knew this would be the place you would come to. It's as though our youth is here, don't you think? As I climbed the hill I half expected to see three young boys lying under that tree, laughing and talking like we used to," Aemi said, gazing fondly at their special cypress tree.

"And fighting," said Caesar with a wry smile. "You and Marcus were always arguing over something or other, don't forget."

It was Aemi's turn to smile now and the silence descended upon them once more.

"What does it feel like?" said Caesar, turning to look at Aemi.

"What?"

"The Toga Virilis. What does it feel like, when you wear it for the first time?"

"Oh, well, it feels the same as any other toga, obviously, but it makes you feel different inside, sort of grown up and proud. Suddenly you notice the boys who have not come of age yet and you feel special."

"Do you feel like a man?"

Aemi looked confused. "A man? Well, yes, I suppose I did. Why do you ask, Caesar?"

"Because I will never know what it feels like, will I? I won't put on my Toga Virilis because I don't have one. Tomorrow I will put on the Toga Trabea and I will be a priest; I will feel a priest, not a man," he said sadly.

Caesar saw a look of pity shadow Aemi's face and turned away.

"You'll still be a man, Caesar, just…different that's all. You and the ordinary were never meant to be, anyway, you have always been different to anyone else I know."

"Tomorrow I will be the Flamen Dialis, the priest, not the man, not Gaius Julius Caesar. No one will see the real me, will they? I will wear those awful clothes, live alone in that awful house, and live my life with those endless rules. I will live the life of a priest, not the life of a man."

Aemi remained silent, and the friends stared out over the city. Torches began to flicker to life in the streets below as the people began to replace the fading daylight with the yellow oily light of lamps. The dull ache in Caesar's heart increased as the hours of the life he loved faded away with the setting sun.

"I wish my father was here," he said.

"I know."

The boys sat in silence, companions of their own inner pain of loss. The sound of a snapping twig pulled them back to the present.

Aemi spun round to see who was approaching. "You!" he exclaimed angrily, and scrambled to his feet.

"Marcus!" Caesar jumped up. "What are you doing here?"

"What do you want?" Aemi demanded.

"I've not come to cause trouble," said Marcus, taking a step closer. "I came to be with Caesar. I thought he might want some company, that's all."

"Thank you, Marcus," Caesar smiled gratefully.

"Well he doesn't! He's got me and he doesn't need you," Aemi snarled.

Caesar turned to Aemi and put his hand on his arm. "Please, Aemi, please, not tonight. Marcus was right to come. I can't think of anything I would like more than to be with my two oldest and closest friends one last time."

Aemi scowled at Marcus but made no further objection.

"I thought you'd be here," Marcus said. "We always came here."

"Yes, this place has meant something to all of us over the years," said Caesar. "Come and sit with us, we were watching the sun set."

Caesar resumed his seat and Aemi sat on one side of him, Marcus on the other.

"How are you, really?" Marcus asked.

"A little nervous," Caesar sighed.

"I came to remind you, just like I said I would."

Caesar smiled and patted Marcus's shoulder. "Thank you, Marcus. You came at the right time. I was in danger of forgetting."

"Forgetting what?" said Aemi.

"Forgetting to believe that this will not last forever. That one day I will be free from being a priest. Marcus promised to remind me if ever I was in danger of losing my way."

"Oh, I see," said Aemi.

"Aemi, I meant to ask you earlier. Would you look after Toes for me? I couldn't bare to part with him, and I didn't know who else to ask. He is to be my symbol of freedom, you see."

"Of course I will, Caesar. He can go to my farm in Picentum. I've plenty of horses there to keep him company, and you can visit him whenever you like."

Caesar shook his head. "You are forgetting that I can't leave Rome. The day I see him again will be the day I am free. Will you keep him for me until then?"

"Yes, Caesar, he'll be ready and waiting for you whenever you need him."

"I'll visit him for you, if Aemi doesn't mind," Marcus volunteered.

Aemi scowled, but didn't reply. He had not seen or spoken to Marcus since that fateful day, and Caesar knew, just by looking at him, that Aemi was finding it very hard, being close to Marcus now.

"I'll only go when I know you won't be at the farm," said Marcus. "You won't have to see me."

"That is acceptable," said Aemi begrudgingly.

"Good, that's settled then," said Caesar. "Thank you. Thank you for being here for me, both of you. I will never forget this evening," he said to his friends.

"The sun is about to set," said Marcus, looking out at the dark purple orb, only the top edge visible now above the horizon.

"Then there is only one thing left to do before this day is over," said Caesar, searching the ground behind him. He collected three of the largest rocks he could find and gave one each to Aemi and Marcus. The three friends held their rocks and looked at each other.

"After three," said Caesar.

"One…Two…Three!"

And three rocks spun up into the air, twisting and spinning in the dying rays of the sun before they plunged forever, out of sight, into the darkness of the abyss below.

"These past two months have felt like an age, without having you around," Aemi sighed, patting his full stomach as he watched the slaves clear the last of the dinner dishes away. A cloud passed briefly across his face as he looked searchingly at his friend. "I have to say, though, you are looking a trifle thin, Caesar."

Caesar grimaced, and dismissed the slaves from the room. He waited until the dark, ornately carved door to the dining room was closed before he answered. "So would you be, if you had to live on the spartan diet I get these days. There are so many things I can't eat because they are forbidden foods that I may as well live on bread and water."

"Yes, sorry, I did feel rather guilty tucking into those quails eggs when all you had to eat was soup."

Caesar smiled and settled himself more comfortably onto his couch. "I'll live. To be honest it's a treat in itself just to see you. I never realised just how busy I would be. I can't believe it's been two months since I saw anybody for longer than an hour. Now, tell me, what's going on in the outside world, and don't hold anything back. Living in this mausoleum is like a prison. If it's not religious, I don't get to hear anything that goes on anymore."

Aemi, who lay on the couch opposite Caesar, stretched out his long legs and, rolling onto his left side, rested his head on his hand. "Let's see…well, Sulla is making great strides in the war…

Aemi was interrupted by the steward entering the room. He approached Caesar and bowed low. "Holy One, a message has arrived from your mother. She asks that you go to her at your earliest convenience."

Caesar knew immediately that something serious must have happened if his mother had sent for him, and he felt the colour drain from his cheeks. "I shall leave at once. Send for the litter," he ordered.

Aemi jumped to his feet. "I'll accompany you, Caesar, it's time I went home anyway."

Caesar nodded and led the way from the dining room out into the great hall. A slave appeared holding the Appex, the white conical hat the must be worn by the Flamen at all times when he is outside his own house. Aemi smiled as it was placed onto his friend's head.

"Don't!" said Caesar, with a grimace of distaste. A second slave carried over a thick woollen striped toga and a pair of lace less boots. Caesar stood perfectly still as the slaves quickly dressed him, then he hurried from the house and stepped into the litter that was waiting for him outside the door. The curtains were drawn to shield him from the public's gaze, but the litter itself, adorned with gold and red paint and furnishings, stood out so brightly that people could not help but stop and stare as the litter was carried ceremoniously through the streets of Rome. Tonight, however, Caesar ordered the slaves to hurry, and they set off at a fast walk, with Aemi striding alongside.

It did not take long to reach Caesar's old home, and, as soon as he felt the litter stop he threw aside the curtains and leapt out.

"I'll say good night, Caesar. I hope it's nothing too serious," said Aemi, preparing to walk home.

"No, please stay," said Caesar, who had an ominous feeling about this summons from his mother.

He walked up to the large wooden door and reached out to bang the brass doorknocker. At the last second he stopped, realising, just in time, that he was forbidden to touch the metal. "I need your help," he said, turning to Aemi, who stepped forward and banged the doorknocker hard.

Within seconds the door was opened by a slave, who, upon recognising the master, opened the door wide and bowed low, as Caesar, followed by Aemi, entered the house. One glance at the slave's face told Caesar all he needed to know. The feeling of foreboding increased as he strode into the atrium to be greeted by the steward.

"Holy One," the steward bowed low upon seeing Caesar.

"Where is she?" Caesar asked, looking around for signs of his mother.

"Your mother is in the sitting room, come, I will take you."

They hurried off along the corridor, and Caesar heard the crying before he reached the room. The steward opened the door and Caesar saw his mother, sitting stiffly on a couch at the far side of the room, her face pale and set hard, with his aunt Julia next to her, crying and lamenting, with several pieces of cloth strewn around her, one of which she was using to dab at her tear stained face.

"Mother?" Caesar walked past the steward into the room and stopped in his tracks. On the low wooden table at the centre of the room, stood a silver funeral urn.

Aurelia looked up at Caesar, and, as their eyes met, he saw immense grief reaching to the very depths of her soul. She started to rise from the couch, as did Julia, for it was against the custom to sit in the presence of the Flamen Dialis.

Caesar raised his hand. "No, stay,"

He saw his mother's eyes flit to the urn and back to his face, and a knot of fear tightened his insides. "Mother…who?" he asked, looking from her face to the urn, but deep down inside he already knew the answer.

"Oh, Gaius, I am so sorry," Aurelia whispered, struggling hard to maintain her composure as her eyes welled up with tears.

Julia let out a wail and buried her face into the cloth she was holding.

Caesar walked slowly forward to the table and looked down at the urn. Tiny delicate patterns were inlaid on the top and sides of the handles whilst the main body was burnished to perfection, the flames from the many oil lamps in the room rippling ever-changing light across its surface. He reached out his hand and remembered that he could not touch the metal so he slowly traced the delicate, patterned design, with his finger, only a hairs breadth away from the forbidden metal.

"Father," he whispered, and as his legs gave way he collapsed to his knees in front of the table.

Caesar felt as though he was falling, down, down into a crushing blackness of devastation. Like a drowning man that sank deeper and deeper under the water, wave upon wave of utter misery filled his very soul and he wanted to let go; to keep falling and never come back. In that single moment of realisation that the silver urn held the remains of his beloved father, everything stopped. Everything he knew, everything he trusted; the one person, whom he loved more than any other, had gone from his life, forever. How could he possibly go on? What was left for him if his father could not be there to share life with him? Desolation, utter desolation rose up inside him, and he wanted to scream; the scream of the living torn from their loved ones. The eternal scream of the bereaved facing life without the person they loved, and he wanted to let go, to drift away from life, because to go back would be too painful.

*"Remember who you are,"* his father's voice whispered inside Caesar's head. *"Be the man you were meant to be."*

"Father? Father… is that you?" Caesar's faint cry echoed round the depths of his mind. "Where are you? I can't see you. Where are you?"

*"I am here. I live inside you; you are part of me, and if you live, then I live also. Remember who you are."*

"I can't, Father. How can I go on without you?" Caesar called out in despair.

*"Trust me, Gaius. Look to the light,"* his father's voice was fading, slowly, softly. *"Look to the light."*

Caesar looked up into the blackness that was his mind, and far, far away he saw a single speck of light. He began to struggle, to stop himself falling deeper, swimming towards the light in his mind. The closer he got, the heavier he felt, but he kept on trying, until, just when he thought he could not find the strength any more, he burst back into the light; the light of the living. He gasped involuntarily, sucking in the air as he fought to regain control, then slowly, he opened his eyes and saw the urn before him on the table. Caesar hung his head as the tears began to fall in large droplets onto the floor.

Aurelia looked at her son, looking so young and vulnerable, kneeling there in the voluminous robes of the Flamen Dialis, and she made an instinctive movement to rise so that she could wrap her arms around him and hold him tight, but as she got to her feet she faltered, forbidden by the ancient customs surrounding her priest-son, who could no longer be touched or caressed by anyone but his future wife. Aurelia was helpless; unable to do or say anything to ease the terrible pain she saw that he suffered.

Julia continued to sob in the background, her grief so raw from the still recent death of her husband, compounded now by the unexpected death of her brother.

The door to the sitting room suddenly opened and in walked Young Marius and Marcus.

"Mother!" Young Marius hurried to his mother's side and was immediately enveloped in her arms as she sobbed into her eldest son's embrace.

Marcus followed and sat down next to Julia. "I'm so sorry, Mother," he murmured.

"Aunt Aurelia, my most sincere condolences on the loss of your husband," said Young Marius, as he prized himself out of Julia's arms. He walked over to Aurelia and gave her a kiss on the cheek.

Aurelia nodded her thanks but her eyes remained on the urn, with her son kneeling bereft and alone before it.

Young Marius became aware of Caesar's presence for the first time. He stood erect and bowed formally to his cousin. "My sincere condolences at your loss, Holy One."

Marcus jumped to his feet. He hadn't noticed Caesar either, and he blushed with embarrassment. "Caesar, I..." he stammered, and then blushed again because he had addressed the Flamen Dialis informally. He caught Aemi's eye and looked away; this was one time when Aemi's animosity was of no importance.

"Lady Aurelia, my condolences," said Aemi graciously, walking forward and bowing politely. "If there is anything, anything at all I can do for you, then you have only to ask. Lady Julia," he nodded, in acknowledgement of Julia's relationship to the deceased, and then slipped away to the back of the room.

The sound of Marcus's voice penetrated Caesar's grief and he looked up, suddenly becoming aware of the people now in the room. He wiped the tears from his face with the sleeve of his tunic and rose slowly from the floor. The room fell silent as the Flamen Dialis stood before them.

"How did this happen? When?" He directed the question to his mother.

"Nineteen days ago, in Pisa," she answered shakily.

Through his own grief, Caesar could see that his mother was using every ounce of self-control to keep herself from breaking down and his heart went out to her.

"Your father was recruiting for Cinna's legions when an argument broke out amongst the men. There was a fight and…he was…stabbed. He died two days later. Marcus Pollonius, your father's friend, said,…said that he fought against…against dying every step of the way, but in the end…" Her voice trailed away as the effort of explaining her husband's death proved too much.

"Did Marcus Pollonius arrange the funeral?"

Aurelia nodded. "He brought the…he brought your father home personally. He also brought that package; he says it was meant for you."

Caesar had noticed the large cloth bundle tied with thin rope, lying on the table, but he had assumed that it contained personal possessions of his father. He looked down at it now and wondered what it would contain.

"The ashes will be interred in the Julii mausoleum, I assume?" Young Marius asked.

Caesar flinched at the word ashes, used to describe his father, and he felt anger rise in him as he looked at his cousin, the spitting image of Gaius Marius. "My Father will be interred alongside his ancestors, yes," Caesar answered curtly. "As paterfamilias, it will be my responsibility to arrange the internment, although I will be unable to attend myself; my office forbids it. You understand, Mother?"

"Of course," Aurelia replied stiffly.

"Oh, poor Gaius, my poor brother!" Julia sobbed aloud.

Marcus put his arm around his mother to comfort her. "I think you should return home with us, Mother. You are tired and upset, and it's getting late. Let's give the family some time alone now."

"But I should stay here; Aurelia needs me!" Julia sobbed.

"No, Julia, Marcus is right, you should go home and rest now, and I have Gaius here with me," Aurelia insisted.

"Come, Mother," said Young Marius firmly, and he gently took Julia's arm and helped her to her feet. "You may see Aurelia again tomorrow, but you need to rest now," he urged kindly.

There was more tears and hugs from Julia as she made her farewell to Aurelia and Caesar, and then she was led quickly from the room by her sons, much to the relief of both Caesar and Aurelia. Aemi left soon afterwards, insisting that he be called upon to help in whatever way he could. Caesar smiled gratefully at his friend as he too left the room, leaving mother and son alone at last with their grief.

Caesar took a seat near his mother and they sat in silence for several minutes, each in a world of their own pain and grief. Caesar looked at the urn containing the last mortal remains of the man he had loved so dearly, and the tears trickled down his cheeks freely now.

Aurelia watched her son but remained silent, allowing him the time to grieve freely without interruption. As the tears that had been so close to the surface since the devastating news had been broken, fell silently down the smooth olive cheeks, she made no move to wipe them away.

Finally Caesar moved, resting his head on the back of the chair, which caused his Appex to fall from his head and onto the floor. Aurelia stood up to retrieve it but Caesar held up his hand. "Leave it, Mother, it doesn't matter," he said, his voice devoid of all emotion.

"But the rules…"

"I don't care about the damned rules!" he retorted angrily. "I am not the Flamen Dialis here, I am your son, and I don't care about the stupid hat."

Aurelia sat down on the couch and studied her son. They had seen each other only once since he had moved out of the family home, and then it was only from a distance. She could see that he had grown thinner, even under the mound of baggy priestly clothing he wore, yet somehow, it seemed to enhance his natural beauty, giving him a look of innocence and vulnerability that had not been noticeable before. "You cannot stop being the Flamen, Gaius, however much you would like too," she said gently.

Caesar sighed and turned his head to face his mother. "I know, Mother, and I am sorry I snapped at you," he said. "It's just…now, at this moment, I have never felt so alone, and so…stifled. I want to hug you, but I can't. I want you to hold me and make everything all right again, the way that you used too, but you can't. I want to touch the urn, to feel closer to Father, but I can't! It's so frustrating, Mother, and I hate him for it!"

"Who do you hate, your father?"

"No! No, never him," said Caesar passionately. "I could never hate Father for anything, after all, he was as much a victim in this as I am. There is nothing he could have done to stop Gaius Marius from making me the Flamen. No, it is Gaius Marius who I hate right at this moment. I hate him more than I ever thought possible!"

Aurelia wiped a stray tear from her cheek. "He was so very proud of you that day. He knew how much you loathed the thought of becoming the Flamen Dialis but you bore it with a strength and courage neither of us believed was in you, because you are still so young. You made him proud to call you his son; you made us both proud."

Caesar looked up at his mother and gave a faint smile. "It was hard, I won't deny it, in fact, it still is. I do not believe I will ever truly accept this life I have been forced to lead, and I cannot give up the hope that one day, something will happen to change all this, but, until that day arrives I will be the Flamen Dialis that the People expect and the gods demand."

Caesar bent down to retrieve the fallen Appex from the floor. He picked it up and held it in his hands, straightening the olive twig attached to the side. "I will not let Father down, I promise."

Aurelia smiled in gratitude and relief. "Your father will always be with us, Gaius, in our hearts. His body may be gone but his spirit lives on in you, and little Julia.

You are so like him, you know, and that is something to be proud of, to keep hold of, for in you he has never completely died."

At that moment Caesar would have given anything to be able to hug his mother but all he had was words, and they just didn't seem enough at this moment. In his frustration he got up from the chair and walked over to the table where the package lay.

"Do you know what it is?" he asked, examining it closely.

"No. Marcus Pollonius said that your father intended to send it to you, for your birthday, but he was delayed and the parcel was never sent. Marcus brought it back with him when he brought…" she tailed off as tears welled up in her eyes again.

Caesar nodded and undid the binding that held the package together, and as the tension released, the cloth sprung open, revealing a finely spun bolt of pure white cloth inside. Caesar gasped as he realised what it was, and he let the outer packaging fall to the floor as he pulled out the pure white Toga Virilis of manhood.

Aurelia noticed that a small parchment letter had fallen from the folds of the tunic and onto the floor. She rose from the couch and retrieved it. "There is a letter from your father," she said, holding it out for Caesar to take.

He looked up into her face and shook his head.

"Would you like me to read it for you?" she asked softly.

Caesar nodded, and dropped his gaze down to the toga he held in his hands.

Aurelia unfolded the parchment and her hands shook as she saw the finely written words of her husband once more.

*"My precious son,"* she began. *"My one regret is that I cannot be there to present you with this Toga Virilis personally, as a father should on this special day. It was a duty that I always looked forward to, presenting my son with his toga of manhood, welcoming you into the world of men, yet distance and circumstance prevent us from sharing that moment together. I know, that for you, this day not only means the end of your childhood, but also the end of your life as you knew it, for you will move from boyhood to priesthood, and this means that you will never have the opportunity to wear the toga you hold before you. Though you are prevented from wearing it, keep it as a symbol of your manhood, Gaius. To face your new life as the Flamen Dialis you will need the strength and courage of a man. I have every faith that you will do your duty to your family, and to Rome, and you will do it well. I am proud of you, Gaius, as my son, and, as the man I know you will grow to become in the years ahead. Never forget who you are, Gaius, even in your darkest moments. You have the blood of the Julii running in your veins and it will give you the strength and courage to endure the life that lays before you now.*

*I send with this toga a father's love and respect for a son, that this day has become a man.*

*Hail to you, Gaius Julius Caesar."*

Aurelia placed the letter on the table and quietly left the room.

"Thank you, Father," Caesar whispered, as he heard the door close softly behind him, and then he buried his face into the folds of the toga and wept; for the loss of the father who had come to mean everything to him, for the loss of the life he would never know, and, for the man he could never be.

The day of his wedding had arrived, and Caesar stood in his dressing room as the body slave put the finishing touches to the folds of his toga.

As he waited patiently, Caesar wondered how his young bride, Cinnilla, was feeling at this moment. Would she be excited at the prospect of marrying him or would the thought of the sterile, joyless life she would lead as the Flaminica frighten her and fill her with dread, as he himself had felt only a few months before? A sudden knock on the dressing room door roused Caesar from his reverie, and he signalled for the slave to answer it. To Caesar's delight Marcus stepped into the room, dressed in a new snow white Toga Virilis, his hair and body freshly cleaned and oiled for the celebrations ahead.

"Caesar, I hope you don't mind me calling in, but I wanted to wish you luck on your wedding day," said Marcus as he bowed respectfully.

"Of course I don't, Marcus, come in," Caesar replied with a warm smile. "I am nearly ready," he added, as he slowly turned round so that his slave could finish the final drapes of the toga across his left arm.

Marcus looked around the room, impressed by the intricately painted frescos on the wall and the carved closet doors. "This house is really impressive," he said, going over to examine a painting of Venus reclining gracefully upon a rock, with a harp in her hand. "Your wife will love it here."

"I hope so. We can't move to another house if she doesn't, it comes with job," Caesar laughed.

"It sounds really strange, *your wife*. So much has happened in such a short space of time, hasn't it? I find it hard to take it all in sometimes," said Marcus, perching himself on a nearby stool.

"I know. My feet haven't touched the ground since the day I came of age. It really does feel like a dream," Caesar agreed, and he lifted his foot up so that his slave could slide the boot on.

"What's she like, Cinnilla I mean? I don't believe I've ever met her before."

"Young," Caesar replied, lifting up his other foot. "I hope she is going to cope with this new life she will lead."

"Mmm. Still, after living with Cinna for so long, anything has got to be an improvement," said Marcus.

The hint of sarcasm was not wasted on Caesar and he grinned mischievously. "Careful what you say, Marcus, that's my father-in-law you are talking about."

"Is she pretty?"

"So they tell me, but, as I have never clapped eyes on the girl then I couldn't comment. All I know for certain is that she has a lot of growing up to do first."

"I expect she will grow up to be the most beautiful woman in Rome, with your luck, Caesar."

"My luck! I haven't seen much of that in evidence lately," Caesar retorted, brushing some stray fluff from his tunic sleeve.

"No, I suppose not," said Marcus suddenly looking serious. "But you haven't given up have you? You do still believe that one day you will be freed from the priesthood?"

Caesar waved his slave away, and waited until they were alone before he spoke. "No, Marcus, I haven't given up believing, but, if I am honest, I'm finding it harder to see a way of ever being free again, especially now that I am to be married. Whatever happens, I will have a wife to take care of, and that will limit what I can do."

"Something will happen to change things," said Marcus. "All of this... well, it's wrong! He said in exasperation. "You should never have been made the Flamen. You were meant for other things, great things. I know it."

Caesar was puzzled. "You sound very certain of yourself, Marcus. What makes you so sure that this is not to be my life?"

Marcus blushed and looked at the floor.

"Marcus?" Caesar was sure now that he knew more than he was admitting to.

"Well, I...I saw something, written down on some papers in Father's study, after he died."

"What did you see?" said Caesar, moving over to stand in front of his friend. "Marcus, if you know something then you must tell me now," Caesar insisted.

"All right, but I am not saying it's definitely about you, Caesar."

"Let me decide, now, go on."

Marcus shrugged resignedly. "Gaius decided that we should empty Father's study so that he could have it as his own when he was home, now that he is paterfamilias, so I agreed to help, and I took the job of sorting through the paperwork in Father's drawers. At the back of the bottom drawer I came across a small locked box and I searched for the key, but couldn't find it. Then a few weeks later I happened to find a key hidden under a vase on the shelf. As soon as I saw it, I knew it was the key to the box, so I opened it. Inside was a bunch of papers and a small parchment book. It was very old and wrapped in oilskin, and I think some of the pages were missing. Anyway, I read the letter that was on top of the book and it was written by one of father's freedmen in Arpinium. He was replying to an earlier letter Father had sent him, from the way this one was written, and it referred to the book."

"What did it say?"

"It said that the freedman had looked where Father had told him to, and he had indeed found the book amongst some old papers of my grandfather. He said he thought the book looked incomplete, with some pages missing at the back, and then he went on to ask if Father wanted him to search further a field, because the Sybil's prophecies were no longer stored in Arpinium, but had been moved to another town in the north."

"So what was in the book, Marcus? Did you read it?"

"Yes, at least I tried to, but some of the words were badly faded. It was sort of a rhyme but it sounded strange. It was all about eagles."

"Eagles?"

"Yes, well, I didn't understand it either, so I took the book to show mother and she read it. I asked her what it meant and she said it appeared to be the prophecy, made about Marius when he was a young boy. She wouldn't tell me any more after that, she said it wasn't important. Then your mother came to visit. I overheard them talking about you and the book, and your mother said you were the ninth eagle."

"She said what? Are you sure, Marcus?"

"I think so, I mean she said it as I walked into the room, and I noticed that she had that book on her knee. I think they were talking about the Sybil's prophecy, and your mother thinks that you are mentioned in it."

Caesar sat in silence for a moment, taking in all that Marcus had said. "Where is this book now?" he asked.

"Mother has it, I suppose. I haven't seen it since that day. You don't sound surprised, Caesar. Did you already know of this prophecy?"

"I knew of its existence because Father told me about it. My parents believed that I was mentioned in the prophecy, but, as no one knew it had been written down, they could never be certain."

Marcus gasped as a sudden look of realisation crossed his face. "Caesar! That's why Father took against you isn't it? That's why he made you the Flamen!"

Caesar frowned, deep in thought.

"Listen, Caesar, if Gaius Marius believed you were the one mentioned in the prophecy, and, that in some way you threatened him, then that would explain why he went to so much trouble to have you ordained as the Flamen! Your mother said she thought that you were the ninth eagle, so that means that there were more than the seven eaglets mentioned in the prophecy. Marius only ever spoke of the seven eaglets, that represented the number of times he would be Consul, but why not the others? What if they don't represent a situation? What if they represent people? Your mother said that she thought *you* were the ninth eagle, so, who is, or was, the eighth? What did the prophecy say about them, and, most importantly, what does it say about you?"

Caesar didn't reply. His mind was whirling with possibilities and half-truths. How could he even begin to make sense of it all?

He saw a shadow of fear cross Marcus's face. "I do hope I did the right thing by telling you about this, Caesar. I wish I could remember what the prophecy said, but I can't, I'm really sorry."

Caesar smiled and shook his head. "You did the right thing, Marcus, trust me. Now, it is time that I went to claim my wife. We must find time to discuss this matter later. Will you find out where the book is now?"

"I can try," Marcus nodded.

"That is all I ask," Caesar said. "Now, will you be attending the celebrations afterwards?"

"Of course, I wouldn't miss it for anything," said Marcus, walking to the door.

"Then I shall see you later," said Caesar. "Oh, and one more thing," he added with a grin. "You must address me as Holy One, and you wait for my permission before you sit in my presence. And don't forget to bow!"

Marcus turned bright red with embarrassment. He had not shown any deference at all during this visit.

Caesar laughed heartily at his friend's discomfort. "It doesn't matter, Marcus, not when we are alone. Just don't forget later, when we are in company."

"No, no of course not...I'm so sorry...I mean..." Marcus stumbled as he hurried from the room, and he set off down the corridor without a backward glance as the sound of Caesar's laughter rang in his ears.

The wedding ceremony was completed without a hitch, and, with the formal feast ended, the guests mingled, chatting and laughing as the wine flowed freely.

Aemi waited until Caesar had finished a conversation with Lucius Cornelius Cinna, and then sidled over to congratulate his friend. "So, you are a married man, and a priest, all in under a year; who would have thought it, Holy One. Congratulations," Aemi said with a grin.

"Thanks," Caesar replied, pleased to see his friend. "I hope the food was to your liking," he added mischievously.

"Indeed, very good. I must say that I did wonder what kind of provisions you would offer your guests. It is a shame that you can't each much of it, considering it is your wedding party."

"Food is merely a necessity to me now and not something to enjoy, unlike you, Aemi; is that a little belly I see growing there?" he tapped Aemi's stomach playfully.

Aemi pulled a face and laughed. "I must say, your wife is a rather pretty little thing," he said, turning to look across the room at Cinnilla, who was deep in conversation with some family friends.

"Yes she is," Caesar agreed. He had been pleasantly surprised when he had seen Cinnilla for the first time. Although very young, at just thirteen, she was exceedingly pretty. Her creamy olive complexion contrasted sharply to her raven black hair, pale, green eyes, and deep, ruby red lips. There was no doubt that she would be considered a real beauty when she reached maturity. " She seems to have a nice disposition too, which helps," he added.

"Oh, that will change, you wait and see. A few months time and she will be ruling your home with an iron tongue!" Aemi quipped.

"And you would know, would you Aemi, never having a wife of your own." They both laughed in companionable amusement.

"Holy One," said Marcus, bowing respectfully, as he approached Caesar and Aemi.

"Marcus, welcome!" said Caesar warmly. "I am glad you could join us."

"Aemi," Marcus said, nodding to his old friend.

"Marcus." Aemi avoided any eye contact by looking over at Cinnilla again.

"Please help yourself to some food and wine if you're hungry," said Caesar, ignoring the coolness between his two friends.

"Thank you, I will, and congratulations on your marriage. Cinnilla is beautiful, you are a lucky man," said Marcus, as he looked admiringly at Cinnilla.

"Marcus... Marcus, would you join me a moment please?" Caesar's aunt Julia called across the room.

"I'll speak with you later," said Marcus, bowing low, with a wry grin on his face and he walked off to join his mother.

Caesar turned back to Aemi. "I'm glad I've got you on your own; I have some news to tell you," he said, lowering his voice and pulling Aemi over to a quiet corner of the room. He proceeded to tell Aemi about Marcus's visit earlier that day.

Aemi listened intently, his eyes growing ever wider as he heard about the prophecy. "But this is great news, Caes…I mean, Holy One," he said, when Caesar had finished. "This means that what your parents believed was true after all, and it could prove that Marius made you the Flamen to prevent the prophecy from being fulfilled!"

"It certainly would appear so."

"Does this mean that you can somehow get free from the priesthood?"

"I don't know, not yet anyway, but I shall speak with mother as soon as I can. What it does mean is that there is hope. It was not my destiny to be the Flamen Dialis, and Marius chose to defy the gods to satisfy his own lust for immortality. Only they can decide whether I am to remain a priest, or, set me free to follow the path I was meant to walk, but, when or how that could happen, I have no more idea than you."

"Then I pray that the gods are listening and they see that a grave injustice has been done to you. This is no life for you, though you strive to do your best, but I can see what it's doing to you, and I want you to know that if there is anything I can do to help, I will do so with all my heart!"

"I may keep you to that, Aemi," Caesar said with a grateful smile. "But for now I have a wife waiting to get some attention from her husband, and, if I delay for much longer, I will have a very unhappy bride."

"You will let me know what your mother says, won't you?" said Aemi.

"Of course, you will be the first to know. Now, go and enjoy the celebrations before the wine runs out!"

Aemi watched as Caesar walked across to join his wife, and, the group of women that surrounded her welcomed him warmly into their circle. It didn't matter that Caesar was dressed from head to toe in those unflattering priestly garments, he still looked handsome and would always attract the women. Aemi turned his attention to the rest of the room, scanning the faces for a sight of the very pretty cousin of Cinnilla's that had caught his eye earlier.

"She's in the atrium," said a voice behind him.

Aemi turned to see Marcus standing behind him. "Who?"

"Aemilia Lepida. I presume that was who you were looking for?" Marcus replied with a sly grin.

Aemi drew himself up to face Marcus. "As usual you are mistaken, Marcus, and I would thank you to keep your thoughts to yourself," he said haughtily.

Marcus shrugged. "Have it your way. I was only trying to be helpful."

Aemi snorted and looked away.

"I presume he told you about the prophecy?"

Aemi spun round to face Marcus. "Shhh, keep your voice down!" he hissed.

"Relax Aemi, no one heard me!" Marcus retorted. "So... did he?"

"Yes, if you must know, although I am led to believe that you were only able to tell him half a story; now why does that not surprise me?"

"Oh get off your high horse will you, just for once!" Marcus snapped. "All that matters is that there could be a way out for Caesar, and, as his two closest friends, it is up to us to support him any way that we can. Would you rather I had said nothing? Left him bereft of any hope at all?"

Aemi scowled at Marcus then shook his head. "No, I suppose not."

"Well, at least that is something we can agree on. Caesar was never meant to be a priest and I believe the prophecy confirms that, if indeed it is Caesar it speaks of."

"Oh it will be, I have no doubt. If your mad father had not been so obsessed with his reputation, so determined to remove or destroy anyone that would challenge his immortality, then Caesar would not have been incarcerated in this...mausoleum! Caesar would have a life and he would not be standing here today having been forced into marrying another one of your father's legacies!" Aemi said through gritted teeth.

"Oh, I quite agree with you, Aemi," Marcus replied with a smile. "And that is why, I for one, shall do everything in my power to right the wrong my Fa...Gaius Marius, did to Caesar. He knew that Caesar was the one spoken of in the prophecy and he took it upon himself to challenge the gods by trying to stop him from fulfilling his destiny by creating him the Flamen. But, I do not believe the gods will allow Caesar to suffer forever, and somehow, something will happen to free Caesar from these bonds. I am going to ensure that if it is in my power to help him then I will, and I hope that you feel the same, Aemi, whatever your feelings are towards me. There may come a time when we have to work together for Caesar's sake and I hope that you can put aside your personal feelings towards me to help your friend."

Aemi looked thoughtfully at Marcus, and, for a brief moment, Marcus saw a look of intense sadness in Aemi's eyes and wondered if he too regretted the loss of their friendship.

"Aemi, I..." he began, but the look faded as quickly as it appeared, and Aemi's face hardened back to cool indifference.

"For Caesar, I will work together with you, but only for Caesar; do not interpret my compliance as anything else."

Marcus sighed with relief. "Thank you, Aemi, that is all I ask."

"Caesar mentioned a letter from a freedman. Is it true that the copy of the prophecy you saw was not complete?"

"Yes. The letter was asking if the freedman should try to locate a copy of the full prophecy made by the Sibyl. The book we had was written for Marius's father, after the event, but some of the pages are missing. Gaius Marius no doubt wanted to find the prophecy in full."

"Is there any further correspondence from this freedman to say that he found the missing pages?"

"No, nothing, and I have gone through all the papers and letters in his study."

"Then I believe that there is something you can do to help Caesar. Find that freedman and see if he managed to find the original prophecy, written by the Sybil's scribe. If he was not successful then somewhere out there the full prophecy exists, and if we can find that, it may give us a clue to how Caesar can get out of this mess."

"I will see to it straight away," said Marcus with a look of grim determination. "The freedman wrote from Arpinium, but the letter was not dated so I have no idea how long ago he wrote it. I shall find this man, indeed, I shall go first thing tomorrow."

"Good. You must let me know what you find."

"Would you like me to?"

"Of course, as you say, Caesar is in no position to help himself therefore it is up to us, as his friends, to do it for him. I suggest we say nothing to Caesar until we have something definite. If we work together, then it may be that we can bring about an end to this debacle sooner rather than later. There has bee a grave injustice done here."

Marcus smiled. "I never thought I would see the day when we would be talking like this, especially after everything that has passed between us."

Aemi raised an eyebrow and looked sideways at Marcus. "Indeed, Marcus, neither did I."

# CHAPTER FIFTEEN

*"A man of courage is also full of faith."*
*(Marcus Tullius Cicero)*

## ROME 84 BC

*Senior Consul: Lucius Cornelius Cinna (4)*
*Junior Consul: Gnaeus Papirius Carbo (2)*

The sun was setting over the dry, arid landscape of Armenia. The camp torches flickered in to life and the legionaries settled down for an evening of celebrations as Dollabella burst into Sulla's command tent, with Lucullus close behind.

"What a day! What a reception they gave you, Sulla. I have never seen such adoration from the men in all the years I've served as an officer; not even with Marius, and he was always a favourite with his," Dollabella boomed enthusiastically.

"Dollabella's right, Sulla," Lucullus agreed. "The men love you. You have given them victory against a stiff opponent and the spoils from this campaign will make most of the men richer than they could ever imagine!"

Sulla smiled with satisfaction as he stretched out on his couch like a big cat returned to the pride after a satisfactory days hunting. "We deserved to win. The men fought long and hard, sometimes against unbelievable odds, but we did it in the end, as I knew we would. The men deserve their booty and they shall have it, but perhaps not quite as quickly as they would like."

Lucullus handed Dollabella a goblet of wine. "What do you mean? The accountants have been working night and day to add up the total of spoils to be divided amongst the men. Verres says that the pay will be ready within a few weeks and the booty will be paid upon our return to Rome. I'm assuming we will be returning immediately to Rome, after all, you are certain to be awarded a Triumph for this victory, even though relations between you and the Senate are a little… frosty."

"That, my dear Lucullus, is one way of describing the situation, however, I have decided that the men can have half their pay now, and the rest once I am safely back in Rome. The legions will stay together until then."

Dollabella almost choked on his wine. "By all the gods, Sulla, surely you don't intend to march on Rome? The Senate are all but grovelling at your feet and the People would welcome you with open arms for this victory!"

"The legions will be disbanded when I say they will. They are *my* men and *I* decide what happens to them. I don't need you to tell me what I can and cannot do, Dollabella," Sulla replied, his voice dangerously low.

"But we've discussed this, time and time again. The men have had enough; we all have. Your exile has been revoked, and the Senate are willing to come to terms with you, if you'd only listen to their envoys. The letter you sent obviously put the wind up them, and now they are prepared to agree almost anything, so long as you don't march on the city. Please don't drag Rome into another civil war, purely for revenge!"

Sulla's rose menacingly from the couch. "Revenge? Revenge! Of course it's for revenge, Lucullus!" Sulla spat out the words. For so long he had kept a tight rein on his emotions, focussing his hatred towards winning the war against King Mithridates, but, now that he had won, he could turn those pent up feelings of anger and revulsion towards it's source, Cinna, and those that had supported his, and Marius's, reign of terror. Even after Marius's death, Cinna had plotted and schemed against Sulla. Driven more by fear than enmity, Cinna was doing everything in his power to prevent Sulla from returning to Rome to seek revenge, unfortunately for him, however, the Senate now wavered it's support, preferring to try and negotiate a peaceful solution to the crisis that loomed ever closer, for they knew what Sulla was capable of, and once the war was over, they knew he would be turning his eyes on Rome, with revenge in his heart.

Sulla paced the tent like a caged animal. "Revenge is all there is. For my friends that were murdered because they saw a future in me, and not that mad despot Marius, or his puppet, Cinna! Revenge for all the innocents who died because they stood up against them, knowing what those men would do if they gained control of Rome. Revenge for my home and all my worldly goods that were destroyed because they were mine! My wife, my babies, fleeing for their lives, my honour, my dignitas, and all the military and social honours I had been given over the years that were stripped from me as though they stood for nothing! How dare you stand there and accuse me of marching on Rome *purely* for revenge. It is the *sole* reason I *will* march on Rome! It is for revenge that I will make those responsible pay, every last rotten stinking one of them! The time has come when Sulla stops being the victim. No more will I allow others to dictate my fate, my life, and my actions. I have stood by for too long and allowed others to walk all over me, but no more I tell you, *no more*! Sulla has changed, and men will remember Marius as a mere babe in arms by the time I have finished, for vengeance *will* be mine!" Sulla snarled as he slammed his fist on the table. "There are hundreds of senators and knights outside, in this camp, waiting for the day they can return to their homes, to their loved ones, and they all look to me to make that happen for them. Many of these men have suffered great depravation and have run in fear for their lives because of Marius and Cinna. They have lost their homes, their businesses, their families and friends. Do you think they are happy to accept their fate and do nothing? Shrug their shoulders and say '*Oh well, it's what the gods decide.*' They want revenge for all that has happened to them and I *will* give them that satisfaction. Every night when I fall asleep I hear the voices of those murdered innocents crying out for revenge, begging me to put right what was taken from them. It is a debt I owe to the living, and to the dead, and I will pay it, in blood if I have to, but paid it will be."

"But not at the expense of Rome."

Sulla spun round to see who had spoken so brazenly, and found Marcus Aurelius Cotta standing just inside of the tent. He watched, cold, pale eyes burning from the passion he felt to the depths of his soul, as Marcus Aurelius approached.

"Not one of those men would want you to avenge their deaths if it meant the end of Rome, Sulla, and that is what it will cost if you return with destruction in your heart."

Sulla felt his heart racing, and his blood pumping, and he fought against an overwhelming desire to put his hands around Marcus Aurelius's neck and squeeze the sanity from him. Why could no-one else feel the hatred and the passion for revenge that he did? How could they just stand by and deny what had happened? "The Rome I know is already destroyed," he said, through gritted teeth.

Marcus Aurelius placed a hand on Sulla's arm and he held his gaze. "No, Sulla, you are wrong. Rome is still very much alive, in here," he said, patting his heart, "and in here," he touched his forehead. "You have the chance to bring Her back to what she was. Good men have died, and many more still suffer, but you can go a long way to repairing the damage left by Marius and Cinna. Use your head, Sulla. Make your peace with the Senate, return to Rome, and then use the laws that we have to bring justice to the memory of those taken so cruelly from us. You have the chance to make a difference. You have the chance to heal Rome, but, you also have the chance to destroy Her. Which will you choose, Sulla, which will you choose?"

Sulla stood immobile for what seemed an eternity, his face an implacable mask, giving no sign as to what he was thinking, and then, abruptly, he turned and walked to his couch. "Leave me," he ordered, as he flung his arm across his face and turned away.

Two days later, Sulla dispatched Lucullus and Marcus Aurelius to treat with the envoys of Rome.

Barely three weeks after Lucullus and Marcus Aurelius had set out from camp they returned, and the news was not good.

Bathed and refreshed from their arduous journey, Marcus Aurelius and Lucullus stared grimly into the flames of the freshly stoked brazier inside Sulla's command tent, as the slaves handed out fresh goblets of wine, bread and sweetmeats. Dismissing the slaves, Sulla settled down on the couch to listen to the news.

"You have no doubt gathered from our prompt return that our undertaking did not go as expected," Lucullus began wearily. "Cinna is dead."

Sulla started, completely thrown by this news. "Dead. How?"

"It happened just before we arrived in Philippi. Cinna and Carbo had moved all their recruits up to the port of Ariminium, their intention being to cross the sea to Liburnia and set up forward defences against your return to Italy. The first batch of troops crossed successfully but the second hit a storm during the crossing, and, when they reached land, the men claimed that the storm was a warning sent by the gods to deter them from taking up arms against you and their fellow Romans. It didn't take long for the panic to spread, and the men deserted in their hundreds. Carbo could do nothing to stop them and he sent a message to Cinna requesting that he do all he could to calm the fears of the men left in Ariminium. Cinna gathered the men together, and by all accounts tried to bully them into obeying his command, threatening decimation if there was any further desertions, and when that didn't work, he tried to terrify them by warning of what would happen if you landed in Italy with your legions."

Sulla raised an eyebrow but remained silent.

"The men turned on Cinna and threw rocks and stones at him as he tried to speak and then… some of the legionaries drew their swords and cut him to pieces."

"What? The men murdered a Consul of Rome?" Sulla gasped.

"Yes, and if Carbo had been with him I have no doubt that they would have turned on him too," said Marcus Aurelius.

Sulla's face clouded, and his birthmark began to throb a deep purple. "You see this is what Rome has been reduced to! Common soldiers taking it upon themselves to murder their Consul," he stormed. "Marius and Cinna did nothing but show the people that it was acceptable to murder in order to get what you want. Fimbria is another example; murdering his superior officer so that he could have command of the legions. Flaccus was no loss, but he should not have met his end in that way. What is happening to Rome? What use are the Senate?"

"The Senate are in disarray, according to the envoys who are still in direct contact with Rome. Many are against Cinna and Carbo, but their fear of you is even greater. I am told that the letter you sent to the Senate informing them of your plans to return to Rome caused serious division amongst them, and meanwhile Cinna and Carbo disregard anything the Senate orders," said Marcus Aurelius.

"Where is Carbo now?"

"All the envoys could say for certain was that he crossed back to Ariminium with those men who had remained loyal. They believe Carbo has requested aid from Fimbria, but they have lost contact with him, for now at least." said Lucullus.

"Do they know where Fimbria is?"

"No. The last reported sighting was near Byzantium, but that was a few weeks ago now."

Sulla took a sip of wine as he digested this unforeseen turn of events. Cinna dead; another he was deprived of bringing to justice, but at least it would make his return to Rome a little easier. He had already decided which path he would take, and now it would be time to put his plans into action.

"Well, with the Senate in pieces and only one Consol remaining, I see no other alternative but to return to Rome. Someone has to take control before the entire Republic crumbles, for mark my words, as soon as our enemies hear Rome is vulnerable they will descend on our provinces like vultures."

Sulla could see that Lucullus was disappointed at this turn of events and, for a second, he wished he could offer his faithful officer the hope of a peaceful solution that he so obviously longed for, but now was not the time to falter in his intentions. Sulla rose suddenly to his feet, placing his goblet on the table before him. "The gods have shown me the path that I must take and I will not shrink from the responsibility. We are marching on Rome as soon as the legions are organised. We must move swiftly before Carbo and the Senate have the chance to rally opposition against me."

Marcus Aurelius snorted contemptuously. "The Senate couldn't organise a party at the moment let alone stop you from returning to Italy, besides, once they get wind that you are on the move, my guess is that those who have openly supported Cinna and Carbo will flee Rome rather than resist you."

"Then let us hope that they see sense and do just that," said Sulla, his eyes flashed ice cold and his face set hard and unforgiving. "Because if there is anyone left in Rome who was responsible for murdering those innocent men then they will rue the day that they did not run. I am returning to Rome and this time *no one* and *nothing* is going to stop me."

Caesar was spending a rare moment of peace; alone in his study he could indulge in a little light reading that had nothing whatsoever to do with religion, and he was relishing this special moment. His mind drifted briefly to his wife, who was absent, consoling her mother over the death of Cinna, her beloved husband. Caesar was relieved that Cinnilla had shown very little emotion when she had heard about the death of her father, for he had no kind words or fond memories to offer her as comfort.

His reverie was brought to a sudden halt as his steward entered the room and announced that Marcus Marius was requesting an audience. Pleased to be able to take the opportunity to see his friend again, Caesar ordered refreshments and welcomed Marcus into his study.

"Marcus, what brings you here?" said Caesar good-humouredly. "It's good to see you."

Marcus grinned as he bowed to Caesar. "I hope you don't mind me calling in Caes…Holy one."

"It's Caesar in private, remember?" Caesar laughed.

"Yes, sorry, I'll try."

"Please, sit down, the steward is sending refreshments," Caesar said, settling comfortably into one of the chairs.

Marcus took a seat opposite Caesar and waited as a slave entered the study and placed a wooden tray of wine, water and goblets down on the nearby table.

"Thank you, we shall see to it ourselves," said Caesar, dismissing the slave from the room.

"I'll get it," said Marcus, rising and walking over to pour the drinks. "So, how is married life? Is Cinnilla well? I was sorry to hear about her father."

"Good, yes, and I wasn't!" Caesar smiled. "Now, enough small talk, tell me why you are really here, Marcus?"

Marcus laughed as he handed a plain clay goblet to Caesar and resumed his own seat. "You are still the same. Nothing ever escapes you does it?"

"Of course I'm the same, now, come on, tell all."

"All right, well I have come to say good-bye," said Marcus, taking a sip of wine.

"Good-bye?"

"Yes, I am off to join the legions; the Sixth, to be precise, under the command of Lucius Cornelius Scipio."

Caesar was overwhelmed with an intense feeling of jealousy. All the years he had dreamed of the day he would announce to his father that he to was joining the legions flashed before his eyes, but his dreams, and his father, had both died, and all he had left was an emptiness that never seemed to go away. "And when did you decide this?" His voice sounded cold, hard and full of bitterness to his own ears.

"Well, it came about rather suddenly, actually. Scipio wrote to my mother offering Young Marius a post as junior legate and me a place as a junior cadet. He was a good friend of father's and he keeps in touch with mother as often as he can. Of course, Young Marius will go as a legate because of his previous experience in service with Strabo's legions, and, I thought it would be foolish to not accept, don't you think?"

"I see, well, that is good news. I wish you every success," Caesar replied stiffly, but he instantly regretted his words when he saw the happiness drain from his friend's face.

"Oh Caesar, I am sorry, I didn't think! Of course this is going to be hard for you, I should have realised, but I was so excited and I wanted you to be the first to know."

Caesar sighed, "No, Marcus, it is I who should apologise. It's not your fault and you have every right to be excited, I know I would be the same, in your position. I am truly happy for you Marcus; it was a surprise that's all."

Marcus's face brightened. "I know, and it is for me too. Mother was against it at first but Young Marius persuaded her to let me go. That's the first decent thing my brother has ever done for me." Marcus said with a wry smile.

Caesar sipped his water as his jealousy subsided to be replaced by a grudging acceptance of resignation to his own fate. "So, what will your legion be doing? Are you replacing a garrison in one of the provinces?"

"Garrison? Oh, no, Caesar, better than that. We are going to fight Sulla!"

Caesar choked on his water. "Sulla?"

Marcus grabbed a cloth from inside his tunic and offered it to Caesar, laughing as his friend coughed and sputtered. "Isn't it wonderful? Carbo has instructed Scipio to bring his legions up to Arretium to join the main army because Sulla is on the move and all the signs point to his return to Italy. There's going to be a war, Caesar, and I'm going to be in it!" Marcus's eyes danced with youthful anticipation at what was to come.

Caesar could see the excitement written over Marcus's face but all he had was a cold feeling of dread settling in the pit of his stomach. "Is this true? Is Sulla really marching on Rome?"

"Well, if he isn't, then he is doing a good job of making everyone think that he is. He's arrived in Macedonia at the head of five legions and six thousand Calvary. Reports say that he is recruiting more men as he goes. I tell you, Caesar, if he does cross into Italy then there's going to be a massive battle. Carbo is gathering legions to his standard claiming to represent the Republic, and freedom, against the threat that Sulla poses."

"I understand that this is an exciting prospect for you, Marcus, but have you really thought through what this might mean for you, and Young Marius?"

"What do you mean?" Marcus looked puzzled.

"I mean, that you are both the son's of Gaius Marius going to war against Sulla. What happens if you are captured? Do you think Sulla will show you mercy because you are young? He has sworn revenge against all those who supported Marius and Cinna for the murder of his friends. He would love nothing better than to have the two sons of Marius at his mercy."

Marcus laughed. "Captured? I won't be captured, Caesar! Anyway, if I am in danger of Sulla's revenge then so are you. Your father worked for Cinna and he was related to Marius, and, you are married to Cinna's daughter. If that doesn't show Sulla where your family loyalties are then I don't know what will."

Of all the things Marcus could have said, this statement of the obvious was more than Caesar could take. For months he had pondered on the consequences of Sulla's return to Rome, and what it would mean for his family. Everything Marcus had said was true, but to hear the words spoken aloud made the whole nightmare become a very real reality, and the helpless frustration he had felt for so long boiled over into anger.

"My father was given no choice! If he did not comply with what was asked of him then he would have ended up dead, and Marius arranged my marriage, not my father, as you well know. None of us had a choice if we valued our lives, and my father put his family first, whatever anyone else might say. *If* Sulla returns, then he will understand the position we were placed in."

"Oh, and he's going to take the time to ask, is he? Do you think you will be given the opportunity to explain? Come on, Caesar, as far as Sulla is concerned your family were Marian supporters, and that is that. The only thing that can protect you, if Sulla returns, is the priesthood, for you are inviolate, and so is Cinnilla as Cinna's daughter. Perhaps being the Flamen Dialis will be the saving of you after all. Anyway…" said Marcus, taking another sip of wine, "Sulla won't win, so it's not a consideration. We will defeat him before his feet ever touch Italian soil."

"And if you don't, what then, Marcus?"

"We will, Caesar, we have to. If Sulla wins then the consequences for Rome do not bare thinking about. You think Gaius Marius and Cinna were sadistic but it will be nothing to the carnage Sulla will cause in his lust for revenge. It's in all our interests to fight his return, every last man of us, and I intend to be there, to be part of history so that I can tell my grandchildren that I was part of the great war that rid the Republic of her greatest enemy, Lucius Cornelius Sulla!"

Caesar could see that Marcus was wrapped up in the excitement and expectation of the great adventure before him to see anything rationally and so he let his friend ramble on, whilst inside, the coldness of fear for the unknown, and the devastating consequences if Sulla returned, lay heavy on his heart.

The parting was a formal affair-Marcus bowing respectfully one last time to his priest-friend. Caesar watched as Marcus walked quickly along the street and wondered when, or indeed if, he would ever see him again.

As Marcus reached the corner he suddenly stopped and looked back. "I almost forgot. Tell Aemi that I haven't forgotten and I will keep looking, I promise!"

"Keep looking for what?" Caesar shouted, but Marcus just waved his hand cheerfully and disappeared round the corner.

# CHAPTER SIXTEEN

"Veni, Vidi, Vici."
*I came, I saw, I conquered*
*(Gaius Julius Caesar)*

## ROME 83BC

*Senior Consul: Lucius Cornelius Scipio Asiaticus*
*Junior Consul: Gaius Norbanus*

*The newly elected Consuls wasted no time in stepping up the campaign to recruit men for their legions in preparation for the inevitable war with Sulla.*

*Within a month they were able to leave Rome in the care of the Senate as they lead over one hundred thousand legionaries and auxiliaries north to join Proconsul Carbo, and the main army. Fear of Sulla's impending arrival in Italy drove many men to join the consular forces as they marched north. Even though the People still mistrusted Carbo, the new Consuls represented salvation for the Republic, for Sulla was coming home with revenge in his heart.*

*Meanwhile, Sulla sailed from Patrae in Macedonia with one thousand six hundred ships, and an army of over forty thousand men. He landed at Brundisium, in southern Italy, and was joined almost immediately by Caecilius Metellus Pius and Gnaus Pompeius, son of the old general, Pompeius Strabo, together with their legions. Both men offered their allegiance, and their men, to Sulla.*

*The first battle was fought at Canusium, one hundred miles north of Brundisium, between Sulla, with his deputy Metellus Pius, and the Junior Consul, Gaius Norbanus. The Consul's army was all but annihilated with over six thousand men lost in a single day, against Sulla's seventy, and Norbanus fled the field. Sulla followed mercilessly behind, destroying all that lay in his path…*

After a busy day of priestly duties, Caesar had returned home to find Cinnilla absent, visiting her mother, and a free evening all to himself. Taking advantage of this rare opportunity, he went straight to his study. He had been relieved to receive a letter from Marcus, earlier in the day, and, snatching the letter up from his desk, he settled down on the couch and re-read the letter for the third time.

*'…Unfortunately I was ordered to remain in the rearguard so I missed out on the actual battle itself, but, Caesar, it was a glorious sight to behold. All the stories that Father used to tell us about the battles he had fought were nothing compared to actually being involved in the real thing. Feeling the rush of blood in your veins as the trumpets sound the advance is indescribable, and you do not know whether it is fear or excitement that you feel as you watch the rows of legions from each side*

*come together in an almightily crash of swords and screams. Our men fought hard and long but the combined force of Sulla and Metellus Pius proved to be too strong for us. I actually saw Sulla from a distance, sitting on top of a hill on his white horse, directing the battle. He looked so calm and in control, which is more than can be said for my general, Norbanus, for he lost his head completely. Of course for we were defeated and had to withdraw quickly, although my brother, put up a good fight with his cohort, but in the end Norbanus had to order him to withdraw from the field otherwise he would have continued to fight to the last man. We are now inland, near Capua, waiting for the final stragglers to catch up with us before we head off to regroup with Carbo. I must end now, for duty calls. Please send my love to Mother. I have not written to her for fear that news of battles and bloodshed will upset her more than she already is and so I would be obliged if you could tell her that I am well and happy. I miss you, Caesar and I wish you could be here with me, seeing what I see, and living the dream we shared. These are truly exciting times and I am most fortunate to be playing a part in Rome's glorious history. I will write when I can.*

*Your friend always,*
*Marcus Marius.*

Caesar smiled as he finished the letter. He could imagine the frustration Marcus would be feeling at not being allowed to participate directly in the battle because he had always been a fighter. The smile faded from his lips and he sighed as he put the letter into the table drawer and locked it. At least Marcus was there, experiencing the thrill and anticipation of war. He would never get the chance to fight for Rome, stuck as he was in the shackles of the priesthood, and, as much as he would look forward to receiving the letters from Marcus he knew it would be hard on himself, to live his dreams through the eyes of another. The gloomy walls of the study seemed to be closing in on him and he had an overwhelming urge to escape his prison. Minutes later he had summoned his litter, and set off to see Aemi.

When Caesar arrived, Aemi was just settling down to his evening meal. Refusing his friend's kind offer to partake of the food, Caesar settled down onto his couch and watched enviously as Aemi set about tucking in to all the fine delicacies he could now only dream of eating. Numerous braziers and torches lit up the room, giving it a warm, cosy, if somewhat opulent feeling, and as the light reflected of the highly polished silver wear that covered the table, loaded with succulent food, Caesar felt a pang of longing for the life he once had.

"I still find it hard to believe that Marcus is in the legions. It seems like only yesterday that we were down the Campus playing with our wooden swords," said Aemi, picking the dry skin off an apricot.

"I feel the same way, but at least his life is moving on. He is realising his dream, which is more than can be said for me," said Caesar, feeling sorry for himself. "First Marcus; you will be next, and I-I will be left in Rome alone with only my musty old books for company. It's *so* unfair!"

"I know, Caesar, and I do understand. For weeks now I've been trying to see you but you're always so busy. I miss spending time together, and sometimes it feels as though you have gone away too."

"I just wish…Oh, I don't know," Caesar sighed, and took a sip of water from his goblet.

"Are you sure you don't want something to eat? I can get the cook to make you something; anything you like."

"No, thank you, I find it easier to eat at home, at least that way I know I will not be contaminating this, oh so holy body of mine," Caesar grumbled moodily.

Aemi shrugged and reached for an apple off the large silver platter that lay on the table in front of his couch where he reclined leisurely. "The war will be over soon, Caesar, and Marcus will come home again. I heard Scipio's legions have abandoned him en-masse, leaving him and his son alone in their tent to be captured, and Norbanus is running around the countryside with Sulla hard on his heels. Apparently both armies are devastating everything that lays in their path in the hope of starving each other into submission. Marcus will no doubt spend the whole of his war running away from Sulla's army so that I doubt if his sword will see much blood." Aemi chuckled at the thought.

"How do you know all this information?" Caesar asked, amazed at the depth of knowledge Aemi had about the current state of affairs between the consular army and Sulla.

"My clients write to me with news. I have several in Metellus Pius's legions alone, and they keep me informed of progress," Aemi said casually.

"Oh, I see," Caesar nodded.

"Actually, I have been very lucky with the clients I inherited from father. Most have sworn allegiance to me, and I have plenty of men on hand if I ever need any help or advice with business matters. On the whole they don't pester me too much, I suppose I'm too young to be much use to them at the moment."

"Then I know where to come if I want some information about the war," said Caesar with a grin.

"Anytime, Caesar, anytime," said Aemi, with a mock air of superiority.

"That reminds me, talking about information. Marcus asked me to give you a message before he left. He said to tell you that he had not forgotten and he would keep looking. He said you would know what he meant."

"Oh, yes," said Aemi, looking casually at Caesar as he took a bite out of an apple.

"What did he mean?"

"Oh, it was nothing really. I asked him to keep an eye out for a particular kind of horse for my new stud farm; he said he might know someone who could help me, but, obviously he couldn't, and so he will keep looking."

Caesar frowned. The look on Aemi's face and the fact that he admitted to having any communication with Marcus was suspicious. "But you don't speak to Marcus. Why would you involve him in business of yours?"

"We are not friends anymore; we could never go back to the way things were, but we do speak when we need too."

"And this horse is so important to you that you involved Marcus?" persisted Caesar. He knew Aemi was lying.

"Obviously, or I wouldn't have spoken to Marcus, would I?" Aemi replied, taking another bite of apple and avoiding Caesar's questioning gaze.

"No... I don't suppose you would." Caesar continued to eye his friend cautiously, but it was obvious that Aemi was not going to tell him the truth.

"Tell me, Caesar, changing the subject, did you speak to your mother about the prophecy?"

"What...Oh yes, though there is nothing much to add. She says she can't remember what the prophecy said and that I should forget all about it. Mother made it quite clear that she had no intention of discussing the subject again, so, I suppose I will never know now."

"No, I do not suppose you will," Aemi replied, looking thoughtful. "Ah well, don't give up, Caesar, something may yet happen to change your life."

"I shall never give up, not whilst I still have breath in my body. I know, inside me, that this life was not meant for me and that my true destiny lies elsewhere, but just how I can ever be released from the priesthood evades me."

"I was told that if the Flamen's wife died then he could be released from the priesthood, is that correct?"

"It is, yes, but Cinnilla is so young and healthy that I can't see anything happening to her, and anyway, I would not wish the death of my wife over my own personal desires. No, there is no way out for me, I will just have to live the life I have been given and try to accept it." Caesar sighed.

"Cinnilla could die in childbirth. Many women die that way."

"Aemi! Please, I don't want to think about such things."

"I know, but it is a sad fact of life. Perhaps the only way you will be free is for a tragedy like that to happen, if, as you say, there is no other route of escape."

Caesar sighed again and rested his head on the back of his chair. To contemplate the death of his wife was something he shied away from and he wondered if the unthinkable occurred and Cinnilla died, would he use that opportunity to release himself from the priesthood?

Aemi picked at a bowl of sweetmeats, examined several very carefully and finally popped the chosen specimen into his mouth. "You were always so certain of your destiny, Caesar, and I used to envy you that, but it seems that the gods have a different path for us to take after all, and no matter how much you might believe your life lays in one particular direction, they may decide differently. I'm happy for my life to unfold as it will, that way I won't suffer the agonies that I see you go through."

"Then it is I who envy you, Aemi, for you still have that choice. I would give anything to be where you are now, free to decide what you do and when to do it. Your hearts desire can be yours if you choose to take it or not. You have free will; you have freedom."

"Yes, I do, but it came at a price don't forget. I would rather be where you are and have my father back with me than live with the memory of his loss. He was torn from my arms, and nothing, nothing, can ever make up for that day. I see that moment over and over in my mind, even now, and I wonder what I could have done to save him."

Caesar saw the pain of his loss etched on Aemi's face and his heart went out to him in sympathy. "I am sorry, Aemi, I didn't realise that the loss of your father still hurt you so much."

"Well it does, though time is helping to take the pain away, as you must know with the death of your own father being only recent. That's why I could never be friends with Marcus again. When I see him it's a reminder of what his father did to mine and I want to hurt him, the way Gaius Marius hurt me and my family."

"But you can't hold Marcus responsible for the actions of his father, Aemi. Surely you must know that he was as appalled at what happened, as we all were. You were his friend, and what hurt you, hurt him too. Can you not bring yourself to believe that? There is still time to mend the friendship if you wanted too."

Aemi frowned and shook his head. "No, it is too late for that, Caesar, and you say Marcus did not condone what happened to my father yet he has joined the legions against Sulla. If Marcus truly believed that what Gaius Marius did was so wrong then why has he done that?"

"What choice did he have Aemi? Do you think Sulla would pass up the chance to punish the son's of his greatest enemy? Gaius Marius drove Sulla's family from Rome in terror of their lives, his young children smuggled out in an old vegetable cart. Now Marius is dead but his son's still live. If Sulla ever gets his hands on Marcus, or Young Marius, he will not let them live, I am certain of that. Marcus is fighting to save his own life."

Aemi snorted. "Then by rights I should join Sulla's army to seek revenge for the death of my father. The Republic is rotten to the core and it will take a man of Sulla's calibre to return Rome to her former glory. Justice must be seen to be done, and, Sulla is the man to do it!" said Aemi passionately. "Indeed, the more I think on, it the more I realise that is exactly what I should do. You are right, Caesar. I have my freedom and I have the choice, so there's nothing to stop me, is there?"

Caesar slid forward to the edge of his couch, horrified at the turn this idle conversation had taken. "You can't, you mustn't, Aemi! You are too young and…and it is too dangerous. You could get killed!"

"I am a year older than you, and Marcus, the age when I should be considering my military career, and as for it being too dangerous, well you really are scrapping the barrel for excuses, Caesar. Marcus has gone to fight for a cause he believes in so why shouldn't I? And you would go too, if you were able, so don't deny it." Aemi's face was flushed with excitement.

Caesar reddened with indignation, though deep down he knew Aemi's words were justified. As with Marcus, Caesar realised that his resentment stemmed from his own frustrations. First Marcus, and now Aemi was set to leave, abandoning him to the straightjacket of religious life.

"It is easy to pledge your allegiance in the heat of the moment, Aemi, but is this path truly what you would choose?"

"Do you ask because you care for me or is it because you are jealous that I can choose what you cannot?" Aemi retorted angrily.

Caesar stood up and paced the floor, his mind in turmoil, whilst Aemi glowered into his goblet.

"Yes, I admit that I am jealous," Caesar said finally, facing up to his weakness. "I am jealous of Marcus doing what he is doing and I am jealous that you could take the same path, leaving me behind, but, Aemi, I do care for you too, you know that, and I want what is best for you."

Aemi's face softened at Caesar's admission. "At least you are being honest with me and I thank you for it, Caesar, but I am free to follow my own destiny and perhaps I have just found it. Surely you will not begrudge me the chance to find out?"

Caesar sighed and ran his hand through his hair. "No, Aemi, I don' begrudge you this for it is your right, and, as you say, this could indeed be your destiny. I'm sorry for my failings as a friend; my life is set, but yours, well it may just be beginning. I shall miss you," he said with a smile of resignation.

"And I you, but this is a way I can honour my father and avenge his death and if that means joining Sulla, then so be it."

Caesar stared moodily at the red and gold silk curtains that surrounded him as he swayed to the gentle rhythm of the litter. The conversation with Aemi had done nothing to ease he growing sense of resentment against the life he was being forced to lead, and then to top it all, Aemi had told him that Young Marius had been elected as Consul for the forthcoming year, even though he had not even started his political career in the Senate. Everyone he knew was moving on, their lives changing in ways he could never have imagined, whilst his own was nothing but what ifs and maybes. Caesar's mind turned to the prophecy, the little glimmer of light in this sea of black emptiness, but even that was all questions and no answers! The frustration that he had felt for so long steamed and boiled inside him. Was this it? Was this all life had to offer him after all those years of expectation; of waiting to come of age so that he could begin to follow the path he knew was rightfully his? Inside, Caesar clung on to the idea that his was to be no ordinary life; that his destiny was to carry him forward to the take his place amongst the greats of the known world, but how would that ever happen whilst he was the Flamen Dialis?

"Stop!" he commanded. The litter came to a sudden halt and Teubod, his chief escort, stuck his head through the curtain and looked quizzically at his master. "Put the litter on the ground." Caesar commanded.

"But we are nearly home, Master; just a little further…"

"Do not argue!" The litter was lowered slowly to the floor and Caesar yanked back the curtain, placing both feet over the side as he struggled to get out.

"No, Holy One, you cannot walk on this ground, it's not sacred!" Teubod gasped, as Caesar heaved himself out of the litter.

"I have had enough of being told what I can and cannot do!" Caesar exploded angrily. "I will do what *I* want to do and let the gods strike me down for defiling this holy body if they are so inclined, because I don't care anymore!"

Teubod cowered in fear and the litter bearers stared at their master in amazement. That the Flamen should defy the rules that so rigidly surrounded him was unthinkable but they stood by helplessly, unable to stop this religious sacrilege.

"I walk, and I walk alone!" Caesar snapped. "No arguments, Teubod. My word is law, now go!"

The slaves needed no encouragement to leave, hastily picking up the wooden shafts of the litter and setting off at a quick walk towards the Forum. Teubod lingered, hopping from foot to foot but Caesar ignored his faithful servant. The anger inside him was flowing free now and he did not care what the consequences of his actions would be. At that moment nothing seemed to matter any more, and when he finally entered the house he brushed past his wife without a word and entered his study, locking himself in and refusing to answer his wife's pleading sobs for two long days.

The Gaius Julius Caesar that had walked into the study, a confused and angry young man came out a different person. The solitude had allowed him to explore his innermost feelings and confront his demons. Now, he was more reserved, serious and accepting of his fate. The boyhood dreams and ambitions had been left behind in that room to be replaced by a grudging acceptance that he would be the Flamen Dialis for the rest of his life. The past was put behind him and he threw himself into his new life with the grim determination of one who had resolved to make the very best of what he had been given.

*The winter months curtailed the armies of either side from engaging in further battles, therefore Sulla and Carbo contented themselves with concerted efforts to recruit more men to their cause.*

*Carbo used the appointment of Young Marius, as Junior Consul for the coming year to stir the allegiance of men who had once served under Gaius Marius and they flocked to the son of the great man hoping to see in him the shadow of his father.*

*Sulla used his charisma and strength, and when that failed he used bribery, reward and finally threats to win men over to his side.*

*Rome was still reeling from the after affects of the great fire that had swept through the Capitol destroying many of the ancient and revered buildings of the City. This disaster had been followed shortly afterwards by a series of devastating earthquakes that had destroyed many of the buildings weakened by the fire. Ancient Oracles were remembered foretelling the fate of Rome and her people. Stories abounded of women giving birth to snakes, strange birds seen flying backwards away from the sun, and on one particular night, the moon was blood red and hung low on the horizon. All of Italy listened and shook at the stories, and the people cried to their gods that they had been forsaken. The whole country waited in dread for the frosts to clear, for they knew that as soon as the roads were passable, the two great armies would begin their inexorable march towards death or glory and the future of the Roman Republic would be decided once and for all.*

# CHAPTER SEVENTEEN

*"Empire and Liberty"*
*(Marcus Tullius Cicero)*

## ROME: January-June 82 BC

*Senior Consul: Gnaeus Papirius Carbo (2)*
*Junior Consul: Gaius Marius (Jnr)*

*The first great battle of the new year was fought on the banks of the river Aesis, between Metellus Pius, and Carinas, an adherent of Carbo. Both sides fought long and hard, with the battle lasting over several hours, but finally, Carinas's legions, sensing imminent defeat, turned and ran, suffering heavy losses. Carinas rounded up what was left of his army and ran back to Carbo.*

*Whilst Metellus Pius was thus engaged, Sulla was involved in a battle of his own at Signia, against the Junior Consul, Young Marius, and his army. Sulla's men fought with tremendous tenacity and the battle was bitter for both sides. The turning point came when seven of Young Marius's cohorts suddenly abandoned their Consul and defected over to Sulla. Young Marius and his remaining men turned and fled, heading for the nearest town that remained loyal to his cause, Praeneste. Once the majority of men were inside the walled city, the townspeople closed the gates. The unfortunate men left outside put up a brave fight against Sulla's advance party but they were outnumbered and their resistance was crushed. Sulla later wrote in his diary that this battle had cost him only twenty three men dead, whilst his enemy lost over twenty thousand men, and, over eight thousand more were held captive. Praeneste was besieged leaving no way in or out of the city. Young Marius's war was over, and, barring a miracle, so was his life.*

*Telesinus, the Samnite leader, who had joined forces with Carbo, was sent to relieve the siege of Praeneste, but as he drew close to the city he realised that he was in danger of being caught in a pincer movement, between Pompeius and Sulla. Telesinus realised that Praeneste was lost, and so in the spirit of the war-like Samnites, he set his sights further a field, towards a bigger prize, and deftly avoiding Sulla and Pompeius he began to march on Rome.*

"Make way! Make way!" The young legate, Catalus Caesar shouted, as he rode his lathered horse at speed down the central street in the vast, canvas village of Sulla's army. Men and animals leapt to safety as horse and rider negotiated several crossroads that dissected the encampment; a portable settlement of tents, shops and stables. The command tent stood alone on a hilly outcrop, overlooking the camp, and he urged his horse onwards. Within minutes, Catalus Caesar reached his destination, pulling up his horse so sharply that it slid to a halt on its haunches. In one swift movement, he vaulted to the ground and hurried over to the group of officers huddled round a large table covered in maps. Catalus Caesar saluted his general and waited for a response.

"Report," Sulla ordered without looking up at the messenger. His brow was furrowed as he stared intently at the mass of lines and symbols etched on the large sheet of parchment before him.

"Quintus Caecilius Metellus sends greetings, General. He wishes to report that his army has engaged in battle with the combined legions of Carbo and Norbanus, near Faventia. The enemy was routed with the loss of over ten thousand men whilst a further six thousand deserted to our legions. Carbo and Norbanus both managed to evade capture and early reports indicate that Norbanus had fled Italy by ship, whilst Carbo remains, as yet, undetected but we believe he has not left the country."

"Excellent news!" Dollabella whooped enthusiastically. "Good for Metellus!"

Sulla dragged his tired gaze from the map and fixed his piercing, pale eyes on the legate. "Yes, indeed. Norbanus has fled Italy, eh? He never did have a stomach for battle," he added contemptuously. "You say Carbo is still believed to be in Italy?"

"Yes, General. Quintus Caecilius Metellus believes that he may be making his way towards Ariminium with the remains of his army, but, our spies have been unable to confirm that as yet."

Further conversation was cut short by the sudden arrival of a second rider. Mud stained and obviously weary, his horse covered in foamy sweat, Sulla recognised the man as one of his outriders, sent to locate the Samnite army.

Sulla stretched and rubbed his sore back as the outrider approached. He could see from the young man's face that something was wrong. "What news?" he demanded.

The rider saluted hastily. "General, the Samnites have avoided Pompeius's legions and...and they are marching on Rome."

"What?" Dollabella gasped.

"How close are they?" Sulla's face remained an implacable mask of self-control compared to his fellow officers who stood beside him.

"They have set up camp nine furlongs from Rome, General."

"By all the gods!" Lucullus exclaimed. "Pompeius was supposed to keep those treacherous Samnites in view! What is he playing at, the stupid young idiot?"

Dollabella slammed his fist down on the table. "All he had to do was drive them towards us, and we could have finished them off! I told you, you should not have given that young puppy responsibility like that, Sulla. Now look what he's done!"

"Be that as it may, the situation has changed and we have to adapt to it and not waste time on recriminations!" Sulla snapped. He was only too aware of the derision his decision to leave young Pompeius in charge of his own legion had been to his older and more experienced senior officers, and, now it appeared that his confidence had been misplaced after all. Sulla hated being wrong, but he hated having his mistakes broadcast in public even more. He threw an icy glare at Dollabella. "How near to our current position is Pompeius?" he asked the rider.

"Two days march at most, General."

Sulla bent over the map, his eyes frantically scanning the area for answers. "So that makes us the nearest army to the Samnites, though we ourselves are more than a days march behind them," he muttered to himself.

"We'll never reach them in time," said Dollabella. "If they are already camped for the night then they'll be fresh to march on Rome by the morning. We have no hope of engaging them before they reach the city. Rome is lost!"

"Rome is not lost!" Sulla snarled, turning his blazing anger on Dollabella. "I do not lose!"

"Dollabella is right, Sulla. We are too far behind the Samnites to stop them. They will take Rome and hold the city before nightfall tomorrow." Lucullus said.

"Get Balbus here, now!" Sulla shouted at a nearby guard. "Now," Sulla said, turning back to look at his map. "How large is the Samnite army; do you know?" he asked the rider.

"Seventy thousand men, General, and we believe they may be waiting for reinforcements before they attack Rome. Reports say that the Lucaians, led by Albinus, are making their way to join them."

"Then all is lost," moaned Dollabella. "There aren't enough men left inside Rome to defend the city."

"The people might not even realise that it is the Samnites that are advancing on the city until it is too late to do anything about it. Once they set foot inside Rome they won't stop until they have plundered the city wholesale and murdered every Roman they can find, because, let's face it, the Samnites only joined with Carbo because they had a legitimate excuse to kill Romans. They have no real affiliation for either side, and if Rome falls then they will have achieved their only desire, the destruction of their life long enemies," Lucullus said gravely.

Sulla took a deep breath and stared once more at the map laid out in front of him. His mind raced over the possibilities before him but he did not have the luxury of time. Every second that he delayed would be one second closer to the fall of Rome. His thoughts were disturbed by the arrival of Balbus, commander of the cavalry.

Balbus looked enquiringly at the glum faces of his colleagues. "Something up?" he asked.

"Balbus, how many of your men do you have that are fit and ready to ride?"

"Approximately seven hundred, Sulla, though a few more days rest would not go amiss; the horses are very tired."

"We don't have a few days, Balbus. Get your men ready and prepare to move out."

"What now? Why the rush?" Balbus looked at Dollabella and Lucullus for an explanation but they just shrugged their shoulders and looked at Sulla.

"I want you ready and on your way to Rome within the hour. Every man and every horse; I don't care how tired they are, just get it organised."

"You want us to ride to Rome?" Balbus looked astonished. "Will someone tell me what is going on?"

Dollabella opened his mouth to speak but Sulla answered for him. "The Samnite army have avoided Pompeius's legions and have marched on Rome. They are currently camped nine furlongs from the Colline Gate, and we have reason to believe that the Lucaians are coming up to join them before they attack the city. There are approximately seventy thousand Samnites and the Lucaians have ten thousand men. I want you, with the cavalry, to engage the Samnites before they can enter the city. Do whatever you have to, but do not let them enter Rome, do you understand me, Balbus?"

"But they outnumber us ten times over, Sulla! How do you expect us to hold back eighty thousand? We don't stand a chance!" Balbus exploded.

"He's right, Sulla, those odds are fatal; how can they hope to win?" said Lucullus.

"They do not have to win, they just have to buy us time. You won't be on your own for too long, Balbus. With any luck, the People will realise the danger and defend the city. All you have to do is engage them and keep them busy until we arrive, which, by my estimate, will be approximately five hours after you. Hold them until I arrive, Balbus and we can do the rest," said Sulla firmly.

"We will have to ride through the night without a rest and engage in battle almost immediately when we get there," said Balbus incredulously.

"As will we," Sulla snapped. "But you *will* do it and we *will* relieve you, Balbus, this I swear on my honour. All I ask is that you trust me and do your best. Hold them long enough for us to reach you," Sulla could see that Balbus was not convinced that his plan would work, but he had no time for further arguments. "Well, what are you waiting for?"

Balbus nodded and saluted Sulla. "We will do our best to hold them, Sulla, for as long as is necessary." Without further ado, he turned on his heels and ran down the hill towards the main camp, shouting orders as he went.

"This is madness, Sulla!" Dollabella exclaimed. "How can you possibly expect the men to march over a hundred miles and fight a battle against an enemy that has superior numbers to our own and has had the luxury of a few days rest?"

Sulla ignored him and turned to Lucullus. "Where is Torquatus?"

"I haven't seen him this morning," said Lucullus, "But he should still be in the camp somewhere."

"Then find him. Tell him to prepare his men. We move out in two hours." Sulla's look and tone brooked no argument. Lucullus saluted and hurried away.

"Quintus," Sulla addressed the young legate. "Ride to Marcus Crassus, he and his men are camped two furlongs from here, to the east. Tell him to prepare his men and march for Rome. He should catch us up on the way, and tell him, he is to report to me as soon as he does."

Catalus Caesar saluted, and, mounting his horse, galloped off across the camp.

"You're making a big mistake, Sulla," said Dollabella.

Sulla looked at his senior officer and smiled. "You forget, Gnaus, Fortuna smiles on me. That is why I have added the cognomen Felix, the ever fortunate. Balbus will hold the Samnites and we will be there to relieve him. Rome will not fall, not whilst I still have breath in my body."

"I still say that what you expect is the impossible. It simply cannot be done!" Dollabella insisted.

The change on Sulla's face was instant. Gone the smile and the warmth in his eyes, now his face was a pale, hardened mask. "I am Lucius Cornelius Sulla Felix. I make the impossible possible. We *will* reach Rome in time and we *will* defeat the Samnites in battle. Now go. You have your orders!" he snarled.

"Well, all I can say is that I hope your luck holds out, Sulla, because we are all going to need it." Dollabella turned on his heels and walked away to begin rallying his men.

Sulla watched as Dollabella disappeared amongst the tents of the camp and shrugged his shoulders. "That is the difference between men like you and me, Gnaius," he said aloud to himself. "You see the boundaries and you go no further. It is only the truly great men that see no boundaries at all. For us, anything is possible…anything."

The dawn mist lay heavily over the open plains of the Campus Martius, reducing the visibility to a few feet for the young men, the last vestiges of hope for Rome, who hurried about their duties as the cold light of day dawned.

Aemi took command of a cohort and he sat astride his chestnut stallion, in full battle uniform, watching his men scurry into formation. He could feel his heart knocking against the metal restraint of his silver plated curais and his stomach churned with knots of alternate fear and excitement as the time drew nearer to March. He thought of Caesar and wondered what his friend would say if he could see him now? Aemi supposed Caesar would be cool and collected as always, and, no doubt would have taken the whole thing in his stride, but he was not Caesar, and he silently acknowledged that he was scared. Never in his wildest dreams could he have imagined that this day would come. When he was seventeen, the age when most young Roman noblemen joined the legions as a cadet, Aemi had decided to defer his entry. It wasn't that he shunned battle, or the military life, but after his father's death he had found his interest leaning more towards the law courts, where his father had been a renowned advocate in his day. Now, here he was, preparing for battle, leader of a cohort of young men, most of whom had only just left their childhood behind them, and preparing to march against an enemy ten times their number; the last defence to save Rome. Aemi had been given his orders before the first fingers of daylight crept above the horizon. The young army were to remain in marching column until the enemy came in sight, when they would deploy into battle formation, with Aemi's cohort on the left wing. With over two thirds of his men on horseback they would perform the traditional role of the cavalry units in the legions, harrying the enemy and engaging in disciplined charges against the foot men of the enemy.

Aemi summoned his young lieutenants to give them their orders, each of whom had responsibility for one section of men, when the horn sounded to prepare to march. The lieutenants melted back into the mist to take up their positions as the horn sounded two short blasts, the signal to begin the march. The rumble of thousands of feet and hooves could be heard behind the walls of Rome as the young men set forth to confront their destiny with the cries of their mothers filling the air, wailing and praying for the safe return of their sons.

Less than an hour into the march the mists began to rise as the early morning sun dried the dew from the ground. Aemi rode along in silence, the sound of hob nailed boots and horses hooves pounding in his ears. The dust kicked up by so many feet filled the air and was so thick that those with neckerchiefs drew them up over the mouth and nose to stop themselves from choking. Aemi remembered the last time he had seen the unmistakable signs of an army on the move, standing on the walls of Rome, when he was still a young boy. Together with Marcus and Caesar, he had watched the dust cloud formed by the approaching legions of Sulla as he marched to Rome in defiance of Gaius Marius. Now, he found himself in the middle of a dust cloud created by his own army, and he wondered if there were three young boys in Rome, this morning, who had stood on top of the walls and watched in awe, just as he had, so many years ago. Aemi glanced behind to see that his men remained in formation; first the three lines of foot men walking eight abreast and behind them the lines of cavalry, sixty horses, four abreast, to keep to the narrow road that they travelled on.

"Hey, Aemi…Who would have imagined this?" His friend, Gaius Trebonius called out, from the second row of footmen. Aemi smiled and nodded in agreement.

Three short blasts of the horn signalled a general halt and Aemi rode out from the line to see if anything was happening further up ahead.

"Battle formation! Battle formation!" a young cadet shouted, as he galloped past.

Almost immediately, pandemonium broke out, with men and horses moving off in all directions. Aemi took his mark from the century in front of him and shouted at his men to form up on the left. His lieutenants repeated his order down the line and slowly the men formed into the standard battle formation of the roman legions; footmen in the front ranks, cavalry to the sides and rear.

Lucius Appius Claudius suddenly appeared at Aemi's side, his horse already covered in sweat from galloping to and fro along the lines. As second in command, due to his brief stint of duty under Pompeius Strabo, as a cadet, Lucius set to work reassuring the young men that if they stayed together and followed orders they would survive. "Cover the left wing, Aemi," Lucius ordered, as his horse sidled nervously. "We don't know how many cavalry the Samnites are fielding but it will be your job to engage any that threaten our wings, or try to outflank us, understand?"

Aemi nodded.

"If the signal is given to retreat then you are to cover our backs, as will Marcus Junius, over on the right flank. Work together if you have to, but…" Lucius was interrupted by six short blasts of the horn. "The enemy are in sight! Stand fast men, and remember we fight for Rome! May Fortuna smile on you this day, Aemi," Lucius said gravely, and with a salute, he spurred his horse away down the line.

Aemi's stallion sensed the tension of the men and tossed his head impatiently, pawing the ground as Aemi addressed his cohort. "Remember, men, stay with me and work together. If a man falls, leave him. Do not break the line! If we are called to retreat, it will be our job to protect the rear. Does everyone understand?"

"Look over there! Samnites!" a young man shouted from the front rank of foot men, and all heads turned as one to look at where he pointed. Spread along the top of the ridge less than a furlong away, row after row of men appeared, their pilliums held high, metal tips glinting in the sunlight. A murmur of fear ran through the ranks as the full extent of the enemy's numbers became apparent. As far as the eye could see, the Samnites held the ridge, seventy thousand battle hardened men, refreshed and ready to do battle with the outnumbered, and inexperienced, youth of Rome.

"Look at them, there are thousands of them!"

"We don't stand a chance!"

"This is madness; we will surely die!"

"Oh, Mars protect us!"

"Stand firm!" Aemi shouted, refusing to be overtaken by the fear that was gripping his men.

"They are coming! By all the gods…"

"Stand firm and hold the line!" Aemi's stallion half reared as his master shouted. "We are Romans. We are invincible! We will not be defeated! Remember who you are, and, remember that the gods are with us. Fight for Rome. *Roma Victorious*!"

"*Roma Victorious*!" his men cried, and raised their pilliums in the air.

Two sharp blasts of the horn sounded the advance and the young men clasped their tall shields to their chests. Swords were drawn from scabbards and held at the ready, their faces set in grim determination. Aemi held on tight to his prancing horse and prayed harder than he had ever prayed in his life.

It was a massacre. Less than a third of the Samnite army engaged in battle, the rest watched the wholesale slaughter of the young men as though they were spectators at the gladiatorial games. In less than an hour the retreat was sounded and the young men of Rome turned and fled.

Balbus, and his seven hundred cavalry had reached Rome, against all the odds, just as Sulla predicted. Pausing only to water the exhausted men and horses, they swooped down onto the unsuspecting Samnite army, who were gathered near to the Colline Gate, making a concerted effort to break into the City. Balbus and his men did their job well, drawing attention away from the Gate, whilst up on the battlements of the city walls the People renewed their efforts to keep the enemy at bay with arrows, clubs, stones and anything else that could be used as a weapon. Norbanus managed to rally what was left of the youth army and together they slipped through the gates and joined in the battle, Aemi amongst them; slicing, hacking, stabbing, biting, kicking, anything to keep himself alive.

Sulla yanked hard on the reins and his stallion slid to a halt in a cloud of dust. From the top of the hill he could see Rome and the writhing, heaving melee of the battle, centred round the Colline Gate. Dollabella rode up beside Sulla, his bay horse literally dripping with sweat from the enforced march of the past few hours. Sulla's white stallion, its flanks heaving from exhaustion, skittered sideways, its red nostrils flared as it pored the ground excitedly.

"We made it in time!" Dollabella gasped as he wiped the sweat from his eyes.

Torquatus, and several other junior officers were next to join Sulla on top of the hill, and the sound panting men and horses filled the air.

"Tell the vanguard to take refreshment immediately," Sulla ordered one of his junior tribunes. "Dollabella, Torquatus, get your cohorts into battle formation. Dollabella, you take the left flank, and Torquatus stays centre with me. Crassus can take the right flank, when he arrives," he added, looking behind for signs of his senior officer.

"But what about the men…"

Sulla raised his hand to prevent Dollabella from speaking further. "Tell them to take a drink once they are in formation. We don't have time to stop now. Balbus is doing a good job, but he, and his men, need relieving before it's too late," Sulla snapped.

"This battle is too important to rush in to, Sulla, surely you can see that? The whole outcome of the war could depend upon it! You stand to lose everything if it should go against you," Dollabella urged.

Sulla shielded his eyes from the sun as he stared down the valley. It was difficult to ascertain what was happening, with thousands of men and animals kicking up the dust from the dry plain.

"Sulla… what are you going to do?" Dollabella pressed his commander for a decision.

Sulla felt a surge of steely resolve as he saw several of his cavalry officers appear out of the dust cloud, chasing a number of Samnite soldiers on foot. "Order the men into battle formation. We fight, and we fight now!" he said firmly. His horse pawed the ground excitedly and Sulla absently patted the animal's neck to settle it. He knew that he was taking a big gamble by throwing his travel weary men straight into battle but he also knew that Balbus, and the people defending the city, were holding the enemy at bay against tremendous odds. His men were needed on the field now, if he stood any chance of winning the day. Sulla reached inside the folds of his tunic for the small figurine of Apollo that he always carried with him in battle. His fingers found the smooth surface of the amulet and he pulled it out into the light. Putting it gently to his lips he intoned: "Apollo, god of my fortune, do not desert your most devoted servant in his hour of need. You, who have raised me up, look upon me now and show the world that I am most worthy to hold the name Lucius Cornelius Sulla Felix. Hear me, Apollo, and grant me this divine favour."

His prayer done, Sulla placed the figurine safely back into the folds of his tunic, and, with a final glance towards the battle field, turned his horse and rode off to prepare his men for battle.

*The battle raged on well into the night, with both sides fighting for their lives. The men could sense that whoever won this battle would win the war; the victor would hold Rome and all that it stood for. The Samnites had played their hand, proving, by marching on Rome, that they now fought for their interests alone. For centuries they had lived in subjugation of the Romans and it weighed heavy on this war-like, fiercely independent people. The opportunity to destroy the great city of the roman empire that they loathed and the call in their blood for the freedom they so badly desired ran deep, and made them fight the harder for it but, though all the odds were stacked against him, Lucius Cornelius Sulla Felix won the right to add this final cognomen to his name. Apollo listened to his prayer and granted him the greatest of wishes. Although the final fatalities for both sides reached fifty thousand men, Sulla triumphed.*

*Telesinis and Albinus were killed in battle, whilst the other generals, loyal to Senior Consul, Carbo, fled into the night, their army destroyed.*

*The battle was won; the war was all but over. As dawn spread its yellow fingers of daylight into the sky, Lucius Cornelius Sulla Felix entered Rome, the victor.*

"Caesar! It's good to see you," Aemi said, as he rose from his chair to greet his friend.

"I'm sorry it has been a few days, but I came as soon as I could," Caesar replied, nodding his thanks to the steward who had shown him in to Aemi's study. As he waited for the steward to leave, he was shocked to see how pale and tired Aemi looked. "I wanted to see for myself how you were. Please thank your mother for sending me the message to say that you were safe and well."

Aemi quickly turned away to pour some drinks but not before Caesar caught the pained look on his face.

"As you can see, I came through the battle relatively unscathed," Aemi smiled thinly, passing an ornately decorated wooden goblet to Caesar. "I had this made specially for you. I couldn't bare to see you drinking out of one of those plain clay cups any longer."

"That's really thoughtful, thank you. What happened to your arm?" Caesar asked, noting the blood stained bandage wrapped around Aemi's left forearm.

"Oh, that, it's nothing, but Mother would insist on covering it, in case of infection." He turned back to the table and filled a large gold goblet full of wine.

"It's a bit early to be drinking, isn't it?" Caesar commented. His friend's behaviour was very out of character for Aemi rarely drank wine before midday, and always took it well watered to dilute the strength of the alcohol.

Aemi pulled a face, "Please, sit down." As soon as Caesar sat comfortably, Aemi slumped into his chair.

"You look tired."

"I'm exhausted, actually," Aemi replied. He tipped back his head and drank the entire contents of his goblet down in one go.

"Then you should be in bed."

"Couldn't sleep," Aemi shrugged.

Caesar sipped his water as he observed Aemi closely. "What is it, Aemi? What's wrong?"

"Wrong? Nothing is wrong…everything is fine. Everything…" Aemi tailed off and got up to refill his empty goblet.

"Was it so bad?" Caesar pressed, hoping to get Aemi to open up and talk.

"It was war." He turned back to look at Caesar with pain clearly showing in his eyes. "All those stories that we learned as children, the tales of Gaius Marius and the glorious battles he fought, well they missed something out," he said bitterly as he returned to his seat.

"What do you mean?"

"I mean the blood…lots of blood, everywhere; the smell of it clinging to your nostrils, the feel of it on your skin, soaking your tunic; standing in pools of it and thinking it was water, until you looked down and saw that you were standing in a pile of someone's entrails. Pools of blood everywhere…and the screaming," Aemi shuddered involuntarily. "So much screaming." He drank deeply from his goblet again.

"It sounds terrible." It was all Caesar could think of to say. Aemi smiled, but Caesar could see that there was no humour behind his eyes.

"That, my friend, is one way to describe it."

"I'm sorry…I don't know what else to say."

"Don't say anything, please…not now, I…" Aemi shrugged again and finished off his wine.

"You will make yourself sick," said Caesar. "Drowning yourself in wine will not help you to face up to what you went through."

"No, but it makes me feel better!" Aemi snapped. "And don't start one of your holier than thou lectures, because frankly, Caesar, I have had just about all I can stomach for one day." He grabbed the pitcher of wine and filled up his goblet for the third time in as many minutes.

"I'm trying to help you!"

Aemi shook his head. "You don't know how lucky you are, Caesar, safe in your cosy priesthood; locked away from the horrors of battle."

"Aemi, please don't."

"I have to!"

Caesar could see the frustration and anger written all over his face, and he inwardly winced as he saw the tears welling up in Aemi's eyes.

"It's the only way I'm going to get through this. You…you have no idea what I went through. All those poor souls; friends, acquaintances, young men, just like you and I. Some of them had only just come of age and never stood a chance, yet we went out there, believing in the glory of Rome. Like lambs to the slaughter we believed we were invincible because we were Roman! The years of drills and practice on the Campus, like the good Roman boys we were, made us believe we could fight and win, after all, hadn't our legions proved it over and over again? Stay together, they told us, hold the line, but there was no line to hold. They cut us down like axe men in the forests, thousands of them swarming all over us like locusts. We never stood a chance, Caesar, but we kept on hacking and cutting and dying, until finally, the recall to withdraw sounded above the din of battle. By all the gods, Caesar, I swear I have never been so pleased to hear such a sound in all my life, and I ran, we all ran, as fast as we could. I lost my horse early on in the battle; he was cut down from under me…and he is out there somewhere now, on that field of slaughter, and I will never see him again." Aemi paused to take another gulp of wine. "He was the last gift that Father ever gave me…I loved that horse."

"I know you did." Caesar swallowed hard, fighting to keep his emotions in check.

"Now he's gone, just like Father, and all those other poor, naïve, stupid boys that rode out to glory and now lie dead, but, I tell you, Caesar, it was not glorious, it was not exciting; it was terrifying, it was carnage, and I don't think I will ever get those pictures out of my head for as long as I live!" Aemi put his head in his hands, his fingers subconsciously pulling at his hair.

"I can imagine it must be very hard for you."

"No…no, that is just it, you can't imagine, no one can, not until you have experienced it for yourselves. When you fight, you are no longer a man but as savage as a wild beast. You don't have time to think you just act. You slash and stab, killing and mutilating, over and over again. You don't look at the men you kill; all you see is a body and their sword or spear coming towards you. The first time that you see their face is the moment of death; when you look into their eyes that are full of pain and bewilderment and the realisation that they are dying. There is a look, a special look, that you see in your victims eyes the moment that their soul leaves their body and they go dark like pools of deep water with no bottom to them. There's just emptiness, a nothing, and then the body slumps lifeless to the floor. I saw that look, over and over again, as I took first one life and then another and another. I killed those men and it meant *nothing* to me. I took a life and I was glad, glad that it was he and not I. Now I understand why the gladiators put up such a good fight. They don't do it to entertain the crowds- they do it to live. The smile on the victor's face is not happiness for a job well done but relief, for he has lived to fight another day and so they go on, over and over, staring death in the face, wondering if every fight will be their last. But it could so easily have been the other way around for them, they could have died, and it could have been me who died, me lying out on that plain with the rest of them. I stared death in the face and I survived, this time, but what about the next and the next?" A sob caught in his throat.

Caesar instinctively reached across to touch Aemi's arm, but Aemi flinched away and rose quickly from his chair. Caesar watched as his friend turned his back and leaned, hunched and dejected, against his desk.

"You can't live each day of your life wondering if it will be your last, Aemi, for death is all around us, in all walks of life. The best that you can hope for is to live your life the best way that you know how, for only the gods know when your time on this world is ended."

Aemi turned to face his friend and the tears flowed freely down his care worn face. "I tell you, Caesar, it's not until you face your own mortality that you realise just how fragile life is. I touched it briefly, when Father died, but you soon forget. I rode towards the enemy full of excitement and anticipation; I was the leader of men and I would lead them to victory because I was Roman and to be Roman is everything, at least, that's what I believed. How young and naïve was I?" Aemi moved slowly back to his chair and threw himself down with a sigh, wiping his eyes with the back of his hand. "I lead those young men to their deaths. I screamed at them to stay together. 'Hold the line, Stay with me!' I shouted, and they did; they stayed until they were cut down around me. They held that line until the enemy broke through. Oh, Caesar!" Aemi let out a heart felt groan, as though his very soul ached with the sadness of it all.

Tears pricked at the back of Caesar's eyes as he listened to his friend recall the reality of war; a reality that he himself would never experience and he wanted to cry, for the loss of Aemi's faith and innocence and for himself, for the experience he was to be denied forever. But now was not the time for self-indulgence. Aemi needed his friendship and reassurance. There would be time later to mourn his own loss. "All men must suffer after their first battle, Aemi, for the first is the reality of war and you leave the playground of the Campus far behind you, but, you will get over this, I promise you. There is no weakness in what you are feeling. It is natural to grieve for the men that died under your command. You will feel the loss heavily but it doesn't mean that you are a weak man. Your next battle will not be so bad, nor the one after that, and soon you will be hardened to loss and to death. You will make an excellent commander one day, just give it time."

"I wager Marcus did not feel as I do after his first battle. I bet he revelled in it for he was ever the warrior," Aemi said bitterly.

"Don't compare yourself to him. You are both two very different men."

"Do you think he's still alive?"

"I hope so, truly I do," Caesar replied.

Aemi placed his empty goblet on the table beside him and rested his head on the back of the chair, closing his eyes with a deep sigh. "Caesar, can I ask you something?"

"Of course, anything."

"Stay with me until I fall asleep. I don't want to be alone."

Caesar smiled and looked with affection at his friend, whose unlined face showed the true youth of the young man slouched now in his chair, the dark circles under his eyes testament to the torment he had suffered.

"I will stay, Aemi, I promise," he said.

No sooner were the words spoken than Caesar saw the tension visibly disappear from Aemi's body as he fell into a drink induced sleep. He waited several minutes to make sure Aemi was truly settled before he gently covered him with a cloak that was draped carelessly on the nearby couch, and tiptoed from the study.

A surprise visitor awaited Caesar when he arrived home. "Uncle Marcus! How wonderful. I did not expect to see you so soon. Did you come back to Rome with Sulla?"

Marcus Aurelius Cotta bowed respectfully to his nephew, a broad smile lighting up his weary face. "It is good to see you, Holy One. Yes, I arrived with the vanguard of Sulla's army late last night and returned to my home this morning."

"Then I am surprised to see you so soon after being re-united with your family."

"I know, but business comes first, and this, I am afraid, cannot wait. Is there somewhere that we may speak privately?"

"Of course, follow me." Caesar led the way down an intricate labyrinth of cold, echoing corridors, to his study.

After dismissing his secretary with orders to organise refreshments to be sent up from the kitchens, Caesar settled comfortably into a chair. "Please, take a seat, Uncle. We don't have to stand on ceremony in the privacy of my study so no more 'Holy One', it's Caesar, just Caesar." He studied his uncle more closely, as Marcus Aurelius elected to stretch out on the couch. He had weathered well, considering he had been living with the army for so long, but Caesar could see a sprinkling of grey now in his hair, and he looked thinner. His face was still the same as Caesar remembered, round and open, with singularly expressive features but the most noticeable change to his uncle could be found in his eyes. The ever-present twinkle of humour and mischief had gone to be replaced by a haunting sadness and reserve that Caesar had never seen before.

"What a splendid room this is," Marcus Aurelius said appreciatively as he arranged his toga over his legs.

Caesar nodded, but he was too impatient to find out the reason for this visit to engage in small talk. "So, Uncle, what is so important that you risk the wrath of your wife to see me?"

Marcus Aurelius smiled fleetingly before his face clouded as he looked discerningly at Caesar. "Sulla has summoned the Senate to a meeting at the Temple of Bellona this afternoon. Everyone is expected to attend, including the Pontifex Maximus and all the main priests, of which you are included. I came to warn you that it is in your best interests to attend, Caesar."

Caesar frowned. "But why does he want the priests? We don't involve ourselves in political matters in the same way as the Senate, indeed, I am not able to look upon a man in military clothing, let alone become involved in military matters. What possible use would I be to his plans?"

Marcus Aurelius shifted uncomfortably in his chair. "Sulla intends to have the Senate elect him Dictator of Rome now that both the Consuls are…indisposed."

"Dictator? But that office has not been in use for over a hundred years!"

"One hundred and twenty to be precise, but that is his intention, and I cannot see the Senate in any position to refuse him, can you? They need a leader and Rome needs an end to this bloody civil war. Unless the leadership is settled soon the city will dissolve into chaos and the Republic will be lost. Norbanus and Carbo are out there somewhere, and who is to say what they will do in the future. They are weak now, but given time…anyway, for the present, Sulla is the one with all the power and he is capable of returning order to this chaos, but he will not share the power or the responsibility with anyone until he is sure all his enemies inside Rome are defeated. He trusts no man and who can blame him after what happened, hence his decision to be elected Dictator. With absolute power he will be safe and no man can touch him. Oh, I am sure that he will make it appear that it is the Senate's idea to voluntarily give him sole power for he is no fool."

"But surely if the Senate make him Dictator, who will be in a position to control him? With all that authority and revenge in his heart…the possibilities of abuse of that power do not bare thinking about," said Caesar.

"I agree, and therein lies the danger, for you personally, I mean."

"Danger to me?"

"Sulla will expect all the priests to agree his appointment as well as the Senate, and I am sure that nearly all will do so, if they value their lives…but for you there lies a singular problem."

"Oh?"

"You are the son of a man who openly showed allegiance to Gaius Marius and Cinna whilst he was alive,"

"But…"

Marcus Aurelius raised his hand to still Caesar's argument. "I know your father was given little choice…"

"No choice!"

"No choice, I know that, Caesar, but Sulla does not. You are also the nephew of Gaius Marius, and, worst of all, you married Cinna's daughter. All of these connections put you in great danger. Now, I promised your father before we parted, that should this day ever come, when Sulla returned to power with his heart bent on revenge, then I would do everything in my power to convince him that all that happened to you and your father was done under duress, and not through any loyalty to Marius. I know that your appointment as Flamen and your marriage was forced upon you, but, the fact remains that Sulla does not, and he will see you as an enemy to be dealt with, unless I can persuade him otherwise."

"And can you? Do you have that much influence with Sulla?"

"Influence? Very little - no man does. What we do have is an understanding, and, a singular favour he still owes me. I would like to believe that he would listen to me."

Their conversation was interrupted by the arrival of refreshments. Caesar took the opportunity to leave his seat and walk around the room to settle his mind. He had always known that one day his family could be called to account for their ties with Marius and Cinna, particularly after Marius had destroyed so many of Sulla's family and friends. It was inevitable Sulla would seek to redress the balance, but Caesar had hoped that fate would step in and that this dangerous situation could have somehow been avoided. Unfortunately, that hope now lay in tatters, and he recognised the serious implications to himself, and his family, now that Sulla had returned to Rome.

The slave left the study and Caesar returned to his chair. "If Sulla does not listen, what then?"

"Let us cross that bridge, as and when we come to it, in the meantime, you must keep yourself very much out of his way. Go about your duties as normal but do nothing to draw his attention to yourself. There are many more powerful men that deserve his attention first, and they all know who they are, but you are a marked man, Caesar, much as it pains me to say it, and sooner or later, Sulla will turn to you. As long as you do as you are bid, and that includes attending this meeting today, it gives us both time, and that may be the difference between life and death for you."

Caesar bit his lip so hard that he tasted the salty bitterness of blood on his tongue. "So, let me get this straight. I am to vote in favour of Sulla becoming Dictator, giving him supreme power over everyone and everything whilst knowing that, sooner or later, he will turn his attentions to me, because of who I am, and that I might actually die because of it? Why should I do such a thing? I may as well sign my own death warrant now!" he said angrily.

"Because, Caesar, you are an intelligent young man, at least you used to be, and I pray that you use the sense the gods blessed you with. Do as I say, and you may come out of this unscathed. Believe me, Caesar, I have seen into Sulla's heart and it is black with hatred and revenge. He will not rest until every trace of Marius and Cinna has been destroyed, along with any man who is known to have been a sympathiser with either of his enemies, and that includes you, my boy. You are a member of Marius's family; you are husband to Cinna's only daughter, and heir to his fortune. Everything points to your sympathies lying with Sulla's enemies. You have a high position of power and influence as the Flamen Dialis, and, you could use it to raise rebellion against Sulla, if you so chose. His mind will turn to you, sooner or later, so you have to listen to me, Caesar, and do nothing to make Sulla believe you are a threat to him. Do you understand me?"

Caesar made no reply, biting idly at his fingernail as he thought through his options. Marcus Aurelius took advantage of the silence to top up his goblet and then settled back on to the couch.

"I have listened, and I will do as you advise, Uncle, but let there be no misunderstanding between us. I am a man now and I make my own decisions. I will not be dictated to, and I will do whatever I deem is right to protect myself and my wife from Sulla's misplaced revenge. Neither Cinnilla, nor I, deserve to be punished simply for who we are. None of this was our making and I will not stand by and be meekly led where others dictate; on that I am resolved. If I am to die then it will be at a time of *my* choosing, and on *my* terms, for I love respect and honour far more than I fear death, and never again will I allow another to dictate my destiny."

Marcus Aurelius nodded. "That is all I ask, Caesar, and I assure you that I will do all in my power to draw Sulla's attention away from you, and your wife. Should the worst happen, then I will support you in any way that I am able."

Caesar allowed himself to smile. "Then we are agreed, and I will attend the meeting this afternoon."

"Good," Marcus Aurelius sighed with relief as he rose from the couch and placed his goblet on the table. "I look forward to seeing you there, and you should warn your mother about the inevitable fate of Young Marius, for the sands of time have all but run out for that young man."

"I shall attend to it directly after the meeting," said Caesar, leading the way from the study.

They reached the atrium and Marcus Aurelius bowed low in respect. "It is good to see you again, Holy One. You have grown into a fine young man; one that your father would be proud of," he said with a warm smile.

Caesar nodded his gratitude. "I try to be, Uncle, I try to be."

The Temple of Bellona was small compared to Rome's usual gigantean standards, nestled into the outer walls of the great racetrack, the Circus Maximus, which lay in the shadow of the Aventine Hill. Inside, the temple was packed; Senators and priests crammed into the small hall to hear the victorious speech of Lucius Cornelius Sulla.

Sulla sat languidly in his curule chair at the top of the podium, his pale eyes narrowed as he scanned the group of men before him. Some of the senators he recognised but there were many he did not, and he wondered how many of those new faces owed their entry into the Senate off the back of their relationship with Marius, Cinna and Carbo. He felt the colour drain from his face as he thought of his enemies and the destruction those men had brought on Rome, and his heart felt cold, unfeeling and untouched as he steeled himself for what he was about to do. He glanced behind at the row of immaculately attired bodyguards he had handpicked from his legions that morning. Each man had a shiny new gladius strapped to their hip, and a gold pointed pillum at their side, as they stood to attention, as still and silent as the many marble statues that lined the edges of the temple. Satisfied that everything was in order, Sulla turned his gaze back to the expectant crowd and waited for the buzz of voices to slowly die down. He nodded imperceptibly to a centurion who stood off to one side of the podium together with a further twenty legionaries dressed in full military uniform. The centurion saluted and led his men out the back door of the temple.

As silence descended in the temple Sulla addressed the gathering, and as he spoke, his icy orbs flickered around the room, skimming the sea of faces. He kept his speech courteous and to the point, but the tone in his voice was hard, and by the look on his face, few men present were under any illusion that Sulla would not seek to punish those that had turned against him. Sulla completed his opening speech and moved swiftly on to the real reason he had called the meeting today-his election as Dictator, but as he spoke, the sound of men screaming could be heard coming from outside the temple.

A murmur of concern rippled through the men gathered in the hall and a couple of Senators, nearest the doors, opened them to see what all the commotion was about. Two armed guards appeared at the doorway, their pillums crossed in front of their chests, to prevent them from leaving. The Senators looked in consternation at the guards and tried to close the doors, but they were gently pushed aside and the doors opened completely to allow the full horror of the blood curdling shrieks to resound around the inside of the temple.

Sulla watched with amusement the effect this had on the men gathered in the hall. "Gentlemen, pay no heed to the disturbance outside. It is nothing to concern yourselves with. Now, back to business…"

The Senators and priests looked uneasy but no one dared speak out and they continued to listen to Sulla, but with only half an ear, for the terrible commotion that was going on outside in the Circus Maximus was too loud and too terrible to be ignored.

Finally, an elderly senator interrupted Sulla. "Lucius Cornelius, Lucius Cornelius! Please, we would all like to know what is the cause of the disturbance outside in the Circus Maximus? There are no races scheduled to run, or gladiatorial games to draw the crowds, therefore what number of men have been drawn here, and for what purpose? I beg you, put us out of our misery and tell us what is happening!"

Everyone in the temple stopped and held their breath, waiting for Sulla to speak.

Sulla smiled benignly at the old man. "I have already told you, Marcus Flavius, that it is of no consequence what is happening outside in the Circus Maximus, but, as you insist on further explanation, I will give it. I have ordered the…punishment, of a few traitors that were captured during the final battle for Rome. It really is nothing to concern yourselves with," he addressed the whole hall, "For the prisoners are not Roman and therefore do not fall under any law that says they must stand trial for their crimes."

"Who are they then?" A senator in the crowd shouted out above the din of the cries and screams that were getting louder and more terrifying.

Sulla's face hardened, and his eyes narrowed dangerously as he looked at the concerned faces before him. "They are Samnites," he said coldly. "…and they are being punished, not because they saw fit to join Carbo and Norbanus against me, but because as soon as the opportunity arose, they chose to turn their attentions towards Rome."

"Lucius Cornelius, pray, one further question to appease an old man's interest," Marcus Flavius shouted. "Just how many Samnite prisoners are being punished in the Circus at this moment?"

"All of them," Sulla said tersely.

"But there are over eight thousand Samnite prisoners!" cried a senator who obviously had some knowledge of the number of prisoners taken during the battle.

"That many? Well no wonder the noise is so loud," said Sulla dryly.

"And they are *all* being killed, *now*, as we speak?"

"Yes, now, can we please get on with the matter in hand? I am sure my men will dispatch the prisoners swiftly so the noise shouldn't trouble us for too much longer," said Sulla firmly, for he was getting a little irritated by these constant interruptions.

Senators and priests alike looked aghast at what they were hearing, both inside, and outside the temple. Today proved that Lucius Cornelius Sulla Felix was back with a vengeance, and this show of force he was putting on for their benefit could only bode ill for them all, of the things that were still to come.

"We have swapped one set of tyrants for another," a young senator muttered under his breath to his colleague, as they filed out of the temple at the end of the meeting. "Sulla, Dictator! What is the world coming to?"

His friend simply shook his head. "All I know is that by this evening I will be well on my way to Verona. I have urgent estate business to take care of…and it may take me several years to complete it."

# CHAPTER EIGHTEEN

*"It is better to create than to learn. Creation is the essence of life."*
*(Gaius Julius Caesar)*

## ROME: July-December 82BC

Aemi glanced at Sulla, who lay reclined and alone on his couch in the large, ornately designed dining room that was once the pride and joy of Cinna, and wondered what was behind the smug smile of satisfaction that played on his lips? His attention was drawn to Marcus Crassus and Dollabella, who, reclining on a couch together opposite his own, bickered good humouredly about whose legion had taken the most prisoners during the final battle to save Rome. Aemi smiled wryly, and glanced over to his left, to the couch next to his own, and whose occupants, Marcus Aurelius Cotta, and the young but already highly distinguished general, Gnaus Pompeius, were discussing the ongoing siege at Praeneste.

His idle musing was interrupted by Catalus Caesar, who lay on the couch beside him, and, who insisted on comparing notes on their own involvement in the battle. Aemi breathed a sigh of relief as Catalus Caesar was cut short by Sulla, who raised his goblet and signalled for silence. Now, perhaps, he would finally get the answers he had been waiting for.

All day, since the invitation to dine with Sulla had been delivered to his house, Aemi had felt sick with anticipation. What could be behind this mysterious invite? What possible interest could Sulla have in him? Aemi had sought Caesar's advice, but his friend had been none the wiser and could only council caution. Aemi's apprehension increased further when he saw the other guests, particularly young Catalus Caesar, who he had not set eyes upon since the day he had declared a blood feud with Marcus. All these men must have something in common, Aemi pondered, but what? Now, he hoped to be given the opportunity to find out.

"My friends, and estimable colleagues, I wish to raise a toast, to the memory of those beloved to us, here in this room, who perished under the tyranny of Marius and Cinna, and lately, Carbo."

The guests all reached for their ornately carved gold plated goblets and raised them up.

"I swore to the gods that the blood of the innocents spilt during this bloody civil war would be avenged if my cause proved to be the right and true one. It was, and now it is time to honour that oath. To the Innocents!"

"The Innocents!" the guests repeated in unison, and drank deeply.

"Now," said Sulla, returning his goblet to the table in front of his couch. "Not only have I asked you all here today to spend time in your quite excellent company…"

They all laughed heartily except Aemi, whose eyes flitted nervously from face to face, wondering how they could all be so calm and relaxed. What did they know that he did not?

"But, each one of you here has lost someone close to you; be it family, as in the case of young Catalus Caesar and Marcus Aemilius…"

Aemi's stomach turned a cartwheel at the mention of his father, and he glanced sideways at Catalus to see whether Sulla's words had generated the same effect, but Catalus Caesar was looking intently at Sulla, with no trace of emotion showing on his face.

"…or who we considered our friends. Men that we shared our lives with both politically and militarily; men whose spirits I feel are in this room tonight and would, if they could, be sharing in the celebration of the successful conclusion of this war with us now."

"Here, here!" said Dollabella, raising his goblet to salute Sulla.

Sulla smiled, but Aemi was close enough to see that the smile didn't reach Sulla's eyes. They remained cold and lifeless like a snake's. An involuntary shiver ran through his body and he pulled his toga closer around his legs.

"I swore an oath to avenge the death of every man who was a victim in this war; a victim of the malice and greed of Cinna and Marius, in particular. It is my intention to speak with every man who has a grievance against them, albeit that the perpetrators themselves are dead, but there are many men still living, still in Rome to this day, who not only supported my enemies but aided them in committing this most heinous of crimes. These men shall be named and shamed before all of Rome and they *will* be punished. It is, by the grace of the gods, in my power now to repay my debts, both to the living and the dead, and you, who sit here with me now will be the first to have this opportunity. Speak - tell me the names of the men responsible for the pain and suffering and the loss that you have endured and I will give them to you, if they are still living, with my undying gratitude, and permission to do with them what you will, providing, at the end of it, they are dead."

The room was silent as the guests digested this unbelievable offer from Sulla. Aemi did not know whether to laugh or cry with the insanity of the moment. How could any man offer up another human being for slaughter in such a casual manner?

"There is only one man that I claim for myself personally," Sulla continued, "And that is the son of my long time enemy and nemesis, Gaius Marius. I refer to his son, the Consul, Young Marius. He is mine and mine alone. Now, speak, give me names," he said, signalling to a slave who stepped forward and placed a wax tablet and stylus in Sulla's hand. He opened the wax tablet and licked the end of the lead stylus. With a flourish, he inscribed Young Marius as the first name on this list of condemned men. His hand poised to write, Sulla looked up at his guests. "Come on, don't be shy! Dollabella, you at least must have one or two names in mind?" he smiled.

"Indeed," said Dollabella, returning the smile. "Marcus Cassius Longinius; he is the first and he has been a known associate of Marius's for years. I have no doubt that he was behind the legal case they made against Catalus Caesar's father; he and his turncoat brother, Gaius."

Sulla wrote the names down on his tablet. "Good, that has got things moving. Any others that you care to mention?"

"Postumius Albinius-he's one!" Gnaus Pompeius called out, as he ripped some meat off a bone with his teeth.

"Most definitely, though I dare say he'll squirm like a stuck eel claiming he was forced into acting for Marius after he returned to Rome," said Dollabella with a sneer.

"They all will, once they know they are marked men," said Cassius. "They stood and applauded as the heads of the innocents appeared on the rostra day after day and the people will have seen that. Put up a reward for information and you will soon have the names of the men you seek," he added wisely.

"A good idea, Cassius," Sulla nodded and made a mental note.

"But what about the men who genuinely did feel they had no choice but support Marius and Cinna or die? What happens to them, for surely you cannot consider them your true enemies, Sulla?" said Marcus Aurelius, who seized this opportunity to test the water with Sulla.

Aemi knew immediately whom Marcus Aurelius was really referring to and he held his breath in anticipation. This could be the moment that Caesar's fate would be decided.

"What, like that Patrician son-in-law of yours?" Gnaus Pompeius said with an arrogant toss of his head.

"If you mean Gaius Julius Caesar, then yes, he is one example, although there are many more, I am sure, and, for your information, Gaius was not only my son-in-law but my nephew-in-law. Aurelia is my stepdaughter as well as my niece, for I married her mother after my brother, her real father, died," Marcus Aurelius replied haughtily.

"You were still related, whatever twists and turns you have in your family," Pompeius replied with a sneer.

"In answer to your question, Marcus Aurelius," Sulla interrupted, "I would have to be convinced that those men who are named as collaborators were acting under duress and it is not being used as a shield to protect themselves from the truth."

Marcus Aurelius nodded his thanks and did not pursue the point further. He exchanged a meaningful look with Aemi as he reached for his goblet.

"Scipio Asiagenus, is he still alive?" Crassus asked.

"I believe so, though he no longer lives in Rome. I seem to remember he retired to his villa in Pompeii," Dollabella answered.

"He might be retired now, but I know for a fact he and Cinna were very thick when Cinna was Consul. Mark my words, he would have been involved, if any one was," said Crassus.

Sulla wrote Scipio Asiagenus's name down on the tablet. "Marcus Aemilius, what about you? I was great friends with your father and he is sorely missed. Do you have any names for my little list?" Sulla asked Aemi.

Aemi felt himself blushing. "I thank you for your kind consideration in this matter, Sir, but I really don't know the names of any of the men responsible for the murder of my father, other than Gaius Marius," he stumbled with embarrassment.

"What about that brat of an adopted son of his, Marcus Marius Gratidianus? Are you still friends with that Italian scum, or did you finally come to your senses?" Catalus Caesar sneered.

Aemi felt his heart miss a beat at the mention of Marcus and shook his head quickly. "No, no we are no longer…" he paused. The rest of the men looked at him expectantly but Aemi struggled with the words, for he realised what he was about to do; deny his one time friend to a room full of strangers who had revenge in their hearts and murder on their minds. He took a deep breath and forced out the words, "Marcus Marius, one time known as Gratidianus, is no friend of mine."

"Marius adopted another brat as his heir did he?" said Sulla. "I never knew that. So there are still two spawn alive to answer for their father's sins. Interesting." His ice cool, blue eyes, looked at Aemi appraisingly. "Do you want him?"

"Excuse me?" Aemi stammered.

"I said, do you want him? I give him to you to do with as you will; to avenge the death of your father by the hand of his - it is only right and fair after all. Where is this Marcus Marius, do you know?"

It seemed to Aemi that Sulla's eyes looked into his very soul. Aemi dropped his gaze and shook his head. "No sir, I don't know where he is now."

"I do, at least, I know where he was," Catalus Caesar said with a smirk.

"Oh? And why would you have such an interest in this young man? How old is he?" Sulla asked, looking at Catalus Caesar and back to Aemi.

"Seventeen," Catalus Caesar replied. "Marcus Marius and I have a blood feud that is yet to be settled. Unfortunately he had not come of age when the feud came about and so I have made it my business to keep in mind his age and where I might find him when the time is right," said Catalus Caesar, with a proud lift of his chin.

Sulla smiled, and this time Aemi could see mischief and malice in his eyes, where, only seconds before they had been cold and lifeless.

"A blood feud, eh? How…quaint. So, where is he?"

"He joined the legions of Norbanus, as a cadet. He was last seen running away with what was left of his legion after our friend, Gnaus Pompeius here slaughtered twenty thousand of Norbanus's men near Alba Pucentia." Catalus Caesar answered.

"Indeed we did!" Pompeius laughed heartily. "What a day that was. Twenty thousand in one battle; now that is a tally worth boasting about!" he said, with a sly look at Dollabella and Crassus.

Sulla nodded and smiled at the young man sprawled casually on the couch. "You were born to lead, Pompeius, of that there is no doubt."

Aemi watched with contempt as Pompeius puffed out his chest in pride. He reminded him of a prancing peacock.

"So," Sulla said, turning to look at Aemi once more. "We have a little difficulty presented to us in the shape of one Marcus Marius. By rights, you could claim him as your man, in debt of your father's death, but young Catalus Caesar here also has a claim, through the blood feud that exists between them. Assuming he is still alive, which one of you wants him? How shall this be settled?"

"Bring him back to Rome and cut the Marian brat in half!" Dollabella roared with laughter, but Aemi felt a lump of bile rise up into his throat at the thought.

"Yes but he only has one head!" Cassius joked.

"Marcus Aemilius, what say you?" asked Sulla.

"If he doesn't want him, I definitely do!" said Catalus Caesar quickly.

Aemi looked at Catalus Caesar and back to Sulla, who sat patiently waiting for a reply. He swallowed but felt too sick to answer.

"If I may," Marcus Aurelius stepped in. "Traditionally, a blood feud cannot be broken once it has been made between the two parties. Was the oath sworn by yourself and accepted by Marcus Marius?" he asked Catalus Caesar.

"Indeed it was, Sir, and witnessed by several people, including Marcus Aemilius who sits beside me." he replied.

The two young men locked eyes, and Aemi saw the hunger that years of waiting had produced, burning fiercely in the jet-black orbs of Catalus Caesar.

"Is this true, Marcus Aemilius?" Sulla asked.

Aemi tore his eyes from Catalus Caesar and looked at Sulla. "Yes, sir."

Marcus Aurelius cleared his throat. "Then the feud overrides any other crime the young man might have committed, including those of his father. It is my opinion that Marcus Marius should, if he is alive and is captured, be offered to Catalus Caesar first to have the feud settled by combat. If, after they have fought their battle, Marcus Marius proves to be the victor, then he should remain captive, by your own decree, Sulla, and handed over to young Marcus Aemilius to be dealt with as he sees fit, providing of course, as you say, the end result is that he dies. That way both of these young men's honour is satisfied."

Aemi looked gratefully at Marcus Aurelius for giving him a way out of answering Sulla, but at the same time, he realised with a sinking heart that whatever Sulla decided, Marcus was doomed to die.

"As always Marcus Aurelius, you are a master of decision!" said Sulla approvingly. "Let it be as you say. If Marcus Marius lives, then he is yours, Catalus Caesar, but if you die, then he will become the property of you, Marcus Aemilius. Do you both agree?"

Catalus Caesar looked very pleased with the decision. "I agree, Sir."

Aemi merely nodded and looked down at the floor.

"Don't be so downhearted, Marcus Aemilius, you haven't seen Catalus Caesar fight yet; you might still have the pleasure of the Marius brat to yourself!" said Dollabella.

Gnaus Pompeius let out a guffaw of laughter at Dollabella's joke.

Aemi couldn't help but smile as he saw the look on Catalus Caesar's face. For once, the jumped up popinjay had got his comeuppance and Aemi was pleased.

"That's settled then," said Sulla. "Moving on…"

The rest of the evening was spent in the bantering of names amongst the senior men as, one by one they helped Sulla to fill the wax tablet full of the names of doomed men. Aemi was relieved when Sulla finally called an end to the night and he could escape that morbid house of horrors.

He walked down the Palatine and into the Forum, his mind filled with the names of the proscribed men who, at this very moment, lay asleep in their beds all over Rome, oblivious to the fate that was to befall them. His feet finally brought him to the door of Caesar's house. The red brick building loomed before him, tall and imposing and Aemi wondered what it would be like to live in such a soulless place. He shuddered at the thought and then shuddered again, realising why he had come here. Just a few hours before he had boasted to Caesar that he was dining with the Dictator; the excitement and delicious anticipation of being in the presence of a man who held the power of the world in his hand had been an awesome experience and one he had very much looked forward to, even though his excitement had been tinged with fear. Instead, he had been faced with the cold harsh reality of life and death. Sulla had the power over both, just like a living god, and he had played with the lives of living men with hardly a second thought, such was his lust for revenge. One of those men had been his friend; their boyhood days spent playing in the sun, wrestling, arguing, laughing, and getting into mischief. Aemi smiled as he remembered some of the scrapes the three of them had got into over the years and then, just as quickly, tears sprang into his eyes. Where had it all gone wrong between them? There was not one defining moment in his mind, not even the death of his father, for Aemi had felt the chasm of difference widening between him and Marcus long before then. Theirs had been a slow and painful death of a friendship: a friendship that Marcus had tried to cling on to, like a man cast adrift in the sea, clinging to any bit of wood he could find to save him. Was it what they were that had caused the rift? One Plebeian, the other Italian, their lives and values so different in so many ways, yet Caesar had managed to bridge the social gap with Marcus. Perhaps it was their father's hatred and animosity that had driven a wedge between them? Whatever the answer something bigger than the three of them ever imagined had seeped into their relationship, gnawing away until finally, the threads of brotherly love, and allegiance, sworn to last forever, had snapped. They had come to a crossroads in their lives but instead of treading the path into manhood together, as they had always planned, they had been sucked into three different worlds; worlds that could not let their friendship endure. Caesar, as Flamen Dialis, removed from the reality of the world, Marcus, to the legions, to fight for his survival, with very little choice, and he, Aemi, paterfamilias, businessman, would be politician and sometime soldier. In the middle was Caesar, the constant between the three: his friendship given equally to both, his loyalty given to both, his love given to both. How was he ever going to find the words to tell Caesar? What could he say? Was Marcus still alive somewhere out there tonight amongst the stars? Or was he lying dead on a plain, his body at the mercy of the wild animals and birds that would feast on his remains, never knowing the man who had once inhabited that body? Aemi hoped that Marcus was dead for he would be spared the awful future that he would face now if he still lived. His brother, Young Marius, was doomed to die in a rat-infested town, cut off from the rest of the world but what fate would befall Marcus?

Aemi wiped away the tears that ran down his face and pulled himself together. He would have to face Caesar sometime, so better now than have his friend find out from a stranger. He walked up to the tall, wooden studded door and grasping the bronze knocker tightly in his hand, he lifted it up and let it fall, with a deep, resounding bang.

"Well, all credit to you, Sulla. You did what you set out to do even when there were those of us who had our doubts," said Dollabella, stretching languidly on the couch facing Sulla. He alone of the guests that had attended the dinner that evening remained, at Sulla's request.

Slaves busied themselves, silently gliding around the room, clearing away the last of the dishes, whilst the steward supervised the positioning of the oil lamps and refuelling of the braziers.

"I know, but perhaps now you will believe me when I say I will do something. Fortuna smiles on me and rewards her favourite son most graciously."

"Indeed she does; the most generous of patrons." Dollabella nodded in agreement.

"As am I, to men who show me loyalty," said Sulla, looking pointedly at Dollabella.

Dollabella watched as the steward ushered the last slave out of the room and silently closed the door behind him. As soon as they were alone, he pulled himself upright on the couch and glared at Sulla. "Surely you don't think I am any the less loyal than I have always shown myself to be!"

"No, no, of course not," Sulla soothed Dollabella's ruffled feathers. "But I need men around me who are going to believe in me without questioning my actions or my motives. Men who are loyal and trustworthy... men like you."

Dollabella appeared pacified by those words and relaxed against the back of the couch. "Good. I'm glad to hear it."

"Now that I am the Dictator there are going to be some major changes to Rome and my decisions are not always going to be met with approval, particularly from the Senate."

"Humph, the Senate, what do they matter now? You are Dictator. You need no man's approval," Dollabella snorted contemptuously.

Sulla smiled. "In theory, no I don't, but I have no intention of remaining the Dictator forever, even though there was no time limit awarded to the office. Therefore it is in my interests to keep the Senate and the People of Rome on my side."

Dollabella looked surprised. "You'll be putting yourself in great personal danger if you give up your position, Sulla. You leave yourself wide open to attack from your enemies. I would give it serious consideration before you make such a rash decision."

Sulla nodded but felt totally unconcerned by Dollabella's warning. "I have nothing to fear, not now or in the future for what else is there left for me in this life but to die? I have achieved more than I ever dreamed of and there is more, much more, that I will achieve before I hand back the reins of power to the Senate. When that day comes I will embrace my future with open arms and trust in the wisdom of the gods. Let them and the People judge me then when I am naked of power and helpless to resist their will. I will offer myself up willingly on that day and if I am to die for the deeds I believed were right and true then so shall it be."

"I don't know how you can be so unconcerned, Sulla."

"I don't let the little things worry me."

Dollabella merely snorted and made no further comment.

"So, Dollabella, my friend, your loyalty is assured?"

"Absolutely Sulla. Always."

"Loyalty such as yours will be rewarded; you have my word on it. How does the consulship sound?"

"Are you offering me the position of Consul?" Dollabella exclaimed.

Sulla smiled and nodded.

"Why yes, of course I would accept, but, hold on, you are Dictator, there is no need for Consuls for you hold supreme power."

"I am aware that I don't *need* them but all the same, it is in my mind to run the consular elections next month the way it has always been. I intend to rebuild the Republic to her former glory, before these years of endless wars took their toll, and by the time I have finished Rome will be even greater than anyone could ever imagine. That is my task, and that is what I intend to do before I lay down the power bestowed upon me. To do that I will need support from both the Senate and the People of Rome and the consular elections will be a good place to start. I use the word election lightly, because of course the men who are elected will actually be my choice, but, after all, I am the Dictator."

"Oh, I see now!" Dollabella laughed.

"Good," Sulla smiled. "So, as I say, the position of Consul is yours if you desire it?"

"Indeed I do, Sulla, indeed I do!"

"That's settled then. Now, there is a little matter you could attend to for me if you would be so kind."

"Of course, name it," said Dollabella who had the look of a man who would sign his soul away if asked.

"Since returning to Rome I have noticed the extraordinary amount of statues of Gaius Marius erected around the public squares, temples, markets and in particular, the Forum, where I counted five on my last walk. They are both offensive to me and an unsightly reminder to the People of the tyrant who brought this civil war upon us all. I want them removed, every last one of them; every statue, every plaque that bears his name, every reference to that man destroyed."

Dollabella smiled. "It will be my pleasure, Sulla. Leave it to me and I shall attend to it first thing tomorrow morning."

"No, actually I was thinking you would do it tonight."

"Tonight? But it is nearly mid-night!"

"Which gives you six hours to clear them all away before the People start waking and going about their daily business," said Sulla.

"Of course, if that is your wish."

"It is."

Dollabella slid up off the couch and slipped his feet into his boots, preparing to leave.

"And one more thing before you leave, Dollabella. I want the ashes of Marius exhumed from that monstrosity of a mausoleum that was built to house his remains and I want them scattered in the Tiber. Then, I want the mausoleum destroyed. I mean what I say, Dollabella; not one trace of Marius is to be left in Rome, not one!"

Dollabella finished tying the laces of his boots and stood up to go. "Leave it with me, Sulla. I promise that by sunrise tomorrow Marius will be but a memory."

"Thank-you," Sulla smiled in satisfaction. He felt the start of a heavy weight being lifted off his shoulders. Once all visible trace of his enemy was obliterated, and his two sons consigned to eternal sleep, Sulla knew that he would begin to feel easier in his mind that finally, he had managed to reek the revenge he had so badly wanted. "I shall be leaving Rome for a few days, in the morning."

"Oh?"

"Yes, I think it is about time the siege at Praeneste was brought to a swift conclusion so I have decided to pop across and give them the benefit of my advice. Besides, there is someone inside that I would quite like to meet, before I have him put to death."

"Ah yes, Young Marius you mean?"

"Indeed. I think that young man has outstayed his welcome. It is about time he joined his father."

Dollabella smiled grimly. "What of the other brat, Marcus Marius? Are you going to find him too?"

"Oh yes, if he is still alive I will find him and when I do I shall heave great pleasure in handing him over to young Catalus Caesar. It should be quite entertaining!"

"Then I wish you gods speed, Sulla. I shall see you upon your return." And with that, Dollabella left to carry out his orders.

Caesar returned home from the morning duties at the temple, spoke briefly to his wife and then took himself upstairs to the quiet sanctuary of his dressing room. He wanted some time alone with his thoughts, to reflect on what had been one of the hardest weeks of his life.

Locking the door behind him he pulled off the hated priestly garments, leaving them strewn across the floor, and threw himself wearily onto the couch. Almost immediately his thoughts returned to that evening, five days ago, when he had listened, appalled, as Aemi told how Sulla had offered up his friend to die. At first he had felt angry with Aemi for denying Marcus but, seeing the look of utter devastation on Aemi's face, he had realised that he had been placed in an impossible position. Aemi merely spoke the truth for he and Marcus were no longer friends, but all the same, Caesar knew that he would never willingly have offered Marcus up to the terrible fate that now awaited him, if, indeed Marcus was still alive, for he had received no word from his friend for several weeks now. Caesar stared up at the ceiling and silently prayed that Marcus was alive and safe, somewhere far from Rome.

The face of his cousin, Young Marius, edged its way into his thoughts and Caesar felt the heavy weight of responsibility on his shoulders. The ending of the siege of Praeneste, two days ago, was openly celebrated around Rome. Word had quickly spread that Young Marius was dead although the rumours abounded as to how and when this had happened. Caesar had been told only that morning that Young Marius had taken his own life rather than be captured and dragged before Sulla, when the townspeople of Praeneste betrayed him had opened the city gates in surrender. He hoped that there was some truth to this. At least his cousin would have died honourably.

Caesar gave a heartfelt sigh and threw his feet over the side of the couch but he couldn't quite bring himself to get up, not just yet, for to round this week off to a perfect end, he had the unenviable task of informing his aunt Julia that her son was dead. As the closest male relative left alive, Caesar was now paterfamilias to his aunt, and as such he had the responsibility of breaking the news. He had been grateful for his uncle Marcus's warning of his cousin's impending fate and he had wasted no time in telling his mother what to expect. Aurelia had showed her usual fortitude when she heard the news and promised to keep Julia with her and away from prying eyes and loose tongues until they knew for certain that Young Marius was dead. Now that moment was here, and Caesar could not put it off any longer or he would run the risk of his aunt finding out from another source.

With a heavy heart he rose from the couch and searched in the cupboard for a clean toga. He became aware of raised voices coming from downstairs and as he opened the dressing room door he heard the unmistakable voices of Aemi and Cinnilla.

"But I must see him, it's urgent!"

"He is changing before he has to leave again. I am afraid he will not be able to see you today."

"Aemi, is that you?" Caesar called down the stairs.

"I need to speak with you, urgently!" said Aemi, appearing at the bottom of the stairs.

"My husband has urgent business of his own to attend to!"

"Come on up," Caesar beckoned to his friend. "I will only be a moment, Cinnilla, please have the litter waiting for me."

Cinnilla appeared for a brief second, scowled at the back of Aemi as he climbed the stairs and stalked off into the atrium.

"She's in a bad temper today," said Aemi as he reached Caesar.

"Don't mind her, she's worried about how Aunt Julia is going to take the news that her son is dead," said Caesar as he led the way back into his dressing room.

"Marcus is dead?"

"No, not Marcus, Young Marius, you fool!"

"You mean she doesn't know yet? But it's been two days since Praeneste fell, surely she must have heard the news by now?"

"Mother has kept her out of the way until we knew for certain. Now we do, so..."

"Poor you," said Aemi. "Still, I'm relieved it's not Marcus. Look," he said, drawing a small scroll from inside his cloak. "I've had a letter from him."

"Marcus has written to you, but why?" Caesar took the small scroll from Aemi and looked at the broken seal. The crest of the Mariian family was clearly stamped in the wax.

Aemi blushed. "Before Marcus left to join Norbanus we...well we came to an arrangement of sorts."

"Ah, the mysterious purchase of horses for your farm," Caesar said, tongue in cheek.

"Yes, well I'm afraid that I was not quite honest with you over that,"

"You don't say!"

"I know, and I am sorry, Caesar, but let me explain and then I know you will forgive me," said Aemi hurriedly.

"Well?" Caesar sat down on the couch and Aemi pulled up a chair.

"Well, do you remember the message he gave to you, to give me? He said he would keep looking?"

"Yes, and you told me it was a horse."

"Yes, well, he was looking for something, but it wasn't a horse. It was something we didn't want you to find out about."

"Oh?"

"I didn't want to lie but it was important that you didn't know, not until Marcus found it, just in case he didn't find it and..." Aemi blustered.

"What are you talking about, Aemi?"

"The prophecy."

"The what?"

"The prophecy. Marcus went to look for the prophecy, the real one, the complete one."

Caesar was shocked. " I don't understand. How...why?"

"Marcus, well, both of us really, could see how upset you were when you found out that the prophecy existed and Marcus was upset that he could not remember what he had read, and then to find out that your aunt had destroyed it, well it made us think. We knew how much you pinned your hopes on finding it and, well, the priesthood is not you, is it, Caesar? It never was, and so we talked and came up with the plan."

"I see," Caesar frowned.

"Oh, please don't look at me that way, Caesar, we were only doing what we thought was best! Marcus said that one of the letters from the Freedman, to Gaius Marius, was asking if he should try to find the complete prophecy as some of the book he had sent to Marius was missing. He said that he might know where to find it, the one written down for the Sybil, because apparently they are kept somewhere safe, though I don't know where, but this Freedman obviously did. Marcus said there was no further letter from the freedman to say he had found the prophecy and there probably would have been, if he had… Sorry, am I making sense? So…"

"I think so, but slow down and take a breath will you? Good, so the point you are trying to make is, that Marcus decided to look for it instead?"

"Yes, but first he had to find the Freedman and that proved rather difficult. You can see now why we didn't want to tell you all this at the time. There were so many things that could have gone wrong and we didn't want to raise your hopes."

Caesar nodded. "So what happened?"

"Marcus promised to keep me informed but I only ever received one letter from him, until today that is. He found the Freedman, well, his son actually, for the old man had died, but the son remembered his father talking of the prophecy and he told Marcus where to go to look for it."

Caesar's eyes lit up as the first rays of hope began to dawn on him. "Did Marcus say where?"

"No, he didn't write much, you know what Marcus is like, but he did say that as soon as he had the opportunity he would go and look."

"So, did he? Did he find it?"

"Yes! That's why I had to see you this morning, to explain everything. Look, see for yourself!"

Caesar unrolled the small scroll and cast his eyes down the familiar scratchy writing. The letter was brief but Marcus explained how he had found the prophecy hidden in a temple together with all the prophecies the Sybil from Arpinium had made in her lifetime. Unable to remove the original, Marcus had copied it down and …was now on his way back to Rome to deliver it personally to Caesar!"

Caesar leapt to his feet. "But he can't come back! It's too dangerous. If Sulla's men find him…"

"I know, my thoughts entirely, but what can we do? We don't know when he sent this letter because he didn't date it, or where he is now; how can we hope to find him and warn him in time? But that aside, there must be something in that prophecy or why else would he risk his life to bring you a copy? This could be the beginning, Caesar, this could be the sign you have been waiting for!"

Caesar looked at Aemi and his eyes filled with tears. "Oh, Aemi, how can I ever thank you enough, both of you. This is…this is it, I can feel it; One day I will be free from this bondage and the prophecy will confirm it. I have hope, real hope once more!"

"Well, Marcus has got to reach us yet, but yes, it does sound promising doesn't it? I just wish there was some way that we could find him and warn him about Sulla. If he gets caught…" Aemi shuddered involuntarily.

"We must have faith, faith in the gods. Marcus will find some way to communicate with us, until then we must wait and hope that all goes well for him."

"I can't deny that there is no love now between Marcus and I, but I don't wish him ill, either. If he returns to Rome I will help him if I can, but once you have safe delivery of the prophecy I cannot in all conscience help him further. It would be a betrayal of my father's memory and it could endanger my life and my family's. I will sacrifice neither for Marcus."

"I understand, Aemi, and I am grateful for all that you have done for me. I know it must be hard for you," said Caesar with a grateful smile. "I promise you that one day I shall be in a position to repay your loyalty ten times over,"

Aemi shook his head. "I don't want repaying Caesar; our friendship has always meant everything to me, and that is all I need. Marcus and I believe in you, Caesar, we always have, and perhaps something in those words written by the Sibyl long ago will give you back the hope that one day you will be set free to follow the destiny intended for you."

Suddenly the door to the dressing room burst open and Cinnilla rushed in, tears streaming down her face. "Oh, Gaius, Gaius!" she sobbed as she flung herself into Caesar's arms.

"Cinnilla, whatever is the matter?"

"Oh, Gaius, it's awful… awful!" she cried, burying her face into his chest like a frightened child. "It's your cousin…Marius…"

"Young Marius?"

"Yes…they…they have put his…his head…on …the…rostra!" Cinnilla burst into tears again.

"By all the gods, not again!" Aemi exclaimed.

"How do you know this, Cinnilla?" Caesar said, gently pulling his wife away so that he could see her face.

"Your mother…sent a slave…to tell you...Oh, Gaius, your aunt Julia knows…and she is on her way to the Forum!"

"What? She mustn't, the sight would kill her! I must go at once," he said, letting go his hold on Cinnilla and snatching a cloak from the back of his chair.

"I'll come too," said Aemi.

"Are you sure?"

"Yes, you're going to need help," Aemi replied firmly as he made his way out of the door.

"Cinnilla, you must remain in the house. Do not leave until I send word, or I return, do you understand?" Caesar ordered as he threw the cloak hastily over his shoulders.

"But I can help!"

"No, you will do as I say and remain here where it is safe. I will return, never fear," he said kindly but firmly. And with a parting peck on her wet cheek he was gone, following Aemi down the stairs.

Julia had been resting in Aurelia's sitting room when the voices of two young female slaves gossiping about the death of Young Marius, floated through the window.

Hysterical with shock and grief, Julia insisted on making her way down to the Forum to see if the news was true. Nothing Aurelia could say or do could deter her, and she could only manage to dispatch a hasty plea for help to Caesar before she was forced to accompany Julia.

As they reached the edge of the crowded Forum, Aurelia stopped and refused to go any further. "Please, Julia, I am begging you…don't do this to yourself. Come home with me and we can grieve together. Please, Julia,"

But Julia pulled her arm free and hastened into the crowd.

"Julia, no…please!" Aurelia shouted, but she was already losing sight of Julia in the crowd and she had no choice but to follow.

Julia clawed her desperate way through the tightly packed bodies until she finally arrived at the edge of the Rostra, Aurelia beside her, and then she looked up…up to the Rostra towering above her, her eyes drawn up to the thick white pole that stood like a sentinel high above the crowd, to behold the head of her son.

It was Julia's scream, the scream of a desperate woman forced to come face to face with a mother's worst nightmare, that carried itself around the Forum, forcing the crowd to silence, and her nephew, Caesar, to come running.

The people around the two women moved back to give them space, not wishing to impose on the raw, heart wrenching grief of a mother who had just lost her child. Julia was beside herself, and she began to rip at her veil, her dress, her hair, clawing and tearing, and all the time screaming; "*My son*! *My son*!"

Aurelia could do nothing but watch the violence Julia was inflicting upon herself for in such grief there is also great strength, and Aurelia knew that there was nothing she could physically do to stop her. She looked in desperation at the hundreds of faces around her but the people turned their backs or avoided her gaze.

"Help her, please, someone, help her!" she cried, but no one moved, no one spoke, no one dared; they just stood in stone faced silence, afraid to show any compassion, for up on to the rostra, facing the crowd, and watching Julia's maniacal display of grief, appeared Sulla.

The Dictator of Rome stood alone on the stone platform towering above the people and watched, his face an expressionless mask, at the scene of violent grief played out below him. The people's faces were turned towards him now, no longer interested in the spectacle of the head of their defeated Consul, or the grief stricken mother's screams, for here stood the most powerful man in Rome, the most powerful man in the world. His very presence seemed to fill the rostra to the exclusion of all else and his ice-cold eyes flickered unemotionally down to Julia, who was now prostrated on the ground writhing in pain and anguish and oblivious to his arrival.

Aurelia sensed the mood of the crowd had changed and she looked up towards the rostra for the first time, straight into the eyes of Sulla. Such hatred, such malice, Aurelia had never before seen in the eyes of a man; such power exuded from those icy shards that she felt as though her very soul shrivelled from his gaze. For a heartbeat, Aurelia felt as though she might pass out, but Sulla broke eye contact and looked back out at the crowd before him.

Aurelia fell to her knees, feeling weak and helpless but fully aware that Julia was now in terrible danger. "Julia, no! Julia, stop!" she cried, trying to get hold of Julia's flailing arms. Whether through sheer exhaustion or perhaps she too sensed the danger, Julia stopped fighting and fell limply into Aurelia's outstretched arms, sobbing uncontrollably, "My son, my son…What has he done to my son?"

"Your son received the punishment that a traitor of Rome deserves!" Sulla spat contemptuously.

Aurelia cringed in fear at the pure hatred she could feel emanating from his presence and his words.

The sound of a male voice seemed to bring Julia to her senses for she lifted her head to see who had spoken such cruel words. *My…son…was…no…traitor*!" she screamed, lifting her eyes to look up at Sulla.

Sulla remained immobile, his face sat hard as flint.

Aurelia tried to stop Julia scrambling to her feet but she was not strong enough and Julia stood and faced Sulla.

"You…you *murderer*" she screamed. "You killed my son! *Why?*" she cried, and an agonising wail tore itself from within her. "*Why*?"

Sulla ignored her, giving time for Aurelia to stand up and steady Julia, who was swaying with hysteria. Aurelia saw that Sulla's attention had been drawn to someone in the crowd, and she instinctively turned to look for her son.

Caesar slowly made his way to the front of the crowd. "Mother! Aunt Julia!"

"Oh, Caesar, thank the gods!" Aurelia gasped in relief, and suddenly the reality of the situation hit her and she began to cry.

Caesar glanced up at the rostra as Sulla stood silently watching, then back to his mother. "You must leave here, now," he urged in a low but firm voice.

"She won't leave, I have tried!" Aurelia cried desperately.

"Aunt Julia, listen to me," said Caesar sternly.

Julia looked up at her nephew, her sobs catching in her throat, "Caesar, is that you?"

"Yes, Aunt, now listen to me…"

"Oh, Caesar, look…look what they have done to …my…*son*!" Julia let out a high-pitched wail and reached out her arms, seeking his warm comforting embrace.

Caesar stepped quickly out of her reach before she could touch him. He had already broken too many rules today and he didn't want to make things any worse than they already were. He looked round, desperate to find someone to help him and he was relieved to see a young man who lived only two houses along from his mother's.

"I need you to help them, if you are willing?" Caesar said. "Take Julia's arm and help Mother to get her out of here."

The young man nodded and quickly put his arm around Julia's waist to take the weight from Aurelia.

"Come Julia, it is time to leave," said Aurelia softly, keeping hold of Julia's arm.

"*No, no*, I cannot leave my son!"

"Julia, listen to me!" Caesar commanded. " Your son is not here, now you must leave!"

The commanding tone of his voice jolted Julia into compliance and she stopped resisting, falling limply against the young man.

"Get out of this crowd and find two litters to take them home," Caesar told the young man. "Tell them that you are on business for the Flamen Dialis and you should not have to pay."

The young man nodded and with Aurelia's help, he escorted Julia through the crowd, who stood back to let them pass.

Caesar watched as they disappeared into the crowd and then turned to leave.

"Priest, one moment!"

Caesar turned round to face the rostra once again and looked up at Sulla who was now standing directly above him. The cold, calculating eyes of Sulla met the deep, black, fathomless eyes of Caesar.

"You are the Flamen Dialis, judging by your appearance," said Sulla.

"I am," Caesar replied, holding Sulla's gaze with not a trace of fear showing on his face.

"Then why, pray, are you breaking your religious rules of conduct by standing here before me now on un-hallowed ground?"

Caesar could hear the people around him muttering their agreement with Sulla's observation but he ignored them. "The crowd was too dense to allow my litter to pass."

Sulla walked closer to the edge of the Rostra, his eyes never leaving Caesar's face. "You called that woman, Aunt. You are related to Gaius Marius?" Sulla's eyes narrowed ominously.

"Yes. She was my father's sister. I am related to Gaius Marius by marriage."

"And your father's name is?"

"Was, he is dead; Gaius Julius Caesar he was called and I am his son of the same name, a name I bare with honour." Caesar drew himself up proudly to his full, imposing height and saw the sudden look of recognition on Sulla's face.

"Ah yes, the little boy who told me once with such certainty that he was going to be the greatest Roman general that ever lived…and instead you grew up to become a priest!"

"I am honoured that you should remember me," said Caesar courteously, but the flash of anger in his eyes belayed his feelings at Sulla's jibe.

"So, that traitor is your cousin, then?" said Sulla, glancing up at the head of Young Marius. "He should have learned to row before he tried to steer," he said contemptuously and looked back expectantly at Caesar.

Caesar remained silent, using every ounce of self-control he could muster but he refused to drop his gaze.

Sulla snorted and eyed Caesar up and down. "Go home, Priest. Your job here is done."

Caesar held Sulla's gaze for a moment more and then turned to walk away.

"Priest, just one more thing," Sulla called out.

Caesar stopped but did not turn round to face Sulla again.

"If you must break the law, do it to seize power: in all other cases, observe it."

Caesar understood the double meaning of Sulla's words only too well. Smiling, he turned round to face Sulla. "I thank you, Lucius Cornelius Sulla, for your advice. I shall remember it, always." And with a curt nod, Caesar turned and walked back through the crowd who parted silently, bowing respectfully to their high priest, leaving Sulla to watch and wonder.

Caesar arrived home late in the evening, exhausted from the day's trials, to be greeted by his angry wife.

"Where have you been, Gaius?" Cinnilla stormed at him as he walked into the atrium. "I have been waiting all day for you to come home. Anything could have happened to you! And what about your aunt Julia and your mother, where are they? How are they? You promised that you would send me a message; I have been going out of my mind with worry!"

Caesar placed his hat wearily on the table. "If you must shout, can we at least go to my study where it is private." He walked off down the corridor with Cinnilla following close behind.

She slammed the door behind her as she entered the room and stood facing her husband, hands planted firmly on her hips. "Why do you always treat me like a child?" she raged.

"Because you act like one," said Caesar, pouring himself a drink.

"No I do not!" she cried angrily. "I deserve more respect than you give me, Gaius. You never trust me with anything important and you always shut me out. You, with your friends and your family; you make it quite clear that you do not need me!"

"Now that's not true, Cinnilla…"

"Yes, it is! And I want to know why the Pontifex Maximus has sent an urgent message here demanding that you go and see him tomorrow straight after prayers. What have you done to make him so angry, Gaius? I want to know!"

"I committed the most heinous of crime of walking in the Forum," Caesar sighed, knowing that his answer would only enrage Cinnilla even more.

"You did what? Oh, Gaius, it is un-holy!"

"Don't you think I know that?" Caesar snapped.

"Then why did you do it, Gaius? What possible excuse could there be for so blatantly breaking our sacred code of conduct?"

"Mother needed me. I had no choice but to walk because the crowds were too dense to allow the litter to pass."

"So, as usual your family come first, over everything else! Me, I do not matter, and your status as Flamen Dialis is held in even more contempt. When are you going to accept what you are, and show some respect?"

Caesar bit his lip to prevent the retort from slipping out.

"You just think of yourself, always you, you, you. How selfish can one man be? I thought my father was bad, but he pales into insignificance compared to your arrogance. The People look up to you, they respect you, and yet they see you flout our religious codes and what do they think? Why did you ever become the Flamen when it is obvious that you have nothing but contempt, for your position, and for the people you serve?"

Caesar felt his face flush with anger and he slammed his fist down on the table. "I did not choose to be the Flamen! I was forced into it, as you well know, just as I was forced into this marriage. Do you think that I like living in this…this bondage? I hate it, do you hear me, I hate it! I hate the prayers, and…and the chants. I hate the clothes and the *endless* rules, telling me what I can't do and nothing of what I want to do. I *hate* this house and I *hate* this life! There, I've said it. Is that what you wanted to hear…well, is it?"

Cinnilla stood shaking with emotion as tears rolled down her cheeks. She shook her head meekly but didn't reply.

"I am tired of being forced to live a life I hate, tired of being forced to do as I am told," Caesar ranted. "I live a life that is *no* life; I am a man that is *no* man, for I am forbidden to do the things that I have grown up to enjoy; riding, shooting, fighting, I can't do anything that would make me feel worthy as a Roman or as a man. Everything has been taken away from me, so yes, I despise being the Flamen ; I loathe it with every fibre of my being! I was meant to do far better things with my life than this; greater things than you could ever imagine or even begin to understand. I have always had a sense of who I am and who I am supposed to be. I was born to be great, but instead I'm trapped in this…this mausoleum, and all because one man was scared that his place in history would be usurped by a boy. In his evil twisted mind I was a threat to Gaius Marius, to all that he was and all that he could ever be. I would be more, so much more, and I tell you, Cinnilla, he was right! I would have been a threat, a very *real* threat, and he knew it, and I know it, even now, and so did my family. They were scared; they still are, of letting me be who I really am. My father and my mother were always trying their best to protect me. Well I tell you, Cinnilla, I don't need protecting!" Caesar slammed his fist down on the table again and the force sent the goblet of water crashing to the floor. "I am who I am, and nothing and no one will stop me from becoming who I was born to be. Not the Pontifex Maximus, not my mother, not even Sulla the Dictator. My chance to get out of this life is coming, I can feel it, and when it does I shall be ready, and I shall welcome it with open arms. I will do whatever it takes to be free from this life, *whatever* it takes Cinnilla, but I will be free; *I will be free!*"

Cinnilla stood rooted to the spot and stared in mortification at this tirade from her husband, and then she cried out in anguish, clutching her stomach. "I am sorry I have been such a burden and a disappointment to you, Gaius," before turning and running from the room.

Caesar stood open mouthed at the retreating back of his wife. As the anger began to subside the full realisation of what he had said and done hit him so hard that he felt winded and he collapsed back into his chair. "Oh no," he groaned as he put his head in his hands. All the anger that had boiled up inside him like an erupting volcano had spilled out, hurting the one person who had never given him anything but love and support. Cinnilla was the very last person he had meant to hurt in all of this, in fact he was shocked at his own behaviour, for he never realised until now just how much the past two years had been slowly gnawing away inside him. He thought he had coped well with the disappointments life had thrown at him, Gaius Marius had thrown at him, but, all the time it had simmered silently just below the surface of his consciousness, eating away at his self belief, his confidence, the very sense of who he was as a man.

Now all that had changed for Caesar realised that he had never really lost himself, he had just been buried beneath the colourful priestly garb that was his life; the real Caesar, the true Caesar was still inside and he had just found himself again, through that explosion of anger and resentment. Unfortunately, this metamorphosis had come at a price: Cinnilla.

Caesar looked up and wondered where she was and what she was doing now? He had not meant to hurt her. True, this marriage had been forced upon him but Cinnilla's sweetness, her innocence, her trust and devoted love for him had slowly turned the liking he felt for her at the beginning to a fondness, and now, to love. He froze, as the realisation of his true feelings dawned on him. Yes, he loved her, and he had not known it until now.

He jumped up from his chair, his heart beating wildly, and ran into the atrium. "Cinnilla, Cinnilla!" he shouted. He turned to the stairs and ran up them two at a time. "Cinnilla!" Hearing no reply he ran down the long winding corridor to her bedroom, which was next to his own. He pushed the handle, but the door was locked. "Cinnilla!" he called out as he rattled the door trying to get in.

"Go away!" Cinnilla cried.

Caesar put his ear to the door and heard his wife's pitiful sobs coming from the room. "Cinnilla, please, open the door," he said softly, hoping to coax her into letting him in.

"Why should I? You don't want me, you said as much!" she cried out angrily. "Go away!"

"I do, Cinnilla, I do. Listen, please let me in and I can explain."

"No, go away!"

Caesar slid down to the floor with his back to the door and rested his head against the hard, cold, wood. "Cinnilla, I am sorry, I am so sorry I said those things to you downstairs. I didn't mean to hurt you, and I can understand why you are angry with me but please, let me talk to you."

After a few minutes of silence Caesar heard the large wooden key turn in the lock to Cinnilla's door and he got to his feet, as slowly, the door opened to reveal Cinnilla, puffy faced, blood shot eyes, but with a weary smile on her face.

"You do like me then?" she said timidly.

"Oh Cinnilla, I like you, of course I like you!" he said, sweeping her into his arms. "I more than like you, I…I love you."

Cinnilla buried her face into his chest as fresh tears ran down her cheeks.

"Did you hear me, Cinnilla, I love you," Caesar said tenderly, burying his face into her warm, softly scented hair.

"And I love you to," she said sheepishly. "We both do."

Caesar pulled back gently from her embrace and looked searchingly into her face. "We?"

Cinnilla blushed and nodded. "Yes. Me, and our unborn child."

Caesar was flabbergasted. "What, you mean you are…?"

"Yes, I am." A cloud crossed her face. "I am sorry, Gaius, I did not mean to tell you like this, please don't be angry," she said.

"Angry, oh you silly little woman, of course I'm not angry," said Caesar with a smile. "How could I be, especially now," he said, running a gentle hand over her flat stomach. "How long?" he asked, gazing down at her tenderly.

"Two months I think," she said.

"Then the baby will be born the same month as his father,"

"He will be just like his father," said Cinnilla with a smile that Caesar recognised as one of pure joy.

"Then Rome had better watch out!" Caesar joked.

"Oh, Gaius, are you truly happy, about the baby, I mean? I am sorry that you feel the way you do about your life; I never realised you were so unhappy."

Caesar pulled her to him again and held her tightly. "Yes, Cinnilla, I am happy. I am the happiest I have ever been at this moment, and as to what is to come, well, that is in the hands of the gods, and I shall follow wherever my destiny lies. As long as I have you by my side, and our little one, I can face anything," he said, and this time he truly meant what he said, with all his heart.

"And I will be with you, always, Gaius, whatever happens," said Cinnilla, burying her face into his chest. "Always."

# CHAPTER NINETEEN

*'For how many things, which for our own sake we should never do,*
*Do we perform for the sake of our friends?"*
*(Marcus Tullius Cicero)*

## ROME: January- June 81 BC

*Senior Consul: Gnaeus Cornelius Dollabella*
*Junior Consul: Marcus Tullius Decula*

*A strange thing began to happen in Rome; men began to disappear without trace. Knights and senators alike; one minute living and breathing the next, gone. Where were these men? What had happened to them, the city whispered.*

*Then the families of these men were turned out of their homes, their estates and personal wealth confiscated, their slaves sold in the auctions; all taken in the name of the Republic; but as everyone knew, the Republic was now one man: Sulla.*

*Panic gripped the city. What was Sulla up too? What would he do next? The wealthy elite of Rome quaked in their boots for there could be only one explanation; Sulla was exacting his revenge.*

The meeting of the Senate was a solemn affair. Senators were still reeling from the consular elections which had turned out to be nothing but a farce when Sulla had stepped in and declared that for the following year he would have Consuls of his choosing and duly appointed Dollabella and Decula, to the dismay of the Senate and People who had believed, naively, that Súlla would adhere to the constitution of the Republic. The increasing number of men who had simply disappeared without trace was on everyone's mind as the senators settled down to the meeting, and the fear was palpable, as Sulla entered the hall and took his seat, high on the dais.

The business of the day started well enough as hardly any senator spoke for or against the changes to the constitution that Sulla now proposed. Finally, when the strain became too much to bare, one brave young senator rose from the back tier of the House to ask the question that was in everyone's mind.

"I beg permission to speak, Dictator,"

Sulla eyed the young man coolly. "What is your name?"

"Gaius Metellus, Dictator…Sir" he stammered.

"Sulla will do just fine, Gaius Metellus. Well, what is it?"

"Sulla, I believe I speak for all in the House when I say that there is increasing concern over the number of men, both knights and senators, who have been taken from their homes and…and…"

"Executed, is that the word you are looking for?"

Gaius Metellus swallowed and nodded. "Yes, yes… that is the word I am looking for. May I be so bold as to presume that, as these men are being…executed, the word itself implying that they have committed a crime of some sort, that this is being done with your full knowledge and consent?"

Sulla's cold eyes flickered over the room. "You presume right, Gaius Metellus. They have committed a crime and therefore they have been executed."

"Ah, right…well then, may I be so bold as to ask how long you intend to continue with these…executions? How many more men do you intend to…to…"

"Execute? In answer to your question, Gaius Metellus…" Sulla paused as if to give the question some thought. "I don't know." He almost laughed aloud as he saw the colour drain from the young man's face, but then, give him his due, he had been the only one with enough courage to ask the question on everybody's lips, so Sulla simply nodded and smiled.

"Sulla, with respect, we are not trying to free from punishment those men you have already determined shall die, but rather, free from this awful suspense those men whom you have decided shall live."

Sulla had never heard such depth of silence in all his time as a member of the Senate. He could have heard a pin drop as every senator held his breath. He waited just long enough to see several of his colleagues start to squirm uncomfortably in their seats and then he answered, "I have not yet decided."

"Then…then please, Sulla, please tell us who you intend to punish!" Gaius Metellus cried, his face creased with sheer exasperation.

Sulla admired the bravery of the young senator standing alone amongst a sea of white and purple. He cast his eyes over the rest of the room and every man present avoided his gaze. "For you, Gaius Metellus, I will do as you ask, since you are the only man in this room who had the courage to stand up and face me."

Gaius Metellus blushed to the roots of his red hair, and, nodding his thanks, he resumed his seat.

Sulla signalled, and a scribe handed over a large scroll, which he opened. "I have here in my hand a list of eighty names of the men that have been proscribed. Several of them have already been dealt with, as I am sure by now you are all aware, and I shall have their names crossed off the list before it is posted up on the Rostra, immediately after this meeting concludes."

Silence.

"Any man whose name appears on this list will not only forfeit his life, for crimes committed against Rome, but also his estate, and his personal wealth. His family will be required to vacate any property owned by the proscribed man and all slaves will be sold off at auction, together with all confiscated property. The proscribed person will be stripped of his citizenship, as will all his children. No son or grandson of the proscribed man will hold Roman citizenship, and they will be barred from running for any public office during their lifetime. Anyone found harbouring a proscribed person will also be proscribed and suffer the same fate. There will be no exceptions. A reward of two talents will be awarded to anyone, of any social rank, who finds and slays a proscribed person. Proof of their death will of course have to be shown before the monies are awarded; a head will suffice. There will be no limit to the number of proscribed men one individual can claim. The proscriptions do not merely encompass those men who still reside in Rome, but, covers the whole of Italy, therefore any man thinking of leaving Rome to avoid detection had better go much further afield, and never think of returning, for they will remain proscribed until the day they die. As I said, this list will be posted on the Rostra for all to see and will be updated daily. Once all the men on the list have been accounted for the proscriptions will stop. Now, does that answer your question sufficiently, Gaius Metellus?" Sulla asked casually.

Metellus sat open mouthed in complete shock, as did every other senator in the room. He merely nodded to Sulla.

"Good, now, any questions, or do you all completely understand what I have said?" Sulla asked lightly, gazing from face to face.

"But… what about a trial? You cannot condemn a Roman citizen for any crime without a trial!" Proconsul Lucius Cornelius Orestes spoke angrily.

Every head turned to look at Orestes as he spoke, and then, as one, every head turned back to look at Sulla.

"Who says I can't?" Sulla replied calmly. "I am Dictator; a position you gave me freely, is that not so? I am above the laws of Rome, I make the laws of Rome; *I am* the law in Rome!"

"But who decides what crime the man has committed? Who decides if they are guilty of committing the crime levelled against them?" Orestes persisted.

"I do."

"And what if some of the men proscribed are actually innocent; what then? You will be guilty of committing a crime against them!"

The purple marks on Sulla's face began to mottle and darken and his eyes hardened as he fought to keep his anger under control. "You *dare* to talk to me of crimes against the innocent? You, who sat wallowing in Rome on your fat arse when Marius and Cinna entered Rome and committed massacres on an unimaginable scale. What did you do to stop the murder of *innocent men* then? Catalus Caesar, Lucius Caesar, Marcus Antonius, Marcus Aemilius Lepidus, to name but a few. *Innocent men*, who once sat beside you in this House. *Innocent men*, who lost their lives because they opposed Marius and Cinna. *Innocent men*, who stood up for what was right; who upheld the traditions and laws of Rome, who had the courage of their convictions to stand up and be counted, and what did you do, Orestes? You blew with the wind, stayed out of the way, committed yourself to nothing and no one, whilst all around you *innocent men died*! The men proscribed on this list are not innocent, they are murderers, they supported murderers; they are guilty! They deserve to be punished, and by all the gods I will make sure that every last one of them is found and dealt with. There is no, *innocent man*, on my list for every last one has been declaimed by another who saw what they did, who knows their guilt, and who wants to see justice done for the memory of all those truly *innocent men* who died! Now, *I will hear no more*!" Sulla shouted, his face purple with rage and indignation. "The next man who so much as raises an eyebrow will find their name on this list, is that understood?" He glowered from the dais at the cowering men below.

Sulla threw the scroll to the scribe beside him. "Put that on the Rostra, *now*!" He turned to face the senators again. "This meeting is over. The next shall be convened five days from now when the new Consuls shall take up their office. You are all dismissed," he said, rising to his feet, and with one last look of contempt he strode down the dais and out of the door.

The senators remained seated in total silence until the door slammed behind Sulla, and then as one, over two hundred men abandoned their stools and scrambled, pushing and shoving, as they made their way out into the Forum. They had only one thought in their minds as they raced for the Rostra where the scribe had just finished nailing the scroll to the notice board. Was their name on that list?

The dining room was full. Over a hundred men, their animated faces, lively banter, and raucous laughter reminded Aemi of the time his father had taken him to his first big gladiatorial games. The crowds had behaved in the same way; the excitement and anticipation of a well fought, bloody battle, was almost palpable in the air whilst they waited for the games to begin, as Sulla's guests waited now, for they had all received an invitation to dine with the Dictator who had promised an evening of unsurpassed entertainment.

Aemi stood apart from the main body of guests, in the corner of the room, to avoid conversation. Apart from a brief word of encouragement from Marcus Aurelius, who was also a guest this evening, Aemi had hardly spoken. What was there to say, for his worst fears had been realised; Marcus had been captured and dragged back to Rome to face the wrath and revenge of Sulla.

From the moment he had received his invitation announcing the news and the evening celebration, Aemi knew that all hope was lost. Beside himself with grief he had turned to Caesar for comfort, and together the friends had mourned this tragedy, for both knew, that by the end of the night, Marcus would be dead. Aemi had gone over this moment in his mind a hundred times, wondering how long it would be before Marcus was hunted down. From the minute he had betrayed him to Sulla, Aemi had felt nothing but remorse, and a longing to set things right with Marcus. All the hatred and blame he had harboured for so long evaporated when he saw Sulla write his friend's name down on the list of men doomed to die, but, his efforts to trace Marcus, to warn him that his life was in danger, had been in vain, and so he had spent the afternoon in painful reproach and resignation with Caesar.

Now the moment he had been dreading had arrived, and Aemi didn't know how he was going to get through this night. Rumours circulated the room about what form the evening's entertainment would take, but Sulla had kept his guests guessing, promising only that it would be an unforgettable event.

Aemi stopped a passing slave with a tray full of drinks and exchanged his empty goblet for a fresh one. He had decided to get as drunk as possible in the hope that this evening would pass in a forgettable haze. Suddenly, Sulla clapped his hands and called for attention. A flash of light caught Aemi's eye as he turned towards Sulla and he looked past the Dictator, through the open, double doors of the dining room, to the garden beyond. Two lines of legionary guards were marching from either side of the villa, each man holding a long wooden torch in front of him. The bright flames rippled as thick smoke from the burning pitch on the newly lit torches burned away, thin black tendrils, snaking out into the blood red sky of sunset.

Sulla was addressing his guests but Aemi heard nothing, his attention transfixed on the soldiers as they marched past the candlelit gold fountain into the vast open expanse of the garden beyond. They formed a large circle, and stood to attention, their torches held high to illuminate the area around them.

"Now, if you have all eaten your fill, I have arranged a little something, as promised earlier, for your entertainment," Sulla smiled.

Aemi saw the faces of the guests looking at Sulla in eager anticipation, like hungry dogs looking at their masters, waiting to be fed, and he felt his knees go weak.

Sulla led the way, the rest of the guests following close behind as they walked down the steps and out into the garden. The path was lit by torches staked into the ground to illuminate the way as they followed Sulla towards the fountain, for the sun had dipped below the horizon, and the darkness of night closed around them.

Aemi hung back from the main body of guests as they walked across the finely manicured lawn. He was fighting back the anxiety that threatened to overwhelm him and all he wanted to do was to get away from this place as quickly as possible. He remembered Caesar's words and began to mutter them like a chant under his breath, "Stay strong, stay strong," but he didn't feel strong, and he wondered how he was going to get through the rest of the evening. He suddenly became aware that a hand had been placed upon his shoulder. He turned to see Marcus Aurelius walking closely by his side.

"I understand," Marcus Aurelius said under his breath so as not to be overheard, and with a brief squeeze to Aemi's shoulder, he walked on to join the main group who had gathered behind the fountain.

As Aemi joined them, he saw that a large dais had been erected which had not been visible from the house. There were five steps leading up onto the main platform upon which, a single gold and purple velvet chair was positioned.

Sulla mounted the dais and sat down. In front of him, the legionaries that formed the arena stood to attention, holding their torches aloft, whilst a single centurion stood to one side, watching Sulla.

"I am honoured that so many of you could join me at such short notice this evening," Sulla began, smiling at his guests. "You may not all know each other but we all have one thing in common; a man who was an enemy to us all. Gaius Marius was taken from this world before the right and just punishment he deserved could be meted out. I know many of you standing before me feel robbed of the opportunity to see that man pay for the crimes he committed against you, your friends, your families, and against Rome. The untimely suicide of his son also took away any opportunity we had for justice, but, I am pleased to announce that the gods have seen fit not to deny us completely the chance to avenge our dead, for they have placed in my hands the last surviving son of our enemy, Marcus Marius." Sulla nodded to the centurion, who hurried off into the shadows behind the fountain.

"There are those in Rome," Sulla continued, "who ascribe to the notion that the sins of the father should not be brought to bear on the sons… but I am not one of those men. The greatness of the father shines down to reflect on the son. It follows then, that the crimes, the shame, the loss of reputation and the punishment, are his to bear as well."

Aemi heard the sound of scuffling and the clinking of chains coming from behind the fountain, as Sulla spoke, and his insides turned to ice as he realised what was about to happen.

"Tonight, gentlemen, I will prove that I, Lucius Cornelius Sulla Felix, am a man of my word. I promised you revenge and I promised that not one man would be left alive who was guilty for the crimes committed against you. I have kept that promise… for I bring you…Marcus Marius!"

Every head turned to look, as from behind the fountain, the centurion led four guards who were wrestling to keep upright the struggling, manacled figure of Marcus.

Aemi's head swam, and he struggled to remain in control as he saw the pitiful sight of his friend being dragged across the garden towards him.

Marcus fought every inch of the way, until finally, two of the guards grabbed his legs and he was carried the rest of the way before being dumped at the foot of the dais. The Centurion stepped forward and put his foot across the side of Marcus's head to keep him pinned to the ground.

Sulla looked down upon Marcus, his face a picture of hate filled scorn, as his enemy's son lay sprawled in the dirt before him. "Marcus Marius, son of the traitor, Gaius Marius, and brother to the traitor, Consul Gaius Marius." Sulla introduced him to the assembled group.

Several guests stepped forward and spat on Marcus's prone body to show their contempt for the son of their enemy, for what they could not do to Marius they could do to his son, without fear of retribution.

"Stand him up!" Sulla ordered, and the guards hauled on the chains, dragging Marcus to his feet.

Aemi fought back tears as he looked at Marcus. Cuts and bruises covered his arms and legs, some of them fresh for the blood still oozed out of his skin. His body was covered in dirt, his tunic ripped and torn, and one shoulder was covered in dried blood and filth. His hair was matted and unkempt, his face swollen and bruised where he had obviously suffered a beating, but he fought against the guards, shaking them off so that he could stand proud and unbent in front of Sulla.

"Marcus Marius, son of Gaius Marius, enemy of Rome," said Sulla, sitting in judgement before him. "You are guilty of committing crimes against the state. You, and your kin, actively sought my personal destruction, and that of Rome. You are formally stripped of your citizenship, your property and wealth is forfeit. The penalty for your crime is death."

Marcus swayed slightly as the sentence was passed but his chin remained firmly lifted, defiance written all over his young face.

Aemi breathed deeply trying to stave off the rising nausea he felt and wiped his hand across his mouth as his stomach dry heaved. His eyes never leaving Marcus for a second as he willed him to be strong and brave.

"It is you who are the enemy of Rome, Sulla," Marcus spat through swollen lips. "My father committed many crimes but illness was his excuse at the end; what is yours…I"

Before Marcus could speak further the centurion stepped forward and smashed him in the face with his fist, sending him sprawling to the floor as his lip exploded, showering blood on those senators standing nearest to him.

"The sentence is passed," Sulla continued. "But there are two men here with us that also have a claim on your life, besides Rome."

As Sulla spoke, Aemi saw a figure enter the torch lit arena: Catalus Caesar. Dressed in full military uniform, he walked towards the dais, his silver and gold curais and ornamental greaves glinted in the torchlight. The silver studs ornamenting his leather skirt clinked softly as the leather swayed from side to side. Aemi noticed the ornately gilded handle of Catalus Caesar's gladius poking out from the top of the leather baldric that was slung low on his hips, and, in that moment, he realised exactly what the entertainment was going to be. Instinctively, he moved forward to protect Marcus but was prevented from going more than a couple of paces by an iron grip on his upper arm.

"Don't be a fool!" Marcus Aurelius hissed, keeping a firm grip on Aemi's arm.

Even in his desperation Aemi knew that Marcus Aurelius was right. What could he do to help Marcus now? He watched through tear filled eyes as Catalus Caesar faced Marcus.

"Remember me, Marius!" he spat, his voice full of scorn.

"There is the matter of a blood feud to be settled between Catalus Caesar and this man," Sulla addressed the audience. "I have agreed to allow Catalus to satisfy his honour by armed combat."

"There is no honour in this feud and he knows it!" Marcus retorted, spitting a globule of blood from his mouth. "But let him try; I welcome the opportunity to rub his face in the dirt before I die!"

Catalus Caesar's hand reached for his gladius and pulled it half way out of the baldric before Sulla intervened with a raised hand. "All in good time, Catalus, all in good time," he commanded.

Catalus Caesar let the gladius drop back into its holder and scowled menacingly at Marcus.

"I mentioned one other, whose father's death gives him the right to claim your life as forfeit," Sulla spoke directly to Marcus as he beckoned Aemi forward from the group.

Aemi felt physically sick as he moved into Marcus's view for the first time, and the two friends eyes locked together.

"Marcus Aemilius Lepidus had his father ripped from his arms to satisfy the bloody revenge of Gaius Marius. It is now in my power to give the son the opportunity to avenge his father's untimely demise by taking this man's life as forfeit, therefore, I decree that should Marcus Marius be the victor in the forthcoming battle with Catalus Caesar, then he becomes the property of Marcus Aemilius Lepidus. Your fate, however remains the same, Marius, you will die before this evening is ended."

Marcus had not taken his eyes off Aemi once as Sulla spoke, and as Aemi looked at his friend with compassion and sorrow he saw the dawning light of recognition cross his face. In that brief moment, more had passed between them than if they had all the time in the world to talk. Aemi raised his left hand ever so slightly and clenched his fist, a movement that was so insignificant no attention was drawn to it, but Marcus saw it, and he understood. He too raised his left hand and clenched his fist in acknowledgement of the sign; the friendship sign that had been with the three boys since childhood. Marcus nodded and the hint of a smile glinted in his eye before his attention was dragged from Aemi and back to the reality of the fate that awaited him.

"Unchain him," Sulla ordered, and the guards dragged Marcus away from the dais and into the middle of the circle of guards, where they unlocked the padlock holding the chains to Marcus and pulled them free. "Give him a sword," Sulla commanded.

The centurion stepped forward and handed Marcus his own gladius then backed away out of the circle and the guards moved closer together to prevent Marcus from attempting to escape.

"No one is to enter the arena until there is one man left standing," Sulla ordered as Catalus Caesar made his way into the arena.

"Please, join me," Sulla addressed his guests. "You will have a much better view from up here,"

The guests climbed the steps of the dais and arranged themselves on either side of Sulla, who remained seated in his chair. Aemi felt as though his legs were made of lead as he climbed the steps, and, as he looked down into the torch-lit arena, his vision became obscured by the tears that misted his eyes and threatened to break free.

The torches, held by the circle of guards, flickered in the soft evening breeze and cast long silvery shadows on the ground where the two men stood facing each other. Marcus had been given a shield to match the one Catalus Caesar had strapped over his left arm, but he had no other form of protection.

Catalus Caesar began to circle, slowly, and Marcus mirrored the action, keeping the distance equal between them, their eyes locked together, each man searching for signs that the other was about to strike the first blow. Marcus shifted the weight of the gladius in his hand and raised it to waist height. He bent and flexed his knees, keeping his body low for better balance and ease of movement; evenly distributing the weight over his legs so that he could move quickly.

Catalus Caesar made the first move; eager to get the fight under way, leaping forward suddenly, his left arm raised and fell as he brought his gladius down in a chopping motion. Marcus easily parried the blow with his shield and thrust his arm away to deflect the sword from reaching his body. Catalus Caesar followed through immediately with a second, then a third strike, his arm raising and falling as he rained blow after blow on Marcus's shield. Marcus kept his shield close to his body to absorb the impact and protect his chest, stepping back at every blow and regaining his balance quickly. Catalus Caesar made a final, powerful lunge, his gladius smashing down on to Marcus's shield, and as Marcus stepped back he tripped and fell heavily onto his back. He rolled neatly to his right, and then his left, to avoid the blow as Catalus Caesar struck with his gladius, plunging the sword towards Marcus's unprotected body. Marcus rolled to the right again, and Catalus Caesar's gladius plunged into the hard ground, where Marcus had lay only seconds before. Lithely, Marcus jumped to his feet, keeping his body low to avoid any back swipe, his sword held out in front of his body to protect himself as Catalus Caesar spun round to face him and they began to circle each other once again.

This time Marcus took the initiative, lunging forward, one step, two steps, and smashing his gladius onto his opponent's shield, then, quick as lightening, he reversed the stroke and brought the side of his sword cracking down onto Catalus Caesar's unprotected head. He staggered backwards, dazed by the blow, blood trickling from his ear as Marcus pressed home the advantage and lunged his sword at his body, but Catalus Caesar had regained enough of his composure to sidestep the move, and avoided contact with the sword point. He immediately retaliated, slashing down with his gladius, his arm swinging too and fro, left, right, left, right, driving Marcus back across the arena as he tried to avoid the blows. Marcus feinted a step back then shifted his weight onto his front foot and lunged forward, bringing his sword down to make contact with Catalus Caesar's, the sound of clashing iron ringing in the air. Both men leaned all their weight into their swords, each trying to bear down on the other. Marcus proved the stronger man, pushing with all his might as the two swords, locked together, drew ever closer to Catalus Caesar's throat.

At the last second, Catalus Caesar raised his leg high off the ground and thrust his foot into Marcus's stomach. The force of the push sent Marcus flying backwards and he scrambled to regain his balance. Catalus Caesar followed, slashing with his sword, Marcus blocking again with his shield. Just before he hit the guards forming the wall of the arena, Marcus twisted his body suddenly, and as he did so he slashed down at the unprotected side of Catalus Caesar's arm. The metal met the soft yielding skin and sliced into it, and Marcus quickly pulled his gladius away, deepening and lengthening the gash. Blood immediately spurted from the open wound, drenching Catalus Caesar's hand and gladius in warm sticky liquid. Marcus brought his sword down again but Catalus Caesar neatly sidestepped and backed away, glancing at the wound to see how bad it was.

Marcus lunged again, seeing the momentary lapse of attention, but missed his mark and struck a glancing blow on his enemy's shield. Catalus Caesar retaliated immediately, parrying the blow with his shield and lashing out with his gladius.

Their arms moved as a blur, lunging, driving, thrusting, and stabbing, as they moved around the arena. Aemi could hear their laboured breathing from the immense physical exertion they were under.

Catalus Caesar was showing signs of growing frustration and desperation in his actions as he slashed and parried, twisted and turned, whilst Marcus remained controlled, channelling his aggression into actions that were effective; making every blow count.

Catalus Caesar let out a shout of rage and charged blindly at Marcus, intent on using brute force over skill to gain victory. At the last moment, Marcus nimbly sidestepped and Catalus Caesar was unable to stop in time. He hurtled into two of the guards, sending them flying sideways as he sprawled face down on the ground, winded.

"Now, get him now!" Aemi said under his breath, willing Marcus to take advantage of the situation, completely forgetting what the consequences for himself would be if Marcus was the victor.

Marcus remained standing to one side, taking advantage of the minutes rest as his adversary scrambled slowly back to his feet.

Catalus Caesar hurtled once more towards Marcus, his gladius slashing wildly, left, right, left, right, the force of his attack driving Marcus back once more. As Marcus twisted, Catalus Caesar's gladius came crashing down on the side of his shield, and then with a twist of his sword, flipped the shield out of Marcus's grasp, ripping the leather thong from his arm with the force of the movement, and sending it spinning into the air to land outside the arena. Catalus Caesar let out a cry of delight and slashed down with his gladius towards Marcus's exposed head. Marcus managed to duck and dodged sideways, spinning his body round as he did so, he side swiped his gladius and managed to hook the edge of Catalus Caesar's shield. Using all his body weight Marcus pulled his sword back sharply and succeeded in pulling the shield from his arm. The minute the shield hit the floor Marcus kicked it out of reach, a triumphant smile on his face.

"Now we're equal!" he panted.

"We will never be equal, you Italian scum!" Catalus Caesar snarled, shifting his gladius into his other hand as he mirrored Marcus's every move.

Catalus Caesar struck again, feinting a cutting movement before changing it to a low, sideways slash. Marcus was not quick enough this time and the blade slid between his ribs, ripping flesh and breaking bone as Marcus twisted his body off the blade. Blood immediately spread across his tunic turning the dirty grey cloth a dark red. Catalus Caesar followed up his attack, slashing at Marcus's head, but this time he was not so lucky and he missed his mark, as Marcus spun away. Turning on the spot, Marcus managed to get behind Catalus Caesar and he lashed out with his foot, kicking him in the lower back and sending him sprawling once more to the ground.

This time Marcus pressed home the advantage; leaping forward he slashed downwards with his sword, but Catalus Caesar rolled onto his back, bringing his gladius up to meet Marcus and blocking the blow. As Marcus raised his arm to strike again, Catalus Caesar rolled sideways, and as he did so, he slashed back low with his sword and sliced open Marcus's calf. A deep, gaping wound appeared, and blood poured down his leg, filling his boot and seeping out onto the ground. Marcus staggered backwards, gasping in pain, giving Catalus Caesar time to clamber to his feet.

Aemi's stomach lurched as he realised Marcus was badly injured. The loss of blood from the wound to his chest was taking its toll and the wound on his calf was bleeding profusely, weakening him more by the minute. Aemi knew that if Marcus did not disable Catalus Caesar soon, it would all be over.

Marcus made one last desperate attack. He lunged forward, feinting a stab to the chest before changing direction and slicing sideways and upwards. The tip of his blade made contact under Catalus Caesar's upper arm, slicing the soft flesh, and then Marcus dragged the blade downward, slashing open the unprotected skin. Catalus Caesar screamed in pain but continued to fight and their swords met with a crash above their heads. Again, each man pushed against his gladius in this locked embrace, as slowly, the swords came down to face height, then throat height.

"Prepare to die Marius!" Catalus Caesar hissed, as he pushed the swords towards Marcus's unprotected throat.

"It's not over yet!" Marcus cried, pushing back against the swords and forcing them towards his opponent's throat.

Catalus Caesar pushed back with his arms, breaking the deadlock and separating the two men once more. Quick as lightening he brought his gladius down and stabbed forwards. Marcus leapt backwards to avoid the blow but his injured calf folded under him, throwing Marcus off balance. That was all the opportunity Catalus Caesar needed and he took it. Keeping the gladius low, he lunged forward, thrusting towards Marcus's stomach. Unable to bring his sword up in time to protect his body, the smooth, bloodied blade of Catalus Caesar's gladius ripped through Marcus's skin, driving deep into his intestines, and pinned Marcus to the sword.

The enemies stood eye to eye, Marcus unable to move, Catalus Caesar gripping his gladius tightly. The crowd strained, watching every movement, every sound, waiting for the two men to move.

"This…is for my father!" Catalus Caesar cried, and he drove his gladius deeper in to Marcus's body.

Marcus gasped in pain, unable to move, unable to do anything, pinioned to the sword.

"And this…is for all the other innocent men killed by your father!" Catalus Caesar ripped the Gladius upwards, tearing into Marcus's intestines.

Marcus made no sound this time, his eyes rolled as he fought to remain conscious. Blood trickled from his mouth as his body began to haemorrhage from the fatal blow.

"And this…is for my honour!" Catalus Caesar took a step back and tore his gladius from Marcus's body.

Marcus crumpled to the ground, unable to move, clutching at his stomach as blood gushed out in torrents from the gaping hole left by Catalus Caesar's sword.

Catalus Caesar turned to face the dais and held his gladius aloft, the blooded, dripping blade casting a long shadow before him in the torchlight, stretching along the ground and up the steps of the dais, to Sulla's feet.

Aemi stood motionless, staring in horror at the sight before him.

"My father, and my family honour, is avenged!" Catalus Caesar shouted triumphantly to the guests on the dais.

Sulla stood up and walked slowly down the steps. The guards parted to let the Dictator pass into the arena and the guests followed behind.

"Congratulations," Sulla said, patting Catalus Caesar on the shoulder. "A magnificent fight, Catalus, very entertaining."

"Thank-you, Sulla," Catalus Caesar smiled exultantly. Several of the guests came forward to congratulate him, whilst others stared down in disdain at the dying form of Marcus.

"He is still alive," Dollabella said, examining Marcus more closely.

"Is he? Oh, good," said Catalus Caesar, turning to look down at Marcus. "I rather hoped he would be."

"What do you intend to do with him?" Sulla asked casually, as he gazed down at Marcus, who remained perfectly still clutching his stomach, his breath coming now in faint gasps, his eyes misty and unfocussed as death drew ever nearer.

"With your permission, Sulla, I would like to remove him from here. I intend to offer him up to the gods as a funeral offering for the memory of my father…piece by piece," Catalus Caesar sneered, and bent down to look Marcus in the face. "I am going to keep you alive long enough for you to understand what is happening to you," he hissed venomously, spittle landing on Marcus's face. "I am going to take you apart, piece by piece, Marius. You think you suffer now, but that is nothing to what you will suffer, believe me," he said, tracing one slim, bloodied finger along Marcus's chin. "And then, I am going to rip out your heart, and burn it. There will no Elysium for you, my friend, no passage across the waters of eternity, just darkness, eternal darkness."

"Wait!" Aemi stepped forward through the crowd to face Catalus Caesar across the body of his friend. "You have satisfied your honour and avenged the death of your father by becoming the victor this night, but Marius is still alive. I therefore ask, Sulla, that I may have the honour and satisfaction of dealing the final blow to this man so that my father and family honour are given satisfaction, as you promised."

"But he is still mine to do with as I will!" Catalus Caesar exclaimed.

"You shall have him, when I am done. Take his body and sacrifice him to your gods, but I claim my right!" Aemi said firmly, looking at Sulla as he spoke.

"Marcus Aemilius has a fair argument, Sulla," said Marcus Aurelius, stepping forward. "The duel was to the death, but Marius is still alive. Clearly Catalus Caesar is the victor, but in the interests of fairness, by dealing the final blow, Marcus Aemilius would satisfy his honour in this matter and all will be well."

Sulla looked down at Marcus and Aemi held his breath, hoping that Sulla would grant his request and give him the opportunity to save Marcus from being further brutalised in the only way he could, by killing Marcus himself.

"I grant you your request, Marcus Aemilius," said Sulla finally. " I too have been denied my revenge in the past and I understand your need to satisfy your honour. Deal the final blow for the memory of your father. Catalus, you may have the body to do with as he will when Marius is dead."

Catalus Caesar scowled at Aemi but dared not argue with Sulla.

"Thank-you, Sulla, you do not know what this means to me," said Aemi, fighting back the tears. Sulla patted Aemi on the arm and turned away.

The group moved back to give Aemi space and the centurion moved forward and handed Aemi his dagger. Swallowing hard, Aemi took it, glancing over at Marcus Aurelius as he knelt down beside Marcus. Marcus Aurelius nodded, giving nothing away by his face, but Aemi understood and was grateful for his intervention with Sulla.

He looked down at Marcus, who was barely alive through the loss of blood, but still conscious. Aemi tightened his grip around the handle of the dagger and positioned it over his chest. He leaned over and put his mouth next to Marcus's ear.

"Friends," he whispered, and, as he felt Marcus's head twitch in recognition, Aemi plunged the dagger down into his friend's heart.

Caesar allowed himself to breath again as the litter bearers hurried along the road, away from Sulla's villa. He closed his eyes and laid his head back against the cushions, breathing deeply as his heart thumped against his chest. Wiping his hand across his brow he saw that it was covered in cold sweat. The full force of what he had done finally hit him as he felt the litter angle slightly upwards as the bearers turned to climb the Aventine Hill, and he felt suddenly sick with fear. What had he done? By all the gods, what had he done!

He thought back to two days previously, when his uncle, Marcus Aurelius Cotta, had broken the news that Sulla wished to meet him. Knowing, from the moment Sulla returned to Rome, that it had only been a matter of time before the Dictator looked in his direction, Caesar had been horrified, and then filled with rage, when Marcus Aurelius had informed him of Sulla's plans. Cinnilla, as the daughter of a proscribed man, was no longer eligible to hold the post as Flaminica. Her status as a Roman citizen was to be withdrawn, and her dowry confiscated, but, worst of all, Sulla was going to order Caesar to divorce his wife, in order that he could remain the Flamen Dialis. The ensuing argument with his uncle, with Caesar refusing point blank to concede to Sulla's demands, ended, what had been quite possibly, the worst month of his life. First the death of Marcus, a grief that would be slow to heal, then

Aemi leaving Rome, unable to cope with the part he had played in the death of their friend, and now he was expected to abandon his wife to an unknown fate so that he could continue to live the life he hated more than death itself. Caesar had no choice but to attend the summons, when it arrived, and he had gone to see Sulla full of intrepidation, but determination. The meeting had been much worse than he could ever imagine, and Caesar had fled in fear of his life.

"You there, hold up!"

Caesar heard the shout, and immediately the litter bearers stopped. So this was it. Sulla had finally come to his senses and sent his guards after him. Now he would be dragged out into the street and executed on the spot for his defiance. Caesar instinctively flinched as the curtain of his litter was pulled aside.

"Caesar! Oh, goodness, you look ill!"

Caesar opened his eyes and saw Aemi's grinning face peering through the curtains. "Thank the gods!" he sighed with relief.

"What's happened? You look awful, are you sick?" Aemi asked, his voice filled with concern.

"There's no time to talk. Follow me to mother's house and I'll explain everything. Foreword!" Caesar ordered the bearers, and Aemi quickly withdrew his head as the litter moved off.

A short time later the litter stopped and Aemi pulled aside the curtain. "We're here," he said, stepping aside to allow Caesar to get out.

Caesar ordered the litter bearers to collect Cinnilla and to bring her to him, then hurried to the front door, thumping his fist against the thick oak casing. "Open the door, quickly!" The sound of a key turning and bolts drawing preceded the door being opened and Caesar rushed past the door slave and into the atrium with Aemi hard on his heels.

"Mother! Mother!" Caesar called out, glancing down the corridors that branched off from the atrium for signs of his mother. The steward suddenly appeared, hurrying across the peristyle garden.

"Where is Mother?" Caesar asked impatiently.

"In her work room, Holy One," the steward bowed low as he spoke.

"Fetch her, quickly and tell her to come alone, we will be in Father's old room," Caesar called over his shoulder as he disappeared along the corridor towards the study.

"Will you please tell me what's going on?" said Aemi, closing the door behind them.

"Wait for mother, then I will be able to tell you both at the same time," Caesar said as he looked around the study. "I need a drink!"

"Shall I call someone?" Aemi asked, moving to the door. Caesar nodded distractedly, and Aemi left, returning a few seconds later. "It's done," he said.

The door opened and Aurelia walked into the room carrying a tray with goblets and a water pitcher. "Caesar, what a pleasant surprise, I was not expecting you today," she said, placing the tray on the table. "And Aemi, are you back in Rome to stay or is this a passing visit?" she smiled, greeting Aemi with a familiar peck on the cheek.

"Mother, this isn't a social call, I'm afraid," Caesar said, biting his lower lip. "I have something important I have to tell you. I think you better sit down," he said nervously.

Aurelia gave a quizzical look at her son and then at Aemi, who shrugged and took a seat next to Aurelia. "Has something happened, Caesar? It is not bad news I hope?"

Caesar paced the floor, biting his fingernail; a sure sign of his agitation that his mother and Aemi both recognised.

"Caesar?"

"Mother, I have done something today; something that I'm afraid may have very serious consequences for me, and my family."

Caesar saw the colour drain from Aurelia's face. "What has happened?"

"I…I had a meeting, with Sulla, this morning. It…well, it didn't go very well, and as a consequence, he…he has threatened to have me killed."

"He's what!" Aemi and Aurelia exclaimed together.

"But what happened? What did you do to make him say that?" Aemi asked.

Caesar ran his hands through his hair and paced the room. "Putting it succinctly, I defied him. He ordered me to divorce Cinnilla and I refused."

"Divorce Cinnilla? But, I don't understand," Aurelia cried.

"I did wonder what he might do about her," Aemi muttered under his breath.

"He ordered me to divorce Cinnilla because her father has been proscribed, therefore she forfeits her Roman citizenship, and, her position as Flaminica," Caesar explained.

"But how has it ended in Sulla threatening to have you killed, Caesar? What did you do to make him so angry?" Aurelia cried.

"I refused to divorce Cinnilla, that's all. I stood up against him and he got angry. I tried to explain that I was bound by the laws of the sate, we married inconferatio, remember, so divorce is forbidden, and my religious office, which again states that the Flamen cannot divorce his wife, but he wouldn't listen. Sulla says *he* is law now."

"Oh no!"

"And he threatened to have Father proscribed for being a traitor to Rome by siding with Marius. He said he could take everything we own and have you thrown out onto the streets to beg for your living."

Aurelia looked as if she was about to faint and Aemi leant down and placed a comforting arm around her shoulder. "But you told him, Caesar, surely you told him that your father had no choice in the matter?"

"Of course I did, Mother, but I don't think he believed me. Sulla kept saying that we all have choices and that Father could have done things differently, if he'd wanted but…"

"That is not true! What else could he have done? Go against Marius and end up dead, like all those other poor men?"

"I told him that, Mother, and I also said that if he ordered me killed then he would be no better than Marius."

"You said that to Sulla?" Aemi gasped.

Caesar set his jaw in defiance. "I did, and I meant every word of it. Cinnilla is a victim of Sulla's revenge and I will not be party to her punishment as I don't recognise his proscription law; I told him that as well!"

"Oh, Caesar, you fool!" Aurelia cried, anger written all over her face. "You stupid, stupid fool!"

Caesar blushed at his mother's admonition but he was not about to apologise for what he had done. "Sulla is the fool, Mother, for backing himself into a corner where he had no choice but to threaten to have me killed if I refused his order to divorce Cinnilla, and that made him appear as vengeful as Marius; a comparison that he did not take too kindly to," he added with a wry smile.

"By all the gods, Caesar, do you want to die?" Aemi retorted angrily. "Comparing Sulla to Marius is the worst possible thing you could have said; you know how much they hated each other!"

"I know, and perhaps I was a little reckless there, but I still stand by what I said. His law is wrong, and unjust, and, I will not betray my wife, not for Sulla, or any man."

"Did he order you to leave the priesthood as well?" Aemi asked.

Caesar looked uneasy, avoiding his friend's gaze.

"Well? Answer the question, Caesar!"

"No. He said I could remain as the Flamen as long as I divorced Cinnilla." Caesar mumbled, turning his back and making pretence of pouring a drink.

Aemi walked over to face Caesar. "Did you tell him how you came to be a priest in the first place? You did tell him what Marius did to you, didn't you? Caesar?"

"I couldn't," Caesar relied testily.

"But why not? Surely by telling Sulla the truth you might have been able to come to some arrangement? The only reason he asked you to divorce Cinnilla was so that you could keep your office as the Flamen!"

"I would not compromise my dignity and honour." Caesar snapped. "I will not beg to be relieved of the priesthood. He thinks I was given the position as a favour from Gaius Marius. He thinks that I want to be the Flamen, and that I chose the priesthood over a military career. I will not give him the satisfaction of knowing that I was forced into it against my will."

"*Oh for goodness sake, Caesar*!" Aurelia cried. "What difference does it make how you became the Flamen. The point is that you could have tried to reach some compromise with Sulla that would have prevented this…this disaster from happening to us…to all of us!"

"Sulla does not compromise."

"No, and neither do you!" Aurelia shot back angrily. "You and your damned pride! I always knew it would get you into serious trouble one day and now look at you; running from Sulla with the threat of death hanging over you, and what about Cinnilla? Have you given her a thought in all of this, or is it all about you, as usual?"

Caesar glowered at his mother but he made no answer.

"What does it matter what Sulla thinks of you, as long as you are alive? You should have told him the truth." Aurelia berated her son.

"You wouldn't understand, Mother!" Caesar shouted angrily as his frayed temper finally snapped. "He laughed at me, he held me in scorn. He remembered what I had said to him as a young boy and he looked down on me as though my words meant *nothing*, when you know that they meant *everything*, to me! I did not tell Sulla the truth because he would have seen me as weak and I couldn't bear that!" He pushed Aemi out of his way as he strode to the far side of the study and stared out the window, fighting to control his temper.

Aurelia made a move to leave her seat but Aemi silently signalled for her to stay where she was.

Caesar took a deep breath to calm himself and turned to face his mother. "I used to look up to him, Mother. Sulla is what I dreamed of being for so long; he has everything I want, *he* is everything *I* want to be, and couldn't have! How could I grovel at his feet, pleading to be freed from the priesthood; how could I look him in the face after that? My dignitas would be in tatters, Mother; I would be worthless as a man!"

"So how was it left between you? What is Sulla going to do now?" Aurelia sighed.

Caesar could see from the look on her face that she didn't understand but he was too tired to argue his point. "Proscribe me, I suppose. It's his only option after what I said. He cannot possibly allow me to live now, and proscribing me is easy, considering my close links with Marius. I'm surprised he didn't kill me then and there; I half expected his guards to come charging after me when I left, but they didn't."

"It won't be long before he acts, if I know Sulla," Aemi said, his face etched with worry.

"So what are you going to do?"

"Leave Rome, Mother; get as far away as I can and then wait for as long as it takes for Sulla to either abdicate or die, whichever comes first."

Aemi nodded. "I can't see that you have a choice. It won't be long before Sulla's guards are knocking on your door."

Aurelia bit her lip and looked frightened. "And Cinnilla, what about her? Caesar please, you must go back and see Sulla. Explain everything to him; make him see that you are as much a victim as your father was. Swallow your pride and tell him that you did not choose to be the Flamen and that you are prepared to step down from the position, anything, as long as you and Cinnilla can be together, and you remain alive!" Aurelia pleaded.

"I cannot do as you ask, Mother."

"Don't be so stubborn!" Aurelia burst in to tears. "Think of your family. Think of your unborn child; *please Caesar*!" she sobbed.

Caesar remained unmoved. "It's too late, Mother, nothing can be done for me now. I knew exactly what I was doing, and what the consequences might be but I still chose that path and I will not grovel at Sulla's feet, nor will I ask anyone else to plead my case."

"You are going to have to make your mind up about what you are going to do, Caesar; time is running out," Aemi said, glancing with compassion at Aurelia before moving over to the window and peering cautiously through the gauze curtain.

"And what do you propose to do about Cinnilla?" Aurelia asked tearfully.

"If she runs away with me she could die. Will you look after her for me, until I return, Mother?"

Aurelia made no reply but simply nodded and wiped the tears from her careworn face.

"Until *we* return," said Aemi, stepping up to stand beside his friend.

"We?" Caesar asked in surprise.

"Well of course I'm coming with you, you don't think I'd leave you when you're about to start the biggest adventure of your life, do you?" Aemi smiled.

"But, it's too dangerous, Aemi. If you come with me then you forfeit your life as well, under the proscription law."

"I know, but I am coming with you, and that's my final word!" said Aemi firmly.

Caesar smiled and sighed with relief. Having Aemi by his side would certainly make the next few weeks, months, possibly years that he would be away from home, all the more bearable. "This means a lot to me, Aemi," he said.

Aurelia looked gratefully at Aemi and wiped her eyes, her face set in grim resignation. "I will go and wait for Cinnilla in the atrium. There is nothing left for me to say." She rose slowly to her feet with Aemi's help and walked to the door. "You will need some fresh clothes, and some money, if you are leaving," she said sadly. "I will arrange it."

As soon as the door closed behind his mother, Caesar pulled the hat from his head and threw it into a corner of the study, followed quickly by his toga. He watched as it slid into a pile on the floor at his feet, then bent down to pull off his boots, flinging them one at a time across the room.

"What are you doing?" Aemi gasped, as he watched Caesar getting undressed. "You can't do that!"

"Who says I can't?" Caesar replied with a grin. He slipped off the belt from his waist and let it drop to the floor. "I can't tell you just how good that makes me feel," he said, flopping back down into a chair, as Aemi stared in horror at the clothes strewn around the room.

"But…but…" he stammered.

"But nothing. The moment Sulla proscribes me my position in the priesthood is lost, and, for all I know, my name has already been added to the list in the Forum, therefore I see no need to continue to wear these appalling clothes for one moment longer!" Caesar laughed out aloud. "Do you realise what this means, Aemi? I'm free! I am no longer the Flamen; I am Gaius Julius Caesar, citizen of Rome, well, for now at least. I can wear what I like, go where I like, eat what I like and touch what I like!" He jumped up and reached for his father's gladius, which lay on the desk. He gazed at it for several moments, running his finger gently along the smooth metal blade before testing the balance and feinting a forward slice. The sheer happiness of the moment threatened to overwhelm him; all thoughts of the consequences of his actions disappeared as he stepped back into the life he had dreamed of for so long. "I am finally free!" He whooped with the joy.

Aemi burst out laughing. "This is madness, Caesar. You shouldn't be celebrating, after all, you could be dead at any moment!"

Caesar paused for a moment and looked at Aemi. "But I would die a free man, and surely that is cause for celebration?" He started to chuckle once more and the chuckle grew into a laugh, a loud, joyous laugh that filled the room.

The door burst open and Cinnilla flew into the room.

"Gaius, please tell me what has happened! It is something terrible, isn't it?" she cried as she flew into Caesar's arms.

Aurelia entered the room carrying a pile of clothes, and immediately busied herself organising them on the table as Caesar gently guided Cinnilla to the couch and began to explain, as best he could, all that had happened.

Cinnilla listened through her tears and mounting distress, as Caesar struggled to make his wife understand the calamity that had befallen them. "You are leaving me?" she said finally, as her safe little world crashed around her feet.

"Yes, my love, I have to," Caesar said softly, gathering her to him and holding her gently in his embrace. He felt her little body shaking against him as she sobbed silently and, for a second, a burning rage filled his heart, that he had been forced to cause so much pain and anguish to the person he loved above all others.

"Caesar, I'm afraid we must think about going; it's too dangerous to stay here for long," Aemi said under his breath.

Caesar nodded and buried his face into his wife's soft, sweet smelling hair. All anger subsided, replaced by a longing for this moment to never end, and the determination that, one day, he would hold her in his arms again. "I love you, Cinnilla," he whispered. "I love you more than anything, please believe me."

Cinnilla looked up into his eyes and he saw everything she wanted to say shining in those dark, tear filled pools.

Caesar drank every last detail of her into her mind so that he would never forget and hugged his wife one last time. "I have to go now," he said, releasing his grip and rising to his feet. "You will remain here with Mother. You will be safe here, and I will send for you as soon as I can."

Cinnilla nodded as the tears fell from her eyes and coursed down her beautiful creamy soft cheeks.

Caesar turned to his mother. "I…I am sorry, Mother. I never meant to hurt you - any of you, please understand that."

"There are spare clothes for you to change in to, and some money…it's not much, but…"

Caesar felt the tears welling up in his eyes as he looked at his mother She seemed so small and vulnerable to him now and he felt a deep shame at what he had done to her. He opened his arms and after a moments hesitation Aurelia stepped forward and his strong embrace enveloped her. Caesar held her tightly to him, breathing in her scent that reminded him so much of his childhood. "Ah, Mother, you have no idea how good it feels to hold you again," he murmured into her hair. "I have missed you so much." Mother and son remained together for several moments; each receiving strength from the other, until Aemi gave a small cough, indicating that time was running out.

Caesar slowly released his grip and moved away, taking one last look at his mother before turning to look at his wife who remained seated, silently crying into the folds of her dress. "You will see me again, I promise you," he said to both the women in his life. "I love you, Cinnilla, don't ever forget that I love you."

And then, scooping up the new clothes from the table, he was gone, the door closing firmly behind him as he stepped forward to his new life.

The two fugitives escaped from the city at nightfall and reached the horses Aemi had organised to be left for them in a small grove, a mile outside the city walls. Aemi busied himself strapping the packs onto the mule before untying and mounting his horse, but Caesar remained standing, staring back through the darkness towards Rome.

"Will I ever see her again?" he asked, thinking wistfully of his beloved city, and his family, trapped behind those high stone walls.

"Perhaps, one day, when Sulla is dead," Aemi said.

"It's funny," Caesar mused. "Yesterday morning I would never have imagined in my wildest dreams I would be leaving Rome, leaving the priesthood, my family, my life behind. Look at me now, no longer the Flamen, a fugitive of Rome, and about to ride a horse once more, that is, if I can still remember how," he said, stroking the animal's neck.

"But you are free, Caesar, surely that is worth something?"

"I dreamed of this moment, but I never imagined I would pay such a high price for my freedom," he said sadly.

"Some things are worth it," said Aemi encouragingly. "Now you can begin the real adventure, follow your true destiny. Remember that Marcus died trying to bring you the prophecy, Caesar. I know we don't know what it said, but what Marcus did must give you hope for the future. You are not destined to die by Sulla's hand, that much is certain. The gods have given you your freedom with their blessing so seize it with both hands; seize it for Marcus, if nothing else."

Caesar looked through the darkness at his friend and smiled. "I will, Aemi, I will. Now, if I can get on to this animal we shall see if I can still remember how to ride." He held onto the mane with one hand and swung his leg up over the horses back, landing lightly onto the saddlecloth. "Oh, this feels good!" he said, settling himself comfortably.

"Are you ready?" Aemi asked, turning his horse's head away from the direction of the city.

"As ready as I'll ever be," Caesar said, and digging his heels into the horse's sides, the two friends set off at a gallop.

# CHAPTER TWENTY

*"Glory follows virtue as if it were its shadow."*
*(Marcus Tullius Cicero)*

## ROME: June-September 81BC

The warmth of the early summer breeze filled the room with fragrance from the flowers in the ornamental peristyle garden that was once the pride and joy of Cinna, and the light, silk curtains, wafted languidly, in and out of the open double doors, gently caressing Sulla's sandalled feet, as he looked long and hard at Marcus Aurelius Cotta, his eyes narrowed in silent contemplation. "All right, Marcus, I believe you, but, if I find that you have been lying to protect Caesar then your own life will be forfeit, regardless of the friendship we have enjoyed over the years," he said, returning to his chair.

Marcus Aurelius inwardly breathed a sigh of relief and smiled weakly at Sulla. "You have my word that I had no idea he had left Rome until I spoke to his mother this morning."

"And she can't, or, won't tell you, where he might have gone?"

Marcus Aurelius shook his head and brushed away a fly that landed on his cheek. "No, none. She said that he came to tell her what had happened between you and then he left; she hasn't seen or heard from him since. She is as upset about her son's disappearance as you are, Sulla."

Sulla grunted his disapproval. "I am not upset, Marcus, I am angry at this young man's wilfulness, and his blatant defiance of my orders. He just stood there before me, as you do now, and simply refused to divorce Cinna's child. Not a flicker, not a flinch did I get out of him, just pure defiance! The boy must have a death wish, I swear, for I made it perfectly clear that I would not be defied, yet it made no impression on him at all!" Sulla said angrily.

Marcus Aurelius shifted uncomfortably from one foot to the other. "I can only apologise for his behaviour, Sulla, and ask that it does not bring down repercussions on the rest of the family as a consequence to his youthful impetuosity…"

"I would call it more than youthful impetuosity, Marcus, and will you just relax! You babble on and on like an idiot," Sulla interrupted.

"Yes… I know…sorry, my nerves do get the better of me, sometimes. Well, all I can say is, Caesar has always been a trifle stubborn and wilful at times. The only person he ever really listened to was his father, and that was only in the last few years before he died. He was never at home very much, you see, always away with one legion or another, and Caesar was too strong-minded for his mother. It's such a shame that Gaius Julius did not have more of an influence on his son; it might have prevented most of the trouble that happened before he died."

"What do you mean?" Sulla asked, taking a sip of wine as he listened to Marcus Aurelius rambling on.

"Well, most, if not all of the trouble I'm referring too stemmed from Gaius Marius's extreme dislike of the boy, which became most apparent after Marius returned to Rome with Cinna. His mother, Aurelia, said that Caesar had brought it all upon himself, you see. He had this belief that he was destined for great things, from a very young age, and, I'm afraid his arrogance increased the older he became. Unfortunately, he chose to confide his dreams to Marius one day, and whatever he said upset Marius to such a degree that he refused to have the boy near him after that, in fact I would go so far as to say that Marius hated the mere mention of Caesar's name."

Sulla nodded, intrigued by this fresh insight into Caesar's relationship with his enemy, Marius. He thought back to the first time that he had met Caesar. "Mmm, I remember meeting the boy when he was quite young and I must admit to finding him precocious, even at that age. So what happened after that?"

"Well, none of us could understand it at the time, although Aurelia did think that it might have something to do with a prophecy, if I remember rightly," Marcus shrugged, "But, as you can imagine, after that little episode it made things very awkward for Gaius Julius and Aurelia, what with Marius being married to Julia, Gaius's sister, and the boy was kept well away from his uncle after that…oh, I do apologise, I've rambled on and on!" said Marcus Aurelius, blushing with embarrassment.

"No, not at all, Marcus, in fact, take a seat," said Sulla, waving Marcus forward to a chair opposite his own. "A prophecy you say? How very intriguing."

Sulla poured Marcus Aurelius a goblet of wine and settled back in his chair. "This prophecy you spoke of, Marcus, tell me more about that," he said casually.

When Marcus Aurelius finished his story, Sulla looked very thoughtful. "And who did they believe the other person mentioned in this prophecy was, do you know?"

"Yes, the boy, Caesar."

"Indeed! And was he aware of this prophecy at the time?"

"Not a first; they didn't want to give the boy any more reasons to hold on to this belief of his great destiny because of the trouble it had caused them already."

"Does he know about it now?" Sulla asked.

"Yes, in the end his father had to tell him of its existence, although no-one was certain what it was supposed to have said, only Marius knew that. Caesar clearly knew they were hiding something from him, and I think it was the only way they could keep him safely away from Marius. They were terrified of what he might do to the boy, you see. Not that it made any difference in the end, of course, because Marius found a way to get to Caesar anyway. I had left Rome by then, and Gaius Julius wrote to me. Marius forced Caesar into becoming a priest, and Gaius Julius had been told in no uncertain terms what would happen to him, and his son, if Caesar refused. He was given very little choice: none of them were."

Sulla stood up and paced thoughtfully around the room. Once or twice he glanced at Marcus Aurelius, looking for any signs that what he had been told was a lie, but he sat calmly in his chair, sipping wine. No, this intriguing story was true, or, at least Marcus Aurelius believed it to be, either way, there was more to this young man, Caesar, than met the eye.

Sulla returned to his chair and smiled at Marcus Aurelius to put him at ease. "So, you would have me believe that Marius saw this young man as a rival, to what, his reputation?"

Marcus Aurelius nodded eagerly. "Yes, or something important enough that he forced Caesar into the priesthood. Unfortunately there is no way of knowing what the prophecy said. The only copy, found after Marius's death, was destroyed."

"Oh, how so?"

"Marcus, Marius's adopted son, found some letters and a book, so I am led to believe, that contained part of the prophecy, though not all of it. He showed it to Julia, of course, and she destroyed it."

"So Caesar and his family are none the wiser?"

Marcus Aurelius shook his head. "No, not that it mattered by then anyway because Caesar was the Flamen Dialis, and his father was dead. Aurelia said it was best to forget it ever existed; after all, Caesar could never leave the priesthood now so what did it matter? Caesar would disagree entirely, of course, for he was forced into the priesthood against his wishes, and obliged to marry Cinna's daughter, although, I have to admit that the young couple have grown very fond of each other, from what I have seen in the short time I have been back in Rome."

"Well he refused to divorce her, if that is any measure of his feelings towards her!"

"Indeed," Marcus Aurelius blushed. "As I said, none of it was his choosing, or his father's. Marius really left them with no choice; it was his way or die. Caesar hates the priesthood more than anything, but he does his duty, and the People admire him for it."

"Yet he had the chance to tell me the truth when he stood before me and he said nothing," Sulla mused, wondering just what this Caesar was all about?

"Well, I can't think why not," said Marcus Aurelius, looking puzzled. "I would have thought he would have jumped at the chance to let you know how he really felt at being the Flamen Dialis. You must believe me when I say that both the priesthood and the marriage were forced upon the boy, and his father. They had no option but to agree to it. They were related to Marius, but that was as far as their relationship went, I can assure you. That family was ruled by fear and hatred, just like the rest of us. Marius trapped them, and they took the only course of action possible that would allow them to live. Surely you can understand that?"

"Mmm," Sulla wasn't convinced. "But if you look at it a different way, Gaius Julius benefited greatly from his relationship with Marius. A son in the priesthood is considered a great honour, especially one with the supreme social standing of the

Flamen. Marriage, to the daughter of one of the wealthiest men in Rome, who was at the height of his power and influence, oh, and a cushy little number, recruiting men to fight against me, for Gaius Julius. Even you can see how it looks, Marcus."

Marcus Aurelius grew pale as Sulla spoke. "Yes...No...I mean, yes, I can see how it might look, Sulla, but no, it wasn't like that, I promise you! The last time I spoke to Gaius Julius he was as a drowning man, with no hope of rescue for he knew that his situation was hopeless. I made a promise to him, before we parted, that I would tell you the truth. Gaius Julius and his family were not traitors, to you, or to Rome. They were as much a victim in all of this as Catalus Caesar, or...Antonius Orator, or any of the other men who fell foul of Marius's madness. The *only* reason Gaius Julius conceded anything was to protect his son. He believed that Marius was looking for an excuse to be rid of the boy because he saw him as a threat, and he found the perfect opportunity, with the death of the old Flamen Dialis. By incarcerating the boy in the priesthood, particularly with all the onerous rules surrounding the Flamen, Marius could be assured that Caesar would never be free to threaten his reputation, or his place in history. It was the perfect solution to what he viewed as a very real, very possible threat to all that he had accomplished, and he was not prepared to give up his place in history to a young rival, however insane that idea might seem."

"So far, so good, Marcus, but explain away the marriage to Cinna's daughter. If Marius was bent on revenge how do you explain this? He could have married Caesar to a pauper, but instead he chooses the pretty young daughter of one of the richest families in Rome. I hardly see that as punishment!"

Marcus Aurelius shrugged. "I can only imagine that he wanted to tie the family closer to your enemies. Marius probably knew that if his plans to destroy you were unsuccessful then you would return to Rome one day and exact revenge on your enemies, as he had done so with his. It wouldn't surprise me if he hoped you would see Caesar as your enemy and kill him too. He had no legitimate excuse to murder the boy, much as I am sure he would have liked to, but this way, Marius gambled that you might do it for him."

"So he laid a trap for me, is that what you are saying, Marcus? I ensure his immortal reputation by destroying the one person he believed challenged it?" Sulla laughed. "Well I wouldn't put it past the old goat to do something like that. He would get a thrill from thinking I had helped him to his place amongst the great men of the world without even knowing it!" Sulla frowned. "And it appears that even beyond the grave Gaius Marius has had his wish fulfilled after all, for I have been forced to proscribe Caesar, and his marriage played an important part in his downfall, just as Marius foresaw." Sulla mused.

Marcus Aurelius nodded but kept silent.

Sulla drank deeply from his goblet. "The fact remains, Marcus, that Caesar defied me and I cannot let that pass unpunished," he said firmly.

"I understand, of course, Sulla, but he poses no real threat to you whatsoever. Could you not find it in your heart to forgive him?" Marcus Aurelius pleaded.

Sulla pondered on these words for a moment. Had he known the truth when he met Caesar then things could have turned out differently for both of them, but instead, the priest had openly defied him and Sulla could not be seen to be weak. Why, he wondered, did Caesar not explain that the priesthood was forced upon him? Sulla's mind drifted back to their meeting in the Forum, the day young Marius's head was displayed on the rostra. He had ridiculed Caesar about choosing to become a priest and he had not denied it then, either. Why? What was it that stopped this young man admitting that he was a victim of Marius's obsessions? He remembered the proud, stubborn look on Caesar's face as he had stood before him in this very room and the total lack of fear that had caused such anger and frustration for Sulla. Could it be that the young priest was too proud to admit that he had been bested by Marius? Sulla remembered the little boy who had stood before him with such conviction all those years ago. "I am going to be the greatest Roman General the world has ever seen," he had said, and Sulla had been amused, and Gaius Marius had scowled. Now his hopes and ambitions lay in ruins because of Marius. What was it about Caesar that had induced such rage, such vengeance, and such hatred against one so young? What did Gaius Marius know that the rest of them failed to see?

"Tell me, Marcus. Before Caesar was, as you say, forced into the priesthood, did he still have ambitions for a military career?" Sulla asked.

Marcus Aurelius smiled. "Oh yes, he never really changed from that little boy that you met all those years ago, in fact he drove his parents mad with his total conviction that one day he would achieve great things. At first they put it down to boyhood fantasies, but, as the years went on he never seemed to waver, and if the truth be told, I think that even now he still has that...conviction, you would call it, that one day he will be free to follow his destiny, although I do not imagine for one moment that he believed his freedom would come at such a price."

"No, I don't suppose he did," said Sulla smoothly.

"I don't think that knowing about the prophecy helped either. If I know Caesar, it would have driven him to distraction, knowing that somewhere out there his future was foretold, and, judging by Marius's reaction, I would say that Caesar had a glittering future ahead of him. That is probably why young Marcus risked his life to return to Ro..." Marcus Aurelius stopped and blushed, shifting uncomfortably in his chair, but Sulla was quick to perceive that Marcus had spoken out of turn.

"Is this Marcus Marius you are referring too?" he asked directly, his clear pale eyes fixed on Marcus Aurelius with a piercing gaze.

"I, ah...yes...young Marcus Marius...yes," Marcus Aurelius stammered.

"Well, come on, spit it out."

"All I know, and its very little really, is that Marcus Marius was on the run, after Norbanus was defeated, and he came across the prophecy, the original prophecy, hidden in a temple vault I believe."

"Go on," Sulla prompted.

"I don't know where this temple was, Sulla, but I do know that Marcus Marius had been looking for this prophecy for some time; he was friends with Caesar you see."

"Yes, I'm beginning to," said Sulla slowly. "Tell me, Marcus, how do you know this? Did you have contact with Marcus Marius?" he added, looking suspiciously through half closed eyes.

"Me? Oh, no, no of course not!" Marcus Aurelius exclaimed.

"Then who told you?"

"It was…it was Aemi, I mean, Marcus Aemilius Lepidus, but everyone calls him Aemi. He told me, the night Marcus Marius died."

"I think it's time you told me everything, Marcus, and I mean *everything*!" Sulla said, his voice as hard and cold as frozen ice.

By the time Marcus Aurelius had finished talking Sulla did indeed know everything. The close friendship between Marcus, Aemi and Caesar, and the subsequent enmity that ensued after Marius murdered Aemi's father, the search for the prophecy and Marcus's attempt to return to Rome. Sulla listened in stony silence, his face portraying no emotion as Marcus Aurelius frantically tried to talk his way out of trouble. When he had finished, Sulla sat for several minutes weighing up the evidence. He could see Marcus Aurelius trembling in fear and anticipation as he waited for Sulla to speak. Finally, Sulla rose from his chair and slowly began to pace the floor.

"So, Aemi, as you call him, was friends with the youngest Marius after all?"

"Yes, no…I wouldn't go so far as to say they were friends any more, too much had happened between their families for that, but they were united in their friendship for Caesar."

"So, this young priest inspires love as well as hate for those who know him. A dangerous combination, don't you think, Marcus?"

Marcus Aurelius merely nodded.

Sulla looked thoughtful. "So, why did Aemi demand that he be allowed to deliver the final blow to finish off Marius's miserable little life? Was it out of hatred, as I imagined it to be, or something else? Tell me."

Marcus Aurelius sighed and took a deep breath. "Because… because he did not want Marcus to suffer any longer."

"That was a very hard, very honourable thing for him to do under the circumstances," Sulla said. "He showed real bravery that night, for I would never have guessed his true feelings towards Marius."

Marcus Aurelius nodded. "It was hard," he said.

A twinkle came into Sulla's eyes and a mischievous smile spread across his face. "And I would like to bet that Aemi is out there somewhere, right now, with Caesar, helping him to evade capture, am I right?"

Marcus Aurelius blushed and looked at the floor.

"It's all right, Marcus, I can guess your answer," Sulla said, returning at last to his chair. "An interesting tale you have told me tonight. You have given me much to think about." He took a long draught of wine and studied Marcus Aurelius over the rim of his goblet. "But, the fact remains, Caesar defied me and he will be proscribed," he said, placing his goblet firmly down on the desk before him.

Marcus Aurelius jumped at the sudden movement. "Yes, but surely now that you know the truth there might be some way to put this right? These are two young, innocent lives, Sulla, please, reconsider your decision." he pleaded.

Sulla shook his head, his jaw set firmly now. "No, it's gone too far for that, Marcus. Caesar must be held accountable for his actions, he is a man now and so is his friend, although I am inclined to overlook his foolishness because of the high regard I once held for his father. I cannot be seen to be weak, Marcus. Caesar will have to be punished."

"Being merciful is not a weakness, Sulla, indeed, many see it as a strength, I…"

"No," Sulla interrupted, "But then who said I was merciful, Marcus? I make enemies and I destroy them. That is who I am."

"Is Caesar your enemy?"

"He defied me!"

"But he is not your enemy, Sulla!"

"That, my dear Marcus, is for me to decide," Sulla said firmly. "Now, I have business to attend to and I must ask you to leave. It has been…enlightening, and entertaining in places too. It has been a long time since I had such an enjoyable chat. You can see yourself out." Sulla snatched up a scroll from a nearby table and began to read the contents.

"Please, Sulla, just one more minute, I'm sure…"

"Are you still here?" Sulla asked, in a dangerous tone, as he continued to read.

Only when the door closed behind Marcus Aurelius, did Sulla stop reading. He bit his lip, staring intently at the empty chair and remained in silent contemplation for several minutes. Finally, Sulla rang the small, gold plated bell at his side and a slave appeared as if by magic. "Take this message to Dollabella," he ordered. "Tell him to add Marcus Aemilius Lepidus to the list; he will be found with the priest, Caesar."

Aemi took one look at Caesar, lying slumped across his horses neck, and saw that he was fading fast. "We have to find proper shelter," he said, scanning the barren countryside for signs of life. A faint light flickered high up on the hillside, through the darkness, and Aemi turned the horses towards it. "There may be a farm up ahead. We can ask for help there; perhaps they have medicine, or at least will know where I can buy some. Hang on, Caesar, it won't be long now."

It had been two weeks since they had escaped Rome in the dead of night; two hard weeks of riding through the night and hiding out in derelict barns during the day to avoid detection. Their progress had been slow, the journey long, as they headed for the Sabine Hills where Aemi owned a small farmstead that they would be safe enough to stay until they could decide what to do next. Unfortunately, a mosquito had bitten Caesar three days ago and it wasn't long before he was complaining of feeling unwell. By Aemi's reckoning, they still had another two days of hard riding before they reached their destination but it was clear Caesar was becoming dangerously ill, and he needed urgent treatment if he was going to survive.

The first fingers of daylight stole across the star lit sky as they approached the farm along a narrow mud track that wound its way round the steep hillside. The door of the house suddenly opened and a surly, middle-aged man appeared, holding what appeared to be an old pillum in his hand. Although he wore the rustic, plain clothing of a farmer, he walked upright, with his shoulders back and chest pushed forward. He had an air of quiet confidence that was evident to Aemi.

"He must be a veteran," Aemi muttered to Caesar as they approached the dry stone wall that circled the property.

The man eyed them warily as they approached. "What do you want?" he demanded, as Aemi and Caesar halted beside the closed gateway to the farm.

"My friend here is sick," said Aemi, sliding down from his horse. "We are looking for some shelter and food for a few days to allow him to recover. We can pay you," he added, hoping the mention of money would tempt the farmer into agreeing, but the farmer remained silent, staring at Caesar. "We mean you no harm," Aemi tried again. We are on business for Marcus Aemilius Lepidus of Rome; he owns a farm not far from here and we were on our way there when my friend fell ill."

"Ay, I know it," the man said, walking closer to get a better look at the strangers.

"All we ask is some shelter and a little food. As soon as my friend is well enough to ride we shall be on our way. Our mule went lame a while back so we are unable to carry many supplies. Will you help us?" Aemi said.

"What be your names?" the farmer asked gruffly.

"I am a freed-man. I take my name from my master, Marcus Aemilius Lepidus. My friend is also a freed-man, from the house of Julius Caesar."

"Caesar, you say?" the farmer asked, looking closely at Caesar who was by now barely conscious, his head drooping heavily on his chest. "What's wrong with 'im?"

"He has a bite that has got infected but we have no medicine to treat it. All he needs is a few days rest and he'll be fine."

"Mmm, well, you can stay in that barn over there, but only for a few days, mind," said the farmer, pointing to a low roofed stone building across the yard from the house. "I don't like strangers on my property, now, show us your money," he said, opening the gate.

Aemi took out his small leather pouch and produced several gold coins. The farmer's hand whipped out and grabbed the money before Aemi could do anything.

"That'll be my payment," said the farmer, thrusting the coins into his trouser pocket.

"But that's far too much!" Aemi exclaimed angrily, for the farmer had taken three times what Aemi had planned to offer him.

"Take it and go then," the farmer grunted, shoving his hand back into his pocket to remove the money. "But there aint another farm closer than a days ride, and I don't think your man will make another hour on that horse," he said.

Aemi glanced at Caesar and saw that the farmer was right. He was barely conscious and had taken no notice of the farmer since they arrived. "All right," Aemi nodded begrudgingly. "But I expect hot food for that price!"

"As you wish," the farmer said, and he opened the gate to let them pass into the yard. "Your animals can stay in the barn with you. I'll bring some food when you're settled," he said, and walked back towards the house.

Aemi led the horses to the barn and helped Caesar walk to a large pile of dry, sweet-smelling hay where he collapsed, exhausted. "You really need a doctor, Caesar," he said, looking worried, for Caesar looked very pale and drawn.

"A good sleep will help," Caesar muttered. "I'll be fine tomorrow, and anyway, your farm is not too far away now is it?"

"No, two more days ride should do it," Aemi said, arranging the hay around Caesar to make him more comfortable. He glanced around the barn and wrinkled his nose in disgust. The stench of animals and their faeces was pungent and mixed with the dry, musty odour of the old wooden barn Aemi had to force himself not to gag.

"Oh for a nice warm fire," Caesar murmured, shivering.

"It's not that cold," said Aemi. "Here, put this around you." He took off his cloak and draped it over Caesar who lay back gratefully into the soft hay.

The rickety barn door opened and a small boy appeared carrying a tray, which had a water gourd and a small loaf of bread on it. He placed the tray down on the ground and stated warily at the men. "Fatha says there will be some stew for you, once it's made," he said.

"Thank you for your kindness," said Aemi as he approached the boy to collect the tray. "What's your name?" he asked kindly.

"Quintus."

"Quintus; a Roman name,"

"I'm named after my fatha, Quintus Lutatius," the boy answered, stepping back away from the tray and eying Aemi suspiciously.

"Is your father a freed-man?" Aemi asked.

"No," Quintus shook his head. "Why do you ask that?"

"Oh, I assumed your father had been a slave to a nobleman of that name," Aemi said as he stood up.

"My fatha was no slave," the boy retorted. "He served as centurion in the legions and he took the name of his general, when he retired and became his client. This is his land."

"Your father's?"

"No, Quintus Lutatius Catalus Caesar, our patron; it's his land. Why do you have a gladius strapped to your waist?" the boy asked, looking with interest at the ornate sword hanging from the baldric, slung low on Aemi's hips.

"For protection," Aemi said, quickly covering the gladius with his cloak and cursing under his breath. He knew that if the farmer saw it he would realise Aemi was not a freed-man. Only a very rich man would own such a fine sword. "Now, thank your father for us. We will be quite at home here," Aemi said, ending the conversation and returning to Caesar.

Quintus stared at the men for a moment longer and then ran from the barn, slamming the door behind him.

"That's blown it," said Aemi, sitting down next to Caesar. "He saw my gladius; now his father will know we've been lying to him."

Caesar shrugged and wrapped the cloak tighter around him. "Get some rest then, before he comes and throws us out," he said, rolling over on to his side.

"Don't you want to eat?" Aemi asked, tearing of a chunk of the bread from the tray.

"No…I'm too tired."

The sun reached its zenith and began the slow afternoon descent when Aemi woke with a start. He rolled over to take a look at Caesar and immediately scrambled to his feet, for Caesar lay on his back, sweat covering his body, his head thrashing back and forth whilst his lips twitched silently.

"Caesar, Caesar!" Aemi called softly but urgently, shaking Caesar's outstretched arm. "Caesar, wake up."

Caesar moaned and rolled restlessly in the hay but showed no signs of waking. Aemi covered Caesar with the cloak that had fallen from his restless body during the night and leapt off the hay. He threw open the barn door, and, spotting the farmer out in the field, he ran across the farmyard and vaulted over the wall.

"What you want now?" The farmer scowled as Aemi approached, breathless and frantic with worry.

"I need a doctor; my friend has got much worse and needs help!"

"What's up with 'im?" the farmer asked, leaning on his hoe.

"Fever, and I can't wake him. He's really ill!"

"Let me see." The farmer trudged slowly back across the field towards the farm as Aemi ran on ahead to rejoin Caesar. When the farmer entered the barn he took one look at Caesar and nodded. "Malaria," he said.

"Malaria, are you sure?"

"Seen it lots of times, specially in Africa."

"You were in Africa?" Aemi asked as he wiped Caesar's hot forehead with a piece of damp cloth.

"In the legions," the farmer muttered.

"Can it be cured?" Aemi looked worriedly at his friend as Caesar moaned and rolled onto his side.

"Sometimes, sometimes not," the farmer answered bluntly.

"Then I need to find a doctor."

"Maybe."

"Where can I find one? Please, you have to help us!" Aemi said desperately.

The farmer looked long and hard at Caesar and then turned his gaze on Aemi. "Tell me who he really is and then I'll decide," he said.

Aemi tried to look innocent. "I told you, we are on business for…"

But the farmer cut him short. "Then you sort your own mess out," he said, and turned to leave.

"No, wait, please!" Aemi scrambled to his feet. "Alright, I'll tell you. He is Gaius Julius Caesar, and, I am Marcus Aemilius Lepidus. We are not freed-men. I'm sorry I lied."

"Gaius Julius Caesar you say? Aint he a relative of Gaius Marius?"

"Yes, Marius was his uncle," Aemi nodded nervously, not sure if admitting the connection to Marius would serve to make matters even worse.

The farmer lay his hoe down on the floor and walked to the corner of the barn where he pulled several empty sacks down from a shelf. "He needs to be kept warm even though he has a fever," he said, placing some of the sacks over Caesar.

"Thank you," said Aemi gratefully.

"I served with Marius in Africa. He was a good man; the best in his day."

Aemi nodded.

"You will find a doctor, of sorts, down in the village, two hours ride from here. Head west at the crossroads and follow the track down into the valley, you can't miss it."

"Thank you!" said Aemi, running over to his horse and grabbing the bridle from a hook on the wall. "Keep an eye on him while I'm gone. I'll be as quick as I can," he said hastily, securing the bridle to the horse's head. He rummaged in his pack for his bag of money and hastily secured it inside his tunic before leading his horse out into the yard. Vaulting nimbly onto its back he dug his heels in, sending the horse straight into a canter. With a mighty leap, the horse cleared the wall and set off at a gallop along the narrow path, heading back down the hillside.

The farmer stood and watched as the young man disappeared round the bend in the track and shook his head. "You won't get far if you ride like that on this ground," he muttered prophetically before he turned and headed back to the barn to watch over Caesar.

Aemi found the village after a breakneck gallop through the steep Sabine Hills and down to the valley below. The doctor was located, and a herbal remedy, purported to be the best treatment for Malaria, purchased at an exorbitant fee. The farmer had been proved right and Aemi's horse had gone lame after bruising a foot on the uneven, sometimes treacherous ground, it had travelled along to get to the village. As luck would have it, a small messenger station was positioned on the edge of the village, and Aemi was able to trade in his lame horse for a small but sturdy mule. With the medicine safely tucked in his tunic, Aemi set off on the long journey back to the farm, hoping and praying that this medicine would work and save Caesar's life.

"Are you telling me that there is *nothing* we can do?" Aurelia snapped in frustration as she paced the floor of her living room.

Julia and Cinnilla sat together on the large couch, close to the warmth of the brazier, and glanced at each other as Aurelia swept past them.

"I have tried talking to Sulla but he simply won't listen. All he sees is Caesar's stubbornness and defiance, and he will not allow that to go un-punished. I warned Caesar what would happen and he refused to listen to me. What else can I do?" Marcus Aurelius replied.

Aurelia snorted with disdain. "Yes, well, it's easy to say I told you so, after the event, but what do we do? There must be some way to make Sulla see sense. He cannot proscribe an innocent man!"

Marcus Aurelius shook his head. "Sulla has changed beyond recognition from the man he once was; he is hard now, and ruthless, and he rarely listens to anyone. He can do as he pleases, as Dictator, and there is nothing we can do to change his mind, Aurelia, particularly as Caesar ran away."

"Well, can you blame him? What choice did he have, Marcus? At least by leaving Rome he stands a chance of staying alive!"

Marcus Aurelius sighed and raised his hands in supplication. "I understand why he left, Aurelia, of course I do, but in all honesty, if Caesar had swallowed his stubborn pride then he would not be in this predicament, would he?"

Aurelia pulled a face and turned away, continuing to pace the room in agitation.

"Caesar stood up for what he believed in, and, I for one am proud of him; we both are," said Cinnilla, gazing down at the newborn baby she held, tightly swaddled, in her arms. She gently stroked the baby's cheek and then looked up at Marcus Aurelius. "Whatever happens to Caesar, at least he has had a taste of the freedom he so badly desired. He would have hated to have died trapped in the priesthood, so, all we can do is hope and pray to all the gods that they will protect him from Sulla, and keep him safe, so that one day we can be reunited again."

"You mustn't worry, Cinnilla, I am sure Caesar will be fine," said Julia reassuringly. She smiled at the baby as it snuffled and let out a small cry in its sleep. "He is young and strong, and certainly clever enough to keep out of harms way."

"Julia is right, Cinnilla," said Aurelia. "Caesar has his wits about him and enough sense to keep his head down until this trouble passes."

"Sooner or later the proscriptions will stop, and I am sure that those who have managed to escape detection will soon be forgotten about," Marcus Aurelius confirmed confidently.

Aurelia did not look convinced but she kept quiet.

"What about the Pontifex Maximus?" Julia said, as she poked her little finger into the baby's hand.

"What about him?" Aurelia asked.

"Well, could he not help, after all Caesar was one of his priests?"

"Well, could he?" Aurelia asked, turning to Marcus Aurelius.

He shook his head. "I doubt very much that he would agree to get involved, especially as Caesar is proscribed; people don't want to become involved, in case Sulla turns on them."

"But I could ask him?" Aurelia was desperate to find a way to help her son. She had waited every day for news but there had been nothing, good or bad, to indicate where he was or if he was still alive. She fought back the urge to scream with the sheer frustration of it all and focussed instead on the face of her granddaughter, baby Julia. The peace and serenity on her tiny face reminded Aurelia that she had to remain calm and focussed if that little child was ever to meet her father.

"You could try," Marcus frowned. "But don't go raising your hopes, Aurelia."

"And the Vestal Virgins," said Julia.

"The Vestal Virgins?" Marcus Aurelius looked puzzled at this singular comment.

"Why not? They are women of the College after all, and I am sure that they would be very good at asking for clemency; they are so nice," Julia said dreamily.

A smile spread across Aurelia's face. "Sometimes, Julia, you are worth your weight in gold!"

Julia returned the smile. "Am I dear, that's nice."

"Then that is what I shall do," said Aurelia resolutely.

"Aurelia, I don't..." Marcus Aurelius began, but Aurelia cut him short.

"Uncle, sometimes you have to concede to a woman's intuition, and mine tells me that this is the right thing to do. Now, are you going to help me save my son, or not?"

Marcus Aurelius rolled his eyes as he conceded defeat. "Yes, all right, I will help you, but I do not hold out much hope in this scheme of yours."

"Good, that is settled then," said Aurelia purposefully. "Tomorrow, we see the Pontifex Maximus and the Vestal Virgins. If I can convince them to help us then Caesar still has a chance."

Cinnilla looked up at Aurelia with tears in her eyes. "Thank you, Aurelia," she said.

"He is my son, Cinnilla, and I will do anything in my power to help and protect him. You are a mother yourself now and you will understand that nothing and no one can come between a mother and her child, not even the Dictator of Rome!"

"Now, you must be very careful of Sulla, Aurelia. Do not underestimate him. Just because you are a woman does not mean you can expect to be treated more leniently," Marcus Aurelius warned.

"I can be just as dangerous and stubborn, as you well know," Aurelia replied, her dark eyes flashed with defiance. "We will succeed, Uncle, I know it."

"Look out Cinnilla," Marcus Aurelius laughed. "If your daughter is anything like her father and grandmother then you will have your work cut out when she is older!"

Cinnilla chuckled and looked down at her baby. "I don't mind," she said. "I don't mind at all."

It did not take Aemi long to realise that he was being followed by the five horsemen, who, whilst keeping their distance, kept him in view as he wound his way along the narrow hillside tracks towards the farm. He stopped his mule behind a clump of rocks at the top of a ridge and looked back down the hillside, scouring the scrubland for signs of the riders. He spotted them at last, as they came out from behind a small copse of trees; five men, riding well bred horses. Aemi's heart sank as he realised who they were: Sulla's men, and they were on his trail.

Kicking his heels sharply into the mule's sides Aemi set off at a lolloping canter. He swore at the animal and urged it on faster with a flick of his reins. Oh, to have a fleet horse right now! How could he possibly outride the men on this ancient old mule? Aemi turned off across the rocky grassland and the sure-footed animal found its way easily through the hidden rocks and clumps of gorse. He banked on the fact that the men would not want to risk laming their horses and would stick to the track as much as possible, giving him some much needed time to get back to the farm.

Urging the tired mule on as best he could, Aemi finally reached the safety of the farmyard and the farmer appeared at the barn door. "How is he?" Aemi gasped, hurrying into the barn.

"No change," the farmer said, eying the sweating animal enquiringly.

"My horse went lame," Aemi explained as he knelt down beside Caesar, who lay inert on the straw, pale and feverish.

"Caesar, Caesar it is me, Aemi," Aemi said, gently lifting Caesar's head and resting it on his knees. "You must drink some of this," He ripped off the top from the medicine bottle with his teeth and held it up to Caesar's mouth. Caesar opened his eyes a mere fraction but they appeared to Aemi to be lifeless and unseeing. "Caesar, please, open your mouth," Aemi urged, forcing the top of the bottle between Caesar's lips. A foul smelling, green liquid, ran down the sides of Caesar's mouth as Aemi tilted the bottle but he saw Caesar swallow and then cough.

"You will kill 'im, doing it like that!" the farmer said gruffly as he watched Aemi's frantic attempts to administer the medicine.

"I don't have time!" Aemi snapped. " I was followed. There will be men here any minute. I have to get this down him and then we must leave."

"Men, what men?" the farmer asked, walking to the barn door and looking out to the open fields beyond.

Aemi realised that there was no point trying to keep up the pretence anymore. "It is possible that the Dictator, Sulla, has proscribed Caesar, which means that there is a two talent price on his head, and those men intend to claim it if I'm not quick enough. We must leave now, or you could get into trouble for harbouring a proscribed man."

The farmer grunted and to Aemi's surprise the corners of his mouth cracked open into a smile. "I aint scared of no trouble, Master Marcus," he said, swinging the door closed as he spoke. He walked to the back of the barn and began to scrape away the straw from the floor with his boot. "Seems to me the world has gone mad since old Marius died, the gods bless 'im. I don't have much time for that Sulla; never did have when I served with 'im in Africa, and don't care much for him now, so don't you worry. Now, give me a hand," he said, as he bent down to the floor.

Aemi joined the farmer and watched as he scraped away dry dirt from around a circular iron handle that was now visible on the ground.

"I made this," the farmer said, beginning to pull on the handle. "When the Italians were on the rampage, a few years back." He struggled to pull on the handle and Aemi leant a hand, pulling with all his might. Suddenly there was the sound of crunching dried wood and a cloud of dust and dirt flew up in the air covering everything nearby. Aemi coughed and spluttered as he peered down at the floor realising that what they had pulled on was the handle to a trap door. The farmer peered down the dark hole and the smell of damp filled the air.

"Aemi, Aemi!" Caesar called out weakly.

"I'm here, Caesar," Aemi called as he ran back to join his friend.

"Where are we? Oh…my head!" he groaned.

"You are sick, Caesar, but you will recover. I have medicine, good medicine for you," said Aemi, replacing the fallen sacks back over Caesar's body to keep him warm.

"Sick? Where…where…" Caesar tried to speak.

"Hush, don't fret yourself; we are safe, but, Caesar, you have to try to get up for me. We need to move you to a better place. Can you help me?"

"Move?"

"You will need a candle to light your way down there," the farmer said, scurrying past Aemi to the door. "You get 'im moving and I'll be right back." He slipped through the barn door and disappeared.

"Come on now, Caesar, I need your help. Try and stand, please!" Aemi placed his arm around Caesar's waist and tried to haul him up to a stand. Caesar groaned as he moved but Aemi could feel him trying to help even though he felt disorientated with the fever. "Now, Caesar, you must try and walk. Hold on to me and walk!" Aemi said as he took a step forward.

Slowly, very slowly, they made their way across the barn towards the trap door. Aemi heard the barn door open. "Thank the gods you're back, I could do with the help. I can't get him down there on my own," he gasped as he struggled to hold Caesar.

"I shouldn't worry about that, if I were you."

Aemi froze with fear. It wasn't the voice of the farmer that had spoken.

"You won't be going anywhere, Marcus Aemilius Lepidus."

Aemi slowly turned round to face the speaker, still supporting Caesar, who was barely conscious now.

"And Gaius Julius Caesar!" the man said, walking forward into the barn. "I've been looking for you."

# CHAPTER TWENTY-ONE

*"I love the name of honour more than I fear death"*
*(Gaius Julius Caesar)*

## ROME: September-November 81BC

A strange procession of people made their way into the ornately designed atrium of Sulla's villa. The doorkeeper stared open-mouthed, and the steward, who had heard the commotion, stopped dead in his tracks at the sight that met his eyes.

Standing at the head of the group, Aurelia looked simply stunning. Her raven black hair was swept up into shiny gossamer ringlets that framed her beautiful face. Her smooth olive skin, languid eyes of the deepest, darkest velvet, and full, blood red lips, gave her the appearance of a woman ten years younger. Her dress was simple but impeccable in design; falling in graceful folds around her chest, her tiny waist embraced by an ornately embroidered belt, and then a cascade of silk that floated to the floor in a myriad of colour and light. Next to her stood Marcus Aurelius Cotta, his best toga gleamed stark and pale in its newly bleached freshness. Behind them stood the Pontifex Maximus, high priest of Rome, dressed head to toe in a magnificent gold and purple toga, and finally, behind him stood six women, covered from head to toe in plain white linen, their faces covered by the thinnest of gossamer veils to protect their modesty, for no man was allowed to openly gaze at the face of a Vestal Virgin.

"Tell Lucius Cornelius Sulla that we wish to speak with him," Aurelia said haughtily, addressing the steward.

Unable to believe his eyes, the steward merely nodded and scurried off down one of the many corridors that led off from the atrium. A few minutes later he returned. "I regret to inform you that Lucius Cornelius Sulla is not receiving guests today." The steward blushed slightly as he glanced across at the Vestal Virgins.

"Then please inform your master that we will wait here until he makes time to see us. We need to talk with him on an urgent matter," Aurelia replied stiffly, and she made her way to one of the many chairs dotted around the room and sat down.

"But Mistress," the steward pleaded, "My Master cannot see you today. You must make an appointment!"

"We do not have time for this!" Aurelia retorted. "Go and tell your Master that we will not leave until he has seen us."

The steward bowed, and hurried back down the corridor again.

"Aurelia, I really do think that it might be better to arrange an appointment, as the steward suggests. We won't do any good if we upset Sulla." Marcus Aurelius looked worried as he stood by her chair.

Aurelia looked defiant. "I am not leaving until I have spoken to Sulla. This could be my only chance; Caesar could be dead by tomorrow."

"Marcus is right, Aurelia," the Pontifex Maximus joined them. "Sulla does not take kindly to being told what to do."

"And neither do I. Now, you all agreed to come here today to help my son, so please, have faith. We will speak to Sulla."

The steward failed to return, and, after a while, the Vestal Virgins took seats close to Aurelia, around the edge of the atrium.

Time ticked away. The Pontifex Maximus paced the floor, back and forth and then, to while away the time, he studied the beautiful frescos painted on the walls. Marcus Aurelius admired the beautiful statues and flowers that filled the peristyle garden, next to he atrium, and the Vestal Virgins whispered amongst themselves, their veils softly rippling on their breath. Aurelia remained sitting, bolt upright, her hands clasped in her lap, her face determined and her eyes fixed on the corridor down which the steward had long since disappeared.

A slave, carrying a long torch, entered the atrium, eying the visitors warily as he began to light the numerous wall scones and oil lamps positioned around the room, as darkness fell outside, but there was still no word from Sulla.

Finally, just as Marcus Aurelius was about to insist that they leave, the sound of footsteps could be heard coming down the corridor and the steward appeared.

"Lucius Cornelius Sulla Felix has a few moments to spare before his next engagement; if you would all like to follow me," he said.

"Finally!" Aurelia exclaimed, rising stiffly to her feet. The rest of the group joined her, and one by one, they filed silently down the corridor after the steward. They walked in silence as they wound their way through a vast labyrinth of corridors; their way illuminated by the many torches that hung at regular intervals on the walls. Finally, the steward turned right and stopped at a pair of ornate, ebony wood doors. He knocked once and waited to be admitted. Silently, the doors swung open as though pulled by invisible strings, and a dazzling light flooded the corridor around the group. The steward stepped forward into the room and they followed him into the light.

The entire room was made of marble; from floor to ceiling, white marble glittered and reflected the hundreds of torches and oil lamps that illuminated the vast space. Down the centre of the hall, huge marble pillars formed a colonnade on either side, and, at the far end of the room, there was a large, white dais. Four large braziers illuminated the dais, so that it looked like a golden platform hovering off the floor, and there, seated on a chair of pure, glittering gold, sat Rome's Dictator, Lucius Cornelius Sulla Felix.

Marcus gently lowered Caesar to the floor and stepped in front of him, resting his hand on the handle of his gladius. "You will have to get past me first!" he said through gritted teeth.

The man walked forward a pace. "Now then lad, there's no need for this," he said, his voice a harsh rattle in his throat.

The barn door burst open and two more men entered, dragging the farmer with them. "We found im in the ouse," one of the men said.

"Stop yer struggling!" The first man to enter the barn was obviously the leader and he snarled at the farmer.

"Who are you, and what do you want?" Aemi shouted, drawing the man's attention away from the farmer.

"I think you know who we are," the leader sneered. "But let me formally introduce myself. I am Cornelius, Captain Cornelius, to my men, and I have been sent by Sulla to find you. Now, you can do this the hard way, or the easy way, but *either* way, you're coming with us, got it?"

"Who says so?" Aemi tried to sound brave, whilst he gripped the handle of his sword tightly and prayed that he would not be forced to use it.

"I do, and that's good enough!" Cornelius growled ominously.

"We can't leave, my friend is sick. If you move him he'll die," Aemi shouted, glancing down at the unconscious form of Caesar as he spoke. He saw Cornelius's eyes flicker to Caesar.

"What's wrong with him?" he asked.

"Malaria."

Cornelius moved closer to get a better look at Caesar."How long has he been like this?" he asked.

"Since yesterday, and he seems to be getting worse," Aemi answered.

"The lad could die," the farmer spoke from behind Cornelius.

Cornelius spun round to look at the farmer. "He's going to die anyway...but not just yet," he sneered. He turned back to Aemi. "Sulla wants you both back in one piece, don't ask me why. My job's to find you and return you to Rome...alive."

Aemi saw an immediate way to postpone their capture. "Then you can't move him, unless you want to incur the wrath of Sulla!"

"What about our money?" One of the men holding the farmer demanded angrily. "If we don't deliver, we don't get paid, and I aint losing my share of two talents for no one!"

"Shut yer mouth!" Cornelius ordered. "You'll get yer money!" But when he looked back at Caesar Aemi saw the concern on his face.

"I'll pay you," Caesar suddenly spoke, his voice barely audible.

"What did he say?" Cornelius asked, stepping closer.

"I said...I'll pay you," Caesar whispered.

Cornelius frowned.

"If you leave us be," Caesar added.

Cornelius shook his head. "Now, you know I can't do that now, can I?"

"Why not?" said Aemi, realising what Caesar was trying to do. "Who is to know that you found us? No one knows we are here, other than your men, and the farmer, and he won't say anything, after all it is a crime to aid a proscribed man, isn't it?" Aemi looked at the farmer, who nodded is agreement.

"I haven't seen no one," he said in confirmation.

Cornelius rubbed his face thoughtfully and Aemi could see that he was wavering.

"How much…am I worth?" Caesar spoke slowly. Aemi could see that every breath he took was a supreme effort and he knelt down beside Caesar and propped him up against his shoulder.

"Two Talents…each!" one of the men said, letting go of the farmer's arm.

"I told you to shut yer mouth!" Cornelius shouted, turning angrily on the man.

"Yes, but he's right, isn't he? Who knows we found em, eh?" the man retorted. "They could be anywhere by now. We can't move im can we; look at the state of im! Sulla's orders were to bring im back alive, and he'll be lucky to last the night, look at im!"

"Least this way we get our money," the other man, who still had hold of the farmer, agreed.

The barn door flew open and two more men entered, dragging the boy, Quintus, with them. They pushed him roughly to the floor and he fell, sprawling at his father's feet.

"Why you…!" the farmer exploded angrily, and shaking off the grip of his captive, he hurled himself at the men who had mistreated his son.

Fists flew as the farmer laid into the men, punching and kicking. The man who had been holding on to the farmer leapt onto his back and grabbed him round his throat with his huge meaty hands. Young Quintus managed to roll out of the way as his father came crashing to the ground with the man still hanging on, trying to strangle the farmer. Cornelius stepped forward, drawing a dagger from his waistband and dragged his man off the farmer's back. The farmer remained on the ground, gasping for air.

"Wait!" Aemi shouted, realising that Cornelius was about to kill the farmer. "No!" He lunged forward and grabbed the hand with the knife in it and held on for dear life, trying to pull Cornelius away from the farmer.

Cornelius whipped round in blinded fury and made a lunge at Aemi but one of his men managed to grab his arm just in time. "No, not im! You can't kill im!" he shouted, pushing Cornelius away.

Cornelius glared at Aemi, his chest heaving with the exertion, and then he spat in contempt on the floor. "Next time you won't be so lucky," he snarled, then he turned back to the farmer still laying on the floor and kicked him hard in the stomach. "You move a muscle and you're a dead man, hear me?" he shouted angrily.

The farmer nodded, groaning as he clutched his stomach. Cornelius brushed the front of his tunic down with his hands and then glanced back at Caesar who had managed to prop himself up against an old water butt, one arm protectively around young Quintus.

"The price just went up," Cornelius snarled. "You pay for them too, or they die."

Quintus whimpered and pressed his body closer into Caesar's for protection.

Caesar nodded. "I'll pay."

"Good, that's settled then. Pay up and we leave. We never saw you, understand? If you get yourselves caught by someone else, and you so much as breath a word of this, I swear, you'll be dead long before Sulla sets eyes on you again."

Caesar nodded again. "How…much?" he asked.

"Three hundred thousand sesterces," Cornelius said.

"How much?" Aemi gasped.

"You heard. Pay up now or they die, and he can take his chances!" Cornelius said looking at Caesar.

"I don't…have…now," Caesar tried to speak, then he waved Aemi to him and whispered in his ear. Aemi nodded and stood up.

"Caesar only has half the money here with him now but he will write you a promissory note. Take it to his banker in Rome and he will pay you the rest."

Cornelius frowned, disliking this arrangement.

"It is the best we can do!" Aemi insisted.

Cornelius turned to his men. "Well, what do you think?" he asked them.

"It's your decision, Captain, but I say take it," one of the men answered. "At least we get something for our troubles."

The others nodded their agreement and Cornelius turned back to Aemi. "All right, you got yourself a deal. Now, hand over the money and get that note written, before he pegs it!"

Aemi went over to the saddlebags lying in the corner and rummaged around until he pulled out a large money pouch. Next he found a small wax tablet and stylus, which he took over to Caesar. He quickly scratched some words onto the wax and then handed the stylus to Caesar, who signed it. Aemi walked back to Cornelius and handed over the money and the tablet. Cornelius stuffed the money pouch in his trouser pocket and glanced quickly at the words on the tablet. Satisfied, he tucked the tablet inside his tunic and turned to his men. "Right, you lot, let's go. I want to be in the bar by nightfall."

His men turned and filed out of the barn. Cornelius turned back to Aemi. "It's been a pleasure doing business with you," he said with a grin, and then he too turned on his heels and walked out of the barn.

Aemi breathed a sigh of relief. "That was too close!" he said.

The farmer struggled to his feet, rubbing his neck, which was red and swollen, with visible finger mark bruising appearing. Aemi turned to look at Caesar and let out a gasp of dismay. "Oh, no, Caesar!" He fell down at Caesar's feet and looked despairingly at his friend. The exertion of talking had been too much for Caesar and he now lay motionless as though dead. The farmer hastened over to them and knelt down.

"He's not…?" Aemi asked, unable to speak the dreaded words.

The farmer shook his head. "No, not quite but he's very sick. Quintus," he said, pulling his son from under Caesar's arm. "Go to the house and prepare your bed. Get fresh blankets and light a fire."

Quintus jumped to his feet and ran off to do his father's bidding.

"Come on, help me get 'im up," the farmer ordered Aemi, and between them they managed to get Caesar up onto his feet.

"I don't know how to thank you," Aemi said as they carried Caesar from the barn towards the house.

"No thanks are needed," the farmer said gruffly. "Any friend of Gaius Marius is a friend of mine, and anyway, he saved our lives; now it's my turn to try and save his."

Sulla watched as the strange looking procession of people walked slowly down the centre of the hall towards him. A smile touched his lips as he thought how absurd they all looked, but he quickly composed his face back to a blank mask, as the group came to a halt at the foot of the dais. The steward bowed to Sulla, and waited.

"You may leave us," Sulla's voice echoed round the cavernous hall and the flames of the brazier jumped into life as though startled by the sound in the otherwise silent room.

As the steward walked away, Marcus Aurelius moved to the head of the group and bowed respectfully to Sulla. "Dictator, thank you for admitting us to your presence," he said formally.

"Your persistence could not be ignored," Sulla replied, making his voice deliberately cold and hard. "But my time is limited; I have other engagements to attend this evening."

"Then we will be brief," Marcus Aurelius replied.

"That would be most appreciated," Sulla nodded. "So, what can possibly be of such importance that I am not only graced by the presence of his Holiness, the Pontifex Maximus, but also our revered Vestals?" Sulla addressed himself to Marcus Aurelius but Aurelia took a step forward.

"They have come at my request, to help me plead for the life of my son."

Sulla's icy gaze switched fell on Aurelia and he looked appraisingly at her. He saw the beauty of this middle-aged woman and he was impressed. He admired her deportment and composure, obviously Patrician, he thought, and she looked somewhat familiar although he could not place where he had seen this woman before.

"And you are?"

"I am Aurelia, daughter of the late Gaius Aurelius, and wife of the late Gaius Julius Caesar."

"So, she is your niece?" Sulla ignored Aurelia and addressed Marcus Aurelius.

"And my step-daughter. I married her mother after my brother, Gaius, died,"

"I see," Sulla looked hard at Aurelia. "And the son you wish to plead for is?"

"Gaius Julius Caesar, the Flamen Dialis of Rome," Aurelia replied.

"*Was* the Flamen," Sulla corrected. "A proscribed man is automatically removed from any public office he may hold," he added coldly.

"That is your law," Aurelia said.

The hint of sarcasm that accompanied that comment was not lost on Sulla. "Yes, it is," he replied, his eyes flashing dangerously. "And as such, I have to inform you that you are wasting, not only your time,but mine as well. The proscription stands and there are *no* exceptions."

Aurelia took a deep breath and Sulla was amused to see the flash of fierce spirit deep within her black eyes. "You pride yourself on being a fair and just man, and yet you would proscribe my son; condemning him without even knowing the truth! Where is the fairness in that? Where is the justice?" Aurelia's body shook with the emotion as she faced up to Sulla.

"Who said I was fair and just?" Sulla retorted, his eyes narrowing to mere slits as he looked at Aurelia. He didn't know whether to laugh in her face or crush her, instantly, for daring to be so insolent.

"The proscriptions are for those men that would have done you harm, and worked with your enemies to that end. The proscriptions are your revenge for the deaths of all those innocent men who died under the tyranny of Gaius Marius and Lucius Cornelius Cinna; men, whose only crime was to stand up for what they believed in, and they believed in you, Sulla. My husband told me that you were considered a fair and just man by many men in Rome, men who subsequently died because they believed in you. I do not know you as a man, Sulla, but I did value my husband's judgement, and that of my uncle, who stands beside me now, and, who believes the same of you. I am here to plead for the life of my son because he is innocent of any crime. He does not deserve to be proscribed because he is not your enemy, nor has he ever been. My son has many faults, pride being the greatest, and it is his pride, and stubbornness, and loyalty to those he loves, that has moved you to proscribe him. He stood up for what he believed in. Does he deserve to die for that? I say he does not, and neither do the people who stand here before you now. Hear what they have to say, Sulla, and if, after you have heard them, your heart is still turned against my son, then I shall walk away and accept your judgement, but, as a mother, I appeal to you as a father. Would you stand by and watch your son loose his life when you knew he was innocent of any crime? I think not, and that is what I ask you to consider now. Do not have my son killed, Sulla, for you will have the blood of an innocent man on your hands."

Sulla had not taken his eyes off Aurelia as she spoke, and when she finished he continued to stare at her as though he was looking right through her, into a different world. Something in her words had struck a chord in his heart. Could she really see past him, in his guise as Dictator? Did she really see the man underneath, the man who had tried to be fair and just, and not the man circumstances had forced him to become? But would allowing that side of him to show be seen as a weakness?

"Dictator," the deep resonant voice of the Pontifex Maximus pulled Sulla back from his thoughts. "With your permission, I would like to speak."

Sulla nodded, taking the opportunity to compose himself for Aurelia had unsettled him, in some strange way.

"As High Priest of Rome, and father to many priests and priestesses, I am saddened that we have lost two of our most prominent priests, particularly now when the People are in need of much reassurance in their lives. I acknowledge your right as Dictator to enforce any law that you might deem necessary, and I do not challenge your proscription of Gaius Julius Caesar," he added hastily. "But the lady Aurelia, and Marcus Aurelius, came to me and explained the very singular circumstances surrounding Caesar's appointment to the position of Flamen, and, I must tell you that it sheds a very different light on the position of this young man, and his wife. These circumstances may aid you in reviewing your decision to proscribe him, should you so wish. If I may explain?" he asked.

"Go on," Sulla replied.

"As you are aware, it was always the prerogative of the College to nominate and elect a new man or woman into a vacancy within the priesthood. These were men and women who professed a calling to the religious life; men and women who were willing to devote their lives to the service of the gods on behalf of the People of Rome. We call these people, the chosen ones, for we believe that their purity of heart, and their willingness to forgo earthly desires, is a calling, given to them by the gods. With the arrival of Gaius Marius and Lucius Cornelius Cinna as, ah…leaders of Rome, there came an abrupt change to the traditional and recognised way of appointments in the priesthood. When the vacancy for the Flamen Dialis arose, I was summoned to see Marius and Cinna, and informed that there would be no election for the Flamen's replacement for they had a candidate in mind; the boy, Gaius Julius Caesar. I was given no opportunity to argue against the appointment, nor was I allowed to speak to the boy before his inauguration into the College. I was therefore unable to ascertain the true vocation of the boy, or his suitability to one of the highest positions within the priesthood. I have since been informed by his family that in fact the position of Flamen Dialis was forced upon him by Gaius Marius, although, I have to say that to his credit, Caesar has always conducted himself with the highest propriety, and his devotion to his work cannot be faulted, indeed, the same can be said for his young wife." The Pontifex Maximus paused, and Sulla shifted in his chair, resting his chin on his hand.

"I have given the matter much thought since I have been made aware of the true circumstances of Caesar's appointment to the Flaminate, and, after consultation with my learned colleagues we have all agreed on one thing. Gaius Julius Caesar was illegally appointed as the Flamen Dialis, and we believe that Jupiter Optimus Maximus, the god that he serves, has shown his disapproval in this matter. We, as a college, failed in our duties to the gods and the People of Rome by allowing this young man to hold a senior position in the priesthood, when it was clear that at no time was he consulted in the matter, and the wishes of the gods were ignored. I am informed that he never once expressed a calling for religious life, and, as such, he could never be considered as one chosen by the gods. It is the opinion of the College that Jupiter Optimus Maximus made his anger felt at this appointment by the recent destruction of his temple on the Capitol. Many have since foretold of dark days befalling Rome; that the gods are angry with us, and the People look to us for answers, answers, which until now, we were unable to provide. We are all of the same opinion that it is the appointment of the Flamen Dialis that has brought much of the troubles to Rome.

Sulla, if I may be so familiar, the gods will not be defied, and Gaius Marius tried to do just that by forcing Caesar into the priesthood. I do not understand what would drive a man to such lengths that he would dare to challenge the gods, but the fact remains that he did, and Caesar should never have been appointed to the priesthood. As for the College, we accept responsibility for our failings, and we ask for your understanding and forgiveness." The Pontifex Maximus concluded his speech and bowed low in obeisance to Sulla.

Sulla sat up straight in his chair and surveyed the group thoughtfully. They in turn waited with bated breath for him to speak.

"If you are to believe the story, as told by the family of Caesar, then you are right to admit to your failings as a College, for the religious welfare of the people is in your hands, and you failed them. You failed the People of Rome and you failed the gods," he said sternly.

The Pontifex Maximus hung his head and looked repentant.

"I say again, *if* you are to believe this tale from Caesar's family."

"It is no tale, Sulla, I can assure you of that," Marcus Aurelius stepped forward to join the Pontifex Maximus.

"Assuming then, that what you believe is true, are you telling me that Jupiter Optimus Maximus destroyed his own temple because he was angry at the appointment of Caesar as the Flamen Dialis?"

The Pontifex Maximus nodded. "The gods have many ways in which they may communicate their feelings to men; through omens and auspices..."

"Yes, yes, I know all that," Sulla snapped impatiently. "But to destroy a temple!"

"If it was the god's intention to punish us for allowing one not of the calling to serve as his priest then what better way to prevent him worshipping than to destroy the temple," the Pontifex Maximus replied.

Sulla could see the sense in this argument and he nodded in acceptance.

Marcus Aurelius seized the opportunity to speak. "Sulla, is this not proof enough that Caesar was a victim of Marius and that he is no enemy to you?"

Sulla ignored him as he continued to gaze thoughtfully at the Pontifex Maximus. "You put forward a convincing argument but how does this in any way affect my decision to have Caesar proscribed?"

"If I may," Marcus Aurelius stepped in. "Caesar's proscription was based solely on the premise that he was the Flamen Dialis."

"How so?" Sulla asked.

"You declared that Caesar's wife could no longer serve as the Flaminica because her father had been proscribed and you therefore asked him to divorce her in order that he could remain as the Flamen Dialis, is that not so?"

Sulla nodded.

"And Caesar refused to divorce her. But what neither of you knew then was that Caesar and his wife were not lawfully the Flamen Dialis and the Flaminica. He was no more entitled to stay as the Flamen, under religious laws, than was his wife, under the proscription laws. Caesar defied you, I accept that, but his defiance was actually as irrelevant as your request asking him to divorce his wife so that he could remain in the priesthood. This situation could all be resolved if you accept what we are saying, Sulla. You would not lose face by pardoning Caesar; after all, your argument was based upon a situation that did not actually exist, well, not lawfully anyway. You could say that the Pontifex Maximus has ruled Caesar's position as the Flamen illegal, and he and his wife can return to private life and remain married. Knowing what you know now, surely a pardon would be the right thing to do for all concerned?"

Sulla remained perfectly still, apart from his eyes, which flickered from face to face. The revelation that Caesar was not lawfully the Flamen did add a different perspective to the situation, but above all of this, Sulla could not forgive the arrogance and sheer stubbornness and lack of respect that Caesar had shown him during their interview. If he were seen to capitulate now, then where would it end?

"Lucius Cornelius, may I speak?" the senior Vestal Virgin stepped forward.

Sulla nodded, pushing his thoughts to one side as he faced the vision of godlike loveliness that stood before him. Whoever married this woman, once her thirty years of service as a priestess was over, would be a very lucky man, he mused as he looked through the thin, gossamer veil at the beautiful face hidden beneath.

"We, of the Temple of Vesta, appeal to your clemency in this case. We have found Gaius Julius Caesar to be of the highest character in both word and deed. He is a good man who did not deserve the punishment meted out to him by Gaius Marius, for indeed, it was a punishment. The boy had no religious leaning and no desire to become a priest. The position of Flamen Dialis is one of many rules and curtailments, which we know he found extremely hard to accept, but he did, most of the time, and with good grace, and he served Jupiter Optimus Maximus well. Surely it shows the measure of the man that he was able to carry out his duties diligently and without complaint. There is much to be admired in him, and we ask for you to show compassion and understanding in what we perceive to be an extremely difficult situation, for all concerned." The Vestal Virgin inclined her head graciously to show that she had finished speaking and moved back to join her sisters.

"Sulla," Marcus Aurelius stepped forward now, his hands stretched out in supplication. "We cannot express enough our gratitude that you have spared us a moment of your valuable time, but I beg for just a moment more. You have heard from Caesar's mother, who appeals to you as a father, and asks you, no, begs you, to reconsider the judgement against her son. You have heard from our esteemed Pontifex Maximus, who has given you the opinion of the College in the religious matter of Caesar's appointment as the Flamen Dialis. You have heard the Chief Vestal speak highly of Caesar's character, and her plea for clemency. Now I wish to speak as the uncle of Caesar; as one who has known him all his life, and a finer, intelligent, more loyal young man I could not wish to meet. Yes he defied you, but does that not convince you of the measure of the man? Above all else Caesar has loyalty and respect for his family, a quality that truly makes him Roman. He is young, barley nineteen, and for the past four years he has lived a tortuous existence as the Flamen Dialis. He has unwittingly become the victim of Marius, as you yourself have suffered by his hand, but whilst you were able to fight back, Caesar could only accept his fate and hope that one day, somehow, he would be freed from his burden. By allowing Caesar to live you are showing the People that you are a wise ruler, a fair ruler, a…"

"Enough Marcus!" Sulla exclaimed in exasperation. He shook his head slowly and ran one hand through his thinning hair. "Have it your way and take him…"

Aurelia gasped and threw her hands to her face.

"Only bear in mind…" he said, leaning forward and pointing a finger at the group, "… that the man you are so eager to save will one day deal the death blow to the cause of the aristocracy, which you have joined with me in upholding; for in this man Caesar there is more than one Marius!"

Aurelia looked incredulous, unable to take in what Sulla had said. "My son…my son is pardoned?" she stammered.

Sulla sat back in his chair and looked down at Aurelia, a hint of a smile played across his lips. "Yes, your son is pardoned."

A thousand unspoken words passed between them as Aurelia stared into Sulla's eyes, tears of gratitude welled up and spilled down her cheeks. "Thank you, Lucius Cornelius, thank you," she said.

"Pontifex Maximus," Sulla said, turning aside. "You have a new Flamen Dialis to appoint. I shall leave it in your capable hands; you shall have no interference from me."

The Pontifex Maximus smiled gratefully and bowed low.

"Marcus Aurelius. You are obviously feeling the strain from being away from political life for so long," Sulla said with a wry smile. "May I suggest you get yourself back into the law courts and practice you oration on someone else, other than me, in future?"

Marcus Aurelius bowed. "Whatever you say, Sulla."

"Good, now, if you will all excuse me, I have an engagement to attend for which I am no doubt late. The steward is waiting outside the door, he will show you out."

The group bowed respectfully to Sulla and began to make their way down the hall.

"Marcus, a word," Sulla called.

Marcus Aurelius returned to the dais.

"When you find Caesar, send him to me."

"Yes, Sulla, of course." Marcus bowed again and walked back down the hall to join the waiting group.

Once outside the villa the Pontifex Maximus and the Vestal Virgins climbed into their waiting litters, and, with heartfelt farewells and thanks from Aurelia and Marcus Aurelius they were taken away, back to their homes in the Forum.

"Oh, Uncle, I cannot thank you enough for what you have done," Aurelia sighed, linking her arm through his affectionately as they commenced the short walk home.

"It was truly a group effort," Marcus replied with a smile. "We just wore him down into seeing sense, that's all."

"Well I hope I never have to live through anything like that again!" said Aurelia with a shudder. "The problem now, of course, is that we have no way of finding Caesar to tell him that all is well and he can come home," she added worriedly.

"I have already thought of that," said Marcus Aurelius. "I imagine that his plan was to lie low until it was safe enough to leave the country. Aemi has properties all over Italy, and my hunch is that they are hiding out in one of them. Tomorrow, I will send messengers out to those properties, and I am sure that sooner or later, the word will reach them that it is safe to return. Have no fear, Aurelia, you will see your son again before too long."

Sulla was disturbed yet again by a knock on the dressing room door.

"Enter," he called irritably.

Dollabella came in to the room, carrying a small animal skin pouch in his hand.

As soon as Sulla saw what he was carrying his face lit up. "You have it?"

Dollabella nodded. Sulla dismissed his slave, with orders to send apologies that he would be unable to attend his dinner engagement, and then he led the way to his study. Once inside, Sulla locked the door, lit a couple of oil lamps, which he placed on his desk and sat down, looking expectantly at Dollabella.

"Here," Dollabella threw the pouch across the desk to Sulla. "Catiline insists that this is all there was. He swears this was all Marius had on him when he was captured and now he's squealing like a stuck pig because he knows you are on to him. His only excuse for keeping it was that he didn't think you would be interested in a scrappy piece of old parchment."

Sulla made no reply; his heart beat in excited anticipation as he pulled the pouch towards him.

"What's in it anyway?" Dollabella asked as he walked over to a side table and poured them both a goblet of wine.

"Marius's nemesis," Sulla muttered, his fingers lightly tracing the front of the pouch. The oil lamps flickered as though a soft breeze had passed over them and Sulla started, peering into the dark, shadowy corners of the study as though he expected to see an apparition appear before him.

"Marius's what?" Dollabella handed one of the goblets to Sulla.

Sulla shivered and pulled his toga close around him. "Tell me, Dollabella, do you believe in destiny?" Sulla asked, taking a deep draught of wine to steady his nerves.

"Destiny?" Dollabella grunted as he sat down opposite the desk.

"Yes, destiny. Do you believe that a man's destiny is planned by the gods from the moment they are born; that there is a path laid out for them to travel?"

Dollabella frowned. "I'm more an opportunist myself," he said after a moments thought. "Seize the moment, I say. I don't give much thought to what lies ahead; getting through the day is enough for me. Why do you ask?"

Sulla reclined back in his chair, feeling the warming effects of the wine as it coursed through his body. "For myself, I have total belief in the gods and their designs on men. Many times I have placed my life in the hands of Fortuna and she has always repaid my faith in her. I consider myself to be one of Fortuna's favourites, and whilst I have her patronage I know that I cannot fail."

"Well, you have done some rash things in your life, that's for sure, but as to whether it is Fortuna who looks after you, I couldn't say. Some men are simply born lucky; some are not. Is this the will of the gods or the choices a man makes as he progresses through life? I don't know."

"So you don't believe that the gods can plan a man's entire life? That he is born to be what he becomes, be it a tailor, a legionary or…the greatest Roman of all time?"

Dollabella shook his head. "Where's the choice then? Does a man have no choice in the outcome of his life? Can the tailor not become the legionary if he so chooses? If his life is already set for him by the gods then what is the point of having what the philosophers call, free will?"

"Perhaps, the choice a man makes is already decided, even before he knows that he even has a choice? Perhaps, it is already laid out in his destiny?" Sulla countered.

"Oh I don't know," Dollabella shrugged. "It's all too deep for me."

Sulla smiled as he sipped his wine. Poor old Dollabella; intellect was never his strong point, but put him in command of a legion and the man was a master. What did destiny hold for him, Sulla wondered. What was his own to be? Was this his destiny, to be the Dictator of Rome, or was there still more to come? Perhaps this was all there was; he had reached the pinnacle of his life's achievements and now he would begin the slow decline, as a waning star, just before the first rays of the sun pierce the darkness of the night. How does a man know when he has reached the place he may have spent his whole life getting to? How do you truly know what your destiny is? Caesar knows, a small voice inside his head answered, and Sulla jumped with a start. He looked down at the pouch before him. Caesar's destiny was written down on a piece of parchment inside that pouch.

"Dollabella," he said suddenly. "I hate to cut this short, but I have a mountain of work still to get through before my day is done. I thank you for your help today, I am most grateful."

"Oh, well I will leave you to it," said Dollabella, getting to his feet. "Are you sure there's nothing else I can do for you before I go?"

"Well, now that you have finally managed to find Catiline, and retrieved this package, I believe you two have some…unfinished business?" said Sulla with a smile.

"Of course. It's as good as done. Right, well I'll see you tomorrow then?"

"Yes, tomorrow," said Sulla, and he waited until Dollabella had gone before he picked up the pouch and opened it.

Inside, Sulla found two small folded squares of parchment. He placed both pieces side by side on the desk in front of him. One of them had the name, *Caesar*, written across the front and he opened this one first. It was a hastily scribbled letter to Caesar and was signed at the bottom by Marcus Marius. Sulla read the letter:

*'Caesar. I do not want you to be angry with Aemi and I when you have read this letter for you must understand that we only ever acted in your interests, because we are your friends…'*

Sulla scanned down the page, avoiding all the preliminary chatter, until he found what he was looking for. *'I have made a true copy of the prophecy and there are four verses to it, yet Father only had three verses in his possession. Caesar, you were right to believe in your destiny for you are going to be a great man one day. Don't take my word for it but read it for yourself. Oh, I wish I could be there to see the look on your face, Caesar but for the moment that is impossible, so I will content myself with the knowledge that once you have read the prophecy you will have hope once more. Now you can have faith in your dreams, my friend, for I believe one day they will become a reality. It is your destiny to be amongst the greats; your name will be spoken alongside our hero Alexander; forever fixed in the annuls of history. I hope and pray to all the gods that I am there to share it with you. Please send my respects to Aemi; tell him that I valued our friendship and that I kept my promise.*

*Your friend always,*

*Marcus.'*

Sulla put the letter down on the table. Marcus Aurelius was right; Caesar did inspire friendship and loyalty by those who knew him well, but would he inspire the same passion of hatred in men too, one day, for love and hate were to be found on opposite sides of the same coin after all. Sulla gazed down at the second square of parchment and slid it towards him. Slowly, he unfolded the parchment and smoothed it out on the table in front of him. The writing was much neater this time; Marius obviously had plenty of time to make the copy, safe in the confines of the temple. Sulla took a deep breath and began to read.

*Nine eaglets can I see,*
*And seven times you shall be,*
*Consul over mighty Rome,*
*More than any other man,*
*Greatest of them all, bar one.*

Here Sulla saw that Aemi had scribbled a note next to this verse.

*'I think the eagles are people; meaning Father is the greatest eagle, excepting one other.'*

Sulla smiled to himself. He was sure that Caesar, if he had read this, would have been able to work that much out for himself. That note was a typical Mariian trait: stating the obvious! Sulla read on.

*The eighth eagle shall full grow,*
*And give you pain and much sorrow,*
*Your end he will conspire to make,*
*Your very body try to break.*

Sulla started in surprise. Could he possibly be this eighth eagle? After all, he was younger than Marius, and years of enmity between them that had culminated ultimately with both men determined to destroy each other. Sulla thought back to what Marcus Aurelius had said, about the suddenness with which Marius had turned against Caesar, and realised that the same thing had happened to himself. Had Marius recognised Sulla as the eighth eagle and had tried to destroy him before the prophecy could be fulfilled? He looked down at the scribbled note Marcus had made next to this verse and saw that he was not the only one to think that, for Marcus had scribbled; *'I think this one is Sulla.'*

Sulla took a sip of wine and then he bent forward over the table to read the next verse.

*The ninth young eaglet, far behind,*
*From noble birth shall grow to be,*
*The greatest eagle of them all,*
*A hairy king of land and sea.*

Sulla read the several notes that Marcus had written beside this verse:

*'I think the ninth is you. Far behind means younger, I think, and you are of noble birth.'*

Sulla nodded in agreement. Marcus's perceptions did seem to make sense.

*'What convinces me this is you is the Hairy King. Your family name is Caesar, meaning a full head of hair. I think that, Hairy means Caesar, and you are going to be a king!'*

Again Sulla nodded. The Sybil's often spoke in riddles, which of course left things wide open to interpretation, but what Marcus concluded made sense to Sulla. So, if it was Caesar, then his destiny was to grow to be the greatest eagle of them all, greater than Marius or Sulla could ever imagine. Was it possible that this young man had known from an early age that this was the destiny awaiting him? Marius obviously thought so, or why would he have gone to such great lengths to stop him? Why, Sulla pondered, did Marius not kill Caesar when he had the chance? This was a question that would never be answered, but it gnawed away inside Sulla. Surprisingly, he felt no jealousy when he realised that Caesar, if indeed he was the one of the prophecy, would surpass even his own great achievements. If it was not meant to be for him, this accolade of the 'Greatest of Romans', then he was still content with his lot. He would not defy the gods through vanity or greed like Marius. He would accept their decision and be content with what he had. So, what did the future hold for Caesar? Sulla read the final verse.

*No Rome for two so one must die,*
*The third through treachery follows,*
*The fate of Rome lies in their hands,*
*The eagles bring much sorrow.*

Sulla noted, with wry amusement, that Marcus had made no note next to this verse, but then, what could he say, for if the prophecy was to be interpreted correctly, the third eagle, Caesar, would die through an act of treachery. So, after reaching such great heights, Caesar was going to be murdered! He re-read the last verse. It was true, Rome had not been big enough for both he and Marius to co-exist peacefully and as fortune favoured Sulla, Marius had died. It was also true the fate of Rome had lain very much in their hands. Their desire to destroy each other had all but destroyed the Republic. The eagles did indeed bring much sorrow.

Sulla stood up and walked over to the small table to re-fill his goblet with wine. What if Marius had never seen the Sybil? What would the future have held for them then, for surely Marius's actions towards himself and indeed to young Caesar had been brought about by his desire to prevent the prophecy from being fulfilled? Would he be standing here now, in his magnificent villa, Dictator of Rome? Was this their destiny, to be wrapped up together, Sulla, Marius and Caesar? Sulla poured the wine and returned to his desk, sitting and pondering on these questions when his musings were disturbed by a knock on the door.

"Come," Sulla called.

His steward entered the study and bowed. "Please forgive the intrusion, Master, but there is a young man outside who says you wish to see him."

"Oh, who might he be?" Sulla frowned, for he did not recall sending for anyone.

"Gaius Julius Caesar," the steward replied.

"Indeed, well, bring him to me," Sulla commanded and waiting until the steward left the room, he scraped the parchment together, along with the pouch, and crammed them into his desk drawer, out of sight. He was a picture of composure and indifference when, a few minutes later, Gaius Julius Caesar arrived.

Radiating youth, and a noble elegance that Sulla had not noticed on his previous encounter with Caesar, the young man stood before him, bathed and shaven, his olive skin oiled and supple, his tousled blonde hair cut short and neat. Tall and lean, but with a muscular frame and exquisite Patrician features, Caesar was the image of a young god. Yes, Sulla thought, as he studied him intently, you are everything I imagine the, 'Greatest Roman of them all,' to be.

The young god spoke; his voice deep and melodious, soft in tone yet belying a hidden power that would one-day serve him well on the battlefield. "You asked to see me, Dictator."

"Indeed I did. Please, sit down."

Caesar took a seat opposite Sulla's desk and sat, composed and calm, not a shred of fear on his face.

"So," Sulla said, resting back casually in his chair so that his face was hidden in shade. "You survived."

Caesar nodded. "I am grateful for the clemency you have shown me, Sir," he replied.

"You have your friends and family to thank for that," said Sulla with a hint of a smile. "They can be very…persuasive."

"But the decision rested with you, none the less, and you have my gratitude."

"Indeed," said Sulla, amused at the gravity of the young man. "Let it not be said that I am an unreasonable man, unlike, for example, your uncle, Gaius Marius. Do you think he would have pardoned you, if he had been in my position?"

Sulla watched intently as Caesar took his time to answer the question. He tried to read the young man's face, but it remained an impenetrable mask.

When, at last Caesar spoke, it was considered and precise. "No, I do not believe he would. Gaius Marius was as immovable in his opinions as he was in his decisions, and the proscription would have been enforced."

Sulla nodded. "And do you perceive that as a strength, or a weakness, in a man?"

"A man should have principles upon which he should guide his life. Dignity and honour are the making of a man, for what is he without those qualities? A man's opinions are his own and it is his right to voice them. A man's decision, however, is a different matter, for it can affect the lives of others when made. He should have a clear idea in his mind as to what he wishes to achieve when he makes a decision, especially when it affects other people. He should honour that decision, and see it through to the end, however, should circumstances change upon which the original decision was based, then a man should be prepared to re-evaluate, and, if necessary, amend that decision. He should have the courage of his convictions to change his mind if it is the right thing to do, for himself, or for others. My uncle's failure was his inability to adapt to change. It is your strength."

Sulla nodded, secretly impressed by Caesar's succinct way of speaking his mind. "I can see that your reputation for oratory skills is well deserved for your mind is both clear and precise; I like that in a man, however, flattery does not become you, Caesar."

Caesar merely inclined his head in acknowledgement of Sulla's praise as if the comments were of no consequence to him. "I do not speak to flatter you, Sir, I merely acknowledge the facts. You proscribed me based on the information you had at the time. This information subsequently proved to be incorrect. Fortunately for me, you were gracious enough to listen and accept the words of the people who pleaded for my life, and you reversed your decision. It is my failing that I myself did not explain matters to you better when we last met."

"So, why did you say nothing when you had the chance to speak up for yourself?" Sulla asked, intrigued with the honesty of this strange young man.

"Pride," Caesar replied simply.

"You were prepared to die rather than admit that you had been forced into the priesthood, is that it?"

Caesar nodded. "I was afraid that you would see me as a lesser man because of it," he admitted.

"But you were a child; you could not have stood up to Marius!" Sulla said irritably.

"I know, but I still saw that as my weakness and failing."

"You have a very high opinion of yourself, young man," Sulla said sarcastically. "Greater men than you have failed against Marius; what makes you so very different?"

Caesar shrugged. "So I have been told. All I can say is that I am who I am."

"And who exactly are you, Caesar? What was it about you that sent Marius into a frenzy of hatred and revenge?" Sulla leant across the desk, his face illuminated once more by the flames of the oil lamps, and his cold, piercing eyes, fixed on Caesar as he waited for a reply.

"I can only answer that I am who I am. Gaius Marius's reaction towards me was born from his fear of inadequacy, and his longing for immortality amongst the great men in history, not through anything I did to him. It was his failure as a man that led to his twisted bitterness."

Sulla studied Caesar's face but there was still nothing to give away how he was really feeling inside. The longer he watched Caesar, the more intrigued Sulla became. "Are you always like that?" he asked harshly.

"Like what?"

"So cold, so unemotional, so…passionless?"

Caesar raised a single eyebrow, the first sign of feeling he had shown since he arrived. "That is merely your perception of me and not one my friends would share."

"No, your friends obviously see more to you than I do, for they are prepared to die for you, their love is so great."

Caesar blushed. "I have loyal friends, yes."

"So loyal that one did die, trying to bring you a copy of a prophecy, is that not so?" Sulla asked shrewdly, his eyes fixed on Caesar as he realised he had found a chink in his armour.

Caesar made no reply.

"Was it worth a life, this…prophecy?" Sulla asked.

"I would rather not have lost my friend because of it," Caesar retorted.

"But you did, didn't you?" Sulla baited him. "And you still have no idea what the prophecy might say? Do you even know for certain that it is you of whom the prophecy speaks? After all, that is what the last few years of your life have been all about isn't it, this…prophecy?"

"I have never seen it," Caesar said through gritted teeth.

"No, I know you haven't," Sulla smiled icily, whilst his pale eyes stared, scornful and full of contempt. "Would you like to know what it says?" Sulla asked suddenly, and was taken by surprise when Caesar merely shrugged.

"I believe it would only confirm what I already know. Whilst it would gratify my curiosity and answer many questions, it will change nothing."

"Oh, you…you are priceless!" Sulla burst out laughing at the audacity of this young man. He banged his fist down on the desk and shook his head in disbelief.

Caesar looked taken aback at this sudden explosion of energy, but he remained silent. At last, Sulla's laughter died away, and he wiped a stray tear from his cheek. "You are one of a kind, Gaius Julius Caesar," he said with a sigh. "And I respect you for it, though the gods only know how you infuriated me with your pig headed stubbornness and foolish pride! However, you have a future to seek now that you are free from the priesthood, and, I admit that I let you go with a sense of some trepidation, not for myself you understand, but for Rome. Still, I am not one to stand in the way of the gods for I am no Marius, but I cannot let our last encounter go completely unpunished." All the laughter had drained from his face and he looked hard at Caesar. "You defied me, Caesar, and showed no respect for me as Dictator of Rome. I have allowed you your freedom so go and follow that destiny you always believed in, but, you will get no further help from me, nor will you be able to rely on the large dowry that came to you upon your marriage to Cinna's brat. I am confiscating the dowry, as the money was part of Cinna's estate. Accept this punishment, Caesar, and you walk away a free man. What do you say?"

Caesar sat silently, and Sulla could see that he was weighing up the offer carefully before reaching his decision. For a moment, Sulla thought that Caesar was actually going to refuse, but then, just as he was about to break the silence, Caesar nodded.

"I accept," he said.

"I thought you might," Sulla smiled knowingly, and then, in an instant, the smile was gone. His face grew hard and cold as he looked at Caesar. "Then our business is concluded. Go and seek your destiny, Gaius Julius Caesar. I hope it is everything you hoped for… but, do not think of returning to Rome, for though I have been merciful today, I may not be so tomorrow. Stay away from Rome, Caesar, for you and I should not cross paths again in this life."

Caesar nodded and stood up to leave.

"What will you do now?" Sulla asked as an afterthought.

"I believe my uncle Marcus can arrange for me to serve as a junior officer to Marcus Thurmus, governor of the Asian Province. I shall begin my military career there, with your permission?"

"You have it," Sulla nodded. "Marcus Thurmus is a good man; you will learn much from him, providing you keep a check on your pride!"

Caesar smiled, nodded his thanks and walked to the door.

"Tell me, Caesar, what do you think Gaius Marius would think of my decision to set you free?" Sulla asked.

Caesar paused as he opened the door and then he turned to face Sulla once more, his face grave in expression. Their eyes met one last time; the ice cold blue, against the black fathomless depths; meeting as equals for the first and last time.

"He would turn in his grave…if he had one." Caesar replied.

A look of smug satisfaction crossed Sulla's face. "Yes, he would, wouldn't he."

Gaius Julius Caesar left Sulla's study, closed the door, and walked away to begin the start of his new life. Destiny was calling and Caesar went on his way, with the sound of Sulla's triumphant laughter echoing down the corridor behind him.

In the underground cavern of a small temple, situated on the edge of S…….., in northern Italy, a novice priest sat alone, surrounded by piles of old and dusty scrolls; a single brazier, his only source of heat and light. His job was to sort through the archive of Sibylline prophesies that the recently deceased High Priest had hoarded over many years. His death had heralded a new era in the religious life of the temple, starting with the complete cataloguing of every prophecy held in the archive to date.

The young priest sighed, shivering with cold for the brazier coals were burning very low, giving out very little heat or light. He pushed the scrolls around absently, looking for any individual pieces of parchment that had become separated from the whole through the carelessness of previous men who had rummaged through the archives. His hand alighted on a small square piece of yellow, faded parchment that appeared to have been torn from a larger book some time in the past. He picked it up and examined it in the dim light of the brazier, and read the faded words:

*One brings glory, tyranny and death,*
*The Second hailed Dictator.*
*The Third a crown upon his head,*
*Will herald great disaster.*

The priest squinted in the gloom and held the parchment closer to the brazier to enable him to read the small, barely legible writing. As he strained to make out the words, the edge of the tinder dry parchment touched a small coal sticking out from the side of the brazier. The heat from the coal, though not strong, was sufficient to set light to the parchment, and a bright yellow flame flared into life, spreading across the page. The priest, realising what had happened, jumped to his feet to keep the fire from spreading and quickly threw the parchment into the brazier for safety. The page lay still on the glowing embers of the dying fire as the sides began to twist and curl from the heat. The priest watched for a moment and then shrugged for it was too late to save the piece of scroll now. He resumed his place amongst the pile of ancient parchment on the floor and continued with his work.

Slowly, the black crispness of destruction spread across the final verse of the prophecy, devouring the words as it went.

*This Third will walk among the gods,*
*The greatest Roman of them all,*
*And with his death will come the end,*
*For with it, the Republic falls.*

With a last, dying, flare of light, the fire devoured its prey, reducing it to a small pile of ash on top of the coals. With one final puff, the flame was extinguished, and with it, the destiny of Rome was consigned to oblivion.

# GLOSSARY

**Atrium** Reception room. Waiting area/large hallway of a roman house.

**Auctoritas** The political and public influence a man possessed.

**Client** A person who would swear to look out for the business interests of a senator. The senator would become the patron and in return for services rendered he would help the client financially or otherwise if the client asked for help. The number of clients a patron had, the higher his **auctoritas** became.

**Dictator** Supreme ruler of the Roman empire. All powerful.

**Dignitas** Pride (dignity) moral values and reputation of a man. Highly valued. In Sulla's case he was prepared to go to war when the Senate injured his dignitas by refusing to believe he had been abducted by Marius.

**Knights** Wealthy men one rank below senators. Businessmen and gentlemen from the provinces. Young Plebeians who had not reached the age to enter the Senate.

**Flamen Dialis** Senior priest of Rome. Seriously restricted by religious sanctions on what to eat, wear, touch, and do on a daily basis, The strictest religious position in the priesthood.

**Forum(Romanum)** The business centre at the heart of Rome. Many major temples, banks, and businesses were based here, together with the Senate House and the Rostra.

**Insula** Latin for island. A tall building often surrounded on each side by a road and split into business and living accommodation. Limited space within the city walls meant that only the wealthy could afford villas, the majority of the population lived in high-rise apartments or insula.

**Italian Allies** Italy consisted of hundreds of different tribes of people all united under the leadership of Rome. The majority did not have Roman Citizenship and were in many cases considered second-class citizens although there was very little difference between and Italian and a Roman. In repayment for Rome's protection, Italian men were used to supplement the Roman legions in the auxiliary units.

**Legate** A military officer in the legions.

**Lictor** A public servant of the Senate employed to escort senior magistrates when on official duty. The number of lictors denoted the status of the escorted senator.

They wore red tunics and carried 'fasces'-an ancient symbol of birch rods tied together by a leather thong, which symbolised the power of Rome.

**Legion** A single legion consisted of 4,800 men and divided into ten cohorts of 48 men. Each cohort was divided further into sections of 8 men. Each legion had 120 cavalry and was identified by their own standard, which bore the company name and number. The minimum length of service for a legionary was ten years after which they were awarded a small piece of land to make a living from.

**Mos Maiorum** The unwritten constitution of Rome. A general understanding by everyone that this was the way things were done, what was acceptable and what was not. It formed the basis on which past and future actions were based and to go against the Mos Maiorum was considered sacrilege.

**Names** A Roman male had up to three names at birth. A first name e.g Gaius, and a family name e.g. Julius. Sometimes a third name was added to distinguish which branch of the family they came from e.g. Caesar. On reaching adulthood, a man could add other names, called a cognomen, to distinguish him as an individual. Usually the name was based on a peculiarity, e.g. Strabo meaning cross eyes, or Felix as in Sulla's case, meaning lucky. Women would have a female version of the male name e.g. Cinnilla, whose father's family name was Cinna.

**New Man** Men who joined the Senate with no previous family history of governing Rome. The old established families looked down on the new men, believing them inferior and it was considered an insult to call someone a new man.

**Optimate** The Senate was divided into two main political factions. The Optimates, generally men from ancient Patrician and Plebeian families who believed in the traditions of Rome and disliked change and the **Populares**, many of whom were new men, or Plebeians, who were open to new ideas and innovation. Sulla was welcomed into the Optimate party who opposed 'new men' like Gaius Marius, who belonged to the Populares.

**Paterfamilias** The senior male of a Roman family. His word was law and nothing could be done without his consent. He had the power of life and death over his family and could not be challenged by anyone. He arranged marriages for his children and divorce was common. On the death of the father, the eldest male son would become paterfamilias, as in Aemi's case on the death of his father.

**Patrician** The original aristocratic ruling families of Rome after the last King was deposed and Rome became a Republic. Consisted roughly of twenty families who were traditionalist in outlook and considered themselves the height of nobility in Roman society.

**Pedagogue** A teacher for children.

**Plebeian** Any Roman citizen not Patrician. To distinguish themselves above the common masses the rich plebeians entered themselves into the Knight social class which enabled them to join the Senate and enjoy a political career equal to the Patricians. With the decline in Patricians due to low birth rate, there became little distinction between ancient Plebeian and Patrician families and they intermarried. Only the family name gave any indication to their social background. The common people of Rome were known as Plebs.

**Plebeian Assembly** Twelve Roman citizens of Plebeian birth, elected by the people to represent them on issues of government. They had the power to pass new laws but the Senate often opposed them. No new law could be passed without the Senate's consent and this often caused political arguments.

**Praetor** See Senate.

**Roman Citizen** A man, woman or child who was either born in Rome to Roman parents or who was granted citizen rights by the State. A person had more rights, protection from the law and state benefits than a non-roman citizen. They also had the right to vote.

**Senate** The governing body of Rome. In Caesar's day there was roughly 300 senators active in the Senate. To be eligible to join, a man had to be of high birth and meet the minimum wealth requirements. The Senate was headed by two Consuls who were elected annually. The Cursus Honorum was the political ladder of magisterial positions that lead to the consulship. The lowest rank was the Quaestor, of which there were 20 men. Aedile was next with 4 men and then Praetor, of which there were 8 men. A Praetor acted as a judge and was given a province to govern after his term in office. When this was completed he would be known as a Pro-Praetor. All ranks were denoted by various purple stripes on their togas and the presence of lictors if they held high office. All men were elected annually into position and the elections were generally corrupt and rife with nepotism.

**Subura** The poorest and most densely populated area of Rome. Generally populated by people from many different nationalities. Wealthy Romans stayed away from the area as it was considered highly dangerous and rife with disease.

**Tribune of the Plebs** A member of the Plebeian Assembly. They had the right to veto any law proposed by the Senate and were often open to bribery both from the people and senators alike.

**Triumph** A General who had lead a successful major battle would be awarded a triumph by the Senate and People of Rome. The General would lead his legions through the city with great pomp and ceremony, showing off the treasure and slaves that they had captured for the glory of Rome.

**Tribe** A Roman citizen was born or placed into a tribe of which there were 35. Thirty-one were rural and four, urban. As a member of the tribe you were allowed to vote in elections. Newly created Roman citizens were placed into an appropriate tribe to their name and circumstances. A non-Roman citizen could not be a member of a tribe, vote, or have any say in the government of Rome. This was a fundamental cause for the start of the Italian Civil War.

**Veteran** Generally referred to a legionary who had served 10 years in the legions and had retired. Many lived for years away from Rome and Italy and often chose to make their last province their new home when they retired. These veterans could be called upon to fight for Rome if war broke out in their province and was a way of Rome being able to spread their culture and civilisation to far reaching provinces.

**Wax Tablet** Two, square wooden frames bound together down one side to allow the frame to open and close, as a modern day book. Inside the frame was covered in wax. The writer would inscribe words using a bone stylus (stick) and then closed the tablet to protect the writing. The tablets could be re-used by melting and smoothing the wax.

CPSIA information can be obtained at www.ICGtesting.com
Printed in the USA
BVOW041719060912

299662BV00002B/29/A